BOOKS BY MEREDITH ANN PIERCE

The Darkangel Trilogy
The Darkangel
A Gathering of Gargoyles
The Pearl of the Soul of the World

Treasure at the Heart of the Tanglewood
The Woman Who Loved Reindeer
Where the Wild Geese Go

the
Firebringer
Trilogy

the Firebringer Trilogy

Birth of the Firebringer
Dark Moon
The Son of Summer Stars

Meredith Ann Pierce

50 YEARS SFBC FANTASY

Published by arrangement with
Firebird
A Division of Penguin Group USA, Inc.
375 Hudson Street
New York, NY 10014-3657

First SFBC printing: June 2003

Visit the Firebird website at www.firebirdbooks.com

Visit the SFBC website at www.sfbc.com

ISBN 0-7394-3570-1

PRINTED IN THE UNITED STATES OF AMERICA

the
Firebringer
Trilogy

Contents

Birth of the Firebringer

To Drew and Jill

Contents

Beginning

When Alma created the world, most of it she made into the Great Grass Plain, which was not a flat place, but rolling like a mare's back and covered all over with the greencorn and the haycorn and the wild oats, knee high, so that when the wind stirred it, billowing, it looked like a mare's winter coat blowing. And that is why some called the grasslands Alma's back. It was not the truth, for the Mother-of-all was not the world, but the Maker of the world.

With the stamp of one hoof, she made the Summer Sea, running shallow and warm even in wintertime. And with a little dig of her other heel, she raised the Gryphon Mountains upon its northern shore. Ranging north from there spread the dark Pan Woods, tangled and close, where only the blue-bodied goatlings roamed. Somewhere to the eastern north lay the Smoking Hills, where the red dragons denned, and due north across the Plain lay the Hallow Hills, a sacred place to the children-of-the-moon.

And that was all that was known of the world to the people I shall tell of in this tale. They lived in a great valley on the northern verges of the Woods. To the gryphons, they had always been a'ítichi, the enemy, and the pans murmured and gestured among themselves of the ufpútlak, four-footed walkers. The plainsdwellers, being near cousins to those of whom I speak, called them simply southlanders. But they named themselves the unicorns, which means the "one-horned ones," for each bore upon the brow a single spiral shaft as sharp as river ice and harder than hoof-breaking stone.

I am one of the fellows of this tale—I will not tell you which I am, though I promise that by the end of the running you will know me. My tale touches how the Firebringer came to be born among the unicorns, *and what his coming meant to Aljan, son of Korr. But to start my tale, I must begin a little before the Firebringer, on a day near winter's end when Jan was six years old, nearly half-grown, though still counted among the colts. It had been a long, cold, dull winter, and the prince's son longed fiercely for the fiery storms of spring.*

Stormwind

2

Stormclouds were rolling in out of the southeast. They darkened half the sky. It had been storming all day over the Gryphon Mountains, far on the horizon's edge. He had been watching the lightning there off and on since midmorning, flickering like great, violent fireflies, and he wondered whether the rain would spend itself before reaching the Vale of the Unicorns.

Jan paused on the trail heading upslope through the trees. He lifted his muzzle, his nostrils flared. The savor of moist earth and evergreens filled him. Winter was done, the snow gone from the ground, but it was not yet equinox. No new shoots sprouted on the slope, no new grass yet scattered among the stubble in the valley below. The year was just now struggling into birth, still in its storming month, the time of cold gales and showers before spring.

Jan lowered his head and shook himself, feeling his mane settle along his neck. He pawed the leaf mold with one cloven heel, swatted a pair of stinging gnats from his flank with his tassel-ended tail, and wondered where Dagg was. He and his friend had a standing agreement to meet on the hillside whenever a storm was in the wind. Jan nibbled at a fly bite on one shoulder, fidgeted. Then the sound of hoofbeats made him wheel.

Pale yellow and dappled with gray, Dagg was like most unicorn colts, the color of his sire. Jan was not—the prince's line never ran true, not since the days of Halla, four hundred summers gone. It was their mark, and set them off from all the herd, that no prince's heir might ever be a match for him, so while Korr was as black as the well of a weasel's eye, Jan, his son, was only sable, a rich dark brown like the color of earth. He spotted Dagg coming toward him through the trees.

Dagg neared and nipped at Jan, shouldering him, and the prince's son shied, kicking. They chased each other off the narrow trail, nickering and fencing with colts' long, unsharpened horns that dashed and clattered in the heavy, storm-awaiting stillness. Then Jan broke off, dodging back to the path, and sprinted toward the hillcrest.

"Hist, come on," he cried over one shoulder. "The storm's nearly here."

They sped upslope then through the patches of sunlight and shadows of the trees. Jan threw up his head, letting his long legs stretch. The wind fingered his mane and played through the shag of his winter coat. He felt young and strong and full of his own power. The rush of air laid back his ears. In another moment—in another moment, he would fly. Then he felt Dagg pulling up alongside him from behind and dropped back to a trot. They had nearly reached the top of the slope.

"Your father'll dance thunder if he finds out," Dagg said after a moment, "that we've come up this high, and with stormwind from the east."

Jan shook the forelock out of his eyes and nickered. Colts were forbidden to stray from the valley floor, away from the ready shelter of the grottoes there. The Gryphon Mountains rose barely a day's flight to the eastern south, and a gryphon could fly far with stormwind at its back. The unicorns lost foals every spring when the gryphon formels, the females, were hatching their ravenous young. Jan shrugged and laughed again. "We'll be back long before we're missed."

"Aye, and what if we meet someone up here?" Dagg asked him. "Then we'll catch a storm for sure."

"We won't," Jan told him. "With the rain so near, they'll all be under hill."

A great thorn thicket sprawled across their path. They began skirting it.

"But what about gryphons?" Dagg added uneasily. "They're bigger than unicorns." The yellow colt had dropped his voice. He crowded up against Jan's flank.

Jan shook him off. "Wingcats only hunt the east side of the Vale. We're in the west. And my father the prince lives here—they'd never dare."

Dagg looked dubious.

Jan snorted and sprang away. "Know what I'd do if I ever saw a gryphon?" The prince's son reared, pawing the air. "I'd give it such a blow, it'd never rise again! I'd . . ."

Then all at once he caught sight of something: motion, a shape. Choking off his words, he dropped to all fours and gazed ahead through the thick of the trees. The hillcrest lay not far upslope. They had nearly rounded the thorns. When Dagg started to speak, Jan shushed him with a hiss.

"What is it?" breathed Dagg.

Jan shook his head. He edged forward, peering. All he could discern through the undergrowth was a vague form, some animal. It was large and stood in shadow among the trees. A cold sensation touched Jan's breast. Neither he nor any colt he knew had ever seen a gryphon, but the singers spoke of great hawk beaks and wings, talons, cat's eyes, and hind limbs like those of the saber-toothed pards that roamed the Plain.

Dagg pressed against him, making him jump. "Can you make it out?"

Jan shook his head again and crept closer, putting his hooves down soundlessly. With so many trees blocking his view, he still could not determine any outline he recognized, and strained instead for a glimpse of vivid green and gold—the colors of a tercel, a gryphon male—or of blue and tawny—a formel.

The creature on the hillside shifted its stance. Jan froze and felt Dagg beside him flinch. Jan felt the stinging gnats at his flank again and did not swat. They waited long seconds. He edged his eye slowly around a treebole and caught a clear view of the hillcrest at last through a gap in the trees.

It was . . . another unicorn. Only that. Another unicorn. Jan snapped his teeth together and could have kicked. Of course it would be one of his own people. Of course! He had forgotten the lookouts. This crest commanded a view of the east. The prince must have ordered watches to scan the stormwind, because it was spring now. Gryphons never came in winter. He should have remembered that. Jan stood absolutely still.

Dagg nudged him urgently. "What's there?" he whispered. "Can you see it now?"

"One of ours," Jan muttered. "My father's . . . oh, it's Tek."

He stopped again, recognizing the other suddenly, for the lookout had stepped from the shadows into the sun. She was not the solid or dapple or roan of other unicorns, but paint: pale rose splashed with great, irregular blots of black.

"What, the healer's daughter?" Dagg was asking, his voice beginning to rise as though he no longer cared whether they were discovered or not. "We're done for storming then."

"Hist," Jan told him, eyeing the lookout still.

She was a strange one, so he had heard. He hardly knew her. A fine warrior, all agreed, but very aloof and always alone—just like her mother, Jah-lila, who was the healer's mate but did not live among the herd. The wild mare who lived apart, outside the Vale. Jah-lila the midwife, the magicker.

Jan eyed the young paint warrior Tek through the trees; and as he did so, a part of his mind that he usually kept tightly guarded, opened— and a plan came to him, insinuating itself into his thought like swift, smooth coils. Jan felt his pulse quicken and his dark eyes spark.

"Hist," he said again to Dagg. "Let's test this lookout's skill." He shouldered the other back into the shadow of the trees. "I have a game."

☙

Jan kept his voice beneath a murmur and whispered the whole of his plan in two sentences. Then he and Dagg parted, and Jan lost sight of the dapple colt among the firs. Quickly, quietly, he himself circled back to the lookout knoll. Peering from behind a bit of ledge and scrub, he caught sight of Tek again. She stood facing away from him, her head turning slowly as she scanned the wall of cloud rolling in from the southeast. Jan waited.

And presently he heard a noise downslope. Tek's ears swiveled, pricked, but she did not turn. Jan watched intently, but as the sound died Tek's ears turned forward again. She scanned the sky. Jan breathed lightly, one breath, two; he held his breath. Then the noise came again, closer, clearer this time. Tek's ears snapped around. Jan champed his teeth. But again the sound ceased and quiet followed. The prince's son settled himself to wait.

The sound came for a third time, suddenly, much nearer, a low, throaty mewling such as the storytellers said gryphon hatchlings made. Jan found himself tense and shivering; his skin twitched. How real it sounded—Dagg was the best mimic of all the uninitiated foals. Tek's head now had whipped around, her frame gone rigid. A rustling started in the thorn thicket. Jan had to duck his chin to keep from nickering. The half-grown mare on the lookout knoll stood head up, legs stiff.

Silence. Jan saw Tek's green eyes searching the brush. She touched the ground, pawing it gently, her eyes narrowed and her nostrils flared. Jan heard more gryphon cries downslope—just exactly as they sounded in the lays. Tek's forehoof dug into the earth. He edged closer, keeping himself concealed. The young warrior's movements fascinated him.

He heard Dagg rustling in the thickets again, and saw Tek bowing her head to polish the tip of her skewer-sharp horn deftly against one forehoof. He had seen half-growns as well as the full-grown warriors doing that before battle. Then suddenly a sharp yell, like that of a wounded wingcat, rang out, and the sound of bushes crashing. Jan could almost believe it was a real gryphon blundering downslope. Tek sprang away, into the trees, so swift Jan almost lost her in a blink, for she ran silent, and gave no warning cry.

Jan shook himself. He felt elated—it had worked! Satisfaction slithered through him as he emerged from the trees and mounted the lookout knoll. He heard Dagg circling the crest of the ridge, giving cries now like an injured tercel, now like an angry formel. No sound came from Tek, and the prince's son wondered if his friend was even aware yet of her pursuit. He hoped so. He needed the lookout kept away long enough for him to watch the storm.

Jan stood on the crest of the knoll. The clouds before him were sweeping in fast. He felt the cool, muggy air beginning to lift, a faint breeze teasing along his back. It grew stronger suddenly, blew, smelling of rain. The thunderheads rolled, black foaming waves that scudded toward the sun. Unseen lightning illumined them in glimmers, like mosslight glimpsed beyond cavern bends.

Thunder sounded in a low growling that crashed all at once like a hillside falling. Jan felt the concussions against his body, and threw back his head to let the thick, cold, wet wind buffet him. He watched the shadow of the storm travel over the Pan Woods below him till a bank of cloud extinguished the sun. The world went gray. Birdfoot lightning gripped the sky.

The clouds loomed high, almost above him, over the Vale. As he gazed up into their wild, dark roiling, it seemed to Jan he could see— almost see—*something*. The sweep of them was like stars turning, like billowing grass, like mighty flocks of birds wheeling, like unicorns dancing, like . . . *like*. . . . He could not say what it was like. He only knew that when he gazed at the storm and lost himself, feeling the whirling turbulence of its power, his heart rose, carried away, soaring, and all the world rode on his brow.

Below him, a few lengths down the slope, Jan heard a whinny from Dagg suddenly and knew that his friend was caught. Above the muting of the wind, Jan heard Dagg's shouts of laughter, his protestations, and now Tek's voice, stinging with anger. Jan snorted and shook his head, only half listening. A dark exhilaration still fired his blood as he watched the dance of stormclouds swallow up the sky.

A pair of hunting eagles, huge ones, dipped out of the clouds far in the distance over the Pan Woods. They were in his sight for only a moment, stooping swiftly into the cover of the trees. He caught only the poise of their wings crooked for the dive and their size, great enough to carry off a young pan between them.

Just before they reached the trees, a blaze of lightning flashed. The deep green of the foliage reflected off their tawny bodies for an instant, turning the near one greenish, the far one almost blue. They plunged into the forest then. Jan lost them amid the canopy of trees.

Almost at the same moment, the sound of breaking brush distracted him. He turned in time to see Tek shoving Dagg out of the trees into the clearing of the knoll. Dagg was laughing so hard he staggered. The half-grown mare clamped the nape of his neck in her teeth and hauled him back as he made halfheartedly to bolt. She stood taller than either he or Jan, and had been initiated a full two years ago. Her young beard was already silky on her chin.

"Gryphons—save me!" shouted Dagg, struggling some, but laughing harder. "I told you it wasn't my game. Ouch! Not so hard—it was Jan's. The whole of it was Jan's."

"I know that very well, Dagg son-of-Tas," replied his captor through clenched teeth. She released him, and Dagg collapsed to the carpet of fir needles at the wood's edge. He rolled there, hooting. "I have heard of the games you two are so fond of." She turned now toward Jan. "And you, prince-son. By Korr, *you* at least should know better."

Jan tossed his head, laughing in his teeth, and shrugged. His father—no, he would not think of Korr. The prince was far below, seeking shelter in the Vale from the coming rain, and Jan was free of him for a little while at least. Free. He sprang down from the lookout knoll and trotted to Dagg, eyeing the hairless patches on his friend's neck and flank.

"Are you hurt?"

Dagg groaned, laughing still. "Hale enough. She champs *hard*. By the Beard, Jan, you should have seen her when she realized I wasn't some storm-riding gryphon."

Dagg rolled his eyes, ears akimbo, nostrils flared, and tossed his head like one who had just trod upon a snake. Jan put his head down, helpless with mirth. He laughed until his legs felt weak.

"Both of you have borne yourselves like brainless foals," the young mare snapped. "You, Jan son-of-Korr, haven't you grace enough to speak when you're spoken to?" Jan ignored her. Her tone crackled. "I am talking to you."

She marked that, when the prince's son neither answered nor turned, by nipping him smartly on the shoulder. Jan jumped and wheeled. Disbelief, and a sudden odd heedlessness uncoiled in him. No one had ever set teeth to him, not in earnest, but his father. No one had ever dared. He felt the blood surging in his head. His ears grew hot.

"You champed me!" he cried.

Dagg on the ground had swallowed his grin.

"You set teeth to me."

"Aye, and I'll do so again the next time you ignore me. What have you to say for yourself?"

Jan stared at her. Not even a word of regret—the arrogance! The astonishment in him turned to rage. He'd let no one, not even the healer's daughter, treat him like a foal. He plunged at her, his head down, before he was even aware what he was doing—perhaps a slash across the flank would teach this half-grown better manners. Tek countered with her own horn, fencing him expertly, and threw him off with a sharp rap on the head.

Jan staggered, startled. He had always been the victor, the easy best in the mock battles among the uninitiated colts. Now—first bitten, then baited, then parried in three blows. Jan regained his footing and stood stunned, humiliated. A cold little voice in the back of his mind teased and taunted him, but he shoved it away, shoved everything away. His breath was coming hard between clenched teeth. Tek had not fallen back even a step.

Dimly, he came aware that Dagg beside him was speaking. "Jan. Hear me. She's half-grown." His friend started to rise. "Colts don't spar with warriors. List, come on, let's . . ."

Jan ignored him, flattening his ears. He was not a colt, not just *any* colt. He was the son of the prince of the unicorns, and he would not be beaten off a second time. Tek snorted, shifting her stance. She squared to meet him. He lowered his head, gathering his legs.

"Enough!"

The word rolled hard and deep above the rising wind. Jan pulled up, startled, spinning around. Tek glanced past him, and he glimpsed her falling back now in surprise. The prince of the unicorns stood before them on the lookout knoll, black against the grayness of the storm. Lightning clashed, throwing a blue sheen across him. Jan flinched at the suddenness, feeling his rash temper abruptly vanish, like a snake into a hole. He gazed uneasily into his father's dark and angry eyes.

"Leave off these foals' games," ordered the prince. "You, Dagg, son of my shoulder-friend, off home with you—at once."

Jan felt his friend beside him scrambling to his feet. Dagg bowed hastily to the prince, then wheeled and was gone. His hoofbeats on the slope grew faint.

"You, Tek, healer's daughter, begone as well."

"Prince," Tek started, but he shook his head.

"Rest sure, young mare, I put no blame on you in this."

"Korr, prince," she said, "I am on lookout. . . ."

He tossed his head then. "Never mind. No gryphons will be flying once the rain comes. Now off, or you will be soaked."

Tek bowed her long neck to the prince, then wheeled and bounded away like a lithe deer through the trees. Korr waited until the gusting wind had swept the sound of her heels away.

"Foal!" he burst out then, and Jan flinched beneath his father's rebuff. "Witless thing! Have I not expressly forbidden any colts so high on the slopes, and warned all against interfering with the lookouts?"

Jan eyed his hooves and mumbled assent.

"Can you not understand gryphons may slip into these woods under cover of cloud in two bats of an eye? A moment's distraction . . ." He broke off with a strangled snort.

Jan hung his head. His father spoke the truth; he remembered the hunting eagles, how swiftly they had fallen from cloudbottom to treetops while Dagg had been baiting Tek. What if, rather than hawks, there had come wingcats instead? Jan picked at the turf with his hoof.

"It was just a game," he murmured, more to himself than to Korr. "We meant no harm."

"Your *games*," muttered Korr. "But enough."

The black prince launched down from the lookout knoll and gave his son a shove to turn him.

"Be grateful this storm's brought no gryphons, young princeling, or you might well have made feast-flesh for some formel's hatchlings—or Tek might, or Dagg. Hie now! Get you home."

Gryphons

3

Jan sprang down the slope, his pace abruptly quickened by a few hard nips on the flank from his father. He galloped blindly, careless of the hillside's steepness, reckless where he set his hooves. The prince ran beside him, herding him away from the sheer drops, the loose rock shelves.

Jan ducked, dodging through the trees. He wished he could fly, fly away and outpace his father. His breast was tight, his eyes stinging. All he had wanted to do was watch the storm. Nothing, no ill would have come of it if it had not been for Tek. Arrogant half-grown! Jan wished the pied mare bad footing.

How he hated the young warriors, half-grown, already initiated—hated, yet in the same breath envied them. He was weary to death of colts' games and foals' playing, and longed to the center of his bones to be allowed to sharpen his hooves and horn and join the Ring of Warriors. *Why* had Korr held him back from Pilgrimage last year, despite his pleading?

Deep down, he knew. And thinking of it brought a bitter taste into his mouth. There was in his nature a grievous fault. He could never do as he was told, as others did. He always plunged ahead without thinking, forgetting the Law—or deliberately breaking it. He was a vexation to everyone, a bitter disappointment to Korr, and secretly he wondered if he would ever learn to bear himself as befitted the prince's son.

Jan plunged down the steep hillside. A stitch had grown between his ribs. It ached like a wound. He and his father left the wooded slope for the rolling meadow of the valley floor. The sky above was wholly dark. Jan felt a great drop splash against his back, soaking into the long hairs of his winter coat. Another drop struck him, and then two more.

The air was thick suddenly with falling water. He heard Korr snorting in disgust.

They headed across the open meadow toward their cave halfway up the near slope of the Vale. Korr sprang onto the rock ledge before the cave mouth, Jan scrambling up behind. The entrance to the grotto was narrow. In the gloom beyond, Jan saw his mother, Ses, cream colored with a mane as amber as autumn grass. She was heavy in foal.

Korr moved two steps into the cave, tossing his head, and the water slung from his long, jet mane. Jan crowded in behind, out of the rain, though he knew by his father's abrupt, forceful movements that he was angry still. The prince of the unicorns shook himself, and Jan ducked, but he could not avoid the spray short of retreating into the rain again. His mother stood back out of range.

"A wet day for bathing," she laughed when Korr was done. "How clement of the weather to soak you both so handsomely." Her light, sure tone seemed to mollify her mate a little. "Jan, come out of the door now; you're wet enough. Korr, let him by."

Jan saw his father glance over one shoulder at him. The prince advanced a pace, no more, cleaning the muck from between the toes of his hooves with his horn. "I found him up on the high slopes again," he said shortly, "near the lookout knoll."

Jan saw his mother's eye grow rueful for a moment, but then she smiled. "But he always goes up there. You know that. He always has."

"It's forbidden," his father snapped. "And not just to Jan—to all the colts. It's too dangerous, especially when the storm's from the southeast." Korr gave a snort. "He had Dagg with him. Bringing others into his Ringbreaking."

His father started on another hoof. Jan had to shrink past him along the wall. He saw his mother glance at him, then felt a few strokes of her rough, dry tongue against his neck, pressing out the damp. He hadn't dared to shake off yet, and now his mother's gentle tolerance was suddenly more than he could bear. He broke from her, from Korr, and clattered away from both of them, deeper into the cave.

Around the bend at the back of the hollow, a little pool of earthwater lay, still as stone, reflecting the dim light rounding the corner. Pale toadstools and lichens scattered the walls and shore, casting faint illuminations. Jan threw himself down on the pebbly bank and lay there wet and miserable. Staring at nothing, he listened to the voices of his sire and dam.

"If that were all," his father's deep voice said, "if that were all, I might let it pass. But Ses, the colt has no sense. He and Dagg weren't on the ridge just to watch the storm."

Jan heard a sigh. "More games?"

Silence a moment. Korr must have nodded. "They were baiting the lookout, drawing her away with gryphon cries. What am I to do with him? That's willful trespass . . ."

"Be patient with him," the prince's mate was saying. Then, softer, "He was born under a dark moon."

Jan dropped his head to the bank and felt his heart clench shut like teeth. He wished she wouldn't defend him—he wished there weren't the need. There was the sound of someone shifting. Jan imagined his mother lying down beside her mate, helping to sponge the rest of the moisture from his coat.

"He's moody, high-spirited."

"Unruly," the prince returned. "A hothead."

"Like you."

"Love, he's not a colt anymore!" Jan flinched at the force of his father's anger.

"He is until you let him join the initiates." His mother's sudden vehemence surprised him. "How often has he begged you to let him go on Pilgrimage?"

Jan heard his father's snort. "How can I, now? Do you think he'd make a warrior? He's nearly half-grown, and still he acts like a spoiled weanling. That wildness . . ." Jan hardly caught the last. What had his father said: *"frightens me"*? No, he could not have heard it right.

"Just let him prove himself," his mother murmured. "More than anything, he wants to prove himself."

Their voices grew softer, dropping into quiet unintelligibility beneath the drumming of the rain. Jan stretched his forelegs in front of him, laying his head along their length. Born under a dark moon. *Dark moon,* she'd said. He stared off into the darkness, with its wan lichenlight, brooding.

❧

He must have dozed, for the next thing he knew was that the grotto had grown a little lighter, and the sound of the rain had stopped. He lifted his head from his knees, blinking and feeling stiff from sleep. He had dreamed something—he was aware of that, but could not remember what. He never remembered his dreams. Jan plucked a pale toadstool from the shore and ground its musty, woody flesh across his teeth, trying to remember. From the light reaching him around the bend, he guessed it must be midafternoon.

The dream had been something about the water, or something in the water. Something swimming in the lichenlight, like a longfish, or an eel. Had it stood up before him, the white thing in the water? Swaying and flickering like . . . like . . . he could not say what. The image faded from him even as he strained for it. But he remembered he had shuddered, squirming as he looked at it, unable to turn away. And it had spoken his truename: Aljan, *dark moon.*

When he had been very young, scarcely weaned, he had begun to have such dreams: dreams of snakes and stinging worms that woke him struggling, screaming night after night, till others of the herd began to mutter that the prince's son must be accursed. Korr, in desperation, had sent for the healer's mate, Tek's mother, Jah-lila, to come and steal away Jan's dreams.

He had been so little then, it had been so long ago, and he had not seen the wild mare since. She rarely ever came into the Vale, and then always secretly, silently, like a shadow barely glimpsed; and she was gone again in an hour, about whatever business a magicker's business might be, of which she never spoke. He remembered only dimly that time she had come to him, while his parents had stood back silent, troubled, out of the way. Dark rose in color, Jah-lila had knelt, lying down beside him, gazing into and through him with her black-green eyes.

"Ho, little hotblood," she had murmured. "Such a fighter, such a dreamer! Eat this now, and breathe in this. Sleep . . . *dreamless* . . . sleep."

She had given him bitter herbs to eat and chewed sweet herbs herself, breathed upon him and let him breathe her breath. He had slept then, at once, deep and restfully. And since that time he had never been able to remember his dreams.

Jan finished the last of the woody toadstool and sipped from the dark cave pool beside him. The water was cool, tasteless. He watched the ripples widen and still. When the surface grew eye-smooth again, the lichens reflected there like a scatter of rose and pale blue stars. From the outer chamber, he heard his mother murmuring, as she had used to do for him, a lullaby to her unborn foal:

> *"Hist, my lambling, quiet now,*
> *Lest a waiting wingcat hear*
> *With ears up-pricked and eyes aglow—*
> *Hush! Let him not find you, little pan.*
> *Still your cry, lie soft, and sleep."*

Jan felt himself just slipping into sleep again. He clicked his teeth, stifling a yawn, when all at once something caught his eye. He blinked.

The surface of the cave pool beside him was dancing. The images of the lichens trembled there. Sounds like something scraping, then sliding reached his ears. The pebbles beneath him shifted and seethed. There came a sudden rumbling roar in which the whole cave shuddered. Chips of stone from the ceiling fell. Dust rose in the air like winter fog.

He heard his mother whinnying, his father snorting, choking on dust. Jan scrambled to his legs and dashed into the forepart of the grotto. A great rock shard from overhead smashed to the floor barely a pace from him. He shied and, as he did so, glimpsed Ses dodging out the cave's entrance into the light.

He sprang to follow, then stopped himself in a sudden panic. Where was Korr? Jan wheeled, casting about him through the dimness, through the dark, crying his father's name. Then he heard the prince's deep voice, "Go on!" and felt Korr's massive frame shouldering him through the cave mouth into the outside air.

Jan plunged through a rain of earth. Stones, some large as skulls, crashed with the rest. The rock ledge ahead was nearly buried. He saw his mother moving heavily down the muddy, sliding slope to solid ground on the valley floor below.

Jan felt a great concussion and wheeled to see Korr shying from a boulder's path. It smashed to fragments. Jan felt a splinter dig into the flesh of his thigh. He stumbled, the soft earth sliding beneath his hooves. Muddy soil and pebbles pelted him as he struggled to rise—then his father's teeth closed over the nape of his neck, half dragging, half hauling him out of the muck.

Jan's legs gave beneath him as he reached the valley floor. The pain in his injured leg was fierce. Ses was standing well back, out of the path of the slide, and he was aware, dimly, of other unicorns dashing from their caves, crying out in consternation, galloping toward them over meadow and slope. Jan tore his gaze back to the grotto.

He saw the last of the rain-softened earth cascading down the slope, the broken stone and fragments of the great, smashed boulder . . . and then, above that, a flash of green, dusty blue, and gold. Two gryphons, a mated pair, perched on an outcropping above the cave. With an uprooted sapling, they levered root and soil, sending it surging down the hillside.

Gryphons. Jan felt cold talons seize his heart. He remembered the flash of color, the two wingèd forms he had glimpsed from the lookout. Not eagles, *gryphons*—who had slipped into the Pan Woods beneath his very gaze.

Jan heard his father trumpeting a war cry. Then a second cry sounded, joining Korr's. Turning, Jan saw Dagg's father, Tas. Other battle yells rose on the air: stallions trumpeting full and deep and wild, high clarions from the mares. Jan saw the wingcats dropping their lever, beginning to scramble up the hillside as Korr and a half-dozen others charged the slope.

Jan staggered to his feet, moving to join them, but Ses swung in front of him, barring his path. "No, Jan," she told him. "Let the warriors have it."

He tried to dodge her, but his bad leg made him slow. She caught him by the nape of the neck.

"Let go," he cried. "They made to trap us. They wanted to kill Korr!"

He struggled furiously. His mother's strong, square teeth only clasped tighter. "No," she panted. "You're not a warrior."

"But I will be," Jan shouted, fighting harder. "This spring I'll be initiated. . . ."

"Not *yet*," Ses answered. His bad leg gave as she forced him to the ground and stood over him. Jan clenched his teeth, his ears burning with wrath. There was nothing he could do.

He watched the hillside. The two gryphons had reached the crest of the unwooded slope. Now they reared upon their hind limbs, beating their wings, but the draggled pinions seemed unable to get a purchase on the air. Jan felt his blood quicken as he realized the warriors would catch them.

The larger gryphon, the formel, launched into the air and hovered unsteadily, her blue wings laboring. Her mate's wings, still streaked with mud, seemed as yet too heavy to fly. With a shout, the prince of the unicorns charged and drove his horn into the tercel's side.

Cat snarl rising to a falcon's scream, the wingcat lashed back. Jan heard his mother's little snort of breath as the prince of the unicorns went down—but then he rolled and was up again in a moment, hammering the gryphon with his hooves.

The unicorn warriors ringed the tercel. Tas seized one talon; others stabbed at his great, green wings. The gryphon fought, raged, broke free of their circle at last and retreated, one pinion dragging. The formel stooped and feinted in the air above.

Jan saw the wounded tercel rise, his wingbeats ragged. He hovered, struggling, above the warriors' heads. Jan saw his father backing, his hindquarters bunched. Korr leapt, catching the wingcat in the belly. The tercel shrieked, wrenching away. The formel clutched him in her claws.

The unicorns watched their uneven flight, the gryphons staggering through the air toward the south. They trailed low over the ridges ringing the Vale. The tercel's wingbeats slowed suddenly, grew more erratic.

The formel labored to bear him up. They barely cleared the lookout knoll.

Then the wounded wingcat stiffened. His green-gold pinions thrashed, stretched taut. His body sagged in the formel's grasp and a long, hoarse scream rose from his mate; her wings beat strong and frantically. Jan could not discern whether she would not release him even then, or whether his talons still clutched her so tightly she could not pull free. Together they plunged into the trees beyond the ridge.

The unicorns were coming down the slope. Korr leaned against Tas, blood running down the prince's neck. He bled from a gash above one eye. Jan realized Ses no longer stood above him. He rose with difficulty and stood, three-legged, putting no weight on his injured leg.

"Where's the healer?" Jan heard Tas calling, as he and the prince reached the bottom of the hill. Ses went to Korr. Other unicorns were moving forward. They drifted around him. Jan alone stood still.

"No, it's a scratch," his father was saying, but the prince's voice was breathless, all thunder gone. Someone brushed past him, and Jan caught a glimpse of Teki, the healer, moving toward Korr. Fear, like a sea-jell, lay cold on Jan's breast.

He felt someone else slip up beside him. "Are you hale, Jan? Your leg's bleeding."

Jan shook his head, blinking hard, and did not turn.

Dagg seemed to take no notice. "By the Circle, I never thought I'd see a real one, a gryphon! I never thought they'd dare come here. And after the prince . . . !"

Jan drew in his breath and held it then, for he felt somehow he might begin to shake, or fall, if he so much as breathed. Ses and Tas were supporting Korr back upslope a little way, toward better light. Teki followed them, his distinctive white and black coloring catching the sun. The valley floor was slipping into shade.

". . . you go with them?" he heard Dagg saying. "The healer should look at you, too."

And suddenly Jan did not think he could bear to be near another living creature, even Dagg. He wheeled, bolting away from his friend, and struck out across the meadow toward the near wooded slope. He had no earthly notion of where he was going, but he had to be alone.

Outcast

4

Jan sprinted toward the wooded slopes, his thoughts in a roil. He felt the others were looking at him, as though his guilt somehow blazed visible. But more than that, he feared Korr knew. It was *his* fault gryphons had slipped into the Vale, his fault his father had been wounded.

How badly? Jan shoved the thought away and galloped harder as the floor of the valley turned upward. The splinter of stone in his thigh muscle gouged him, but the shame he felt stung him more. He was unworthy—he had always known. Unworthy of Korr or to be called the prince's heir. *Why* was he so different from others? He clenched his teeth against the tightness in his throat, and fled into the trees.

It was late afternoon. The clouds above had spent themselves and were pulling apart like wet seed tufts. Swatches of the yellow sky shone through. Jan climbed a little way, then rested, surveying the wood about him bleakly. Droplets glistened on the fir needles; the cedar bark was damp. The sun hung westering, and everything smelled clean.

His injured leg had begun to ache in earnest now. The thigh muscle felt strained. Jan nibbled at the wound, working the splinter free, then spat it out, tasting blood: It had cut his tongue. He climbed on. When he reached the lookout knoll, he found Tek standing there and halted, startled. She wheeled.

"You," she cried, her eyes bright, throat tense. "And what brings you back, prince's son—come to gaze on the sunset after the storm?"

Jan stood, hardly knowing what to say. "I came to be alone," he managed.

She studied him. "I saw what befell," she said. Her voice was husky. "From across the meadow—the gryphons. I'd just emerged; the others were all still under hill. I saw a form of green and gold, then one of

tawny blue come down the far hillside, dragging a great tree limb. They
began to lever up the rock and earth above your grotto. I gave a cry—I
don't think anyone heard—but I was too far away to join the warriors."

Jan gazed at her, but could think of nothing. "My father's
wounded."

Tek nodded. "My father was sent for."

Jan eyed his hooves. The breath caught in his throat. "It's my doing," he mumbled.

Tek threw up her head, eyes flashing. He thought at first it was with
anger. "You?" she cried, and he realized then it was with astonishment.
"*I* was the one posted lookout." Her voice grew tighter, almost choking.
She gasped between clenched teeth. "But I let myself be tricked away . . .
oh! Just like a foal not yet a warrior. Just like an uninitiated foal."

Jan started to interrupt. "No. I saw them from afar. I thought . . ."
But then he choked himself off, realizing what she had said. *Initiation.*
The spring rite of Pilgrimage lay less than a month off.

Each new year, as soon as the forage had sprung upon the Great
Grass Plain, the prince of the unicorns led a chosen band to the sacred
well of their race. A few of the band were warriors, acting as escorts;
the rest, initiates, those fillies and foals adjudged worthy of drinking
from the well. In doing so, they would cast off their childhood and join
the Ring of Warriors.

Jan and Dagg had hoped to join the Circle this season, together,
though Dagg was younger than the prince's son. Jan's parents had held
him back from Pilgrimage the spring before—it was not uncommon.
His mother had said gently that he needed another year of colt's play.
Korr had told him more curtly that his hot head needed to cool.

Jan felt a sinking in his chest. Korr would hold him back again—
the thought stung him more sharply than shame. He would be scorned,
thought of forever not as the prince's son, but as the young firebrand
who had let the gryphons in and was not fit to be made a warrior. And
he knew what became of those who never drank of the well in the sacred
rite of passage. He had heard the fate of Renegades in singers' tales.

They ceased to be unicorns. Banned from the herd, they saw their
horns rot to the skullbone and fall away, their heels lose their fringe of
feathery hair and their ears their tufted tassels. No fine, soft beards ever
sprouted along their chins. Their cloven hooves grew together, each into
a single toe: strange solid hooves that left round imprints in the dust.
Renegades grew old before their time, and died young.

Jan started suddenly, coming back to himself. He saw Tek's green
eyes on him from the lookout knoll.

"He'll hold me back," he blurted out. "My father will keep me from the rite again."

Tek's gaze had lost its hardness. She nodded a bare trace and said quietly, "Aye, princeling. I think he may."

Anguish welled in Jan. What could he do? Despair enveloped him and he felt himself sliding down its dark throat toward nothing. The prince would make no announcement. Nothing would be said at large— he would not be publicly disgraced.

But everyone would hear of it. His unworthiness would be revealed at last. It would be known—it would be known! Panic gripped him. Jan wheeled, clenching his teeth to keep from crying out, and bolted away into the trees. Tek called after him, but did not follow. Her shouts soon faded.

He found himself running along the ridge and plunged over the hillcrest down the wooded slope. He was on the far side now, the side that faced the Pan Woods. This was forbidden territory, even to warriors—but no matter. Better to wander the rest of his days in the goatling woods than to go back disgraced and face another year denied the Ring.

He halted suddenly and bowed his head, running the tip of his horn along the outer edge of each forehoof once, twice, a half-dozen times in short, unpracticed strokes. This, too, was forbidden. Colts were banned from sharpening their hooves and horns. By Law, only the warriors were allowed.

But he was an outcast now, a Renegade, and must be his own Law. And if the pans came upon him in the woods, he meant to draw their blood before they dragged him down. He ran on then, blindly, fleeing a great, looming fear he could not name. He wished the earth might open and swallow him.

Without warning the ground beneath him shifted, gave way suddenly, and he was plunging. Rain-soaked soil crumbled about his legs and he slid headlong, dropping abruptly, and landed with a jolt that knocked the breath from him. Something tumbled past his head, struck him a glancing blow behind the ear, then thudded softly to the dirt beside him. A stone.

The place was very dim; he could scarcely see. Straining for breath, he shook his head. It was exceedingly quiet. The fall of earth and rock had made almost no sound. He lay a few moments, his legs folded awkwardly beneath him, a little stunned, and not at all certain what had just happened.

His head cleared. His breath came back, and Jan was able to take in his surroundings. He lay on a heap of earth in the narrow opening of a cave, a mere crack in the hillside, very close and dark. Glancing up, he saw some of the roof overhanging the grotto's mouth must have collapsed when he stumbled across it. And a good thing, too, he realized with a start, or else in his blind gallop he might have run right off the cliff.

He picked himself up warily, still giddy with relief. None of his bones seemed to be broken. Only his bad leg hurt. He stood now half in, half out of the cave, and the sky behind him was brightening to flame. What rags of cloud were left were infused with red. A little of that light reflected off the lip of the entryway.

Jan peered ahead of him into the dimness, but could make out nothing. He listened, hearing nothing. The narrow space smelled old and goaty. But presently, his nostrils quivered as a new scent reached him, strange and musky—not one he recognized. Jan frowned, breathing deeper, and limped forward a few paces into the earthy darkness of the cave.

His eyes had grown accustomed now, and he discerned the uneven wall opposite the one near which he stood, the continuation of the grotto's crevice back into the rock. He started forward again—but halted suddenly. A large mound lay at the back of the cave, just before where the chamber narrowed to a crack too close and dark to see beyond.

The half-light from the outside had grown warmer, redder as the unseen sun dropped lower in the sky. Jan's vision improved: tawny fur and azure feathers. The musky odor swam in his head. At the back of the grotto, not five paces from him, lay some animal. . . .

His heart contracted, jerking him back. Jan recognized a gryphon curled upon its side, wings folded, limbs drawn against its body. Its head was turned to one side, beak tucked beneath one wing. Its eyes were closed.

Its furred and feathered side rose, fell softly with each breath. There was blood upon its feathers, its talons rust colored with blood. Its wings looked battered, its fur muddy and wet. It lay still and bedraggled, like a newly pipped hatchling, as though the earth itself had just given it birth.

The formel. Jan started backward again as he realized. This was the formel of the pair that had attacked them—but she was dead! She must be. He himself—they had all seen her plunge out of the sky beyond the lookout knoll, surely to her death? He wondered now, his thoughts spinning. Perhaps she had struggled free of her dead mate at the last moment. Perhaps the drop had not been so great as it had seemed.

All at once a new thought brought him up short: Even his father had been deceived. If Korr had so much as suspected one of the pair had survived, he would have sent warriors to comb the woods and hunt it down. Once again Jan's mind sprinted. If this wingcat were allowed to escape safe home, next storm she might return, bringing others of her kind, well assured how easily they might strike against the prince of the unicorns and live.

Jan eyed the sleeping formel. All thoughts of his self-made exile vanished; his coltish boasts to Dagg vanished as well. The wingcat was three times his size. Alone against her, he had no chance; but if he ran like wildfire, he might just have time to raise the alarm in the Vale and summon the warriors before dusk. Jan backed slowly toward the egress of the cave.

The sun must have moved very slightly in the sky. The light on the cave wall shifted. A ray of red sunlight eased across the gryphon's eye, and Jan felt himself go rigid. The formel stirred, sighing heavily, then coiled herself tighter in her napping ball. Jan in midstep waited, waited, *waited*. The wingcat did not stir again. Jan put his hoof down very carefully and raised the next.

"Jan!"

He started. The voice echoed so loud in the close, oppressive stillness that for a moment he could have sworn it had sounded just beside him.

"Jan!"

He realized then it was a long shout, coming from the outside. Someone was calling him from up the slope. The call came again, nearer this time: Dagg. Dagg had come looking for him. Jan stood frozen in the dusky dimness barely ten paces from the sleeping wingcat. He wished feverishly that his friend would hurry and pass on, give up the search, or else be still.

"Jan!"

This last shout was closer, louder, more insistent. He saw the formel's ears twitch once. Her cat's eye opened slowly, fixing on him— then snapped wide. He felt as if the air had vanished from his throat.

"Jan!"

Dagg's voice had grown impatient, anxious now. The wingcat started up. Jan shied and scrambled back from her, feeling his hindquarters come up hard against the wall. He stared at the gryphon. The gryphon stared at him.

"Come hunting, little princeling?" the gryphon said. "Found me out in my cave just as we found you out in yours, my mate and I."

The formel moved, leaning forward into the sunlight. Her pupils constricted into slits. Jan felt his heart galloping inside his ribs.

"Your father killed my mate not this hour past," she told him quietly, tentatively, cat-and-mouse. "Your father is a mighty warrior, is he not? Kilkeelahr was a mighty warrior as well, among my people, was my mate."

Jan was aware of the hard stone wall pressing his flank and side, of the sweat beneath the long hairs of his coat. Cold fear had begun to numb him.

"But he fell out of favor with the high clans," the formel murmured, singsong, seductively. "Fell out of favor, did my mate. But I dreamed a dream. A white salamander spoke to me. So I proposed this foray, to kill the black prince of the unicorns, and buy our way back into power with glory."

The light of dusk played across the colors of her eyes as she spoke, poured in and among them like water, making them gleam. Gazing into those eyes, Jan felt his mind slacken. It seemed he could see mountains, canyons, many gryphons in the formel's eye. Her voice took on a cutting edge. He hardly noticed.

"Why ever did you *itichi* come here? Northern plainsdwellers, asking no one's leave to settle. Our leaders have had enough of you; it will not be many years before all the clans are united and Isha grants our prayers for fair winds. Then we will come in a body and harry you out."

The light in the formel's eye shifted and spangled. Jan saw flocks of gryphons swooping and fighting, tearing each other's nests, pashing each other's eggs and carrying off one another's young—things such as he had never seen or heard in ballad or lay.

"Why do you trouble the demesnes of the gryphons? This was *our* land before you stole it."

Around the iris of each of her eyes circled a narrow band of gold: a thin, bright ring that went round and over, over and round. Jan felt his limbs melting away. There was a serpent in the gryphon's eye, he realized slowly, a snake and a hawk that danced and circled one another. The formel's voice lilted, drifting in and out of his thoughts.

"Your father escaped our plans and cut down my mate. This night the pans will feast on him—on me as well, they would have, had I not torn myself free among the trees. . . . But do not think you will escape *me,* little princeling."

The hawk snatched the snake in its talons. The serpent coiled about the falcon's feet and stung it in the throat. The falcon screamed, clutched at its prize and rose in the air, to carry the serpent, still writhing and stinging, away.

"I have a nest of hungry hatchlings. Do not think you will escape
me...."

"Jan!"

That other voice cut across his senses like a slap of cold sea-water.
Jan started, coming to himself. The cave stood narrow and solid about
him. The wingcat crouched, eyeing him, and Dagg was calling him from
somewhere up the slope.

He heard the formel clucking in frustration as she saw him wake.
Only then did he realize what she had been doing—mesmerizing him
while she crept close enough to spring. The distance between them had
halved. Jan saw the formel's pupils dilate, ruby colored in the flame-
colored sunset. She sprang.

Jan dodged, his bad leg giving under him, and his knees struck the
stone floor of the cave. The gryphon shrilled as she missed her strike,
coming up hard against the wall. The narrow grotto echoed with her
cry. The lunge had taken her past him. Jan skittered to his feet and spun
around, vaulting over the staggered gryphon. With a surge of speed he
never knew he had, Jan sprinted for the egress of the cave.

Battle

5

Jan bolted for the mouth of the cave, clambering over the heap of fallen earth, and suddenly stopped short. There was nowhere to flee. The ground a pace ahead of him dropped away in a sheer precipice. He caught a flash of green and gold among the tops of the trees below: the dead tercel.

Then he heard a rush in the cave behind him and sprang hard to one side just as the beak of the formel snapped empty air. A narrow goat trail appeared from nowhere, threading the cliffside before him. Jan dashed along it. The gryphon shrieked, scrambling after him, her wings thrashing. He heard her talons scathing the soft, wet rock.

"Jan!"

The cry rang out from the slope above. He saw Dagg standing near the lookout knoll.

"Fly!" Jan shouted. "Dagg, fly!"

Behind him the gryphon screamed and rose into the air. Dagg stood staring, too astonished to move. The goat trail had vanished. Jan threw himself up the steep, rocky slope, the ground crumbling and sliding beneath his hooves. His injured leg wobbled like a dead tree limb.

"Shy!" shouted Dagg.

Jan shied, stumbled, and fell to one side, too late. The formel's talons dug into his shoulders. Jan thrashed wildly. He heard Dagg crying out—alarm or battle yell, he could not tell—as the wingcat hoisted Jan aloft. They hovered just below the hillcrest, almost eye to eye with Dagg.

Jan kicked and twisted, and felt one heel strike home. He kicked again, harder—again. The formel shrieked and snarled, holding him away from her. Then Dagg was charging, rearing, lashing out with his forehooves. The formel pulled back from the hillside, straining to rise. Jan felt dizzied, as though he had been dancing in circles. His vitals turned. The world below him was sinking, sinking by hoofspans away. Beneath, Dagg yelled, flailing desperately, but the formel had managed to rise beyond his range. Her wings heaved and struggled. Jan's senses swam. He knew beyond all hope that he was lost.

Then another unicorn burst from the trees. She sprang past Dagg, her wild, ringing battle yell snapping Jan back to himself. Tek lunged at the gryphon with head down, her horn aimed. Jan felt the formel tense and twist away as the skewer grazed her side. She writhed.

Tek came to earth. She lost her footing and went down. Dagg charged and leapt, missed, leapt again. Jan glimpsed his friend's unsharpened colt's horn draw blood from the formel's flank. She stamped him hard across the forehead with her lion's paw. Dagg fell to earth, rolling, then staggered to his feet, shaking his head.

Jan twisted in the gryphon's grasp, throwing his head back, trying to bring his own horn into play. He felt it glance across her throat. She screamed again, grappling with his horn, holding him with only one claw now. Her talons grated against his shoulder blades.

Jan felt his head wrenched painfully, and at that moment nearly slipped from her grasp. They fell a few feet in the air, the gryphon trying again to seize him. Jan felt his heels brush the crest of the hill. Tek came charging up the slope and wounded the formel in the shoulder, from behind.

The wingcat staggered in the air, whirling to bat Tek's horn away. Jan pitched forward. His knees struck earth. The gryphon's weight came down and knocked the breath from him. He could not gather his legs beneath him.

"Run!" shouted Tek. At first Jan thought she was talking to him. Then he saw Dagg before him on the hillcrest, blinking at the blood from a long scratch on his forehead. "Away. Give the alarm," Tek was calling. "Go!"

She reared and brought her forehooves down on the fallen gryphon, but was driven back by the great, thrashing wings.

"You're too small to aid me here. Fetch help!" cried Tek. She whirled on Dagg and struck him across the flank with the flat of her horn. "Haste, away!"

Dagg bounded over the hillcrest, shouting the alarm.

The wingcat rose to her hind legs and scrambled to turn. Jan felt himself clutched again; she dragged him with her. As she and Tek faced each other now, the formel began backing away. Tek pursued her, slowly, over the brow of the hill. The young warrior's head was down, her horn ready. The gryphon held Jan between herself and Tek.

The formel edged backward through the trees. Jan caught a glimpse of open space behind. The Vale spread out below them. Dagg's distant cries told him his friend had nearly reached the valley floor. As the gryphon edged toward the end of the trees, Tek feinted and sidled, seeking to drive her back into the wood. But the wingcat screamed, snapping and holding her ground.

The slope opened treeless behind them. Jan felt the formel spring backward once, twice. He was dragged along—and they were airborne again. Jan struggled furiously, for if she got him away from the ground this time, he knew he was lost.

The formel's wings caught an updraft, beating hard. Tek sprang from the hillside, seeming to fly herself for a moment. Jan still thrashed in the gryphon's grasp, but could not break loose. Tek passed beneath them—too low, and cold anguish filled Jan as he realized she had missed her lunge.

Then the wingcat lurched downward suddenly, losing her hold. Her talons tore across his shoulders. He slid free and dropped to the rocky slope. Jan bolted to his feet, wheeling about, and saw Tek skidding downhill with the gryphon's tail caught fast in her teeth.

Tek scrambled to brace herself. She turned, her forelegs splayed, weight thrown back on her hindquarters like a wolf cub playing tug-at-bone. Jan saw her head shaken from side to side, the sinews of her long neck straining, her forehooves lifted from the mountainside as the wingcat fought to flee.

Abruptly, the formel faced about, tearing herself loose. The half-grown mare ducked and dodged. The gryphon struck at her with beak and talons. Eyes half shut against the buffeting of those massive, blue-gold wings, Tek feinted clumsily twice, three times with her horn, but missed each time. Jan saw lines of blood against the pale rose of her neck and shoulders.

He yelled, bounding downslope, and sprang between them. Rearing, he struck the gryphon with hoof and horn. Anger welled in him. Why wouldn't Tek fight? She merely stood, her head bowed, backing slowly downslope while the relentless formel boxed and buffeted her. Jan drove the gryphon back.

"No!" Tek shouted furiously, and shouldered him roughly aside. She snatched the formel in her teeth again, by the wing this time, dragging her forward, past Jan and farther downslope. Below, behind them in the Vale, Jan heard Dagg's alarm cry taken up by other voices.

And he understood then, suddenly. It was a trap, a game. Tek was baiting the gryphon, holding her until the warriors arrived. Jan bounded after the pair of them. If Tek would drag, then he would drive.

He reared and fell on the formel's furred and feathered shoulders. She wheeled, freeing herself from Tek, and struck at him with her great, hooked beak. Jan fell back, feinting at her. He had seen young warriors do that when they sparred.

"Stay back!" Tek shouted. Jan circled downslope, drawing the gryphon after him, toward Tek. "You're too small. You're not a warrior," she cried. "Get behind me. Get back!"

She interposed herself between him and the gryphon. Her backward stepping forced him farther downhill. Too enraged to think of escape, the wingcat lunged after them, screaming and snapping. In the distance behind, he was aware of war cries, the drumming of hooves upon the slope.

"Let me by; let me fight," Jan yelled at Tek. He dodged, trying to slip past her. Tek sidled and kicked at him one-footed to keep him behind.

"You haven't the skill," she snapped, parrying a feint from the formel's claw. She kept herself squarely between the gryphon and Jan. "If she catches you again, she'll carry you off. She can't lift me—stand back! You're in my way. Keep b. . . ."

Her words bit off suddenly. Jan saw a stone skid from under the young mare's heel. She sprawled sideways, head up, her throat exposed. The formel's beak darted, and Jan cried out, vaulting forward before he could even think. He was aware of yelling, keening some terrible war chant.

And suddenly, unicorns, others of his people were surging around him. He glimpsed Tas snorting and plunging, and Leerah his mate. Tek had found her feet again and was fighting like a hillcat. The formel was a fury of screams and talons. Jan saw Dagg charging amid the fray, tearing at the gryphon's wings.

Then someone was rearing, fighting beside him—massy and powerful, blacker than storm. His mighty voice thundered, "Alma, great Alma! Stand at my shoulder, O Mother-of-all!" Other warriors took up the cry. The formel shrilled. The sky above spanned amber and amethyst. The sun in the west was fire.

Jan saw his father rise to stand against the sky, a poultice of chewed medicine wort above his eye now beginning to flake and fall away. A gash. It was only a gash! Jan felt relief flooding his limbs. Korr glanced at him, and Jan saw a gleam he had never seen there before.

His heart lifted, soaring. His aching limbs felt suddenly wondrously strong. Pride, pride lit his sire's eye! He let go a war chant, sang wild and high. He was redeemed. It made him giddy. A deeper trumpet sounded from the prince of the unicorns.

Then it was over, all at once, too suddenly. Jan realized dizzily the fight was done. He came to a halt, and let the careening world around him steady. Unicorns ringed the fallen formel. Fur and feathers lay on the ground.

Dagg stood across from Jan, panting and grinning. His father nearby him pawed the earth gently with one forehoof. Beside him Leerah, pale with dark red dapples, nudged the dead formel with her horn. Tas bent to clean the blood from a nick in his mate's neck.

Jan shook his head and snorted. The fire in his blood had not yet stilled. Tek stood two paces from him, putting no weight on her near foreleg. On the others, Jan saw only a few feather cuts and bruises, a slash or two. He was astonished how unscathed they all were. He ached to the very bone.

Jan turned then to look at his father. The look of approval had not faded from Korr's eye. "Have I not always said," the prince was saying at large, "what a clever colt I sired—to spot the gryphon that got away when none of the rest of us saw? A fighter, too."

The warriors snorted, stamping their assent. Jan's ears burned. Korr was deceived. The prince knew only half the truth. But at that moment, Jan would not have enlightened his sire for all the world. He shook himself. And, if he had not entirely earned his father's goodwill, he was resolved to do so faithfully from this day forward. No more Lawbreaking. He swore it.

More quietly, his father was asking him now, "Are you hale?"

Jan nodded. "Aye." His voice was hoarse from yelling. "And you?"

The prince nodded. "I'll mend. Come, then." He turned, and Jan went beside him. "Teki the healer should see to those cuts."

Jan felt a throbbing in his wounded shoulders then. His side felt bruised. His hurt leg bore his weight only unsteadily. Slowly, he and his father started down the slope. Below them, on the valley floor, Jan saw others waiting. His pale dam, Ses, her round belly heavy and ripe, stood among them.

Glancing back over his shoulder once—he realized then how much his shoulders hurt at the slightest move—Jan saw Tek coming carefully, three-footed, down the slope, flanked by Tas and Dagg. Upslope, he caught sight of Leerah and the rest of the warriors lifting the dead formel onto their shoulders to bear up the hillside and cast over the cliff.

The Lay of the Unicorns
❧6❧

Each month the unicorns gathered at dusk to dance in a Circle under the full, dusky moon. They were the only race they knew of that did so. For when Alma made the world, she fashioned all the other creatures first, out of earth, wind, water, and air—then invited them to dance. But the pans turned wordless away from her, and the gryphons flew to find mountains to nest in, and the red dragons burrowed deep into the Smoking Hills, and the wyverns laughed.

So Alma created the unicorns after her own shape: sleek-bodied and long-limbed for swift running, wild-hearted and hot-blooded to make them brave warriors. Then she took from the cycling moon some of its shining stuff to fashion their hooves and horns and make them dancers. So the last-born and best-beloved of Alma called themselves also the moon's children, and each month danced the ringdance under the round, rising moon.

Equinox fell on the night of the full moon that spring. Jan stretched out beneath its pale, smoke light falling from among a river of stars. The ground beneath him was springy soft and thawing with the year. His shaggy winter coat, not yet begun to shed, kept out the coolness. He stretched his limbs among the fine shoots of new grass that threaded amid the old.

Lifting his head from his knees, he gazed at the other unicorns assembled in the wide, rough Circle on the valley floor. Some were standing lazily, three-footed, regaining their breath. Others bowed their heads to nibble the new grass. Murmurs of talk and nickers of laughter drifted on the still night air. The moon had risen a quarter of the way toward its zenith, and the dancing was over now.

Jan lay inside the Circle with the other initiates. He gave Dagg beside him a nudge with his hind heel, murmuring, "Wake," for on the low rise jutting near them at the Circle's heart, Khraa the king had gotten to his feet. The tales were about to start.

Jan's grandsire was old and did not seem it. Strong-built like his heir, but leaner, Khraa stood upon the ledge, pale gray as cloudcover, with a coal-dark mane and hooves. He was the king, and would have ruled the unicorns in a time of peace. Even now he retained his place as high justice, head of all ceremonies save those of battle, and would rule as regent during the coming absence of his son.

But Korr the prince led the unicorns now, for the children-of-the-moon were at war, and had been at war for four hundred years.

"O unicorns," cried Khraa the king, "here we stand under the rising moon, midwiving in the birth of the new year with our dances and our songs. The dancing, it is done, and the singing is to come. On the morrow's morn, our young fillies, our young colts will slip away unseen upon their Pilgrimage through the dark Pan Woods, over the Great Grass Plain, and across the crumbling shelf-land of the sleeping wyverns—let them not wake—until they come upon the Mirror of the Moon, our sacred well, there to perform their rite of passage."

The gray king paused, drawing breath. All the unicorns had lain down now. Night stretched dark and bright around them. Jan listened to the king.

"The time has come," he said, "for singing the Lay of the Unicorns, which tells of the beginning of this war and how our race was driven from its territories by treachery and forced to abandon the Moon's Mere—long, it was a long time past. Singer, come forth! Let the story be sung."

Khraa slipped silently from the ledge then and lay down beside his mate. Jan spotted the healer lying within the Circle. Even by moonlight he could make out the great black patches patterning the other's white coat, the dark spot encircling each eye so they stood out huge and seemed never to blink. But the one who rose from the grass at the king's nod was not Teki, but another lying beside him.

"Who is it?" whispered Dagg.

The young mare mounted the rise, her black and rose coloring pale ghostly under the moon. Jan hardly recognized her at first. It had been nearly a half-month since the battle of the gryphons—his shoulders were healed—and he had not seen Tek, save in far glimpses, since then. He had not realized before this that the healer's daughter was a singer of tales.

"Hail," she cried out, her voice low, harsh-sweet, "I'll sing you a tale of when Halla was princess of the unicorns, and a rare princess was

she. This was while her father Jared was yet alive and king, and in the
time when queen or king still ruled the unicorns.

"And this was long after the great Serpent-clouds had scoured the
Plain. And this was some after the war with the haunts had been fought
and won. And this was just after the spring fevers had carried off Halla's
first mate, and her two younglings, a twin filly and foal—but before she
had taken Zod the singer to husband as her second mate, while the
unicorns still lived in the Hallow Hills by the sacred well, in and around
the milkwood groves that now are called the Wyvern Wood. Because
of the things I shall tell of in this tale. Because of the coming of the
wyrms."

"What's milkwood?" murmured Jan, to himself. He had never wondered it before.

"Hist," Dagg told him. "I want to hear."

Tek changed her stance a little on the rocky platform, facing now
a slightly different quarter of the Circle.

"It was summer, midsummer, the solstice," she sang, "and winter a
long time gone. But winter touched the hearts of the unicorns still, for
the herd was shrunk and saddened at the death of so many fine warriors
and weanlings, the young with the old, from a spring plague that year,
the princess's own nurselings among them. Zod the singer was just
coming into the full glory of his voice, and aging Jared, Halla's father,
was king.

"Then Halla, dawn-colored like fire, stood beside the moon's pool,
sad in contemplation, asking Alma why That One had seen fit to steal
away the flower of the unicorns."

Jan felt another wondering. "What's fire?" he said aloud.

"I don't know," hissed Dagg. "It comes from lightning, or maybe
the sun."

Tek had paused a moment in her song.

"Hot," murmured Jan, "so the ballads say. It dances and darts." He
had heard of fire every now and again, in story and song. Fire dwelled
in dragons' mouths. This or that hero was color-of-fire. But Jan had
never seen any, and no unicorn he knew had ever seen any. "What is
it, I wonder. Is it alive?"

"Be still now," Dagg insisted. "I want to listen."

Above them on the rise, under the moon, Tek had changed her
stance again, turned just a little. Such was the singing of the unicorns.
Jan knew that by the time the tale was done, she would have turned full
Circle and taken in the whole Ring of listeners.

"Halla the princess stood at the wellside, when of a sudden she
glimpsed movement across the water, some creature emerging from the

green, cool woods bordering the Mere. It was a pale thing, like a great snake or a salamander, and came sliding out of the forest, lean and wrinkled as a dying toad. Watching, she saw it dip its long neck to the water to drink.

" 'Stop,' Halla cried, before its narrow snout could touch the surface and disturb the stillness of that hallowed pool.

"The creature looked up across the water with its clear, uncolored eyes. It seemed unable to see her well.

" 'This is a sacred place,' Halla informed it. 'Only we, the children-of-the-moon, may drink here.'

"Then the thing flicked its thin, forked tongue very fast between its needle teeth, as in anger. But in a moment, eyeing the dawn-colored princess of the unicorns, it grew softer, seeming to reconsider. It spoke to her in a strange sliding voice that hissed and lilted, hollow and velvety sharp. 'Oh, please, a drink. One drink. I perish.'

" 'Not of this lake,' the king's daughter replied. 'But if you thirst, I will tell you where lies another pool whereof you may drink.' "

Again Tek turned away from him and Dagg, more toward the side as she gazed over the Circle.

"And at those words," the healer's daughter sang, "at Halla's words, the creature at the wellside crumpled, seeming too weak to rise. So Halla walked along the curve of the shore until she came to it and bade it follow. It roused itself with difficulty and came slithering alongside her downslope through the woods.

"She studied it as they went, long and pale as a fish's belly, cold-looking like ice. It seemed smaller in body than a unicorn, with a long, scaled tail that had a sting-barb at its end. It kept two stubby forelegs folded against its body as it slithered. High on its neck, behind the head, a ruff of gills fanned and gaped when it opened its mouth. Its teeth were long, back-curving fangs.

" 'What are you?' Halla asked it.

" 'Oh, please,' it panted. 'Water first. A little water.'

"They reached the second pool. Near the top of a fall of stone shelves, a little spring welled and cascaded forming a pool at the base of the rocks. As soon as the pale creature saw this, it darted past Halla quick as a grass-flick and dropped its long neck to the water, lapping at it and laving it over its head.

"And as it drank, it seemed to grow, its withered sides swelling like a toad that is fat with poison. Then it slipped into the water and writhed about, bathing and whining a high, thin pleasure-song—until it caught sight of Halla on the bank and crept out of the pool, cringing again.

" 'You must forgive me,' it moaned. 'It has been months since I last tasted water.' It was now nearly twice the size it had been before.

" 'What are you?' Halla asked again.

" 'I?' it said, in its strange, sliding voice, preening its wet, gleaming skin. 'I am Lynex, and a wyvern.' "

Jan listened to the singer's voice, clear and dusky under the smoke moonlight. The wyverns were a noxious breed, sprung from the stink of quagmires at the beginning of the world. That was why the unicorns had come to call them 'wyrms': slithery, slippery things. Tek sang:

"But just at that moment, as he was speaking, the wyrm caught sight of the caves and rock shelves beyond the pool, spreading away to the southeast. Streams threaded across those rocks, welling and falling, pale as cloud. And seeing these, the wyvern gave out little sharp barks of glee, sliding here and there over the shelves, muttering.

" 'Ah, but these are just the thing. They would suit perfectly! Not as vast as the dens we left, but we could dig more at need. Perhaps. . . .'

Then he turned on the princess of the unicorns, demanding, 'Who dwells here?'

" 'No one,' replied Halla, mildly.

" 'Ah.' The wyvern sat, considering.

" 'But these lands fall within our territory,' the princess said, 'the unicorns'.'

"The creature glanced at her. 'Quite so,' it answered, more softly now. 'Quite so. I . . . we . . . that is, my people. . . .'

" 'Your people?' Halla inquired.

" 'There are more—a very few. A very few more of us. We have been lost, wandering across the Plain. We wish to settle.'

" 'You seek the unicorns' leave to settle here?'

"The wyvern bowed stiffly down to the dust. 'You would know our gratitude.'

" 'I have not the right either to grant you or to turn you away,' Halla replied. 'My father Jared is king. Tell your leaders to assemble here tomorrow. Bathe and drink. I will bid the elders of the unicorns come to you. Then we will decide.'

"So Halla left the wyrm beside the shelves and pools, and sprang off through the milkwood trees, traversing meadow and dale and grove to gather the unicorns to come parley with the wyrms."

🔥

Tek fell silent in her singing, bowing her head. She changed her stance again, turning more and more away from Jan, taking in others of the Circle. He was aware of Dagg beside him in the dark.

"I wonder . . ." he began, but his friend's sigh cut him short. "That's your trouble," Dagg whispered. "You're always *wondering*. Now quiet. She's starting the second cant." Tek lifted her head. "And next day beside the shelves and pools, parley was held between the sinuous leader of the wyverns and Jared the old king, with Halla his daughter and Zod the singer and a great many others, both wyverns and unicorns, present as well.

" 'How many have you in your band?' inquired Jared of the wyrms.

" 'Not many,' Lynex replied, hollow-voiced and sliding. 'Only a very few. Not nearly enough to fill these burrows.'

" 'He is lying,' murmured Halla between her teeth, close to her father's ear. 'I sent scouts to spy them out. They reported more than just a few. Yet most, they said, were torpid, near death. They look a livelier lot this day. Well-watered.'

" 'We do not wish to intrude,' the wyvern leader continued, 'only leave to stay here a little and rest from our arduous journey.'

" 'When first you spoke with me,' said Halla, stepping forward, 'you said you desired to settle.'

" 'Only for a season or two,' Lynex replied, 'to breed. We must have hatching grounds to brood our eggs.'

" 'Well enough,' said Jared, seemingly very little intent upon the parley. He had slept but fitfully the night before, strange troubles sliding through his dreams, and he was old, grown old before his time—sometimes his mind wandered; no one could say why.

" 'I see a wyvern breeding in a unicorn's belly,' said Zod then softly, an evening-blue unicorn all spattered with milk, 'eating up the children that were there.'

"But the princess ignored his words, for he spoke but softly, near her ear. Zod was a seer of visions and a dreamer of dreams, and often spoke riddles that meant nothing.

" 'How long will it take your eggs to hatch, and how long thereafter before your young may travel?' said Halla to the wyrm.

" 'Not long,' said Lynex, preening his supple skin with a thin, forked tongue.

" 'Well enough,' the king replied.

" '*Not* well enough,' the princess cried. 'How long?'

" 'Oh, a season,' said Lynex, smiling. 'No more than that. Our young thrive fast.'

" 'How many eggs do your kind lay in a clutch?'

" 'Oh, two—three?' the wyrm replied, as if he did not know. As if he were asking her.

" 'No snake I know lays so few little death-beads at one squat,' muttered Zod the singer, more loudly.

" 'We are not snakes,' the wyvern snapped, fanning his hood. A double tongue flicked angrily between his needle teeth. 'We are wyverns.'

" 'Wyrms.'

" 'Peace, Zod,' said Jared the king; then, to the creatures: 'Pay him no heed. We do not. He is a speaker of foolish nothing.'

" 'Wise foolish nothing,' the seer replied beneath his breath."

"Why don't they believe him?" muttered Jan under his own breath now. He could never lie still during the second cant. "Why doesn't the princess heed him—can't she see the wyverns are lying?"

"This is a tale," Dagg hissed at him. "Of course *we* can tell."

"Halla spoke," said Tek. " 'Where will you go when your younglings are ready?' the princess of the unicorns inquired.

"The wyrm hung its head. 'We do not know. We will move on, across the Great Grass Plain, hoping to stumble upon someplace hospitable to our kind, where we might live peaceably, disturbing no one.' "

"Liar," muttered Jan.

"Be *still*," hissed Dagg.

" 'Whence do you come?' said Halla to the wyverns. 'Why have you journeyed across the Plain?'

" 'Ah,' cried Lynex, 'we come from the north, the north and east where once we dwelled in harmony with our cousins, the red dragons. But our cousins cast us off—for envy, we think. We are too beautiful for their liking, though that is not the reason they would give.'

"The wyvern's eyes reddened with rancor.

" 'They said we were too many; they said. . . .' He stopped himself suddenly. 'Ah, but . . . as you see, we are only a very few.'

"Halla stood gazing out over the backs of the wyverns. She swatted a deerfly on her haunch and picked testily at the ground with one forehoof. Now that she scanned, she saw the white wyrms matched the diminished herd of the unicorns nearly beast for beast. 'Not so few,' she muttered to herself.

" 'More than that,' her scout beside her murmured. 'Our lookouts spotted many more than that.'

" 'Are all your people here assembled?' Halla asked aloud.

" 'All that yet are left to us alive,' Lynex replied.

" 'Well enough,' Jared replied. Then turning to Halla and her advisors, he said—seemingly to them, but loud enough for the wyrms to hear—'Harmless enough, they seem. I say we should succor them.'

" 'A moment, Father,' the princess cried. 'They appear to me less harmless than you think.' She turned again to the drove of wyverns. 'What do you eat?'

"And at this, for the first time, the wyverns did not answer at once, but turned to consult among themselves in their soft, sliding whispers.

" 'Fish,' said Lynex, turning, 'when we can get them, small lizards, birds' eggs. But when those cannot be found, we may subsist on grass for a little, as we have done these past months—that same sweet grass which you yourselves eat.'

"Halla eyed their needle teeth.

" 'Aye, fine sharp cusps they have,' murmured Zod the singer, 'for the grinding of grass.'

" 'You have poison stings on your tails,' said Halla.

"Then the wyverns flicked their tails and hissed till Lynex stilled them. 'Mere decoration only,' he replied, brandishing the barbed tip of his tail. 'And no defense against dragons, I fear.'

" 'Then why . . .' the princess began.

" 'Well enough, well enough!' her father cried. 'Let us put an end to this bickering. It grows late, and I am weary.' Before his daughter could protest he continued: 'Hear my judgment. Let the wyverns make dens in the rocks for one season. At the end of that time let us assemble again to parley their further stay.'

"Then Lynex the wyvern king bellied down to the dust. 'You will not regret this largess, O king. We are used to living inconspicuously; we will not disturb you—and we sleep all winter.'

"Coming forward then, he and Jared sealed their bargain with the pledge-kiss rulers give one another. But as her father turned away, Halla saw that the ear above the cheek where the wyvern king had kissed him lay crumpled, stood upright no more.

"Then the wyverns gave a great hissing shout and disappeared quick as a twitch into every burrow and cranny and cave in the rocks, so that at the end of ten heartbeats there was not tip nor tail to be seen of them, nor hardly any sign that they had been there at all.

" 'And now that they are slithered in,' said Zod to no one, softly, 'how ever shall we get them out again?'

"And Halla said quietly to her scout beside her, 'Let us send runners over Alma's back to north and east to find the red dragons. I would know what reason *they* give for the casting out of these slithery cousins of theirs.' "

Shadow Under the Moon

7

T ek paused again and bowed her head. The second cant was done. She stood facing wholly away from Jan and Dagg now, gazing out over the far half of the Circle. The moon had floated well up into the sky, its cool light spilling as pale as water.

"So the runners were sent," chanted Tek from her ledge. Jan heard the faintest echo of her words bounding back from the far hillside. ". . . at Halla's behest and without the king's knowing. Summer paled slowly into autumn, and hardly a scale was seen of the wyverns. They kept to their rock shelves, to themselves, until the unicorns nearly forgot their presence with the feasting and the dancing and the gathering of fall.

"But Halla was troubled. Her messengers did not return, and it seemed that her father made merrier than the rest, strange merriment. His thoughts strayed and rambled. And the ear where the wyvern had kissed him still drooped, so that now he was a little deaf. It uneased her.

"Zod, too, seemed uneasy. Haunting were the lays, all danger and betrayal, that fell from his tongue, mostly for her ears, though the princess did not know him well. And when on cold autumn nights from beneath some spreading fir Halla awoke to a distant, mournful cry, she knew it was the singer at his dreams.

"Winter came, and with it, snow. The wellsprings froze, and then no sight or sound of the wyverns came. They lay curled tight in sleeping knots below ground, so the unicorns supposed—though sometimes wisps of acrid mist rose from the airholes to their dens. It was a puzzle passing strange. No one could make it out.

"Then the unicorns ate of their stores, pawing through the snow to find forage, and chewed the leaves of spruce and fir, warm in their winter shag, thinking nothing of the wyrms—while Zod sang songs of doom all winter and Halla waited for her runners to return."

Tek had turned just past halfway around in her circling. Jan began to be able to see her face again, though she faced still toward the far side of the Circle. The lightest of echoes sang back from the distant slope as she chanted, shadowing her words. The moon hung two-thirds of the way to its zenith. Jan listened to Tek's singing under the moon.

"Spring came. The snows dissolved. Ice that had locked the pools melted, and new grass sprang upon the Plain. Then two young colts disappeared within a day of one another and were not seen again. Searchers combed diligently, but no trace could be found.

"Companions said they had last seen them in the south and east, near the wyvern cliffs, but no sign of wyverns either could be found, and no answer came when the searchers shouted down into their caves. Jared the king said the year was early yet for wyrms to be abroad. No more was said. No more could be done.

"Then a young mare heavy in foal went up to the Mirror of the Moon to bear, but returned not, nor her companion the midwife. They were not seen again. This time the searchers found wyvern tracks and belly marks about the poolside and crystalized droppings under the trees. But still no answer came from beneath the shelves when the searchers called, and no wyverns emerged.

"Jared the king said still the white wyrms were asleep, fast slumbering, and the searchers must have mistook the signs, that the tracks must be those of banded pards, or other grasscats wandered in from the Plain. But when urged by his advisors, he would post no lookouts. So scouts were posted at Halla's word, against the orders of the king.

"Soon some of them said they had seen wyverns moving about the shelves at night. Others spoke of wyverns bathing in the sacred Mirror of the Moon before dawn. Hearing this, the princess grew alarmed, and ordered mineral salt thrown down about the Mere to keep them off.

"But when clear traces were found at last that the wyverns had visited the salt-clay cliffs where the dead are laid beneath the stars and had carried off the bodies of warriors put to rest there, Halla went with this knowledge to her father and confronted him before his counselors."

Tek had turned more around now. The faint, silvery echo still repeated her words.

"At first Jared laughed at his daughter's charges against the wyrms. Then he grew angry when she told him of the watchers she had posted against his word. And suddenly, without warning, he cried out in a voice that seemed unlike his own:

" 'Traitor, traitor, thrice a traitor! My own daughter, my heir, has betrayed me!'

"He got no further, for by this time a great assembly had gathered, and hearing that Halla had set sentries upon the white wyrms, most of the people cried out in her favor, for there was much murmuring now against the wyverns, and much fear.

"But even as they were speaking, a messenger came galloping, tangle-hooved and exhausted. He pitched to a halt before Halla, bowing low.

" 'Hail, princess. I have returned from the red dragons. All summer it took us to find their country across the Plain, and all autumn to persuade them we were not spies. Over the winter, one of our number died, and two are still held hostage. But the dragons have allowed me to return to you, and here is the answer to the question we carried:

" 'The red dragons cast out the wyverns from the Smoking Hills in wintertime and drove them away across the Great Grass Plain, hoping to spell their death. The wyrms had been let live among their hosts as scavengers and carrion clearers. The dragons claim no kinship to them.

" 'But when the wyverns began to breed out of hand and grow past a moderate size, and carry off dragon pups to devour, and rob the earthen tombs—the firedrakes bury their dead in the earth—then the dragons set snares and caught them at their plunder, fell on them and drove them from their burrows with fire.

" 'But Lynex, the wyrms' leader, and some others escaped them. The dragons let them go, thinking surely upon the Great Grass Plain they would die. But Méllintéllinas, who is queen of the red dragons, warns you, Halla, princess of the moon's children, that this Lynex is as subtle as craft and she believes, though she cannot be certain, that he has stolen from their godstone a golden carrying bowl, and in it, the secret of their fire.' "

A bowl. Jan wondered what a carrying bowl could be. He had never wondered it before. He drew breath to speak then, but Dagg beside him in the darkness murmured, "List."

The healer's daughter had turned in her Circle under the moon. The soft songshadow still repeated her words.

"Hearing these things of the wyverns, the unicorns cried out in consternation, but Jared shouted them down. 'Let be! Let them be. Why should we trouble the wyrms? They have done us no harm, caused us no alarm. . . .'

" 'They have stolen our children,' cried Halla, 'both the born and the unborn, and our people, and our dead. They have drunk of the well of the unicorns, and hide in their holes when we call them to task.'

" 'Lies,' cried the king, 'all lies by your followers to unseat me. I know who the true friends of the unicorns are. You have defied me! You have moved in secret against me. Now this messenger of yours brings more lies.'

" 'There is a worm in his brain,' chanted Zod, low like a dirge. 'I have seen it in a dream, and it eats away his reason.'

" 'You traitor,' Jared cried, broken-eared, deaf—and his words still tumbled out in that strange hollow voice unlike his own. 'Usurper. No longer my daughter. Death for what you have done to me! You shall die.'

"And before another unicorn could utter a word or draw a breath, Jared the king reared with hooves and horn poised to strike down the princess of the unicorns. But Halla fended him off, though all unwillingly. She smote him a great blow to the breast with her forehooves and struck him with the flat of her horn to the skull.

"Then the king went down, unexpectedly, to everyone's surprise. He fell like one shot through with poison, and lay at the unicorns' feet, stone dead. Those assembled watched his wilted ear twitch once, twice, and a tiny wyvern crawled forth, long as a foreshank and fat with its feasting. Its forked tongue flickered between needle teeth.

"Halla cried out and rose up to smash the murdering thing with her hooves, but Zod the singer sprang between them, crying, 'Beware, princess. Even newborn, it carries death in its tail. Its spittle is sweet poison on teeth sharp as fishbones, and its breath is a bringer of nightmares. I know; I have seen it, I who dream dreams.'

"But even as he was speaking, a cry went up in the south and east, from scouts flying to bring the alarm:

" 'The wyverns, the wyverns—to war!' "

🝆

Above the Vale, the full moon floated, serenely bright, nearing its zenith. Tek stood in perfect profile now, her voice pitched to carry; she sang out like a bell:

"All about the gathered unicorns, the wyverns now came streaming, slithering like flood rain—many more than there had been at midsummer, many more than the unicorns were. Most of them were little things, no bigger than hatchlings. Quick as kestrels, lithe as eels, they darted about the heels of the unicorns, stinging.

"And snaking at the head of them, Lynex shouted, 'Ah-ha! Ah-ha! Did I not say our younglings thrive fast? Come, prit; come, pet.'

"Then the wyrmlet that had crawled from the dead king's ear flashed to the wyvern king and twined about his neck. And seeing this, Halla rose up, shouting a war cry. Her warriors rallied. The unicorns charged. All day the fighting lasted. Many wyverns were slain, the great ones pierced through the vitals, the little ones trampled underfoot.

"But the warriors were scattered and few. Some were yet heavy in foal or only recently delivered. Many shattered their horns against the wyverns' breasts, for the wyrms were made with a bony plate under the skin and above the heart that could not be pierced. And those that had been stung felt a langor overtaking them, till they sank to the ground, unable to rise."

Jan squirmed in the dark in his place beside Dagg. He champed his teeth, hardly able to bear that Alma should grant all things in season— even defeat for the unicorns. The singer sang:

"Slow and by little, the unicorns fell back, and the wyverns poured after them in fierce hordes until the westering sun hung like a gryphon's eye, and the unicorns fought upon the last slope of the Hallow Hills, upon the verges of the Plain.

"Halla cried out then, 'Is all lost? Hoof and horn prove no match to the barbs of the wyrms. So many lie slain. Another hour and we shall all of us be dead. Is no hope left?'

" 'One hope,' answered Zod, the singer of dreams, for still he fought alongside her, protecting her flank. 'Fly—away across the Great Grass Plain. These wyrms will gorge themselves upon our dead and theirs, and will not follow.'

" 'Run?' Halla cried, staring at him. 'Leave the Mirror of the Moon for them to lap and paddle in?'

" 'The Moon's Mere is now bitter salt,' the seer said, 'and poison to them. You have said yourself, O princess, another hour's fight will see us dead. Better for us to fly now and live, to grow many and strong again, one day to return and reclaim our land—than to die to the last here and now, giving it up to them forever.' "

Jan kicked one leg in silent protest. His young heart cried out, *No. Better to die, die fighting to the last, than to live with the shame.* But that was foal's talk, and he knew it, that no warrior would countenance. The healer's daughter turned some and spoke, soft echoes shadowing her speech:

" 'But how may we ever reclaim it?' cried Halla, like one dying for grief. 'How long must we wait?'

"Then her companion's eyes grew far and strange. 'I have heard in dreams,' so the seer said, 'that it will not come in our lifetime. Our sons will not see it, nor our sons' daughters. But when at last the night-dark one shall be born among the unicorns, then the Mirror of the Moon will grow sweet again, and the wyverns shall perish in fire. Our people shall call him the Firebringer: a great warrior as are you, O princess, and a seer of dreams as am I.' "

"How does he know that?" muttered Jan, hardly realizing he spoke.

"Seers know things," whispered Dagg. "Alma tells them, and they know."

Tek stood now as she had at the tale's beginning, and the moon hung above her at zenith in the sky. And it seemed to Jan, as he lay listening, that that soft songshadow, faint on the very verge of his hearing, still sounded from before him, from the far hillside, though the healer's daughter now faced wholly away from that slope as she sang.

"So Halla, hearing the dreamer's words, ate at last the bitter root of defeat, bowing to the wisdom of the moon, which says that all things wax and wane, even the greatness of the unicorns. She bade her warriors escape and save themselves, flee away into the dusk while the wyverns in the foothills sat howling their glee.

"But glancing back, Halla—the very last to leave the field—saw Lynex holding aloft in his teeth the bough of a tree all ablaze with amber flowers. Beside him upon the ground tested a golden bowl of glowing stones.

" 'What, fly, will you?' cried the wyrm king through his teeth. Then let this pursue you in our stead. Never think to trouble us again, vile unicorns!'

"Then he cast the scarlet brand upon the Plain, and where it came to earth, suddenly the stubgrass bloomed as well with wisps of light that danced and ran before the wind. Clouds of choking dust arose beneath the fury of their passing, and they left the grass behind them blackened in curling crisps.

"Those whom the hot, darting dancers touched screamed wild in pain. Not horn nor hoof availed against them, and any who fled slow or wounded, the flames ran down like pards upon the Plain. The unicorns fled rampant then, terrified, for two whole nights and a day, till spring storms trampled out the deadly flares, and the children-of-the-moon dropped where they stood, to sleep like dead things in the rain."

🌿

The healer's daughter fell silent then, and her echo fell instantly silent as well. Very like her own voice it was, only a little deeper. Jan sighed heavily, studying the ground. The story always ended the same, with the rout of the unicorns. If only. . . . He screwed his knees tighter into the turf. If only, if only—he knew not what. Tek made an ending to the tale:

"I have sung you the Lay of the Unicorns, how we were cast from our lands by wyverns and wandered many seasons, south over the Plain, till at last we came upon a Vale. And here, by Alma's grace, we have begun to grow strong again.

"But we have never forgotten that these are not our own true lands. One day we shall regain the Hallow Hills. Each year some of us must return: quiet, careful, on dangerous Pilgrimage, to drink that drink which makes us what we are, unicorns, warriors, children-of-the-moon.

"The sacred well, the Hallow Hills, are not yet ours again. The Firebringer is not among us yet, but he is coming. He is coming—soon."

Tek stood a moment on the ledge and then descended. Those in the Circle began to stir. Dagg in the moonlit dark beside Jan whispered, "She changed that last."

Jan was still gazing after Tek as she lay down beside her father now.

"She didn't just say the Firebringer was coming. She said he was coming soon."

Jan nodded absently, thinking of something else. "I wonder," he murmured. "Did this valley belong to anyone before we came here?"

Dagg eyed him with a frown. "It was empty. Everyone knows that."

"I wonder," murmured Jan. "Someone told me once . . . it seems. . . ."

This valley was ours before you stole it. Ever since the day of the gryphons, those words had been in his mind. Who was it that had told him that? Every time he strove to picture the speaker, the image slipped from him. It was like a dream he had awakened from and now could not recall.

Khraa upon the ledge had begun to speak, but Jan hardly listened, still trying to puzzle out those strange, half-remembered words: *This valley was ours. . . .*

Dagg was nudging him. "Do you think she's a dreamer? Tek, I mean. Maybe she's foreseen the Firebringer."

Jan felt his skin prickle. For a moment the thought quickened his blood: that the Firebringer might be more than just an old legend, that the prophecy might one day come to pass.

"But do you think," whispered Dagg, bending closer, "she could have meant Korr?"

Jan started and stared at his friend. The feeling of exhilaration passed. The prince's son snorted and shook his head. "Zod foretold 'a seer of dreams.' "

"Yes, but the dreaming sight doesn't always come early," said Dagg. "And your father's coat *is* color-of-night."

Jan looked away. Could that be—his sire, the Firebringer? The idea unsettled him somehow. True, Korr was black and a great warrior, the first black prince in all the history of the unicorns. But his father had no use for dreamers and their dreams. He would have no truck with them at all—except that once with Jah-lila, the healer's mate, who lived outside the Vale.

Jan snorted again. No, it could never be Korr. Impossible! He rolled onto his back and scrubbed himself against the soft, grass-grown dirt. His winter coat was still long and shaggy from the cold months, and he wished it would shed. Spring was early this year, and it itched.

He shook himself then, and settled himself. Dagg beside him had closed his eyes. The gray king had quit the ledge, and all around, Jan heard other unicorns preparing for sleep. He let his breath out slowly; his eyelids drooped.

Above him the moon, mottled and bright, fissured down its middle like a ripe eggshell. Out of it crawled a winged serpent that hung above him in the starry sky, breathing a sour breath upon him and speaking words he could not understand.

Jan's limbs twitched in his sleep; his nostrils flared. Breath caught and shuddered in his throat. Dagg jostled beside him in the dark. Jan rolled onto his other side and breathed more deeply then. His eyelids ceased to flutter. The snake in the heavens flew away.

It was very late. He realized he must have slept, but he could not remember having closed his eyes. The unbroken moon, whole and un-damaged, had tilted a little way down from its zenith. Jan saw a figure standing among the sleeping unicorns.

It turned away, walking toward the Circle's edge, then it sprang lightly over a sleeper and cantered noiselessly toward the far hillside. Jan felt the drumming of heels through the ground and lay wondering. By Law, no one was allowed to break the Circle until the moon was down.

As the figure disappeared upslope into the trees, Jan realized suddenly that it seemed to be heading toward that point whence the echo had come while Tek had been singing. He frowned, shaking his head. The valley stood empty now, the Circle around him still and undisturbed.

It's restlessness, he told himself. *I imagined it.* He felt no drum of heels in the soft earth now. He shut his eyes, shivering with fatigue. And as he slipped again into that country between waking and sleep, it seemed the night air brought to him, just for a moment, a delicious odor like roses in summer. He slept deep without dreams then, till morning.

The Pan Woods

8

The trees leaned close around them as they walked, and bird cries haunted through the gloom. The air was cool, with gray jays and redwings flashing through the wells of light. As Jan watched, golden foxes slunk through the bracken. There a hare crouched, its eyes as black as river stones, beside a skeletal thicket all budded in yellow-green. Deer browsed among the shadows, raising their heads as the unicorns passed, gazing after the newcomers with great, uncurious eyes.

The pilgrims slipped through the still Pan Woods that forested the folded hills as far as the Plain, a day's journey to the west. They had risen at dawn, all those within the Circle, sprung up and shaken the sleep from them, while those forming the Ring around them had lain sleeping still. At a nod from the prince, the initiates had turned, leapt over the sleepers, and stolen from the valley—silently, lest any left behind awaken, breaking the Circle before the pilgrims were away.

They moved in single file now, the colts and fillies behind the prince and flanked by warriors here and there. Over the long train of backs wending before him, Jan caught glimpses of rose and black, the healer's daughter, and sometimes white and black, her sire. Others he remembered from the battle of the gryphons, for Korr chose only the worthiest warriors to accompany the initiates over the Plain.

The Hallow Hills lay far to northward, a half month's running. By then the full moon that had set over the Vale a half hour gone would be dwindled to nothing. By the moon's dark, then, while the wyverns slept, the unicorns would keep Vigil beside the sacred Mere; and at daybreak they would dip their hooves and horns and drink a single sip of its bitter waters.

So much Jan knew of the ceremony at their journey's end. So much and no more. He and Dagg filed on through the trees of the Pan Woods, near the tail of the line. And the morning passed.

They halted near noon to lie up beside a tangle of berry brush. Splendid curtains of sun streamed into a small clearing nearby. Jan and Dagg threw themselves down upon the soft brown carpet of bracken leaf, near the clearing's edge but out of the light, and lay there, not talking. The morning's long walk had tired them.

When Alma first had made the world, so the singers said, she had offered her children the gift of speech. The unicorns took it gladly, and sang their thanks to her. The gryphons took it, and the dragons, even the wyrms. But the goatling pans ran away into the woods, hiding themselves from the Mother-of-all, refusing her gift. And for that, the unicorns despised them.

Jan and Dagg had even seen one once, a pan—a small, cowardly thing. The previous summer they had stolen high upon the slopes, looking for red rueberries to roll in so that, returning to their companions below, they might game them into believing they had been sprung upon by bobtailed hillcats.

But unexpectedly, they had come upon a strange beast: round-headed, flat-faced, and horned like a goat. Its hairless chest was broad and shallow, with a bluish hide, its forelimbs fingered like birds' feet, and the hind limbs shaggy brown with cloven heels. A slight figure, it would have stood only shoulder high to Korr.

It had been crouching when they had come upon it, plucking ripe berries from the ruebush with the long toes of its forelegs; but it had sprung up and dashed away when it saw them, upon its hind limbs alone, like a wingless bird. He and Dagg had chased it, but it had disappeared over the hillcrest and down into the Pan Woods quick as cunning. What an odd, ungainly looking creature. Ugly as old bones.

Remembering, Jan smiled with the easy arrogance of unicorns and nibbled the young buds from the briar beside him. It was Alma's frown upon the goatlings that made them so. Only her favored ones, the moon's children, walked truly in beauty. He swatted at a deerfly that lighted on his rump. The shoots of the bush tasted tender and green.

The handful of warriors stood guard about the dozing initiates, or moved silently among the trees, scouting for pans. Jan watched them idly, and presently he heard a strange sound far in the distance, drawn out and windy, like the whooping of herons. It died down after a few moments, then began again, nearer. And as he listened, it seemed to Jan he could discern a pattern in the cries, calling and replying to one another through the trees.

Dagg was just turning to him, drawing breath to speak, when all at

once Jan cut him off with a hiss. He nodded. Teki and another warrior
had emerged from the trees a dozen paces from them and stood conferring with the prince.

"Something's afoot," murmured Jan, feeling his blood quickening.
"Maybe they've spotted pans."

All morning since they had left the Vale, he had been half hoping
they might stumble upon the pans. They were not colts anymore, after
all. They had nothing to fear. Indeed, it would be a fine game, putting
a few of those timid little blue-skins to flight. The Woods had been so
quiet, the morning so monotonous, with only bird cries for distraction.
Boredom nibbled at Jan with tiny, needle teeth.

"It *is* pans," whispered Dagg. "It must be."

The two warriors had broken off from Korr now and were whistling
the initiates to be up and off. Jan sprang to his feet and shook himself,
laughing with Dagg at the prospect of diversion. The file forming behind
Teki was already trotting away into the trees.

"Step brisk," Jan heard Korr calling, "and less noise."

Jan champed his tongue and hurried into line. Dagg behind him was
doing the same. Since the day of the gryphons, Jan had kept his vow,
following the prince's word always, at once, without questions. His
father's goodwill was too precious, had come too dearly bought to part
with now. Jan swallowed his high spirits and stepped brisk.

The gloom of the Pan Woods enfolded them. Behind them, Korr
was bringing up the rear of the train. Jan pricked his ears, scanning the
trees. Nothing. The Woods were empty, still. He lifted his head, catching
the scent of trees and earth, of shady air. No whiff of pans—not yet.
But it hardly mattered; they could not be far.

He wrinkled his nose, trotting, feeling the waves of anticipation in
him rise. A sense of reckless abandon seethed in him. They were warriors, dangerous and fierce, and on their way into a skirmish. Ears
pricked, nostrils wide, his eyes scanning ahead, Jan listened to the crying
of herons falling away into the distance behind.

&

They kept at a jogtrot into the middle afternoon. The whooping
voices of the herons had long since faded. Jan snorted, frowning. His
anticipation waned; his limbs felt sore. Korr had trotted toward the fore
of the line a half hour gone. Now, as Tek strayed near, Jan could bear
it no more.

"Hist, Tek," he whispered, and the young mare turned. "When will
we come upon the pans?"

She blinked. "Never, Alma be kind, and if we go carefully."

Jan shook his head, not understanding. Dagg had come up alongside him now. "But," he started, "wasn't it because of pans that we broke camp so suddenly?"

Tek glanced at him. "Aye. But no fear, they're well behind us now."

Jan snorted, and astonishment went through him like a barb. "We've been going *away* from them?"

A smile sparked the young mare's eye. "What, did you think we'd sprung up to go seek them?" She broke into low laughter then. "By Alma's Beard, princeling. I never yet met a colt who could so *not* let trouble lie, but always must be up and hunting it."

Jan felt his ears burning. He wanted to bite something. He wanted to kick. "Trouble?" he cried. "They're only pans. . . ."

"Hark you," said Tek then, and her tone had lost its laughter suddenly, become that of a warrior to a foal. "We are not eaters of flesh like the gryphons, nor lovers of death like the wyrms. Nor do we bloody our hooves and our horns save at need."

She eyed him hard a moment more, then broke off and loped toward the head of the line. They had come to a stream. Jan kept his tongue and snatched a drink as they waded across. Fiercely cold, the water ran like ice along his ribs. He lashed furiously at the swarm of tiny water-wings that settled to sip his sweat.

His blood was burning still. Tek's mocking had made him feel like a fool. He was only grateful Korr had not overheard. How could he ever hope to become prince among the unicorns if he could not even remember the simplest rule of Law—one he had been hearing since birth? Warriors were sworn not to battle without cause. His flash of anger cooling now, Jan's whole frame drooped in despair.

As they emerged from the stream, the band slowed to a walk. Jan guessed the watercourse must have marked some boundary. The pans were a scattered people, divided and weak. They ran in little herds called tribes that fought for territory. His father's band must have crossed now into another tribe's demesne.

They walked in silence through the budding Woods. The sun, unseen, sank lower in the branch-woven sky, and the gnats subsided as the air began to cool. The shadows grew long. Jan tried to imagine a race that would make war upon its own kind, and could not. His own people were single, of the Circle. The unicorns were one.

The Woods around them had grown very still. Jan came out of his revery and lifted his head as he realized he had not heard a bird's cry in a quarter of an hour. He scented the air, and an odor came to him, goatlike and salty. He had smelled it only once before. Ahead, two warriors stood halted in their tracks, staring off into the trees.

"Dagg. . . ." Jan started.

But the splinter of falling wood cut him short. A dead cedar toppled groaning across their path. Its tangled roots, still clotted with earth, were stubby, as though they had been bitten through. Initiates whinnied, scattering in confusion. Something struck Jan on the shoulder.

He felt another sting against his fetlock—stones. The air was thick suddenly with flying stones. A sound like the voices of herons again filled the Woods, and pans poured from behind the trees. Some held what looked like rams' horns to their mouths, their cheeks puffed. The long, wavering cries were coming from the *horns*. Jan stared. He had never seen such a thing before.

"Don't scatter," Korr was thundering now above the commotion of horns. "Keep close—we'll soon outrun them. Follow the healer!"

Jan saw Teki rearing, his hide a flash of white and black. He whinnied sharply, then wheeled and charged the fallen cedar. Others flew to follow him. The goatlings, taken by surprise, fell back as the healer cleared the tree and was away.

Dagg bolted then, shouldering past Jan. The pans had ceased their standing volley and begun to charge. Jan rose, ready to strike at them, but Korr sprang to send him after Dagg with sharp nips and a curt command. Only then did Jan realize he and Dagg had stood staring when they should have been flying. The others were all over the tree and gone.

Jan heard a cry from Dagg, wheeled to see a goatling springing from behind a tree. She wrapped her forelimbs about Dagg's neck. He reared, writhing and thrashing, then kicked at another one rushing his flank. Jan yelled, charging, heard the prince's war cry behind him and the thunder of Korr's heels. Blue-bodied goatlings scattered for their lives.

Dagg freed himself and fled for the cedar, soaring over at a bound. Gathering his legs, Jan sprang after. Pans were standing on the other side. Some brandished pieces of pointed wood, strangely blackened and sharp as tusks. Dagg reared again, striking wildly at them. Jan cast about desperately for some sign of the band.

He could not spot them. They had vanished. The Woods stood so close and tangled here they could have been but twenty paces off and he would not have seen them. The clamor of horns deafened him. He could not think, and Korr was still behind them on the other side of the tree.

Jan slashed at a goatling that lunged at him, and suddenly caught sight of something in the gloom—a unicorn. It reared among the trees not ten paces from them, crying, "Follow!" and sprang away. Jan bit Dagg on the shoulder and shouted, "This way!"

He plunged after the other unicorn through a maze of shadows and trees, and heard the sound of Dagg's heels coming behind. Dense thickets closed about them. Jan caught only glimpses of their rescuer, could not even tell the color of the one who ran before. He had no idea who it was.

The land beneath his hooves fell suddenly away, and Jan stumbled into a gully between two hills. He realized he had lost sight of the one ahead of them then, and panic gripped him. He sprinted down the dry gravel wash. Dagg behind him was shouting something, but Jan ignored him, ignored everything, galloping harder. The others could not be far ahead.

"Jan!" Dagg behind him was crying. "Jan, stop. Stand!" All at once, his friend charged past him, veering across his path.

Jan ducked, trying to dodge, but the twisting river course was narrow. He plunged to a halt. "Dagg, we'll lose them!" he cried.

Dagg shook his head, nearly winded, blowing hard. "Wrong way," he gasped. "We've run wrong. Can't you hear them? They're behind."

Jan stopped shouldering, staring at him, then lifted his head and listened. Above the pounding of blood in his throat and the harshness of his own breathing, of Dagg's, he caught sound—far in the distance, just for a moment—of the whinny of unicorns in flight and the loonlike sounding of the horns.

"But how . . . ?" Jan wheeled, beside himself, still panting. His limbs twitched with fatigue. "I was following. . . ." The faint, far sounds were fading now into the utter stillness of the Woods. Dagg shook his head. "Come, haste. We'll have to go back." He started past Jan.

"No. Hold," cried Jan suddenly. "We mustn't. The pans are between us and them now."

Dagg halted in midstep. They stood looking at each other. Above them, the sky was the color of rueberry stains, and the Woods all around had grown dusky, the silence deep. Jan shook his head and tried to think. His blood had quieted at last; his breathing stilled, and so, too, the sense of panic that had gripped him. He turned and climbed the sandy bank of the wash.

"We'll go west," he said. "The Plain lies that way, and it can't be far."

He glanced back over one shoulder at Dagg. His friend sidled, uncertain, gazing at the dark Woods before them with wide, nervous eyes.

Jan turned at once and began shouldering his way through the undergrowth that bordered the wash, giving the other no time to reply. Dagg
had to follow to keep him in sight.

"Let's be off, then," Jan told him. "The sun's low."

Lost

❧ 9 ❧

They came upon a glade just as the Woods grew too dim for them to make their way. Pans had been there, a great many of them, but the scent was old. Another scent fingered in the air as well—pungent, like cedar, and somehow dry. Jan had never met that odor before. He and Dagg emerged into the open. The sky above was purpling. Dagg turned to him.

"What now?"

"We wait," Jan told him. "The moon should be up soon. Once it gets high enough, it'll cast good light."

Dagg fell silent. They gazed about them. In the last moments of twilight, Jan studied the glade. Something about it struck him as strange; he could not quite get his teeth on it. Then he had it. The glade was round. The trees bordering the open space made a perfect Ring, and all the ground cover had been cleared from the interior. He and Dagg stood on brown, bare soil.

In the middle of the clearing lay a Circle of stones. A grayish powder lay in little heaps within, along with a few leafless twigs, oddly blackened. It was from these that the pungent aroma arose. Jan approached the Circle of stones. He stepped inside.

The dust felt soft beneath his heels, incredibly fine. The branches, puzzlingly brittle, crunched and compressed as he stepped on them. Dagg set one hoof inside the Ring as Jan bent to sniff the powdery gray stuff, savoring its acrid, aromatic scent. Dagg fidgeted suddenly and stepped back outside the stones.

"What's wrong?" Jan asked him.

"Don't stand there," Dagg told him. "It's hot."

Jan lifted his head and realized that his friend spoke true. The dust was warm beneath his hooves. But the heat felt good against the night air's chill. "I wonder what makes it so?"

"This is some sort of pan place," muttered Dagg. "Let's wait at the glade's edge."

Jan nodded over one shoulder toward the edge of the clearing. "You go," he murmured. "I'll keep watch."

So they waited, Jan within the Circle of stones, Dagg amid the darkness at the verge of the wood. And while the two of them kept watch, another watched them, unseen, from across the glade—one who had led them there, though they did not know it, for private ends: that the prince's son might see a thing no unicorn within the Ring had ever seen before.

The sky darkened through deep blue to black, then turned a dark silver. The moon rose, huge and brilliant, throwing black shadows through the trees. By its light, Jan saw countless pan tracks crisscrossing the soft earth of the glade—but his and Dagg's were the only hoofprints within the Circle of stones.

Just then, very faintly, Jan caught sound of something, a little run of sliding notes. He started, straining his eyes against the shadows beyond the glade. His heart had gone tight. He could make out nothing through the trees. Stepping from between the stones, he backed toward the wood's edge.

"Dagg," he breathed. "List."

Dagg lifted his head. "What is it?" he said lowly. "It isn't unicorns."

Jan and Dagg melted out of the moon's light into the Woods. Among the shadows now, Jan craned his neck; but still nothing met his gaze across the glade but moonlit trees. The notes came again then, just a snatch. They fluted through the dark.

"It's singing," murmured Jan, suddenly sure, "but no words to it. Like bird's song."

The sound grew clear now, continuous, one clear voice piping wordlessly up and down. Jan and Dagg stood perfectly still. As they listened, it was joined by another voice, and then a third. Three soft, sweet strains trilled in the stillness, drawing near.

Dagg sidled. "It's a night bird. It must be."

Jan shook his head. He felt no fear, only fascination now. "No bird," he breathed. "Hist, I want to listen. I want to know what creature sings so sweet."

Beside him, Dagg went rigid, his nostrils wide. "It's pans," he whispered, strangled. "I can smell them. Fly!"

Jan felt the muscles of his friend beside him bunch. "Stand still," he hissed, "or they'll see you."

Dagg hesitated. But Jan felt strangely, perfectly at ease. He wanted to see—he *had* to see—what would happen next, and he would not have Dagg bolting and spoiling it. The pans were coming into the glade.

They moved in a long file, a whole band of them, and made themselves into a Circle. Crouching and lounging, they faced inward. Jan saw small ones, weanlings the size of hares, and old ones, gaunt and gray-flanked among the rest, not just the slim, strong half-growns and warriors that had attacked them earlier. And then, within the Circle under the moon, three pans began to dance. Goat-footed, high-stepping, they moved and swayed.

"They dance," Jan murmured, with a little start of surprise.

Dagg shook his head. "Only the unicorns dance."

But it was so. The goatlings were dancing there, each dancer holding a flat bundle of marshreeds bound with grass. The reeds were bitten off in uneven lengths and, held to the pursed lips of the dancers, they produced the high, sweet singing. Those watching from the Circle nodded as the dancers passed, glancing at one another, snuffling and making small gestures. Jan felt a tremor down his spine.

"They're talking to each other," he breathed.

Dagg, pressing against him, muttered doggedly, "Pans can't talk."

Jan shook his head. "With the pipes," he whispered. "With their forelimbs." A flash of insight went through him then, hot and sharp. "And they were talking to each other earlier, with their rams' horns in the Woods."

Dagg stood silent a moment, watching the glade. The dancers piped and turned. The watchers murmured, nodding. Dagg shrugged. "Not talking—they can't be. It's just chatter."

Jan shook his head again, but kept his tongue. It *was* speech, he was sure of it. Then that legend of the pans in the old lays must be false. The goatlings were *not* speechless, had not turned away the Mother's gift. The discovery astonished him. He strained his ears to the pipes, his eyes to the intricate movements of those strangely jointed forelimbs, and felt the uncanny certainty that if only he could watch long enough, listen deeply enough, he could come to understand.

Dagg beside him shifted suddenly. "What's happening?"

Jan came back to himself. He realized the snuffling murmur was dying now. A hush followed. One by one the dancers handed their pipes to members of the Ring, and for three moments in turn one strain of the music paused, and then resumed.

The dancers caught up blackened stakes, the male brandishing one in each forelimb like long, straight hooves. Each female held one stake to her forehead like a horn. They snorted, tossing their heads, and pawed at the earth. Jan felt a rush of recognition.

"It's a singer's tale," he hissed. "They're telling it—but without words."

The two females circled lazily within the goatlings' Ring, seemingly unaware of the male stalking them. The music of the flutes grew soft and secretive. Suddenly, the male caught up a branch and threw it down before his quarry. The females whirled, leaping back as if surprised as the other sprang up, brandishing his stakes. The panpipes shrilled.

The mock unicorns lowered their heads and charged, the pointed stakes at their foreheads aimed—but the male batted them lightly away. Once more the females charged and again were put to flight. This time the male pursued them, round the inside of the Ring, until his quarry at last outdistanced him.

The male pan halted, raising his forelimbs, his head thrown back in triumph. The fluting of the panpipes swelled. The mock unicorns straggled away in defeat. The dancers left the inside of the Ring, rejoining their fellows at the rim.

"The ambuscade," murmured Jan. He was shaking, but from astonishment, not fear. "They were telling the others how they put us to flight."

"But," Dagg hissed through clamped teeth, "that isn't how it happened at all!" The interior of the pans' Ring lay empty now. The fluting continued, very soft. "They didn't rout us," Dagg insisted. "We didn't *deign* to fight. . . ."

He had no time to finish, for Jan beside him had caught in his breath.

"Oh," the prince-son breathed, brushing his shoulder against his companion to still him. "Oh, Dagg. What's that?"

A pan had risen from the Ring and now was kneeling beside the Circle of stones. With a sheaf of reeds, she brushed aside the gray powder. A second pan came to the stones and threw down a heap of dead branches. Small lights, like red stars, leapt upward through the twigs.

Then something flickered upon the branches, something bright. Jan stared, overtaken with wonder. The stuff upon the twigs—it moved, it danced. It was the color of his mother's coat, of a setting sun. It flowed like a unicorn's mane, like grass in the wind, like . . . like. . . . He could not say. The branches beneath it blackened and curled. And some began to glow, orange red, then broke at last and fell into a fine, gray dust.

It cast a fleeting light upon the bodies of the pans. They crowded closer, holding their forelimbs to it. Jan saw their bluish hides trickling sweat, even in the chill night air. Mist rose from the flaring stuff, tendrils that to Jan seemed black against the hoary moon, and pale against the sky.

"Prince-son," a voice behind him breathed, "and Dagg. Stand still and do not speak. It is I."

❦

Jan started and wheeled, then felt sudden relief flooding through him as he recognized the healer's daughter. She had slipped up between them in the dark.

"Come away, softly now," she said. "I'll take you to the others. They are not far."

Dagg turned hurriedly to follow her. Jan heard him sighing with relief. But the prince's son had to force himself to go. He wanted to stand watching forever under the moon and the stars. He fell in slowly behind Dagg and the healer's daughter. They skirted the glade. Then without a backward glance, Tek struck out into the dark. Jan sighed, following her. He caught a last glimpse of the pans in their Ring through the trees. A handful of them had begun once more to dance.

"They danced," said Jan, after a time.

Tek looked at him. "The pans? I saw none dancing, young prince."

"Before you came," he answered, "and just now, as we left. They were beautiful."

He stopped short, saying it—for only now as he spoke did he realize that it was so. There had been a strange grace in those upright, two-footed forms, a litheness in those odd forelimbs unlike any grace a unicorn could ever have. Jan saw Dagg eyeing him over the back of the healer's daughter.

"Pans?" he cried. "Those twisted little haunts crept up and fell on us this day, without cause."

"We're in their land without their leave," answered Jan, but so softly he was speaking to himself. That thought, too, was new—it had just come to him. Dagg paid no heed. Jan saw him screwing shut his eyes.

"They're like hillcats. They clutched our manes and tried to pull us down. . . ." Jan saw him shudder.

"Peace," murmured Tek.

Jan turned to her. "Was it you," he asked her, "who led us off? You've been ahead of us all this time?"

The young mare looked at him. "Led you off? I only came upon you a few moments gone, out scouting for stragglers."

"There was another then," Jan told her. "I heard . . . I saw. . . ."

The healer's daughter laughed, but gently. "Thought you heard or saw, perhaps? Come, it's easy to imagine haunts and followers in a dark wood at night."

Jan shook his head; he had not meant that at all—but they had reached the others now. Jan spotted them through the trees ahead, in a glade almost at the wood's edge. He saw the moon shining white upon the Plain not twenty paces farther on. Korr stood with Teki across the open space. The prince shifted impatiently, staring back toward the Woods. He seemed to be attending to the healer's words with only half an ear.

Jan followed Tek and Dagg past the sentries into the glade. Spotting them, the prince broke off from Teki and came forward. Those not standing guard had already lain down among the bracken. Korr nodded Dagg away to join the others. Jan halted and gazed at the dark figure standing before him.

"Struck off to delve the Pan Woods on your own?" the prince said curtly. He stood against the moon, a black shadow against its light. Jan could not see his face. "Did you not hear my order to keep together?"

His father's rebuke felt like the slash of hooves. Jan flinched. "We lost sight of the others," he started.

"Dawdling when I told you to fly."

Jan dropped his head. "We ran wrong," he mumbled, picking at the turf with one forehoof. "But we knew if we went westward we'd reach the Plain."

He heard his father sigh. "Well, I suppose that was clever enough," he conceded at last. "If only you were half so clever at staying clear of trouble as you seem to be at finding it." He snorted again. "Heed what I tell you in future," he added. "And stay with the band. Now find you forage, and rest. The Plain is harder going than the Woods."

Korr turned away then, lashing his tail, though there were no flies now, only night millers and moths. Jan gazed after the prince as he went to stand staring out over the moonlit Plain. His heart felt hollow, filled with an ache too keen to bear. He had lost his father's praise.

"You are a silent one for thought," Tek said to him. With a start, he realized the healer's daughter had not left his side. He said the first thing that came into his head.

"I . . . was thinking of the pans." And saying so, he did think of them. The memory of their beauty eased his heart a little. He turned to her. Her eyes were clear, green stones lit by moonlight. "Was it fire?"

She shook her head, clearly puzzled. "A huddle of pans under the moon was all I saw."

"But . . . ," he started. Then he felt sleep catching at his mane and had to swallow a yawn.

"Enough," the young mare said. "The moon's halfway up into the sky. Time enough for talk tomorrow, on the Plain. Good rest."

She bowed to him, going to seek her place among the sentries. Jan bowed in return and, finding where Dagg had lain, he lay down beside him. His limbs felt loose and empty with fatigue. His thoughts were growing woolly, slow. Even the sting of his father's ire was numbing. Nothing seemed to matter now but sleep.

He closed his eyes, images flaring before his inner gaze like flame. By morning, he could not recall, but that night he dreamed of goatlings dancing under the bright egg of the moon.

The Plain

🌿 10 🌿

When Alma made the world, she made the heart of the world first, which was fire, and then the air above the world, and then the sea that girdles the world, and lastly the land. Woods, mountains, and valleys she made, each where each was fitting. But most of the land she shaped into the Plain—not level, but rolling, a vast expanse of gentle rises and wrinkles and rolls.

Korr kept them moving all day their first day upon Alma's back, loping in long easy strides where the ground was smooth or downsloping, checking to a trot where it steepened or grew rough. The moon, huge and yellow, floated beside them on the horizon's edge in the hour after dawn before it set.

They lay up at noon for an hour's rest in a shallow hollow between two rills. Jan threw himself down beside Dagg, panting. His muscles ached and trembled as they cooled. Then before he had even half caught his breath it seemed, they were off again.

Just before dusk, Korr brought them to a halt. Jan's legs folded under him, his eyelids sliding shut of their own accord. He was asleep before he knew. Later, Dagg roused him, and in the dark after sundown they tasted their first grass since they had left the Vale—tender, green, and marvelously sweet.

The land remained hilly as they moved northward. The Pan Woods and the Gryphon Mountains beyond dwindled in the distance, becoming a dark line on the horizon behind them, then vanished at last. Jan felt his muscles hardening, his flanks growing leaner and his stride rangier as each day rolled on.

It was their third morning out of the Woods. The dew was still thick upon the grass, the sun in the east barely risen over the flat rim of the world. Jan's limbs, still stiff from sleep, were beginning to limber. The band had not yet broken camp.

"Well," Jan was saying as his long, slim horn clattered against Dagg's, "what do you think?"

Dagg parried him.

"Keep your guard up," he heard Tek saying.

Jan countered Dagg's sudden thrust and threw him off. They reared together, shoulder-wrestling for a moment.

"Think of what?" Dagg asked him, struggling.

"About the Firebringer," Jan panted, shifting his weight. "That he'll be the color-of-night, and a great warrior. . . ."

He braced himself and Dagg slipped from him. The two of them rolled, then scrabbled to their feet and fenced a little, tentatively.

"More force, Jan," he heard Tek telling him. "You foot as though this were a dance."

But it was, in a way, he thought as Dagg and he dodged, paused, parried, measured, each advancing and giving ground by turns. But he kept his tongue. Dagg was lunging at him.

"The Firebringer? But that's history. Zod the singer saw him."

Jan fended his friend's slow, hard jabs with a half-dozen light taps.

"More force!" called Tek.

Jan parried harder. "But only in a dream."

"A seer's dream."

"List, *faster,* Dagg," the young mare instructed. Jan glimpsed her sidling for a better view. Dagg pivoted, grazing him. The sudden sting surprised him. Jan knocked his friend's horn away.

"I know," he breathed, throwing himself after Dagg. "But do seers' dreams always come to pass?" Taking advantage of his friend's misstep, Jan rained a volley of feints and thrusts. Dagg was too hard pressed to answer. "Tek?" panted Jan. "Does it?"

"Well enough, let be," he heard the healer's daughter laughing. "Enough hornplay for now. We've a day's running ahead of us yet."

Jan and Dagg fell apart, catching their breath. As Tek turned away, they followed her to the edge of the loose Ring of resting unicorns, away from the clash of other pilgrims, early risen, still learning battle-craft. The healer's daughter turned to Jan.

"Until he come, little prince," she said, "all we may know of the Firebringer is what Zod and other dreamers said of him: that he shall come on hooves so hard and sharp they will strike sparks upon the stone. That his blood shall be of burning, and his tongue a flit of flame. That he may not come until the Circle has been broken. And his birth shall mark both the beginning and the ending of an age."

Jan shook his head, frowning at her words. Dawn wind was rising now. "I thought only Zod had foretold the Firebringer."

The healer's daughter shook her shoulders. "Others have seen him. Caroc foretold he would be born out of a wyvern's belly, and Ellioc that he would not come from within the Ring at all, but outside it—a Renegade. . . ."

"But Caroc and Ellioc were false prophetesses," Dagg said impatiently. "Nothing either of them foretold has ever come to pass. . . ."

"Yet," murmured Tek. Dagg snorted.

"How could a unicorn be born out of a wyvern's belly?" He swatted a blackfly from his haunch. "The only one who ever truly saw the Firebringer was Zod."

Tek stood three-legged, cocking her head to scratch her cheek with one heel. "Oh, truly?" she murmured. "Then I suppose I have not seen him."

Jan looked at her. "You saw . . ." he began. "Where, when?"

The young mare straightened, shaking herself. "Not in flesh. In a dream."

Dagg came forward. "Is *that* why you changed the ending of the lay, the one you sang at Moondance?"

Tek glanced at him, and let go a nickering laugh. "So far, you seem to be the only one to have remarked it." She laughed again, half at herself. "Perhaps the others were all already asleep."

"The Beard," Jan heard Dagg breathe. "I told you she was a dreamer."

The young mare sighed. "No dreamer. Only a little of a singer, and a warrior. I saw the Firebringer on the night all unicorns are dreamers: at my initiation, two years gone."

Jan snorted. "What do you mean?"

Tek looked at him. "You have not heard? I thought all colts found out before the time, though they are not meant to."

Jan studied her, and she was laughing at him with her green, green eyes—taunting him, daring him. But he refused to be baited. He only said, softly, "Will you tell us of it, of initiation?"

She nodded then, shrugging. "I suppose. You'll find out soon enough in any case." And she made her voice low, like a singer's cant. Both colts had to lean closer to hear. "Those who have come far over Alma's back, kept Ring and borne themselves bravely—those whom the Mother finds worthy—will at dawn behold a true vision of their destinies upon the Mirror of the Moon."

Jan's heart missed a step. "Their destinies," he whispered, gazing at Tek. She sighed, her eyes fixed, unfocused now.

"Only a glimpse. A glimpse."

"And you saw the Firebringer."

She had turned a little away from him. "I saw the moon crack like a bird's egg and fall out of the sky, and from the broken shell stepped forth a young unicorn, long limbed and lithe, a runner, a dancer, and black as the well of a weasel's eye. He looked exactly as the old song says:

> *"The silver moon rode on his brow,*
> *And a white star on his heel."*

"But," said Jan; he had to force himself to speak slowly, "if you saw him born. . . ." Excitement flared in him. "Then that can only mean the Firebringer will come among us in your lifetime."

Tek glanced at Jan, then Dagg. She laughed, casting a glance at Korr. "Perhaps. Or perhaps he is already among us, only waiting to be known."

Jan turned to gaze after his father, who stood a little apart from the band, watching the fiery dish of the sun pull free of the horizon. Korr was a mighty prince, a fleet runner, a fine dancer. And he was black, black as a starless night. Did Tek think Korr might be the one—did others think it? Dagg had hinted as much at Moondance, days ago.

Jan felt a rush of longing then. Was there nothing he could do to win back his father's esteem? And though the prince had not a mark of white or silver on him, odd spots, appearing suddenly, were not unknown among the unicorns. One never knew what lay beneath until spring shed.

Tek started away from him, murmuring, "We'll be breaking camp soon."

Jan let go his daydreaming and yawned, shaking himself. Dagg shouldered against him. The grass before them billowed and stirred. As Dagg lowered his head to nibble the tender green shoots, Jan turned to follow Tek. There had been something more he had wanted to ask her. The sun was up, the waning moon in the western sky well past its zenith. Tek was rousing those who were dozing still.

"Hist, Tek," said Jan lowly. The healer's daughter turned. "Where were you off to, night past?"

The young mare frowned and shook her head. "I stood sentry before dawn, if that's what you mean."

She turned and woke another pilgrim. Jan waited till they were out of others' earshot again. "Earlier—before moonrise."

Tek halted and studied him keenly. "Breaking the Ring is forbidden," she told him. "And straying away would be madness at night. There are grass pards on this Plain."

Jan shook his head. "I saw you."

Teki had sung them a lay after dusk, how Alma created her own being from a dance of light in the Great Darkness before time, and the world was but a droplet shaken from her as a young mare shakes bright water from her coat. Afterward, as the others around him had drifted into sleep, Jan had lain restless, gazing off into the dark.

The sentries, at last getting their turn to eat, had torn at the young grass too greedily to keep good watch. Then Jan had caught a hint of motion from the corner of his eye and turned to see a unicorn slipping away from camp, half hidden by the folds and rills of land, then striking out at a fast, silent lope in the direction whence they had come.

He stood gazing at Tek as she eyed him now in the light of broken day. "I have gone nowhere, young princeling," she answered, suddenly formal, then turned to rouse another initiate. "You must have dreamed it."

Jan watched her go. It had been no dream. Tek's own mother, Jahlila, had banished his dreams when he was small. Surely the pied mare could not have forgotten that. He had not been able to see the other's color, night past, by the dim starlight, but the form and the gait had reminded him strongly of Tek.

She moved away from Jan, stepping among the Circle of pilgrims, murmuring for them to rise. Jan gazed after her, feeling oddly unsettled and at a loss. Sleepily, the last of the initiates rose and stretched. Korr's whistle to the band a moment later cut across Jan's thoughts, and they were off once more across the Plain.

🌿

Jan and Dagg ran with Tek, as had become their custom. Other initiates had singled out warriors to be their mentors as well. Jan said nothing more of having seen Tek slip away, and the morning drifted on. As the unicorns loped over the rolling grassland, the sun pulled higher. White clouds began to stray across the wide, blue sky.

After a time, he came aware that Dagg had drifted from them, and now was running a little apart from the band, his gaze fixed intently away. Jan followed his stare, fixing his own eyes on the far horizon and the miles of openness between. *What lay beyond there?* he wondered, the question stirring and murmuring in the back of his mind. *What lay beyond?*

Jan came back to himself with a start, as Dagg before him suddenly stumbled, missing his stride. They both had drifted even farther from the herd. How long had he been running, lost in thought? Jan wondered. The sun seemed higher. Before him Dagg snorted and tossed his head. Jan drew alongside.

"What is it?"

"Look there."

Jan scanned to westward, straining his eyes. Then he saw, suddenly, two figures very far away upon the crest of a roll. They stood splay-legged, heads high as if surprised, watching the herd loping by. They were unicorns.

"Tek!" cried Jan, veering back with Dagg toward their mentor. "Do you see them? What are they?"

He saw the healer's daughter turn and her green eyes narrow as she spotted the figures on the distant rise. She glanced at Jan. "Renegades."

Jan wrenched his gaze back to the pair. They had passed the mid-point of his gaze, and he had to turn to keep them in view. Renegades— those who had deserted the Vale, forsaken Alma and broken the Ring of Law. Outcasts, criminals, infidels. *And I almost became one of them,* he found himself thinking, his mind going back to the day of the gryphons. Jan stared at the figures on the hill.

"Watch," Tek was telling him.

She let loose a long, loud warrior's cry. The pair upon the hillside started and wheeled, vanishing over the crest of the rise. Jan thought he could hear their wild, high whinnies very faintly on the breeze. He saw his father snorting, refusing to acknowledge the Ringbreakers' presence by so much as a glance. The band galloped on.

Time passed. Hours, and then days, almost a dozen of them. Sun-rises and moonsets fell behind them as they ran, and the land seemed to roll away under their hooves. For Jan, their days were all loping, snatched rest, and sparring. The warriors taught them battlecraft, how to stalk, how to follow a trail. The healer told them the properties of herbs and where to find water on the Great Grass Plain.

Their nights were all greedy feeding and singers' tales and sleep. Korr showed them how to find their way using the stars. The whole sky had become strangely tilted now; new starshapes looming before them as they traveled north, the old ones slipping beyond the world's rim behind.

Sometimes at night now, gazing into the pattern of Alma's eyes, Jan felt himself taken from himself, made hollow. If only he gazed long enough, deeply enough, it seemed he might begin to read some great mystery in their turning, something deeper than simply where on the world he stood. As if the stars might, very gently, bear him away.

But despite the unceasing cycle of busyness and rest, busyness and rest, Jan felt a restlessness within him growing. Though he guarded himself very close now, keeping himself always within the band as his father had commanded, more and more he found himself gazing off across the Plain. That strange little voice he could not quite hear whispered in his mind still: *What lies beyond your band, beyond the vastness of the Plain? Come, come away. Come see.*

Sometimes, in the distance behind, he glimpsed a figure that did not stop and stare at them, as Renegades did. And sometimes he caught the far, faint drum of heels after the band had already come to a halt. Only Tek seemed restless, too, though she said no word. Twice more he glimpsed her slipping off into the dark.

Something moved out there, just beyond his range. He felt it to the marrow of his bones. Not all its cunning could keep him from beginning to suspect that something watched him, or awaited him, or both. Its hold on him that had blocked his vision for so long, at last was growing tenuous.

So it kept itself nearby, but circumspect. And the prince's son stayed baffled still, for it dared not risk letting him—letting any of them—learn who it was that ran behind.

Renegade

❧ 11 ❧

T he twelfth day of their travel upon the Mare's back was stretching on toward noon. Jan and Dagg ran with Tek near the middle of the band. A light rain must have fallen the night before, for the ground over which they ran was damp. They had seen no hard rains yet upon the Plain.

The prince before them crested a rise, and Jan saw his father come suddenly to a standstill. At his whistle, the pilgrims plunged to a halt. Jan stood a moment, puzzled; the day was early yet for halting. The sun had not yet topped the sky.

Jan trotted forward, and a few others followed. He halted near his father, who stood gazing down the slope. Then Jan started and cavaled as he saw what had caught the prince's eye. Below them lay a unicorn, pale blue and bloodied, her horn stained red. The great vein of her throat had been torn; talons had scored her flank and neck. Nearby lay a banded pard, gored through one shoulder and the ribs of one battered side staved in from a mighty kick.

No spotted kites yet circled the sky. The blood upon the grass was wet. Jan stared, realizing: It could not have happened an hour gone. He heard his father give a great snort, then, as though he had unwittingly smelled fetor.

"Pard," Korr muttered, starting downslope at an angle, away from the dead. "Renegade."

"See the mistake she made," Jan heard Tek telling Dagg. "She let it clasp her by the throat." Her warrior's voice was flat, dispassionate. Jan wheeled to stare. "If ever one of those springs on you, buck—roll. Don't gore. Use your heels—and run."

Jan turned back to the fallen mare, pity mingling with his horror.

She was so young; she could not have been much older than Tek. And she had died bravely, fighting for her life—*as I once fought for my life,* Jan found himself thinking, *not so long ago.*

Others of the band, he realized, were already following the prince. Though some of the initiates still stood staring, the warriors turned them, hurrying them off, themselves trotting by the dead with hardly a glance.

"But," Jan started, "shouldn't we bury her?"

The prince broke into a lope at the bottom of the hill, whistling the others to follow him.

"But," cried Jan, "she's dead. Shouldn't there be rites?"

His father wheeled. "Less noise," he called. "We move on."

Jan stared in disbelief. They could not simply abandon the dead. It was against Alma's Law. It was shameful. "We can't go yet," he burst out. "A warrior deserves. . . ."

At that, Korr wheeled and smote the ground with his forehooves. "Hold your tongue," he thundered. "*That* is no warrior." He tossed his head toward the fallen mare. "She was a Renegade, and died as all outside the Circle must—unmarked and unmourned. The Law is not for her. Now come."

Others of the band had strayed to a stop, stood watching the prince of the unicorns and his son. Korr wheeled away. Jan stood confounded. A Renegade? But she bore a horn upon her brow. Her hooves were cloven still, not solid round and single-toed. And even if she were a Renegade, what could that matter now? She was a unicorn, and she was dead.

His father gave no backward glance. Jan found himself shouting, "This isn't right!"

But a sharp nip on the flank cut him short. He spun around. Tek shouldered against him, shoving him after the herd.

"Enough," she whispered. "Don't contest with your father."

"No, it's wrong," cried Jan, "leaving her." He threw his weight back, resisting. He felt hot and rash.

Tek bullied him forward, nearly knocking him down.

"Be still, Jan. Just come!" he heard Dagg call.

The prince and the others were cantering away. Dagg lingered, but Teki shouldered against him, turning him. Dagg tried to duck around, dodge back to Jan, but the healer herded him away after the rest. Dagg gazed back over his shoulder helplessly. Jan stared. The others' dust clouded the air. Another sharp nip on the flank brought him back to himself.

"Hie!" Tek shouted. "*Now,* or we'll not catch them till noon."

Jan kicked into a gallop, seething with rage. He and Tek breathed dust, running hard for a mile until they caught the herd. Korr called a halt not long after. Jan threw himself down at the edge of the Ring. At the prince's nod, Teki kept Dagg with him across the Ring, away from Jan. The healer began to sing them a lay.

"I'll tell you now of the Renegades, how each was a unicorn once, but failed initiation, or else was banished for murder or some other crime, or else faithlessly broke Ring and ran away to live wild, godless, Lawless, hated of Alma upon the Plain. . . ."

Jan could not listen. His thoughts were in a snarl. Fury made his jaw ache, his ears burn. His blood felt feverish. After a moment, he pitched to his feet and left the Ring. Tek beside him showed no interest at his going. The others were all either absorbed in the tale or intentionally ignoring him, as Korr was. Jan trotted around a low rise, out of sight of the camp. He had to get away.

The sentry eyed him indifferently, then turned his attention back to the camp. Jan pawed the turf, frustration biting at him. He did not care if the mare *had* been a Renegade. What they had done was dishonorable, simply leaving her, as if she had been no more than a dead gryphon or pan. No! Jan shook his head. She was a unicorn. She had killed a pard at the cost of her life and deserved a hero's death rites.

Something occurred to him then, a possibility he had not considered before. He halted, turning it over in his mind. Did he really need anybody's leave? Anyone might perform the rites. And if he ran quick and light, keeping low behind the brow of the swells before striking out across the Plain, he could be halfway back to the mare before he was spotted—if he was spotted. It was almost like a game.

Jan glanced at the sentry on the hill. The warrior's ears were still pricked to the sound of Teki's voice, his gaze inward turned, not scanning the Plain as it should have been. Jan made up his mind in a rush and plunged into the dry gully across from him, putting another rise between himself and the camp.

He followed the streambed back the way they had come, then clambered up the short, steep bank onto the grass again. Behind him, the sentry was a small, gray figure against the sky, and the fallen Renegade lay only a couple of miles' hard gallop off. Jan sprinted across the Plain.

The Renegade was not difficult to find. Spotted kites had begun to circle now. At home, in the Vale, Jan had seen the rites for the dead, how the fallen were laid upon the outer cliffs with forelegs extended, their heads thrown back, manes streaming and their hind legs kicked out behind. Nearing the spot where the dark birds circled, he told himself he would lay out the fallen mare and be back to noon camp before he could be missed.

Jan topped the gentle rise before the slope on which the Renegade and the pard that had felled her lay—then pitched to a halt, snorting, staring. Someone had been there before him, and whoever it was had been laying out the grasscat as well. The pard lay stretched now, paws folded, a Circle trampled in the grass all around—just as for a warrior.

Jan glanced about him, puzzled, and suddenly uneasy, wondering whom he had interrupted at the rites. He gave a whinny, then another, and listened. No answer came. The legs of the mare had been laid, but her head was not yet lifted. The Circle about her was only half complete. The shadows of the dark birds wheeled and floated over the grass.

He had no time to waste on wondering. Jan descended the slope. He took the young mare's horn in his teeth—carefully, lest it prove brittle. To his surprise, it was strong and hard. Horn in teeth, he lifted her head and laid it so her silvery mane streamed long and knotted on the grass. He had to work quickly. The kites were dropping lower in the sky.

He had just finished the stamping of the Circle about her when he caught the sound of hoofbeats. He whirled, fearing for a moment that it was members of his own band, before realizing that the sound came from the wrong quarter, from the west.

A unicorn topped the rise. He was young, no older than Dagg's young mother, Leerah, and color-of-evening-sky. His mane was long, with feathers tangled in it. He bore a horn upon his brow. A pale orange mare joined him in a moment, then a crimson filly almost half-grown. They stared at Jan. Jan stared at them. They all had horns. The evening blue came a few steps down the slope.

"What do you here?" His words were quiet, odd. A moment passed before Jan understood him.

"I was burying them," he answered. "Weren't you here before?"

The other shook his head.

"We saw the kites," the pale mare said.

The blue was eyeing him more closely now. "You have not the look of one from the Plain," he said. "Nor the speech of one, either. Whence come you?"

Jan gazed at them, startled. "I come from the Vale of the Unicorns. On Pilgrimage."

All three of the strangers started.

"He's a Moondancer," the pale mare muttered. "One of those who drink of the wyvern pool."

Jan glanced at the dead mare, then turned to the one who stood before him. "I didn't start to bury her," he said. "I only finished the rite. Was it none of you?"

The dark blue unicorn shook his head. "Nay. And I know of no one else who runs in these parts this moon. It must have been the Far One."

"The Fair One," the pale mare said, and the filly echoed, "The Red One, the Rare One."

"She is often on the Plain in spring," the blue unicorn added, and Jan realized he must have looked confounded. "She is a strange, dark mallow color, without any yellow or amber in it. She is holy, and very wise. Her hooves are oddly made, for she comes from a far place. And once, it is said, she was not a unicorn."

Jan had to listen very hard to be able to follow. Their speech was strange, like a singer's cant—and much of it he did not understand at all.

"She is known and welcomed everywhere among the Free People," the crimson filly said.

Jan shook his head; he had never heard of such a one. "You have seen her?" he asked.

Now the filly shook her head.

"They say a young prince of the southlands found her, years ago, lost and wandering," the orange mare said. She came a few steps downslope to stand beside the blue. "He told her of the wyvern country far across the Plain, that she might go there in summer, and drink of a miraculous spring that would make her a unicorn."

"What prince was that?" cried Jan. He had never heard of such a deed in song or lay.

"The one whose name means 'thunder,' " the blue one said. "The black one. . . ." He glanced at the mare beside him.

She told him, "Korr."

Jan started like a deer. "My fa. . . ." He caught himself. "A prince of the unicorns would never do such a thing—let drink of the sacred pool one who was not of the Circle."

"Circle?" the red filly asked.

Jan stared at them. "Don't you know? You're Renegades."

"Renegades," the evening blue murmured, tasting the word as though it were strange upon his tongue.

"Weren't you born of the Circle, in the Vale of the Unicorns?"

The blue shook his head. "I was born here, on the Plain."

Jan breathed out hard, feeling as if his ribs had been kicked. They were not of the Circle, had never been of the Circle. They were not runaways from his people at all. They were, instead, of another clan, another—he searched for the word—*tribe* altogether, like the gryphons, like the pans.

Then his skin grew cold. For they were unicorns. They had never sipped of the Mirror of the Moon, yet their horns had not fallen, nor their cloven hooves grown single and round. Wispy tassels tipped their ears, and their heels were fringed with silky hair. They were bearded. He could not seem to catch his breath.

The blue unicorn shrugged. "I have always lived here."

"*I* have heard of this Circle of the southerners," the pale mare said, coming forward now again, "this Ring of War, this Circle of the Moon—and your Vale. My mother fled them when she was no more than a filly." Her words were sharp. "She said you southlanders think much of your Ring, and bind yourselves to it until you cannot see or say or think or do a thing that is not within it."

She tossed her head and snorted.

"Well, we are not bound to your Circle. We come and think and say as we please. We are the Free People."

Jan blinked and stared at her. He had never been so spoken to in all his life. And what was this they said of Korr—that he had broken the Circle, broken the Law, to tell the secret way to the Mirror of the Moon to one who was not even a unicorn. Or what had they said? Who had *once* not been a unicorn? He saw the blue unicorn eyeing the sky. The shadows of the kites had grown sharper, their spirals tighter. They circled lower to the ground.

"The time turns short that it would be proper to remain here," the blue unicorn said. "Soon it will be the kites' time."

Jan's gaze went once more to the fallen mare, pale middle blue against the dark earth of the Plain. Her blood on the grass was dry. She looked as though she were springing free of the Ring that encircled her. He glanced at the dark blue unicorn with feathers in his hair.

"Did you know her?" Jan asked him. The other shook his head. Jan turned back to the fallen one. "We have a song for the dead," he said, "when we lay them out to greet the sky:

> "*Fate has unspoken   one of the Circle,*
> *Pride of companions,   wonted of fame.*
> *Vouch for her valor,   her heart of a hero,*
> *Fellow of warriors,   fallen in battle:*
> *Rally, remember her name.*"

He was no singer, but his voice was young and strong. Jan stopped himself at the last word.

"I don't know her name," he said.

"The Mother knows," said the blue unicorn beside him.

The filly told him, "Álm'harat knows."

Jan turned, drawn up short again with wonder—though he was already so stunned it almost seemed nothing should surprise him anymore—that any dared speak the truename of Alma here, so openly. He had always been taught that those outside the Ring had cast off the Mother-of-all, had forgotten her.

The plainsdwellers joined him at the Circle's edge. He saw them dip their heads, going down on one knee first to the fallen mare, then to the pard. Jan blinked, frowning. It was no gesture he had ever seen before. He bowed his own head to the mare, then after a pause, to the grasscat as well. The plainsdwellers rose.

Then the pale orange mare turned to him and went down again on one knee for a moment before him. Jan drew back, not knowing what to make of it.

"My words were harsh to you before, young stranger," she said, rising. "For that, I ask your pardon. You have honored our dead in accordance with your custom, and that is unlike any southlander I have ever heard of."

"And you have honored her slain enemy as well, as is fitting," the blue unicorn said. "That, too, is unlike what we have heard of southlanders."

"I didn't," Jan started. "We don't. . . ." He stopped and gazed at the three plainsdwellers before him. Then he blurted out, "A gryphon came, a month ago. . . ."

"Gryphon?" the red filly said.

"It's like a pard," cried Jan, "but wingèd." He caught himself. Why was it so urgent he give these strangers only the truth?

" 'Wingcats,' my mother called them," the pale mare murmured. "They don't come here."

Jan drew breath and made his voice as steady as he could. "We killed it—it had attacked us—but we didn't bury it. We cast it over the cliff."

The dark blue unicorn frowned. "That is strange."

"Why do you dishonor your enemies?" the red filly asked. "Was this wingcat not brave?"

"Is all that is true to its own nature not worthy of honor," the evening blue said, "being part of the Cycle?"

A kite passed very close overhead. Jan felt the wind of its passing against his brow. He flinched, frowning. "I thought you said you disdained our Circle. . . ."

The plainsdweller shook his head. "Nay. That is not the Cycle of which I spoke . . . hist. Come away."

A kite had alighted on the grass, across the Circle from them. Jan came with them, following the plainsdwellers up the slope. The sky in the south was dark with cloud. More kites were settling on the grass below. The blue unicorn raised his head, his nostrils wide.

"A storm's in the wind," he said.

Jan glanced at the sun. "I have to go back," he told them. "Noon's almost done."

"Farewell, then, young stranger," the evening blue said.

"Swift running," said the pale mare, "and no pards behind you."

"Light sleeping," the filly bade him. "Far seeing."

"Alma keep you," Jan found himself saying. He was bowing—he almost wished he could stay. They were so strange—unicorns, yet not like his own people at all. He wished he could understand them, grasp more of what they had said to him, but he dared not linger. The band would be breaking camp before long. He could not stay.

The plainsdwellers dipped to their knees in leave-taking, then wheeled, whinnying and tossing their heads, and galloped off across the Plain to the west. Jan shook himself, then turned at last. The storm in the south had drawn nearer. He sprinted northward. Behind him, the spotted kites were dropping from the sky.

He found the gully he had followed before and slipped into its shelter long before the gray speck of a sentry could take note of him. He sprinted along the dry channel's flat, even bed until he was almost to camp. The lookout on the hill above was still attending to Teki's lay. Jan crept past, around the rise. The unicorns yet rested in their Ring, all eyes upon the healer reciting his tale:

"So that is the lay of Aras, the first Renegade, false Ringbreaker, who spurned Halla the princess's rule and forsook the herd. . . ."

Jan spotted Dagg across the Ring, staring off miserably at nothing. Korr's gaze was turned pointedly away from Jan's empty spot. As Jan slipped into place beside the healer's daughter, Tek hardly glanced at him. Teki was singing:

"So he perished horribly, as I have told, for Alma's wrath. And all of this took place after the unicorns had been cast out of the Hallow Hills, but before they came upon the Vale that is now our home. My tale is done."

Jan lay at the Ring's edge, catching his breath. No one even seemed to have noticed he had been gone.

The Hallow Hills

❧ 12 ❧

Teki finished his tale, and the unicorns broke camp. They trotted at first to loosen their limbs. Jan felt wobbly, short of breath—he had spent none of the noon halt resting—and Korr still kept Dagg between him and the healer, apart from Jan. A line of tall, dark thunderheads crowded the distance behind.

By midafternoon they had swallowed the sun, bringing in their shadow a rush of cool, southern air. Jan felt his old wildness at thunderstorms rising. Stormwind riffled his winter coat, lifting the dust, bowing the grass. The smell of water hung in the wind. Then the gusts grew stronger suddenly, buffeting, the dust rising in whirlwinds.

Korr whistled the band to a faster lope, and Jan wondered if he hoped to outrun the storm. If so, it was to no avail, for within minutes rain began to lash at them. The stormshadow around them had grown very dark. Great bolts of blue lightning vaulted overhead.

And then Jan caught sound of something, another sound above the rain. It was a rushing as of many gryphons' wings, a roar like hillsides breaking and plunging away. One moment it sounded faint and far, the next almost upon them, coming and going in the gusts of storm. Ahead of him, Jan saw his father's head come up.

"Gallop!" thundered the prince. "Full gallop, all!"

The band sprang into a run.

"What is it?" cried Jan, drawing alongside Tek.

"Serpent-cloud," she shouted at him. "A great destroyer!"

Jan felt his legs tangle, his breath grow short. The old lays sang of Serpent-clouds, great tunnels of storm that ran down Ringbreakers and Renegades. He cast a wild glance over one shoulder, but could see nothing for the blinding, choking rain.

"Where is it?" he shouted at Tek. "How if it catches us?"

"Fling us to bits," the young mare answered. "So fly!"

They ran. The ground over which they galloped was slick, treacherous with mud. Thunder snorted and stamped. Jan felt the herd around him growing ragged. The eyes of some had begun to roll. Lightning fell to the right and left of them, the band flinching and veering at every crash.

"Shelter!" he heard someone to the fore of them crying. "Shelter ahead!"

Jan felt the pitch of the ground rise under his feet, then curve and fall abruptly away. He vaulted into a gully and then flung himself backward, folding his legs. Tek was scrambling into place beside him. They lay, shouldered into the steep curve of the bank, sheltered somewhat from the driving rain. But above the fury of thunder and wind, he still heard the wild crooning of the Serpent-cloud.

"Where's Dagg?" Jan said suddenly, and flung a glance over his shoulder. "Dagg?"

He searched the downpour, up and down the line of other unicorns crowding the gully. He did not see him. Where was he—had he fallen? Was he still out upon the Plain? Jan bolted to his feet and struggled up over the bank again, shouting his friend's name. Tek scrambled after him.

"What is it?" she cried. "What are you doing?"

The stormrain whipped at his face, his eyes. "It's Dagg!" he flung back. "I don't see him. Da. . . ." But then he saw another thing that drove even the thought of Dagg from his mind.

It seemed that for a moment a lull descended on him. Despite the wind and dark, his vision cleared. The stamp of thunder, the lightning's flare, and the wet pummeling of rain faded from him. To southward he could see a long flail of cloud spinning down out of the thunderheads. It was wholly black, writhing and dancing like a whipsnake upon its tail. Where it touched the Plain, great gouts of earth sprang up and whirled away.

But before Jan, between him and the storm, stood a unicorn, far away on the crest of the long gentle slope down which the band had just run. He could make out nothing more about it, neither its color nor its gender nor its age. The stormwind seemed to make its short, thick mane stream upright along its neck.

The unicorn was singing. Jan was certain of that. His body heard it through the air; it reached his hooves as a kind of trembling in the ground. It made his eyes water, his breast burn—and he wanted to follow, follow without thought, that music, wherever the singer might lead.

The unicorn turned then, westward, trotting away in a dancing stride. The low, magical singing floated back, sweeter, immeasurably sweeter than panpipes to his ears. The Serpent-cloud veered sluggishly. It seemed to hesitate, and then drifted after the retreating unicorn, docilely as a nursling after its dam.

Jan cried out as he realized they were going. He staggered after them a few paces—and the vision ended. The rush of stormwind returned, and the lightning's clash. Feeling the wet hooves of rain upon his back, he blinked and snorted. The water stung in his nostrils, splashing his eyes.

"He's well," he heard Tek shouting beside him. "I saw him take shelter." Thunder swallowed her words. ". . . down the bank by Teki! He's safe."

Jan realized dimly she was telling him of Dagg, and felt her shouldering him back toward the gully.

"Who was it?" cried Jan over his shoulder, once he and Tek were again safely dug into the bank.

"Who?" she cried back. "I saw no one."

"The unicorn," he shouted, "at the top of the rise."

"I couldn't see the top," Tek called back at him.

"You did," cried Jan, suddenly desperate. "You must have."

The wind lashed furiously above them now. Tek bent to his ear. "What are you talking of?" she exclaimed. "I don't follow."

"You do," Jan yelled. "It was in the Vale at Moondance; it sang then, too. And in the Pan Woods—it cried out to Dagg and me and led us astray." The angry timbre of his own voice surprised him. He could not stop. "And it's been behind us, on the Plain," he cried. "You know it has. You keep slipping away from camp to look for it, or talk to it, or. . . ."

Tek did not reply.

"Now it's called away the storm." Jan demanded, "What is it? Who is it?"

"I don't know!" Tek shouted at him. "I don't know what you mean—what you've dreamed here, in the rain. . . ."

The wind tore the last of her words away. The storm had grown too wild to let them talk. She did know. She knew *something* and was not telling him. Frustration burned in him. He turned furiously away from Tek and settled himself to ride out the storm.

Eventually the gale lessened, the rolling thunder receding to north and west. Jan laid his head against the wet bank, aware for the first time how weary he was. Around him, the unicorns lay still. Gradually, the light rain subsided, and at last the sun broke through the parting clouds.

Jan stumbled to his feet, his fury spent. He heard others around him doing the same. He clambered from the gully and up the far bank, shaking off and struggling to the top of the next gentle rise. Dagg stood there. Jan went to him, and no one parted them. The storm seemed to have washed away all memory of the Renegade and Jan's disgrace.

Dagg shouldered him companionably, and the two of them stood gazing toward the west. The thunderheads hung there, small and distant now, edged red-golden by the sun.

"Look," Dagg said.

And when Jan turned, he realized for the first time that they stood in sight of the Hallow Hills.

🦄

The prince's son and the dapple colt stood watching the dusk stream over the far line of hills as the sky behind them deepened past violet to black. The band spent nearly the whole night feasting then, waiting for the ground to grow dry enough to lie upon, and eating all they could; for there would be no feasting on the morrow, the night of the nothing-moon.

Jan alternately browsed and dozed, toying with what Tek had told him during the storm. Perhaps panic *had* misled his eyes; and he had imagined it all—for he had half believed, while they had fled, that Alma had sent her Serpent-cloud for him, to strike him down for having broken the Ring and consorted with Renegades. Jan snorted then. But that was nonsense, surely, and the unicorn leading away the storm, a dream.

He slipped into genuine sleep near the end of the night, and a scant slip of waning moon appeared barely an hour before dawn. Korr roused them. They broke camp before sunup, and day broke over the Hallow Hills as the unicorns loped toward them under the horns of the moon.

Korr called a halt again, still early in the day, not a half hour's distance from the slopes. Jan watched his father scanning, testing the wind. He had ordered scouts ahead to comb for wyverns, for spring was coming in apace that year. Who knew when the wyrms might wake? The initiates he bade rest while they might, for there would be no sleep that night as they kept vigil beside the pool.

When by midafternoon the last of the prince's scouts were safely returned, having found no sign of wyverns, Korr whistled the pilgrims into line, and they entered the Hallow Hills. Their pace, a trot, seemed leisurely after so many days of hard running.

Jan found himself traversing gentle, rounded slopes newly in grass, small groves, and wide, sprouting meadows. The groves of hardwood and evergreen that they skirted looked cool and dense. After a time, Jan noticed that the hills had begun thrusting up in short cliffs. Beneath the dark topsoil, patches of pale chalk showed through.

In the late afternoon, they reached the base of a steep hillside with a narrow trail wending its face. Korr ordered them to climb. The stone proved very soft and crumbling; Jan and Dagg had to struggle to keep their footing while showers of scree from pilgrims above skidded about their hooves.

The last dozen paces of the slope were the steepest. Jan braced himself, shouldering Dagg up over the rim of the cliff, then scrambled up himself. They halted a moment, catching their breath, and Jan found they stood in a grove of hardwood trees with pale, rutted bark on twisted trunks. They were still in leaf, and their foliage had a silver cast. Jan lifted his head with nostrils wide; the scent of the trees was like mare's milk and honey.

As they moved away from the cliff's edge, deeper into the grove, Jan scented water under the fragrance of the trees and peered ahead of him. Then he caught his breath, for it lay before him, through the tree-boles: the sacred pool of the unicorns, the Mirror of the Moon.

And it was round, perfectly round, twenty paces across and shallow near the banks. But it deepened at the heart, falling away in a blue cavern that went down, down it seemed into the heart of the world. No plant, no fish blotted the whiteness of its bottom or banks. No ripple marred the eye-smooth surface of the pool.

Only the flat, flaked sand at the cavern's edge fluttered in its depths like flurried snow. Jan gazed, unaware how near he had drawn. That flickering reminded him of something: birds flocking, a dance of unicorns seen from a high slope, strange stars. They seemed to form a pattern he ought to study, read. But as he started forward again, Tek moved suddenly across his path.

"Hold, prince-son," she said. "It's not yet dusk. Let the warriors prepare."

Dimly, Jan realized he had come to the grove's edge, and Dagg was no longer at his side. Jan shook his head to clear it now, and glanced about him. Warriors were stepping onto the flat, sandy bank and approaching the Mere. Initiates hung back among the trees. Jan's eyes returned to the water.

"Nothing grows there," he heard himself saying.

"Too salt," the healer's daughter said. "But with the coming of the Firebringer, they say it will grow sweet again."

Jan glanced at her.

"Come," she told him, moving away among the trees. "I'll show you the grove."

🌿

It was late afternoon as they walked among the trees. Jan gazed more closely now at their papery leaves: rounds and hearts and slender crescents, with pale undersides that reflected the light. Tek moved before him through the slim, twisted trunks and Jan followed, leisurely. The sun ran in dapples over her odd, pied coat.

"They are called milkwood," Tek was telling him, "because the sap is thick and white, sweet to the taste. The rosehips—the fruit of their flowers—drip it when ripe."

Jan was only half listening. He felt very calm, suspended almost, neither hungry nor tired now. A thick carpet of pale, wispy leaves rustled about his pasterns as he walked. Their light, rich scent hung in the air.

"It is good against toothache, pain in the bones, and some poisons."

Jan halted a moment. "They're dropping their leaves."

Tek nodded. "They do that in spring. To bloom."

Jan drew nearer to one of the trees and saw green buds upon the limbs. A breeze lifted, then fell. The slender, knotted branches shivered, and a flock of bright leaves shimmered down. The scent of resin underlay the waft of honey in the air.

"What will they look like, the flowers?" Jan asked her, trying to see past the green in the buds.

"Deep rose," the young mare answered, "or pale, with five petals, yellow at the heart."

The light wind breathed again, and the whole wood sighed. More leaves flickered, silvery in the sunlight. Jan lifted his head suddenly from the low bough he studied.

"How do you know that," he asked her, "their color and shape? You've only been here once before, and that was at first spring, too."

The young mare smiled, to herself, looking off. "My mother told me."

Jan glanced up. "How does she know?"

Tek's expression never changed. "My mother is a magicker, and knows many things."

"Like how to sing away my dreams," murmured Jan.

"Yes."

The healer's daughter still looked away. He could not see her face now, but suddenly her stance seemed very sad.

"You do not see her much, do you?" Jan ventured, trying to remember the last time he himself had seen Jah-lila. It was only that once, when he was young. "She is hardly ever in the Vale."

Since then, he had only heard of her, in whispers. Tek seemed to be looking down.

"My mother is in and out of the Vale more often than you think," she said quietly. Then, almost sharply, "But you are right. She does not come to visit me." Abruptly, she began to move away. Jan sprang to follow. Tek snorted. "Well, no matter. I do not miss her anymore."

Jan stared at her, not understanding. How could she say that? If his dam had chosen to live apart from him, he would have missed her terribly. "Why is that?" he asked of Tek.

The healer's daughter stopped then, with a sigh, as if realizing that she had said too much, and turned to face him. "Because I am not like her, little prince. When I was young, I used to tell myself, 'When I am grown, I will go to my mother and live as she lives, apart from all others, alone. But no more. I know myself better now. I am only a singer, and a warrior. Nothing will ever make me a dreamer or a magicker."

Then she moved on again, and Jan with her. They walked a little while through the trees.

"Why . . . why does she live apart?" Jan tried again. It was a question he had been wondering all his life, though he had never been able to get from anyone any answer longer than "It is her way." But Tek's reply was equally short; she did not want to talk.

"That is the prince's doing."

Jan halted, staring at her.

"Korr's . . . what do you mean?"

Tek glanced at him. "Some old falling-out between the two of them. I know nothing of it. It was before I was born. But I do know that some of it—most of it, much of it—is because my mother dreams dreams, and the prince will have no truck with dreamers. . . ."

She broke off all at once, with obvious relief, for they had come through the grove at last to the cliff's edge. The trees ended as the land sloped steeply away, then leveled off in a long, descending array of shelfland below. Sparse, stunted brushwood stood in thickets, and rivulets snaked sluggishly over the brittle white rock. Hollows of darkness showed here and there beneath the jutting shelves.

"The wyvern steps?" asked Jan, keeping his voice low. He held himself to the shadow of the trees.

Tek nodded. Her voice, too, when she spoke, was low. "Their dens extend—probably under these cliffs as well."

Jan's glance fell to the limechalk he was standing upon. The toes of his hooves felt strange. "But they're sleeping still," he said. "The wyrms."

The healer's daughter shrugged. "We found no sign of them."

Jan gazed out over the wyvern steps. The stretch of them, away to the southeast, was vast. As he watched, the tint of sky changed, grew yellow, casting a sallow light upon the land. Jan felt a twinge between his shoulder blades. The country before him seemed unearthly still. Nothing moved among the scrub or within the dark mouths of the caves.

"Did you bury her?" Tek beside him said. Her voice was very low. Jan turned to look at her, not following. His mentor's eyes met his. "The mare," she said. "The Renegade."

Jan's forehooves slipped. He scrambled back. A little shower of stones tumbled down the white cliffside.

"I heard your hoofbeats when you slipped away," Tek was saying. "Is that where you went, back to bury her?"

A cold sensation of betrayal slid between Jan's ribs. She had known! He clamped his teeth, staring ahead as bitterness welled in his throat. Now she would give him over to Korr. He refused to care. In his father's eyes he was already hopelessly fallen.

"Aye," Jan answered defiantly. "And if I did?"

"Good," muttered the healer's daughter, looking off now. "I'd have gone with you, but you made such a noise when first we came upon her, I feared notice if we both slipped off."

It took a moment to regain his breath. Jan gazed at Tek. The young mare glanced at him.

"You are not the only one, prince-son, who breaks the Ring and follows his own heart now and again."

Jan could not recover from staring at her. He felt his jaw might brush the ground if he gaped any more. The healer's daughter turned to face him more squarely.

"Little prince," she told him, "I became a warrior as young as I could so that I might be out from under my elders' eyes and run where I willed and do as I pleased. But even before that, whenever my father caught me stepping outside the Ring, he never scolded, but only told me, 'You'll make a warrior soon enough, filly, if you stay at this clip.' "

And she laughed then suddenly, almost lightheartedly. It sounded strange in the stillness to Jan's ears. And she was laughing at him a little, it seemed, baiting him, daring him with her green, green eyes. His limbs felt weak. Abruptly, Jan felt his bravado vanishing.

"Pledge me you won't tell Korr," he whispered, for all at once hope sparked in him again. Perhaps he was not lost, after all. Perhaps in time he could win back his father's grace, if only the prince never learned of this.

The healer's daughter laughed again, more gently. "No fear. I hadn't planned to."

Jan studied her dubiously. She looked at him.

"Will you have my word on it? Here: I, Telkélla, swear."

Jan felt a sudden rush of gratitude then, and just a trace of shame. Among the unicorns of the Vale, one's truename was a secret, given at birth and known only to oneself and one's dam. Not even Korr knew Jan's truename. Yet Tek had trusted him with hers as readily as the Renegades had spoken the name of the Mother. He felt he must repay her somehow.

But Tek was already speaking. "Unless *you* speak of it, no one will ever know. But by the Beard, little prince, you were in such a froth during the storm, I thought you might babble the whole thing afterward."

She snorted, picking at the soft chalk underfoot with one hoof. Jan felt his ears burning, abashed, not quite sure whether Tek was right in thinking he had almost confessed, or because she had mistaken his desperation for terror. She gave another snort, half a laugh.

"You've been keeping yourself so docile of late—save getting yourself lost in the Pan Woods—until you spoke your father back upon the Plain, I was half afraid you'd lost your fire."

And two emotions roiled up in Jan suddenly, like wellsprings rising, overwhelming and obliterating the tranquillity that had filled him since he had entered the grove. The first was fury, fury at Korr for all the helpless frustration he, Jan, had felt during the storm—and before that, beside the fallen Renegade when his father had simply loped away, ignoring him, as though he were *nothing*.

And the second emotion, which was for Tek, he could not even name.

"Aljan," he told her. "My truename's Aljan."

"Dark moon?" the healer's daughter said. "It suits."

He found himself gazing at her—he had been gazing at her for some time now, he realized, and could not stop—caught unexpectedly by the way the patches of black and rose in her coat mingled and interlocked. Not odd, beautiful. The suddenness of his seeing it surprised him. Why had he never noticed it before?

The color of the sky above had grown warmer, redder, and the cast of the wyvern shelves below almost coppery. Tek stood eyeing him with her green, green eyes that caught the light like gryphons' eyes, and all at once Jan felt himself flushing scarlet beneath the skin.

She tossed her head, shaking herself. "Come," the healer's daughter said. "We should go back. It's dusk."

Vigil

❧ 13 ❧

Jan followed Tek back through the milkwood grove. The shadows of the trees slanted long around them, and their shadows trailed dark over the fallen leaves. Then the soil changed from grayish brown at the wood's edge to the white lime sand surrounding the pool. Dagg, already standing before the water, was glancing about anxiously. They slipped up beside him.

Jan saw other pilgrims stepping into the place about the Mere, all facing inward, ringing it round—no outward-facing sentries this night. Alma must keep them while they kept their vigil (might the wyverns not wake). The sky above, fire-streaked with gold, was mirrored in the pool.

Across the water, Korr began to speak. He told of Halla, how she had formed the Circle of Warriors in the first years after the unicorns' defeat at the teeth of the wyverns. She had made the Ring that the herd might not scatter, each running his or her own way across the Plain. It was Halla's wish that the unicorns remain a single people, whole and strong, so that one day—at the coming of the Firebringer—they might return and cast the wyverns from these hills.

But Jan found he could hardly listen. His thoughts wandered along their own path. Tek's words in the grove troubled him. Was she not, as a warrior of the Ring, bound to report him? Yet she had pledged not to. Was her breach then not as great as his?

Only the worthy, the prince was saying, only those who had kept themselves true, did Alma permit to join the Ring. As for the rest, the Ringbreakers, they were lost. As Renegades, they perished on the Plain. *Am I worthy?* Jan asked himself. *I have not been true.* Once he became a warrior, he would no longer have a colt's excuse.

He watched the sunset in the water, the gold in the sky turning to amber, then deepening to red. Streaks of shadow shaded from mauve into purple, then dusky taupe. The dusk wind lifted, stirring the grove, then soughing, died. Jan began to be able to see stars through the dim glow of sky reflected in the pool.

Teki chanted them the lay of Wenfedh, a young warrior newly returned from Pilgrimage, who had died at the talons of gryphon captors rather than forswear the Ring and betray the unicorns. The twilight turned into evening, the sky becoming deep blue and then at last true black between the stars. Silence settled; the unicorns grew still. Strange constellations lay like bright dust upon the surface of the Mere, and Jan watched them.

No moon arose. It was the night of the nothing-moon, when the moon ran mated with the sun under and around the other side of the world. On the morrow's eve, a new moon would arise, newborn, a thin crescent slip. Jan gazed intently at the still, dark water, and his tangled thoughts quieted. The night rolled by, the sky overhead wheeling slowly, ever so slowly, like a lazily circling kite.

The hour swung past midnight. Jan felt no uneasiness, no urge to sleep. His legs held firm, without stiffness, and he measured the dark, surrounding space by the little noises: a restless murmur, the scuff of hooves as someone shifted, a soft snort, a swishing of tail. Each sound fanned out, thinning, filling the night until it rebounded on the dark.

Night waned. The young hours after midnight loomed and passed. Jan found his gaze on the pool had grown deeper. Perfectly steady, he no longer needed to glance away to keep his balance or his bearings. His hooves seemed rooted to the soil, growing downward like the boles of the milkwood trees. Their savor hung on him, pervading the air.

His gaze was fixed upon the Mere, moving steadily farther into that clear deepness. He felt the woods, the others around him all falling away, and knew that he had been searching for a thing that lay hidden just beyond his gaze for a very long time. He came aware of a light, a dim glow slowly brightening that dark infinity of night. And he had existed for an age, an endless universe of time, in darkness, with only the glimmer of stars for a guide.

But now the light was coming. He felt his heart lifting, his breath quickening. The others around him—he could neither see nor hear them anymore, but he felt their kindred anticipation, scented it, tasted it almost, like the dying of the dark. The stars faded. Dawn sky blended from black to indigo, from wine to rose and apricot, then gold.

He saw something, a dark figure, but could not quite make it out. The grove around him still lay in smoky shadow, the reflected sky casting only the subtlest of light. He moved forward without thinking, nearer the water—and the vision moved. He hung over it, staring at it, holding his breath as the dawn grew gradually brighter. Then in the next moment, the vision crystalized, clarified, became—only himself, his own image reflected back at him from the surface of the Mere.

No foreseeings. No destiny. Jan felt his chest tightening until he thought his ribs would fold. His eyelids were stinging, but he refused to blink. His breath had grown ragged. He understood. He had broken from the Ring in the Pan Woods, on the first day of their journey. He had almost forgotten that. Alma had not.

He had consorted with Renegades, buried a Renegade. The Serpent-cloud had been a warning. He should have heeded it, confessed to Korr. If only Tek—but it was too late now. He was unworthy, not fit to be the prince's son, no better than a Renegade himself. The Mother-of-all had cursed him, showed him no fate upon the pool because no destiny could lie before him among the children-of-the-moon.

All around him he heard the pilgrims' voices: gasps of wonder from the initiates, sighs and murmurs as their mentors once again beheld their fates. Jan's nostrils flared. He had been holding his breath. Swiftly and without a word, he broke from the Circle and fled silently away into the trees.

✵

Not then, but only much later—after the pilgrims had finished their beholdings and spoken their oath of fealty to the prince, heard more of Teki's lays, sharpened their hooves and horns and dipped them in the Mere, then chanted and danced to declare themselves half-grown, warriors—only then, about midmorning, did the unicorns discover one of their band was not among them.

The heady scent of the milkwood, which they had been breathing all night, had lulled them, and the languor which always follows visioning had made them slow. Dagg and Tek stared at one another and shook their heads like beasts amazed that they had not noticed him gone before. No one had seen him slip away, nor could tracks be found, for the sand of the bank was all tossed and trampled from the dance.

Korr ordered the clifftop combed, but leaves had already fallen to cover Jan's tracks. They searched and called the long hours before noon, but found no trace. Then, as they met back at the pool at midday, the whole band, Teki took the prince aside and argued with him.

The healer said, hark to the hour. By custom the band should have been back on the Plain by now. Nor might they tarry, for the pilgrims must be returned to the Vale by full moon's time, as was the Law.

And Korr, half wild, said trample the custom and the Law.

And the healer said, was the prince gone mad? Could he not feel the sun, hot as a gryphon's eye overhead? Spring came in apace this year, the grove was nearly in bloom; and it had always been held, for generations on end, that the wyverns awoke when the milkwood flowers. Who knew whether all this stirring and calling had not already wakened them?

And Korr, in a passion, answered him, let the wyverns all perish.

Then Teki said no word, but only nodded over one shoulder toward the initiates, so that Korr might take note of how huddled they stood, scanning the wood, how their skin twitched and their eyes rolled, and they started at nothing. It was the age-old terror of the wyverns, kept alive by the singers for four hundred years, that set them quailing so. Even the prince, despite his thunder, felt it.

Then the healer said, they are frightened, my prince. They fear your son has been stolen by the wyrms and that if we linger, we too shall meet the same. I fear it. Jan is a clever colt, and if he has but wandered off, lost in dreams, then surely he will find his way back to the Plain. But if he has been taken, then he is already lost, and our remaining cannot save him.

And at that, Korr bit down his anger and his fear, and bowed his head. Then he whistled the band into line once more, and they began to depart. But it was a semblance only, this seeming surrender by the prince. He meant but to see them safely to the Plain and then return, for he had vowed to himself, secretly, that he would not leave the Hallow Hills without his son.

But what no one had noticed—not he, not Teki, nor any other of the band—as they began their slow descent down the precarious cliff face, then filed at last out of sight beyond the canyon's bend, was that two of their number still searched among the milkwood trees, never having returned to the Mirror of the Moon.

No one guessed that Tek and Dagg had glanced into each other's eyes, each swearing silently to the other to find their friend despite the hour, despite the prince, despite the fear of wyverns that crawled in their breasts. Wise fear. Rash fools, they had no inkling of the prince's plan, nor had he any notion that a half-grown colt and so young a mare would dare anything so heedless or so brave.

❧

Jan wandered through the milkwood trees. The scent of honey thickened the air. The buds upon the boughs had swelled. More leaves had fallen. He noted it all without interest. He had only a vague plan, to remain hidden in the grove till afternoon when the others would be long gone. At nightfall he would make his way back to the Plain.

He told himself he would become a Renegade. There was grass in plenty upon the Plain, and safety in his long legs if he kept his ears pricked for pards. In winter he could rove southward to the warm Summer Sea, in summer strive eastward or west to places and parts no unicorn had ever seen.

But such thoughts were no comfort to him, for he would be alone, with not even Dagg to share in the game. Always before when he had stepped outside the Ring, it had been but for a moment, an hour. And each time he had been able to return, either nipped and jaded if he had been caught, or flushed with secret triumph if the game had worked. But there would be no returning this time, for Alma had not made him like other unicorns. He saw that now.

Time passed. The sky overhead lightened past dawn into daybreak. He hurried deeper into the trees, fearing lest someone should follow him, try to force him to return. And then he came aware, presently, of another scent edging in among the honey of bursting buds and the subtle resin of bark and leaves. It was faint but pungent, like fir cones, like bitter herbs. He sniffed, trying to locate it, but the odor vanished.

Jan halted, frowning. It seemed he had smelled such a scent somewhere before—not quite the same, but similar. Somewhere. He raised his muzzle and wandered through the trees, until after a time he caught a whiff of it again. This time it held, and he followed it.

The stretch of the grove was greater than he had imagined, tending to downslope, with odd cracks here and there in the earth and little caves tunneling down. There were more of them the farther he went, and the pungent scent had grown stronger now. From several of the crannies, he noticed mist rising. It hung in the boughs of the milkwood trees.

And then he remembered the breath of fire. He and Dagg had seen it, scented it rising into the night sky in the Pan Woods, while the blue-bodied goatlings piped and danced. He halted before a crevice and leaned over, but he could see nothing past the first length of shaft. Bits of gray sod clung to the pitted stone.

But the strange mist, oddly warm and dry, made his eyes smart and his throat feel dusty. So he drew away. And then he knew nothing for a little time. He had no memory of walking; it was as if someone or something familiar bore him along without his knowing.

The next thing he was aware of was that he stood before a cave. It tunneled gradually downward into the hillside, disappearing around the bend. Wisps of scented smoke trailed upward along the ceiling like a slow, misty stream. Jan, peering into the cave's dimness, breathing its earthy air, entered its coolness as in a dream.

Pale limerock walls reflected the daylight streaming in behind. The floor looked worn, as though smoothed by water, its surface rosy crystalline, or green, or amethyst. The color changed as Jan entered deeper, as the angle of the light striking his eye altered. The floor seemed duller, somehow, softer than stone. It clicked like the substance of horn beneath his heels.

Jan picked his way down and around the turns. Every dozen paces or so, some cranny burrowed down from the surface. Wan patches of light lay on the lime walls, glimmered on the crystal floor. The meandering ramp leveled out at last into a broad, straight hall. The light was dimmer here, the walls tunneling farther from the surface overhead.

Jan moved forward, gazing dreamily about. Smaller corridors angled off on either side. All around him lay drowsy still, but even so far down, so deep in the earth, the air was not stale. A faint breeze trickled in with the light. Jan scented the air, still following the smoke tumbling languidly overhead.

He came aware of a faded odor now—it smelled barely, hauntingly sweet. Yet underneath ran a slight stench, like moldering flowers, or damp rotted leaves. The scent itself was not faint, he realized, but subtle. It had taken him a long time to discover it under the keener, more pungent odor of smoke. But it had always been there. And the scent was old, very old, though lingering.

The smoke overhead had begun to grow thicker, wider in its stream. Jan spotted where it bled into the main hall from a side corridor. He followed it. The way was narrow, very dark, and doubling back upon itself. Jan had to pick his path by feel. Then the alleyway sloped suddenly, steeply down, and angled into a larger hall.

High, shallow tunnel windows provided light, while the smoke pooled and tumbled overhead. Jan set off down the broad, well-lighted corridor still in a dream, but beginning to come to himself now, a little. The hall came shortly to an end. Jan saw ahead of him a natural doorway, and a glimpse of chamber behind.

Warm, changing light played on that snatch of wall, the white smoke spilling through the door's archway. Jan approached without volition, unaware of his own motion, as though he himself were smoke, only spilling toward the chamber, not away. He heard some slight movement beyond the door, just at the threshold of his hearing. The scent of rotting flowers had grown stronger. He reached the doorway and gazed through.

Fire lay in a golden bowl, which rested on a ledge of rock beside the far wall. The dish was circular, a pace across, and shallow like a shell. Within it, curling branches of milkwood lay upon a bed of fine gray dust. Those underneath were red and glowing, the ones on top blackened and covered with flickering tongues of flame.

At the foot of the altar lay a heap of dead milkwood branches, and upon the altar face itself, beside the bowl, a little pile of withered herbs. The wall just behind was a broad column of stone, grooved and water-stained.

Water had worn a depression in the wall overhanging the fire. The stone was eaten very thin there, translucent: Jan could see the water through the stone. The little crescent-shaped cistern was full to the brim. As he watched, a clear droplet condensed through a crack in the rim and fell into the flames with a hiss.

He had no idea how long he stood there. Time had become suspended, as it does in dreams. It seemed a long time. The room was warm, Jan realized suddenly, warmer than the cool, shaded corridors down which he had just come, warm almost as the air outside. The air above the firebowl shimmered with heat.

He watched the smoke arise and swirl about the ceiling, some of it escaping through the light well illuminating the chamber's center. It was then Jan realized that he had entered the room, skirting the sun curtain as if by instinct, staying in shadow. He stood, now only a few paces from the firebowl, and felt the last of whatever influence had brought him there dissolve. He was himself again, fully aware. And then a cold, sliding voice behind him said:

"When you have had done admiring my fire, little dark thing, turn around, that I may look you in the eye."

Mistress of Mysteries

14

Jan spun around. The wyvern lay on a bed of great, round stones, a sort of ground, he guessed, for sleeping. Larger than himself, larger even than Korr, the white wyrm reclined, its tail coiled langorously about itself, and forked at the end into three arrowhead stings.

Pearly, like the inside of a seashell, the creature stared at him. Its slender torso was propped on stubby forelegs, broad and clawed like a badger's, but hairless, white-skinned, and translucent in the firelight. Jan could see the fingerbones through the flesh.

The wyvern had three heads. Jan felt a shudder run through him as he realized it. The long, sinuous neck was divided near the base, with the lowest head being also the smallest. On the other side, a higher, thicker branch bore a larger head. But only the tallest, central head had spoken. The other two hissed softly, shifting and swaying. All three were looking at him.

"I said come away from my fire," it told him again, and the second added, its voice lighter than the primary's, somehow younger, "Stand in the sunlight." And when Jan hesitated an instant's breadth, the third head snapped, "Can you not understand a civilized tongue? Be quick."

The creature lay between him and the door. Jan's heart beat hard and slow inside his ribs, and his throat was desperately dry. But strangely, curiosity very nearly overrode his fear. It scarcely resembled anything he had imagined of wyverns from the singers' tales: white and sinuous, yes, but not noxious, not hideous. Very lithe and supple, rather—almost . . . almost beautiful. Jan stepped forward into the light.

"What is it?" he heard the two heads whispering. The primary head poised, eyeing him.

"What manner of creature . . . ?" the second head began, but the tallest laughed.

"A unicorn! I have not seen one alive since my babyhood four hundred summers gone. Speak, unicorn. Tell us your business and your name."

Jan felt his blood quicken. The white wyrms were sorcerers that could fell kings with a kiss. To give one his name, even his usename, would be a dangerous thing.

"Speak," the third, smallest head hissed at him. "Your name."

Sunlight was dazzling him; he could scarcely see for the glare. He shifted his stance till one eye moved into shadow.

"Do not approach," the second head started, but the great one snapped at it.

"Oh, peace," it ordered, languidly. "A little silence."

The wyvern reared up, flexing and extending both powerful, stunted forepaws so that only a toe or two remained in contact with the ground. It was, it seemed, less looking at him now than scenting him. Jan noted the sickle-shaped nostrils, the catfish whiskers, and wondered how well this wyvern could see him out of strong light. He took another sidelong step, getting his other eye out of the glare.

"I have heard," it began, almost companionably, "that the unicorns now live in a valley far to the south. They are ruled by a prince, are they not, a black prince?"

It settled back upon its bed of stones. Its three heads tilted and bobbed. Jan gazed at it and racked his brain. How to get past? He needed a stratagem, for it was huge. He could never hope to best it in a fight.

The wyvern did not seem to mind his silence. "You, too, are dark, little unicorn," it resumed presently. "You would not by chance be some relation of his—his nephew, perhaps? Perhaps his *son*."

If that last word was accented, ever so slightly, Jan hardly heard. His gaze had fixed on the wyvern's tail. Its triple-barbed tip twitched and lashed as it spoke, sometimes coiling and knotting back on itself. Above, its three heads lazily bobbed and swayed. He found their ceaseless weaving fascinating.

"You are admiring my three heads," it said suddenly. The flanking two hissed and intertwined, whispering to each other now. The central one continued mildly. "You know something of wyverns? It is unusual, yes. But I am very old. Only the very old among us grow more than one head."

Its voice was strange, hollow, oddly modulated. It shifted up and down scales weirdly, invitingly. Abruptly, Jan shook himself, on guard against its spells.

"Yes, I am old," the wyvern sighed, "and only the king has seen more years. Lynex has lived to seven heads."

Lynex. Jan felt a bolt go through him. Surely not that same Lynex from the old lays? The wyvern paused, surveying him, he guessed, to see whether its wordspell was having an effect—and felt a small triumph to see its flash of disappointment. But the wyvern hid it swiftly, and resumed.

"I was not sleeping, just now when you entered. Oh, no. I do not sleep much in winter, as others do. Do you know why we sleep the winters by, most of us? Too cold." It shimmered, shrugging. "And not enough food in the cold season, too."

It nodded past him toward the golden carrying bowl. There was no wind in the still chamber, but Jan could feel the fire's heat along his coat in gusts.

"But I am mistress of the wyverns' fire. The king granted me this honor when I was no more than a slip, barely hatched, not long after we won these shelves for our own from you unicorns."

Jan felt a spark of anger then. Almost, it overrode his fear. The other's eyes darted wickedly, as if expecting him to understand something that he did not. The firelight glinted in them, and ran over the walls in watery streams.

"Lynex's reward for my part in the battle."

The wyvern laughed suddenly, throwing back all her heads, her mouths gaping wide, and Jan caught a glimpse of her teeth for the first time: like ice-splinters, or fishes' spines, rows of them.

"There, my little cloven-footed visitor. Now do you understand who it is who commands you to speak—or does my greatness overawe you?"

Jan found his voice.

"You are a wyvern, hatched just before your people drove mine from our homeland through trickery and deceit. *That* is all I know of you."

He saw the other's eyes flash then. She reared again.

"Oh, you are full of contempt, are you, little four-foot, for me and my kind? Because we use stratagems to gain our ends when it suits us."

"Proud beasts!" the second head spat. "Do you think that you yourselves are above such games—that none of you ever harken to the whispers of power?"

The littlest head spoke now in a voice gone suddenly quiet, almost sweet. "Did your own princess not cut down her father, seizing his place four hundred years past, just before we took possession of these hills?"

Jan stared at her, and felt his blood burning. That she could even speak of such a thing! But he had no time to make reply.

"Has your own father not held you back from initiation because he fears you? You are cleverer than he, and see much he cannot or will not see."

Jan clenched his teeth. *Lies, all of it.*

"And does the prince's mate not scheme against him by urging you to follow your own heart, not his commands . . . ?"

"Not so!" cried Jan. "Halla was a brave princess and a true warrior who struck in her own defense against the king, who was mad with a wyvern in his ear and fell dead when the thing had eaten out his reason." He drew breath, shaking with rage. "And as for Ses, and Korr my father. . . ."

"Ah." The wyvern smiled. Very white she looked suddenly, very cool and deadly. Her teeth snapped, still smiling. "So you *are* the prince's son."

❧

Jan choked to a halt, startled, staring. The wyvern's gaze had grown keen now, her eyes like polished stone. The flanking heads growled, deep in their throats, but the main one snaked closer to him.

"Listen to me, Aljan son-of-Korr, did you think I would not know you? That I had drawn you down into my den with a spell of fire to no purpose?"

Her whiskers bristled. The ruff of gills on her three heads spread. Jan felt astonishment flood him. She knew his name, his own truename, and had known it all along. Fear sprang into his mind again, cold as river ice. A wyvern magicker held him in her power.

"I am the mistress of mysteries," she whispered. "I gaze into fire and much I see there. I know your people dream of a great hero, one who would make war on the wyverns and drive us from our dens. . . ."

"The Firebringer," breathed Jan.

"Your name for him is unimportant," the wyvern snapped. "I care only that he is to be color-of-night—a black warrior such as this Korr who rules you now."

"My father," murmured Jan. Did she know, did she speak the truth? Was Korr to be the Firebringer?

"It is he; it *must* be," her third head was muttering. "What other unicorn is color-of-night?"

"And yet, for a long time, I was not sure." The second head mused now, seemingly more to itself than to him. "Though I watched him— and lately I have been at great pains to thwart him—for the patterns in the sky have told me this hero's time is coming, very soon."

The central head was looking at him.

"Yes, I can read the stars," she said, "though their meaning is often veiled. And there are other powers within my skill. When upon my fire I lay certain herbs, I can walk in others' dreams."

"Dreams," murmured Jan, and just for an instant her voice became so familiar, eerily so, he could have sworn he had heard it somewhere, somehow before. "I dreamed once, in a gryphon's eye. . . ."

He remembered now, with perfect clarity, that dreamlike trance.

"Dreamed I saw a fair serpent charming a hawk. Was it you?" He turned to the white wyrm again suddenly. "You who spoke in the gryphon's dream?"

The wyvern laughed. "I have seen many things gazing into my fire. One of them is how close the Gryphon Mountains lie to your Vale. And the gryphons are jealous. Shreel, the blue female—I spoke in her dream of the glory to be had if she and her mate destroyed the black prince of the unicorns."

Jan felt himself shivering, with revulsion, not fear. "We defeated your wingcats," he told her. "Killed them both."

The wyvern shrugged.

"And the pans?" Jan demanded suddenly, remembering now the sting of stones, the whistles of warriors, branches whipping, and horns crying in pursuit.

"I told the goatlings when your pilgrimage would pass." She smiled. "But my powers lie not only in the reading of stars and the directing of dreams. I can call things and conjure things, given time: raise wind and bring weather. . . ." Her long, sinuous necks shifted, swaying. She hummed a little, almost crooning.

"The Serpent-cloud," cried Jan, softly. His limbs prickled, momentarily weak. "You called the storm upon the Plain."

The wyvern's middle head chuckled. "Clever. No. I did not make it—but I did coax one wheeling funnel of darkness to dance your way."

"We outran it," Jan answered, defiant. "It passed us by."

"Well," the wyvern said. "I am almost glad, for that has enabled you to come to me."

She shifted position, coiling herself more tightly about her sleeping-stones.

"Smug unicorns," her third head muttered, "thinking yourselves so secret and so safe. Did you think we do not know what you unicorns do, that you come each year at borning spring into our hills?"

Our hills, *our* hills, she called them.

"Come for your rites by the poison pool," the second head added. "We find your marks, your hoofprints above the banks, traces of your passage along the paths."

The main head rested now upon the stones, seemingly unconcerned, letting the others talk.

"We know about your *Circle,*" the little head murmured, the last word hissed. "How you, all of you, pledge yourselves to it and serve it. And I know the reason you are with me now, young hothead, is that you are *outcast.*"

That last she spat, crackling with contempt. Jan felt his bravado vanish instantly. Shame scathed him like a scourge. It was the truth. She spoke the truth. Her words needed no spell now to catch him in their teeth. The wyvern laughed.

"Yes, little mud-prince, no more your father's heir. That, too, has been my doing, in a way. Your hasty temper hardly needs much prodding, but I have teased it when I willed."

He stared at her, and felt again all at once that wild hotheadedness coiled inside him like a snake.

"Oh, yes, Aljan. I have been watching you for a very long time. Did you think I would not keep one trick in the back of my teeth in case all my others against your father failed?"

She had raised her central head again, and turned it slightly, eyeing him. Beneath that malevolent gaze, Jan felt his resistance vanishing. The two flanking heads chuttered and hissed.

"Do you not remember all the dreams that I have sent you?"

And the memories came then, unclouded, unimpeded at last, and terrifying: a longfish swimming in the water, a winged serpent that hatched out of the moon, salamanders that burst bright into flame—and a dozen others such as he had had before the coming of Jah-lila. But now the passage of time and the white wyrm's words, her burning smoke and Jan's own efforts to recall had at last swept all the wild mare's protections away.

The wyvern's eyes blazed into his.

"*Dreams,* Aljan, to wean you away from the unicorns and win you to my cause, though you did not until this moment know it. The length of your life I have prepared for your coming. And now, at last, at long last, my unicorn, you are here."

🌿

Jan forced himself to speak, forced his lips and teeth and tongue to move, for he felt paralyzed, exactly as he had in the gryphon's cave, as he had in the first moments of the pans' attack. He knew even now that he must fight, fight the urge to surrender to her spells. He could not take his eyes from the white wyrm before him.

"What do you want of me?" he managed.

"Ah," the wyvern said, and her other heads echoed, "Ah." She smiled. All three of her faces smiled. "I know your heart, Aljan the dark moon. And in your heart you are a trickster. Not so?"

He found himself nodding, just barely nodding before he was even aware, and he realized, dimly, he must already have slipped a little under her spell. She settled herself.

"Well, so am I a trickster, a plotter. . . ."

"A betrayer," added Jan—*magicker, liar, dreamstalker*—forcing himself desperately to speak, act, think of his own volition, not hers.

"Yes. I tried to reach your father once, before your birth, Aljan, when Korr was young and not yet prince, and I had perceived only the vaguest of forebodings among the stars."

The wyvern's gaze turned inward now, her necks, her tail knotting and unknotting.

"I tried to send him a dream to ruin him, send him running wild Renegade across the Plain, that this hero-to-be might never come and trouble my people with war; but I could not reach him. His mind was closed to me, safe within your Ring of Law."

Her eyes came back to Jan, a hunter's eyes.

"Your father is no dreamer, Aljan. And so for years I was frustrated, uncertain whether this young black prince was to be our starspoken enemy. And I was unable to strike at him, either, even when his yearly Pilgrimage brought him so *close*."

Her eyes flashed and her three jaws snapped. Jan shivered.

"For the winters here have been freezing chill these last ten years, spring's warmth not in till long after equinox. And though each time he has come I have been awake, here below, I dared not leave my fire untended, nor could I rouse my people from their winter sleep."

Again that flash of eyes, that triple snap.

"But then. . . ." Her tone was silken, and suddenly the scent of woodsmoke in the air seemed sharper, the room closer, the light dimmer and the white wyrm herself even paler and more opalescent. "Then I saw, not many seasons past, a mare in labor under a dark moon: the prince's mate. And I knew this prince would have a son. . . ."

"A dreamer born," the third head hissed.

The second laughed. "One whose mind was not closed to me."

"One who would *not* keep himself safe within the Ring of Law."

She slithered toward him suddenly, rearing up, her cut-jewel eyes measuring him and all her heads weaving upon their slender stalks. Jan stumbled back. The rays of the light well glided over him and glanced in his eyes.

"I want you to play another trick, Aljan. For me—a little trick. Only that."

Jan stared at her. Her shimmer dazzled him. "What manner . . . of trick?" The words seemed to drag from his teeth, so slowly. The effort of speech had become almost pain. His thoughts had blurred, and her voices seemed to wash over him in waves. He listened, only half understanding what she said.

"Our king is old, Aljan, and has no heirs. No need, he says, for he will live another hundred years at least. But I am not content. Lynex lets our people languish. Too much sleep has made them slothful. The poison in their tails is weaker. . . ."

"Some . . ." the second head broke in. The wyvern shifted on her spot. "*Some* even hatch with no stings on their tails at all—blunt tips, nothing!"

Her central head champed its teeth, the little one muttering. "Such freaks would have been eaten at birth when I was young. But the king grows lax. A weak people are easier for him to manage in his age. Well."

Once more she shifted.

"I would make my people great again. I would share fire among all the dens as when first we came here. The wyverns must breed in winter as we once did, and the weak be eaten, if our line is to regain its vigor. Now only the piddling summer eggs hatch, and no fruit comes of an autumn tryst. . . ."

"But only because of the *cold*," the second head hissed. "With fire, I could. . . ." She broke off. "Ah, but the king will not listen to me."

"I want you to return to your father, Aljan," the white wyrm said suddenly. Her eyes had come back from their distance now. The central head spoke. "Explain your absence somehow. Tell them you have seen a marvel, our dens deserted, or all the wyverns dead of plague. Tell them anything, but make them follow."

Jan watched her, helpless now to move or speak. He wanted to run, turn away, shake his head in flat refusal, but his body would not obey. And he was outcast. *Outcast.* He could never go back. She laughed softly.

"It is our king's custom to be first out of the dens in spring, to go hunting and bring back the season's first catch: red meat for his people upon their awakening. But how if I were to seize that right? The people love me, support me. They would proclaim me his heir. Then he *must* listen."

Again her eyes found him.

"You must lead your people away from the poison pool, Aljan. My

people still fear that place—superstitious fools! Lead your father and
his band into the canyon below the cliff. It is a dead end, with sides
too steep for your kind to scale."

She preened herself a moment, fretfully.

"I, meanwhile, will rouse my people. They sleep lightly this year,
with the spring come in so early and so mild." She laughed, all three
heads shaking, their sliding notes hollow and strange. "To kill the black
prince of the unicorns and outstrip my own king in a single stroke. Will
that not be, little trickster after my own heart, the finest game of all?"

❧

Jan stared at her across the well of sunlight. Firelight played over
the minute scales of her delicately tinted skin. They flaked off along
her underside as she slid along the floor. It must be these, he found
himself thinking suddenly, irrelevantly, packed down and hardened for
centuries, that formed the crystalline surface of the tunnel floors.

His captor grew impatient for his reply. She spat, "Surely you can
feel no loyalty to them, pompous unicorns, the very ones that cast you
out?"

The truth in her words mocked at him. No, he was not like other
unicorns, could not keep to the old ways, to Halla's Circle, though his
father's pride and the love of Alma depended on it. The white wyrm
coiled about her bed of stones, looking at him, laughing at him with her
three pairs of cut-jewel eyes.

Jan could not recall ever seeing a creature more beautiful, though
there nagged somewhere at the back of his mind the notion that she
ought to have seemed hideous. Why? For she was pure, admirably pure,
without a twinge of conscience or shame.

"Serve me, Aljan," her little head hissed. "Once we have destroyed
the unicorns, I will let you go—off across the Plain to run wild Renegade if you will. Or even," her voice grew sly, "back to your Vale.
Who would know, with all the others dead, that anything you chose to
tell them was not the truth? *You* would be prince, then, little darkling.
You would rule the unicorns. . . ."

Something struck him then, dimly, through the fog. Why was she
so importunate? And then that, too, came to him—*because time is slipping away. It must be noon by now, or past, and the unicorns preparing
to quit the pool. Because I am the last trick she has against my father.
Without me she will never get him into that dead-end canyon. Her people are afraid to go near the poison pool.*

*And without me to lead the unicorns into her trap, she will never
have her bold stroke to outshine the king, to seize his place in her*

people's hearts and come to power. I am the spark to all her kindling. Without me, her great scheme becomes only ashes and dust. I have only to refuse her, and she shall be undone. I have only to refuse.

But he could not refuse. For she held his name, like a mouse struggling in her teeth. Aljan, Aljan—every time she said the word, he felt himself sink deeper in her power. He was tangled, frozen; he could not get free. Her spells had knotted round him like a snake. But she seemed oddly unaware how nearly he was hers—and then he realized he stood in shadow now. She could hardly see him.

"How may you deny me?" her central head grated. Her tone had grown darker. She hissed with frustration. "Look what I have offered you: power, freedom, the death of your enemies. Unicorns! I know your kind to the marrow of the bone. When I was barely hatched, I fed upon the wit of one mightier than you, foal princeling. Do not tell me I do not know the things that tempt a unicorn."

Her words, like a thunderclap, brought Jan sharp awake. The cold coils that had trammeled his mind fell away. He stared. This one, this great three-headed thing, had been the little slip to gnaw away the mind of Jared the king half a hundred generations gone? She. *She* had done?

A blazing anger rose in Jan, and the last of the white wyrm's spell dissolved in its heat. His jaw tightened; his body tensed. He tossed his head, his nostrils flaring. He was Jan, the son of his people's prince, and not some wyvern's gamepiece. Eyeing her ice-white, reptilian form, he felt himself growing dangerous.

Fire

❧ 15 ❧

"What will you give me?" said Jan suddenly. "What will you give me in exchange for the unicorns?" He picked up his hooves and set them down again, restlessly, for a sense of power had flowed into him. He could not keep still. The wyvern cocked her heads, clearly surprised.

"What I have said . . ." she began.

"No," Jan told her. "My freedom? The leadership of the unicorns? Those things I will have anyway, if I do as you say." He sidled, dancing. "You must give me another thing—to make this worth my game. Another thing, mistress of mysteries."

The white wyrm lay silent, eyeing him suspiciously. Jan knew it must be plain to her that he no longer lay beneath her spell; but it did not matter. He had her. She needed him. She *must* agree.

And if he could stall her, dicker with her long enough to let the unicorns depart the Hallow Hills, if he could keep her from rousing her people for only so long—a weary sense of finality overcame him now— then it did not matter what happened to him after she found out he had been gaming her.

The wyvern shrugged after a moment, her smallest head snapping its teeth. "Oh, very well, little unicorn," she muttered. "What will you have? I will give it to you if I must—only because it pleases me." Her central head added sharply, "But be brief. Our time is short."

Time, time, thought Jan, what thing might he ask her for that would take the most time? A mystery. One of her mysteries—but which? How to read the stars? Only there were no stars, for it was still broad day. How to raise wind and bring weather? But here below, out of sight of the sky. . . .

His gaze strayed to the firebowl, burning red flags in a golden shell.

our skins volatile. Flame would run along our caverns faster than we could slither to escape." A low laugh. "It happened once."

She smiled slyly.

"In the beginning, when first we lived here, the king shared fire among us all. Every chamber had its hearth. Eggs hatched in all seasons, and no one slept. But all the while, the trails were building up—within a few years all our passages were crystal-coated.

"Then one day a torch fell—some servant in the king's room—no one knows. That whole quarter of the warren went up. The king escaped, but many did not. We tore down the ceilings of connecting passageways to seal the wing. It smoldered for days.

"Afterward, Lynex ordered all fire either killed or confiscated, and put it into my keeping as a sacred charge. . . ."

Jan stared unseeing into the dancing flames, and it seemed he could almost see what the wyvern described to him, behold it happening that moment, vivid as a dream.

"But what *is* fire?" he found himself demanding, interrupting the white wyrm. "Where does it come from?"

The mistress of mysteries bent her head to his ear.

"Sunstuff," she whispered. "The stuff of lightning flash in storms. Starstuff—our god. It can kill or quicken eggs to life: a weapon or a friend. It is Magic. It is Power, the source of all our sorcery. We worship it."

She was looking at him from the corners of her eyes.

"One can even see visions in the fire, if one is a dreamer or a sorceror. Look, look into the fire, little unicorn. Look closer. Closer."

Her voice had grown sly, but Jan hardly noticed. He leaned forward. The heat shimmer above the flames was like water rippling, like the stirring beneath the surface of the Mirror of the Moon. The wyvern's mocking laughter haunted softly through the room. She lifted a clump of herbs from beside the firebowl. They were small, withered pods with wispy spires on the underside.

"What are those?" he asked.

"Rosehips," the wyvern said, "the fruit of the milkwood tree. We gather them in autumn." She tossed them onto the fire. "They give a sweet smoke to bring one dreams."

Jan watched the round seed cases fall among the burning twigs. Soon they began to smolder, to send up thick, twining tendrils of smoke, pearly white mixed with bluish gray. The pale smoke had the heavier, milder fragrance, smooth and soothing; the darker, thinner threads had the keener scent. It stung his eyes.

Jan realized he had leaned far forward over the rosehips even as the wyvern had moved back out of their vapor. His face, his throat and nostrils tingled. A trembling began in the center of his limbs, made him feel at once weak and utterly unbendable, rooted to the stone. The sensation spread to his chest and ribs.

His senses were growing very acute suddenly. Before, he had not noticed the sound of fire. Now it fascinated him—a thick hissing, almost a thrum, like sea surf, a slow, arresting roar. He began to distinguish licks of color in the flames, greens and reds, pale violets. They flickered and danced.

Behind him he heard the three heads of the wyvern arguing.

"Why have you told him our secrets, of fire?" That was the second head, impatient but controlled.

"No matter." The central head, softly. "He's no more than a prit, a child. And he'll have no time to make use of what we've given him, even if he understood. . . ."

"And why the rosehips?" the little head cut in. "Their influence is always uncertain. They may put him in such a stupor he'll be no use to us at all."

"What choice had we?" the great head snapped. "We are out of time. And how was I to know he would be strong enough to throw off a wordspell? Only the fire seems to have any power over him."

"I say pounce on him now and be done," the third head muttered.

"*Patience*. We've other plans for him."

Jan did not mind their words. He knew he ought to, somehow, but he could not manage it. The wyvern's voices remained a faintly distracting background noise.

"Hist, be still." That was the second head again. "He's not quite under yet."

Under what? Jan wondered briefly, and could not care. He had the feeling that he must watch, watch very carefully now, as if this were the most important lesson of his life and he must memorize it all the first time, for it would not come again.

Yet at the same time he was vaguely aware that presently he must act. Watching the fire was important, surpassingly important, but it would end soon. He mulled over what he might be expected to do then, and had not a clue. No matter. A plan would come to him, or not, just as it chose. Things were moving so slowly now. There was time enough.

"I say slay him," the third head hissed. The thin, sharp sound of its voice fizzed on the air. "Our eggs are but a day or two from hatching; perhaps only hours. Red meat to nourish our little prits—and meat improves with age."

Jan admired the glow of the charring rosehips. They did not seem to burn. *Winter eggs,* he thought. *Little poison-prits.* Heirs to the king that would have no heirs. What had Lynex done, all these hundreds of years? *Pashed all the eggs of his mates to bits before their hatching.*

"*Fah.*" The wyvern's second head scoffed at the third. "If we killed this unicorn now, I can well guess where the greater part of the flesh would go—down your greedy gullet."

"Only a little," the little head sniffed. "What could be spared. The winter has been long. I'm ravenous."

The second head did not reply. Jan listened without interest. The fire was absorbing his whole attention. But he had begun to feel that time was starting to slip away. He sought to rouse himself from the torpor now creeping over his limbs, tried to lift his head away from the heat, but the vapors were making him slow. His limbs refused to move. He made to speak—how slowly the words formed in his mind.

"Is this. . . ." He had to pause, draw a breath heavy with smoke. His throat burned. "Is this the only fire the wyverns have?" He could not seem to turn his head. The words did nothing to lift the spell.

"Yes," the wyvern's central head replied, raising its voice, "save for the king's. He keeps his own small torch with him. The king, you see, must never sleep." She laughed, mocking. "And he thinks to keep himself safe from my magic that way. But his puny brand does not make half the flame my firebowl does."

Jan felt himself falling back into the fire, felt it consuming his thoughts. He had scarcely been able to drag his mind away to listen to the white wyrm's reply. Behind him, the heads were arguing, hissing and snapping.

"Fool, would you undo all that we have worked for? Once we have taken the prince of the unicorns and his band, there will be plenty of red meat—for our hatchlings and your greedy mouth as well." A simper, a smile. "I shall see that the king gives us this one, though, this little dark one specifically. Only the best meat for my prits."

He knew then that his time truly was out. But his muscles were melting, his head drooping, chin bowed to his chest. The heat grew fierce. His body prickled with sweat. An updraft from the coals lifted his forelock, flinging it back gently from his brow. He closed his eyes.

Even with his eyes closed, it seemed he could still see the flames— see into them as in a dream; looking deeper and deeper, merging more and more into their changing dance. Searching for something. Searching as others had been searching—for him.

He came aware then, in a twinge that was not sufficient to wake him, that others had been searching for him, many others of his band.

But that was hours ago. Now there were only two. Two searching above ground, below ground. It was all the same.

"Just a few moments more," the great head was murmuring, "and the rosehips will make him a slave to our command."

Jan's nose was now well back from the lip of the bowl, below the rising smoke. The air he breathed felt cooler, more clean. His senses seemed to be clearing. The heat upon the rest of his face intensified. He laid his ears back along his skull.

His thoughts had grown dim. He felt his horn's tip touch the far rim of the bowl, and realized distantly that bright flame must be licking its long, spiral shaft. He felt no pain, only heat like the sun. The white wyrm's triple laugh echoed, sounding oddly faint and farther than it should have. Jan's consciousness was ebbing, his ears muffled in wool, his limbs slipping away.

"Not long now," the wyvern was murmuring. "See how he faints over the flame."

❧

Jan came to himself suddenly at a soft, crackling hiss. The scent of singed hair filled his nostrils. He felt a sharp pain across his brow and realized as he started up that his forehead had touched the curved lip of the bowl, his heated sweat turning to steam. The pain made him suddenly aware of himself again, gave him the use of his limbs. He heard the wyvern sliding toward him across the crystal floor.

It came to him then, all in a breath, what must happen now. The wet, stained wall above the firebowl gleamed, the pearly, translucent pocket in its stone catching the firelight like a gryphon's eye. It seemed to glow. Beneath the wyvern's subtle, pervasive sweetness, beneath the pungency of rosehips and flame, the scent of water had grown suddenly strong.

Without another moment's thought, he sprang forward, rearing, bracing his forehooves on the altar's edge. The branches in the bowl of fire had died again to coals, the blackened rosehips crumbled to ash. Jan champed his teeth, clenching shut his eyes against the updrafts of heat, and brought his horn down in a hard blow against the wall above the fire.

"Hold!" cried one of the wyvern's heads. Another cried, "What does he do?"

The thin stone shattered like an old seashell. Chips of crystal flew. Jan felt bits striking against his forehead, his closed eyelids. The point of his horn struck the hard stone at the back of the crescent pool.

"Stop!" the wyvern shouted. "Are you mad?" He heard the soft scratch of her belly scales upon the floor.

Jan opened his eyes and shied to one side as water rushed from the breached cistern. The hot coals below sizzled, overwhelmed. White licks of fire leapt roofward, vanishing, as bits of twig and dead embers rode the surge, washing over the rim of the firedish and spilling to the floor. The rest swirled sluggishly about the bowl.

The chamber stood all at once in smoky dimness. The white wyrm gave a triple shriek. Jan turned his head. She sat transfixed, her pale form indistinct in the sudden gloom. Her voices rang out again, strangled.

"What have you done?" cried the central head; and the second, "He has killed the god! All our magic, all our power—gone." The third head shouted, "Murderer!"

The wyvern lunged. Jan sprang away, his limbs still giddy from the rosehips' breath. The wyvern missed him by two paces—then he realized it was not he she had sprung at. She darted to the altar, searching frantically among the sodden twigs. But the fire was dead past saving. Her three heads turned on him like goshawks. He made out the glinting of her cut-jewel eyes.

Too late he realized he had missed his chance—he should have fled while she had been distracted. Jan found himself in a corner, one wall crowding against his flank. The white wyrm reared before him, her whiskers bristled, her gill ruffs spread. Her necks stretched wide; her pale jaws gaped. Her teeth like broken birds' bones gleamed.

Jan squared himself to fight.

Poison

⦾ 16 ⦾

Jan faced the wyvern across the narrow space, her body poised, her eyes colorless in the hazy dimness. His blood felt slow and heavy from the rosehips' breath. She snapped at him. He dodged, the wall crowding his flank. The wyvern smiled, her rosy, double tongues darting among her needle teeth. The fingers of her foreclaws twitched.

"Oh, did you think to thwart me, Aljan?" she whispered. The chamber echoed in the dark. "Then you misjudged. So my fire is gone, and my magic, too. But I am angry now, Aljan." Her heads hissed, sizzling. "And there was always more to me than magic."

He was lost. He knew it. He had neither the size nor the strength to defeat her, and she had him cornered. But he would fight. He was a warrior, the prince-son of the unicorns, and he meant to go down fighting. There would be no songs to mark his death; and none of his people would even know. But he had saved Korr and the others of the band. It was noon—they were safe out of the hills by now, and none of the rest of it mattered.

Above him the wyvern loomed. She came toward him slowly. Then suddenly behind her, beyond the entry to the chamber, Jan heard a scrabbling of earth and a wild, high shrill. The note was echoed by another—the battle whistle of a warrior. The white wyrm started, snapping around. Jan heard a clatter of hooves on the crystal floor. The wyvern reared, recoiling, as a form—two forms—glanced through the well of light.

He caught glimpses then of rose and black, of dusty yellow shading into gray. He heard the snort of breath and the sound of struggle. The mist of rosehips rose in his mind, and he was a long time recognizing Tek and Dagg.

They were fighting in and out of the suncurtain now. He saw his shoulder-friend lunge, miss, and lunge again. The wyvern's long, sinewy necks darted, teasing them. Her jewel eyes glinted. Tek reared, panting, but could not seem to land a blow. The wyvern dodged, her hide throwing off brilliant flashes in the sunlight: blue-green, amber, yellow, mauve.

"The light," Jan heard himself crying, and his voice sounded different—deeper?—or as if there were another voice in it besides his own. "Drive her into the shade," he cried. "These wyverns have no eyes to pierce the dark."

One of the wyvern's heads turned, her whiskers bristling, her nostrils flared, and struck at him. Jan shied, circling the shaft of light. He came around and faced the wyrm. Tek and Dagg had forced her out of the sunlight. Her back now pressed the wall.

Dagg stumbled. Jan saw him lose his footing on the crystal floor. The wyvern lunged, snarling, and struck him a glancing blow with one badgerlike forepaw. Dagg rolled, scrambling to his feet, then suddenly lunged and caught the wyrm's smallest head by the throat. The wyvern shrieked. On the other side, Jan glimpsed Tek fastening into the second head's ruff. The central face rose over Jan.

"Well, little darkling." She was hard-pressed, but she mocked him still. Her claws took powerful sweeps at Tek and Dagg. "So it is only you and I now, again."

Her breath came short, though her eyes were jeering. The smallest head continued to shriek.

"Your friends fight well—but even if they kill both my little heads, you will still have *me* to deal with."

From the tail of her eye, Jan glimpsed the whipping and coiling of the wyvern's necks. Tek and Dagg were being shaken, their forehooves lifted from the ground.

"Yield to me. You cannot win." The wyvern held her main head high, just out of reach. She laughed. "Betray your friends—*now,* Aljan, before I shake them off."

The smoke of rosehips still mingled in his blood. Despite himself, Jan felt her wordspell taking hold again. Her cut-jewel eyes had fixed on him. Pale, with an inner fire they shone, marvelously, malevolently inviting. And he knew that she was lying; yet it didn't seem to matter. Jan felt himself growing lost.

"Yield, little princeling. Yield," she whispered, moving toward him. "Help me to slay your friends. Even these two will be of use to me against my king. And if the prince of the unicorns is lost to me this year—well, perhaps you will stay with me, and we will try another spring."

Her hollow voice was sweet, soothing. Jan stumbled away from her, and she shook her head.

"Do you think to fly?" She laughed. "You cannot escape. The world's a Circle, Aljan. You will always come back to me in the end. *Come.* You know that in a moment you will come. . . ."

Then something slipped underneath Jan's heel. He felt it give like rotten fruit. A sweet stench filled his nose, and his heel felt suddenly wet and warm. He lost his footing on the slickness, falling. More shells gave under him, cutting his flank. He had stumbled amid the bed of eggs. The realization came to him as he struggled up. Gray globes crowded about his legs.

"My eggs!" the wyvern shrieked. "You fool. Come away. You will breach them!"

She writhed then, fighting toward him. Tek and Dagg held on, bracing to hold her back. Jan kicked at the eggs encircling him, tripping his limbs—he could get no footing. He plunged, trampling, but could not get free. The ground here was a shallow dish, and new eggs rolled constantly about him.

"Stop!" cried the wyrm. "You have killed my fire. Leave me my eggs."

She shook herself, furiously. Tek lost her grip and was thrown. The white wyrm staggered Dagg with a blow. He dropped her head; his legs folded. Jan hardly marked it. He stood astonished, the sick-sweet savor choking him. All about him lay fragments of egg. Broken shell ground underneath his heels. His legs were wet to hock and knee. Only one egg remained unbreached. The wyvern lunged for it. Jan sprang between her and the egg.

"Let me have it," screamed the wyrm. "What good is it to you?"

"Wyverns!" Jan thundered back at her, and it was his new voice again, resonant and strong. "I know your kind to the marrow of the bone—for you have been in my head for a long time now, uninvited guest. Did you think I would not know the things that tempt a wyvern?"

He felt the egg against his fetlock and kicked it very gently—not enough to breach it, only enough to make it roll. He kicked it again, carefully, backing toward the near wall and keeping his eye on the white wyrm the whole time; for a stratagem had come to him.

The wyvern slithered after him. Beyond her in the dimness he saw Tek getting unsteadily to her feet, Dagg shaking his head as though stunned. Jan came up against the wall behind the wyvern's nest, and held the egg between his hind heel and the stone.

"Give it to me," the wyvern said.

"What will it buy me if I do?" Jan asked her, quietly. His limbs trembled and he was breathing hard; but despite it all, he felt strangely light-headed—for he had her, had her in his teeth now like a pard, and that sure sense of his power made him flush. He met the wyvern's eye. "What will your last egg buy?"

The wyvern watched him, shifting uneasily. Her third head flopped weakly, whimpering. Her second head gasped, bleeding from the gills.

"Name what you would have," the wyrm queen spat. "Your free-dom. Your companions' lives—your father's life. Give me the egg, and I will say nothing, will not raise the alarm till you are clear of these dens."

"I did not come here of my own will," murmured Jan. A quiet rage was filling him. The egg felt smooth and fragile beneath his heel. "You brought me here with a spell of fire. All my life you have troubled me, till the wild mare had to sing away my dreams, the good ones with the bad. . . ."

The wyvern strained, writhing. Her fingers clawed her belly scales. "You have had your vengeance, and more," she cried. "My fire, my golden god is gone. All my little prits but one. Leave me that. Only that. And go."

Jan shook his head. He could not trust her. He felt the slight give of the shell beneath his hoof. The wyvern's breath hissed, trembling. The prince's son snorted. "The word of a wyvern is as good as a lie."

"How might I pursue you or give the alarm?" the wyvern demanded. "I must hide the egg before it hatches. With only one left, I dare not risk discovery. The king must never. . . ." She broke off angrily. "Give it to me. You must. Give it to me *now*."

Jan stood three-legged, eyeing her. Behind her, Dagg had gotten to his feet. Head up, Tek glanced at him, at Jan, at the wyrm. Her hoof dug a shallow scratch on the crystalline floor. Jan motioned her back from the wyvern queen.

"You might have spared yourself," he said, "if only you had let me be. Your eggs, your fire would still be yours. I did not ask to come here."

The wyvern hissed. Behind, Tek was moving too slowly.

"Tek, Dagg, get to the entryway."

The young warrior glanced at Dagg. Still he stood, shaking his head.

"Now," barked Jan.

Tek turned to Dagg and shouldered him. They circled toward the entry. The wyrm's heads turned, watching them, her eyes blazing. Jan took his heel from the egg and moved aside. Tek and Dagg were at the door.

"The egg is yours," Jan told her, halfway to the entry now himself. "Take it and use it as you will against your king. I am a unicorn. The games of wyrms are nothing to me."

The wyvern's heads snapped back around. Her main head's eyes bored into his. Those of her second fixed on the egg. She drew breath fiercely. "Godkiller," she muttered at him. "Hoofed monster. Murderer."

He saw her body begin to shift, the hindquarters bunching, and cavaled, nervously, aware that she was planning something but not quite sure what. Though the wall still crowded him, he was out of reach of her teeth now, even if she lunged. But he dared not take his eyes from hers. Her wounded head wailed shrilly. The others hissed and gargled.

"The stings," he heard Tek cry out suddenly. "Jan, the stings!"

The wyvern twisted her lower half. He heard the sweep of scales across the floor, glimpsed the long tail lashing. There was no retreat, no room to run—the wall was at his back. He sprang hard forward, the only way she had left to him—and the sting-barbs whipped beneath his hooves.

He closed his eyes, ducking his head. His knees and forehead collided with the wyrm. She shrieked. His brow burned in a thin arc of soreness where the firebowl had touched it. He did not realize at first that his fire-tempered horn had pierced the bone of the wyvern's breast.

The claws of the wyrm's fingers raked his cheek. Jan struggled free; he stumbled back. The white wyrm reared up, up, looming above them all like a massive white tree—and then she toppled, pitching forward. The three of them shied and scattered. And as the dead wyvern came to earth, her third head struck the last egg, pashing it.

Jan found himself standing panting by Dagg. The two of them stared at the fallen wyrm. It lay quivering, the necks twisting and twining still while the tail thrashed madly, like a murdered snake. Jan turned away. He shuddered. He felt battered, bruised to the bone. Beside him he saw Dagg champing his teeth as though they ached.

"Are you hale?" he heard Tek asking them. Her voice was low. The chamber was very still, save for the slither of the wyrm.

"Hale enough," Jan murmured. The sweet flush of power had faded from him.

Tek snorted. There was blood on her neck and shoulders where the wyvern had cuffed her. "We heard your voice coming up from the ground, and the white wyrm baiting you," she said. "We followed it down."

"Aye," said Jan, "I know it," for he did know. He had seen it in the fire: companions searching for him, above ground, below. Tek glanced at him keenly, surprised. He turned to Dagg then, as he realized his friend had been eyeing him as well.

"Why did you slip away?" Dagg asked. "Was it a spell she put on you?"

"Yes—no," said Jan. How to explain it? He himself scarcely understood. It had been half her spell, and half something within himself.

Dagg's eyes had grown more puzzled still. "If it wasn't," he whispered, "if it wasn't that. . . ." He glanced at Tek uncertainly, then back to Jan. "You'd only to ask me, and I'd have gone, too."

Jan felt his throat tighten suddenly. He drew breath to speak, but Tek cut him off.

"Hist, come," she said. "Another time. Let's be gone from here. The others must be halfway out of the hills by now, and who knows whether our noise may have wakened the wyrms?"

Jan felt his blood quicken then. She had given Dagg's shoulder a nip to turn him, and then sprang after him herself. Jan followed. Beside the wall the dead wrym lay twitching, its long necks and tail knotting and unknotting.

"Mind the stings," he heard Tek murmur. "They're poison still."

Dagg gained the hall, disappearing through the natural doorway, then Tek. But just as Jan reached the threshold, he glanced back into the darkened chamber, at the white sunray and the trampled eggs, at the drowned altar and the writhing wyrm.

And he felt a prick in his left hind heel—a nettle sting, no more. And looking down, he saw the longest, middle point of the wyvern's tail just grazing his fetlock. He stared at it, uncomprehending. The white wyrm shuddered and at last was still.

Jan's legs had carried him through the doorway's arch and out into the hall before he was aware—not a half pace behind the others. He could hear them just ahead, but his gaze was fixed over one shoulder at the chamber, a hollow of darkness behind.

The stinging in his fetlock had begun to burn. Then panic surged in him, and disbelief. The wyrm was dead—how could she strike? How could a dead wrym's sting be poison still? Perhaps—perhaps Tek had been mistaken, and there was nothing to fear. But it was useless, trying to game himself. For he had begun to feel, unmistakably, the warmth of poison spreading upward from the wound.

※

They galloped up the curving corridor. Light wells cast wan illuminations in the gloom. The crystal resin underfoot muffled the clatter of their hooves. Jan's heel felt hot and weak, the smoke of rosehips in his blood balmy and cool. The corridor stretched on before him, and he realized they had already passed the sloping side alley down which he had come. Tek and Dagg must have found their way in by another path.

Jan found himself hard-pressed to keep abreast of Tek. Their pace made it impossible for him to limp. Hot pain crept upward into his thigh muscle. The cooling smoke in his blood seemed to mingle with the venom, easing it a little. Jan shook his head and tried desperately not to think of it. There was nothing to be done for it now.

The pathway over which they ran had leveled some. Fewer light wells illumined the gloom. Dagg's form was a paleness in the dimness ahead. The fire had reached Jan's hip joint now. Each stride was agony. All around them was stillness and the dark. The harshness of their breath, the muffled tatting of their hooves only deepened the quiet.

Jan champed his teeth, too weak now to keep up with Tek. He fell back, his nostrils straining. His breath was coming very short. The venom burned slowly along his back toward the shoulder blades. His back legs were stumbling. Up ahead, Dagg came abruptly to a halt. Tek did the same. They moved forward cautiously then, heads lifted, nostrils wide. Jan stumbled after them.

They entered a great hall, with archways to many side chambers opening along the far walls to left and right, but few light wells pierced the high, dim ceiling. Their footfalls echoed in the vast, deserted dark. Jan felt the immense weight of earth pressing down from above, and his skin tremored and twitched. After a moment, he realized the subtle smell of rotting flowers had grown much stronger here. His eyes grew more accustomed to the gloom.

And he saw the wyverns then, vague glimpses through the dark doorways opening into the hall. They lay in heaps, dozing, sharing their warmth. Coded into weird shapes, pale pearl in color, they barely seemed to breathe. The hall rustled with their soft sighing. Jan felt the poison in his breast dripping against his heart, working down his fore-limbs, inching up his neck.

He stumbled into Tek and gasped in surprise. She shushed him. They had entered a narrow exit tunnel. The floor here rose, veering, the slope growing steep. Jan stumbled again, the sound of it loud in his own ears. Leaning against Tek, he staggered upward along the rising tunnel.

"What is it? What's wrong?"

Jan heaved himself over another shallow ripple in the floor and struggled on. He saw Dagg glancing back.

"I've been stung," Jan panted, looking at neither of them. The panic had left him, and the disbelief. He felt only despair. "The wyvern stung me on the heel."

He heard Dagg's quick drawn breath, felt Tek's teeth closing over the nape of his neck. His knees were giving way.

"Dagg, help me," he heard Tek hissing through a mouthful of his mane.

The two of them supported him between their shoulders, kept him from leaning, sinking. Jan sagged, but still he fought to gather his legs and make them obey. The poison had reached his head. His thoughts were made of water now, shifting and spangling. He could not keep his head up, gazed dully at the ground. His eyes felt glazed.

The tunnel canted upward, up, tipping crazily. More and more light poured into the passage. It hurt his eyes; he had to squint. He heard Tek and Dagg laboring to breathe, felt their sides pressing against his own. The tunnel's entrance passed overhead. He felt a sudden rush of light and air—it seemed to beat about him like wings. They were outside, and the daylight was blinding.

He felt Tek beside him shying suddenly, and felt her sharp hiss of surprise. Dagg sidled, whickering. Jan dragged his head up and peered through the blaze before him. The sky was a vault of blue flame all around. The edge of the milkwood grove twenty paces distant looked smoky and cool.

A figure stood before them at the wood's edge, looking shadow-colored against the bright glare of the sky. Very graceful and long of limb—Jan knew this unicorn. It was ... it was ... the poison eating up his mind had burned the name away.

The figure was coming toward him now. He wanted to go to it, but his limbs were made of shifting earth, of wind, and refused to bear his weight. He realized he was falling, slowly, and could not feel the ground beneath him, so that even as he came to rest upon his side, it felt as though he were falling still. The blood in his body danced with heat, and he gazed with one eye at the fire-white sun, floating above him on a blue lake of sky.

Dreams

The grassy ground where he had fallen felt hard and somehow distant. Jan closed his eye to the brightness of the sun and the shadows of unicorns standing above him. Darkness and fire, then, and for a while he knew nothing but that his blood was burning and he was growing weaker, very weak, like a newborn foal.

At last he began to see again, as through a haze, and hear muffled sounds; but still, there was a distance. A red mare—Jan recognized her somehow, but could not say from where. It was she, he realized, who had stood at the wood's edge. Her coat was deep rose, the color of milkwood flowers. Her eyes, like Tek's, were green.

Jan sensed the fear and tension in her. Her shoulder blades were tight with it, her mouth gone dry. He had entered into her somehow, as in a dream, and could feel her every sensation as if it were his own. She had left the others now and was descending into the wyverns' dens, through the hall of sleepers, through the tunnels and turns. She moved deliberately, as if she knew the way.

Jan felt himself returning to his companions then. Tek was standing over something that lay near the cave's entrance, shadowing it from the sun. She was trembling—strange, for the day was warm—and her teeth were clenched. Dagg returned to her with a branch of rosebuds from the grove. He and she chewed them urgently and crushed them beneath their heels. The taste upon their tongues was pungent sweet.

The red mare rejoined them. Something huge and loose and pale shimmered as it trailed on the ground behind her. She held a fold of it in her teeth: the skin of the three-headed wyvern. Upon it lay a golden bowl. Jan felt the wyrm's blood sting the red mare's skin, her own sweat smarting in her eyes. They were dragging the skin behind them now, all three of them. It had become very heavy for some reason. They sweated and struggled. Wyrm's blood tasted bitter in their mouths.

Then he glimpsed himself upon the wyrmskin, lying beside the golden bowl, and realized it was he they bore through the milkwood grove. Even as they worked, he was aware of an image of himself in their minds, dying. That puzzled him. He had forgotten all about the wyvern's sting.

The heat of his blood rose, and he wished he could be cool again. His mind seemed to be floating still, a few paces above his own body. The eyes of the dark colt below him rolled and fluttered beneath their lids. His breath came short. His limbs twitched now and again as though he dreamed.

Jan felt his awareness lifted away then, from his body, from the milkwood grove. He glimpsed the rest of the pilgrim band at the edge of the Hallow Hills, Korr arguing once more with Teki, then with others. He watched the prince turn back toward the hills, the others going on reluctantly, to wait a little distance out on the Plain.

The grasslands fanned out before him in their vastness, and Jan felt himself skimming, as from a great height, like a bird, southward toward the Summer Sea. The unicorn valley loomed suddenly before him, and he saw his mother, heavy in foal, trotting restlessly about the verges of the birthing grove. Later, he saw the unicorns in a great Circle, wailing, "He is dead, he is dead!" and dancing the funeral dance used only for those of the prince's line.

His thoughts shifted then, altering entirely. For a moment, he became a gryphon, two gryphons, slipping into the Pan Woods under cover of cloud. Then a pan crouched two-footed among the shadows, with others of his kind. A band of *ufpútlak,* four-foots, was filing by—unicorns, by the scent of them. The pan fingered his fire-hardened stake. Trespassers. Then a banded pard sprang from the grass upon the Plain. A blue mare shied and kicked her in the ribs. Jan watched, merging into them, sometimes the mare and sometimes the pard.

Jan's blood grew hotter then, writhing hot, and he felt his distant body twitch and moan. Thirst burned in him. He saw a swirl of many beasts, dust-blue herons enacting their courting rites beside the Summer Sea. He saw creatures with stiff paddles for limbs and broad, flat tails, blow-holes on their brows, and unicorns' horns growing from their mouths.

He saw the sinuous red dragons tunneling their Smoking Hills; gryphons flocked on broken mountainsides, screaming to drive out the hated unicorns. He saw the wyvern king drowsing deep in his own chamber, guarding a flickering torch and brooding subtle, seven-stranded thoughts.

But the last beasts he saw were not wyverns, nor dragons, nor gryphons, nor pards. They stood upon two legs like goatlings, but their lower limbs were straighter and less shaggy. Among them moved many unicorns, but solid-hoofed and without horns. The two-foots bound them with cords and set them to dragging great loads on wooden discs that rolled like eyes.

He caught sight of one of the hornless ones, a red roan mare, very long-limbed and clean-moving: a young beauty. Her dark mane stood upright along her neck. Her body was draped and tangled with cords. She balked, snorting. The two-foots rushed and struck at her, shouting, dragging at the cords until she reared up screaming and flailing.

The glimpse melted away. The whole world had begun to fill his eye. He merged into forests, and the wind riffled his branches. Trees rose and died; new seedlings grew. Then he was grassland, rolling and measureless. Kites wheeled above him, circling a dead Renegade.

He was sea, suddenly—green, surging, and salt—a river of ocean that girdled the world. And then he was earth, massive and still, under-lying the forests, the grasslands, even the sea. He was fire, liquid stone, moving under the earth and forcing the crack. Its heat felt like his own blood, simmering.

Then he was air, a turbulent sky, heavy with clouds that blotted the sun. Great stormcells roiled toward the upper thinness, and then, blanch-ing cold, spilled their moisture in torrents of wind-whipped rain. A band of tiny, single-horned creatures fled before him.

Jan felt himself spinning, stretching down from the clouds. He whirled, skimming the Plain, slinging up great gouts of earth and joying in the destruction. *I, too,* he heard the storm thunder. *I, too, am part of the dance.*

Storm faded, dissipated. The sky cleared. The sun sank and stars appeared. Jan felt himself among the stars, high over the earth. And the stars were moving, all things about him in the velvety blackness moving. And someone was beside him. Though he could see nothing of it, he was aware of a presence stretching away from him on all sides. It sur-rounded the stars, and was within the stars, and *was* the stars.

"What are you?" he heard himself asking. He was not afraid. "Who are you?"

"Your guide," the presence answered, and her voice was so familiar to him, Jan felt unexpectedly weak with relief. But he could not say from where or when he knew her.

"Where are you?" he asked. "What are you called?"

A pause in which the whole universe seemed to wait.

"You name me." The answer came from everywhere, within him and without.

"Alma," he breathed.

"Aye," the presence answered. "Come. I will show you a thing."

At her words, he felt himself buoyed farther from the world, lifted higher among the stars. The air about him thinned and vanished, but he felt it go without distress—though were it not for the venom in his blood, he would have frozen. He gazed down and saw white mist enveloping the world.

"Tell me now," the presence said, "what do you see?"

"I see the world," Jan told her, "bright as seafire. It is round, a swirl of colors, turning upon itself like someone dancing."

"And?"

"And," answered Jan, "I see the pitted moon before it, ghost-lit, dancing above the world."

"And?" With a smooth, windless motion, they drew back even farther from the planet and its moon.

"I see the world and the moon," said Jan, "dancing around a pain-bright sun, with other worlds and moons of amber, mauve, and lichen-green, both larger and smaller, some nearer and some farther away."

"And now?"

They pulled back rapidly. The sun grew very small, a yellow glint among the other, whiter stars. The gulf between the pricks of light was black as nothing. The burning stars floated like firefish in the void.

"I see the sun, small as a star among other stars, some blue-white, some rosy, some red-yellow."

"Your sun *is* a star," the presence told him. "And?"

They moved back now in a headlong rush.

"I see," said Jan, softly, "the stars in a great swirl, slowly turning like some vast, spiral flower; and in the distance, I see more starflowers, some blue, some red—many of them, and all turning."

"So," the presence told him, "now you have seen more than any living creature from your world has ever seen."

Jan gazed at the fiery pinwheels arrayed around him, all leisurely spinning. He watched what seemed a long time, saying nothing, until at last he felt himself beginning to descend. The swirls of stars below grew greater, brighter, enveloping him. He struggled, uselessly.

"But," he cried out, "is there not more?"

The presence was still beside him, had never left him. "Infinitely more, Aljan," she told him. "And you shall see it all, one day. But now our time is short."

Jan cast a long, longing glance after the bright, turning swirls, contracting to the size of stars among the other stars. They were nearing his own sun now, with its own little dance of worlds. The closeness of their passing beside the yellow star made Jan's blood sizzle. He and his guide hovered above the swirling, blue-white planet, its moon overlying it like a disc upon a disc.

"Why have you shown me this thing?" he asked.

"What have I shown you?" countered his guide.

"You. . . ." He faltered. "You have shown me the great dance, the Cycle—the one the Renegade spoke of, the one beyond even our own moon and sun. You have shown me the stars' dance."

"Aye," the presence said. "And what is my Dance?"

"It is motion," Jan told her, "energy, turning."

"It is rest and stillness also," she replied.

"Is it life, then?" Jan answered. "All things that live."

"Life, aye," the presence nodded. "And . . ."

"And?" Jan murmured.

"The wyverns also are part of my Cycle, and murderous gryphons and wheeling kites. Fire which can destroy and the Serpent-cloud which flings all things to dust."

"Death, too," ventured Jan, "is in the Dance."

A little silence then.

"Why have you brought me here?" Jan started. "No one of my people ever has had such a vision as this."

"Ah, so you see this for a vision." The presence smiled; he felt her smile. "Well, you are a dreamer, well used to dreams."

He denied it with his thoughts. "I never dream."

The presence laughed. "Jah-lila took away the waking memory of your dreams. This day you have won them back again."

Jan shook himself. "Tell me why. . . ."

Again the presence's quiet laugh. "So importunate! But is this not what you have always wanted, to apprehend the workings of the Dance? You have looked for it only half knowing, and found it only in little bits: in the roiling of stormclouds and the workings of fire, in the fluting of pans dancing under the moon—in the depths of danger in a gryphon's eye. In the rolling vastness of grasslands that call out, 'What lies beyond me? Come see!' "

Her voice had grown so familiar now, as though she knew him to the marrow of the bone. He had not known even a god could read his inmost heart. "What are you, then?"

"I am Mystery," she told him, "that goads intelligent beings to understanding. I am Curiosity. I am Solution. I am what is, demanding to be known. Those things that you have always been asking, I have answered now, a little."

"No!" cried Jan. "You have given me only questions, a thousand more."

"Good," the presence laughed. "Spend your energies seeking their answers, not on colts' games and trickstering." Jan flinched a little beneath her bluntness. "Understand things, Aljan," his guide told him, "by learning to think as they do: enter in. Study the world and see how it works—make it work your own ends, if you can."

"But what are my ends to be?" Jan burst out.

A long silence. At last she said, "I leave that to you."

"Then why was I alone chosen to see these things?"

"Many have I given this vision to, Jan," she said. "Though none till now have I let return."

"But I will return."

He felt her nod of affirmation and fell silent then. He could think of nothing. He understood nothing.

"Come now," his guide replied, a little mocking. "You cannot be so dumbstruck as all that. Have I not whispered all your life that you were born to see great things?"

Jan felt his mind constrict. "Great things," he murmured. "Will I . . . will I see the coming of the Firebringer?"

"You have already," his guide returned. "The Firebringer is among you now."

"Is it . . . ?" Jan stumbled to a stop. He hardly dared say it. "Will my father be the one?"

The presence seemed to turn away a little then. "Perhaps," she said, indifferently. "Who knows?"

"You do!" cried Jan.

The goddess laughed. "Aye. I do that. But that is not yet yours to know."

"My people need a Firebringer," Jan insisted. "To rout the wyrms. The Vale is growing too close for us, and the gryphon said. . . ."

"I know what the gryphon said."

A sudden urgency burned in Jan. "Her people hate us. They are planning to fly against us and drive us from the Vale. . . ."

"Have you told your father that?" the presence interrupted.

Jan shook his head, startled. The gryphon had charmed him—he realized that now—telling him while he gazed into her eye as in a dream. He had not remembered until this moment.

The goddess said, "But if you won back the Hallow Hills before that time, the gryphons could have your Vale and welcome; there would be no need to war." It was as if she had spoken his own thoughts back at him. "Is that what you were beginning to say?"

"My father is a great warrior," Jan answered her. "He could rout the wyverns from the Hallow Hills. But the legend says he must have fire. The wyverns' dens would go up in a blaze if. . . ."

"There are many kinds of fire, Aljan."

Jan hardly heard. "But my father knows nothing at all of fire. I am the only unicorn who knows—but I know nothing, hardly anything!"

"Then you'd best make a study of it, hadn't you?" the presence remarked. "You've only a few years' time before the gryphons fly. List, now," his guide said suddenly. "The time grows very short. Ask me what question you will, and I will answer."

"I . . ." started Jan. He could feel the vision's end looming, and burst out with the first question that came to him. "Why do the gryphons hate us?"

"You already know the beginning of that."

"Why do the pans speak so differently from us, then?" He struggled. Time slipped from him. His body burned.

"Again," the goddess told him, "you may find that for yourself. Hist, be quick."

"Then, then . . ." stammered Jan. He racked his thoughts for some riddle worthy of a god. "Why must we bind ourselves to the Circle of Warriors?"

"Who tells you you must? Not I. I do not make kings, or Rings of Law. Those things are yours to make, or to unmake, just as you choose."

"Why does my mother tell me to follow my own heart, not Korr's?"

"Ask her," the goddess said.

"Who is the Red Mare the Renegades spoke of?"

"Ask her."

Jan felt himself beginning to fall. He struggled desperately to remain aloft. "But why does your voice sound so familiar to me? I have never met you before in dreams."

"Whom do I sound like?" the presence demanded, bearing him up for a moment more.

"Like Jah-lila," said Jan, "and like Korr. Like Ses my dam and like Khraa the king. Like Tek and Dagg—Tas, Teki, Leerah. . . ."

"Who else?"

"Like the three-headed wyvern," Jan replied. "Like the gryphon in the cave, like the fluting of pans, or Renegades crying, like. . . ."

"Like?"

"Like sea, like earth shifting, like wind and like fire."

"And?"

"Like myself," said Jan, coming suddenly breathless to a halt. He had quit struggling. "Like me."

"I *am* you," the Mother-of-all replied, "and much, much more besides. I am everything you have ever known and that has ever been. I surround you all, and am within you, and am you. You are my kindling; I am the Fire. I am the Circle. I am the Dance. Learn to know me. Come." A moment passed. "The time's at hand. You must return."

Then he felt what had been supporting him vanish. He was descending in a rush toward the bright, pale-blue world and the gray pitted moon before it. The world grew large, more varicolored. Its gray companion, within its disc, also increased. Jan felt himself falling toward the heart of the moon.

"Alma," he cried out. There was no need. The presence had not left him. "Did you not tell me I would return to the world?"

The other nodded in his mind. "Aye. Back to the Hallow Hills and your three companions."

The moon loomed, burning silver in the white light of the sun. Perfectly round, it seemed to lie upon the surface of the world like a lake of still, bright water.

"But Alma," cried Jan, "the moon. . . ."

"Nay, Jan," the goddess told him, departing now. "The Mirror of the Moon."

He felt a splash and heard the sound of it. Then he was aware of three unicorns: Tek, the red mare, and Dagg. They had staggered from the woods, dragging the wyvern skin. Stumbling under its weight in the midafternoon sun, they waded out into the water.

He felt the wet slosh about their knees, and the strain against their teeth and jaws. The wyrmskin on which he lay touched the surface and buoyed up. Cool liquid spilled in at the slack places, bathing him. The fire in his blood swabbed out.

He heard the angry hiss of water mingling with the wyrm's blood on the skin, and the air was suddenly thick with acrid steam. He heard whinnies of alarm, then snorts and choking. The wyvern skin fell abruptly slack. It floated. The golden bowl slid off and sank.

He could not get his eyes open, could not see what was happening. He struggled weakly to raise his head. There was thrashing in the water nearby him: he heard gasps, and then two, three dull thuds upon the sand. The acrid air around him hung suddenly, utterly silent, until the harsh vapor invaded his senses at last. He knew nothing more.

Homecoming

18

Jan came again into awareness slowly. He felt himself floating, the coolness of water against one side, and the soft, sinuous membrane bearing him up. The sun on his other side was warm and drying. He opened his eyes and blinked. Raising his head with difficulty against the yielding surface of the skin, he saw he lay on the sacred pool, near shore. The sun overhead shone midafternoon.

He floundered off the floating hide and onto the white sand of the shallow bottom. His limbs no longer burned with fire. The golden bowl lay submerged, sun-gleaming, a half pace from him. He got to his feet and champed his teeth. His nose and heel were plastered with chewed milkwood buds. The taste of water in his mouth was sweet. He bent and took a long drink from the pool.

Lifting his head, he spotted the others. They lay on the bank, fallen in midstride. Jan felt his heart go cold a moment, but then he saw the rising and falling of their sides: they were alive. He waded toward them, and halted in the shallows beside the red mare.

He recognized her now. She was Jah-lila, Tek's mother, the lone unicorn—she his father had called once, long ago, to come sing away his dreams. Jan bent and nudged her with his nose. She stirred then, snorting, and rolled to get her legs under her, but did not rise.

"Well glad I am to see you alive, prince-son," she told him at last, then shook her head, as if groggy still. She managed a laugh. "The Mirror of the Moon is strong proof against poison."

Her voice was very like Tek's, but fuller and a little more deep. Jan nodded, eyeing her, feeling strange and unsurprised.

"I heard you singing on the night of Moondance," was all he could think of to say.

The wild mare nodded. "Aye. I was singing a charm on you, little prince, to keep you from seeing me. But my power over you is all ashes now." She sighed, still smiling, and gazed away. "No ears but yours were meant to hear that song, but I think Tek heard it, too, for she came looking for me." Jah-lila glanced at him.

"She looked for you in the Pan Woods, too," said Jan, "and again upon the Plain. But she never . . ."

The other laughed, gently. All her moves were careful and unhurried. "I did not mean for her to find me—or for you. But of course it was mostly your father I meant to . . ." But Jan hardly heard.

"You called out to me in the Pan Woods," he said suddenly, "and led us away from the others to the goatling's Ring." The realization jarred him. "You began to bury the Renegade."

The red mare nodded. "I did those things."

Jan bit his breath, stopping himself. "The Serpent-cloud," he said. "You led the storm away."

The healer's mate smiled. "So you saw me then, too?" She sighed, laughing. "Already you were stealing back your dreams."

A little silence then.

"Why did you come?" he asked, at last.

"On account of you," Tek's mother said, studying him now. The green in her eyes was very dark. "I meant to stand unseen among the milkwood at Vigil and sing back to you what I had taken once, at your father's bidding—for none may behold his fate upon the Mirror who cannot dream."

She shook her head.

"I told your father that, when first I sang you, that you must have back your dreaming sight before you got your beard. But he did not wish it, argued against it. He is very much afraid of dreams, ever since, a very long time past, a wyvern tried to speak to him in one."

Jan felt his skin prickling.

The red mare said, "He did not send word to me, as I had bidden him, when you were to go on Pilgrimage. Your mother did that."

Jan gazed at nothing, striving desperately to remember what the wyvern had said: *I tried to reach your father once . . . when Korr was young and not yet prince . . . tried to send him a dream to ruin him, send him running wild Renegade across the Plain. . . .* The red mare gazed back at Jan, her quiet tone gone rueful now.

"But I could not be with you on this night just past. I had to run a long way across the Plain with that storm in my teeth before it blew itself to nothing. It has taken me all this time returning."

Jan shook his head. His mind was full. He could not take in any more. "You could have given me back my dreams in the Vale, at Moondance."

🦌

Lying with folded legs beside the water there, I shook my head. "No. I took your dreams by the dark of the moon, and so by the dark must they return."

Would he understand that? I hoped so. The ways of magic are limited, and strange. Then I told him a little more of the truth, speaking slowly, that he might follow me.

"But there is another reason I held back. On a night many years past before ever you were born, prince-son, when first I felt the weight of a horn upon my brow and my body becoming a unicorn's, I stood beside this Mere, beholding a dream. It told me I must one day return to the Hallow Hills, and deliver a unicorn safe out of a wyvern's belly."

I stood up then, shaking the sand and damp from me, unsure how much of what I had said he had been able to grasp. The young prince continued to stare at me, and for the first time he seemed to realize how my black mane stood up in a brush along my neck and that my tail fell full and silky as a mane. No beard grew silken on my chin, no feathery fringe about my heels. He saw my hooves then, which are round and single as the day I was foaled, for all that a horn now sprouts on my brow.

For I was not born among the unicorns. In that, the Renegades were right. I come from a place far to the western south, beyond the shallows of the Summer Sea. But I fled away in time, and found the unicorns in their Vale. Their beauty, when first I saw them, was so great I ached to join them. But I held back, sick with longing, for I was not like them—until I learned of a sacred well across the Plain that makes the unicorns what they are, and a young prince told me the way.

But that is another tale.

"What are you?" whispered the prince's son, falling back a pace to gaze on my beardless chin and single hooves.

I tossed my head. What could I tell him? He wanted it all in a word, and I myself only barely understood what it was I had been, and was now, and was yet becoming. Still, I tried to answer him.

"I am the midwife," I told him, "who stands between the womb of Alma and the world. I do not make, but I help what has been made to be born."

Did that make sense to him? I studied his face, but what he made of my words I could not tell. I tried again.

"I am a dreamer, and a little of a magicker. There is a race of two-footed creatures, Aljan, great movers and builders. They keep many burden-beasts to haul and carry for them." I could not quite keep the bitterness out of my voice as I said the last. "I was such a bearer once, until I came away."

Then the young prince surprised me. "I saw you," he told me, soft, and did not draw away from me, as others do. "I saw you among the two-foots in my vision." And I knew then, for him to have seen that, he must be a far-dreaming seer indeed. He looked at me. "But your coat was another color, then. It was roan."

I smiled a little. "The blossoms of the milkwood which I ate made my coat this color, and the bitter waters of the Mere gave me a horn."

"So you are the Red Mare the Renegades spoke of," Jan answered quietly. "They said my father helped you somehow."

I nodded, remembering. "He was very like you then—wild, hot-headed, and proud, though not so clever or farseeing by half. Though it was against all custom, he told me the way to the unicorn's Mere and, in doing so, broke the Ring of Law and opened himself to a wyvern's spells. I kept them at bay, barely."

The young prince stood, not seeing me, looking inward then. I told him, "And afterward, I sang much of that memory out of your father's mind, just as I once sang away your dreams. One day perhaps I will give it back to him—if he will have it back. He is not a seer, Jan, and has no understanding of magic and dreams."

The other's dark eyes pierced me then, urgent and fire bright. "Give me the tale," he whispered. "I must know. Sing me the tale."

"I *will* give you the tale," I replied, turning away. "But not just now. Another time."

The prince's son said nothing then, watching me.

"Are you not cold, little prince, with your coat still full of water?" I asked him. Behind me I could hear Tek beginning to stir. "Shake off," I said, turning to rouse her. "The afternoon grows late."

Jan shook himself. He *was* cold. The water from his coat showered onto Dagg, who stirred and at last got groggily to his feet. I roused my daughter. She stood up, draggled and chilled, and shook herself. Jan came near us, and though from time to time I caught his eyes darting guardedly at me, full of questions—a thousand questions—he seemed willing to curb them, for now.

"Drink," he told us, bending again to the pool himself. "The water's sweet."

"Sweet?" I heard my daughter say as she waded out into the Mere. "I tasted it this dawn. It's bitter salt."

Jan shook his head, gazing at her again as he had gazed at her for the first time in the milkwood grove, with new eyes. "Sweet now. Taste it."

When first I had sipped of the Moon's Mere, years ago, it made me ill. Then I could stomach no more than a half-dozen swallows before I began to shiver and sweat, and stagger a little in my walking, so strange had been the taste, so mineral. But now as I bent my head with the others to drink, the water was cool and without taint. It washed the bitter taste of the wyrm's blood from my mouth.

Jan felt his strength beginning to return. He no longer felt hollow, famished, though he had not eaten in more than a day. The water alone seemed to satisfy him. The rosebuds plastered to his nose and heel had long since sluiced away. His fetlock still felt sore from the wvyern's sting, his brow tender from the firebowl's burning. But even those aches were beginning to fade. His forelock fell thickly into his eyes.

"It is," Dagg was saying, raising his mouth from the water. "It is sweet."

I heard a little noise behind us suddenly and turned, glimpsed something drawing near through the milkwood trees. Then the prince of the unicorns emerged from the grove. I and two of the others started. I had not been expecting him. Only Jan seemed unsurprised.

His father stood a moment, open-mouthed, and stared at us, seeming almost more astonished to see me than he was to see his son. But it was Jan and the others he spoke to in the end, ignoring me as though I were some haunt or dream.

"What game is this?" he snorted, stamping his hooves as he always did whenever he was baffled or made uneasy. "Where have you been, the three of you? Traipsing these groves at some colts' play while your elders and companions ran themselves to rags hunting you."

He was all terrible thunder and princely affront. I started to speak, but the princeling stepped past me. He would need no mediator ever again. Approaching, he stood before his father without flinching and said, "No games. Tek, Dagg, and I have been killing *that*, lest she rouse the wyrms to fall upon us all."

He nodded toward the wyvern skin, which lay still floating on the pool. My daughter and Dagg dragged it from the water and spread it out upon the sand. The prince fell silent then, staring at it. Jan turned away, and I stood off with Korr a few moments, telling him from my daughter's account what had befallen his son in the wyvern's den.

The young prince and his two companions meanwhile had raised the skin and shaken off the sand. They let the wind lift it streaming into the air and laid it upon the low branches of the near milkwood trees.

Like a great pennant, a banner, it blazed and shimmered in the hot spring sun.

I left off with Korr, and he said no more to Jan, either in praise or in rebuke. I think it puzzled him to have suddenly a son who neither trembled at his frown nor needed his approval to feel proud. Instead the prince of the unicorns gauged the sun.

"Come," he said at last. "We must be off. The hour is late, and the others wait for us upon the Plain."

"I'll leave you then," I said, shaking the silence from me.

Korr stared at me. "You'll not run the journey home with us?" he began.

I shook my head. "Someone must go before you, and sing the tale." I gave him no time to argue with me. "Farewell, my prince, my brave daughter, Dagg."

And oh, the look Tek gave me then, as if to say, "Off again? Off again, Mother, and only just met." Would she ever guess why I had left her to be raised in the Vale by the one who calls himself my mate, or ever trust that there are reasons for everything I do? I glanced from her to Jan—then shook such thoughts from me. I could not stay.

To the young prince, I said, "I'll leave you with your father now, prince-son, but one day, in a year or two years' time, you must come away with me. I'll teach you things a prince should know."

He barely understood me. I did not mean him to. That day was yet a long way off. Then, giving to none of them time to stay me or make reply, I tossed my head and wheeled away, galloping off through the flowering milkwood trees, until their boles and the distance hid me from their view.

❦

Nothing of note befell them in the Hills after I left them. I have never asked the prince's son how much he told his father of his game of wits with the wyvern queen or of his vision in the womb of Alma—little, I think. Nor have I troubled to discover how they spent their half month returning over the Plain, save only that it was a good running and swift, without mishap.

I reached the Vale two days before them, and told the whole herd assembled how the prince's son had saved the pilgrim band from wyvern's jaws by battling their queen to the death below ground. The old king Khraa was much impressed, fairly burst with pride, calling his grandson a worthy heir.

But I noticed the gray king looked older than when I had seen him last, barely a month ago. He moved with a stiffness in his bones. Alma was calling him. He and I both knew it, and nothing lay within my power either to stem that call or stay his answering.

When the prince-son, his father, and the others returned home, two hours before sunset on the day of the full moon, that night each month which the unicorns of the Vale call Moondance, I was already a half day gone. Many of the mares the pilgrims had left in foal the month before now had new foals or fillies at their sides, Jan's mother among them. And the king was dead.

❦

So when the prince led his pilgrims home at last, he found, not a gathering of welcome, but one of mourning. Dagg's father, Tas, took Korr apart to tell him of the gray king's death. They had buried him the day before, unable to wait upon his son's return, for the wheel of the world must turn, and time with it.

Hearing of his father's death, Korr bowed his head and did not speak. Then he went off to the burial cliffs with a small circle of the highest elders to be made king before sunset, for the herd had been nearly two days without a king and were uneasy for want of one.

Jan stood amid the milling crowd, feeling lost and uncertain. Friends greeted the new-made warriors with joyous shouts and jostling. Others stood off quietly, recounting the death of the king. But in all the crush of kith and strangers, Jan caught no glimpse of his own dam, Ses. As he stood scanning for her, Dagg's mother came up beside him.

"Your mother bade me tell you she would wait for you at the wood's edge, there."

Leerah tossed her head. Jan gave her a nod of thanks, then sprang away across the valley floor. He mounted the slope, passing his own cave, and headed toward the line of trees. He saw his mother then, waiting at the wood's edge among the long, dusky shadows. Her form was the color of beeswax, of flame. A filly not more than two weeks old stood pressed to her flank.

"What will you call her?" Jan found himself saying. He had come to a halt. The filly started at the sound of his voice, pressing closer to the pale mare's side. His mother smiled.

"Lell," she answered. "We'll call her Lell."

Jan came closer. Dark amber, the filly watched him. Her brushlike, newborn's mane was blonde. Her brow bore but the promise of a horn, a tiny bump beneath the skin.

"Well met," he heard his mother saying, "my bearded boy. You'll have fine silk upon your chin by summer's end."

Jan felt a rush of pride. Already, he knew, the feathery hairs were sprouting along his jaw.

His mother said, "How was your pilgrimming?"

He shrugged, suddenly shy. "You have heard it all already from Jah-lila." She nodded and laughed. He said nothing, looking off. "I had a dream," he said at last, "upon the Mirror of the Moon. I dreamed the unicorns in mourning, crying, 'He is dead. He of the line of Halla, dead!' " He looked at Ses. "I thought they wept for me."

His mother laughed again, but very softly now. "I knew you would return to me. Korr feared you would fly off breakneck at the first opportunity—run wild Renegade across the Plain. But I did not."

Jan frowned. "Why would he think that? My place is here, among the Circle." Already he had forgotten ever dreaming himself outcast.

Ses nodded, murmuring, "You are prince now of the Ring."

Jan gave a little start, then sighed. He had forgotten that. "Mother, I have seen other Rings than ours. I have seen gryphons that were brave and loyal after their own kind of honor, pans dancing to reed voices under the moon, and Renegades who were not hornless, solid-hoofed or godless things."

"Aye," she told him. "That is an old mare's tale, about the Renegades."

"And I have seen a Cycle that is wider than all our smaller Rings," said Jan, "and includes them, and surpasses them. A place waits for me in that wider Ring, too. I have seen it, and cannot wake or sleep dreamless of it ever again."

He saw a slow smile light his mother's eye. "Then I am glad," she said. "All that ever I have wished is to see you follow your own heart, and no other."

She came forward and stood against him, laying her neck about his neck. Jan saw his sister, Lell, begin to suckle, butting his mother's side. He leaned against his dam, watching. After a time, he felt her warm, dry tongue stroking his shoulder. He drew back.

"What are you doing?" he began.

"Getting the dust off you," she replied. "Truth, how did you get so much into your coat? You look as though you've rolled in it."

Jan stood off and shook himself. He *had* rolled in dust. His winter coat had shed upon the Plain, coming off all in an evening in thick mats of hair. And the color beneath had been darker than the old, not a trace of sable to it. For he was black as his father beneath the shed. The color at last ran true.

But he had felt strange in his sleek new coat, like a trickster, somehow—like a thief. So he had rolled in dust to hide the color from others' eyes a few days longer. But there could be no more hiding now. He was home. He shook himself again. Dust rose like smoke from the glossy blackness of him, and hung in the still, sunlit air between the shadows.

His mother gave no indication of surprise. "And what is that upon your brow?"

He realized then he had shaken his forelock back as well. He had not meant to. He had been letting it fall thickly into his eyes this last half month. But there could be no taking that back, either. He went to stand before his dam.

She studied the new hairs, pale as hoarfrost, growing in a thin crescent where the rim of the firebowl had burned him. He had seen them for the first time only that morning, in a pool in the Pan Woods. But he had felt them these last dozen days, growing.

"Show me the heel where the wyvern stung you."

Jan lifted his hoof and held it crooked that she might see the fetlock better. Since they had left the Hallow Hills, he had kept the spot daubed with mud on the healer's advice; but they had waded streams in the Pan Woods that day, and he had forgotten to replace the mud. The new hair covering the little spot was pale as well.

"I am the Firebringer," he said. He had not realized it until they were long out of the Hallow Hills, halfway home across the Plain. He had said nothing to anyone, till now. "I . . . I always thought it would be Korr."

Ses laughed then. "My son, I love your father well, but he is no seer of dreams."

Jan gazed at her. He could not fathom her unsurprise. Again she laughed.

"On the night of my initiation, long ago, I saw myself give birth to a flit of flame. And I have never doubted for a day what that must mean."

Then Jan said nothing for a while, for he could think of nothing. His sister Lell left off her suckling, and crept around her mother's side to look at him.

"Look," he heard Ses saying. "I see Korr across the Vale, coming back with the elders from the kingmaking." She looked at him a moment, and then off. "The sun's almost set. We should go down."

She started forward, out of the trees' shadows. He did not follow. She halted, glancing back at him.

"Do you come?"

He shook his head. "You go," he told her. "In a while."

He watched his mother descend toward the valley floor, Lell stumbling after her on long, still-awkward legs. They joined the crowd and made for the rise at the center, which Korr was now mounting. His shoulders were daubed with the red and yellow mud of the grave cliffs, that marks the new-made kings among the unicorns. Jan turned and headed upslope through the trees.

He made his way to the lookout knoll and stood only paces from the wood's edge there, from the treeless swatch where he and Tek had fought the gryphon more than a month past—it seemed a very long time ago. Jan gazed down at the milling unicorns, deep blues and scarlets mostly, a smattering of ambers, here and there a gold, a gray.

"There you are," panted Dagg, coming up the slope. "I've been looking—everyone has."

Jan nodded, not turning. He scrubbed himself absently against the rough bark of a fir. His new coat itched.

Dagg snorted and shouldered against him. "What are you doing up here?"

"It's a good spot," Jan answered. "I can watch the dance from here."

"Watch it?" cried Dagg. "You're always *watching* things. You never enter in."

"I do," said Jan. "I'm a better dancer than you."

"You are not."

They fell on each other, nipping and shoulder-wrestling. They snorted, panting—and broke off abruptly at the sound of a low, nickering laugh. Jan turned to see Tek watching from the trees.

"How did you find us?" demanded Dagg.

Tek shrugged, emerging from the trees. She turned to gaze toward the unicorns below. "I have long known all your haunts and hollows. They were mine but two years gone."

Jan and Dagg came to stand beside her. The dusk deepened. None of them spoke. The evening sky grew red.

"We should go," Dagg said.

Jan caught him back. "Not yet."

The sky above was hinting into violet. Tek turned to Jan. "They want to make you prince before the dance," she said. "It was why I came."

Jan looked at her. "Will it matter to you, when I am prince?"

He heard Dagg's laugh. His friend shouldered against him. "I never cared when you were princeling, did I?"

Tek shrugged, eyeing him with half a smile. "Princes put no fear in me."

Jan almost laughed, then caught himself. The mark of Alma rode heavy on his brow. "But what if I were more?" he said. "More than prince—would it matter?"

Dagg looked at him. "Korr's not dead yet," he said.

Then Jan did laugh. He caught Tek studying him.

"What are you talking about, little prince?" she said quietly. "Tell us."

The prince of the unicorns looked down, away. His white heel pricked him in the dark. He picked at the fir needles underfoot with that hind, cloven hoof. "Tomorrow."

Above them, the sky shaded from wine to indigo, lying smooth and cloudless as still, clear water. Night settled. A line of silver peered over the slope across the valley from them, and the dark blue of the sky grew suddenly smoky and more light. The few stars pricking the canopy above paled. Jan watched the rim of brightness edging over the hills.

"Moon's up," he heard Dagg saying. "They'll be starting the dance."

Jan drew his breath. "Full moon tonight," he murmured. "I'd forgot."

The herd below had begun to turn, slowly, a rough, wide Ring drifting now deasil, now widdershins about the rise in the valley floor where the new king stood. Tek wheeled on Jan suddenly, gave him a smart nip on the shoulder, then bolted from beside him, tearing down the slope. Her light taunt drifted back:

"First down shall have the center of the dance!"

Jan sprang after, and heard Dagg barely a half-pace behind. They galloped breakneck, shouldering and kicking, as they raced to overtake her before she reached the bottom of the slope.

Full Circle

🌿 19 🌿

So it was not Jan, but I that night who watched the dancing from above. Though the others thought me gone, I had kept myself hidden on the far wooded slope where I had stood the month before. Thus I saw the pilgrims safely home, and the making of Korr into the king.

The Circle on the valley floor below me grew gradually thinner, its members fanning outward to form a greater, more circular Ring. The young prince, my daughter, and their shoulder-friend rejoined the dance now moving deasil, steadily deasil, beneath the circling moon.

I departed, and left them to their dancing. And I have come among you these many years after, you who dwell upon the Plain and call yourselves the Free People, you who know so little of your southern cousins, the unicorns of the Vale.

I have told you this tale to remind you of them, for though you have forgotten it, all unicorns were once a single tribe, just as—though you may doubt it—my people, who dwell beyond the Summer Sea, were once like yours. But this tale marks only the first night of my telling. Come to me tomorrow evening, and I will tell you the rest.

Dark Moon

For P.G., in the hope of things to come

Contents

Before

)

H*e was the youngest prince the unicorns had ever known, and his name meant Dark Moon. Aljan son-of-Korr was swart as the well of a weasel's eye, the night-dark son of a night-dark sire, with keen, cloven hooves and a lithe, dancer's frame, a long horn sharper than any thorn, and a mane like black cornsilk blowing. While still counted among the colts, young Jan had won himself a place in the Ring of Warriors. Upon the death of his royal grandsire, Jan had seen his own father declared the king and himself—barely half-grown—made battle-prince.*

During time of peace, Korr the king would have ruled the herd, but because the unicorns considered themselves at war, it was to Jan, their prince, that the Law gave leadership. His people's bitterest enemies, the wyverns, dwelt far to the north, in sacred hills stolen from the unicorns many generations past. Vengeful gryphons held the eastern south, barely a day's flight from the great Vale in which the exiled herd now made its home. And hostile goat-footed pans inhabited the dense woodlands bordering the Vale.

Such were the uneasy times during which this young prince came to power. I am his chronicler, and yestereve I spoke of his warrior's initiation, during which the goddess Alma marked him, tracing a slim silver crescent upon his brow and setting a white star on one heel in token that one day he must become her Firebringer, long prophesied to end his people's exile and lead them triumphant back to the Hallow Hills.

Tonight, I resume my tale little more than a year after Jan's accession: it was the afternoon of Summer's Eve. The morrow would be Solstice Day, when thriving spring verged into summer. Jan stood on a lookout knoll high above the Vale, rump to the rolling valley below, black eyes scanning the Pan Woods spilling green-dark to the far horizon, beyond which the Gryphon Mountains rose, flanking the Summer Sea.

Solstice

☽ 1 ☾

Cloudless sky soared overhead, blue as the sweep of a gryphon's wing. Breeze snuffed and gusted through the dark unicorn's mane, warm with the scent of cedars sprawling the slope below. Sun hung westering. Jan shifted one cloven heel and sighed. He was not on watch—no sentries needed this time of year: gryphons never raided past first spring. But the herd's losses had been heavy that season in fillies and foals carried off by formels—the great blue gryphon females—to feed their ravenous newly hatched young.

Brooding, the prince of the unicorns surveyed the folds of the Pan Woods before him. It was not the number of recent raids which troubled him most, but their manner. Always in springs past, wingcats had come singly, at most in mated pairs. This year, though, many of the raids had included more than two gryphons. A few had even consisted solely of tercels—male gryphons—no female at all. Jan snorted: clearly at least some of the spring's forays had had little to do with a formel's need to feed her chicks.

"Alma," the young prince whispered, and the wind stole the name of the goddess from his teeth. "Alma, tell me what I must do to defend my people."

Only silence replied. Jan's skin twitched. With his long fly-whisk tail, he lashed at the sweatsipper that had alighted on his withers. Vivid memory came to him of how, only the year before, the goddess had marked him with fire, granted him the barest glimpse of his destiny—and spoken not a word to him since. Standing alone on the lookout knoll, he felt doubt chill him to the bone. He wondered now if the voice of Alma and her vision had been nothing but a dream.

A twig snapped in the undergrowth behind him. Jan wheeled to spot a half-grown warrior emerging from the trees. Pale dusty yellow with dapples of grey, the other shook himself, head up, horn high. Jan backed and sidled. Like a fiercely burning eye, the copper sun floated closer to the distant horizon. The other snorted, ramped, then whistled a challenge, and the prince sprang to meet him. Horns clattered in the stillness as they fenced. A few more furious strokes, then the pair of them broke off. Jan tossed his head. Grinning, the dappled half-grown shouldered against him. The prince eyed his battle-companion Dagg.

"Peace!" Dagg panted. "What brings you brooding up onto the steeps so close to dusk?"

Jan shook himself and nickered, not happily.

"Gryphons."

Again his shoulder-friend snorted, as though the very thought of gryphons stank.

"Bad weather to them," Dagg muttered. "Broken wings and ill fortune—praise Alma spring's past now and we're done with them for another year."

Jan nodded, champing. Dusk wind lifted the long forelock out of his eyes, exposing the thin silver crescent upon his brow. Gloomily, he picked at the pine-straw underhoof with his white-starred hind heel. Beside him, Dagg shifted, favoring one foreleg.

"How's your shank?" Jan asked him.

The dappled warrior blinked grey mane from his eyes and slapped at a humming gnat ghosting one flank. He flexed the joint.

"Stiff yet, but the break's well knit. Teki the healer knows his craft."

Behind them, the Gryphon Mountains stood misty with distance. The reddened sun above the Pan Woods had nearly touched the rim of the world. Lightly, Jan nipped his shoulder-friend.

"Come," he told him. "Sun's fair down."

Dagg shook him off and fell in alongside as they started through the evergreens that forested the Vale's inner slopes. Amber sunlight streamed through the canopy. Just ahead, a pied form moved among the treeboles. Jan halted, startled, felt Dagg beside him half shy. A moment later, he recognized the young warrior mare Tek. Her oddly patterned coat, pale rose and black, blended into the long, many-stranded shadows.

"Ho, prince," she called, "and Dagg, make haste! Moondance begins."

Jan bounded forward with a glad shout, reaching to nip at the pied mare's neck, but light as a deer, she dodged away. Tek nickered, shook her mane, back-stepping, laughing still. The young prince snorted, pawing the ground. The next instant, he charged. This time, the pied mare reared to meet him, and the two of them smote at one another with their forehooves, like colts. Tek was a lithe, strapping mare, strong-built but lean, a year Jan's senior—though the young prince was at last catching up to his mentor in size. They were of a common height and heft now, very evenly matched. He loved the quickness of her, her sleek, slim energy parrying his every lunge and pressing him hard. With Tek, he need never hold back.

"So, prince," she taunted, feinting and thrusting. The clash of their horns reverberated in the dusky stillness. "Is this the best my pupil can do? Fence so lackadaisical this summer by the Sea and you'll never win a mate!"

Jan locked his teeth, redoubled his efforts. On the morrow, he knew, he, Tek, and Dagg—and all the other unpaired young warriors—must depart upon their yearly trek to the Summer shore, there to laze and court and spar till season's turn at equinox, when most would pledge their mates before the journey home.

Tek clipped and pricked him. Jan glimpsed Dagg standing off, absently scrubbing a flybite against the rough bark of a fir, and whistled his shoulder-friend to join in the game—but just then, more quick than Jan could blink, the young mare lunged to champ his shoulder, taunting him with her wild green eyes. In a flash, he was after her. Jan heard Dagg's distant, startled shout at being left behind as the young prince plunged breakneck downslope through treeboles and shadows. The last rays of red sunlight faded. Moments later, he burst from the trees onto the Vale's grassy lower slope.

The hour was later than he had reckoned, the round-bellied moon not yet visible beyond the Vale's far steep, but turning the deep blue evening sky to gleaming slate in the east. On the valley floor below, the herd already formed a rudimentary circle. Ahead of him, the pied mare pitched abruptly to a halt. Lock-kneed, snorting, Jan followed suit. Korr, the king, stood on the hillside just below them. Jan tensed as his massive sire advanced through the gathering gloom.

"Greetings, healer's daughter," Korr rumbled.

"Greetings, my king," Tek answered boldly. "A fine night for Moondance, is it not?"

Jan felt himself stiffen at the black king's nod. He barely glanced at Jan.

"It is that," Korr agreed, "and a fine eve to precede your courting trek." The healer's daughter laughed. Pale stars pricked the heavens. The unseen moon was washing the dark sky lighter and yet more light. "Faith, young mare," Korr added in a moment, "I'd thought to see you pledged long before now."

Jan felt apprehension chill him. He had always dreaded Tek's inevitable choosing of a mate. The prospect of losing her company to another filled the young prince with a nameless disquiet—the pied mare would doubtless be long and happily paired by the time such a raw and untried young stallion as he ever won a mate. Restless, he pawed the turf, and his companion glanced back at him with her green, green gryphon's eyes.

"Fleet to be made warrior, but slow to wed, I fear," she answered Korr. "Perhaps this year, my king."

The eastern sky turned burning silver above the far, high crest of the Vale.

"But I will leave you," she continued, "for plainly you did not wait upon this slope to treat with me."

Tek shook herself. Korr acknowledged her bow with a grave nod as she kicked into a gallop for the hillside's base. Still paces apart, Jan and his sire watched the healer's daughter join the milling herd below.

"A fine young mare," murmured Korr. "Let us trust this season she accepts a mate."

Jan felt a simmering rush. "Perhaps I'll join her," he said impulsively.

Korr's gaze flicked to him. "You're green yet to think of pledging."

Jan shrugged, defiant, eyes still on Tek. "I was green, too, to succeed you as prince," he answered evenly. "But perhaps I shall be Tek's opposite: slow to be made warrior, yet quick to wed."

The sky in the east gleamed near-white above the far slope. Korr's expression darkened. "Have a care, my son," he warned. "You've years yet to make your choice."

The young prince bristled. Behind them, Dagg cantered from the trees and halted, plainly taken by surprise. He glanced from Korr to Jan, then bowed hastily to the king before continuing downslope. The young prince snorted, lashing his tail. The king's eyes pricked him like a burr.

"Be sure I will choose when I know myself ready," he told Korr curtly and started after Dagg.

His sire took a sudden step toward him, blocking his path.

"If it be this year, my son," he warned, "then look to those born in the same year as you. Fillies your own age."

Astonished, Jan nearly halted. By Law, not even the unicorns' king might command their battle-prince. Angrily, he brushed past Korr. "Do you deem your son a colt still, to be pairing with fillies?" he snapped. "A bearded warrior, I'll choose a *mare* after my own heart."

He did not look back. White moonlight spilled over the valley floor as the herd before him began to sway, the great Ring shifting first one way, then the other over the trampled grass. Jan's eyes found his mother, Ses, among the crowd. Beside the pale cream mare with mane of flame frisked his amber-colored sister, Lell: barely a year old, her horn no more than a nub upon her nursling's brow. Korr cantered angrily past Jan, veering to join his mate and daughter as the dancers found their rhythm, began to turn steadily deasil.

Jan hung back. Dagg's sire and dam moved past: Tas, Korr's shoulder-companion, like his son a flaxen dun dappling into grey; Leerah, white with murrey spots, danced beside her mate. Jan spied his granddam Sa farther back among the dancers. Dark grey with a milky mane, the widowed mate of the late king Khraa whickered and nodded to her grandson in passing, placing her pale hooves neatly as a doe's. Jan dipped his neck to her, but still he did not join the Ring.

Other celebrants swirled by, frolicking, high-stepping, sporting in praise of Alma under the new-risen moon. The circling herd gained momentum, drawing strength from the moonstuff showering all around; the white fire that burned in the bones and teeth, in the hooves and horns of all unicorns, placed there by the goddess when, in fashioning her creatures at the making of the world, she had dubbed the unicorns, as favored sons and daughters, "children-of-the-moon."

Tek swept into view, pivoting beside the healer Teki. The black and rose in her coat flashed in the moonlight beside the jet and alabaster of her sire. Tek's riant eyes met Jan's, and she tossed her mane, teasing, her keen hooves cutting the trampled turf, daring him to join her. Daring him.

In a bound, the young prince sprang to enter the Ring. Bowing, Teki gave ground to let Jan dance beside his daughter. The two half-growns circled, paths crossing and crisscrossing. Dagg drifted near, chivvying Jan's flank. Jan gave a whistle, and the two of them mock-battled, feinting and shoulder-wrestling.

Tek's eyes flashed a warning. Jan turned to catch Korr's disapproving glare. Reflexively, the young prince pulled up. Then, blood burning beneath the skin, Jan shook himself, putting even more vigor into his step. Moondance might have been a staid and stately trudge during his father's princely reign—but not during his own! Dancers chased and circled past him in the flowing recurve of the Ring. He found his grandmother beside him suddenly, matching him turn for turn.

"Don't mind your father's glower." The grey mare chuckled. "It nettles him that it is you now, not he, who leads the dance."

Jan whinnied, prancing, and the grey mare nickered, pacing him. They gamboled loping through the ranks of revelers until, far too soon, the ringdance ended. Moon had mounted well up into the sky. All around, unicorns threw themselves panting to the soft, trampled ground, or else stood tearing hungrily at the sweet-tasting turf. Fillies rolled to scrub their backs. Dams licked their colts. Foals suckled. Stallions nipped their mates, who kicked at them. Jan nuzzled his grandmother, then vaulted onto the rocky rise that lay at the Circle's heart.

"Come," he cried. "Come into the Ring, all who would join me on the courting trek."

Eagerly, the unpaired half-growns bounded into the open space surrounding the rise. Behind them, their fellows sidled to close the gaps their absence left, that the Circle might remain whole, unbroken under the moon. Jan marked Tek and Dagg entering the center with the rest.

"Tonight is Summer's Eve," he cried. "The morrow will be Solstice Day. Before first light, as is the Law, all unpaired warriors must depart the Vale for the Summer Sea, there to dance court and seek our mates. There, too, must we treat with the dust-blue herons, our allies of old, who succored our ancestors long ago. But mine is not to sing that tale. One far more skilled than I will tell you of it. Singer, come forth. Let the story be sung!"

Jan descended the council rise as the healer Teki rose to take his place. The singer's black-encircled eyes, set in a bone-white face, seemed never to blink. Jan threw himself down beside Dagg as the pied stallion began to chant.

"Hark now and heed. I'll sing you a tale of when red princess Halla ruled over the unicorns. . . ."

Restlessly, Jan cast about him, searching for Tek. He spotted her at last, nearly directly in front of him, eyes on her sire. Contentedly, Jan settled down to listen to the singer's fine, sonorous voice tell of the defeated unicorns' wandering across the Great Grass Plain. After months, Halla's ragged band stumbled onto the shores of the Summer Sea, watched over by wind-soaring seaherons with wings of dusty blue.

"So Halla, princess of the unicorns, made parley with these herons, to treat with them and plead her people's case," Teki sang, turning slowly to encompass all the Ring beneath his ghostly gaze.

" 'These strands are ours,' the herons said. 'And though the browse here may seem good in summer, little that is edible to your kind remains during the cold and stormy months of winter.'

" 'We do not ask to share your lands,' the red princess sadly replied. 'Not long since, we consented to the same with treasonous wyverns, only to find our trust betrayed and ourselves cast from our own rightful hills. Now we seek new lands, wild and unclaimed, to shelter us before the winter comes.' "

Tek tore a clump of leaf-grass from the ground beside her and shook her head. Jan watched the soft fall of her parti-colored mane against the graceful curve of her throat. Her green eyes caught the moonlight. Jan felt again the flush of warmth suffusing him. Truth, never had a mare lived—not even red Halla—more comely than Tek. As the singer lifted his voice again, Jan wondered if that long-dead princess of whom the other sang had had green eyes.

" 'We will go in search of such a place for you,' the blue herons said. 'Our wings are strong and the winds of summer fair. Your people are spent from your long wayfaring. Sojourn here for the season beside our Sea while we seek out a place such as you describe.' "

Teki sang on, finishing the lay with the herons' discovery of the grassy Vale at the heart of the Pan Woods, verdant in foliage, its steep slopes honeycombed with grottoes to lend shelter against wind and rain, the whole valley uninhabited save for witless goats and deer. Exultant, the unicorns had claimed the Vale, securing at last a safe wintering ground: their new home in exile until the foretold coming of Alma's Firebringer would one day lead them to reclaim their ancestral lands.

Listening, Jan found his thoughts straying to the fierce, furtive pans, whose territory he and his band must on the morrow begin to cross in order to reach the Summer Sea. Bafflement and frustration over the worsening gryphon raids crowded his mind as well, mingled with thoughts of the distant wyverns and this fitful, generations-long impasse his people termed a war.

Heavily, Jan shook his head. The moon upon his forehead burned. Somehow, he must find a way to conquer all these enemies and return his people to the Hallow Hills. Legend promised that he could do so only with fire. Yet he possessed no fire and no knowledge of fire, no notion of where the magical, mystical stuff could be found—not even the goddess's word on where to begin.

Alma, speak to me! he cried inwardly.

But the divine voice that had once guided him so clearly held silent still. Despair champed at him. Teki quit the rise, his lay ended. Jan sighed wearily and stretched himself upon the springy turf. Dagg sprawled alongside him, head down, eyes already closed. Before him, Jan saw Tek, too, lay down her head. The moon, directly above, gazed earthward in white radiance. Jan shut his eyes. Others all around, he knew, already slumbered.

He felt himself drift, verge into dreams. Tangled thoughts of his people's adversaries and his own impossible destiny washed away from him. Even memory of Korr's harsh, disapproving stare faded. In dreams, the young prince moved through mysterious dances along a golden-shored green sea. Before him galloped a proud, fearless mare, her name unknown to his dreaming self, though she reminded him of none so strongly as the legendary princess Halla—save that this nameless, living mare had a coat not red, but parti-colored jet and rose, and green, green gryphon's eyes.

SUMMER

☽ 2 ☾

Tek tossed her mane, wild with the running. Wet golden sand scrunched between the two great toes of each cloven hoof. Alongside her, companions frisked through cool green waves. Summer sea breeze sighed warm and salt in her nostrils, mingling with the distant scent of pines. Ahead of her, the prince loped easily along the strand, his long-shanked, lean frame well-muscled as a stag's. She loved the look of him, all energy and grace. What a stallion he would make when he was grown! Tek laughed for sheer delight.

High grassy downs bordered the shore. Jan led the band toward the maze of tidal canyons known as the Singing Cliffs. Wind fluted through their honeycombs like panpipes, a plaintive, sobbing, strangely beautiful sound. Above their soughing rose the shrieks and ranting of the seabirds which nested there.

Far overhead one speck among the myriad began spiraling earth-ward. Head up, the pied mare halted alongside Dagg as the prince whistled his band to a standstill. Other specks glided effortlessly down, blue as the sky in which they sailed. Soon they dropped low enough for Tek to distinguish long wings and slender necks, sharp, bent bills and lanky, web-footed legs.

In another moment, they began alighting on the sand. One heron, taller than the rest, her eye roughly level with Jan's shoulder, fanned her feathery head-crest to reveal deep coral coloring under the dusty blue.

"Greetings, Tlat, far-roving windrider," Jan hailed her. "Peace to you and to your flock."

The leader of the herons clapped her bill and studied Jan with one coral-colored eye. Behind and around her, her people bobbled, folding their elongated wings with difficulty.

"So. Jan," she called in her high, raucous voice. "The prince of unicorns returns."

"Yes, I am returned," the dark stallion answered. "Last year found me no mate, so this year I must try again."

"Ah!" the seaheron cried. Bobbing and clattering, her people echoed her.

"How fared your own courting this past spring?" Jan inquired as the herons subsided.

Obviously pleased, Tlat groomed her breast. "Ah!" she piped. "The crested cranes—tried to steal our nesting grounds again this year. Ah! We drove them off."

The prince nodded solemnly. Breathing in the tangy sea breeze and feeling the deep, steady warmth of sun upon her back, Tek bit down a smile. Every year the same report. Though the cliffs held ample nesting sites for all, the ritual clash between herons and cranes continued spring after spring. Tlat gabbled on.

"Now the nests are built, the hatchlings fat and sleek with down. My own brood numbers six! My consorts and I press hard to feed them all."

Behind her, several of the smaller birds, males, began to step in circles, ruffling and fanning their crests. Tek counted half a dozen of them: one consort to father each chick? Jan bowed to them.

"My greetings to your mates, and to your unseen young as well. I trust we will meet when their wing-feathers grow?"

"Yes! Doubtless!" screamed Tlat proudly. "But we cannot stay. Our squabs cry out to us from the cliffs, and we must not let them hunger. Greetings and farewell!"

Tek glimpsed the red chevron on the underside of each pinion as the windriders shook out their wings.

Bowing, Jan replied, "The herons have been our allies for generations. We do not forget the debt we owe. Our courting dances will be the more joyous for your greeting."

"Good!" screeched Tlat. "Beware the stinging sea-jells washed up on shore today. Though they are delicious to our kind, we know you find them unpleasant."

The heron queen stretched her neck and stood on toes.

"Welcome, children-of-the-moon! May your summer here prove fruitful—though how odd that your kind takes but a single mate. Unicorns are strange beasts." Abruptly, the stiff wind caught her, plucking her away almost before the pied mare could blink. Other seaherons followed, rising light as chaff. Tek joined Jan and her fellows in bowing again to the departing herons.

"Good winds and fair weather attend you," the prince called after them. Tek was not sure they could hear him above the thrash of surf and eerie crooning of the Cliffs. The windriders had already dwindled to mere motes overhead. A moment later, she lost sight of them, swallowed by the fierce blue, cloudless sky.

Stinging sea-jells did indeed lie beached downshore as the windriders had warned. Jan kept his people out of the waves until the next tide swept the bladderlike creatures with their trailing tendrils away. Summer passed in a headlong rush. The young prince felt himself growing, bones lengthening, muscles massing. He was ravenous and glad of the freely abundant forage. The sky held mostly warm and fair.

He devoted a good part of his day to chasing the other young half-growns and setting them to races and mock-battles, dances and games. Herons brought news of shifts in the wind so that Jan could whistle his band to shelter in the tangled thickets well before any storm. What time he did not spend tending the band he passed with Dagg, exploring inland at low tide along the Singing Cliffs, stopping now and again for a furious round of fencing.

Tek's admirers, he noted testily, were even thicker this year than last. Yet she seemed to pay them as little heed as ever. Once or twice, he even noted her ordering some overly bold young stallion smartly off. More and more, the young prince observed, the healer's daughter sought him out, teasing him away from the band—even from Dagg—to run with her along the wet, golden beach, dodging through dunes, or up onto the highlands above the cliff-lined shore.

Though he knew she could only be doing so to gain respite from bothersome suitors, Jan found himself increasingly willing to be led away. The pied mare's every word, her every move fascinated him. He loved to brush against her smooth, hard flank in play or simply prick ear to the cadence of her voice.

Long summer days ambled lazily by, the starry evenings fleetingly brief. With each passing moon, the high sun of summer gradually receded toward the southern horizon. Now it shone nearly directly overhead at noon. Nights lengthened: soon they would overtake the days in span. Equinox, marking the summer's end, crept up on the young prince unawares.

He and Tek chased across the high downs above the shore, wind whipping their manes and beards. Overhead, herons soared, diving like dropped stones into the shallows of the Sea, fishing for squid. Tek laughed, plunging to a halt at cliff's edge. Frothed with foam, the surging green waters below shaded into ultramarine at the far horizon. Shouldering beside her, Jan was surprised to find himself now taller than she. Had he truly grown so in these last swift months?

Tek tossed her head. The rose and black strands of her mane stung against his neck. The Gryphon Mountains stood barely within sight across the vast bay, but Jan spared them scarcely a thought. Never had unicorns summering upon the Sea been troubled by raiders. Wingcats attacked unicorns only within the Vale, and only at first spring. Spotting his shoulder-friend on the smooth beach below, in the thick of a group of sparring warriors, Jan felt a sudden chill.

"We should go back," he said. "We've left Dagg."

The healer's daughter shrugged. "He is with companions"—she eyed him coolly—"and seems content."

Jan snorted, champing. "We leave him much alone these days." Even so high above the shore, he still caught the faint click of parrying horns. Wind gusted and sighed. Farther down the strand, another knot of young half-growns frisked, fishing fibrous kelp from the waves and playing tussle-tug. Salt seethed heavy in the wind. Abruptly, Jan turned to Tek.

"You are ever luring me off these days, even from our shoulder-friend. Will not Dagg's company do as well as mine to keep your admirers at bay?"

Tek laughed. "Dagg may be my shoulder-friend as well," she answered, watching him aslant. "But he is not the one I am courting, prince."

Jan felt surprise slip through him like a thorn. He stared at her. She could not have knocked the wind from him more thoroughly if she had kicked him.

"What, what do you mean?" he demanded. "I'm far too callow—"

"Are you?" the healer's daughter asked. "So speaks your sire! But what say *you?*" She sidled, teasing, nipping at him with her words. "Three times before have I come to the courting shore—each time only to depart unpaired. The first two summers, I was newly initiated, just barely half-grown. Last year, it was the one on whom I'd set my eye who was just freshly bearded, unready yet to eye the mares. This year, though, while young yet, he has wit enough to know his own heart—and I count him well grown."

She shouldered him. Jan looked at her, unable to utter a word. A sudden fire consumed him at her touch.

"Hear me, prince," the pied mare said, "for I begin to chafe. Long have I waited for you to catch me up." She shied from him, circling, leading him. The dark unicorn followed as by a gryphon mesmerized. "Surely you do not mean to make me wait forever?"

Trailing after Tek, Jan felt himself growing lost. Her eyes drew him in like the surging Sea. In their jewel-green depths, he saw of a sudden possibilities he had never before dared contemplate: Tek dancing the courting dance with him under the equinox moon, the two of them running the rest of their days side to side, unparted by any other—and in a year or two years' time, fillies, foals. . . .

"I—I must think on this," he stammered, stumbling to a stop, and cursed himself inwardly for sounding like a witless foal. Tek only smiled.

"Think quickly, prince. Equinox falls in only six days' time. Five nights hence, we dance the dance." She snorted, shaking her mane. The scent of her was like roseships and seafoam. "Remember my words," she said saucily, "come equinox."

She sidled against him, nuzzled him, her teeth light as a moth's wing against his skin. Jan shivered as Tek broke from him, flying away across the downs, skirting the cliff's edge and heading for the steep slope angling down toward shore. Dumbstruck, the prince of the unicorns stared after her. By the time he had gathered both wit and limb, she was already gone.

◆

"So you've decided," the dappled warrior remarked. Jan and he trotted along the narrow strand flanking the Singing Cliffs. Tide was out, affording them passage. The sea breeze hooted and sighed through the twisting canyons.

The young prince halted, unable to mistake his shoulder-friend's meaning. "How did you know?"

Dagg whinnied. "I've known since spring. I wish you both joy."

His mirth had a strangely painful ring. Hearing it, Jan became suddenly aware that Dagg had no young mare like Tek with whom to spend his hours and dream of one day dancing court. Jan shook himself. The thought of making the pledge himself and leaving Dagg behind, unpaired, made his skin taut.

"Hist, nothing's decided until the eve of equinox!" he cried, shouldering against the younger stallion. "Come, you've time yet to make a choice—any number of mares would spring to pledge with you. What of that filly I saw you sparring with the other day? The slim, long-legged blue . . ."

"What—Gayasa's daughter, Moro?" Dagg laughed again, in earnest this time. "She's barely got her beard; she was only made warrior this spring past—far too young." He shook his head. "And so am I. Another year."

Turning, he broke into a trot. Jan loped after him. "It doesn't have to be," he said urgently.

Dagg halted, stood gazing off across the green and foaming waves. "She's not among us," he said at last. "She's not yet here for me to pledge."

Jan frowned, not following. The dappled warrior turned.

"Do you recall," he asked quietly, "the night of our initiation two springs past?"

Jan nodded slowly: the night when initiates to the Ring of Warriors became, for one brief instant, dreamers, to whom Alma granted glimpses of their destinies.

"Tek says she saw the foretold Firebringer," continued Dagg, "moon-browed, star-heeled."

The young prince shook the forelock out of his eyes, digging nervously at the shell-embedded shore with his left hind heel. *Aye, marked as the Firebringer,* he thought miserably, *but without so much as an inkling of where I'm to find my fire!* Dagg glanced at him.

"You yourself beheld visions of the goddess's Great Dance."

Jan shrugged and sidled. *And only darkness since: not even a whisper of a dream.*

"What did you see?" he asked his friend suddenly. "You've never said."

Dagg closed his eyes. "I saw a mare," he said, "small, but exquisitely made, high-headed, her coat a strange bright hue such as none I've ever seen. Each Moondance, I've scanned the assembled herd. . . ." He opened his eyes and turned to took at Jan. "Even though I know my search is hopeless. Her mane stands upright along her neck. Her tail falls silky as a mane. Her chin is beardless, no horn upon her brow. Each hoof is one great solid, single toe."

The young prince stared at him, dumbstruck. Dagg nodded.

"Aye. She's not of the Ring, Jan," he whispered. "She's a renegade."

Frowning, Jan shook his head. "You and I both know those legends of outlaws losing their horns when banished from the Vale are only old mares' tales."

Dagg stood silent. Again, the young prince shook his head.

"Yet, if not a Plainsdweller," he murmured, "what manner of mare could this dream creature be?"

The dappled warrior snorted, shrugged, his pale eyes full of pain.

"I've no notion. I only know she is my destiny—and I'll never find her in the Vale."

They both stood silent then. The breeze through the near Cliffs hummed and shuddered. Cranes wheeled screaming among the herons overhead. Tide came foaming in, wetting the two unicorns' cloven hooves, eating away the beach. The prince's shoulder-friend leaned hard against him.

"Jan, don't wait for me," he said. "Alma alone knows when I'm to find my mate. You've already found yours. Don't hold off. Don't spoil your own happiness—and Tek's—because I can't join you this year in the pledge."

Jan turned to study his friend. Favoring one foreleg, Dagg forced a grin. Half-rearing, he smote at the dark unicorn smartly with his heels. Jan whistled and shied, fencing with him, grateful and relieved. He felt as though he had tossed a hillcat from his shoulders. Wheeling, Dagg sprinted away. Jan sprang to follow, and the two galloped back along the seacliffs to rejoin the band.

On the night before equinox, the firefish were running: small, many-armed creatures that swirled luminous like stars through the great bay's pellucid water. They filled its breadth with a blaze of rose and pale blue light. The herons celebrated the advent of the firefish with noisy whoops, diving from moonlit air into the midst of those swarming near the surface of the waves, tentacles entwined, about their own strange courting rites.

Other windriders skimmed low, their bent bills laden with tangled, suckered arms as they snatched prey from the combers. Their eerie, loonlike cries and staccato splashes sounded through the cool, motionless air. For once, the Singing Cliffs held silent, no wind to wake their ghostly song. Jan and Dagg stood at the edge of a tangled thicket, watching herons and firefish and foaming sea as evening fell.

"Moon's up," Dagg told him.

The huge, mottled disk hung just above the far Gryphon Mountains to the east, dwarfing them, paling the stars. Its light made a long path of brightness across the placid bay. Jan nodded. Dagg fell in beside him as he turned and trotted through the verges of the thicket. Jan's ears pricked. Above the herons' distant plash and cry, the quiet rush of waves along the shore, he heard the sounds of unicorns gathering: snorts and shaking, the dunning of hoofbeats, a restless stamp.

He and Dagg emerged from the trees. Horn-browed faces turned expectantly as the dark prince loped to the center of the dancing glade, a circular, open space at grove's heart, trampled clean of vegetation by generations of unicorns. He halted, chivvying, his own blood running high. His restless followers milled and fidgeted, anxious to declare their choices in the dance. Jan tossed his head.

"This is the night we have all awaited," he told them. "Let those who know their hearts choose mates tonight, pledging faith to one another in the eyes of Alma for all time!"

With a shout, eager half-growns sprang into vigorous, high-stepping cadence, prancing and sidling before their prospective mates. Jan watched the moving river of unicorns, chasing and fleeing their partners in an endless ring. Dagg cantered past twice, three times—but where was Tek? He did not see her. Frowning, the young prince scanned the russets and blues of the others until a flash of pale rose and black revealed the pied mare. She seemed to be deliberately skirting the fringe, ducking behind other warriors to conceal herself from him.

The young prince plunged into the dance. The healer's daughter quickened her pace. With a surge of determination, he sprinted after her. All around him, companions circled, manes streaming, heels drumming. The moon rose higher until the youngest warriors, wearied and unpartnered still, dropped out to stand at the edge of the grove, only watching now. He glimpsed Dagg among them, pulling back, panting, sparing his once-broken foreleg just slightly.

Jan redoubled his pursuit of Tek, dodging through the remaining half-growns. In pairs, some of these had started to slip away, mares leading, stallions following, chasing off into the trees. Jan listened to their whistled laughter, their hoofbeats fading. Deep under cover of darkness, they would dance their own, more privy dances under Alma's eyes alone.

The crowded rush had begun to thin, more than half having slipped off or dropped away, unpaired. Yet still the healer's daughter eluded him. The young prince snorted, wild with frustration. How could she manage it, threading so nimbly among the others, always just a few teasing strides ahead? Once more he started to quicken his gait—then abruptly stopped himself, for all at once, he understood. He must stop trying to catch her, cease striving to run her down like some rival in a race—for this was not a race, he realized suddenly, nor any sort of contest at all. It was a dance.

They moved in a circuit. He could not lose her, and whether it was he who overtook her, or she who circled forward to catch him from behind, what did it matter? Laughing, he let himself fall back into the flowing ring of unicorns, and all at once, she was beside him, the two of them prancing and frisking, chasing and circling one another. Others around them faded from his thoughts. He and Tek formed their own circle at the heart of every larger circle and cycle and dance.

They had left the grove, he realized. The sound of the other celebrants faded behind them as he and Tek loped deeper into the trees. The murmur of sea and shore drew nearer. The shimmer of sealight glistened beyond the shadows, mingled with the pale gleam of moonlight.

Tek moved ahead of him, still beyond his reach, but only trotting now. She glanced over one shoulder, nickering, her green eyes lit by the moon. In another moment, he would catch her and pledge his vows, hear her pledge hers in return. Then they would be conjoined for life, their bond unshakable in Alma's eyes. It was what he had always longed for. He knew that now, and the knowledge warmed him like a fire.

Storm
) 3 (

Jan stirred in the grey light of morning. He lay on dry, sandy soil under knotted, smooth-barked shore trees. The beach lay only a short way off. Sky had grown heavy and overcast, dark slate in color. No longer calm, the grey-green sea frothed, foaming along the strand. *Storm in the wind,* he thought. Even now, at slack tide, the sea was running high.

His head rested upon another's flank, his neck lying along her back. He savored the warmth of the other's side against his own, her breaths even and light. Tek woke and, lifting her head, leaned back against him, caressing his strong-muscled neck with her own. Gently, he nipped her. She laughed, gathered her limbs, and, shaking the sand from her, rose. Jan did the same, nuzzling her.

"My mate," he murmured.

Again the pied mare nickered, shook him off. "Enough, prince! All night we danced, and I am spent. We must rejoin the others and take our leave of the dust-blue herons."

Jan sighed. By custom, the newly paired warriors must be gone from the courting shore by noon of equinox day. He stretched his limbs. Time enough to dance with his mate again when they reached the Vale some three days hence. He smiled, languid still, as Tek started away through the trees.

"What sluggards we have been," she called. "Half the morn is lost!"

Jan laughed, trotted to catch her up. The trees were sparse enough to keep the shore in view. The sea was truly wild this morn. Wind gusted, frothing the waves to spume. The beach had been eaten almost away by the rising tide. Dense clouds thickened the sky. Across the broad bay, great purple thunderheads boiled above the Gryphon Mountains. The air smelled humid, heavy with the coming rain. Abruptly, the dark prince halted. Against the soughing of wind and the crash of sea he heard high, keening screams—too sharp and full-throated to be herons' cries. Tek's ears pricked.

"List," she started. "What . . . ?"

The strident calling intensified. Jan's heart contracted suddenly as he caught the piercing whistles of warriors taken by surprise. Dagg's voice bellowed orders from the beach.

"Gryphons! Haste—rally: make ring! Wingcats are upon us—"

With a shout, Jan charged past Tek, heard the drum of his mate's heels only a half-pace behind. The trees fell away as he burst from the grove to behold his whole terrified band ramping on the wind-whipped shore, sea foaming behind them, while a dozen screaming gryphons circled above. Jan shied, staring, stunned. Never had such a thing been recounted in story or lay, that gryphons should attack unicorns upon the shores of the Summer Sea. Wingcats only raided the Vale—and only at first spring!

Before him, the young warriors scrambled to form a ring. Dagg whinnied orders, hurrying them into rank. Skirling gryphons dived. The flock consisted mostly of lighter, smaller males: the tercels' jewel-green feathers and golden pelts stood out against the storm-dark sky. Only four of the raiders were the larger females—blue-fletched formels with tawny hide. Jan shook his head: these were not mated pairs! Nor, so late in the year, could any hungry hatchlings yet remain in the nest.

Fiercely, the unicorns reared and jabbed at their attackers. Sprinting past her mate, Tek sounded her war cry. Furiously, Jan trumpeted his own. He dodged a green-and-gold tercel's swoop—then, quick as storm-flash, leapt after and felt his horn slash golden hide. The gryphon shrilled. Jan whinnied in defiance. Tek, he saw, had safely reached the ring. He himself was beside Dagg a moment later.

"They fell on us without warning," the dappled warrior panted, rearing and stabbing at a swooping formel. She pulled up before meeting his horn. Dagg smote the ground in frustration. "Just moments before you arrived!"

"No taunts? No challenges?" Jan asked him, then shouted at a young warrior starting after a low-flying tercel to get back into line and not break ring.

"Nothing!" Dagg answered, wheeling to drive off another formel diving from behind toward the center of the ring.

Jan grazed her wing, champed a cluster of feathers in his teeth. He yanked hard, trying to pull her down but, shrieking, she tore free. Dagg gouged her belly, and she slashed at him with one claw.

"It's war, then," Jan said grimly. "Not just hunting."

Across from them, he glimpsed Tek repelling a tercel that dropped toward a mare who had stumbled. Around her, the ring of warriors ramped and jostled, badly crowded by the tight formation. Above them the circling gryphons darted, stooping to slash, then lofting away. The young prince snorted in disgust. A traditional defense was proving useless. Nearly impenetrable to grounded foes, the band's outward-facing ranks availed little against adversaries that darted from the air, attacking the unicorns' unprotected hindquarters at the circle's heart.

"Get to the trees!" he shouted as yet another formel plunged toward the ring's center. "Haste! Break ring! Get into cover of the grove!"

"Jan, what—" cried Dagg, aghast.

"Fly!" ordered the prince. What he urged was unprecedented, he knew—but clearly facing an airborne foe required fresh tactics. "They can't swoop to attack us among the trees!"

Rising wind nearly ripped the words from his teeth. He saw his mate nipping and hying her fellows, driving them toward the trees. Dagg and too many of the others simply continued to stare. The dark prince whirled and shouldered the young stallion nearest him, striking him across the rump with the flat of his horn to send him off. The half-grown mare beyond bolted as well while the wingcats redoubled their attack.

"Move!" he cried.

The dappled warrior seemed to swallow his consternation at last as the ring, now hopelessly broken, scattered toward refuge in the grove beyond the dunes. For an instant as she fled past him, Tek's puzzled gaze met his. Clearly she did not understand his strategy, even as she carried out his commands. Dagg started after her. Jan himself did not follow, watching as the two of them hung back a bit, forming a rearguard for their escaping fellows. They were the last to disappear into the trees.

"The prince! The unicorn prince!" one of the tercels cried.

Other wingcats took up the chant. The wind off the sea had grown so strong that Jan saw his attackers wobbling precariously as they banked and turned, breaking off their pursuit of the retreating unicorns. The relentless sea surged at his back. As a dozen wingcats beat toward him from above the dunes, he knew he could never hope to win past them to the grove.

"Alma aid me," he whispered. "Stand at my shoulder, O Mother-of-all!"

The Singing Cliffs rose to his left. Their honeycomb of wind tunnels and tidal canyons shrieked in the rising stormwind. Jan noted with relish how the wingcats strained and labored through the air. Whipping gusts tossed and batted at them. Earthbound, he himself was not so hampered.

As the first gryphon to reach him stooped, the dark unicorn dodged, sprinting away down the beach. The angry cries of his pursuers rose behind. The tall Cliffs opened before him. Jan ducked into their twisting maze. The air around him hummed, vibrated. Wind sheered and shuddered through the turning canyons, whistling like warriors, like birdsong, like reed flutes of the woodland pans.

His path looped and folded back upon itself. Powerful air currents buffeted treacherously. Rounding a bend, Jan glimpsed a wingcat formel being dashed by the gale against the cliff's side behind him. She crumpled, falling, and her companions screamed, increasing their speed. Long, keening wails rose on the stormwind as the churning air grew furious, laden with scattered, stinging rain.

Glancing back again, Jan saw more gryphons swept against the cliffs. The tremendous gusts barely reached him in the canyons' depths. Elated, the dark prince sped on while his remaining pursuers struggled to keep aloft despite the pelting rain. Drops fell more heavily, pounding down. Another tercel smashed into a ledge. Blue lightning split the heavens, casting a cold sheen like moonlight across the cliffs.

Tidewater spilled into the canyons suddenly. Jan found himself running through seawater up to his pasterns, flinging sheets of spray with every step. Only three gryphons remained in pursuit, green tercels all. Their shrieks tore at his ears. The cliffs sang, shuddered with stormwind. He heard the hammering of waves just beyond the canyon wall.

More seawater poured into the chasm. Halfway up his shanks, its depth impeded his gallop. Rain pummeled down. The tempest howled. Jan plunged on, limbs straining against the turbulent water's pull. The canyon ran straight now, without a bend. If he did not find a way out of the Cliffs soon, he realized, he might well drown.

The cliffside opened abruptly before him. Jan glimpsed beach and storm-filled sky. Only a single gryphon's voice trailed him now, the others all lost, or dashed to their deaths, or given up. Seawater crashed into the opening, the swell up to his knees, its undertow fierce. Furiously, Jan fought his way through the inrushing tide. The gryphon behind him shrilled in fury, so close the sound sliced the prince's ears.

Suddenly he was free of the cliffs, in a tidal trough deep with running sea. Firm ground lay within sight, a rocky beachhead only a score of paces beyond. Jan plowed toward it through the foaming surf. Again the gryphon's savage cry. The dark unicorn felt talons score his back, a razor beak striking the crest of his neck. He ducked, dodged sharply.

Great green wings slapped the waves to either side. The raptor's grip tore into his flesh, fastening upon his shoulder blades.

Screaming with pain, Jan bucked and reared. Lion's claws hooked into his flanks, forcing him down onto all fours again. With a surge of unsought strength, Jan galloped breakneck, thrashing. Broken shells and beach gravel ground beneath his heels. The wingcat's grip slipped, balance faltering. The sea drew back, momentarily shallower—then a huge green wave twice Jan's height broke, overwhelming the young stallion and his attacker both.

Jan felt himself trod down as by a mighty hoof, the breath knocked violently from him. His knees, his ribs grated against the tidal trough's stony bed. He felt the gryphon torn from him by the surge. Struggling against a powerful current, he broke surface, snatched a breath. The black sky above roiled as rain-pebbled waves swept him under again.

Choking and snorting, he flailed madly to keep afloat. He glimpsed the Cliffs—much farther off than he had expected—and strove frantically to swim back to land. But the tow only pulled him farther out to sea. Something green and gold washed onto the distant rocks. The surge dragged it back before flinging it higher. This time it lodged, sodden and unmoving: the body of the gryphon tercel, broken by the waves.

Jan lost sight of shore. Rolling hills of water bobbed all around. Merciless wind whipped, its driving rain blinding him. Again a wave-crest broke over him, forcing him down into churning depths. Again he fought his way up, but more weakly this time. Something drifted against him in the darkness under the waves, brushing his flank. Long tendrils twined about his limbs, pricking him with needles of fire. Sea-jells! Rucked up from deep ocean by the storm.

Panicked, the dark prince floundered, gasping, choking. But the barbed streamers only entangled him further. Their burning poison began to numb him. Vainly, he searched for land. The sea heaved. Storm-wind buffeted. Presently, the sea-jells released him and floated on. Strange drowsiness stole over him. His burning limbs twitched, heavy as stone. Then his eyelids slid shut as he sank beneath the cold and furious sea.

Search

☽ 4 ☾

Tek hunkered down, rump to the driving rain. No gryphons had pursued them into the trees. Dagg hunched close, his nearness shielding her. Tek wished it were Jan flanking her as well—but in the confusion of flight, she had lost track of her mate. The pied mare shuddered. Wind and storm were now so furious she could scarcely see the other warriors huddled among the treeboles of the grove.

At last after what seemed an age, the gale spent itself. Black clouds parted, scudded away across the sky. The clean-washed air seemed dazzling, charged. And cold. The brilliant, midafternoon sunlight held no warmth. The first draft of autumn breathed unmistakably across the shore. The pied mare shook her rain-soaked pelt. Dagg trotted off to round up stragglers. Tek headed the other way, eager to discover Jan—but as she nipped and shouldered her scattered fellows back toward the rest, she felt a beat of fear.

"I don't see him," she called, glancing anxiously through the half-growns following Dagg. The prince's shoulder-friend cavaled.

"I'd hoped he was with you."

Drenched and weary, the battered young warriors milled around them. Tek noted bruises but few gashes, none deep. Most simply seemed badly shaken. Frowning, she lashed her tail. Where was the prince? It should have been he, not she and Dagg, to gather the band.

"Would he have gone scouting?" the dappled half-grown asked.

The pied mare shook her head. Why would Jan search for wingcats on his own when companions would have made the task far safer? The young warriors fidgeted.

"Ho," she called to them. "Which of you sheltered beside the prince?"

Half-growns shifted, glanced at one another. No one spoke. Tek snorted.

"I say regroup on the beach," Dagg offered. "Jan's most likely already there."

Tek whistled the others into line, unease edging into full-blown worry. She doubted her mate would rush to examine a battlesite when all trace of the fray had surely been obliterated by storm and tide. Trotting briskly to the head of the band, she called back, "Dagg, take rearguard."

They picked up a few more stragglers among the trees—but the beach lay deserted, half-eaten by storm. The gale-high tide had only partly receded. The pied mare gazed in dismay at the cast-up sea wrack, the carcasses of dead sealife. She spotted a dark shape lying beached upon the shore and froze, her heart beating hard. Then her terror subsided as she recognized it for what it was: a black whale calf, dead. Roughly the same size as a half-grown unicorn—but not Jan. Not Jan.

Tek champed her teeth, sent the others off to comb the strand. The unicorns fanned out, calling their prince's name. She kept several of the keener-eyed on watch, scanning the sky, not daring to trust the gryphons safely gone. When one of the lookouts whistled, Dagg and the others came galloping back to where she and the sentries stood craning heavenward.

"Wingcats?" he panted.

"Nay," she answered. "Look at the pinions' length: seabirds, not raptors."

"Herons!" cried Dagg. "We can enlist their aid in finding Jan."

As the slender forms of the seabirds dropped within range of her voice, Tek hailed them.

"Succor us, O herons! Your allies have need of your airborne eyes."

Gingerly, awkwardly, the flock alighted, their leader, Tlat, touching down to the damp sand first, followed by her consorts and the rest. Tek noted a number of gangling half-growns among them, uncrested, barely full-fletched. They gazed at the unicorns with round, curious eyes. Beside her, Dagg snorted and sidled impatiently. Tek hissed at him to be still, then whistled the others to keep their hooves firmly planted, lest the flighty windrovers take wing in alarm.

"Ah!" cried the heron queen, bobbing and dancing. "Where is your prince, pied one? Where is the unicorn Jan? First storm of fall has blown, and we have flown our young from the cliffs at last to teach them to forage on their own. Whale meat! Sweet squids! And to show them the unicorns before you must depart. Equinox is past. Fall glides in. You must be off, we know. But where is Jan? I would show him my brood."

Scarcely able to contain her urgency, Tek forced herself to hear Tlat out and to bow her neck respectfully.

"Your many young are beautiful, Queen Tlat, strong-limbed and finely feathered. May their crests grow brilliant. Would that my mate were here to see them. But he is lost to us. We do not know where he is. We were set upon by gryphons just before the storm. Now we cannot find Jan."

"Gryphons!" shrieked Tlat, hopping backwards. "Stormriders, yes."

Her people fluffed and began clapping bills, some dancing in agitation. One young bird started to whoop, and one of Tlat's mates stalked over and pecked it to silence. Tlat preened, fanning her crest, and looked at Tek one-eyed.

"We saw the cat-eagles, yes! Approaching across the bay—we longed to send you warning, but the wind was already too strong. We dared not leave our cliffs. So they attacked you? War! War! Marauders."

She stabbed at a crab digging itself out of the sand near her toes, cracked its shell, then tossed its contents down. More bill-clattering from the flock. Tek fought for composure in the midst of the cacophony.

"We regret you were unable to bring us warning," she replied, striving to recapture Tlat's attention. The queen of the seaherons stood turning her head from side to side, eyeing the dead crab first with one eye, then the other. "But we ask your aid now. The herons are our fast allies, and we value the deep friendship between our two peoples."

"Friendship," clucked Tlat. "Allies, yes! How may we aid you?"

"Lend us your wings and your eyes," Tek urged her. "Help us to search for my mate, our prince."

"Prince's mate!" the heron queen cried. "Look for your mate—yes. We will! We will help you seek the prince of unicorns!"

With a scream, Tlat unfolded her slim, lengthy wings and fanned the air. The seawind—now no more than a breeze—caught, lifted her. Dipping her long neck to catch up the empty crabshell in her bill, the heron queen rose. Her consorts and children and the rest of her people followed, soaring aloft, shouting, "Find the prince! The prince!"

One of her consorts skimmed near to pluck the crabshell from her bill. It was snatched from his by another bird and passed from beak to beak throughout the flock. Tek stood on the beach, gazing after them, mystified. Another fear had begun to gnaw at her like a biting fly: that Jan perhaps lay wounded among the trees, invisible from the air.

High above, the herons broke and scattered, some skimming up the beach, others down, and many inland, sailing low over the tops of the trees. Shaking herself, Tek whistled her own followers into a similar sweep, desperately hopeful that they would find her young mate soon.

❦

The seaherons spied no trace of Jan that day, nor the next day, nor the next, though they found nearly a dozen gryphons dead in the honeycombs of the Singing Cliffs. Had the remainder carried the prince away? Rising panic held Tek's heart in its teeth at the thought that she might have become the prince's mate but for a night, their wedding dance the last joy of him she would ever know. As heron messengers returned each night, Tek found it harder and harder to stave off despair.

On the third day, Dagg ceased to speak, all optimism dashed. Other members of the band remained painfully silent: angry, grieving, stunned. Tek felt all her wild hopes dying. The day ended in storm, not so violent as that of equinox, but bone chill, beating down the seaoats to rot and whipping the foliage from the trees. When the following cold, grey morning dawned, Tek, herself frozen past any feeling but exhaustion, forced herself to speak.

"He is gone," she told the band. They stood subdued before her, silent. "Surely the gryphons took him. They have killed our prince in open war. We must return to the Vale and bring word of this to the herd."

Dagg bowed his head. None of the others so much as raised a voice in protest. With a start, Tek realized that they had all despaired days ago. Only she had clung to the stubborn dream that Jan might still live. Outrage filled her at her own foolishness.

When the seaherons came again, Tek bade them farewell, thanked them woodenly for their hospitality, and praised again their lank, gawking children. Pledging to return the following summer, she expressed the unicorns' unending gratitude for their allies' diligence in the search. Plumage drooping, crests flattened to the skull, the typically raucous herons only nodded. Tlat even solemnly returned Tek's bow before soaring away with her flock.

Numb, Tek whistled her own followers into line. They straggled after her from the sandy shore, climbed the downs, traversed the coastal plain, and entered once more into the dark Pan Woods, having failed even to discover and carry back to the Vale their prince's bones to be laid with proper ceremony upon the altar cliffs beneath the sky.

What will I tell his father? What will I tell the king? The refrain repeated itself relentlessly inside the pied mare's skull as she led the band dejectedly homeward. Dagg brought up rearguard. They could not bear to face one another. Tek groaned inwardly, wretched. All the while the image of Korr, dark and brooding, loomed before her.

Fever

) 5 (

The rhythm of the waves woke him, their gentle wash against and across him soaking his pelt. He felt the cold sting of air briefly, then another wave. The dark unicorn opened his eyes to find himself lying pressed against wet sand. Another swell sluiced over him. Choking, he rolled to his knees, pitched shakily to his feet.

He stood on a low, flat beach, the sand silver-white. No cliffs or downs flanked the shore, only dunes—and beyond them, dense thickets of trees. The dark unicorn blinked in confusion. He did not recognize the grey sea and white sand. He had come from a place of green waves, golden shore. He remembered a storm.

Weakly, the dark unicorn shook himself, staggered. Beach grit abraded his skin. His withers and back were scored by deep wounds, his limbs and belly patterned with raw, raised welts. His mind felt poisoned, numb. The salt air breathed against his wet coat, chilled him to shivering. The waves foaming placidly against his pasterns and shanks felt soothingly warm.

Turning, he gazed cross the calm, grey expanse: no longer storm-tossed, the sky above pearly with a thin overcast of cloud. The wind shouldered against him insistently, full of salt and particles. He faced away from the sea, climbed laboriously higher onto the beach. His hooves sank deep into the soft, dry sand. He set his rump to the wind's relentless, gentle gusts and bowed his head. The sting-welts ached. His shoulders ached. Heat burned in him, guttering against the cold.

"Fever," he muttered.

Feebly, he slapped the draggle of wet mane from his eyes and gazed at the trees beyond the dunes. Trees would shelter him, provide forage.

Maybe water. The gummy, salt taste of his own tongue constricted his gorge.

"Water," he told himself dully. "Find water."

Aye, a soft voice answered now. *Get out of the wind and cold. Find shelter. You've drifted a long time.*

The dark unicorn blinked. No speaker met his eye. The windswept beach lay empty, deserted. Strange. The words had seemed to come from within. Feverchills danced along his ribs and limbs. Still muddled, he shook his head.

"Water first," he croaked. "Then . . . find the others."

He remembered companions vaguely: unicorns like himself. What were their names and whence had they come? Somehow he knew the golden, cliff-lined strand he recalled was not their home. Yet neither was this flat expanse of silvery shore.

Find the fire, the inner voice said clearly.

Glimmers of warmth and tremors of cold gusted through him. The dark unicorn shook his head.

"Fire?" he muttered.

He had forgotten his own name. Small grey-and-white seabirds wheeled overhead: dark hooded, with darting pinions. The strange voice commanding him sounded half like the sighing of shore wind and half like their high, piping calls.

Behold.

The dark unicorn started, stared as a brilliant red streak arched burning across the sky in the far, far distance. A dark wisp of vapor or dust blossomed up leagues upon leagues away, beyond horizon's western edge. Long seconds afterwards, a faint concussion reached him: the earth trembled.

Head west, the inner voice instructed him. *Along the shore.*

The dark unicorn staggered, nearly fell. Standing took almost more effort than he could muster. "What is my name?"

West, the voice reiterated. *When you have found my fire, you will once more know yourself.*

The voice faded, faint as a gull's trill on the wind. The dark unicorn blinked dizzily. Shelter, food, and water—he must find them soon, or he would die. Painfully, he dragged his hooves across the low, white dunes, heading westward toward the distant, tangled trees.

Home
☽ 6 ☾

The sky spanned clear, the air crisp with the breath of fall. Tek shook her head. Had they been but three days crossing the Pan Woods, returning from the Summer Sea? It felt like dozens. Solemn half-growns straggled around her as they emerged from the trees onto the Vale's grassy lower slopes. Tek beheld the waiting herd below: mares and stallions, fillies and foals milling expectantly. Her heart froze as she spotted Korr, the king; his mate, Ses; and their yearling filly, Lell: princess of the unicorns now. The pied mare shivered, glad Dagg had come forward to walk alongside her.

"What has happened?" thundered Korr as they reached the bottom of the slope. "We awaited your return days since! Why do you, healer's daughter, head the band instead of Jan? Where is my son?"

Heartsick, she met Korr's gaze.

"Jan is not among us," she answered. "Gryphons took him. He is slain."

The dark stallion's eyes widened. Around him, the whole herd started, shying. Tek heard shrill whinnies of astonishment. Before her, the king reared, snorting wildly.

"Gryphons?" he demanded. "On the Summer shore?"

Tek nodded and listened, mute, while Dagg recounted the wingcats' attack, unicorns and herons searching, finding only dead gryphons among the cliffs.

"They've killed our prince," he concluded, voice hard. "It's war. When spring returns, we must strike back."

"Aye, vengeance! War!"

The whole herd took up the cry, whinnying and stamping in a frenzy of mourning. Korr tossed his head, pawing the air and smiting the ground. Ses wept softly. Lell looked frightened, anxious to suckle, but her mother fidgeted, too distracted to stand still. Withdrawn into herself, Tek scarcely heeded the clamor until all at once, Korr spun on her.

"So, healer's daughter," he demanded furiously, "how is it you alone keep silent? All around you mourn and rage against the gryphons' treachery, yet you stand there cold."

The pied mare stared at him.

"I have been three days weeping in the Pan Woods, king—as have all the band—and three days before that searching the Summer shore. I've wept me dry. I've no more tears to spill. My mate is dead! What more would you have of me?"

She found herself shouting by the end of it. She wished that she might shout until she dropped. The king drew himself up short, eyes white-rimmed suddenly.

"Your . . . mate?" he whispered.

Baffled, Tek nodded. "Aye."

"My son?" cried Korr, voice rising. "My son—your mate?"

"Aye!" Tek flung back at him, angry and confused. "We danced the courting dance and pledged—"

Only then did she realize Dagg had begun his recounting on equinox morn, never mentioned who had paired with whom the night before. The king continued to stare at Tek, his breathing hoarse.

"You?" he choked. "You beguiled my son?"

"He chose me," Tek answered. "And I him."

Abruptly, she remembered the preceding spring: Korr's odd but unmistakable disapproval whenever he had glimpsed the two of them in each other's company.

"Seducer!" screamed the king, bolting toward her through the press of unicorns. "Cursed mare. Daughter of a renegade!"

Tek shied, crying out in astonishment. She had to scramble back to avoid Korr's hooves as Dagg and his father, Tas, lunged to turn the huge stallion. Korr shouldered into Dagg, nearly knocking him to the ground. Tas, as tall as Korr, if leaner, threw his full weight against the king's side and forced him to a halt.

Other unicorns crowded forward: her own father, Teki, as well as the king's mate, Ses, and Dagg's young dam, Leerah. The healer's daughter looked on in consternation with the rest of the herd as the king, still shouting, strove to plunge past those who boxed him in.

"Temptress! Betrayer! Because of *you* my son is dead!"

"What are you saying?" Tek gasped. "I loved your son!"

"Liar! Outlaw's get. Four summers unpaired, you lay in wait to destroy him!"

The pied mare shook her head in dismay as the king fought on, struggling to reach her, the look in his dark eyes murderous. Not even Ses could still him.

"Alma will wreak her revenge—"

"Enough! Enough of this, my son."

Startled, the king whirled, and the uproar around him abruptly ceased. Those blocking his path fell back a pace as Sa, the old king's widow, emerged from the crowd.

"What means this frenzy?" Dark grey with a milky mane, she faced him, her expression full of pain and dismay. "You revile your slain heir's widow as if *she* were your foe."

The grey mare's son stood panting. His dam waited.

"Speak," she said. "Why do you fly at one who has done you no injury?"

Panting still, Korr turned on Tek. Clearly he longed to fall on her even yet. Alert, watching him, the pied mare held her ground.

"No injury?" he growled. "You left my son to die upon the shore." The king gazed with open hatred at the healer's daughter. "You should have stayed with him! Died with him—died *for* him. You were his . . . his mate!"

He choked on the word, as though it tasted filthy in his mouth. Fury sparked in Tek. She felt her eyes sting, her ribs lock tight. She had thought she had no tears left to shed.

"*My son, you shame me.*" Once more she heard the grey mare's fierce rebuke. "You shame yourself and the office you hold. Tek is blameless in Jan's death. Have done, I say."

Swiftly, pointedly, she turned away. The king's jaw dropped. The herd milled in astonished silence. Abruptly, Korr wheeled and bolted across the Vale. Unicorns scattered from his path, then stared after him, stunned. Tas glanced at Ses, but the king's mate shook her head.

"Let him go," she murmured. "Only time can cool him."

Tek shuddered. She felt the pressure of Dagg's shoulder solidly beside hers and leaned against it gratefully.

"Pay him no heed." The dappled warrior spoke gently. "Our news came too suddenly. He's mad for grief."

"Come, child"—the late king's widow turned to her—"my granddaughter now by Law. You are spent from tears and journeying. Rest in my grotto, until the dance."

Trembling, Tek closed her eyes at the thought of Jan's funeral train to be danced at dusk: a great slow procession used only for those of the prince's line. The mourners, all smutched from rolling in the dust and hoarse from wailing, would call out, "He is dead! He is dead! He of the ancient line of Halla, dead!"

"He was my prince," she muttered as she stumbled after Sa through the crowd toward the grey mare's cave. "And faithfully I fulfilled his command—to get the others to the trees." Her father, Teki, nuzzled her. Dagg flanked her other side. Tek swallowed hard. "Now Korr despises me."

"Not so!" Dagg insisted. "How could he?"

They had reached the far slope of the Vale and started to climb. Sa glanced back as though to assure herself that they followed. The crowd behind them had begun to pull apart, the sound of their lamentations floating upward on the still morning air, making the pied mare shiver. The dappled warrior snorted.

"Korr's always favored you highly. Truth, many's the time he's treated you better even than his own son!"

The healer chafed her gently, reassuringly. "The king will relent."

But Tek shook her head, heaved a great sigh, painful against the crushing tightness of her breast. "Nay. Never. I *should* have stayed on the beach with Jan. I wish I had died instead of him."

Firekeepers

☽ 7 ☾

Days blended one into another, sometimes stormy, sometimes fair, but always cold. Fever consumed the dark unicorn. Often, he lay shuddering among the trees, too weak to rise. The mysterious voice spoke clearest to him then, urging him westward along the strand. It almost seemed that he himself were made of fire. More than once he came to awareness amid surroundings he did not recognize, certain that hours or days had passed of which he had no memory. Time wandered by in a dream.

Evening fell. Sun sank in a fiery blaze beyond the western horizon, the sky to the east grown dark as bilberries. Stars burned overhead, thinly veiled by fog. The full moon peering above the waves shone ghostly bright. Frowning, the dark unicorn stumbled to a halt. An amber glow flickered in the distance before him. As he left the strand and headed toward the dusky glimmer across the dunes, he caught a whiff of acrid, pungent scent. The sound of chanting reached his ears.

"Dai'chon!"

One clear voice sounded above the rest, calling urgently, ecstatic, echoed by a chorus of other, deeper voices.

"Dai'chon!"

It was no tongue the dark unicorn recognized. He halted on the rim of a deep pit in the dunes, as though the hoof of some unaccountably vast being had dug a trough in the sand with a single sweep. Perhaps two or three dozen creatures hunched in a circle at the bottom of the pit. Smaller than unicorns, they were shaped like pans, with round heads and flat faces, their upper limbs not fashioned for the bearing of weight.

Their smooth, nearly hairless bodies were swathed in something that was neither plumage nor pelts. The dark unicorn's nostrils flared. It smelled of seedsilk. He stared, fascinated by these two-footed creatures' false skins. All of them knelt around a fire, its bright, reddish flames dancing over blackened driftwood. Grey tendrils of smoke curled upward through the misty air. The dark unicorn shivered.

"Dai'chon! *Dai'chon!*"

Chanting, the two-foots faced a stone embedded in the deepest part of the pit. The sand there was scorched, fused into glass. Deeply pocked and charred, the stone resembled a small, dark moon. The black unicorn recognized readily enough what it must be: a sky cinder. Such heavenly gifts were formed of a substance both harder and heavier than true stone, a substance that resounded with a clang when struck or stamped upon.

Before the sky cinder, a tiny figure stood, pale crescent marking the breast of its dark falseskin. Grasped in one black forelimb rose a long, sharp stake. From the other hung a vine, its end frayed into a flail. The figure's limbs and torso resembled a two-foot's, but its neck was thicker, longer, a brushlike mane cresting the ridge. The muzzle of its face was long and slim, like a hornless unicorn's, with white teeth bared and red-flecked nostrils savagely flared.

Smoke rose from those nostrils. Astonished, the dark unicorn snorted, his own breath congealing in the cold, damp air. Strangely rigid, the little figure never moved. It smelled of fire and skystuff, not living flesh. Some object created by the two-foots? It must be hollow, he realized, its belly filled with burning spice.

Before it, the foremost of the two-foots rose and bowed. Green falseskins draped her. A crescent of silvery skystuff glinted upon her breast. The four kneeling nearest her were also females, the dark unicorn perceived by their scent, the remainder all hairy-faced males. Puzzled, the young stallion frowned. Why so many males, so few females? And where were their elders, their young? The eldest male, though grizzled, did not look much past the middle of his age.

"Dai'chon!" the green-clad female chanted, and the other two-foots echoed her, "*Dai'chon!*"

Forelimbs upraised, she beckoned her four companions, who rose. One by one, the males approached them, bearing seedpods and spicewood, dried foliage, and much else the dark unicorn could not identify. These the females laid carefully, as though in offering, at the feet of the little figure smoking before the sky cinder. What could the purpose of such a strange object be? the dark unicorn wondered.

The eldest of the males stepped forward with a great bunch of ripe, fragrant rueberries. The dark unicorn's belly clenched at the sight and scent of food. He leaned after it longingly. Reaching to receive the gift, the moon-breasted female glanced up. Suddenly her eyes widened, and

she gasped. The dark unicorn froze. Drawn by the delicious heat of the
two-foots' camp, he realized with a start, he had emerged unawares from
the mist and shadows into the light of the fire.

The other females lifted their eyes. The males forming the circle
before them turned. Abruptly, their chanting ceased. For five wild heartbeats, two-foots and unicorn stared at one another. Then the male
crouching nearest the dark unicorn sprang up and bolted with a cry.
Screaming, the leader's four companions dropped their offerings and
fled. With shouts of fear, the remaining males scrambled after them,
dashed desperately up the steep sides of the sandpit and vanished into
the fog.

The dark unicorn stood dumbstruck, dismayed. The camp below lay
in disarray. Only the green-clad female remained, transfixed. The young
stallion shifted nervously, nearly staggering from hunger and fatigue.
Tossing the forelock back from his eyes, he switched his long, slim tail
once against his flank, uncertain what best to do or say. Below him, the
other's gaze darted from his mooncrested brow to his steaming breath
to his fly-whisk tail. Catching the firelight, the dark skewer of his horn
glinted.

Behind her, the black figurine with its hornless unicorn's head stood
wreathed in smoke, its chest emblazoned with a silver crescent, the
hornlike skewer clasped in one forepaw, the frayed vine dangling from
the other. The two-foot leader's words came in a rush.

"Dai'chon," she whispered, crumpling to the ground. "Dai'chon!"

She pressed her forehead to the sand. Confused, the dark unicorn
gazed at her. Had she collapsed from fear? Unsteadily, he descended
the pit's sandy, glassy slope and nosed her gently. The black hair on
her head smelled clean and very fine, like a new colt's mane. Trembling,
she raised her head. Carefully, he tried to repeat her words.

"Taichan," he managed, but his mouth found the strangely inflected
syllables almost impossible to frame. He tried again: "Daijan."

"Tai-shan?" the other said suddenly.

She touched the moon image upon her breast and gazed at the pale
crescent underscoring the horn on his brow.

"Tai-zhan," he tried, finding that a bit easier. "Tai-shan."

The creature before him listened, rapt. The dark unicorn snorted,
not pleased with his awkwardness. The two-foot language was full of
odd chirps and grunts.

"Forgive me," he told her, reverting to his own tongue. "I mean
you no harm."

The crackling blaze of the fire drew him. He stepped nearer, trembling with cold. The two-foot made no move to halt him, only gazed at him as though spellbound. Dried fruit, fragrant seedgrass, and other offerings lay strewn about the sand. Hungrily, the dark unicorn eyed the tempting stuff.

"May I share your forage?" he asked. "I've found little but bitter bark and shoreoats for . . . for many days."

His thoughts remained tangled, his memory confused. He could recall nothing from before his emergence from the sea. Still kneeling before him, the other made no reply. Unable to resist, the dark unicorn bent his head to a branch of thornfruits at his feet. Tough and leathery, they nonetheless smacked more succulent to him than the tenderest spring grass. He found himself tearing into the prickly rounds, unable to stop. He scarcely noticed when the green-clad two-foot softly rose and drew nearer.

"Tai-shan," she said gently, as if caressing the word. "Tai-shan."

She held something out to him in one graceful, smooth-skinned paw. The thing smelled like nutmeats, but sweeter, and resembled a large brown seedpod. He had never seen such a thing before. Curious, he bent to take the flattened oblong and ground it between his teeth. Honey. It tasted of honey—all sugary and waxless and free of angry, swarming bees. It also tasted of the crisp kernels of hazel trees, but without the fibrous shells. Deliciously warm, the thing was crusted on the outside, softer within.

She held out another of the honey nutpods, offering it, too. Eagerly he accepted, and the next she fed him, and the next. Picking among the scattered leavings of her followers, the two-foot leader brought him grasses, fruits, herbs, followed by a long drink of clear water from a vessel hollowed out of wood. Ravenous, the dark unicorn ate of the firekeepers' strange, rich provender until he thought he would founder. His first full belly in weeks and the delicious heat of the dancing blaze made him suddenly, unutterably drowsy. He could not have kept his eyes open a moment more or taken another step if he had wanted to.

His knees gave. He stretched himself out on the warm dry sand. The two-foot seated herself beside him. He felt her gentle touch along his neck and laid his head upon her flanks. She stroked his cheek and chin, combing the long, nimble digits of her forepaws through his matted mane. The dark unicorn closed his eyes. Beside him, the bright flames crackled and hissed. Weeks ago, the mysterious voice had bade him seek out fire, and he had done so. Perhaps now, presently, he would also discover his name.

"Tai-shan," the gentle two-foot crooned, stroking him. "Tai-shan."

Tai-shan awoke to find the fog had lifted. Morning light streamed around him. The leader of the firekeepers sat beside him still. Her followers had returned during the night, he realized with a start. Still clearly in awe of him, they moved about their campsite furtively, keeping beyond the fire. Garlands of withered flowers and grass festooned him. He nosed them, puzzled. Those offerings that had formerly rested before the sky cinder now lay about him. The two-foot leader beckoned to one of her female companions.

"Daïcha," the other murmured, bowing, and hastily withdrew.

She had placed something resembling a great bird's nest on the sand before him. Tai-shan rolled to his knees and shook himself. The nest-thing was filled with nutpods, fruit, seaoats and dune grass, dried kelp and tender twigs. Once again he ate ravenously. The eldest male spoke respectfully to the two-foot leader. She answered, shaking her head. The dark unicorn listened carefully, but the only phrase he recognized was the one the other female had used: daïcha. He concluded that such must be his rescuer's title or name.

His own name, so it seemed, was to be Tai-shan, the name the daïcha had given him the night before. He felt stronger now, his fever diminished. His head was clearer, though he still remembered nothing of who or what he had been before emerging from the sea. The dark unicorn rose. Beyond the fire, two-foots froze in alarm, but their leader called to them in a calm, steady voice, and none bolted.

Tai-shan turned and climbed to the top of the dunes bordering the pit. He gazed seaward, trying to gain his bearings. A great whale lay beached upon the strand, the largest he had ever seen. Some of the two-foot males milled about it. Abruptly, the dark unicorn realized what lay below was not a whale at all. Whale-shaped, aye—long and streamlined with a ribbed belly—but it smelled of waterlogged wood, not stinking whale.

Curiosity roused, Tai-shan trotted toward it. The male two-foots on the strand cautiously drew back as he sniffed the thing's wet, barnacle-encrusted underside. Other two-foots stood on the flat, canted back of the thing. One of them disappeared through a square hole into its depths, and the dark unicorn understood with a shock that the place was hollow, like a shell.

This great wooden thing was a shelter, a kind of cave. Tai-shan marveled at the firekeepers' ingenuity: wood crafted into shelter, seed fibers matted to make false skins, logs hollowed into water traps, strips of treebark laced into nestlike containers, delicious foods hoarded like the troves of treefoxes—and fire! Truly a strange and inventive people.

He smelled rain presently. Glancing back toward the dunes, the dark unicorn caught sight of clouds blowing in. The breeze had picked up. Anxiously, he lashed his tail. Must he take to the woods again, trusting their thin cover to keep the worst of the wet off him? He shivered, still very weak. Away from the two-foots' fire, he had already begun to feel chill.

Topping the dune, he saw the two-foots in the pit below also gazing at the sky. The *daïcha* clapped the undersides of her forepaws together and spoke to her female companions. The eldest male barked orders at the rest. They began hastily to gather up all their strange belongings. Reverently, the *daïcha* carried the small, black figure up the crater's slope, followed by her folk.

The salt breeze stiffened, heavy with the scent of rain. Cresting the slope, the two-foots hurried past him, down toward the caveshell on the beach. The breeze began to whip, carrying spatters of moisture. The fire sizzled, crackling. Worried, Tai-shan watched its flames beaten down, growing smaller and smaller beneath the falling drops. Rainwater killed fire, he realized suddenly, and without fire, he could never hope to survive the coming winter on this barren, forbidding shore.

On the beach below, the *daïcha*'s companions clambered up onto their caveshell's back. Their goods, he saw, had already been loaded and carried below. Most of the males remained milling on the beach. The wet wind gusted, dampening them all. Behind him in the deserted pit, the dancing flames sizzled and died.

Before him on the beach, the *daïcha* carefully handed the little figurine up to two of her companions on the caveshell, then boarded herself, assisted by the grizzled male. Tai-shan blinked suddenly, realizing. Though the fire in the cinder pit was clearly doomed, that within the smoking figurine, now being carried away in the reverent grasp of the *daïcha*'s companions, still burned. This fire was to be kept sheltered in the caveshell, safe from the killing damp. It was this fire he must follow, then.

The dark unicorn loped to the foot of the dune. The males gave ground as he crossed the beach to stand before the caveshell. The *daïcha* called down to him, beckoning with her forelimbs. Tai-shan hesitated, gauging the distance between them. The wind whipped harder, rain beginning to fall in earnest now. The *daïcha* called again. The young stallion sidled, measuring his strength. At last, bunching his hindquarters, he sprang onto the flat, tilted back of the caveshell.

The slick wooden surface boomed beneath his hooves. For a moment, the caveshell rocked precariously. He had to scramble for his footing until it steadied. The remaining two of the *daïcha*'s female companions screamed and scattered while the males on the shore cried out in consternation. But the *daïcha* laughed in delight, stroking the dark unicorn's neck and leading him toward the rear of the caveshell. A low barrier edged the shell's perimeter. Tai-shan had little fear of sliding off. Still, the cant of the wooden surface disconcerted him. He moved unsteadily, unused to the feel of slanted deck underhoof.

At the caveshell's tail end, the *daïcha* disappeared through a narrow ingress. Following, Tai-shan found himself in a small wooden chamber. Scattered about the floor lay soft falseskin pads stuffed with rushes, upon which the other females huddled. The chamber was warm, the air heavy with the savor of spicewood and smoke. Before the opposite wall, the black figurine stood, breathing fire. Bowing before it, the *daïcha* murmured, "Dai'chon."

Tai-shan lay down against the near wall. The *daïcha* knelt beside him, chafing him with a soft, dry falseskin, smoothing the damp from his coat like a mare licking her foal. The sensation was delightful. Sighing, he closed his eyes. Presently he heard her companions moving cautiously about the chamber. He scarcely marked their activity, any more than he heeded the grunting and shouting of the males on the beach beyond.

Sleep had nearly claimed him. His surroundings seemed vague and distant now. Stormwind gusted. Rain drummed against the chamber's walls. Beneath him, the floor shuddered. Much splashing and clambering and shouting from without. He heard a low grating like distant thunder. None of the two-foots in the room gave any sign of concern. Only half-waking, he ignored it all.

The tilted floor seemed to right itself momentarily, becoming more level. Then it began rocking gently, very gently, smoothly tossing and rolling like treetops in a summer breeze. Such an odd dream to be having, the dark unicorn mused. It felt like drifting in the sea. He let his thoughts dissolve into the hypnotic swaying of wooden planking beneath him, the soothing rush of wind outside, the plash of nearby sea, and the gentle creaking of rain-soaked wood. He slept.

❧

Tai-shan awoke with a start. The deck beneath him was swaying in earnest: pitching and tipping. It was no dream. Alarmed, he lifted his head. The *daïcha* was not within the wooden chamber. Two of her companions dozed on falseskin pads across the narrow space from him. The dark unicorn struggled to gather his legs under him as the caveshell's floor shifted and tilted. He no longer detected the quiet patter of rain. Time to return to the beach, he realized.

Maintaining his balance with difficulty on the slowly tossing, gently rolling surface, he passed through the chamber's egress and emerged onto the open expanse of the caveshell's back. The sky had indeed cleared. Only stray puffs of cloud now flocked the heavens. It was midafternoon. To his astonishment, he beheld a great tree growing from the caveshell's back, webbed with vines. Male two-foots swarmed the webbing. Others standing below hauled on the dangling ends.

Tai-shan stared, fascinated. The caveshell lurched and heaved. He spotted the *daïcha* on the far side of the tree, conferring with the eldest male. Cautiously, the dark unicorn started toward her, then pitched to a halt with a horrified cry. The beach had vanished. The caveshell was bobbing in the middle of the sea!

Whinnying, he reared. Male two-foots dropped their vines and scattered, shouting. The wooden surface beneath the dark unicorn's hooves bucked violently. He nearly fell. Panicked, he sprang to one edge of the caveshell's back. Open sea lay beyond, deep and blue-grey. The caveshell pitched the other way, sending him skidding toward the opposite side—sea there as well. Nothing but grey waves moved all around, empty and calm.

With a scream of consternation, Tai-shan wheeled. The caveshell tilted precipitously, hurling him against the near rail. He kicked at it. One hind leg tangled in a tarry coil of vine. Frantically, the dark unicorn pivoted, twisting and plunging. He lost his footing and went down. He heard the eldest male barking orders, but his ears were too full of his own terrified whinnies to heed.

"Tai-shan! Tai-shan!"

The *daïcha*'s frantic cries penetrated his frenzy only dimly. Twisting and bucking, the dark unicorn glimpsed her struggling toward him. The eldest male had hold of her forelimb, seeking to keep her back, but she shook him off angrily and came toward Tai-shan slowly, speaking gently now in her lilting, unintelligible language.

"Tash, 'omat. Bikthitet nau. Apnor, 'pnor. . . ."

None of the other two-foots moved. Panting, heart racing still, the dark unicorn stood shuddering. The *daïcha* leaned against him, stroking his neck and chest. Her touch trailed lightly along his flank, then down his haunch. He tensed as he felt her grasp the vine that so painfully encircled his pastern. Then he realized she was worrying it, using her nimble, long-fingered paw much as a unicorn might use her teeth to loosen the vine and pull it free.

"Tai-shan," the two-foot lady crooned. "Tai-shan."

Still stroking him, she gestured beyond the rail, beyond even the blue-grey curve of sea. With a shock of wild relief, the dark unicorn spotted what he had missed before: land—just at horizon's edge, a narrow ribbon of shoreline stretched. He felt the jaws biting down upon his heart ease. The caveshell was not simply adrift, hopelessly lost. The shore remained—barely—in sight.

Tai-shan's balance swayed. Fever burned in him still. Wearily, he sank down. Later perhaps, when his strength returned, he could spring over the rail and swim for the strand. Doubt chilled him suddenly. Did he dare desert the caveshell—leaving the fire behind? Exhausted, his mind fogged, he shook his head. Time enough to ponder that later. For now, resting his chin along the top of the low rail, he lay quiet. The sun felt warm along his back. The *daïcha* called to her companions, who approached with food. She sat beside him as he ate.

It occurred to him then for the first time that her people did not seem the least disconcerted at their caveshell's now resting in the sea. Strange. Baffling. Perhaps they *wanted* it to be in the sea—but why? Presently, at the eldest male's direction, his two-foot minions unfurled a great falseskin from the tree. It belled out like the huge, round belly of a pregnant mare.

The image emblazoning it resembled the strange, fire-breathing figure before which the *daïcha* and the other two-foots had bowed: dark-limbed, its body like a two-foot's, a crescent moon upon the breast, a skewer in one forepaw and in the other, a trailing vine, yet its head that of a hornless, beardless unicorn with blood-rimmed nostrils and glaring eyes.

By late afternoon, Tai-shan had come to realize that the caveshell was moving, the distant shoreline changing. The great falseskin caught the sea breeze like a gryphon's wing and pulled the caveshell along parallel to the strand. Gradually it dawned on him that his hosts and their entire shelter were sliding westward without themselves taking a step. The dark unicorn lay amazed.

Later, the wind fell. The grizzled male gave orders, and most of the younger males descended into the caveshell's belly. Moments later, Tai-shan spied long, slender limbs emerging from the vessel's side. A hollow booming began, like the beating of a mighty heart. The slim, straight limbs dipped, shoved backward, rose, and dipped into the sea again. The caveshell was using its many legs to crawl like a centipede across the waves.

At dusk, the wind returned, and the caveshell's limbs withdrew. The steady booming ceased, and the males emerged from below to unfurl their windwing again. As the air darkened and chilled, the *daïcha* rose. Tai-shan followed her carefully back to her wooden chamber.

Inside, basking in its fire-warmed air, he listened to the great tree creaking and straining outside, its taut vines rubbing against each other as the windwing heaved and burgeoned. The gentle lifting and falling of the caveshell seemed almost restful now, much as he imagined the rocking motion of a mother's walk must feel to her unborn foal. No panic troubled him, now that he realized the firekeepers were traveling, taking him with them. He wondered what their destination might be.

Snowfall

) 8 (

Tek had always known fall as a time of feasting in the Vale: a season for fattening on sweet berries, ripening grain, tallowy seeds and nuts. This year, however, the healer's daughter felt no joy. The air's pervasive chill cut her to the bone. Much vegetation had been nipped by early frost, and storms blew in every other day, roaring across the Pan Woods to rot what little provender remained and force the unicorns to spend full as much time huddling underhill as they did foraging for food.

The pied mare shivered, watching the swirl of grey clouds overhead. All the herd seemed to share her gloom. Somehow, many muttered, the children-of-the-moon had displeased Alma. Now the Mother-of-all was making her displeasure known. Tek snorted at so much witless talk. Yet as regent, Korr did nothing. Still wrapped in grief, the king barely uttered a word even to Ses. Jan's young sister Lell, the new princess, was a mere nursling: many seasons must pass before she might lead the herd in anything but name.

The pied mare sighed, keenly aware of the loss of her mate. Jan would never have tolerated his people's superstitious champing. Instead, he would have set them all to gleaning every scrap of available forage before first snow. Angrily, Tek shook her head. Her breath steamed like a firedrake's in the wet, chilly air. Another storm approached.

Korr's silence and Lell's youth left the late king's widow, Sa, as the sole voice of authority among the unicorns. Tirelessly, the grey mare ventured abroad, recounting what had been done in seasons past when winter came early and hard, what foodstuff helped best to deepen the pelt, thicken the blood, and form a rich layer of fat. She urged her fellows to be out and about early each morn, despite the cold, to forage all they might on whatever they might, and spent long hours combing the hillsides of the Vale for browse.

Standing in the entry to the grey mare's cave, Tek cavaled, lifting and setting down her heels in the same spot to get the stiffness out of her legs. It was such a foraging expedition that the late king's widow headed now, reconnoitering the Vale's far slopes with a band of young warriors not half her age, searching for berry thickets and honey trees. The healer's daughter hoped to see them safely back before the storm broke.

Hoofbeats above drew her half out of the grotto, craning upward, expecting Sa—but it was Dagg. The dappled half-grown slid down the last of the steep slope and crowded past into the dim grotto's shelter. Dagg shivered, shouldering against her and stamping for warmth.

"So," she asked, "how was graze on the high south slopes?" She knew that Dagg had, at the grey mare's urging, set out early that morning to scout that particular ridge. She herself had roved the lower south slopes with a third band the afternoon before.

"Lean," Dagg answered dejectedly. "We found little but bramble."

The pied mare murmured in sympathy. Dagg twitched, lashing his tail.

"We've got to find more forage!" he burst out. "We've enough to feed the herd for now, just barely. But none among us is putting on any flesh—none, that is, but you."

He glanced at her with open envy. The healer's daughter shifted, unsettled by his gaze. Her belly had indeed begun to swell ever so slightly—but it was not fat, as would surely grow plain to see as soon as the weather grew colder, forage scarcer, and her ribs began to show. She wondered anxiously if it could be gut worms or colic—but she did not feel ill. And though none of what slender fodder she found seemed to be going to fat, still her girth, day by day, infinitesimally increased.

She had not wanted to trouble her father, Teki, as yet. The usual round of minor complaints among the herd consumed his time: bites and scrapes, strained tendons, thorns. Soon enough, she speculated with a shudder, more major ills would claim his attention, brought on by cold and lack of feed. Moreover, the healer had his teeth full simply gathering the many herbs required for the coming winter, most of which were proving even scarcer than the forage this year. Some days, she knew, he searched from daybreak to dusk, and still returned with only a few poor sprigs.

Shouldering against Dagg, the pied mare sighed. She wished her mother, Jah-lila, were here to advise her. The Red Mare was a loner, a midwife and magicker who lived apart from the herd. Some called her the child of renegades, yet she herself was no renegade—despite Korr's wild charge—for since coming among the herd before Tek's birth, Jah-lila had never been banished. Rather, the Red Mare now lived in the southeastern hills beyond the Vales by her own unfathomable choice.

Calling Teki her mate, she had left her weanling daughter in his care years ago, that Tek might be raised within the Vale. At long inter-vals, Jah-lila still ghosted through, never announced, as often as not to consult with the pied healer but briefly and be gone within the hour. Sometimes the young Tek had not even glimpsed her, merely caught scent of her dam in Teki's grotto upon returning home at day's end. The pied mare shook herself. No use wishing.

"It's only that I don't run myself ragged, as you do," she told Dagg, dragging her mind back with an effort to the dappled warrior beside her.

Her words were true enough. She could not seem to run as nimbly as she had before: her burgeoning belly got in the way. Again Tek shook herself—and dismissed her own mysterious condition with a shrug.

"With luck, Sa and her band will have found something in the Pan Woods," she added, hoping. She worried less for herself and Dagg than for the herd's fillies and foals. It was they who would suffer heaviest from the coming winter's lack. And after the young, it would be the elder ones, the mares and stallions Sa's age.

Dagg nodded vigorously, facing about now in the limestone grotto, the cave the old king's mare had long inhabited with her mate. Since the death of Korr's father, the grey mare had had no one to help her warm the empty space until now. Since returning from the Sea, the healer's daughter had sheltered with Sa. During Tek's absence, Teki had accepted a number of acolytes: young fillies and foals not yet ini-tiated. The pied stallion was busily teaching them his craft—and though she felt more than welcome, the prince's mate sensed ruefully that lodg-ing in her sire's now-crowded grotto would only have put her under heel.

"When do you expect Sa to return?" Dagg asked her, coming to stand beside her at the cave's narrow entryway.

A flutter of white feathers drifted from the sky. The pied mare snorted, her breath curling and smoking like cloud. "Soon, I hope."

"First snowfall," Dagg muttered. "Birds' down."

More lacy flakes gusted past, whirling and dancing. Tek watched the rapidly thickening flurries with dread, thinking of the cover it would provide, concealing what remained of the Vale's dwindling supply of foodstuffs, making the unicorns' foraging even harder than before.

Would Korr respond? she wondered. Would the advent of winter at last bestir the king?

Hoofbeats roused her, a dozen sets, coming not from the hillside above this time, but from across the flat below. Dagg whickered, and Tek peered ahead through the ashen turbulence. Dying day grew greyer by the moment. In another few heartbeats, she spotted Sa, the rest of the band scattering, each to his or her respective grotto. The grey mare trotting up the brief, steep slope toward Tek and Dagg whinnied in greeting. Healer's daughter and dappled warrior fell back from the cave's entrance to allow her passage. Once within, the grey mare stamped, shaking the snow from her back and mane.

"What news, kingmother?" Dagg asked. "Did you discover forage?"

The grey mare chuckled.

"Did we indeed! A thicket of tuckfruit ripe as you please—neither birds nor pans have found it yet. We ate till I thought we would burst! Tomorrow I'll lead the rest of you to it."

Tek whooped, half shying as Sa reached playfully to nip her neck. The grey mare frisked like a filly, and the healer's daughter whickered, amazed how suddenly her mood lifted at the prospect of a full belly of sweet, greenish tuckfruit. Come the morrow, they would feast for the first time in days! She ramped, scarcely able to restrain her exuberance. Dagg chafed and chivvied her, laughing himself now. With the certainty of at least a day's ample forage ahead, all thought of both the herd's troubles and her own slipped unmissed from her thoughts.

Landfall

)9(

The firekeepers' settlement sprawled along one bend of a broad, cliffed bay, rank upon rank of their timber dwellings crowding the slopes above. Tai-shan stood gazing in astonishment as the caveshell angled toward land. A crisp, clean breeze slapped at the billowing windwing. Other caveshells glided by, their own windwings whitely belled.

The *daïcha* stood alongside him, her green falseskins fluttering, the silvery crescent upon her breast flashing in the late afternoon sun. A throng of two-foots milled upon the nearing beachhead. As the caveshell ground ashore, they surged and shouted. Laughing, the *daïcha* lifted one graceful, hairless forelimb and gestured in greeting.

Tai-shan heard gasps, cries of wonder and alarm as he leapt to join the *daïcha* on the strand. Half the spectators seemed ready to flee at the sight of him—the rest shouldering forward for a better view. A company of two-foots pressed back the jostling crowd, using long, straight staves tipped with glinting skystuff. Each such male wore a burnished head-covering, also of skystuff, topped with a purple plume. Beyond them, the throng waved and cheered.

"Greetings!" the dark unicorn called to them in his own tongue. "Greetings to you, noble two-foots!"

The *daïcha* cried out a long phrase ending in "Tai-shan." The crowd took up the word, chanting his name as the *daïcha* led him up a stony path between the tall wooden dwellings. Green-plumed two-foots armed with skewers, not staves, escorted their green-clad leader and her companions along the rising path. The dark unicorn walked alongside. Solid ground felt strange beneath his hooves after so many days at sea. More two-foots—held back by the purple-plumes—crowded the narrow way.

"Tai-shan! Tai-shan!" roared the crowd.

The tumult grew deafening. Two-foots leaning from openings high in their timber dwellings' walls flung brilliant seedpods, withered flowers, and shavings of aromatic spicewood onto hard, flat cobbles of the path. Through the shower of offerings, the dark unicorn gazed in amazement at the vast settlement. Fire burned everywhere, glowing in blackened hollows of skystuff, crackling upon treelimbs set in niches, and dancing in hanging boxes of semitransparent shell.

The sun sank lower, edging toward dusk. The petal-strewn path, he saw, climbed toward a magnificent dwelling that crested the slope. A barrier of timber surrounded the place. As they neared, green-plumes rushed forward to shove at a pair of heavy wooden panels mounted in the timber wall. These pivoted inward, creating an entryway. Sun slipped below horizon's edge. The air grew dark and chill. As the *daïcha* led him through the entryway, the dark unicorn glanced back at her people's immense settlement spilling the shadowed hillside below, the whole slope ablaze with little flickers of captured fire.

The commotion of the crowd abruptly muted as the huge wooden panels boomed shut. Tai-shan found himself in an open, cobbled space lit by burning brands. Around him, the *daïcha*'s train milled expectantly until an ornate panel in the nearest dwelling swung open and a male two-foot strode out, accompanied by more of the purple-plumes. He appeared young and vigorous, darkly bearded and attired in falseskins of deep violet and gold. A circlet of skystuff gleamed among the black curls crowning his head.

"Emwe! Emwe, im chon," the *daïcha* cried gladly.

She and her fellows dropped to the ground. Startled, the dark unicorn cavaled—then stilled his hooves as he remembered that the two-foots used this crumpled posture to show homage. This purple-clad male—the *chon*—must be the settlement's ruler, he concluded in surprise. Who, then, must the *daïcha* be—his sister? His mate? Facing the two-foot ruler, Tai-shan dipped his long neck in a bow.

The *chon* clapped the undersides of his forepaws together, and the crouching two-foots raised their heads. Baring his teeth, he beckoned to the *daïcha,* who hurried to him. He enfolded her in his forelimbs for a long moment. When he released her, she turned, talking to him excitedly and gesturing toward Tai-shan. The other's eyes widened as he took note of the dark unicorn for the first time. Tai-shan tossed the forelock out of his eyes, and the other exclaimed in astonishment at the sight of his moon-marked brow.

"Dai'chon!" he whispered.

Gently, the *daïcha* corrected him: "Tai-shan."

The *chon* called out a sharp command. Purple-plumes hurried to snatch firebrands from wall niches and hold them near. Tai-shan stood in a ring of fire. The *chon* strode forward and circled the dark unicorn, peering at him in obvious fascination. He exchanged animated comments with the *daïcha,* who stood back, watching anxiously. Disconcerted, Tai-shan pivoted to remain facing his host.

Emwe. Emwe, im chon. He struggled to repeat the *daïcha*'s greeting, but as before, the unpronounceable words came out whistled, garbled: "Am-wa. Umuwa m'shan. . . ."

The two-foot ignored his words, staring pointedly at the dark unicorn's cloven hooves. Tai-shan cavaled uneasily. Without warning, the *chon* stepped forward to lay one forepaw against his chest. The other he ran swiftly along the dark unicorn's back to the croup. Tai-shan jerked away with a startled snort. The other's peremptory manner astonished him. Only the *daïcha* had dared to touch him before—and he realized now it was her touch alone that he welcomed. His skin twitched.

Clucking, the other made to approach him again, but the dark unicorn dodged, shaking his head vigorously. The *chon* halted, eyes keenly narrowed suddenly, lips pressed tight. Then with a barking sound that might have been laughter, he stepped back from the ring of fire to rejoin the *daïcha.* She seemed relieved. Once again, he embraced her, speaking warmly to her. She smiled and nodded. Abruptly, he turned to quit the yard, and his purple-plumes, still bearing their torches, accompanied him through the great shelter's paneled entryway.

The *daïcha* beckoned her female companions and her green-plumes to her as she led Tai-shan across the darkened yard to another, smaller building. The lighted interior felt luxuriously warm, the tang of fire pervading the air, and the musty, sweetish scent of vast quantities of dried forage. The young stallion sneezed, unused to such a savor of abundance so late in the season. His nostrils flared suddenly. He halted dead.

"Unicorns!" he exclaimed. The musk, spicy scent of his own kind hung all around. "Unicorns!"

Only silence answered. Not so much as a slap of mane or a stamp replied. Nevertheless, a rush of euphoria filled the young stallion's breast. Surely these must be the lost companions he had sought so long. "Where are you? Show yourselves!"

Once again, only silence. The *daïcha* was urging him onward. Eagerly, he followed, hoping she might lead him to his fellows, though his memory of them and of his former life remained dim. They proceeded down an aisle between two rows of wooden compartments—all empty, though the scent of unicorns remained strong. Oddly, he scented mostly mares—here and there, a whiff of filly or foal—but no mature males, none even old enough to be called half-grown.

The *daïcha* halted before the last compartment, one far roomier than the rest. A two-foot in green falseskins had just finished raking out the old, yellow grass thickly carpeting the floor. A companion stood throwing down heaps of fresh. The dark unicorn breathed deep, finding at last the scent he had missed. Though this space, too, stood unoccupied, it had lately housed a stallion, young and vigorous and in full prime.

The *daïcha* swung open the compartment's front panel, and the dark unicorn entered. Forage and water were brought to him. Tai-shah ate greedily: berries and fodder, nutmeats broken from the shell, all crushed, blended together somehow, and steaming. Afterwards, the *daïcha* drew a bristly clump of spines through his coat. They felt like a thousand tiny birds' claws scrabbling, scratching away the grit and seasalt and old, sloughed skin.

The dark unicorn sighed deeply, sank down at last and closed his eyes. Softly bedded and sumptuously feasted, solicitously groomed and well sheltered against the cold, he let his thoughts drift back to his last glimpse of the firekeepers' dark dwellings spilling the slopes below, illuminated by spots of flame like a hillside strewn with burning stars. He had never known such luxury. On the morrow, he would seek out the other unicorns that abode here and learn from them of this strange and marvelous haven to which he had come.

Companions

☽ 10 ☾

Snow fell in gusts, bitterly cold. Tek stood on the valley floor while around her jostled most of the unicorns from the southwest quarter of the Vale. The pied mare shivered, even in her thick winter coat, dense now as a marten's pelt. They had come upon no more windfalls like the tuckfruit—days ago, and like her fellows, she had no layer of fat to keep out the cold. Sa brushed against her. Dagg appeared out of the press and halted along her other side.

"What do you think the king intends?" he asked her softly.

The healer's daughter shook her head. It was the first assembly Korr had called since the courting band had returned from the Sea, weeks past. Around them, the herd milled expectantly, huddled for warmth. Tek caught snatches of conversation, speculation. She spotted runners standing ready to carry the king's word to the far reaches of the Vale. Seasoned warriors all, she noted, especially chosen by the king. Beside her, the pied mare heard Dagg snort.

"Were Jan among us still," he muttered, "those runners would include half-growns as well."

She nodded. "True." *Jan might even have traveled to the far reaches of the Vale himself to spread the news,* she mused.

Faintly, the healer's daughter smiled, remembering. Her young mate, the prince, had been fearless of change: ever one to break with precedent when precedent failed to serve. The newer warriors had all adored him—though old traditionalists, she knew, had greeted Jan's innovations with consternation. And none so markedly as Korr. Bitterly, she sighed. How different the king was from his son!

A sudden stirring swept the crowd as, through the diffuse grey of falling snow, Korr's massy, storm-dark form appeared. His mate and

Dagg's father, Tas, flanked the king. Her own sire, Teki, brought up the rear. The crowd parted as the procession neared, and with a shock, Tek spotted Lell pressed close to her mother's flank.

The flame-colored mare moved slowly, shielding her filly with tender care. Alongside walked Leerah, Tas's mate, lending her shoulder, too, against the biting wind. The amber filly stumbled, racked with cold. The king never so much as glanced behind. Tek gazed at Korr, angry and aghast—for his daughter's presence could only be by king's command. Ses would never willingly expose her tiny nursling to such weather. The brow of the king's mate was furrowed, her jaw set.

The pied mare sidled uneasily. Abruptly, she realized she should have melted back into the crowd at the king's approach: too late now to do so unseen. She stood her ground, and Korr passed directly before her, spoke not a word, merely leveled at her his ferocious stare. Tek's heart clenched. Grimly, she lifted her chin, refused to flinch beneath the dark stallion's gaze. In a bound, he mounted the council rise and turned, looming above them like a thunderhead.

"Unicorns!" he called. "Children-of-the-moon! Since I learned the harsh news of my son's death, you have seen me but little. I was deep in grief, struggling to fathom why Alma should claim my son, your prince, bereaving us all."

Korr's fine, deep voice penetrated even the muffle of wind and snow. Glancing about her, Tek glimpsed a thin young mare shushing a companion, an old stallion pricking his ears. Long starved for the sight of their king, the unicorns quieted, listened attentively.

"My son was a fine warleader, was he not?" continued Korr. "A bit rash and hotheaded, to be sure—but quick in wit and great in heart, a courageous warrior! You loved him well."

A cry of agreement went up. The healer's daughter watched a cluster of spindly half-growns a few paces off, snorting and stamping in assent. Beyond them, a gaunt pair of elders nodded. A rush of gratification welled up in her. They *had* loved Jan—even the older warriors whom the young prince's reformations had so often confounded. The king raised his head.

"Aye, you loved him. As did I. But what of Alma?" The great stallion's tone abruptly darkened. "How must Alma have felt to see my son's wildness, all his princely verve and quickness of mind—though never ill-meant—used but to bend her Law and flout her will and tempt us, her best beloved, along untried paths, kicking aside her time-honored practice as though it were worthless nothing?"

Tek felt a frown furrow her brow. What was this talk of Alma and the Law in the selfsame breath? "Alma does not make the Law," she murmured. "The Council of Elders makes the Law and always has—"

"Could such have been the will of Alma," the king inquired, still facing the herd from the rocky rise, "to see her anointed prince, my son, flagrantly leading her children astray?"

Tek snorted, baffled. Was the prince of a sudden to be deemed the anointed of Alma?

"Only the prophets are anointed of Alma—" Dagg started beneath his breath, but the king's words cut him off.

"No!" Korr thundered, his voice rebounding from the far hillside. "Such blasphemy could *not* have been the goddess's will. And so she swept away my son—as she will sweep away all who fail her trust."

The dark stallion wheeled, stamping, tossing his head, full of fury now. The healer's daughter watched him, astonished. She heard Sa beside her champ her teeth. Beyond Dagg, a young warrior mare—ribs showing—was standing stock-still despite the cold. Beside her, a couple of half-starved colts poised motionless, as though caught by a wyvern's glare. Her own limbs felt stiff. Hastily, Tek shook herself. All around her the herd stood frozen as if mesmerized. "First Alma sent her gryphons," ranted the king, "but we paid no heed. Then she seized our prince, my son. Now she has sent this harsh winter to chastise us!" The pied mare listened dumbstruck, appalled.

"Jan was a brave prince, my own get, and I loved him," the dark stallion cried, "but he was wrong! In his pride, he defied Alma. In destroying him, the goddess speaks clear warning: we must turn back! We must return to the old ways and the true worship of Alma. Only if we once more devote ourselves unswervingly to her will can spring return and again bestow upon us her blessings."

Beside her, she felt Dagg snorting in disgust, glimpsed the troubled look on Sa's face deepen into dismay.

"Old ways—which ones?" she heard the grey mare breathe. "And true worship—what on earth can my son mean? Is now even the weather to be ascribed to Alma?"

Nearby, an old mare, clearly exhausted and perilously thin, swayed as though any moment her limbs might give way. Tek lashed her tail furiously, scarcely able to contain herself.

"Uppermost in our minds ought to be not who among us worships most fervently," she hissed, "but how many fillies and foals will see this killing winter through!"

Yet save for a few stamps and uncertain glances among the crowd, most still remained attentive to the king. She caught sight of one haggard stallion murmuring accord. The shivering mare beside him nodded.

About the foot of the rise, the seasoned warriors who were to act as the king's runners cavaled restlessly, snorting and tossing their heads in agreement.

The pied mare half shied. Truly alarmed now, she searched the faces of those flanking Korr upon the rise. With relief, she noted again the fierce, if unvoiced, disapproval of Ses, and her heart went out to Lell, cold and miserable, shuddering against her mother's side. Behind them, Tek saw her own father, Teki, standing silent, his expression profoundly saddened. Tas, however, stood nodding calmly, as did his mate. Tek felt another surge of indignation. Were the pair of them so blind in their loyalty to the king that they actually supported this folly?

"In following my son," Korr proclaimed, "we have all become Ringbreakers and renegades. But no more! Thus I say to you in the name of my daughter, the princess Lell, that from this day forward, any who breach Alma's sacred Law shall be banned."

A ripple passed through the crowd. Tek saw warriors, half-growns starting as though abruptly awakened.

"Banned?" Sa beside her gasped.

"But banishment in winter means death!" Dagg exclaimed.

The king's dam shook her head, one cloven forehoof striking at the frozen ground, her tone quietly outraged. "The herd has *never* imposed exile, regardless of the crime, between first snowfall and spring. What 'old tradition' is this?"

At the foot of the rise, the king's warriors circled. Tek suddenly froze. Korr no longer surveyed the entire assembly. His stare now fixed squarely on her.

"Be it known," he thundered, "Alma tolerates not even the slightest infraction. Tread with caution, I charge you all—or be cast from the herd!"

Tek felt Sa's astonished start, Dagg's indrawn breath, and held herself rigid, refusing to quail. Though he had spoken no word directly to her, had not even called her by name, Korr's meaning could not but be evident to all: let the healer's daughter stumble in even the tiniest regard, and he would find a way—any excuse, or no excuse—to banish her. The crowd shifted, murmuring.

Tek felt her fury spark. Did the dark stallion truly believe fanatical devotion to Alma had power to alter weather, grow forage beneath the snow, and avert gryphon raids in spring? How neat it all was! Korr had but to declare himself the mouthpiece of Alma, and displeasing him became defiance of the goddess herself. Now he would have them all believe that the Law—indeed, even custom—was fixed immutably by the goddess's behest. And was "tradition" to be anything the king now said it was, even if he had just this moment invented it? Angrily, she eyed the band of seasoned warriors who, at the king's nod, had begun to ascend the rise.

"Behold my newly appointed Companions," he cried to the herd. "They are Alma's eyes and ears among you now!"

Gazing about, Tek noted alarm on the spare, hungry faces of many. One older mare looked badly shaken, the lean young half-grown beside her merely puzzled. The pied mare shivered. Yet one stallion she had noticed nodding earlier still evidenced rapt attention. A convert, she realized uneasily. A bitter taste came into her mouth. On the rise, the king's warriors arranged themselves in a double phalanx. Sa snorted indignantly.

" 'Companions,' indeed!" she mused beneath her breath. "More nearly a personal guard. What does my son intend them to protect him from—the truth?"

Tek shook her head. No king or queen in all the history of the unicorns had ever appointed—or needed—a personal guard. As by pre-arrangement, the king's Companions started to stamp and cheer. Still none among the herd spoke out. Colts shrank against their mothers. Half-growns found their mates. Dawning throughout the crowd Tek glimpsed expression of anger, betrayal, and fear. Flanking the king, his guards whinnied and shouted enthusiastically, but few others joined them. How many, she wondered, while unwilling to risk voicing questions or protests aloud, nevertheless harbored grave doubts? How many had begun to share her own suspicions? The pied mare shivered uncontrollably.

"The king," she whispered, so soft she herself scarcely heard, "is well and truly mad."

"You have heard my will," the dark stallion cried, "which is Alma's. Remember it!"

Tek watched him vault from the rocky rise. The herd shrank back from him. Korr seemed imbued by a cold and desperate energy. His train followed more cautiously, picking their way down the icy, slippery stones. Trotting briskly, the king headed back through the ever-thickening snowfall toward his grotto across the Vale. His Companions remained behind on the council rise, necks arched, chests thrown forward, legs stiff. Slowly, as though stunned, the assembled unicorns began to disperse.

"He hasn't any food to give us," she heard Sa beside her murmur, "so he has fed us lies! Some of us have even swallowed them, and now feel full and well-fed, though in truth we are famished still." She eyed the king's guard upon the rise with open contempt. "When no food can be found to fill an aching belly, a scrap or two of arrogance contents some very well."

Fidgeting, Dagg stood gazing after the king's retreating train. "I can't believe my sire and dam approve this," he burst out. "I can't believe anyone could!"

One of the Companions on the rise turned to gaze at Dagg. Tek hurriedly shushed him, but fuming still, the dappled half-grown ignored her.

"And your father, Tek!" he cried. "The healer raised not a word of protest, though plainly he did not agree."

A second Companion had joined the first, their heads together, now conferring.

"Has our king lost all reason—?"

"Peace; hold your tongue, you young foal!" Sa ordered suddenly, sharply.

Tek turned, startled. Beside her, Dagg fell silent, stared in confusion at the grey mare. She had spoken far louder than necessary. Above them, the two warriors watched. Abruptly, the grey mare wheeled.

"Come with me," she commanded crisply, "both of you. I've a word to say regarding how fitly to comport yourselves in your loyalty to our king."

Astonished, Tek followed as the king's dam trotted away from the rise through the throng of dispersing unicorns. Dagg fell into step at her side, his expression baffled. As soon as they were out of earshot of the king's Companions, Sa halted, turned.

"Pray forgive my shortness, Dagg," she told him gently. "That was for show, to save my son's pack-wolves the pleasure of correcting you. Take heed, for the wind has changed, and if you cannot scent it yet, you will."

Dagg champed his teeth. "Aye, the wind *has* changed," he managed gruffly. "It stinks."

"Hist, lower your voice!" the grey mare cautioned, dropping her own to the merest whisper. "We dare not speak freely anymore—for some, no doubt, will seek favors from my son by reporting dissent."

"Since when was dissent a crime among the unicorns?" Dagg hissed angrily, though taking care now that his voice did not carry. "Since when was speaking one's mind to be feared?"

"Since *now*," Tek spat. The vehemence in her words plainly surprised him. "It's one of Korr's new 'old traditions.' *'Alma's will'!*"

She snorted, shaking her head. Her breath steamed, rising like dragons' breath. She shifted, wincing, for her swollen belly pained her. She heard Dagg's beside her growl. Shuddering, she longed for the wind-sheltered warmth of the grotto she shared with Sa—but she knew they had all best use what scant daylight remained to forage, else they would shiver the cold night through, unable to sleep for hunger. The grey mare nodded.

"I fear you are right, Dagg," she said softly. "Grief seems to have stolen my son's reason." All around, the dispersing unicorns drifted, pale haunts through the ashen snowfall. Sa looked at them. "Clearly, we have much to do."

Dagg glanced around him, frowned. "To do?"

The healer's daughter snuffed. "We must scout out the rest of the herd, of course," she answered, "and uncover our allies."

Dagg shook his head, still lost. "Allies?" he asked, then abruptly blinked, voice dropping to a whisper, truly hushed now for the first time. "Defy Korr, you mean? Disobey the king?"

Tek shrugged. "Who knows?" she murmured. "We cannot know what is possible until we count who and how many his opposition are."

"Young warrior," Sa said tartly, "you seem to forget: my son is not the ruler of the unicorns. Lell is our princess now, though not even she can make or unmake the Law. That is the Council's prerogative." The old mare smiled grimly. "If enough of the herd so demand, the elders— of whom I am one—might choose another regent."

The dappled half-grown let out his breath. Clearly, he had never even considered such a thing. Yet that of which the king's dam had just reminded them was true: it was the Council who—quietly, unobtrusively, year after year—made the Law, declared the succession, and invested warleader or regent with power. If they chose, the elders could rescind that power. Tek's own heart thumped. The Council could depose the king.

"It's settled, then," she said after a moment. "Dagg and I will scout the herd. But—" she added, glancing a warning in his direction and lifting her chin slightly toward the king's distant Companions.

The dappled warrior nodded. "We must proceed with the greatest caution, aye."

"That we must," Sa agreed. "But not you, Tek. You must avoid entanglement in this above all."

Tek started, stared. "How so?"

The grey mare shook her head. "Dear one," she said, "did you not mark the way my son looked at you?"

Bitterly, the healer's daughter laughed. "All the herd marked it."

Sa nodded. "Aye, he has singled you out to his wolfish 'Companions' and all the rest. They and others will be watching you close, and what could be more disastrous for you than to be accused of subversion?"

"No more dangerous for me than for you," Tek answered hotly.

Dagg snorted beside her. The snow was falling thick as mare's milk now. Their breath steamed around them like wafts of burning cloud. "Nay, Tek. Far more dangerous for you," Sa was saying. "I am the king's dam after all. Do you truly think that even grief-maddened as he is, my own scion would turn me out into the snow? And Dagg was your mate's shoulder-companion from earliest colthood. I doubt Korr would do him serious harm for anything short of open rebellion."

Again she shook her head.

"But you, my child. Though once Korr appeared to esteem you, at times even above his own son, his feelings towards you have greatly changed."

Stubbornly, the pied mare ducked her head. "I'll not be warned away," she said. "I'll not let the pair of you charge boldly into wolves' teeth without me alongside."

Dagg shouldered her gently. She leaned against him, grateful for his support. The grey mare sighed ruefully.

"Very well, child, I cannot stop you. But have a care! In your present state, I fear the king's ire can only increase as the winter months go by."

Tek shook her head, puzzled yet again by Sa's words. She sensed the same reaction from Dagg.

Once more she said, "How so?"

The king's dam snorted, eyeing the young mare's gently swollen belly.

"My dear, have you not yet realized?" she answered dryly. "You are in foal."

Moonbrow

☽ 11 ☾

Tai-shan savored his new life in the fire-warmed enclosure, well pleased with the layer of winter fat at last beginning to sheathe his ribs. Whenever the weather held fair, the green-clad *daïcha* accompanied the dark unicorn to the open yard that he might frisk, leaping and galloping fiercely. Yet—maddeningly—he caught not so much as a glimpse of others of his kind. Gradually their scent within the enclosure's vacant compartments grew old.

The chill, dark afternoon was growing late, the *daïcha* just leading him back toward shelter. The weather had turned much colder than the morn. Ice slicked the squared cobblestones where formerly puddles had lain. His breath steamed like a dragon's in the bone-dry air. All at once, Tai-shan pricked his ears. Abruptly, he halted. The muffled sound of hooves and far-off whistles reached him.

With an astonished whinny, the dark unicorn wheeled and bolted across the yard toward the sound. He scarcely heard the dismayed exclamations of the *daïcha* behind him. His own heels rang sharply on the icy stones. The low, calling whickers grew louder as he ducked down a narrow passage between two buildings. Emerging, he beheld another, far more spacious yard, unpaved, and surrounded by a barrier of wooden poles. Beyond milled a group of unicorns. Tai-shan's heart leapt like a stag.

"Friends," he cried. "I have found you at last!"

The others turned in surprise. They were all mares, he noted, save for a couple of well-grown fillies, and all quite small. Their coloring was disconcerting, dull shades of brown mostly, not at all the hot sunset reds and skywater blues of the fellows he only dimly remembered.

Among these strangers' subdued, earthy hues, one mare alone stood out. Slender, clean-moving, her coat a vivid copper that was full of fire.

"A stallion!" he heard her whisper.

A companion nodded, murmuring, "Aye, a stallion—here! And mark the color of him."

"So dark—near black."

"He *is* black . . ."

Tai-shan trotted toward them. "I am a stranger here," he called. "Can you tell me what place this is?"

None of the mares replied, though one of the fillies exclaimed, "Look! Upon his brow—"

The coppery mare shushed her. The dark unicorn halted, puzzled. Beyond the wooden poles, the mares shifted nervously, eyeing him with mingled curiosity and alarm. Several seemed on the verge of bolting. At last, cautiously, the tall coppery mare started forward. Her companions cavaled and whickered, calling her back, but she shook them off.

"Who—what art thou?" she demanded of him, seemingly poised between boldness and terror. "Whence comest thou?"

The dark unicorn blinked. The other's odd manner of speech was new to him, softly lilting. He found himself able to understand it only haphazardly.

"I am . . . I am called Tai-shan," he began, aware all at once that he still could recall no name other than the one the *daïcha* had given him. "I come from . . . from far away—"

"Moonbrow?" the young mare interrupted. "Thou art the one our lady hath named Moonbrow?"

Tai-shan frowned. Was such the meaning of his name? "You speak the two-foots' tongue?" he asked.

"Two-foots!" the other exclaimed. All at once, she burst out nickering.

"Why do you laugh?" the dark unicorn asked her.

"Thou calledst our keepers 'two-foots'!"

"Keepers," the dark unicorn murmured. Short for *firekeepers,* doubtless. "You speak their tongue?"

The coppery mare tossed her head. "Nay. No *da* can manage that. But I reck it some."

By *reck,* he guessed she must mean *understand.*

"*Da,*" he said. "What is . . . ?"

He choked to a halt suddenly, noticing for the first time what he had missed before: the mare across the wooden barrier from him was hornless. No proud spiral skewer—not even a nursling's hornbud—graced her brow. He half-reared, exclaiming in surprise, and saw that her fellows behind her were just the same: foreheads perfectly flat. Their manes stood upright along their necks like the manes of newborn foals. Like fillies', their chins were beardless. Stranger still, their tails were not tufted only at the end, but were instead completely covered by long, silky hair. Beneath smooth, unfringed fetlocks, each hoof was a single, solid toe.

"You are no unicorns!" he cried.

"Unicorns?" The coppery mare cocked her head, pronouncing the word as though it were new to her.

Tai-shan stumbled back from her, staring. "What manner of beasts are you?"

"*Daya,*" the other said. "I and my sisters are the sacred *daya* of Dai'chon."

He heard footfalls behind him and glimpsed the *daïcha* hastening toward him. At the same moment, a commotion among the mares caused him to turn again. Beyond them, another of their kind was just entering the enclosed yard through a pivoting panel in the barricade of wooden poles. This was a stallion, as hornless as the mares. His coat was reddish umber, shanks black below the knee. He wore an odd kind of adornment about his head, made of fitted links of shining skystuff. A silver crescent resembling the *daïcha*'s spanned his brow. The pair of two-foots accompanying him each grasped a long strap attached to the muzzle of the thing.

"Our lord cometh!" one of the fillies cried.

"Hist, away!" her elder sister urged the coppery mare.

Behind him, Tai-shan heard the *daïcha* draw her breath in sharply. Catching sight of him, the umber stallion pitched to a stop. His two-foot companions halted in seeming confusion. The *daïcha* hastened forward, calling out to them and waving one forelimb as though urging them to depart. Eyes wide, the two-foots began tugging at the long straps, but the hornless stallion planted his round hooves, stiff-legged, refusing to budge. Head up, he stared at Tai-shan. Abruptly, the umber stallion let loose a peal of rage.

"What meaneth this? Who dareth to approach my consorts?"

The dark unicorn snorted, confused as much by the other's hot and angry tone as by his strange way of speaking. Before him, the mares screamed and scattered, thundering away toward the opposite end of the barricaded yard, all save the coppery mare, who cried out to him hastily.

"Peace, my lord. Naught unseemly hath occurred. This is Moon-brow, that our lady hath . . ."

"Moonbrow?" the other snarled. "The outlander that hath usurped my stall?"

Tai-shan frowned. The meanings of several of the other's words he had to guess at. *Outlander* must mean one from outside the two-foots' settlement. Perhaps *stall* referred to the wooden enclosure in which he now sheltered. Ignoring his escorts, the umber stallion stamped and sidled.

"Wouldst claim my harem as well?"

Tai-shan shook his head. He had no idea what a *harem* might be.

"I seek nothing that is not my due," he called across the barricade. "I long only to learn what place this is—"

"A place where thou'lt find no welcome, upstart!" the stallion spat, eyes narrowed, his small, untasseled ears laid back. "Stand off, harlot," he shouted at the coppery mare. "Thou'rt pledged to me!"

Trembling, the coppery mare began to back away. Once more, the *daïcha* called sharply to her fellows. They tugged with determination at the straps of the stallion's headgear, but he shook them furiously off.

"Trespasser!" he flung at the dark unicorn. "Thief!"

Tai-shan ramped and sidled for sheer bafflement. "What is my trespass?" he cried. "I assure you, I am no thief. . . ."

"Dost challenge me?" the other shrilled, rearing. "I'll brook no such outrage!"

With shouts of surprise, his two-foot companions lost their grip on the straps as all at once, the stallion charged. Confounded, Tai-shan sprang back.

"Peace, friend," he exclaimed. "I seek no quarrel. . . ."

"No quarrel!" the other roared. "Our keepers should have cut thee, not made thee welcome, freak! *I* am First Stallion here!"

His words made no sense to Tai-shan. Across the yard, the two-foot escorts cried out in alarm as the umber stallion thundered toward the dark unicorn. Tai-shan tensed: the wooden barrier between them was only shoulder high, an easy leap—then abruptly he realized it was the coppery mare, not he, who stood directly in the other's path. With a startled cry, she scrambled aside—too slowly. The umber stallion champed and struck at her savagely.

"Hie thee back to thy sisters, strumpet!" he snarled. Then to Tai-shan, "Be grateful a fence standeth between us, colt, else it would be to thee I'd give this drubbing."

Cornered against the barrier, the coppery mare cried out, unable to dodge. Tai-shan saw blood on her neck where her assailant's teeth had found her. She stood on three limbs, favoring one bleeding foreleg. With a shout, the dark unicorn leapt the barrier and sprang between them, shouldering the umber stallion away from the coppery mare.

"Leave off!" he shouted. "She has done you no hurt."

Behind him, he heard cries of amazement. The place seemed full of two-foots suddenly, running and calling. The *daïcha*'s voice rose commandingly above the rest. At the far end of the yard, the panicked mares galloped in circles. Green-clad two-foots ran to contain them. The umber stallion fell back from Tai-shan at first with an astonished look, then seemed to recover himself. Viciously, he lashed and flailed at Tai-shan, who braced and struck back, striving to hold his ground lest he himself be driven back and trapped against the barrier.

"Nay, do not defend me, Moonbrow," the coppery mare gasped, limping painfully out of the umber stallion's reach.

The *chon* burst into the yard suddenly. Tai-shan heard him shouting above the tumult, the clatter of footfalls as his purple-plumes rushed forward with their long, pointed staves. Screaming, the flatbrowed stallion lunged and champed Tai-shan on the shoulder, drawing blood. The dark unicorn struck him away with the flat of his horn.

"Moonbrow, have done!" the coppery mare called to him urgently. "Thou darest do him no injury. He is sacred to Dai'chon!"

Tai-shan glimpsed the *daïcha* dashing forward to intercept the charging purple-plumes. She waved her forelimbs, crying out frantically to the *chon*. Taking note of her, apparently for the first time, he barked an order and threw up one of his own forelimbs. Lowering their staves, the purple-plumes strayed uncertainly to a stop.

Eyes red and wild, the umber stallion wheeled and plunged once more at the dark unicorn. Tai-shan reared and threw himself against the other's side, catching him just as he pivoted. The flatbrow's hindquarters strained, forehooves pawing the air. The dark unicorn lunged, shifting his whole weight forward hard until, hind hooves skidding, his opponent crashed to the icy ground.

"Hold," the dark unicorn cried, springing to press the tip of his horn to the other's throat. "Enough, I say!"

Eyes wide, the fallen stallion stared up at him. The other's red-rimmed nostrils flared. His breaths came in panting gasps. He made as if to scramble away, but Tai-shan pressed his horntip harder.

"*Peace,*" he insisted. "I sought no quarrel with you, nor did this mare."

Across the yard, the other mares had quieted. They stood silent, astonished. The two-foots as well. Eyes still on the umber stallion, Tai-shan stepped back, horn at the ready.

"Be off," the dark unicorn snorted. "And do not think to trouble this mare again while I stand ready in her defense."

With a groan, the defeated stallion pitched to his heels and limped away. His two-foot companions came forward cautiously to catch hold of his headgear's trailing straps. Other two-foots hied the mares from the enclosed yard through the pivoting panel. They disappeared down a passage between two buildings. The crestfallen stallion allowed his escorts to lead him after the mares without further protest. Tai-shan turned back to the coppery mare.

"Are you hale?" he asked her. "Did he do you much harm?"

The other gazed on him in seeming wonder. "Naught but a bruise and a gash, my lord Moonbrow," she murmured. "No more than that."

Warily, another two-foot edged toward them along the wooden barrier. The young mare snorted.

"Sooth, lord," she exclaimed, "ye must be winged, to have sprung such a height with such ease—and from a standing start!"

The dark unicorn shook his head, amazed. These hornless *daya* must be puny jumpers indeed if they found such low barriers any impediment.

"Tell me," he asked her, "why did you suffer that other to use you so? No warrior of my race would have stood for such—"

"Warrior!" the young mare whickered. "Lord, I am no warrior, only the least of the First Stallion's consorts—so new he hath not even claimed me yet. Only the First Stallion is warrior here, and he hath reigned four years running, defeating all comers at the autumn sacrifice—yet ye overcame him in a trice. . . ."

Drawing near, the two-foot clucked. The mare turned meekly, as from long habit, and started to go to him.

"Wait!" Tai-shan exclaimed. "Will I see you—you and your sisters—again?"

The coppery mare hung back, seemingly torn between the desire to stay and an obligation to accompany the two-foot. He clucked again. The coppery mare shrugged.

"If our keepers so will."

The overcast hung very low and grey. Feathery flakes of snow, the season's first, had begun to float down through the darkening air. Reluctantly, the coppery mare turned to follow her two-foot escort.

"Hold, I beg you!" the dark unicorn cried. "Tell me your name."

For a moment, glancing back over her shoulder, the other's chestnut eyes met his. She nickered suddenly, despite the obvious pain of her injured leg.

"Ryhenna, my lord Moonbrow," she called back to him, "that meaneth *fire*."

She limped slowly, three-legged, beside her escort toward the opening in the wooden barrier across the yard. Tai-shan turned to find the *daïcha* deep in debate with the *chon*. She stood directly before him, forepaws resting on his upper limbs, which encircled her middle. Purple-

plumes surrounded them. The ruler listened, frowning, seemingly reluctant to accede to whatever it was the *daïcha* was insisting upon. The
dark unicorn saw him twice shake his head.

In a bound, Tai-shan sprang over the wooden barrier again and was
surprised once more to hear exclamations of astonishment from the two-
foots. The *chon* and the *daïcha* both turned, startled. Tai-shan whickered
to the lady and made to approach. The ruler's clasp about her tightened
protectively. His purple-plumes tensed. At his sharp command, they
raised their pointed staves and hurried to block the dark unicorn's path.

Tai-shan halted with a puzzled snort. Turning in the *chon*'s grasp,
the *daïcha* protested. Reaching out one forelimb to the dark unicorn,
she continued talking to the *chon*. The two-foot ruler eyed the young
stallion suspiciously, but at a cautious nod from him, his purple-plumes
fell back, staves still at the ready. Tai-shan went forward to nuzzle the
daïcha. She crooned to him and stroked his nose.

Releasing her, the *chon* laid one forepaw briefly upon her shoulder,
then turned and strode away across the yard in the direction the mares
and the stallion had taken. His purple-plumes marched after him. Dusk
had fallen. The snowfall was coming down more thickly now. The *daïcha*'s female companions arrived, carrying firebrands. Tai-shan held
himself still as, by their flickering light, the lady ran her slender forepaws gently over his nicks and bruises. She dabbed them with a pungent
salve from a hollow vessel that was the color of soft river clay but rigid
as stone.

The *chon* returned, striding across the yard once more with his
purple-plumes. He bore in one forepaw the same silvery adornment the
umber stallion had lately worn. The long, trailing straps had been removed. Its dipping, crescent browpiece gleamed, flashing in the darting
firelight.

The *chon* handed his prize to the *daïcha,* who accepted it with a
delighted laugh. Curious, the dark unicorn bent forward to examine the
thing more closely. It smelled of skystuff and bitter oil. Holding it up
in one forepaw, the *daïcha* caressed his muzzle and cheek. Tai-shan had
no notion what the purpose of such an odd device might be, yet he felt
not the slightest misgiving as, moments later, the lady of the firekeepers
fastened it securely about his head.

Winterkill

☽ 12 ☾

The first weeks of winter had proven arduous. Sa shivered hard, frigid wind gusting her flank. She moved painfully, limbs aching. Sharp little crystals of ice seemed to have formed in her joints, making them ache. In all her many years she could not remember a winter so cold.

The weather worsened by the day. Forage grew steadily scarcer and ever more difficult to uncover beneath the hard-frozen snow. King's scouts no longer reported newfound forage to the herd at large. Korr alone decided who should learn of such. Those who gained his favor were led to the spots: those who earned his displeasure were left to fend for themselves.

The grey mare clenched her jaw. The shame of it: her son playing favorites when a mouthful of withered grass might mean the difference between starvation and survival this winter! Unicorns were dying now, herdmembers frozen or starved to death—nurslings and weanlings first, followed by the oldest stallions and mares.

Sa shook her head grimly as she picked her way over the rocky trail, eyes alert for any patch of green among the constant grey. Next it would be the older, uninitiated fillies and foals. Then the half-growns. Finally the warriors in their prime. The weather remained too harsh even to permit the proper funeral dances for the dead.

The grey mare's innards rumbled hollowly. She had not eaten since the afternoon before. Hunger had driven her high up the slopes, far from the constant wailing in the valley below: mothers discovering their young dead in the night, warriors stumbling across aged sires and dams too weak to rise. The Council of Elders had been devastated: three of its members already dead, five others gravely ill.

Korr ordered the herd assembled daily now, holding them for hours, captive to his rantings. He spun wild tales of the will of Alma, who mercifully punished her beloved followers for their transgressions. It was all absurd. Exposed to the elements, unable to move about for warmth, the herd listened to their mad king's tirades under the vigilant eye of his chosen Companions—"wolves," as many now called them when out of range of their ever-pricked ears.

Yet others, weak and weary, starving and cold, swallowed down the king's words as though they were sweet graze. The grey mare snorted, shaking her head. To be sure—standing dumbly rapt took far less energy than plowing through the cold, pawing hard-packed snow in search of forage, or breaking the hoof-thick ice of streams to snatch a sip of freezing water, Sa mused bitterly.

Her vitals growled again. Thinking not of her own ills, but of Tek's, Sa felt her brow furrow. As the pied mare's belly continued to swell, she kept more and more to herself these days, foraging far from others' eyes, wary lest they deduce her condition and bring the news to Korr. His eye, Sa noted when it fell upon the healer's daughter, remained dark and full of fury still. At Korr's rallies, Sa insisted that Tek stand between her and Dagg, in hopes of disguising the younger mare's burgeoning belly from the king's watchful gaze. Did he know? Did he guess? She could not tell.

The grey mare's only consolation was in noting that her granddaughter Lell was no longer forced to attend: Ses's influence, surely. Silently, Sa thanked the flame-colored mare for standing up to her mate. Korr had stopped referring to the nursling princess almost entirely, no longer calling upon his daughter's title as the source of his authority. It was all Alma now: often it proved impossible to discern if the will he spoke of was the goddess's or his own.

Fortunately, she, Dagg, and Tek had managed to scout out a few others of rebellious mind. Approaches had to be cautious, much discussion slipped into brief spaces, since the king's wolves maintained close tally on who associated with whom. To her surprise, many of the old traditionalists who had so resisted her grandson's innovations now spoke with longing of the "fair old days" of Jan's brief reign.

And yet—infuriatingly—most of the herd continued meekly to submit to Korr's tyranny. They followed as in a daze, too weak or ill or spiritless to turn away. Disgusted, the grey mare snorted and pawed the frozen earth. Did these poor fools not realize that every waking moment must be devoted to forage if any were to survive to see the spring? With or without Council approval—and despite the king's fanatical personal guard—steps must be taken and *soon* to quell her son's worsening madness, or he would starve them all.

A flash of green caught her eye suddenly. Sa halted along the rocky trail. The cliffside fell away sheer to one side of her, more than a dozen stridelengths to the slope below. Not far beneath the dropoff, clinging to the cliff, rose a tiny spruce, its slender trunk leaning out over open space, its spindly branches tipped with dark, succulent needles, half a dozen mouthfuls at least. The grey mare gazed at the tempting forage, all thought of Korr's madness and the Vale's dire plight slipping from her mind as her empty gorge cramped in an agony of hunger.

Cautiously, she moved to the edge of the precipice and leaned out, nostrils flaring to catch the delicious, resinous savor of the greenery. Her long neck reached scarcely halfway to the little fir's tender tips. No wonder no unicorn had yet managed to claim his prize! Carefully, she inched nearer, straining. The pungent scent of pinesap made her dizzy for a moment. Her hooves skidded. She jerked back from the icy drop-off, tossing her head hard for balance, and managed to catch herself.

Think! She must think. How to get at that marvelous food, the first she had encountered since wolfing down a few old, dried thornberries and the bitter thorn they had hung upon the day before. Not until after she had finished had she stopped to consider—and realized she ought to have taken half back for Tek.

She had returned to the grotto that evening to find her grandson's mate huddled shivering—having turned up nothing that day. Now, standing at the edge of the precipice, gazing out at the little spruce, the older mare steadied her resolve. She would pluck the fir, but she would eat none of it. Not one twig! Her belly growled again in protest, but she champed her teeth against the grinding pain. Tek's unborn needed this nourishment far more than she.

Wind gusted harder, nearly overbalancing her on the treacherous ice. Her bones ached. She cavaled awkwardly to regain her equilibrium. She would need to use the greatest care—but she *must* get the branch. A mere scrap in summer, its foliage made a rare feast in these lean times. Sa champed her teeth again, against the aching stiffness in her joints this time. Once more she approached the cliffside's edge and leaned out.

She reached once, missed, reached again—striving to grasp the branch where it grew slender enough to break. The thin bough wavered in the wind, almost within range of her teeth. She braced her hooves and tried again. The wind whistled, numbingly chill. The icy stones of the cliffside clicked, cracking with the cold. The branch bobbed so near she felt it brush the whiskers of her nose. She snapped and missed.

The wind soughed, tugging, shoving at her. The little branch nodded and danced. She had it! All at once, she had it in teeth. The grey mare felt a rush of triumph as she strained the final infinitesimal distance to capture the elusive twig. Moisture rushed to her mouth. Scabrous, aromatic bark abraded her tongue.

Then without warning, the icy surface beneath her gave way. She jerked in surprise, hooves skidding. The treacherous wind whipped her mane stinging into her eyes. The limber branch tore free of her grasp and sprang away. She tried to rear back, scrambling wildly, but could find no purchase on the crumbling stone. Then she was hurtling headlong through empty space. The hillside below rushed up to meet her.

Ryhenna
) 13 (

Winter deepened. Snow fell almost daily, piling in great drifts beside
the two-foots' wooden dwellings and along the high timber wall. Now
when the *daïcha* led him from the warm enclosure, Tai-shan trotted at
once through the cobbled passage into the wide, unpaved yard where
the coppery mare and her flatbrowed sisters waited. Rather than
springing over the barrier of poles as he had done before, he schooled
himself to wait until the *daïcha* had swung wide the wooden panel to
let him pass.

"Ryhenna!" he had cried out joyfully, trotting forward toward her
on the day following their first meeting. A long strip of white falseskin
wrapped the young mare's injured foreshank.

"Emwe, im chon Tai-shan," she answered boldly. "Greetings, my
lord Moonbrow."

Whickering, the dark unicorn shook his head. The silvery adornment
felt odd about his muzzle still, but he was fast growing accustomed to
it. It jingled softly when he moved. "Speak, I beg you," he bade Ryhenna. "Tell me of this place."

Their conversation proceeded in fits and starts. Every other sentence, it seemed, he had to ask her to explain some unfamiliar word or
phrase. The two-foots' vast settlement, he learned, was called a city,
this walled complex housing the *chon* and his retinue, a palace. The
daya themselves dwelled in a shelter known as a stable. By the time
daylight waned and the *daïcha* beckoned him to return with her to his
quarters, the dark unicorn's head was spinning.

As the days passed, he asked Ryhenna to teach him as much as she
knew of the two-foots' odd, guttural tongue. Gradually, over the passage
of weeks, he began to pick up other phrases on his own: *tash* for "no";

homat for "stop"; *apnor*, "enough"; *himay*, "stay" or "stand still." To his rue, the *daïcha* remained as oblivious as before to his clumsy attempts at speech—but failure only sharpened his resolve to persevere. Eventually, he vowed, he would make himself understood. Chafing, Tai-shan practiced and bided his time.

Among the flatbrows in the yard, it was mostly the coppery mare to whom he spoke. Her sisters remained unaccountably shy, casting their gazes aside deferently when he spoke. Yet all seemed eager to gambol and frisk. Though most were full-grown mares, not one had any more skill at arms than a nursling filly—but they gladly learned the dances and hoof-sparring games he managed to recall from the haze of his past, and they taught him their own versions of nip and chase.

Theirs seemed an utterly carefree existence, their every need met by willing two-foots, who appeared to ask nothing in return. Meanwhile the *daya*, he noted, followed their keepers' lead in everything, coming promptly when called, going docilely where directed. Indeed, he did not recall ever glimpsing any of the *daya* moving about the palace grounds without a two-foot escort. Truly an odd arrangement.

While nervous of speaking directly to him, Tai-shan noticed, the *da* mares spoke much of him among themselves. One morning he overheard two mares and a filly discussing him when they thought his attention elsewhere. Unobtrusively, the dark unicorn listened.

"Our new lord seemeth a far sunnier consort than our last."

"Indeed! So even-tempered, so gentle and mannerly."

"A great one for sport."

"Ah, child, but how long ere he tireth of these gambols and seeketh better sport?"

Light, nervous laughter.

"Soon, I hope!"

"To be sure, child. Give it but a whit more time—"

"Aye, though wonderfully well-grown, he *is* a very young stallion."

"And hath lately languished ill."

"Sooth, his jumping beareth witness that he recovereth apace!"

More nickering.

"That it doth."

"Patience, sisters. By my reck, we shall all stand broody to his stud by spring."

Tai-shan had not the slightest idea what they could mean. So many of their odd words were unfamiliar to him still. Yet he hesitated to ask for an explanation and in so doing reveal his eavesdropping: more often than not when he singled one out, she merely fidgeted like a filly, exclaiming, "Sooth, lord! Ye honor me too much."

Only Ryhenna seemed to possess a bolder spark, addressing him frequently as "thou," a term he surmised to be for use between equals and friends, rather than the more formal "ye" her sisters used. His questions often sent her into peals of mirth. Exasperated, the dark unicorn gave up trying to scowl, for the other's laughter was infectious and before long, he, too, was nickering. Ryhenna told him all she knew of the marvelous city beyond the palace gate.

"Our gentle keepers are mighty sorcerers," she said, punching through the knee-high snow blanketing the yard. The strip of white falseskin wrapping her foreshank had been removed only that morn, though she had long since ceased to limp. "The keepers' mastery of heavenly fire hath enabled them to build all thou seest that sheltereth both themselves and us, their *daya.*"

Tai-shan trotted beside her. Their white breath wafted and steamed.

"But where do the *daya* go in spring, after the snow melts?" he asked her. Surely once the weather warmed, her kind must leave this cramped and barren place—perhaps they roamed the grassy slopes beyond the city until the return of winter snows? Ryhenna turned to him, puzzled.

"Go? My lord Moonbrow, the *daya* do not go. We remain here under our keepers' care."

Tai-shan blinked, surprised. "Always—even in summer?"

The coppery mare nodded. "In sooth," she answered proudly. "Our lives here are enviable: fed, groomed, sheltered, and exercised by the *daïcha*'s minions. Why should we wish to leave?"

Dumbstruck, the dark unicorn snorted. His breath swirled in the curling mist between them. Across the yard, Ryhenna's sisters whickered and chased. Tai-shan gazed about him at the walled grounds of the *chon*'s palace. A pleasant enough idyll for a season, he supposed—and far preferable to winter's privations and killing cold—but after the thaw at equinox? To be shut up atop this high, rocky cliff while all around the open hills greened and fragrant meadows beckoned to be raced across and rolled in?

The coppery mare shook her head.

"Dwelling within the *chon*'s palace is our privilege as bluebloods, sacred to Dai'chon."

Dai'chon. That word again: the one the *daïcha* and her minions had chanted upon the beach before the sky cinder. The same word both she and the *chon* had exclaimed at first sight of him. Tai-shan frowned. He had heard it upon the lips of *daya* as well as two-foots since and never yet asked Ryhenna what it meant. He was just drawing breath to do so when a look of sadness passed over the coppery mare's features.

"Others, of course, are not so blessed as my sisters and I," she murmured.

"Others?" Tai-shan forgot all about his intention to ask Ryhenna for the meaning of the word *dai'chon*. "There are other *daya* besides you and your kith—do they dwell in the city beyond?"

During the long uphill procession from the bay to the palace crowning the cliffs, the dark unicorn had caught not so much as a glimpse or a whiff of any four-footed creature besides himself—but then, the crush of two-foots and the confusion of new surroundings had been so great he had been aware of little beyond the tumult and the shower of dried petals and shavings of aromatic wood. The coppery mare shrugged.

"They are only commoners, of course. Of no consequence."

"Commoners?" Tai-shan pressed, moving nearer. "What are they?"

Again the coppery mare shrugged, moving off. "Merely common *daya*—those not sacred to Dai'chon."

Before he could question her further, the *daïcha* called out to him from the wooden barrier's gate. Across the yard, other two-foots clucked to the *da* mares. Ryhenna trotted obediently toward them. The dark unicorn stood gazing after her as she joined her sisters and followed the two-foot escorts from the yard. Behind him, the *daïcha* called again.

That evening, alone in his warm, straw-bedded stall after the *daïcha* had feasted and groomed him, Tai-shan reflected on the coppery mare's words. Who were these "common" *daya*? Were their lives different from the pampered comforts enjoyed by himself and the sacred bluebloods? In truth, despite its luxuries, now that he had regained his vigor, the unending sameness of life within the confines of the palace grounds had begun to wear on him.

Almost all he knew of the city beyond, he realized, came to him through Ryhenna—yet today she had hinted that she herself had never even ventured beyond the palace gate. Had any of her sisters? Surely some of them must—yet all save Ryhenna remained too shy to converse with him. The dark unicorn snorted. His only direct knowledge of the settlement below was little more than a confused and fading memory. Desire seized him suddenly to explore the two-foots' city of fire and behold with his own eyes whatever mysteries it might hold.

Wych's Child

☽ 14 ☾

Tek waded through the drifting snow, her rump to the biting wind. Sa had not yet returned to the grotto, and with the early dusk not far away, the pied mare grew anxious for her. Tek shivered hungrily as she picked her way across the slope. Late afternoon was very dark. Stumbling across the grey mare's body at the foot of a sharp drop took her by surprise. Sa lay smashed on the icy stones, one foreleg splayed, her head and neck twisted at an impossible angle. Tek halted, staring in horror. High up the cliff, she spotted the place where the other must have lost her footing. A little fir tree, hardly more than a sprig, grew out of the rock.

Grief overwhelmed Tek. The sky above her seemed to spin. She sank down, nuzzled the grey mare's body, already stiff with cold. Wind gusted, heavy with snow. It dragged against the cliff-side, moaning. Surely a snowstorm was in the wind. She knew that she must rise, must return soon to the shelter of the caves. Dusk was fast approaching, and if she were caught by storm, she might never find her way back. Slowly, with effort, she gathered her cold-numbed limbs and rose. Someone must bear news of Sa's death to the king, she realized with a groan. The thought chilled her even more than the wind.

Motion behind her made her start and wheel. Downslope two of the king's Companions came into view. They halted in surprise. Stallions both, one was dark, midnight blue with a pale, silvery mane. He looked to be of the same generation as Korr. The other, perhaps a year or two older than Tek, was middle blue and spattered all over with eye-sized blots of black.

"It's Tek," he muttered to his fellow, "the Red Mare's—the wych's child—"

The older Companion cut him short. "Alma's beard," he exclaimed. "Look—the king's dam, Sa!"

Still numb with grief, Tek fell back as the two stallions climbed hastily to stand over the grey mare.

"Dead!" the younger one exclaimed.

The heads of both Companions snapped up. Their glances flicked to her from the carcass at their feet. The dark, midnight blue leveled an accusing gaze at Tek.

"What do you know of this?" he demanded.

Tek's mouth felt thick and dry. "I . . . she must have fallen."

"Did you see it happen?" the younger, spotted one snapped, advancing uphill.

Tek shook her head. "Nay, I—"

The older stallion, too, came forward. "Why did you let her climb that dangerous cliff?"

"I wasn't with her—"

The younger stallion snorted.

"Why not?" the older, the dark blue, interrupted. "These slopes are steep."

"And forbidden to any but king's Companions," his comrade added.

The pied mare blinked. No such proscription had been announced. She backed another step as the pair continued to advance. She could barely make them out now for the snow and the gathering dark. Heads together, the two began conferring in low voices, never taking their eyes off Tek.

"If she wasn't with her, she *should* have been. Sa was an old mare."

"It's a crime not to protect the king's dam."

"Crime?" Tek's jaw dropped. What new laws were these? The two stallions ignored her.

"Aye, but if she's lying?" the spattered younger one asked. "What if she *was* with the mare?"

"What are you saying?" Tek demanded sharply. The snowy wind moaned. The air was grey and dark.

"Everyone knows you're a wych's child," the midnight blue said. "Your dam was born beyond the Vale."

"Korr banished her for magicking."

"My mother lives in the southeast hills by her own choice," Tek exclaimed. "She was never banished!"

"She enchanted Jan the prince when he was no more than a weanling," the younger stallion insisted.

"To protect him from wyvern sorcery," Tek snapped, outraged. Her mother, the Red Mare, had ever used her mysterious arts for the good of the herd.

"You're no better than your wych mother," the older stallion growled. "You seduced our good prince from the path of Alma."

"Liar!" Tek burst out, astonished, stung. How dared the king's lackey spit such filth at her?

"Traitor," the other stallion continued. "You ran away when the prince was assailed by gryphons, leaving him to his death."

"Untrue!" shouted Tek, half choked with wrath.

Her words echoed off the cliff. The king's Companions tossed their heads, champing. The two of them continued toward her across the slippery, rocky ground. Tek could do little but retreat upslope. The narrowed eyes of the spotted Companion glinted at her from their mask.

"Ringbreaker—you ran. Everyone knows it! It's common knowledge."

" 'Common knowledge' to those who were not there!" She wanted to fly at him and skewer him. She wanted to trample him underhoof.

"You befriended our king's dam," cut in the other, older unicorn, "that you might share her cave and eat her forage when your own sire cast you out. Her kind heart was her own undoing."

"What do you mean?" cried Tek.

The other bared his teeth. "That you lured Sa here, to dangerous cliffs, on the pretext of finding forage. That you were with her at her death and failed to inform the king."

"Perhaps you caused her death," the younger guard pressed.

"Never!" gasped Tek. "I had only just come upon—"

They gave her no time to finish.

"A cunning tale. The mare is cold. She's been dead hours."

"I wasn't with her!"

"The king will decide."

"Come with us," his younger companion said. "Come willing, or we'll compel you."

Panic gripped Tek. If she went with these two now, she realized, she was as good as dead. They had the king's ear, and their groundless accusations would carry far more weight with him than any truth. Then the king might do whatever he wished. Banish her, even attack her. Who was to stop him now? Under the watchful eye of the king's wolves, the whole herd would stand silent, cowed.

The two stallions stood waiting. The spotted one's eyes gleamed, gloating. Tek wondered what forage he expected in exchange for giving her life to the king. The dark blue stallion motioned impatiently with his head.

"Come," he told her. "It grows dark, and the sooner this is dealt with, the better."

"The sooner you will feed, you mean," grated Tek.

A cold rage such as she had never known seized her, displacing fear: it would not be simply her own life lost, she realized in a rush, but that unborn within her as well.

"You lying wolves!" she cried. Through the gathering darkness, the rising wind and snow, they were little more than blurs to her. "Those of you who still have your wits, yet willingly follow him are worse than Korr! I carry the late prince's get in my womb. Therefore harm me at your peril!"

Eyes wide, both stallions studied her midsection uncertainly.

"Her belly's swollen," the older blue murmured.

His companion tossed his head as if to dodge a meddlesome fly. "Great with hunger—just as ours," he snorted. "All the mares that conceived this fall past have miscarried, the weather's been so foul and the forage so slight—*her* doing. Wych," he snarled. Then, louder, "Wych!"

He started forward, but the older blue nipped his shoulder to stay him. "List! What if what she says is true, that she carries the late prince's heir? That would make *her* more fitting regent than Korr. . . ."

Hearing him, the pied mare started, appalled suddenly at how hunger and grief had dulled her wits. She had never once since discovering her pregnancy considered that as the late prince's mate and mother of his unborn heir, she herself held a better claim to the regency than Korr. The king therefore could only view her burgeoning belly as a threat, invalidating as it did his young daughter's claim and making him, as Lell's regent, into a usurper. For an instant, surprise blinded her.

To what lengths, Tek wondered starkly, would his chosen Companions go to protect both their leader's—and their own—unfounded authority? All at once, in wild alarm, she realized how rashly she had spoken. Her words, intended to keep these two at bay, were having the opposite effect. Their eyes—particularly those of the younger Companion—had grown even more hostile, and though she was a trained warrior, young and strong, one of the finest, she knew that, big-bellied now and half-starved, she had not the slimmest hope of matching two such strapping opponents. The pair glanced at one another.

"She lies. She's a wych," spat the younger, his spots shifting and shuddering as his skin twitched with cold. "If she carries a foal, it can't be that of our late prince! Yet she'll claim so to the herd—if we let her. She'll sway them with her lies and turn them against the king."

The other appeared dubious, but also alarmed. Despite the dimming light and thickening snow, Tek spotted the thin rim of white circling his eye.

"What are you saying?" he whispered.

The younger Companion set his teeth. "That we settle the matter without troubling the king. She's clearly guilty of the grey mare's murder. And she abandoned the late prince to his death by gryphons—that's as good as murder."

His eyes upon the pied mare narrowed. He dropped his voice yet lower still.

"We'll say she resisted, tried to flee when we made to stay her."

Fury filled Tek. She felt reckless, bold.

"Would you kill me?" she spat, coming forward. She snorted, teeth set, anger throttling her. "Alone on this hillside without witnesses to thwart or even question you? Who would be murderers then?"

The older blue fell back a pace. The spotted Companion champed impatiently, ignoring her.

"Nonsense! None would dare dispute us. We're the king's chosen Companions, empowered to act in his name."

"Then the worst you may do me is banishment," growled Tek. "You have heard that sentence from the mouth of Korr himself!"

Halted now, the older Companion shifted from hoof to hoof, tail switching one flank, clearly in a quandary. His eyes flicked from his fellow to Tek. Angrily, the younger stallion champed him.

"Coward! Are you afraid of a mare?"

"A wych," he whispered. "A wych, you said."

"The prince's mate," cried Tek. "Mother of his heir."

"Are you not starving?" the spotted Companion demanded of his comrade. "Tell me how much forage we found today—scarcely a mouthful! Think of the feast we'll be shown if we do this for the king. . . ."

"Renegade! Lawbreaker," shouted Tek. "All the herd will know."

The older stallion sidled, still undecided.

His younger companion hissed, "Korr alone need know the truth of it. He'll thank us for serving his interests and sparing him need of dealing publicly with the seducer and betrayer of his son. Are you with me? Then hie!"

Nipping his companion hard on the neck, he lunged toward the pied mare, his horn lowered. With a cry, Tek reared to fend him off. She had the advantage of slightly higher ground but knew her belly would make her slow. With a deft twist of the head, she caught and deflected the black skewer aimed squarely at her breast. Hard blows from both forehooves dashed its owner away. He stumbled upon the slippery, icy rock, skidding downhill.

His comrade, the dark blue, still cavaled uncertainly. Tek gauged him with a glance and decided he would not charge. Below, the younger stallion regained his footing and was lumbering upslope toward her again. She lunged, head down, forcing him to dodge—clumsily, because of the slope. Their horns clashed and grated. She grazed him along the neck and leaned into the thrust. Blood spattered. Ferociously, Tek parried his stabs, jabbing and slicing.

How long can I sustain such a pace? she wondered wildly. *Summer last, sleek and well-fed, unburdened by pregnancy, I could have sparred all day and never lost my wind.*

Already her breaths came painfully short, steaming white clouds on the air. Her assailant grunted and heaved, hard-pressed to hold his footing on the steep hillside, unable to fight his way upslope past her. Twice more her forehooves drove him back. Abruptly, he backed off, eyes blazing. Tek dared not follow, afraid to put his comrade behind her lest, despite his earlier hesitation, he move to attack at last. Panting, the pied mare held her ground.

All at once, the spotted stallion charged again and tried to bull his way past her. Head ducked, shouldering at her, he strove to knock her off her feet. Tek lunged, her forelegs bent, knees pressed against his heavy shoulder. Hind legs locked, he leaned uphill, fighting to keep from overbalancing. Desperately, the pied mare braced her own hocks and shoved with all her might.

She felt him topple. With a scream, he crashed onto his side, rolling and tumbling away down the ice-slicked slope. He managed to right himself—yet still he plunged, limbs folded, unable to slow his hurtling descent. At last, at the distant treeline, he slammed to a halt. Tek watched, full of wrath still, gasping for breath. She hoped all his limbs were broken. She hoped he never rose.

A snort and movement to one side of her made her whirl. The other's comrade was coming forward. Hastily she scrambled back, readied herself for another clash—then realized he had no wish to engage her, only to peer over the steep slope's edge to where his fellow now lay, struggling weakly. The older stallion stared a long moment at the writhing form far below before returning his gaze to Tek, his eyes glassy.

"Wych," he whispered. "You truly are a wych! No mare in foal could overcome a stallion in full prime. . . ."

She stood panting hoarsely, desperate for breath. Had she allowed him even a moment to consider, he surely would have seen how close to spent she was. She doubted herself capable of another such frenzied effort as had allowed her to overcome her first, rashly foolish assailant.

"Would you be the next?" she demanded. The blue stallion flinched. Her voice seemed thunderous. "Make but one move to harm the life I carry, and I'll pitch you over the side as easily as I did your comrade."

A faint whinny came from far down the slope, weak and strangled with pain. The blue glanced toward his injured companion, then warily back at Tek. The snowfall had become smotheringly heavy, the wind rising even higher and more fierce. Was it dusk yet? The pied mare shook her head, dizzy with panting. The afternoon had grown so dark she could not tell the hour. The dark blue unicorn glared at her, then with a champ of helpless fury, turned and started picking his way cautiously down the steep, slippery hillside toward the younger stallion below.

"Flee while you may, wych," he spat at her. "I must see to my comrade. But be warned, the king will send my fellows to hunt you down."

Grey snow whipped between them in the dusky air, and for a moment Tek half expected him to change his mind, come charging back up the slope. She let no trace of fear show in her eye, making herself breathe slow and deep. The other's injured fellow whinnied again. Angrily, he turned from her and continued gingerly down. Weak with relief, Tek wheeled in the opposite direction and fled.

City of Fire
☽ 15 ☾

Tai-shan shook himself full awake with a start. The warm enclosure was very still. Shadows slanted steep around him. All the lamps had been doused hours ago. Since resolving the evening before to explore the two-foots' city of fire, he had little more than dozed the long, slow night through. He leaned to tug with his teeth at the peg fastening the gate of his stall, swung it open with a nudge.

He trotted down the aisle between empty stalls. The wide wooden closure of the shelter's egress stood ajar. A thin mewl of protest sang from its hinges as the dark unicorn shouldered through. The courtyard outside lay deserted in the predawn darkness. A near-full moon hung low in the sky, barely topping the timber wall.

Tai-shan galloped hard, hooves ringing hollow on the frozen cobbles. He sprang and cleared the wall, clipped one hind heel painfully on the rough upper edge. Too long he had been lazing, feeding over-well in the palace of the *chon*. Time to be done with that! Coming down on the other side of the wall, he shook himself, full of energy. His breath steamed, curling in the frosty air. The layer of fat beneath his pelt kept out the cold. The stone-paved path sloping away from him lay empty and snow-covered, ghostly white. He trotted toward a distant glimmer of firelight.

Through a small, square opening in the wall of one of the wooden dwellings lining the cobbled way, he glimpsed a firelit room. The heat of the place was fierce. Two-foots bustled about, their falseskins folded back to reveal forelimbs coated in a fine, white dust. The stoutest punched at a substance resembling pale mud while her assistants plopped pawfuls of the stuff onto dust-covered flats. They pressed berries and nuts into each gooey pat before thrusting the flats into small stone chambers that were full of fire.

A savor of honey, oil, and grain pervaded the air. Tai-shan watched, fascinated, as the soft blobs sighed and expanded, then dried, hardened, and began to turn brown. The dark unicorn's jaw dropped. What lay forming in the heated vaults were honey nutpods! As the two-foots retrieved the flats from the firechambers, Tai-shan shied away from the hole in the wall, his senses reeling. These two-foots created their own provender by means of fire! He would never have guessed such a thing to be possible.

Once more, he trotted down the cobbled path. Lamplight bled through a crack between wooden panels covering one of the square wall-openings in another shelter he passed. Halting, the dark unicorn nosed at the shutter, eased it back and peered cautiously through. A pair of two-foots knelt in the chamber within. The elder, a bearded male, kneaded a pale, doughy substance resembling the grain paste, but grey instead of white. It smelled like river silt.

Carefully, the elder male smoothed the silt into the shape of a hollow vessel. The dark unicorn had seen the two-foots' stone jars used to store unguent, oil, and drink—but what possible use, he wondered, could exist for a jar made of mud, too soft to hold even its own shape for long?

Beside the bearded male, his assistant, a smooth-cheeked half-grown, stood bundling himself into a thick falseskin. Carefully, his elder handed him the wet mud jar, and the half-grown ducked with it through an egress to the outside. Tai-shan let the wooden shutter swing softly shut. He trotted to the edge of the building and peered around.

The young half-grown stood in a small yard before a conical structure of stone. Heat rippled the air above. Another firechamber, the dark unicorn guessed. The young two-foot opened a port in the chamber's side, placed the soft vessel of mud within and slammed the port. More vessels stood alongside the chamber, Tai-shan noticed. Stamping his feet against the cold, the half-grown bent to catch up a pair, then turned and hastened back toward shelter. The jars clinked solidly against one another as he did so, the sound sharply musical.

Once again the dark unicorn's mind raced. Had these hard vessels already been in the chamber of fire? Had flame somehow transformed the yielding clay as it had the grain paste? Were the firechambers themselves—indeed, the very streets of the two-foots' city—made of stone at all, or of blocks of heat-hardened clay? Tai-shan shook his head, marveling at the vast and complicated city around him. Had fire been the tool to create it all?

The sky above him was lightening, the moon nearly down. Strange tracks in the snow beside him caught the dark unicorn's eye. One set was clearly that of a *da*, the other, that of a two-foot. But two deep, narrow ruts scored the snow alongside, one on either side of the paired tracks. Tai-shan cocked his head. Frowning, he studied the parallel grooves, unable to make out what could have made them.

Dawn came swiftly. The stars above paled and began to fade. The dark unicorn followed the strange tracks as they turned off the main thoroughfare onto a narrow, winding side-path. His ears pricked to the sound of foot-traffic somewhere nearby. Rounding a curve, he found himself in a great open space, crowded with stalls. Stacks of painted tile and heaps of sweet hay, bolts of brilliant falseskin and fat brown sacks of grain, rows of fire-clay vessels and strings of pungent, edible bulbs filled the air with richly varied scents. Tai-shan's nostrils flared. Before him, two-foots milled, the odd tracks he had been following obliterated beneath their trampling heels.

Intent upon their own tasks, the two-foots spared scarcely a glance for the dark unicorn. Wandering speechless between the stalls, he beheld a two-foot male, flushed and sweating over a red-hot rod of skystuff. With a heavy implement, the two-foot pounded the rod, reshaping it into a flattened skewer. The dark unicorn beheld other wonders, all engendered by fire: fresh herbs withered and preserved by parching on heated stones, brittle honeycomb softened and fashioned into burning tapers, muddied falseskins stirred clean in steaming cauldrons, and stinking, bubbling vats in which pale hanks of seed fibers steeped to vivid shades of vermilion, golden, bronze-green, and midnight blue.

The sun broke over the hills. More and more two-foots crowded into the square, surveying the contents of the stalls and conversing with their overseers. Goods and little disks of silvery skystuff changed hands. An oddly familiar scent reached the dark unicorn. Smoky and sweet, it clung to his nostrils. Turning, hunting it, he nearly stumbled over a very old two-foot who crouched upon a patterned falseskin spread upon the paving stones. Baskets of spicewood shavings and dried flower petals surrounded her, and figurines of blackened skystuff.

Tai-shan recognized their form: the body of a two-foot with the incongruous, flatbrowed head of a *da*. Fragrant smoke rose from the red-rimmed nostrils. A crescent moon blazoned the breast of each figure, most of which stood fiercely poised, brandishing in one forepaw a long, flattened skewer and in the other a tuft-ended vine. Tai-shan noticed, however, that a few of the figures were different. The skewer had become a horn upon the *da* head's brow, the vine a unicorn's tail sprouting from the base of the two-foot torso's back. The crescent moon-shape appeared not upon the chests of these different figurines, but upon their brows.

Selecting a curl of spicewood from one of the baskets, the elderly two-foot cupped it in one forepaw and struck a sliver of skystuff against a stone. Sparks flew up, bright as fireflies. The dark unicorn stared, incredulous, as the spicewood curl began to burn, sending up a fragrant, smoky plume. The two-foot unfastened a hinge in the belly of the unicorn-headed figure before her and thrust the crackling curl inside. Smoke rose through the figure's nostrils.

Tai-shan stood dumbstruck, staring. The two-foots could *make* fire! For all his hosts' mastery of the sorcerous stuff, it had never once occurred to him that they held the secret of its creation. Fire was the greatest mystery his people knew: it glanced through storm-tossed heavens; its substance formed the sacred sun and stars. Generations of unicorns lived and died without ever glimpsing an earthly flame. Yet these two-foots could summon such at will. Tai-shan stood trembling—for it was a power he knew his kind could never share. Lacking nimble forepaws, no hoofed creature such as himself could even hope to manipulate skystuff and flint into striking a spark. No unicorn could ever kindle fire.

"Dai'chon!" The exclamation brought Tai-shan back to the wintry square. The two-foot firesmith had caught sight of him. Her eyes widened. She started up. "Dai'chon!"

"Emwe," Tai-shan replied haltingly, pronouncing the difficult inflections with the greatest care. He bowed courteously. "Emwe ki Tai-shan."

Greetings from Moonbrow—with Ryhenna's help, he had deciphered enough of the two-foots' tongue to attempt a simple phrase. Fervently, he hoped he had spoken clearly. A rush of triumph overtook him as he saw comprehension light the other's eyes. Dropping her flint and the sliver of skystuff, she sank to her knees, pressing her forehead to the patterned falseskin. Tai-shan frowned, puzzled by her response. Muffled sounds came from the elderly two-foot, like moans.

"Pella! Pell'!" *Look, behold.* He heard gasps all around him suddenly, shouts of dismay and cries of what sounded at first to be his name. Yet when he pricked his ears, he discovered that many of the two-foots were calling out "Dai'chon" instead of "Tai-shan."

That baffled him. He had no idea still what the word could mean.

"Emwe!" he cried out boldly as two-foots began to cluster around him. "Tai-shan nau shopucha!" *Moonbrow greets you.* To his consternation, many fell back at the sound of his voice and, like the old female, crumpled to the ground. Were they so surprised to hear him speak?

Others, by contrast, pressed forward eagerly, forelimbs extended as to caress him. The dark unicorn sidled.

"Tash," he cried out quickly. "Homat!" *No, stop.*

Mercifully, they seemed to understand. Others were sinking to their knees now. An onlooker tossed one of the tiny disks of silvery skystuff at him. It clattered onto the cobbles near his hooves. Tai-shan danced away, half shying in surprise. More disks of skystuff followed, along with bits of spicewood, dried flower petals, berries, and nuts.

"Homat!" the dark unicorn cried again: *stop.* "Apnor!" *Enough.*

Instantly, the shower of offerings ceased. The dark unicorn cavaled. Before him, two-foots melted back, allowing him passage. Almost all had fallen to their knees by this time. The rest stood gaping. Tai-shan bowed his long neck to them all and hurried on. None followed. Relieved, Tai-shan slipped through the crowd. The possibility of admirers swarming after him, pelting him with gifts, made his skin twitch.

Dodging around a stall, he nearly collided with a *da* standing before a massive wooden bin heaped with tubers. They smelled musty of starch and earth. A webbing of vines lashed the *da* to the bin, which creaked and swayed atop a pair of great wooden disks caked with muddy snow. The dark unicorn stared. Dragging such a strange contraption, Tai-shan wondered, could this *da*—or another similarly burdened—have cut the odd ruts which had first led him to the square?

"Dai'chon!" the *da* exclaimed, falling back with a start. "Great lord, ye walk among us. So it *is* true. At last. At last!"

Dull brown like other *daya*, this *da* looked much thinner and shabbier than the bluebloods he had met in the palace of the *chon*. Odd marks crisscrossed the deeply swayed back, and one skinny flank bore a crescent-shaped scar. The *da*'s posture, formerly weary and slumped, changed to joyous cavaling as the scrawny neck bowed reverently.

"Nay, friend," the dark unicorn answered. "You mistake me. I am called Tai-shan."

Still bowed, the other exclaimed, "Ah, lord, by whatever name ye choose, your faithful know you at a glance."

As Tai-shan shook his head, the *daïcha*'s adornment rattled loosely about his face. The *da* before him wore a similar device, the dark unicorn noted, one fashioned of brown strips of hide, not links of burnished skystuff.

"I am a stranger to this place," Tai-shan told the other. "Tell me, what is this great burden you drag?"

The other whickered. "Truth, it is nothing, lord. I haul it gladly, in your name."

"What is it that you haul?" Tai-shan asked, scarcely following the other's reply.

The *da* shrugged humbly. "Whatever my keepers put in the cart: firewood, grain sacks, jars of oil. Bolts of fabric. Foodstuff. Dung."

"Why is that?" the dark unicorn persisted. The point of such labor escaped him.

"Our keepers have need of such goods," the other told him. "We *daya* cart for them."

Tai-shan frowned, eyeing the chafed spots on the other's raw bones where the vines had rubbed. The cart looked heavy. Amid the myriad clashing odors of goods and two-foots all about, he caught scent of the *da* before him at last, a warm, musty aroma close to that of unicorns. Yet though clearly older than half-grown and not past prime, the flat-brow had the air of neither stallion nor mare: genderless as a beardless newborn or the very, very old.

"Of course, my lord," the other was murmuring, "the burdens of gelded commoners need not concern you, dwelling so far above us as ye do, First Stallion to your own sacred brood mares in the stable of the *chon*. . . ."

Tai-shan's frown deepened. Many of the other's phrases were new to him.

"Gelded?" he asked. The word had an ugly ring.

The flatbrow's head cocked, as though the explanation were self-evident. "Fillies and foals are born in equal numbers, my lord, as ye know—but only the finest colts become breeding stallions." He sighed. "As for the rest, we are made geldings."

Once more the dark unicorn shook his head, still not following. "These . . . these geldings," he said. "You get no young?"

The other glanced sadly away. "Nay. We lose all interest in the mares after the priests cut us."

Tai-shan fell back a step, staring. "Cut you?" he stammered. "Cut you?"

The one before him nodded. "Aye, underneath. Back between the legs. Then they mark us upon the flank with fire. Thus we are gelded and given the brand. Then our servitude begins."

The dark unicorn snorted, gagging. His nostrils filled with the imagined screams of mutilated foals. His senses reeled. Could such a shameful thing be true?

"But why?" he demanded hoarsely. "Your claim makes no sense—why maim innocent colts?"

The gelding *da* stared back at him, plainly alarmed and baffled by the dark unicorn's response. "Such is the geldings' lot, my lord, just as mares are for brood and stallions for stud—by your own decree! It is the will of Dai'chon."

Appalled, Tai-shan backed away from the gelded *da*. What was this infernal *dai'chon* with which *daya* and two-foots alike seemed to have associated him? No, he would not believe a word the other said—it went against his every impression of the gentle *daïcha* and her folk. The flatbrow's words could be no other than a cruel jest, a haunt's tale to play upon a stranger's ignorance—and yet before him loomed the heavily loaded cart, the crescent scar upon the stranger's flank, that odd, blank odor of genderlessness.

Shouts from behind distracted his attention. The dark unicorn whirled. The crowd of two-foots he had fled only moments before had followed after all. Tai-shan sprang away into the hustling, jostling press. He wanted only to find his way out of the crowded square and be gone from this place. He had gotten no more than a dozen paces before eager followers closed around him from all sides, most falling to their knees as before.

"Tai-shan!" some of them called out, and others echoed, "Dai'chon!"

The two words, so similar in sound, slurred and blended together. The dark unicorn ramped and sidled. Surrounded by kneeling two-foots, Tai-shan could find no opening through which to flee. All at once, screams and shouts of alarm arose from the back of the throng. Violet-plumed two-foots shouldered through the crowd, shoving their kneeling fellows roughly aside with long, sharp-tipped staves.

Scrambling to their feet, many fled, but others only fell back a few paces, staring sullenly, as the purple-plumes cleared a path from the edge of the square. Beyond, a broad thoroughfare climbed toward the *chon*'s palace, visible on the hillcrest above. Down this avenue, a glittering raft approached, mounted on poles and borne upon the shoulders of eight brawny two-foots. Atop the platform sat the *chon*, resplendent in falseskins of purple and gold. He glared at the crowd.

A heavy cart stood stalled directly in his path. Laden with blocks of fire-baked clay, it canted to one side, one of its wooden disks caught between two paving stones. The *chon* gestured impatiently, and purple-plumes wielding flails sprang forward, striking both at the pair of *daya* hitched to the cart and at their two-foot escort as well. The crowd cried out in protest. Many surged forward, but purple-plumes with staves held them back. Eyes rolling, the gelded *daya* strained mightily, but were unable to heave the trapped cart free.

"Homat! Homat!" *Stop*, Tai-shan cried—but his words were lost in the hubbub of the crowd. Leaping past the armed purple-plumes, he lent his own strength to that of the frightened *daya* as, shouldering the cart from behind, he felt it lurch free and roll ponderously out of the *chon*'s path. The crowd surged and began to cheer.

"Tai-shan! Dai'chon!"

At a sharp order from the *chon*, the purple-plumes with flails turned them on the crowd. Others, still clearing the *chon*'s path, shoved and struck their fellows with such violence that some at the front of the press were knocked to the ground. The dark unicorn fell back in consternation as the purple-plumes created sufficient space for the *chon*'s conveyance to be set upon the ground.

"Asolet!" roared the purple-plumes. "Asolet!" *Silence*.

The crowd quieted as the *chon* rose and stepped from the raft. Brow furrowed, forelimbs folded across his chest, he stared at Tai-shan. The dark unicorn sensed the other wished to approach, for he shifted from foot to foot, his bearded chin thrust forward, mouth set. Murmuring, the crowd watched. Tai-shan bowed his neck to the two-foot ruler.

"Forgive me, *chon* of the two-foots," he began in his own tongue. His store of words from his hosts' odd, clicking language was still far too slender for him to attempt it now. "I see my absence from the palace has troubled you. . . ."

Still the other hesitated, eyeing him warily and without comprehension—indeed almost, the dark unicorn thought uneasily, as though he had not spoken at all. The two-foot ruler approached him cautiously. He made loud clucking sounds. His manner seemed both determined and afraid.

"Bim," he growled, slowly and clearly, as though addressing a wordless nursling or a half-wit. "Bim, Tai-shan!"

Frowning, Tai-shan held his ground. What was the other saying to him? Though the two-foot made no move to touch the dark unicorn, clearly he wanted Tai-shan to do something. *Come*, perhaps? Return to the palace, most likely. The young stallion took a few steps in that direction. Both the *chon* and his purple-plumes holding back the shifting crowd sighed in obvious relief.

"I beg you to pardon the commotion my presence here has caused," Tai-shan offered. "I had no notion. . . ."

The *chon* ignored him, already climbing back onto his conveyance. The brawny bearers crouched to lift it, when shouts halted them. Tai-shan turned to see several purple-plumes striding from the crowd into the open space before the *chon*. One dragged an elderly female roughly by one forelimb. Another two carried a heavy bundle between them. This they tossed with a clash onto the cobbles. Figurines of blackened skystuff spilled from the patterned falseskin. The dark unicorn recognized the old firemaker suddenly, along with her wares.

One of the purple-plumes knelt before the *chon*, speaking urgently. The ruler's frown deepened as his eyes turned briefly to Tai-shan before coming to rest on the tangled heap of figurines. He barked an order, and a kneeling two-foot snatched one of the figures from the pile, held it up before his ruler's gaze. This was one such as the dark unicorn had seen in the past: a hornless *da*'s head atop a two-foot's frame, skewer and frayed vine grasped in the forepaws, crescent moonshape upon the breast.

Next, the kneeling purple-plume lifted one of the newer kind, the sort of figurine Tai-shan had not seen before today, with its unicorn's head and tail, moon blaze upon the brow. The *chon*'s eyes widened. He snatched the new figurine from the kneeling purple-plumes and stared first at it, then at Tai-shan. With a cough of rage, the *chon* hurled the unicorn-headed figure onto the cobbles. Shoving his kneeling minion aside, he pulled other, similar figures from the heap. These, too, after a brief inspection, he cast down in disgust.

Murmurs ran through the crowd. The *chon* growled another order, and the elderly female was dragged before him. Uttering horrified cries, she collapsed at his feet, hiding her face with her forepaws. Brandishing one of the unicorn-headed figures, the *chon* stood over her, shouting. Tai-shan stared in astonishment, unable to follow the other's tirade.

Onlookers shifted, rumbling, trying to push past the purple-plumes' pointed staves as the *chon* grasped the old female's falseskin and dragged her upright. She wailed and cowered. Impatiently, he shook her, as though demanding some reply. At her timid shriek, he flung her to the pavement once more. Outrage flared in the dark unicorn's breast. Did these two-foots bear no respect for their elders? Was their leader allowed to abuse his people so?

"Tash! Apnor!" *No, enough*, he cried. "Homat!" *Stop*.

But the *chon* did not so much as turn his head. Once more, Tai-shan knew, the tumult of the milling, agitated throng had drowned out his voice. Desperately, he clattered across the cobbles to stand between the angry *chon* and the cowering firesmith. Another cheer rose from the crowd.

"Desist, I beg you," the dark unicorn exclaimed. "How has this old one offended you?"

Eyes wide, the two-foot ruler fell back before Tai-shan—and the dark unicorn realized he had spoken in his own tongue, not the *chon*'s. Clearly, the other could not understand his words. Behind Tai-shan, the aged female wailed and wrung her forepaws. Gently, the dark unicorn bent to touch the old firesmith, hoping to reassure her—but with a shriek, she shrank away, lurched to her feet and, ducking under a purple-plume's staff, disappeared into the crowd. More cheering. The astonished look upon the face of the *chon* changed rapidly to one of fury. His purple-plumes leaned against the surging, cheering throng, which had begun to chant alternately "Tai-shan!" and "Dai'chon!"

The *chon* roared orders, and purple-plumes dashed forward to surround the dark unicorn, their pointed staves braced and ready. Tai-shan wheeled to stare at them as shrieks of alarm and angry shouts rose from the crowd.

"Tash! 'Omat!" the dark unicorn shouted at the *chon* through the deafening noise. "Call off your minions. I mean you no harm. . . ."

Tai-shan's skin twitched as something brushed his near flank. A similar sensation slithered about his throat. Vines! At the *chon*'s command, the purple-plumes were casting vines to ensnare him. With a whinny of disbelief, the dark unicorn reared. He kicked desperately at the two-foot holding the vine that encircled his hind heel. The kick knocked the other to the ground. The vine slackened. Tai-shan danced, and the cruel pressure against his pastern eased.

All at once, his head was jerked violently around. Three purple-plumes gripped the free end of the vine about his neck, using their combined weight to anchor him while another pair flung a second vine about his throat. It tightened suddenly, throttling him. Choking, unable to breathe, the dark unicorn lunged at the three purple-plumes nearest him. Two dropped their vine and managed to dodge, but the third, slower than his fellows, suffered a slash across the ribs. With a yell, he sprinted away, clutching his bleeding side.

Tai-shan shook his head vigorously, trying to slacken the remaining vine. He needed air! The purple-plumed pair held on, hauling on the vine to keep it taut. The dark unicorn ducked and lunged at them. They dodged. Others darted near and tossed another noose. Tai-shan reared, flailing, to keep them back. His limbs were growing numb. Coming down on all fours again, he staggered.

The crowd heaved, thundering wildly. The dark unicorn saw, but could not hear, the *chon* bellowing orders to his minions. One of the purple-plumes strode toward Tai-shan with forelimb cocked, his sharp-tipped staff held level with his ear. Shouts and shrill cries from the crowd all around. The dark unicorn realized dimly that the *chon*'s advancing minion meant to hurl the pointed staff at him. Black spots wandered across his vision. Weakly, he shied as the purple-plume's forelimb tensed.

A shout from across the square halted the two-foot in his tracks.

Whirling, he lowered his staff. The *chon* and the others also turned. The crowd began to stamp and cheer. Tai-shan spun unsteadily to behold the *daïcha* hastening down the cleared path, flanked by her own, smaller company of green-plumes. Though they bore no staves, slung from the middle of each dangled a flattened skewer.

For a sickening moment, the dark unicorn thought the two armed groups would clash—but then the *daïcha* signaled her own followers to a halt while she hastened on alone, her expression one of outrage and fear. Straining for breath, Tai-shan stumbled toward her drunkenly. The throng was ranting, screaming now, the *chon* continued to roar. The dark unicorn felt his limbs buckle, his knees strike the paving stones as the *daïcha* wrenched the still-taut vine from the purple-plumes' grasp.

As from a great distance, Tai-shan heard her frantic cries, felt her nimble digits clawing at the vines cutting into his throat. He tried to speak, but could get no air. The world had grown very still and dark. All around him, the frenzied noise of the crowd diminished to a whisper. "Dai'chon! Tai-shan!" were the last sounds he heard.

Swift-Running

☽ 16 ☾

Dusk had fallen by the time she reached the Vale. The deep snow and heavy cloud-cover, which had seemed so dark by day, now faintly glowed in a shadowy half-light that was brighter than true night: enough to find her way by, barely. Wind and snow continued to blow. Heaving, half-frozen, Tek stumbled into her father's cave, nearly trampling a grey roan filly lounging just within the narrow entryway. The healer himself lay at the back of the crowded little cave, surrounded by his other acolytes, half a dozen fillies and foals well past weaning but too young yet to be called half-grown. The young ones looked up in surprise as the black-and-white stallion broke off the lay he had been reciting. Tek recognized it from even such a brief snatch: "The Mare of the World."

"Daughter," he exclaimed. "Is someone ill? Wind outside will be a blizzard soon."

The pied mare shook her head. The sudden warmth of the grotto's small, close space unbalanced her. She swayed where she stood.

"Sa is dead," she panted. "Fell . . . on the slopes. I found her. Two of the king's Companions say I murdered her."

Teki pitched to his hooves. His acolytes scattered. The pied mare sidled in agitation.

"They know I am in foal."

The healer's eyes widened. "Hist," he said over his shoulder to one of the fillies, "keep watch and let me know at once if you see king's Companions or any other."

Tek's eyes sought his, searching his face as he came forward to stand breast to breast with her. His nearness warmed and steadied her.

"Now tell me, daughter," he continued, "did any see you come into the cave?"

The pied mare shook her head.

"Good. Snowdrift will soon cover your tracks."

Champing, the healer ducked his head, deep in thought. Expressions curious and alert, five of his acolytes stood huddled to one side: three reds and two blues, the grey once more posted at the entryway.

"Mark you," he instructed them all. "What now befalls must remain our secret. Breathe no word of it, not to your sires and dams, not to anyone. We never saw Tek this night. She did not come here. You understand?"

Solemnly, the acolytes nodded. Standing so near him, Tek noted all at once how small the healer was. More slight than most unicorns, Teki's value to the herd had always lain in his knowledge of herbcraft and lore rather than prowess in battle. What the pied mare had not fully realized before now was that she stood taller at the shoulder than he. Being longer both of rib and shank, her robust, lank-limbed frame was of altogether a different sort than his.

How odd, she mused, her thoughts careening wildly. Unicorn colts almost always resembled their sires more than their dams, not only in the color of their coats, but in size and build as well. Yet, though pied like the healer, her colors did not precisely match his, being rose and black, not white and black. And though they had always gotten on famously from the day her dam had left her in the healer's care, their temperaments, too, were dissimilar: Tek's passionate and bold, Teki's contemplative. Indeed, it struck her now that were a stranger to view them at this moment, side to side, surely that one would never guess them to be scion and sire.

Strange, she mulled. *I never noticed this before.*

"You must flee, daughter," Teki was saying, glancing up. "Nowhere in the Vale is safe for you now. And this is the first place the king's wolves will come sniffing when they find Sa's grotto empty."

The pied mare felt her skin grow cold. Teki called a name, and the grey filly at the entryway pricked her ears.

"Go at once to the cave of Leerah and Tas. Fetch their son here as quick as may be. But mark you!" he called as the filly wheeled. "Do not say why I need him. Be certain Leerah and Tas know nothing of Tek's presence here. Though Dagg is our ally, his sire and dam remain loyal to the king. Do you heed?"

Hastily, the filly nodded and dashed off. A blue foal stepped to take her place at the entryway. Gravely, the healer shook his head.

"Flee?" Tek pressed him. "Father, where am I to go? The king's wolves will hunt me down even on the far side of the Vale. If I hide on the shelterless outer slopes, I will freeze. The Pan Woods beyond are full of vicious, hungry goatlings, and the Great Grass Plain too distant to even hope for. . . ."

Her breath ran out, her agitation rising. The Vale was her home, the children-of-the-moon her people. She could never live content in the solitude beyond the Vale as her mother did—beyond the reach of the Ring of Law as the Plainsdwellers did. If she fled now, she would be declared a renegade and barred forever from return. Jan's heir could never inherit.

"Come, daughter." The healer turned and herded his acolyte away from the rear of the cave. "Eat of this herb. It will fortify you against exertion and the cold."

Tek stared at the little clump of withered leaves drying on the low ledge bordering the grotto's wall, each three-lobed leaf nipped to a spiky point. The musky, bitter scent wrinkled her nose. Her skin grew taut, for she recognized the grey-green clump: an herb so perilous that even her father—for all his healer's skill—had always eschewed it. Though it temporarily masked hunger and numbed one to cold, its aftereffects were ravenousness and utter exhaustion.

Sometimes those who ate of it fell into such deep slumber they could not be roused. Others, tasting repeatedly of the herb, grew stark-eyed and wild, spooked by every bird and leaf, their ribs standing out like the bones of dream-haunts. Soon, even if they wished to renounce the herb, an irresistible craving compelled them to seek it out and devour it again and yet again. Eyeing the shriveled leaves, the pied mare shuddered.

"Would you poison both me and my unborn?" she whispered.

"List, daughter," the healer returned. "No more than two mouthfuls, and only that small sup because we are desperate."

He snorted unhappily, and the chill in Tek's breast eased to realize that he regarded her sampling the herb with as little relish as did she.

"Your dam, Jah-lila, brought these sprigs to me," he continued softly, "summer last while you were courting at the Sea. She would not tell me what purpose for them she planned, only that I should know their use when the hour befell. I suspect now that her seer's gift must have foretold your need to her."

His tone grew urgent.

"Great risk attends, to yourself as well as to your young—but even greater risk if you refuse it and remain here, or if you flee and have not strength enough to outrun your pursuers. I pray you, make haste and eat!"

Full of trepidation, Tek reached to nibble first one mouthful, then another of the shriveled wort, desperate enough to undertake even this to protect her unborn. The herb's bitter taste made her mouth draw, puckering her lips tight against her teeth. Her eyes watered. Her nose stung. Teki stood watching her. Presently she felt a tingling invade her limbs, moving in waves along her ribs. Her shoulders twitched. The grotto felt uncomfortably warm. She cavaled, lashing her tail, a sensation like summer flies swarming her flanks. What lay in her womb seemed to quicken and shift. The grey filly stumbled through the cave's entryway, and Tek jumped like a deer. Dagg followed, shaking heavy snow from his winter shag. He stared at the pied mare in surprise.

"What's amiss?" he asked. "Tek, I see white rimming your eyes."

Tek fidgeted, her heart racing. The herb kept it hammering against her ribs. She champed, trying to wash the unsavory taste from her mouth, but her tongue had turned to sand, her lips too numb to let her speak. Her throat closed up as she tried to swallow. Dagg's puzzled look changed to one of alarm.

"What's happened?" he demanded.

Quickly, Teki sketched the events of the previous hour. Dagg's eyes grew wide.

"How fierce is the storm?" the healer asked.

Dagg shook his head. "A true blizzard. The drifts will be deep before the night is done."

"Good." At a startled look from the dappled warrior, the healer added, "Tracks will be obscured and pursuit much hampered. You must be off, daughter, for I see the herb has begun its work."

Tek shook herself, sweating, unable to stand still. The heat in the cave oppressed her. She longed to be out in the battering wind, to cool herself by rolling in snow. The unborn young within her stirred and struggled. Her eyes felt glassy. Her mind seemed unable to hold any single thought for more than an instant before it buzzed away like a gnat.

"What ails her?" said Dagg.

Both he and her father seemed to be moving with maddening slowness. Still standing within the cave, she felt as though she were hurtling at a headlong run. Teki gave a reluctant sigh.

"I have given her swift-running."

"Ghostleaf!" Dagg exclaimed, giving the herb its more common name. The dappled warrior stared at Tek in dismay. The pied mare glared back at him. She felt skittish and resentful without real cause. The eyes of Teki and his acolytes distracted her. She wanted only to run, to lose herself in endless, heatless flight.

"But where is she to go?" asked Dagg.

"To her dam, Jah-lila," Teki replied. "Tek must seek out the Red

Mare in the southeast hills beyond the Vale. Not even I know exactly where she dwells. . . ."

Tek scarcely listened, scarcely able. Already, in her mind, she bounded effortlessly through wind and drifts in the semidarkness of snow-lit night toward the far southeast tip of the Vale and the wild hills beyond. She had spent all her nursling days there at the Red Mare's side until, weaned, she had followed Jah-lila on the long trek to the Vale. Why had her mother done it? Why cast her away into the healer's care?

Reared within the great valley's sheltering slopes, Tek had never returned to the southeast hills since that distant time: herd-members were forbidden to traverse the Vale's boundaries on their own. Now she eyed the cave's egress impatiently, chafing to be gone, eager to once more run breakneck over the southeastern hills, free of kings and Rings of Law.

"Then how will she ever find the Red Mare?" Dagg was asking the healer.

Teki shook his head, his movements troubled, stiff. His acolytes milled nervously. Again, the healer sighed. "She may not. In such storm, anything may befall." Dagg stood speechless. The pied stallion glanced at Tek. "But she must try. You, Dagg, I would ask to accompany her— though I will give you none of the running herb. I doubt you will be able to pace her far, but I beg you to stay with her as long as you can."

"Of course!" snorted Dagg, wheeling. "Come, Tek. We must lose no time."

The healer leaned to nuzzle the young mare he had reared long years with brusque, awkward affection. She fidgeted away: the herb made her chary of any touch. Sadly, Teki gazed after her with ghostly, black-encircled eyes.

"All rests now upon the shoulders of the goddess."

"Hist!" cried the foal standing lookout. "I see figures, but whether the king's or others, I cannot tell."

"Off with you!" Teki exclaimed. "At once! If the Companion who attacked Tek survives, I will doubtless be summoned to attend him. Out into the storm quickly, daughter—Dagg. Go now, and you will not be seen."

Tek bolted through the cave's entryway into the cool, stormy night. Snow lay deep; the wind gusted fiercely—yet neither seemed to impede her. She sprang up the Vale's icy hillside easily. Glimpsed only dimly through the falling snow, figures converged on Teki's cave below. Dagg had already fallen behind, panting with the exertion of the climb. How slow he was! Tek bit back a wild laugh. Giddy pleasure at her own miraculous strength surged through her. Let the king's wolves think the pied wych vanished without trace in a storm of her own conjuring.

Suddenly she was among the trees, the lower slopes of the valley lost from view. Her breath steamed; her heart sprinted. She wondered how long before the effect of the herb wore off. Morning, Teki had said. Was she to run all night, then, without tiring? Without feeling the cold? The prospect thrilled her. So must mighty Alma have felt prancing across heaven, tossing her mane and digging immortal hooves into the turf of the world, casting up mountains with every step.

Tek sped on through the snowy scrub and trees, skimming the hill-crest rimming the Vale, heading south and east. She heard Dagg crashing through the underbrush in back of her, plowing gamely through knee-deep snow to catch her up. She wondered how long she must endure his floundering escort, poor mortal, as he battled wind and slope, snow and the cold to exhaust himself in her wake.

I am the Mare of the World, she thought: *she who ran dusk to dawn, besting the sun in his race for horizon's edge, to become the moon that rules the night and wards all unicorns. . . .*

Laughing, the pied mare galloped on through the frigid, stormy night, lost in godlike velocity, dream motion, preternatural speed.

Nightmare

☽ 17 ☾

The dark unicorn twitched, shuddered in sleep, the dream unfolding before him as real as real. He beheld a pied mare bounding through wind-whipped snow, her pace hurtling, effortless. Breath spurted from her nostrils in jets of white cloud. A dappled companion plunged determinedly along her snow-filled tracks, his own gait staggering with exhaustion, ribs heaving in ragged gasps. He ran with a limp in one foreleg, as though the pain of some old injury, long healed, now recurred to plague him. He fell farther behind the pied mare at every step.

The dreaming stallion shifted, striving to move closer to the scene before him. He recognized this pair somehow, despite the distance and the dark, though whence he knew them or who they were—friends, foes—he could not say. Above them, a narrow gorge loomed, threading a path through the high, icy slopes of the great valley through which they fled. A howling pursued them, though whether of wolves or the gale the dreamer failed to discern.

Abruptly, the dappled runner lost his footing, struggled to rise, and went down again. He vanished from view in the whirling, blinding snow. Wild-eyed, the pied mare climbed on, sparing not a backward glance. The slender canyon before her was already so deep in drifts as to be nearly impassable: another hour would see it snowed under till spring. The pied mare pulled farther ahead now, where the dreaming stallion could not follow. Stormy darkness swallowed her as she disappeared into the pass.

🐚

Tai-shan woke with a start. He lay deep in soft hay. The wooden walls of his stall within the *chon*'s stable surrounded him. Firelight flickered, casting shadows. It must be evening, he realized groggily. His throat throbbed, burning. The muscles felt bruised. He swallowed painfully, remembering the strangling vines with which the purple-plumed minions of the *chon* had trapped him that morning in the square. Gasping, he struggled to roll to his knees, get his legs under him.

"Tai-shan!"

The *daïcha*'s soft voice brought him full awake. She knelt beside him in the hay, caressing his cheek and neck.

"Tash. Homat. Bithitet nau." *No. Stop. Calm yourself.* He was amazed by how much of what she said he was now able to understand. "Himay." *Stay still.*

She murmured on, other phrases he could not follow. With a square of white falseskin dipped in herb-scented liquid, she gently sponged the raw, oozing chafe marks encircling his neck. As the cool, pungent scent filled his nostrils, the dark unicorn felt the tightness in his throat begin to ease. Gratefully, he breathed deep. Still crooning, the lady dabbed the crusting scabs with tingling oil.

Wild longing filled Tai-shan to be able to respond to the *daïcha*'s words in kind. Just that morning, he recalled, before the arrival of the *chon*, he had managed to make himself understood to the aged firesmith and other two-foots in the square. But as he drew breath now to speak, his injured throat contracted hard. His neck felt wrenched. Half-stifled, he tossed his head, striving for air. A bitter disappointment filled him. The painful swelling would have to subside, he realized, before he could once more hope to replicate the *daïcha*'s gargled, clicking tongue.

Champing in frustration, he rose. The *daïcha* withdrew, slipping through the stall's gate to rejoin her green-garbed assistants who clustered there. Restlessly, Tai-shan circled the little enclosure, his breathing labored. *Why?* The outraged question burned in him, unaskable. Why had the *chon* ordered his minions to attack when he, Tai-shan, plainly had offered their leader no harm, only sought to stand between him and the frail old female?

A stirring among the *daïcha*'s retinue made the dark unicorn turn. A male two-foot approached, bearing a steaming wooden hollow. His falseskin bore a decoration of purple and gold. With a brief bow to the *daïcha* and her followers, the purple-badged male began emptying the hollow's contents into the stall's feeding trough.

Moisture came to Tai-shan's mouth as the savor of steamed grain, chopped fodder, and dark, sweet canesap reached him. His belly rumbled painfully. It had been nearly a day since he had eaten last. The *daïcha* stood looking on with a puzzled frown. All at once, her nose wrinkled. Hastily, she caught the forelimb of the purple-badged male.

With one forepaw, she brought a dollop of the mash to her lips. Her eyes widened. She spoke sharply to the purple-clad two-foot.

He bowed his head respectfully but stood firm, refusing to be ordered off. Tai-shan heard the word *chon* pass his lips several times. The dark unicorn eyed the provender in his feeding trough suspiciously. Obviously it came from the two-foot ruler—yet no *chon*'s minion had ever brought his feed before. Did the *chon* intend this gift as a peace offering? If so, what could the *daïcha*'s objection be—that the ruler had not come himself to deliver it?

At last, the lady broke off. Angrily, she wrested the wooden hollow from the male and emptied the remainder of its contents into the trough, then thrust the hollow back into the other's grasp before striding purposefully off, gesturing her companions to remain behind when they made to follow. Tai-shan heard her utter the word *chon* herself a number of times before she reached the shelter's egress—as though she meant to seek him out that very moment.

Gingerly, the dark unicorn sampled the fare before him, grinding the water-swelled grain between his teeth, crushing the tart, chewy berries and crunching the nuts. They had used honey, he decided, as well as cane. The mash was delicious. Eagerly, he bent his head to the trough. Swallowing proved painful still, but he was almost too hungry to care. The barest hint of bitterness undershadowed the sweet.

"My lord Moonbrow!"

The unexpected voice of Ryhenna snapped the dark unicorn's head around. A green-garbed two-foot proceeded down the aisle between stalls, leading the coppery mare on a tether.

"Ryhenna," the dark unicorn whistled in surprise, able to manage his own, fluting language well enough, though his throat still felt raw. Never before had he seen her—or any *da*—within this shelter, though obviously it had housed more than a few before his arrival. "What brings you here?"

The young mare tossed her head, crowding up against the gate of the stall. Before her, the two-foots fell back.

"I and my sisters are to be housed with thee now, by the *daïcha*'s command," she told him. Behind her, Tai-shan glimpsed her fellows being led into adjacent stalls. "O my lord," Ryhenna murmured, eyeing the bruises and abrasions about his neck, "tell me what hath befallen thee. The rumors have been wild! Such rushing about among our keepers this morn—stablehands beaten, stalls searched. When thou camest not among us in the yard at noon, I knew not what to think."

The dark unicorn shook his head and sighed. He had had no inkling what an uproar his absence from the palace would cause.

"I ventured into the city . . . ," he began.

"Into the city?" Ryhenna exclaimed. "Alone, before dawn? But the gate is barred, my lord."

Tai-shan cocked his head. "I went over the wall, of course. How else?"

Was such not the way *daya* departed the palace grounds when no two-foots were about to unbar the gate? The coppery mare simply stared at him.

"Over the wall?" she whispered. "My lord, thou'rt divine—no mortal *da* might ever hope to clear a wall so high! And to wander alone through the City of Fire. . . ." Her tone mingled admiration and dismay. "How fearless thou art! What wonders thou must have beheld—"

Frowning, the dark unicorn snorted. "Ryhenna," he asked her, "have *none* of the *daya* here ever ventured forth into the city?"

"Never, lord!" the coppery mare exclaimed. "The city is forbidden to the sacred *daya*."

Tai-shan gazed at her in astonishment. Beyond her, more of the mares with whom he sported daily in the yard were being led into stalls. They glanced at him shyly, gladly, but said nothing. The *daïcha*'s followers, even the one holding Ryhenna's tether, stood off to one side now, murmuring quietly among themselves and watching him. The dark unicorn shook himself. The fire-warmed enclosure felt suddenly very close and still.

"Aye, I saw many wonders in the city," he told the coppery mare. The tightness in his throat was growing painful once more. "I met a peculiar kind of *da*, Ryhenna. One that called itself a gelding. It told me two-foots maimed it as a foal. I saw a firescar upon its flank and welts from blows across its back. I saw other *daya* cursed and beaten, encumbered to heavy loads by webbings of vine."

The coppery mare nodded, shrugged. "To haul and carry for our keepers—such is the gelded commoners' lot. Ours is a lighter service: sacred mares for brood and stallions for stud."

The dark unicorn blinked. "Brood?" he echoed. "Stud?" He had heard the odd words somewhere before.

Ryhenna nickered. "The taking of mates and getting of young," she laughed, "according to our keepers' pleasure."

Tai-shan stared at her, open-mouthed. "Are you saying the two-foots choose your mates for you?"

"Of course," the coppery mare replied. "Did we choose one another? Nay, for what mare hath wisdom enough to choose her stud, nor any stallion his mares? Our keepers choose."

"How do they dare?" the dark unicorn burst out hoarsely. "What gives them the right?"

Ryhenna drew back from him, surprised. "They have every right, my lord," she replied. "Our lives belong to them. The keepers *own* us, Moonbrow."

The dark unicorn shook his head, unable to believe his ears. His limbs had begun to feel strangely heavy and numb. An unpleasant warmth stole through him. The cloying taste of sweetmeal clung sticky to his mouth. He shook himself. The coppery mare fidgeted.

"What are you saying?" Tai-shan demanded of her. "Are the *daya* prisoners here? Do the two-foots hold you against your will?"

"Our will?" Ryhenna exclaimed. "Lord, we have no will. All *daya* must bow to the will of Dai'chon."

"What is this . . . Dai'chon?" the dark unicorn began. He felt flushed suddenly, and very thirsty. The coppery mare seemed not to have heard him. Her voice grew distant.

"Dai'chon directeth us to serve our masters. Thus hath it been for time out of mind. We know no life other than this."

Tai-shan turned toward the hollow of water that always hung filled and fresh beside the feeding trough in one corner of his stall. The scent of sweetmeal lingered in his nostrils, sickeningly sweet. The water in the hollow looked cool and inviting. Moving toward it, he stumbled. His own clumsiness amazed him.

"The keepers provide for our every need," Ryhenna was saying. "They feed, house, and protect us. . . ."

"Choose your mates for you," the dark unicorn muttered. "Trap you with walls, bind you to carts. Beat, brand, and geld you . . ."

"Nay! Not *us*, Moonbrow," Ryhenna protested. "Only commoners suffer so, and what do they matter? We sacred *daya* never haul or carry."

With an effort, Tai-shan turned to study her. She seemed perfectly in earnest, her amber eyes upon him clear and troubled. Behind her, her fellows milled whickering in their stalls, ears pricked. The dark unicorn staggered. The *daïcha*'s followers eyed him keenly.

"How then, Ryhenna, if you do no work," Tai-shan mumbled, his lips sluggish, tongue unaccountably thick, "do the sacred *daya* . . . serve their masters?" He had trouble completing the thought. "What do you . . . give the two-foots, in return for your keep?"

He grew dizzy. His vision blurred. Ryhenna seemed no more than a chestnut shadow. His legs collapsed under him, settling him heavily to the soft straw bedding of his stall. The depth of his abrupt fatigue astonished him. The bittersweet mash lay in his belly, weighty as a stone. The *daïcha*'s followers murmured gloomily. Soft, puzzled cries came from Ryhenna's sisters. The coppery mare leaned toward him over the gate of his stall.

"We give up our lives for our keepers, Moonbrow." Her words were the last he heard before darkness muffled all. "We die for them."

Magicker

☽ 18 ☾

Morning was half gone, bitterly cold, the sky above grey overcast. Not a breath of wind stirred. Not a feather of snow fell. The blizzard had blown itself out hours ago. Tek floundered through chest-high drifts. Wild, rolling hills beyond the Vale surrounded her. She had lost track of Dagg sometime the night before. Her limbs, no longer weightless, swung woodenly. The unborn in her belly lay motionless, still as the frozen air.

Keep going! she told herself, half rearing to shoulder through the next great swell of snow.

She must find her mother, Jah-lila, the Red Mare, soon, or she was lost. Wolves had been trailing her since daybreak. At first, the ghostleaf singing in her blood, she had easily outrun them. Now, the herb long spent, she staggered, hooves dense as meteorstone, near the end of her strength. Her pursuers' cries floated eerily above the rolling meadow: eager yips interspersed with long, trailing notes. They were nearer now, much nearer than before. Trees marked a canyon many paces ahead of her. The pied mare struggled toward it.

Casting over one shoulder, Tek glimpsed the first of the pack. A second and then a third burst from the scrub into open meadow behind. They bounded through the deep snow, joyous harks rising into wails. Frantically, Tek hurled herself against the drifts, fighting toward the forested cliffside, but her strength was gone. She stumbled, dragged herself up, collapsed again. She realized she would never reach the trees.

A figure burst from the canyon ahead of her: a deep cherry color as brilliant as mallow-flower against the trackless snow. Too large for a wolf, the red figure plunged toward her, black mane flying, traversing the meadow with a will. Dazed, staring, the pied mare strayed to a stop.

"Keep coming!" the other cried.

Tek plowed on toward the tree-sheltered canyon. The other unicorn charged past her, straight at the wolves. Tek swung around, astonished.

"Go!" the other ordered.

The pied mare plunged on. The wolves behind were howling, in full cry now. Did the Red Mare mean to meet them all? Pausing as she reached the shelter of the cliffs, Tek saw her dam pitch to a halt beside a pile of drifted snow. Twin branches rose from it, stark and leafless against the whiteness of the field. Half a dozen similar mounds clustered nearby. Tek herself had wandered through the midst of them only moments before. Furiously, the Red Mare began to dig.

Tek stared, baffled. The coming wolves bayed. Every few moments, the Red Mare lifted her gaze to gauge the distance between herself and the closing pack. All at once, Tek realized that what the other excavated was not a snowdrift at all but the carcass of a great deer, twin antlers rising like leafless branches from the snow. Others of his kind lay all around—a whole herd stranded, frozen. They could not have lain winterkilled long. The last flurries of the dying blizzard had barely covered them.

The Red Mare scraped and pawed at the snowbound stag. The wolves were very near. Jah-lila leapt away just as the leading three reached her. Snapping and snarling, two fell upon the carcass. Only the foremost bothered to pursue the dark red unicorn even a few strides. Jah-lila pivoted and lunged, horn aimed. The wolf dodged, turning, loped back to the carcass as the last of her packmates arrived. They fell ravenously upon it, tearing the half-frozen flesh to pieces, which they fought over.

Thus would they have done to me, given the chance, the pied mare thought, heart beating like a bird inside her ribs. *Or the king's wolves.*

Her dam plunged toward her across the meadow. Drawing even with Tek at the canyon's mouth, she tossed her head, motioning the younger mare to follow.

"Ho, daughter! Well met," she cried. "Come. My grotto lies not far above. Sooth, what a canny filly I bore, to recall the way home after all these years!"

Limbs tottering, Tek fell in behind Jah-lila, already climbing the steep hillside through the dark and barren trees.

❦

The cave was deliciously warm. The narrow entryway turned back upon itself, kept out the wind and snow. Sunlight, too, faltered—but the grotto was not dark, for the upper walls and ceiling of the interior were covered with tier upon tier of fan-shaped lichens and mushrooms. They glowed in luminous blues and reds, soft yellows, pale mauves—here and there a faint, brassy green. They emitted warmth as well as light. Shivering, Tek stared. She had forgotten the ghostlight of her mother's grotto.

A huge heap of fragrant, dried grass occupied half the cave. The pied mare blinked, dumbstruck. How had such a vast store found its way here? The most any unicorn might carry was a mouthful at a time. Surely the grotto contained enough fodder for a dozen unicorns to feast the winter through without ever needing to venture outside for forage. How had Jah-lila acquired it all?

Exhausted, Tek shook her head. More than a day and a night had passed since she had last known food or sleep. She heard Jah-lila stamping in the entryway, shaking the snow from her pelt. A moment later, the Red Mare rounded the turn. In smaller alcoves adjoining the grotto's grass-filled main chamber other provender lay: bark and berries, spruce boughs, roots, seedpods, and nuts. Their tang made the pied mare's knotted stomach burn.

"Lie down, my child," her dam bade her.

Tek's legs buckled like shafts of old, dead wood. Her cold-locked muscles ached in the musty warmth of the cave. She had forgotten to shake off in the entryway, felt the snow on her beginning to melt. Lying down beside her, her dam passed a warm, rough tongue over Tek's shaggy coat, stroking her dry.

The pied mare closed her eyes. Her mother had changed little in the years since Tek had last seen her—coat still a brilliant mallow red such as no other unicorn possessed. Much about her mother set her apart, the healer's daughter mused. Jah-lila's black mane stood upright along her neck instead of falling silky to one side. Long, silken strands sprouted the whole length of her tail, not just at the end. Hers were a beardless chin, untasseled ears, and fetlocks unfringed with feathery down.

But most of all, Jah-lila's black hooves set her apart. They were oddly round: solid and uncloven, not like Tek's own split hooves—not like the divided hooves of other unicorns. It was those hooves Tek remembered best from her fillyhood. She had never realized how unique they were until she had followed her mother to the Vale and first seen the cloven heels and bearded chins, tasseled ears, fly-whisk tails, and fringed fetlocks of others of the herd.

Tek stirred, uneasy. Why had the Red Mare done so? Why abandoned her weanling to Teki's care and returned to the solitude beyond the Vale? Tek tensed, remembering how as a tiny filly little older than

Lell, she had overheard the vicious whispers of her Vale-dwelling fellows, hissing that Jah-lila was not and could never be a *true* unicorn, since she had not been born among the herd, but in some far, unimaginable place. Red Mare. Renegade. Magicker. Tek's eyes came open with a start.

"Eat," Jah-lila instructed, nudging a heap of sweet-smelling fodder toward her.

Eagerly, Tek champed at the withered grass. Unpalatably dry at first, it soon grew sweet in her mouth, more savory than rueberries, sweeter even than beeswax and honey. The trickling of water nearby reminded her that her mother's grotto housed a spring. Thirst overpowered her. With an effort, she rose and followed the sound. The tiny stream at the back of the cave tasted warm compared to the frigid snow outside. In summer, she knew, it would have tasted cool. She drank deep.

"Rest, child," her mother murmured as Tek returned. "You need rest badly now—but do not sleep. You must not sleep until certain herbs for which I have sent arrive."

Sent? Tek scarcely knew what her mother could mean. Had the Red Mare acolytes, as her father Teki now had? All the Vale—herself included—had long believed Jah-lila lived alone, without companions.

"I," Tek started, stopped. Despite herself, her eyelids drooped. Sleep dragged at her. Her womb felt lifeless, her thoughts a blur. "Jan is dead," she managed. "Gryphons killed him. We pledged to one another at courting time. . . ."

"Peace," her mother soothed. "My dreams have already told me. I know that you are in foal to Jan and that the king runs mad for grief. I know that Sa, who sheltered you, is dead."

Tek stared at her, eyes wide suddenly. In truth, her dam's powers must be greater than she had guessed. The magicker smiled.

"Rest easy. Last night's blizzard has sealed the Vale. None of Korr's minions may pursue you now till spring."

Tek felt a surge of relief. A great heaviness had settled on her. Fatigue washed over her in waves. She wanted only to sleep. A sudden smarting brought her out of her doze with a jolt. After a moment's confusion, she realized the Red Mare had nipped her.

"Forgive me," the other said firmly, "but I am in deadly earnest. You must not sleep until the healing herbs arrive. Meanwhile, my dreams have brought me other news which may serve to keep you awake: they tell me that at the grey mare's funeral this day, Korr means to declare himself the Firebringer."

Tek turned to stare at her. "Firebringer?" she exclaimed, her grogginess fading for the moment. "Alma's chosen prophet?"

"Aye, Korr will usurp his son in that office as well—though the marks upon his brow and heel be only smears of white lime."

Despair swept over Tek. What did any of it matter anymore?

"Let him call himself the Firebringer if he will," she murmured dully. "Who shall contest him—Jan? Dead. Sa, dead. Dagg, lost. I and my unborn, forever banished."

"Jan is not dead," Jah-lila corrected gently. "Your mate lives. This, too, have I seen in dreams."

Tek started, stared, heart suddenly pounding.

"What are you saying?" she demanded. "Jan . . . Jan alive?"

The Red Mare nodded. "Alive, but captive—many leagues from here. A race of two-footed sorcerers holds him in the city where I was born a hornless *da* so many years ago."

My daughter stared at me as we lay side to side in the luminous warmth of my ghostlit grotto. The tiers of mushrooms and lichens lining the walls glimmered faintly, casting a moving pattern of light across her rose and black markings. Wild hope and confusion and disbelief played similarly across her face. Her fatigue seemed, for the moment, held at bay by the prospect of learning of her lost mate. I had hoped as much.

"Da?" my daughter murmured, frowning. "What is a da?"

"The daya *resemble unicorns," I told her carefully, measuring her, "though they live much briefer lives. Most are dead by the time a unicorn beareth her second foal."*

Memory of that long-past time and far-off place recalled once more to me the da *dialect of my youth, and I slipped into it now as easily as blinking. Tek lay watching me intently, hungrily.*

"Daya have no horns, nor beards, nor tufted tassels upon their ears," I continued, "nor fringe of fine feathery hair around their fetlocks. They are mostly dull brown in color. Their manes stand upright along their necks. Their tails are full and silky, their hooves great solid, single toes."

Still Tek gazed at me. "They sound like what legends in the Vale call renegades," she began, "those creatures unicorns fear to become if we break the Ring of Law, becoming outcasts. . . ."

She choked to a halt. I nodded.

"Aye, daughter, they sound very much like me, for though I now bear a horn upon my brow, I've no beard as thou hast, no eartip tassels, no fetlock feathers. My mane standeth along my neck, and my hooves are uncloven. Nonetheless, I am a unicorn of sorts. And I was a unicorn

when I bore thee, though not when thou wert begot. Before, when I lived in that sorcerous City, I was a hornless da *like all the rest, held captive by the keepers of fire."*

"Firekeepers?" my daughter answered. "What are they?"

"The enemies of all daya: *two-footed creatures something like the pans in shape—" I saw Tek shudder at the mention of the goatlings inhabiting the vast woodlands not far from my cave. I hastened to add, "—though in sooth, pans are as different from firekeepers as* daya *are from unicorns. These keepers hold my former people prisoner, slaves to their treacherous god. . . ."*

As succinctly as I could, I described to her the wretched lives of the city's daya.

"I was able to escape that accursed place," I told her. "Drinking of the unicorns' sacred moonspring far to the north, I was transformed. Had I never found my way to that miraculous well and drunk thereof, I should be a da *still."*

Tek's face was drawn now with shock, her inner thoughts as plain to me as though she had shouted them: her dam, not born a unicorn? Her mother, transformed from some degenerate, hornless freak by the sacred wellspring that was the birthright of all unicorns—a birthright I did not share? She shuddered now to realize that the strange, garbled rumors she had heard all her life must hold some truth after all: Jahlila the outcast, the "renegade"—not a true unicorn at all!

"Who knows of this?" my daughter whispered.

"Teki knoweth," I told her. "To Jan once I gave the barest sketch, on his initiation day. Now thou, too, knowest. And Korr."

"Korr?" The pied mare looked up, astonished. I nodded.

"It was he who showed me to the moon's sacred wellspring—though such was against all custom and his people's Law."

Tek's eyes grew rounder yet. Clearly she had never thought the black king capable of even contemplating any breach to the Ring of Law.

"After fleeing the City," I said, "I escaped inland. Upon the Plains, I encountered Korr, the young not-yet-prince of the unicorns, a single-horned stallion far more magnificent than any da. *His father, Sa's late mate, Khraa, was prince then, and Khraa's mother the queen. Korr, then newly initiated, used to travel alone outside the Vale, on fire to see what lay beyond, burning to contemplate the world.*

"Though not strictly forbidden then as they are now, such expeditions were no less frowned upon in his day—but who dared gainsay the prince's son, destined to become prince himself in time? When he stum-

bled across me during one such youthful sojourn, I was yet a hornless
da, *wild and desperate from my harrowing flight.*

"He mistook me for a renegade at first: one of his own people who
had either deserted or been banished from the herd. Of course, thou
and a few others well know that such outcasts do not lose their horns,
thus ceasing to be unicorns—but Korr believed and still believes the
old legends, as many do. Thus he shunned me, but at length I convinced
him I was no renegade, that I came from neither his Vale nor the Plain,
but from a far and different place.

"Learning of my flight from that imprisonment, he took pity on me
at last, telling me of his own proud, free race and urging me to join
them. He guided me to the sacred well, where I drank. And when, afterwards, I felt a horn sprouting upon my brow, I trusted that accompanying the princeling Korr upon his return to the Vale, I might find
refuge there.

"And yet my strangeness lingered, a strangeness which no new-
grown horn could dispel. Our travails in reaching the sacred well—in
summer, when poisonous wyverns roved everywhere—had been terrible.
Korr's guilt at transgressing an age-old custom began to weigh upon
him. He feared for his future as prince, I think, should it become known
that he had consorted with a once-hornless 'renegade,' betraying his
people's secrets to her.

"In the end, he abandoned me, forbidding me to follow or try to
find him. But I did follow, reaching his marvelous Vale. He pretended
not to know me then. I called Teki my mate, for propriety's sake, though
we have never sojourned together by the Summer Sea, nor joined ourselves one to another as you and Jan have done by the pledging of
eternal vows. Ours has been a partnership of colleagues and companions, not mates.

"Teki taught me his healer's art, the ways and history of the unicorns, and I shared with him as much of my own lore as I might:
starcraft mostly—he is no magicker. Briefly, I shared his grotto, but
quickly saw how greatly my nearness, even as the healer's supposed
mate, troubled Korr. Though the leaving of his strange, wild folk held
much pain for me, I quit the Vale with the reluctant blessing of my
'mate' and settled here, in the hills, to raise thee.

"How sorely was I tempted to keep thee selfishly at my side, for
though this life in the wilderness hath its rewards, it is lonely, Tek. In
the end, I could not wish such desolation upon thee. The hardest thing
I have ever done was to lead thee back to the Vale when thou wert
weaned. And until this autumn past, Korr hath always watched over
thee, from a distance, hath he not? Even favoring thee highly, for mem-

ory of me—and for his guilt's sake at abandoning me upon the Plain. My daughter, at least, hath lived welcome among unicorns, a joy I fear I may never share."

I fell still at last after my torrent of words, and my daughter lay in stunned silence, as though not knowing what to say. A long time passed as we lay there, face to face beneath the warm, shifting glimmer of lichenlight. At last, my daughter found her voice.

"If Teki who raised me is not my sire," she said simply, "then who?"

Her jewel-green eyes were watching me. Dared I tell her the truth? Dared I not? At last, I said: "A renegade—not a Plainsborn unicorn, but a true outcast, one who roved the Plain after quitting the Vale. A Ringbreaker, outside his people's Law."

Her gaze fell. I could not tell now what emotion lit her eye. Could she herself yet tell? Perhaps not. I dared to hope only that in the end, she would not hate me. I glanced impatiently toward the egress of the cave, anxious for the arrival of the restorative herbs my child and her unborn so desperately required. Luckily, she remained alert for the time being—no sign yet of her slipping into dangerous sleep. Nothing to do but wait. Returning my gaze to Tek, I found my daughter once more watching me.

"But what of Jan?" she whispered. "You said he lives—a prisoner in that sorcerous place, that city where you were born."

I nodded, relieved to have skirted so nimbly such dangerous ground. Blame my daughter's fatigue—and her overwhelming hunger for word of Jan above even her own history.

"Why did you not bring word?" Tek asked, her voice deathly quiet still. "Why did you not come to the Vale with word Jan was alive?"

I snorted. "And what good is my word in the Vale?"

"Korr has always respected your word!" the pied mare exclaimed.

"Feared it, rather, by my reck."

I saw my daughter's eyes widen. Clearly she had never considered that Korr might be afraid of anything.

I champed my teeth. "In his present state, I much doubt Korr would credit any news I uttered."

Tek fell silent a moment, mulling that. Her eyes flashed suddenly. "You might have come to me, at least," she said savagely, "told me of your suspicions my mate yet lived!"

I sighed. "I dared not. Korr had turned on thee so swiftly, so thoroughly, I feared my presence would only madden him further. And what better pretext to quarrel with thee—even do thee harm—than consorting *with an outcast, self-exiled, a magicker, dream-walker, foreigner: your own dam?"*

Tek fell silent again, considering.

"If my mate remains a prisoner," she said at length, "then no mat-ter the distance, with or without Korr's help, I must go to him, rescue him!"

Her eyes were on fire suddenly. Vehemently, I shook my head.

"Even were this the mildest of winters, daughter, thou couldst never hope to complete such a trek."

I sensed outrage welling in my daughter's breast. Her thoughts once more showed plain upon her face: was she not a warrior, as fleet as any, and with more stamina than most?

As gently as I could, I said, "Starved as thou art and exhausted by flight from the Vale, thou must needs spend the balance of thy time at rest, recovering thy strength if thou art ever to bring safely to term what lieth unborn within."

To my midwife's eye, her pregnancy was now so obviously precar-ious that the least misstep might precipitate a miscarriage. Relief flooded me to see her reluctantly admitting the prudence of my words: she must do nothing further to endanger her as-yet-unborn filly or foal. Clearly her unborn's peril was very great. Yet dismay remained on her features for only a moment. Abruptly, my pied child's expression hard-ened.

"You must go, then, if I cannot." Once more she looked me in the eye. "You know how to reach this city of fire and where within the settlement its sorcerers are holding Jan—"

"I'll not leave thee," I answered sharply, surprised at my own ve-hemence. My daughter's dire condition had unsettled me more than a little. "Come spring, Korr will send searchers. He cannot but suspect where thou hast fled."

Across from me, Tek shook her head stubbornly. Alarmed, I risked greater candor.

"Daughter, without the herbs I mean to give thee in the coming months, thou wilt surely miscarry—or die in travail. Either may still occur. I must attend thee. I dare not go." Gratefully, I watched her sober. "Be easy," I hastened to add. "All shall be well. It is within my power to aid thine unborn mightily, making up for time and nourishment lost."

Tek lay clearly in a quandary now, her thoughts evident. "What is to be done?" she exclaimed. "Jan must be freed and returned to us— before his mad father destroys us all."

"Jan is safe enough where he is for the present. He's no hope of

*surviving outside the City till spring thaw, in any case. I am already at
work to aid his escape. Once the grass is sprung, we must see which
way the wind blows—but enough of this, daughter!"*

*I stopped myself suddenly, pricking my ears to sounds from without
the cave. My pied companion's poor battered frame had begun to droop.
It seemed she could keep her eyes open no longer.*

*"We will talk more of Jan soon," I assured her. "We have all winter
to plan. Presently I will let thee sleep. But first, healing. Look: the herbs
for which I had sent have now arrived."*

❧

Lifting her sagging head and dragging open heavy eyes, Tek heard
movement in the grotto's entryway. All at once, an unmistakable odor
filled her nostrils: salty and goaty. The verges of the Pan Woods lay
not far off. Panicked, the pied mare was just gathering her limbs to
scramble up with a warning cry of "Pans! Pans!" when her dam snorted,
whickering.

"Peace, daughter. These goatlings are come at my request."

From around the curve which hid the entryway, two young pans
appeared, both females, huddled beneath shaggy drapes: one bearskin,
by the smell of it; the other, boar. Tek's nose rankled. She stared at the
loathsome, spindly creatures as both dropped their cloaks by the entrance. Catching sight of the pied mare, they grimaced, baring their
square little teeth—or was such the pan way of smile? The elder goatling grunted and twittered at Jah-lila, gesturing with hairless forelimbs
as she spoke. The Red Mare replied with similar twittering, incompre-
hensible to Tek.

"What," she gasped, "what do such creatures purpose here?"

"They dwell here," her mother calmly replied, slipping back into
the unicorn way of speech, "under my care." Smiling now, the Red
Mare glanced warmly at the young pans. "I found these starving at
wood's edge one day, years past. Their dam had been killed by a cat
and their people fled. I have sheltered and raised them, suckling them
like fillies. The elder already spoke enough of their odd, guttural speech
for me to follow. It is not so unlike that of the two-footed firekeepers.
And I have learned more in conversing with other goatlings in the
wood."

Tek shivered at the thought. Pensively, her mother sighed.

"But since many quirks of the face and forelimb also hold meaning—and most of these I can at best only approximate—I fear I still
speak Pan but poorly. It has been far easier for these two to learn Unicorn. They call me 'ama' now, which means 'mother' in their tongue.

They are my acolytes: herbalists and midwives. It is they who gathered our grotto's winter provisions. The taller is Sismoomnat, the younger Pitipak. They have been eager to meet you and gladly scoured their home woods this day for the rare and perishable herbs you must take before you sleep."

Eyeing the ugly, upright goatlings, Tek felt her skin tremor. Despite her dam's reassuring tone, the pied mare could scarcely restrain her urge to bolt. Only overwhelming fatigue kept her reclining as the pair of pans approached, laying before her a great clump of ferny, withered fronds. They crouched then, openly curious. The younger one, nearest to Jah-lila, laid one slender forepaw on the Red Mare's neck and stroked her companionably. Jah-lila nuzzled the young goatling easily as one might a filly. All at once, Tek felt her revulsion beginning to fade. She could scarcely catch her breath for wonder.

"Greet-ings, Tek, Jah-ama's daughter," the elder, Sismoomnat, pronounced carefully, her birdlike inflection strangely melodious. "Welcome to our home. We have brought you ama's herbs. Ama has told us you would find your way to us before the win-ter was out. We are so glad that you have come, and that at last we may behold you. Welcome, foster sister. Wel-come home."

Sweetmeal
☽ 19 ☾

Awakening, the dark unicorn felt sluggish, strangely fatigued, though he was aware he must have slept long and deep. His mouth felt gummy, dry. It was morning now. He remembered vaguely leaving the palace grounds and wandering the city. How long ago? He stirred, trying to gather his clumsy limbs. With great effort, he heaved himself up and stumbled to the water trough, drank—but his head did not clear. All he longed for was to drift. He sensed movement and turned—very slowly. Ryhenna stood in the stall opposite his, her look one of apprehension. Her sisters occupied other stalls.

"How dost thou fare, my lord?" she asked. "Thou didst sleep so late, I had begun to fear. . . ."

The dark unicorn blinked, tongue fumbling over the words. "Tired," he told her. "Very tired."

A hazy memory came to him of green-clad two-foots leading the mares into the warm enclosure. His head nodded, thoughts slipping away. Time passed. A sound at the end of the aisle roused him. The dark unicorn swung himself slowly around to see the *chon*'s purple-badged minion coming down the aisle, carrying a steaming wooden hollow. It bore the delicious fragrance of sweetmeal. Tai-shan moved forward eagerly as the two-foot emptied the steaming meal into his trough.

Followers of the *daïcha* accompanied the male two-foot, but the hollows they carried contained only dry grain, which they poured into the troughs of the other stalls. As Ryhenna and her sisters dipped their noses to the feed, it occurred to Tai-shan to wonder why the mares should receive fare different from his own. He struggled to speak, but

the same dulling sense of drowsiness he had suffered the previous evening was stealing over him again. He lay down heavily, numb.

Across from him, the coppery mare lifted her head from her trough.
A worried expression furrowed her brow as she gazed at the dark unicorn. Tai-shan's vision blurred. Sleep dragged at him. He would speak
with Ryhenna later, ask her about the feed, about what troubled her.
Soon. Just as soon as he had rested and his mind grew clear.

❦

Time drifted by. He could not say how long. Weeks perhaps. His
injured throat seemed to heal in moments. The dark unicorn was only
dimly aware of winter passing, waning. It would be spring again soon.
Ryhenna and her sisters remained stabled with him within the warm
enclosure, but Tai-shan never mustered energy enough to ask the coppery mare what plainly continued to disturb her. If only he were not so
sleepy all the time! Sweetmeal was all the two-foots fed him now.

The *daïcha* returned at intervals to gaze at him, talk to him, stroke
his neck. She seemed unbearably sad somehow. Messengers from the
chon often called her away. The *chon* himself never appeared, though
the ruler's purple-plumed minions stood constant watch outside the
warm enclosure's egress. They no longer allowed the lady to lead Tai-
shan to the yard for exercise along with the mares. The dark unicorn
raised no protest. His strange, all-pervasive lassitude made any effort
impossible.

But troubling dreams began to invade his sleep: a Vale shrouded
deep in drifted snow, winterkilled unicorns lying frozen, others starving.
He saw a night-dark stallion, stark-eyed and fanatical, haranguing the
cowed, exhausted herd, a crescent-shaped smear of white mud marking
his brow. Equally fervent companions surrounded him, their fellows
moving in a pack through the crowd: harassing and bullying, demanding
answers.

"Where is she, the pied wych? Did you help her to escape?"

About whom were they speaking? The dreaming unicorn could not
begin to guess. All he saw seemed familiar somehow—yet memory
slipped away from him the moment he woke.

Soon he no longer slept the nights through. Restless, unable to recall
what frightening images had tangled through his sleeping brain only
moments before, he often remained awake the balance of the night,
reluctant to return to the unremembered country of his dreams. Morn-
ings and afternoons, he dozed. Ryhenna, though clearly distressed,
seemed hesitant to disturb him. As spring approached, his reveries grew

more vivid. Often now he remembered snatches: before him in dreams, the moon-browed stallion reared.

"I am your Firebringer!" he shouted. "Come spring, we must find and slay the pied wych who seduced my son. Only thus may we gain Alma's blessing for our war against the gryphons!"

The decimated ranks of unicorns groaned. Half looked as though they would not survive till spring—much less make war. Appalled, the dreamer recoiled. If only these dying unicorns had possessed fire, he realized, they could at least have combatted the cold!

Though the fearful images still faded rapidly upon waking, their foreboding lingered. By night, Tai-shan grew increasingly restive, and soon became too restless to doze the day away. Gripped by a vague yet mounting anxiety, he paced his stall for hours, ignoring queries from Ryhenna, whose concern now clearly verged upon alarm. Then, very near the start of spring, a vision came to him: he saw the unicorns' mad ruler ramping before the starving herd.

"By Alma's divine will, I command you—speak! Who among you aided the wych?"

His bullies nipped and harried the silent, sullen crowd. The black unicorn stamped, snorting. Impatiently, he reared—and suddenly his torso began to flatten, shrink. His lower limbs rapidly thickened and changed. For an instant, he stood with the body of a two-foot, moon-blaze white upon the breast, his hornless unicorn's head glaring wildly, teeth bared, hot breath smoking in the cold. Then the head, too, abruptly altered and shrank, becoming the dark-bearded face of the *chon*.

The bullying pack had all sprouted violet plumes from their brows. In another moment, they, too, had transformed into two-foots. The unicorns before them grew bonier, coats colorless drab, manes thinned to bristles, horns broken and falling away—until they had assumed the shape of flatbrowed, beardless *daya,* flinching beneath the bite of the purple-plumes' flails. The dreamer tried to cry out, "Apnor, 'pnor!" *Enough, enough!* in the two-foots' tongue—but coils of vine were strangling his voice.

Without warning, two-foots and *daya* melted from view. The dreamer found himself high on a peak overlooking the Vale. A great storm brewed overhead, black thunderheads churning and roiling. Merciless strokes of lightning flashed like the hooves of an angry god. Before their fury, tiny figures fled—but whether unicorns or hornless *daya,* the dreaming stallion could not say.

The stormclouds swept on, topping the snow-bound crags bordering the Vale and gusting out over the wild southeast hills. Winter snows melted, clearing a frozen pass through the crags. Suddenly, it was spring. Still spilling torrential rains, the stormclouds battered the wilderness, loosing mudslides and flash floods.

Wolves coursed the hinterlands, catching hares, foxes, ptarmigan, deer—even hapless pans foraging the verges of their Woods. The dreamer twitched. The dream wolves shifted, turned into bony haunts hunting down some unseen quarry, crying out above the stormwind in long wailing harks that sounded more like the belling of hounds than the voices of unicorns:

"Where is she hiding? Where can she be? We must track her down at the king's command!"

Still the dreamer had no notion about whom they spoke. On a cliff-side above, watching as they pounded by, stood a roan *da* mare. The moon lay like a pool of silver at her feet. She bent to sip from it, and her color darkened, intensified to true cherry mallow. A black horn thrust like a skewer from her brow. Lifting her head, she faced the dreamer, gazing at him with her black-green eyes.

"Little did my former masters guess," she said, "that the fare whereby they sought to tame thee would only open thy dreams to my warnings at last. Behold."

The red mare vanished into the rain. Beside where she had stood, the perfect disk of the moon lay flat upon the ground. It tipped upright, balanced erect on its edge and became a mare. Mottled like the moon, her color deepened from ash and silver to black and rose. Heavy in foal, her sides hugely swollen, she trotted restlessly, her labor pains begun.

Below her, the circling haunts raised their muzzles, turned. Baying and whinnying, bones rattling like hail, they bounded across the meadow toward her. Alarmed, the dreamer thrashed, struggling to vault down from his mountain fastness and stand between the bloodthirsty haunts and this unknown mare. But walls of timber sprang up around him; vines suddenly ensnared him.

"Where is the midwife?" the dark unicorn shouted.

With a mighty effort, he burst the vines and vaulted the wall, clipping one hind pastern painfully against its rough upper edge. Plunging down the mountain's side, he found himself running with ghostlike slowness, floating almost, as though he were swimming. Then he realized he *was* swimming: stormrains had risen in a furious floodtide. An ocean now parted him from the pied moon mare.

"Too soon," she moaned, gasping, unmistakably in travail. "Before my time . . ."

"Summon the midwife!" he cried out again. The pied mare snorted hoarsely, in grave distress. The red one could have aided her—but was nowhere to be seen. Frantically, the dreamer struggled across the endless watery gulf. In the distance before him, the moon mare shuddered, collapsing to her knees. Bounding up the sheer cliffside, her skeletal pursuers closed around her.

"The time of the Mare of the World betides!" the dark unicorn thundered—and wrenched awake as one hoof struck the near wall of his wooden stall with a report like a thundercrack.

The warm enclosure around him was all dimness and shadow. Little white tongues of fire within the lampshells by the distant egress burned low, fizzing in the silent air. Tai-shan struggled to his feet, heart racing, the clear memory of his dream hurtling through him still. Who were the figures he had seen there? He knew them all somehow—though he could no more recall who and what they were to him than he could recount his own true name. Ryhenna, shaken from sleep, peered at him across the darkness from her own stall.

"Moonbrow!" she exclaimed. "My lord, what aileth thee?"

"I must get home!" he cried, staring about him.

He scarcely recognized his present surroundings, the vision still coursing through his mind. The dream of that faraway Vale and the unknown mare seemed so vivid, so real, it was the *chon*'s comfortable stable that felt unfamiliar—unnatural—to him now. Surely no unicorn was ever meant to be housed in such a place: fed, groomed, and tended by sorcerous two-foots; head compassed in silver; mind, will, and energy sapped by luxury.

Across from him, the coppery mare murmured, "Home? My lord, *this* is thy home!"

Tai-shan shook his head. The adornment slapped against his muzzle, jingling.

"It isn't," he answered. "My home lies far away from here. It is a great Vale, I think, nearly surrounded by woods. I must find it! My people are unicorns, not *daya*. I have stayed too long."

Ryhenna gasped. "Nay, my lord," she protested, "thou must remain! Thy presence among us is the will of Dai'chon."

The dark unicorn stopped short. That baffling word again. "Dai'chon," he muttered, cocking his head. "What is this Dai'chon of which you speak?"

Ryhenna gazed at him blankly a moment, uncomprehending, then gave a nervous nicker. "Dai'chon is the one true god, of course! Master of the celestial fire, all-knowing and all-powerful—it was he that made our keepers and gave them dominion over *daya* and all the world. Why didst thou reck the *chon* keepeth this vast stable? We bluebloods here are sacred to Dai'chon."

The dark unicorn stared at her. "The two-foots' god—'Dai'chon' is a *name?*"

Ryhenna nodded. The dark unicorn's mind buzzed. Until this moment, he had thought it merely another indecipherable word.

"Dai'chon . . . ," he mused, tasting the syllables on his tongue. Dai'chon had been the first word the *daïcha* had ever spoken to him. "It sounds very close to the name the *daïcha* gave me—Tai-shan." The dark unicorn shifted, suddenly remembering: "That morning in the square—half the crowd cried out 'Dai'chon!' to me instead of 'Tai-shan.' "

Again Ryhenna's nervous laugh. "Not by chance, my lord, for thou greatly resemblest the god. The *chon* is little pleased."

The dark unicorn wheeled. "Resemble—? What do you mean?"

Ryhenna tossed her head and snorted, surprised. "Hast thou not seen Dai'chon's image, my lord—as black of body as thou, but with limbs and torso of a keeper and the head of a *da*? He carrieth the crescent moon upon his breast, as thou dost upon thy brow, and thy tail is unlike the full, silky tails of *daya,* more like a whip or flail."

The dark unicorn felt his limbs go cold. He recalled the image before which the *daïcha* and her followers had bowed that first night upon the beach. He recalled similar figurines seized by the *chon*'s purple-plumes in the square as well as the unicorn-headed figurines that had so enraged the *chon*. The coppery mare spoke on.

"When the great streak of fire hurtled out of the sky on the first day of fall, the *daïcha* declared it a sign from Dai'chon and set out in search of the firegod's gift."

Memory welled up in the dark unicorn's mind of standing soaked and exhausted upon a silvery, windswept beach and seeing a red plume of fire plunge out of heaven.

"Weeks later," Ryhenna told him, "the *daïcha* returned with thee, calling thee Tai-shan. From the first, *daya* and keepers alike have whispered thou art the very image of Dai'chon: his steed, perhaps—or his messenger?"

The coppery mare watched him as she spoke, as though in hope of either confirmation or denial of her words.

"Many," she continued, "even dare to say thou art the god himself, openly calling thee 'Dai'chon' in defiance of the *chon*'s edict and bowing down before images of thee instead of those of the real Dai'chon. Perhaps it is the *daïcha*'s fault in calling thee a name so close to the god's—for now the people have confused the two, and the *chon* is furious." A moment later, as in afterthought, she added, "Furious, too, that thou hast delayed so long in taking up thy duties as First Stallion."

"What do you mean?" the dark unicorn asked again, baffled. He had lost her thread.

Ryhenna snorted, tossed her head.

"The First Stallion exists to get foals and fillies for the sacred stable," she exclaimed. "Yet I and my sisters frolicked daily with thee for weeks, and thou madest not the slightest advance."

Tai-shan shook himself, staring at the coppery mare. "You mean the *chon* intends you—you and your sisters—to be . . . my *mates?*"

Ryhenna stamped impatiently. "Of course. What else might I and my sisters be to thee? The *chon* is anxious for thee to sire more horned marvels such as thyself—not steal the people's worship from their god."

Tai-shan fell back a step, appalled.

"What are you talking about?" he demanded hotly. "Surely the *chon* knows—must guess—I have always meant to depart as soon as spring arrives, to seek my homeland and my people once more. I must leave this place!"

"No! The *chon* considereth thee no more than a strange sort of *da*," the coppery mare replied. "He will never let thee go."

"Ryhenna," the young stallion told her, "I am no *da* but a free unicorn. How may the *chon* hold me if I mean to be gone?"

"By the same means he holdeth all my race," the *da* mare answered softly. "With ropes and tethers, locked stalls and barred gates. With whips and bits and hobbles—and with tainted feed that taketh away even thy will to rebel."

Her eyes flicked to his empty feeding trough. Following her gaze, Tai-shan felt a sudden chill.

"Tainted?" he said slowly, stupidly. "Tainted feed?"

The coppery mare avoided his eyes, her voice a whisper. "The sweetmeal the *chon* ordered for thee is laced with dreamroot. A healing herb, it speedeth the mending of wounds and numbeth pain—yet it can also induce trance, making the rebellious docile to the firekeepers' will."

The realization reverberated inside his skull like a thunderclap. The black unicorn stood trembling, stunned. The stable around him seemed to grow darker. Wind moaned beyond the warm enclosure's draft-tight walls. He felt buffeted, cold.

"So many times," the *da* mare whispered. "So many times I longed to tell thee—yet feared to rebel against my captors and my god."

Violently, Tai-shan shook himself. "The *daïcha*," he gasped. "The *daïcha* would never . . ."

"The *daïcha* hath no choice in the matter! The *chon* is her master as well as ours." Ryhenna shook her head, speaking more forcefully now. "The dreamroot he ordered lest thou go abroad in the city again, inciting heretical adoration."

Despite his belly's insistent rumbling, the dark unicorn felt his gorge rise. He'd not touch another mouthful of that tainted meal! Tai-shan ramped and sidled, scarcely able to contain his agitation. His mind raced.

"I must find a way to flee this place!"

Ryhenna ignored his protests. "Nay. Escape is impossible. Put it from thy mind. Repent thy rebellion and accept the will of Dai'chon. If thou wilt not, my lord Moonbrow, then I fear for thee in sooth. Even now, it may be too late."

"Too late?" the dark unicorn murmured.

Ryhenna looked at him hard. "I fear Dai'chon's judgment upon thee, my lord! Surely to entice the people's heterodox worship in defiance of the *chon* cannot have been the purpose for which Dai'chon sent thee among us."

"I am no envoy of this Dai'chon," the dark unicorn protested. "The two-foots' confusion of me with their god is none of my doing!"

"Such mattereth nothing to Dai'chon," the coppery mare snapped. "One may hide one's inmost heart from one's fellows, Moonbrow, but mighty Dai'chon recketh all. Twice yearly he cometh to judge the sacred *daya*. None can ever hope to escape his judgment—not even thou! I have seen his vengeance. It is swift and terrible. Dost thou not understand thy peril? The equinox is coming!"

Tai-shan shook his head, not following. "The equinox?"

Ryhenna came forward, pressing against the gate of her stall, her voice urgent. "On that day, every spring and fall," she answered, "a great procession of townsfolk ascendeth at dawn from the sea to the palace gate. Passing within, they proceed to the white clifftops overlooking the sea. In the fall, the priests cut the young foals who are to become geldings and the First Stallion defendeth his harem against all comers. In spring, Dai'chon judgeth the herd and chooseth who must follow him. Those *daya* the priests then drive forth to the kingdom of Dai'chon. . . ."

"Drive forth?" Tai-shan interrupted. "You mean they are exiled, sent into the wilds beyond the city?"

"Not banished," Ryhenna hissed. "*Sacrificed*: herded over the cliffside into the sea!"

The coppery mare fidgeted, unable to stand still.

"A place in that select company is considered the greatest of honors, a glory outshining all. I think the *chon* would rejoice to see thee among that company—for without progeny to redeem thee in his eyes, thou art more trouble to him than thou art worth. Yet the people adore thee. Were Dai'chon to claim thee, however, the folk could raise no protest. It is an *honor* to die for Dai'chon."

The dark unicorn could only stand staring, amazed at her sudden fire. His belly growled again. He ignored it angrily. Ryhenna eyed him with wise, sad eyes.

"My lord Moonbrow, thou hast but one real hope of returning from the white cliffs alive: fulfill thy role as First Stallion. What other choice dost thou have? Even a life imprisoned is better than no life at all! Sire progeny upon thy brood mares. If thou wilt not, I fear Dai'chon will claim thee at equinox."

Tai-shan shook himself. His skin twitched. Fear beat against his heart. "You think this Dai'chon means to kill me?" he breathed.

His stablemate nodded.

"Our dams tell us as nurslings that unlike the common *daya,* those sacred to the god do not truly die—that though our bodies may fall, we bluebloods house within ourselves a spark of Dai'chon's fiery breath that mounteth the sky in triumph and gallopeth rejoicing to the pastures of Dai'chon."

Ryhenna whickered without a trace of humor.

"But last year I glimpsed his chosen rotting on the rocks below the cliffs, food for scavengers. Though I hide it from my sisters, surely Dai'chon must reck my faithless, doubting heart, for I wonder if we bluebloods do not die like other beasts, and have no souls."

For long moments, the dark unicorn could only gaze at the coppery mare. Then slowly he shook his head.

"I'll not lay myself before the mercy of this terrible god," he told her grimly. "Ryhenna, I mean to quit this place ere spring."

"Too late, Moonbrow," the coppery mare whispered. "It is already spring. The procession from the sea hath even now begun. This morn is the morn of equinox."

Only then did Tai-shan note the hour. The little tongues of white fire in the distant lampshells by the enclosure's egress burned pale and wan. Dawn had broken. He had never noticed the darkness greying, the shadows within the stable thinning. He heard Ryhenna's sisters stirring sleepily within their stalls. Ryhenna told him: "This day, Moonbrow, must thou face the judgment of Dai'chon."

Travail

☽ 20 ☾

Standing at the grotto's mouth, the pied mare gazed out over the rolling hills. White snow still blanketed the land—but the smell of spring was in the wind. The two young pans, Sismoomnat and Pitipak, had remained in attendance throughout the winter, making only brief forays at Jah-lila's behest to gather medicinal herbs on the verges of the Pan Woods, barely an hour's lope away. To Tek's delight, a layer of fat had at last begun to sheathe her ribs, and her winter coat had thickened luxuriously. Her dam urged her to eat as much as possible to provide her unborn with all the nourishment she could.

Yet heaving her enormous girth about, Tek wondered at the strange herbs collected by the pans. Surely they did far more than merely sharpen appetite: with spring barely arrived, her belly was already bigger than many mares' near or even past their time. Yet months remained before she was due. Progeny conceived at summer's end never arrived until spring was well underway—unless they came too soon. Tek suppressed a nervous shudder. Earlyborns almost invariably died, often taking the mare with them.

But Jah-lila continued to assure her all was well. Tek herself felt hale and rested, and her young seemed vigorous. Indeed, the pied mare almost suspected her unborn must have two sets of heels, so often did she feel the kicks. Her unborn must be growing crowded in the womb, she realized, eyeing her moon-round belly. Tek groaned. She did not know how much more her sides could be expected to swell. She could barely stagger about as it was.

Nevertheless, her most pressing fears sprang not from her pregnancy, but from the certainty that once the snows of winter melted, Korr would send his Companions through the pass in search of her. Surely he must guess where she had fled. Resolutely, the pied mare thrust such bootless thoughts away. Her mother, she knew, kept careful watch. Tek suspected some of Sismoomnat and Pitipak's foraging expeditions were as much to scout for signs of the king's wolves as to gather bark and herbs.

Whenever the pan sisters returned, Jah-lila questioned them at length in their own tongue, a strange mixture of clicks and hisses, guttural grunts—even gestures that were, in actuality, words. How long had the Red Mare been treating in secret with the pans? Tek wondered. It astonished her how rapidly she herself had come to accept her foster sisters. Their gentle, affectionate natures were much at odds with the unicorns' long-held view of pans.

Before her flight, the pied mare had, like her fellows in the Vale, believed goatlings to be witless, speechless brutes. Now for the first time, she realized that discourse between her own people and the pans might be achieved: a negotiation of safe passage through the Pan Woods during spring pilgrimage and autumn trek, perhaps? Tek had mulled over the possibilities all during the waning months of winter.

And if truce could be reached between races that shared no common tongue, what might then follow between those that did? Perhaps parley—even peace—with species with whom the children-of-the-moon were in conflict: namely, the gryphons? And what of those with whom the unicorns were openly at war: the hated wyverns?

Standing at the entrance to her mother's cave, surveying the far Pan Woods, the pied mare shook her head, unwilling to take her wild musings further. They felt dangerously new and untried, reminding her keenly of Jan. She had always thought him an extravagant dreamer. Only now did she begin to wonder whether his more fanciful speculations might, after all, turn out to be of practical use.

Dusk drew on. Tek watched the gathering shadows travel over the snow-shrouded hills. Far in the distant meadow below, a small band of shaggy boar plowed their way through the deep snow. Tek shuddered, thinking of the wolves that had pursued her across that same meadow, months ago now. She paced restlessly before the grotto's opening, a vague sense of unease nipping at her.

She wondered where Jah-lila could be. After dozing the afternoon away in the warmth and pale glow of the cave's phosphorescent mushrooms, she had awakened only shortly ago to find both her mother and the young pans gone. Surprised, she had strained to her feet and taken up her vigil at the cave's egress.

The burden in her belly shifted, bearing down. The unaccustomed pressure made walking difficult, yet she could not keep still. Clumsily, she lumbered down the path leading from the cave—but quickly lost her breath. Her unborn seemed to weigh against her lungs. She stood lock-kneed for a few moments, panting, before moving on. Twilight deepened. The air grew dank and chill. She saw nothing of either the pans or Jah-lila. The boar in the far meadow had disappeared into the trees.

A ferocious storm was brewing to the northwest, she noted, ambling laboriously along the path. Darkness seethed and roiled over the distant Vale. Blue-white flashes illuminated the rapidly rising thunderheads. Dense and incredibly black, the clouds built with a preternatural swiftness.

The storm was spreading this way, she realized, catching the first whiff of freshening breeze. Stormclouds devoured the setting sun. *Best get underhill,* she told herself, swinging ponderously around. This was sure to be a violent blow. She hoped Jah-lila and her pan fosterlings would return to the grotto soon, hating to think of any beast caught out on such a night. The path back along the hillside's curve seemed steeper than she recalled.

Breathless, heaving, she had taken no more than a dozen steps before a crushing pain overtook her. Tek halted with a sharp outbreath of surprise. The pressure in her belly deepened suddenly into a pang. It passed quickly, but left her weak. Though the evening air was chilling fast, a fine film of sweat pricked her beneath her thick winter shag.

Alarmed, she had managed only ten more paces when a second pang constricted her, forcing her to exhale and drop her head. A low moan escaped her. This pain, too, was brief, though more protracted than the first. The pied mare's thoughts spun. Something must be badly amiss. She and Jan had pledged on the autumnal equinox, only half a year before. Her young would not be full term till near the start of summer, more than two moons away. Cold fear gripped her.

Desperately, Tek staggered toward the distant cave. Her urgency only precipitated another pang, which nearly pitched her to her knees. Wincing, she forced herself on. She must get out of the cold and the coming rain, back to the hidden grotto's shelter and warmth. Doubt chilled her. Could she even reach the cave? The path seemed endless, the grotto nowhere in sight. Another pain.

Rounding a bend in the hillside at last, she saw Sismoomnat, the elder of the pan sisters, standing in the grotto's egress, casting about worriedly, a bundle of newly gathered bitterbark still clasped in her forepaws. Was Jah-lila with her? Tek did not see her dam. Gasping, she managed a wounded warrior's whistle just as another spasm, the most severe yet, swept hard through her. She stumbled, crying out, heard

Sismoomnat's answering hail and the rapid two-footed patter of the young pan's heels. A moment later, she felt the other's nuzzling touch as her mother's acolyte surveyed her with a few quick sniffs and glances.

"How goes it with you, sis-ter?" Sismoomnat asked gently, her flat, goatling brow furrowed with concern.

The pressure began to abate, not completely this time. Tek was barely able to raise her head and speak.

"Something . . . is wrong. Sharp pains . . ."

She felt the other's tongue tasting the salt of her sweat—more than a gesture of affection, the pied mare knew. A midwife could tell much by a taste.

"Come," the goatling urged her. "Walk while you may. Storm nears. Jah-ama is not yet home. We must make haste to shel-ter."

Drenched in sweat, Tek stumbled along the narrow path. Its gradual incline seemed almost insurmountable to her now. Though the pain had eased somewhat, she still had to halt, panting, every half dozen steps to rest. The cold wind cut into her coat. Sismoomnat leaned against her, supporting Tek with her own frail goatling's strength.

The cave's mouth loomed. Sismoomnat whistled shrilly through her teeth. Her sister, Pitipak, scampered from the grotto's mouth and hurried toward them. Tek put down her head. Her belly clenched again. She felt as though a relentlessly tightening band encompassed her. She heard the soft guttural cries of the younger pan, felt hairless forepaws caressing her. As she struggled through the cave's entryway, the warmth and windlessness of the ghostlit chamber hit her like a blow. She lost her footing, nearly fell.

"On-ly a few more steps," Sismoomnat murmured.

Pitipak darted ahead, shoving a thick bedding of dried grass into the pied mare's path. Tek collapsed onto it gratefully.

"What . . . what is it?" she gasped, in agony again.

"Birth pangs," Sismoomnat replied calmly.

Panic shot through the pied mare, redoubling the clenching jabs. "No! The foal isn't due . . . for months!"

The two pans had sunk to their haunches beside her, one on either side, buttressing her lest she heel over completely. Tek struggled feebly, but found herself too weak to rise.

"Too soon!" she panted. "I'll . . . lose the foal!"

She stared around her at the grotto full of roots and herbs—if only she had known which ones to take! A healer's fosterling, she held some knowledge of the worts that treated wounds and other ills, but none at all of those used in the midwife's art. Wild with frustration and pain, she half whinnied, half groaned. Where was Jah-lila? If the Red Mare were here, she would know what to do.

"Peace, sis-ter," Sismoomnat soothed, stroking the pied mare's neck and mane. "You need no herb to delay this birth. The pains are ear-ly, but Jah-ama has prepared for this. Have no fear. She will return from her task ver-y soon. Till then, we will aid you. She has instruct-ed us tho-roughly in mat-ters of mid-wifery."

The goatling's nimble forepaws smoothed and kneaded Tek's heaving sides with firm, steady strokes. The ache remained excruciating. Shuddering, the pied mare sensed the younger pan bustling about under her sister's direction, fetching this herb and that. A bundle of bruised and fragrant leaves was thrust beneath her nose. Sismoomnat urged her to breathe deeply to dull the pain. Tek tried futilely to deepen her rapid, shallow panting—but the pangs were coming harder and faster now.

The pains crowded out all else. She felt the unborn within her shifting, shifting with maddening slowness, as though overly cramped within her tightly constricted womb. Tek writhed and rolled, unable to find any position that could relieve the unrelenting contractions. Outside, the downpour grew deafening. Violent flashes of lightning seared her vision even through her clenched eyelids. Roaring thunder rumbled unendingly as though the mountain were preparing to fall.

Her mind glazed, only dimly aware how late the evening had grown. The birth was taking too long. In the Vale, she knew, most mares accompanied the midwife to the birthing grounds in the morning, were safely delivered by noon, then returned before dusk. But this arduous labor had already lasted hours without issue. A monstrous sense of foreboding gripped her. After a time, she realized it was full night.

No moon shone outside. Even without the storm, she knew Alma's heavenly daughter would not have lit the sky—for tonight was moondark, the time of the nothing moon, when the pale moon mare ran paired with the sun on the other side of the world. This was the night each month when unicorns of the Vale huddled underhill, hiding from haunts and spirits: a time of hazard and evil influence, the hour of freaks and miracles.

Superstitious nonsense, all of it, Tek tried to tell herself, contracting and crying out yet again. The young within her, striving so gamely to be born, would not come forth. At last her strength gave out. She could not even moan anymore. *Breech birth.* The realization rolled through her like the thunder. Neither she nor her foal would survive this travail. Mad Korr would have his victory after all.

Hollow hooffalls suddenly, barely audible above the booming of thunder and the clatter of rain. Tek smelled the sweet, spice scent of her dam shaking off in the entryway.

"Daughter!" Jah-lila's voice called, full of urgency and dread. "I came with all speed but could not outrun the storm. Curse the work that called me from you this day. . . ."

The pied mare could not answer, could not even open her eyes. She lay on her side exhausted, unable even to twitch an ear. No curiosity stirred in her to wonder what task had kept the midwife so long from her side. Jah-lila had come too late. Tek knew no herb could save her now. She waited only for death.

"Haste!" her mother was saying. "Sismoomnat, Pitipak—rub your forelimbs with bitterbark."

Someone lay gasping hoarsely nearby. Dimly, Tek realized it was herself and clenched her teeth against the sound.

"Reach, Sismoomnat," she heard her mother saying. "Aye, slow and smoothly—reach deep."

The pied mare felt a sudden pressure moving through her, gliding upward toward the womb. She kicked reflexively, but someone was kneeling on her hind legs, pinning them. She smelled her mother's rain-soaked scent, felt her reassuring nuzzle.

"Peace. Peace, daughter," she murmured. "All will be well soon. Soon."

Tek thrashed feebly, too weak to drag herself away.

"Have you got firm hold, Sismoomnat?" the Red Mare was saying. "Pull, then—pull hard!"

Something slipped struggling from her womb. Tek felt a rush of blood-warm fluid.

"Well done!" she heard Jah-lila exclaim. "Well done, my fosterling. Now, Pitipak, you must do the same: reach deep and pull, exactly as your sister did."

Tek felt again the sliding reach, the clench and pull—and her womb emptied suddenly, the sense of unbearable distention abruptly gone. She felt herself subsiding, her heartbeat slowing, pulse beating fainter, fainter yet. Weariness smothered her. She knew she must be dying now, only distantly aware of the young pans' joyous cries.

"Behold, Jah-ama!"

"So vig-orous—and so well grown!"

"Rejoice, daughter," the Red Mare whispered in her ear. "In thy progeny and Jan's brought hale into the world."

A sensation of warmth stole over her. The pied mare managed a wordless sigh. Her young lived. She had accomplished the task she had set herself in fleeing the Vale: to see Jan's offspring safely born. Her own life scarcely mattered any more. Surely her magicker dam could rear an orphaned filly or foal—even a suckling newborn—as she had the two young pans. Utterly spent, Tek drifted toward beckoning darkness.

The foreboding that had gripped her earlier, she realized drowsily, portended not the stillbirth of her progeny, but only her own end and that of this aged and withered season, now passing with great gnashing and thundering away. Winter's deathgrip was broken at last. By morning, the torrential rains would have battered months of snow and ice into muddy slush. Tomorrow would dawn the equinox, first day of the new and long-awaited spring.

Equinox

☽ 21 ☾

The dark unicorn stood on a vast clifftop. Swept clean of snow, devoid of vegetation, the broad, flat expanse before him lay fetlock deep in straw, withered flowers, and the sweet-smelling shavings of spicewood. Behind, the *chon*'s great timber palace stood. All around, a sprawling press of two-foots stamped and swayed.

"Dai'chon!" they chanted. "Dai'chon!"

The *daïcha* stood to one side of the crowd, flanked by her female companions and her green-plumes. The great crescent of skystuff gleamed silver on her breast. Behind her, the sacred *daya* of the palace milled, coats brushed to gleaming, manes intricately braided. Tai-shan spotted Ryhenna among the rest, her color all coppery fire. She huddled, miserable-seeming.

"Dai'chon!" the crowd shouted. "Dai'chon!"

Tai-shan remembered the arrival of green-garbed keepers to the warm enclosure scarcely an hour before, hustling the *daya* and himself from stable to clifftop through the surging press of celebrants, many of whom had fallen to their knees at the sight of the dark unicorn. Tai-shan cavaled and shook himself as petals and wood shavings, seedpods, and whiskered ears of grain continued to rain down. Even here in the open, the thick, soft carpet of tindery stuff underhoof scarcely muffled the din. The noise on the clifftop was deafening.

"Dai'chon!" the crowd roared. "Dai'chon!"

Before the throng stretched an open space, empty save for a great dais of stone. Offerings heaped its base: provender of every kind, bolts of vivid falseskin, coffers of glinting river stones mixed with little disks of skystuff. Jars of oil and the dark, fragrant juice of crushed berries gave off a sharply aromatic scent. Beyond the platform stretched more open space until the clifftop dropped abruptly away.

"Dai'chon!" ranted the throng, stamping rhythmically. "Dai'chon!" The *chon*'s purple-plumes held back the crush. Of the *chon* himself, the dark unicorn saw no sign. He stood trapped, purple-badged minions holding twin tethers to the silver halter imprisoning his head. An impassable sea of two-foots surged to one side of him. To the other lay only clifftop and empty air. Stormclouds roiled to the east at horizon's edge, devouring the rising sun.

"Dai'chon!" the crowd thundered. "Dai'chon—"

Without warning, silence fell. The rhythmic stamping abruptly ceased. Two-foots stood panting, covered with sweat in the cool morning air. Tai-shan's ears twitched. The stillness seemed to reverberate. Even the restless *daya* quieted. The only sound upon the clifftop now was that of seabirds and the foaming crash of unseen breakers dashing themselves to spume upon the rocks far, far below.

With one accord, the throng parted. A glittering raft, mounted on poles and borne upon the shoulders of eight brawny two-foots, emerged from the press. Hushed onlookers sank to their knees as it passed. Tai-shan recognized the conveyance as that which he had once seen carrying the *chon*—but the figure now seated upon it bore little resemblance to the firekeepers' king. Drawing even with the dais, the raft's bearers halted. Its occupant rose and stepped regally onto the high stone platform.

The dark unicorn stared at the creature now turning to face the crowd. Garbed all in black, it carried in one forepaw a vinelike flail, in the other a sharpened skewer. A white crescent moon emblazoned its breast. Yet though its body was that of a two-foot, the head resting upon those square, wide shoulders resembled a *da*'s, all black, with fierce, staring eyes and flared red nostrils. Black mane bristled down the arched and oddly foreshortened neck.

Before it, the great crowd of two-foots cowered. Across the open space from him, Tai-shan saw the coppery mare gazing at the dark figure in open terror. Yet despite its fierce appearance, the monster's head seemed strangely stiff, the eyes shadowy hollows. The ears did not swivel. Its lips—pulled back to bare square, white teeth—appeared frozen. The dry, red tongue within the gaping mouth never moved. The neck remained rigid. To turn its head, the dark unicorn saw, the figure had to pivot its whole torso.

At a peremptory gesture from the black-clad figure on the platform, the *daïcha* rose and approached. Tai-shan watched as she collapsed to her knees, folded her forelimbs across her breast, and bowed her head.

The glowering godking brandished its skewer and cracked its vine. Lifting her forelimbs, the lady called out to the *da*-headed thing. The dark unicorn could decipher only a few phrases: "Emwe, Dai'chon," *hail, godking.* "Undan ptola," *by your will.* She seemed to be reciting both a greeting and a pledge.

Dai'chon answered nothing, only nodded its stiff, ponderous head. With a low bow, the *daïcha* withdrew, gesturing to her green-garbed followers. One by one, they led the sacred *daya* before Dai'chon. Pulse hammering, the dark unicorn sidled. His breath came in restive snorts. He could not stand still. No opportunity for escape had yet presented itself: his only choices were plunging over cliff's edge or trampling the kneeling crowd.

The parade of *daya* before the godking went on and on. Most passed by without a pause, but every so often, Dai'chon snapped its flail, and the keeper then before the dais halted, allowing Dai'chon to scrutinize that particular mare or stallion more closely. The watching crowd seemed to hold its breath.

Usually, the godking cracked its vine a second time; the *da* was returned to the *daïcha,* and the watchers heaved a heavy sigh. Sometimes, however, Dai'chon pointed toward the halted *da* with the skewer, and the kneeling throng murmured with delight as the *daïcha*'s minion then led his charge to the side of the stone platform nearest the cliff. The half dozen *daya* there pranced gaily, tossing their heads. Their keepers were hard-pressed to keep hold of the tethers. Tai-shan stared angrily, helplessly at the joyous *daya*: all blissfully unaware that they celebrated their own approaching death.

Ryhenna was among the last to pass before Dai'chon. The dark unicorn tensed, heart between his teeth, as the godking cracked its flail, signaling the keeper who held the coppery mare's tether to halt. Ryhenna stood wild-eyed before the platform, so plainly terrified that the dark unicorn half expected her to bolt. But Dai'chon snapped its vine at last and allowed her to pass. Able to breathe again, Tai-shan sighed deep with relief as the coppery mare rejoined the other, unchosen *daya.*

The last of the sacred *daya* was led before Dai'chon. With a snort of surprise, Tai-shan recognized Ushuk, the former First Stallion, whom he had defeated upon their first encounter, months ago. The godking seemed barely to notice the umber stallion, remarking his passage without so much as a crack of the flail. Crestfallen, Ushuk faltered in his gait. The *daïcha,* too, seemed puzzled. Her companions glanced at one another.

With halting step, the umber stallion allowed his escort to draw him on, but he gazed back uncomprehendingly at Dai'chon, plainly unable to believe the god would pass him by. The dark figure on the dais gave him not so much as a second glance. Instead, Dai'chon turned toward Tai-shan. Fixing its strange, shadowy eyes on the dark unicorn, the godking snapped its whip.

The whole crowd started. The purple-badged keepers holding the twin tethers of the silver halter stood riveted, clearly astonished by the godking's summons. Again, impatiently, Dai'chon cracked its vine. Tai-shan saw the *daïcha*'s look of puzzlement change to one of alarm as the *chon*'s minions began to tug him toward the stone platform. The lady took a step forward, as though to intervene, then caught herself. Champing and dancing, Tai-shan suffered himself to be led forward. What choice had he? There was nowhere to run.

His keepers halted before the dais. The lowering face of the godking glared down at him. Cavaling, the dark unicorn laid back his ears. Slowly and deliberately, Dai'chon held out the skewer. The crowd gasped in dismay. A single, bitten-off cry rose from the *daïcha*. Tai-shan saw her standing as though stunned, one hand to her lips. Her companions behind her murmured wide-eyed, some shaking their heads.

Suddenly, the *daïcha* was striding forward. She looked both angry and afraid. Halting before the dais, she cried out to the godking in exhortation and appeal. She seemed to be pleading with the figure above, very vehement. Tai-shan backed and sidled, pulling the *chon*'s purple-badged minions with him. The godking, still clutching its skewer and flail, stood with forepaws upon its hips. Slowly, silently, it shook its head at the *daïcha* and gestured once more with the skewer toward the dark unicorn.

Obediently, the pair of keepers tried to guide their cavaling charge toward the half-dozen chosen *daya* waiting on the far side of the dais. Snorting, Tai-shan braced himself, set his heels. The *daïcha* cried out again, desperately. She looked as though she might rush up the stone ramp flanking one side of the platform to confront the godking face to face.

Angrily, Dai'chon gestured toward a knot of purple-plumes, who started forward as though to pull the lady back from the dais. Drawing their weapons, her own green-plumed followers hastened to intercept them. With a shout, the *daïcha* threw up one forelimb to halt her followers, shaking her head. Both parties milled uneasily, the purple-plumes clearly reluctant to lay hands upon the lady, even at the order of Dai'chon, the green-plumes seemingly unwilling to clash unless their leader were more explicitly threatened. The godking turned once more toward Tai-shan.

"Flee, my lord Moonbrow!" Across the yard from him, Tai-shan saw Ryhenna rear up suddenly among her fellows. "Flee *now*—ere the god ordereth his *chon*'s guard to drive thee over the cliff!"

All around her, *daya* shied in confusion. Startled two-foots scattered. Their cries amid the sudden commotion halted Dai'chon, his skewer and flail half-raised. Ramping and flailing, the coppery mare plunged through the sacred herd. In the same instant, Tai-shan wrenched free of his keepers' grasp and wheeled to face the sacrificial *daya*.

"Run! Run, all of you!" he shouted. "Only death lies beyond the drop. Flee for your lives!"

Between the platform and cliff's edge, the sacrificial *daya* danced anxiously, tossing their heads violently and rolling their eyes. They seemed more afraid of him than of their own captors, the dark unicorn realized in dismay. Two-foot keepers stroked and soothed their skittish charges. At an impatient gesture from Dai'chon, Tai-shan saw his own pair of keepers starting toward him. With a peal of rage, the dark unicorn flew at them. Shouting, they scrambled away through the scattered hay and wood shavings. Behind, the sacrificial *daya* shied. Keepers grasped halter leads in both forepaws, struggling to hold them.

On the stone platform before them, Dai'chon cried out. Tai-shan spun around, startled to hear the godking's voice for the first time. It was low-pitched and strangely muffled, like a cry from deep underhill. The godking gestured with its skewer, and several of the purple-plumes cast aside their staves, rushing Tai-shan with forelimbs outstretched to catch his tethers. The dark unicorn charged them, lashing with his forehooves. The purple-plumes dodged, crying out in fear. Across from him, many of the *daya* around Ryhenna had already bolted. Others now fought their tethers, screaming to break free.

Tai-shan saw the *daïcha*'s green-garbed followers striving desperately to hold and calm what *daya* they could. Their lady stood poised, as though uncertain. Then all at once, she rushed to snatch a tether from her minion's grasp. Shouting, she struck the frightened mare across the flank, sending her careening away after the others that had broken free. Calling sharply to the rest of her followers, the *daïcha* dashed among the remaining *daya,* waving her forelimbs and hying the last of the skittish beasts to bolt. The throng about the palace surged to their feet and erupted in chaos as stampeding *daya* hurtled through their midst.

Tai-shan circled, making to herd the sacrificial *daya* away from cliff's edge. Dai'chon's muffled shouts and angry gestures continued. More of the *chon*'s purple-plumes responded, some turning to chase fleeing *daya*, others coming on toward Tai-shan. At a shout from the *daïcha*, her own green-plumed guards hastened to form a line before

the advancing purple-plumes to prevent their reaching the dark unicorn.
Ushuk thundered past just as the green-plumes closed ranks.

"Blasphemer!" the umber stallion shouted, storming toward Tai-
shan. "How darest thou defy the will of the god?"

The dark unicorn ducked and fell back, too surprised at first to
defend himself.

"*Homat!* Ushuk, stop!" Tai-shan heard Ryhenna crying. She, too,
had broken through the *daïcha*'s line of green-plumes. "Did thy first
encounter with black Moonbrow teach thee nothing? Thou'rt over-
matched!"

The umber stallion responded with a growl. "Cursed mare, to join
this *punuskr*—this demon—in defiance of Dai'chon. Thou shalt share
his fate!"

Again he flew at the dark unicorn. Once more Tai-shan dodged and
fell back, sidestepping the abandoned conveyance resting on the ground
before the godking's dais, its bearers long since fled.

"I served the godking joyfully all my days," the umber stallion
cried, his eyes wide and bloodshot, the snorted spray from his nostrils
flecked with blood. "In the end I proved unworthy, and he cast me aside.
Yet still I worship and adore him. *Dai'chon undan ptola*—the godking's
will be done!"

Ushuk lunged, flailing recklessly at Tai-shan. Unwilling to use his
horn against a flatbrowed adversary, the dark unicorn reared and threw
one shoulder against the other. Ushuk's hind hooves skidded on the
soft, slippery carpet of wood shavings. One pole of the *chon*'s raft
caught his legs. Thrashing, the umber stallion toppled. Tai-shan heard
the *daïcha*'s horrified cry as, squealing in pain, Ushuk struggled up from
the chaff and tinder, one foreleg shattered.

"Himay," he heard the *daïcha* calling. "Ushuk, himay!" *Stand still.*

The dark unicorn recoiled in dismay. The limbs of *daya* must be
fragile as deer's! Ushuk staggered, blundering on three limbs back
through the ranks of the green-plumes still holding off the *chon*'s
purple-plumed guards. At a snarl from Dai'chon on the platform above,
purple-plumes surrounded the injured stallion.

"Tash—'omat!" the lady cried: *No—stop!*

Ignoring her, the godking made a furious gesture. One of the *chon*'s
minions lifted a thin slice of skystuff to the great vein of Ushuk's throat
and drew the blade across. The umber stallion collapsed with a shriek.
He thrashed for a moment, blood spattering the bone-dry tinder. Then
he lay still. The dark unicorn stared, stunned, unable to take it in. With
a healer's care, Ushuk's limb might have mended! Shaken and sick,
Tai-shan backed away.

Behind him, he heard Ryhenna scream. Whirling, he saw Dai'chon kneeling on the platform's edge, Ryhenna's tether grasped in one fore-paw. Trembling, the coppery mare tugged and tried to back away—but she seemed almost paralyzed with fright. The godking spoke soothingly in its strange, hollow-sounding voice. It pulled her head closer. Eyes rolling, the coppery mare whinnied shrilly as, crooning, the godking placed the point of the long, sharp skewer to her throat.

"Tash! 'Omat!" shouted Tai-shan, vaulting onto the high stone plat-form.

He lunged to catch the skewer's length against his horn and bat it away. With a cry, Dai'chon fell back, releasing Ryhenna. The dark unicorn reared. Growling, the *da*-headed creature slashed at him. Tai-shan parried, sweeping his horn to once more knock aside the blade. The godking ducked, dodged. Tai-shan felt his horn strike a solid blow and leapt back astonished—for the other's neck was hard as wood, with none of the give of mortal flesh. The sound of the blow rang hollowly, like a hoof-stamp on a rotten log. Dai'chon staggered. The head upon the creature's shoulders wobbled. A moment later, it fell. Tai-shan cried out. His blow had held neither aim nor force enough to have severed his opponent's gorge—and yet Dai'chon's strange, stiff head toppled with a hollow thump to the dried petals and wood shavings littering the dais. Dumbstruck, the dark unicorn stared at the creature before him. Though beheaded, it still possessed a head: a round, two-foot head upon a squat, two-foot neck. An ordinary firekeeper stood before him, one whose real head had been concealed beneath a hollow artifice of wood. The unmasked keeper glared at Tai-shan, black eyes furious, his own teeth bared as fiercely as the carved teeth of the wooden godhead had been. The dark curls of the other's hair and beard were slick with sweat. An instant later, the dark unicorn recognized him.

"The *chon*! The *chon*," Ryhenna below him cried. "No god at all!"

Similar screams came from the stampeding *daya*. Shrieks and wails rose from the scattering two-foots as well. Eyes wide with betrayal, faces drawn with shock, the commonfolk of the city scrambled to flee. Yet the two-foots of the palace reacted differently. The *daïcha*'s com-panions and her green-garbed followers, plumed guards of both colors as well as the *chon*'s purple-badged underlings, while clearly outraged at their ruler's unmasking, did not seem the least surprised to discover their mortal leader impersonating a god. Even the *daïcha*, the dark uni-corn realized in astonishment, had known all along.

A stinging welt across one shoulder brought Tai-shan sharply around. The *chon* had lunged at him again, slashing with the skewer and lashing with the flail. The dark unicorn dodged, back-stepping. Ryhenna's cry came almost too late.

"My lord Moonbrow, the edge!"

Wheeling, Tai-shan sprang away barely in time. The *chon* had sought to drive him backward over the stone platform's brink. Shouting, the two-foot ruler pursued him across the dais, cracking the stinging lash. As the dark unicorn ducked, the lash coiled itself about his horn. With a heave of neck and shoulders, Tai-shan jerked it from the two-foot's grasp and slung it spinning off across the clifftop into the empty air beyond. It hung a moment against the gathering stormclouds, before vanishing. Growling with rage, the *chon* redoubled his attack with the blade.

" 'Ware the *chon*'s guard!" Ryhenna cried.

Tai-shan glimpsed a handful of purple-plumes breaking through the *daïcha*'s green-plumed defenders to rush the dais. Ryhenna dashed to the foot of the platform's ramp, blocking their path. The purple-plumes fell back in confusion as the wild mare reared and struck at them. Tai-shan returned his attention to the *chon,* countering the other's lunges and blows, parrying each feint and thrust. The nimbleness of this puny, upright creature astonished him. Though the *chon* possessed not nearly the strength of a full-grown unicorn, the sweep and agility of his forelimb gave him great range. Tai-shan had never fenced such a dexterous foe. The dark unicorn plunged, pivoted, ramped, and dodged.

His hooves grew hot. Churning and plunging through the dry stuff strewn about the platform, he felt his heels striking the flinty stone beneath. Flashes of white and amber light leapt from his hooves. More flashes showered down as his horn grated against the skewer of the *chon.* Sparks! Sparks of fire were falling from his horn as it struck against the skystuff—more springing up from his hooves as they skidded on the stone: sparks such as he had once seen leap from the tools of the two-foot firesmith. Now his own hooves and horn were doing the same! Astonished, the dark unicorn stared.

"Look! Look!" Ryhenna below him cried. Many of her fleeing companions had halted, gazing in open wonder at the bright rain falling from his hooves and horn. "Here standeth the true Dai'chon, full of the divine fire!"

Lighting upon the platform's thick carpet of dry hay, withered flower petals, and aromatic wood shavings, the sparks began to smolder. Black stormclouds were fast sweeping in across the sea. A warm, wet wind picked up. Bits of burning chaff gusted from the dais to the open space below, catching in the dried stuff there. A thick pall of smoke rose, filling the air with cinders. Plumed two-foots of both colors tore off their outer falseskins and flailed at the spreading flames.

Choking, the *chon* covered his mouth and nose with one forepaw— yet still he fought. Tai-shan clashed and countered, gasping for breath, until in a furious assault, he drove the two-foot ruler to one knee and disarmed him with a parry that knocked the skewer from his grip and sent it, like the flail before it, spinning away into the emptiness beyond the cliff. The dark unicorn ramped before the defeated *chon,* whose bloodshot eyes glared back at him, full of hatred still.

"Tash! Tash so bei!" The *daïcha* rushed past Ryhenna up onto the platform to interpose herself between the dark unicorn and the *chon.* "Tash bei im chon!"

Tai-shan knew she must be saying, *No, don't kill him. Don't kill my king.*

Fury burned in the dark unicorn. At that moment, he wanted nothing other than to skewer the treacherous two-foot ruler—but the *daïcha* stood suppliant before him, and he owed her his life. Forehooves touching the ground once more, Tai-shan shook himself. A kind of silence fell around him. With great difficulty, summoning all the agility of lips and teeth not made to frame such speech, he strove to pronounce clearly the words of the firekeepers' tongue.

"Undan ptola, daïcha," he told her. *As you wish.*

The other's eyes widened. She gazed at the dark unicorn as though unable to believe her ears. The purple-plumes below the dais stood halted in wonder. The green-plumes, too, had heard. They stood staring. Beyond them, the *daïcha*'s companions sank to the ground, two of them weeping. On the dais, ashen-faced, the *chon* shook his head.

"Tash," he gasped. "Tash—ipsicat!"

Tai-shan did not recognize the second word, but he could guess its meaning: *No. No—impossible.* The *chon* made as if to rise.

"Tash! 'Omat!" the dark unicorn ordered. *No. Stop.* "Himay." *Keep still.*

The *chon* choked out something else, too fast for Tai-shan to follow. What was he saying now, the dark unicorn wondered, that *daya*—even miraculously horned, outland *daya*—ought not be able to speak?

"Jima'pnor!" *That's enough,* the dark unicorn commanded, cutting the *chon* off as he spoke. "Asolet." *Silence.* Again the other made to rise, but the dark unicorn stopped him with a feint of his horn. "Tash bim!"

He did not know the phrase for *Come no nearer* and so had to settle for *Do not come.* Tai-shan stamped angrily, galled by his lack of words.

"Ipsicat!" the *chon* whispered again. *Impossible*. Then, gesturing with his forelimb, he shouted suddenly, "Punuskr!"

Tai-shan recognized the term: *demon*. A string of epithets followed, too rapid for the dark unicorn to decipher. From the other's furious tone, however, it was clear they were dire threats. The *chon* motioned to his purple-plumes, shouting.

"Bei so! Bei so ahin!"

The dark unicorn needed no translation to tell him the *chon* was shouting, *Kill him. Kill him now!* But the purple-plumes at the foot of the dais stood motionless, eyes wide with awe. Several fell to their knees, gasping, "Dai'chon!"

The cry was taken up among the green-plumes, a ragged chant. "Dai'chon! Dai'chon!"

Upon the dais, the *daïcha* sank to her knees as well, bowing her head and crossing her forelimbs over her breast. Below, her green-plumes did the same.

"Emwe," she murmured. "Emwe, Dai'chon!"

Below them, the whole clifftop seethed in confusion. Wildfire leapt and crackled. Stormwind had picked up, fanning the flames. Screaming *daya* dashed madly about. Frightened two-foots cowered or tried frantically to flee, but the passageways beside the palace had become so crowded as to be impassable. The palace itself was on fire now. Heaped about the base of the dais, offerings kindled and burned.

A scream from Ryhenna caused Tai-shan to wheel. Fire from the burning offerings had set her mane alight. With shrills of terror, the coppery mare bolted. The dark unicorn sprang after her, vaulting down from the dais through a veil of fire and smoke. He sprinted behind her, crying her name.

"Ryhenna, stop!" he shouted. "Turn—you'll run over the edge!"

The smoke and cinders grew so thick, he could not see her. Then he caught a glimpse of coppery flank. The smoke parted suddenly—just as the earth vanished beneath his heels. Ryhenna hung in the air before him. He glimpsed realization in her eye, felt horror clutch like a many-toed suckerfish at his own breast.

He tried to wheel, to regain solid ground: far too late. His legs flailed only empty air. Ryhenna plunged helplessly beside him. The roiling white sea dashed upward toward them. A great crack of thunder sounded, accompanied by a bitter odor and a blue-white flash. Lightning had struck the clifftop behind—above them now. They were falling.

So, too, did I fall, a voice whispered to him, *not so long ago. It seemed to take forever—though I fell toward frozen earth, not foaming sea.*

The dark unicorn twisted, astonished, still capable of astonishment even now. The quiet voice was infinitely familiar to him—surely the same that had spoken half a year before to him standing nameless upon the strand.

"Who are you?" he cried out.

Your own granddam, of course, the whisper replied. *Who else would I be?*

Memory stirred in him, hazy and distant still. "Sa? My father's dam?"

The hurtling wind whistled past his ears. *Once I was Sa. I am part of Alma now.*

"You told me to find the fire. But the fire was within me," the dark unicorn gasped. "It was within me all along!"

The sky around him seemed to nod in affirmation. *Ever since your initiation pilgrimage, two years past, when I touched your hooves with fire in the Pan Woods, and then your horn in the wyvern's den.* He remembered suddenly, clearly, standing upon the banked coals of a goatling campfire and later bathing his horn in the firebowl of a wyvern sorceress. The air sighed. *I have been waiting such a long time for you to discover that spark within.*

Falling, he answered bitterly, "I've set the clifftop alight with that spark. They're all trapped. Now two-foots and *daya* alike will perish—"

No one will perish, the voice murmured. *Any moment, my Red Mare's conjured rain will douse that blaze. The fire you have kindled in their minds, however, will burn a long time after this day. Your spark will transform the city. The power of the* chon *lies in ruins now. The* daïcha *will lead the firekeepers from this hour forward, and Dai'chon come to be worshiped in a new and gentler way. It will take time, to be sure, but it will come—because of you, my Firebringer. Did you think it your destiny to dance fire solely among the unicorns?*

Beside him in the air, Ryhenna screamed and flailed. Droplets pelted them. He thought at first they were spray from the frothing waves below. Then he realized they came from overhead: rain—a driving rain hard enough to damp the wildfire raging across the clifftop above. In that, at least, the goddess spoke true: those trapped on the cliff would live, though he and the coppery mare perished.

"Take my life," he besought Alma, "but spare Ryhenna."

The goddess laughed, very gently, as he and his companion plunged. The storm-tossed sea surged up to meet them. *But I already hold your life, Aljan, son of my son, Dark Moon.*

Moondark
☽ 22 ☾

The pain had passed. A dim haze of morning light filtered into the grotto, augmenting the wan lichenlight of the cavern's walls. The pied mare lay quiet, unable to focus her thoughts. A delicious drowsiness enveloped her. Her mouth tasted smoky-sweet of rosehips. She had no memory of chewing the herb, only of hours of travail the evening before. She was alive, and the knowledge astonished her.

Warm, dry hay had been heaped around her. Sismoomnat, the elder of her foster sisters, crouched nearby, stroking her neck and crooning in the oddly musical, half-grunted language of pans. The goatling held a clump of dried seedgrass near the pied mare's nose, offering it to her. Tek managed to turn her head away. She had no desire as yet for food.

The young pan vanished from beside her, to reappear holding fore-paws cupped before her. Tek's response to the smell of water surprised even herself: slurping the delicious contents of her foster sister's palms in a single sup. Twittering with pan laughter, Sismoomnat brought her another drink, another, and another yet. Dozens of swallows at last assuaged the pied mare's thirst.

The muffled sound of her mother's voice reached her then, muttering low and urgently. A strange aroma pervaded the cave: a faint, slightly bitter savor, as of chewed roots or bark. Tek tried weakly to raise her head, and Sismoomnat helped, lifting the pied mare's cheek to rest on her shaggy flank. Their dam stood across the grotto, in the shadows where few of the faintly glowing lichens grew. The Red Mare swayed, lock-kneed in trance, chanting softly: "Brothers-in-ocean, sisters-in-the-waves: swift-coursers, far-rovers, aid us! Two of our kind are in gravest peril. Dreams speak to me of this."

Tek had no notion what her mother might be doing—petitioning some unseen listener? The Red Mare's chanting continued, endless, monotonous. Tek's perceptions grew foggy. Even the slight effort of resting her head on Sismoomnat's flank exhausted her. She felt herself drifting into sleep.

Something nipped at her, rustling the hay. The pied mare jerked awake, struggling feebly. Her limbs did little more than twitch. Sismoomnat stroked her neck and murmured soothingly, then gently turned the pied mare's head, holding it so that Tek could view her own side and flank. Her belly, relieved now of its months-long burden, seemed oddly flattened to her eye, grown accustomed to the huge swell of her pregnant side. The younger pan, Pitipak, crouched near the pied mare's hindquarters, stroking something which nestled against Tek's belly.

"Seek them for me, my sisters-in-ocean!" Her mother's soft, urgent chanting continued. "Already you are coasting the Summer shore, traveling to the sacred shoals off the Gryphon Mountains to calve. My fellows are struggling not far from you. Aid them, my brothers-in-the-waves."

Tek paid scant attention, gazing instead at the young pan beside her, who sang and murmured while she herself stared blearily, trying to focus her eyes. A warm tide of relief flowed through the pied mare suddenly as she spotted the tiny, newborn unicorn lying suckling beside her. She felt exhausted and euphoric and utterly light. The little creature struggled, shifting the hay. Tek felt its toothless gums again, nipping insistently at the teat. Deeply, she sighed.

Not ill-omened, she told herself. *Miraculous. Full of mystery and joy.*

But was it filly or foal? She could not tell. The heaped straw and crouching form of Pitipak obscured her view. Her nursling seemed to shift and blur. The pied mare blinked. At times her doubled vision saw twin images: one dark, one light, so that she could not be certain of her young's true color.

"Hear me, comrades-of-the-deep," the Red Mare murmured. "My fellows are weary and in need of rescue. Do not let them perish, I beseech you. Buoy them up against the waters that would claim them."

The words continued, urgent, ceaseless—just at the threshold of Tek's hearing. She ignored them, too spent to listen, to puzzle them out.

I must think of a name, she thought languidly. *A truename for my child.*

As dam, she alone could fashion her offspring's secret name and whisper this first and most closely guarded gift into that newborn ear alone, never to be repeated to another unless the greatest of trust lay

between them. Jan had told her his own truename—Aljan, Dark Moon—
on his pilgrimage of initiation, two years gone.

And that was when I knew, she thought, *knew beyond all doubts
and shadows that this young firebrand was the one for me, even if I had
to wait years for him. And he was worth the wait. As this moment has
been worth the wait, to feel our young suckling at my flank.*

"Unicorns-of-the-sea! Unicorns-of-the-sea!" her mother chanted
softly, tirelessly. "Fierce, fearless single-horns—you who are also the
beloved of Alma and who, like us, also call yourselves children-of-the-
moon. Bear my fellows safe to land!"

Tek drifted, as on gentle swells. Sleep was dragging at her. She
could not remain afloat a moment more. *Return to me soon, O my love,
my Dark Moon,* she found herself thinking, as though her mate somehow
floated beside her, able to hear her thoughts. *Return and share my joy
in the birth of your heir.* Sleep rose like a wave and overwhelmed her.
Unresisting, she let herself slip down, down into the darkest depths,
devoid of light and sound and dreams.

Unicorns-of-the-Sea
☽ 23 ☾

The driving rain no longer fell, but stormwind continued to batter. The dark unicorn panted with effort, churning with all four limbs just to keep his head above water. Waves heaved and tossed. Land lay nowhere in sight. He could not tell if the darkness were that of storm alone or of night. It had all come back to him now: his people and their Vale, his title among them—Korr's son, prince of the unicorns. He remembered his journey to the Summer Sea at solstice time, the long months of mock-sparring and wooing. A flush of warmth suffused him as he recalled the courting dance on equinox eve. Memory of Tek blazed up, and wild longing filled him to return to his fellows and rejoin his mate.

Too weary to fight the riptide anymore, Jan lay in a daze as the cold, gusting stormrain began to abate. His limbs felt violently jolted, his ribs badly bruised. After he and Ryhenna had sprung from cliff's edge toward the storm-high surf below, strong ocean currents had dragged them far from shore. Alongside him, whenever the wind fell, he heard the coppery mare's panting breath as she, too, struggled against the fierce, running sea. After a time, her thrashing roused him.

"Don't . . . ," he managed, slinging a wet draggle of mane from his eyes. "Don't fight the waves. Breathe deep, and keep your nose just above water. Use your limbs as little as possible."

Eyes rolling and wide, the coppery mare turned to him with a gasp of relief. "My lord—great Dai'chon—ye stir!"

Jan shook his head weakly. "I am no Dai'chon. Ryhenna, I am Aljan, prince of the unicorns. I have remembered my own truename at last."

"Alj—Al-jan?" she stumbled, still flailing frantically. "But—I saw the divine fire spring from thy hooves and horn. . . ."

Again the dark unicorn shook his head. Breathing hurt his ribs. He had suffered some injury in the fall. The pain weakened him. "Don't swim so fiercely," he urged her. "You'll spend yourself."

Reluctantly, Ryhenna slowed her vigorous paddle. She seemed fearful of sinking without the constant motion of her limbs.

"Call me Moonbrow, as before, if you wish," he said, snorting cold seawater, "though that is not the name by which my people know me."

The coppery mare gazed at him. "Tell me of thy people, my lord Al-jan, Moonbrow," she whispered, "and whence thou comest."

Jan told her of his people, the children-of-the-moon, and of his life among them in the Vale. He spoke until his voice became ragged, rough. Ryhenna's breathing calmed. Her efforts at remaining afloat grew more steady. She paddled determinedly now, no longer desperate, and listened, hushed, as he described the free lives of unicorns.

"Ye have no keepers," the coppery mare murmured, awed, "and yet ye do not starve? Ye find your own shelter against the cold and wet, and defend yourselves from harm? And ye follow your own god, this Mother-of-all, this Alma?"

Jan nodded, talked out, spent. His tale had taxed his waning strength. He let himself drift, treading the waves as slowly as possible, saw the coppery mare watching him, trying to do the same. The grey sea had calmed somewhat, though the sky remained windblown, dark. Abruptly, she turned away.

"I have no such loving god to watch over me," she murmured bitterly. "My god was a sham, naught but a mortal two-foot in a mask. Oh, Al-jan—Moonbrow—if only I might see this marvelous Vale of thine and meet thy fellows and know the blessings of thy goddess Alma, I might die content."

Jan stirred uneasily, thinking of his dreams. He remembered only snatches—of killing winter cold and starving unicorns; his own father with a false moon painted in white clay upon his brow, ramping and shouting as one mad; Tek and Dagg fleeing together through driving snow, pursued by haunts or wolves. The dark unicorn shivered. All around, the cold waves heaved and chopped.

"Where are we?" he heard Ryhenna beside him asking, her voice plaintive. Clearly she was beginning to tire. He himself felt drained and chilled, at the end of his strength. How long had they been in the sea—all day? Was it dusk now? Evening? He saw no stars overhead, but the sky was so dark, he was not sure if it were night or only cover of cloud.

"Near the coast still, rest sure," he answered, forcing his own voice to sound reasoned and calm. "The storm can't have taken us so very far from shore. If only we knew what direction, I imagine we could swim it." Seeing her casting about worriedly, he added, "Sooner or later, we're bound to drift back toward land."

He turned away for a moment, fearful to catch her eye, and told himself that his words were not a lie. He had no doubt that eventually they would wash up on shore—but he knew that could be days, even weeks hence: long after their spirits had leapt free of the world to join with the Mother-of-all, leaving only bloated corpses on the waves.

Great Alma, save us! he cried inwardly, fighting his own panic down.

Jan shook himself, paddling as much for warmth now as to remain afloat. He saw Ryhenna scanning the horizon intently. Underneath her seeming composure, he sensed she was terrified still, nearly exhausted. The sea began to grow rougher again. Waves pitched and slapped at them. As darkness deepened, Jan realized that true evening must be falling at last, that the grey dimness encompassing them before had been only storm-shadowed daylight. The wind rose, gusted, but with no sign of rain.

Time passed. Beside him, he heard Ryhenna's sobbing breaths. His injured ribs ached. His limbs hung numb. He felt his eyelids straying shut. Only for a few moments, he told himself: he would rest, then swim on. Part of him knew that he was drowning, beginning to sink—down, the long way down to the soft, silt bottom, where firefish and sea-jells would pick his bones. But he could not struggle, could not swim another stroke. He had lost track of the coppery mare, unsure whether she still drifted beside him. Seawater filled his mouth and nose.

Into your keeping, Great Alma, he bade the goddess silently, *take me and my companion Ryhenna.*

A splash of spray. Something long and sleek broke the surface alongside him. Jan started, choking, jerking his head once more into the air above the rocking darkness of waves. A tumult in the waters all around. He paddled reflexively, blinking, stared at the gently curving back of the large dark form that had just surfaced before him. The blowhole atop its rounded head spouted a spurt of steaming breath.

Similar creatures—nearly a score—crowded around him and Ryhenna, bearing them up. Across from him, the coppery mare floundered, dazed, only half aware of their rescuers. The dark unicorn could only gaze in wonder as he felt the smooth, shifting surface of the ocean creatures' backs supporting him, lifting him partially free of the waves. His own struggles ceased as, in the depth of his mind, he heard a soft, laughing voice gently mocking him.

Aljan, my foolish colt. Did you really think I'd let you drown?

The seabeast nearest Jan turned to look at him with its bright black eye. The creature clicked and chattered through its steaming blowhole. Its fellows did the same. Across from him, the coppery mare's thrashing had subsided. She lay insensate, swooned. Jan felt himself growing light-headed, faint. He seemed to be floating through dark, star-filled sky instead of sea. Burning sea-jells and firefish swirled, surrounded him like stars. The strange, streamlined creature gliding before him through the darkness clacked and chittered still. From its short, blunt snout—he beheld now, staring—grew the long, twisting spiral of a unicorn's horn.

❧

The dream of stargliding endured for a great span before Jan returned to himself, found himself once more in the night-dark sea. For hours, it seemed, he could do little more than lie exhausted against the slick, pliant backs of the unicorns-of-the-sea. They were mostly dark grey, though a few were silvery with great black spots. Across from him, Ryhenna slept peacefully, sprawled across the shifting backs of the obliging sea-unicorns. Much of the cloud cover above him had blown off now, and Jan was able to see stars. The few ragged, scudding clouds that remained threatened no rain. The breeze had turned unexpectedly, mercifully warm.

Not all their rescuers possessed the tusk-horn, Jan noted after a time. Only about half did, most of whom appeared to be the larger males—and yet, among those with the longest, keenest, and most elegant horns swam two that were plainly females with half-grown calves. One of the group even sported a pair of horns, one spiral skewer sprouting from each side of the jaw. The group's leader was evidently the beautifully tusked young male who had broken the surface first. In the beginning, he only clicked and whistled at Jan, but presently switched to the common tongue of unicorns and *daya*.

"Among my folk," he began, "I am known as A'a'a'...." A string of crackling squeals followed, baffling Jan's ears. The sea creature tossed his head, flipping a shower of spray. "But I realize this designation is difficult for your kind."

The young male swam alongside, bright-eyed, smiling. The dark unicorn could not escape the impression that he was being politely laughed at.

"You may therefore call me A'a."

Despite his bone-wearying fatigue, Jan managed a bow. "A'a," he began, "I am called Aljan. My companion is Ryhenna. We are both deeply grateful for your aid. But I have never seen or heard tell of your kind before. What are your people called?"

"We are narwhals," A'a replied: "Moonspawn, blessed of the Great Mother. We are on our spring voyage east along the silver coast to our calving grounds off the Birdcat Mountains."

Birdcat Mountains. Jan grew suddenly more alert. Might such be the name of the Gryphon Mountains among A'a's people? The dark unicorn felt his whole body quiver. If the unicorns-of-the-sea knew of the Gryphon Mountains, then surely they knew of the Singing Cliffs where the seaherons nested, from which he could easily find his way back to the Vale.

"We sing to one another constantly beneath the waves," A'a continued. "My pod was closest to you when our dreamers harkened Red-One's hail entreating your rescue."

Red-One? Jan blinked. All the narwhals in his view were dark silver, mottled grey, or black. "Who is Red-One?" he asked. "Is that one among you now?"

A shower of staccato clicks marked A'a's laughter. "Nay. She is of your kind," he replied, "though once, like your companion, she lacked a horn. Years ago, we aided her flight from the two-footed boat-builders. We curse their kind! They kill us when they can—though we have never offered them the slightest harm. They steal our tusks and dappled skins, our rich fat and strong, supple bones. They would harness us as they do their hapless *daya,* we think, could they but devise a means."

A storm of angry crackles and squeals came from A'a's fellows, evidently signaling agreement.

"Where does this red mare live?" the dark prince asked as the tumult subsided.

"Inland," A'a replied. "She visits us from time to time, coming down to the golden shore in spring when we are passing by. Sometimes she travels with us a while. We tell her of all the realms undersea that we have visited, and she speaks of the drylands she has seen. Several of us have learned her tongue, and she speaks our own tongue a little, too."

The swells rolled dark and warm around them.

"You are fortunate, O friend of our great friend," the sleek sea-rover added, "to have such an ally to intercede on your behalf."

Jan lay silent a moment, thoroughly confused. A hornless *da* mare, having escaped the two-foots, now living as a unicorn? Surely he could not have heard the other right.

"You say this mare once lacked a horn . . . ?" he began.

The narwhal leader clacked and nodded. "Drinking from a sacred pool guarded by white poisontails transformed her," he replied. "A horn now grows upon her brow."

The dark unicorn snorted, shook his head, still utterly perplexed. Could A'a be referring to the sacred wellspring of the moon, Jan wondered, deep in wyvern country?

"But how could this Red-One," he murmured, only half realizing he was thinking aloud, "many miles inland, know of our plight—and send you word?"

The black narwhal laughed. "Red-One glides through our dreams," he answered. "Her spells conjured the storm that raised the sea above the rocks and enabled your escape from the stinking boat-makers. It was surely a mighty leap to fling her powers so far. We are uneasy for her now, having received no further sending from her these many hours since."

Jan felt a stab of recognition now. Could Tek's dam be the one of whom the narwhals spoke? He had known all his life that the Red Mare was a magicker, able to enter dreams and bring weather. He knew she often traveled far from the Vale on mysterious errands never explained. It had been Jah-lila, years past, who had saved him from a wyvern's sting and hinted at origins far stranger than merely being the offspring of renegade unicorns—outlaws of the Plain—as most of the herd believed.

The sea-unicorns bobbed and whistled. Despite the mildness of the air after the storm, all Jan's limbs felt suddenly chill. Had Jah-lila once been a *da* in the city of the two-foots? Could drinking of Alma's sacred pool deep in wyvern-occupied territory somehow have transformed her? For all its healing powers, could that miraculous well truly change hornless *daya* into unicorns? The prospect both disturbed and excited him.

"I believe this Red-One of whom you speak is kin to me," he said to A'a, "being mother to my mate."

The narwhal leader reared back, startled, his speech degenerating into a series of squeals and staccato raps, by which, Jan supposed, he transmitted this news to his fellows. The dark prince nearly slid from the backs of his rescuers as other narwhals joined in their leader's gleeful dither, jostling and chattering.

Across from him, Ryhenna's supporters seemed to contain themselves better than their podmates, so that the sleeping mare only stirred, but did not wake. Eventually, to Jan's relief, A'a calmed himself and restored order with a barrage of deep, rapid snaps and bursts of rising notes. As the narwhals quieted, their leader once more resumed the unicorn tongue.

"We were unaware of your kinship to Red-One," the narwhal replied. "This news pleases us very well."

"I seek to return to my home," Jan told him urgently, "and I would bring my companion Ryhenna with me, but I do not know the way. . . ."

"Do not fear," A'a replied. "You need only travel east along the silver shore to reach the whistling steeps and the golden sands where the blue skimmers flock. From there, you and your companion will be able to find your way inland, will you not?"

Whistling steeps, golden sands, blue skimmers. Quickly, Jan grasped the most likely translations: Singing Cliffs, the shores of the Summer Sea, and the dust-blue herons.

"Aye," he cried. "We can easily find our way inland from there."

"Good," A'a replied. "We are not far from the shallows—though you will need to travel many days along the silver strand before you reach the steeps. We should be within sight of the drylands by morning. Until then, sleep, friend Aljan, unicorn of the land, for I see you are as weary as your companion. It is time both of you slept. Rest now till we put you safe ashore."

Prince's Get
☽ 24 ☾

Dagg felt exposed, vulnerable now that he had passed outside the Vale. Tepid sun and cool spring air seemed almost sultry. Grazing as he went, he trotted through the greening hills, admiring the delicious shoots and young buds bursting everywhere. His long winter pelt, grown ragged now, had yet to shed. He found himself sweating beneath the shag. Gnats and midges swarmed in droves. He swatted at a biting fly on his rump.

He could not believe how quickly the season had changed. The violent storm at equinox, little more than a month gone by, had banished the hard-frozen snows in a single sweep. Dagg shuddered, thinking of the desperate winter past: Jan, gryphon-killed; mad Korr ordering his son's innocent mate pursued even in her exile beyond the Vale. Then the storm. Common knowledge called Tek's dam, to whom she had fled, a magicker. Could the Red Mare truly have conjured the deluge at equinox—and all that had ensued?

Uneasily, Dagg shoved speculation aside. Those tragedies were over—nightmares from which the herd must now awake. He trotted across pathless, rolling hills of mixed forest and meadow. Deep in his breast stirred the fear that had dogged him all winter since Tek's flight. Had she been able to find her mother, the elusive Red Mare—or had she perished with her unborn in the snows beyond the Vale? Even strengthened as she was by the healer's herb, her desperate run must have cost her much.

A sharp whistle cut through his troubled musing. The dappled warrior halted dead, his nostrils flared. He cast about him with ears and eyes. He stood in an open meadow beside a narrow ravine, gushing now with spring flood. On the cliffside opposite, a figure moved, partially hidden by trees. His heart lifted suddenly as Tek stepped from the forest's edge onto the open hillside.

"Ho, Tek!" Dagg shouted, half-rearing. "Well met!"

The pied mare laughed. She seemed surprisingly hale. Dagg himself was only beginning to recover from the privations of the harsh season past. Despite the recent abundance of sprouting shoots and buds, his ribs still showed. Tek, by contrast, looked sleek.

"Come up," she cried. "I'll meet you."

Wheeling, she vanished into the trees. Dagg splashed across the flooded ravine and started up the rocky trail. A thought struck him just as he reached the trees. Though a tall, strapping mare, Tek had always been lean, slim as a filly, without an ounce of spare flesh. So he recalled her from their years in the Vale, and so she had appeared to him on the hillside above only moments before.

A chill bit into Dagg's breast as he counted the time since the night of courting upon the shores of the Summer Sea. Tek's pregnancy ought to have been far advanced by now, her unborn progeny not due for close to another moon—yet her slender girth made obvious that she was no longer pregnant. Dagg's heart fell. She must have lost the foal.

The sound of hoofbeats along the steep trail made him quicken his pace. Through the trees ahead, he glimpsed Tek rounding the bend. She let out a glad whinny and charged him. Dagg braced, laughing, as she shouldered against him, frisking and nipping. He felt like a colt again, dodging the smarting blows of her hooves and fencing her nimble feints of horn. Panting, the two of them subsided at last, Tek tossing the long black-and-rose strands of mane from her eyes. Dagg marveled at her energy.

"Well, Dagg," she said, a little breathless. "What brings you?"

"You," he answered, chafing against her companionably. "How are you?" he asked her. "How fared you this winter past?"

Tek laughed, stepping back. "As you see. I found my dam and sheltered in her grotto. But you, Dagg—" Her voice sobered. "How fared you and those I left behind in the Vale?"

Dagg cast down his eyes. "So many perished," he answered. "Mainly the old and the very young."

As he thought of Korr keeping huge assemblies standing in the fierce cold for hours daily, sharing only among his favored Companions the secret of where the best forage lay, the dappled warrior's voice grew hard.

"Many starved, who need not have starved. Many died of cold who need not have died. By the end of winter, even the most loyal acknowledged Korr must be mad."

Tek nodded, sobered. "I sorrow to hear of it."

Dagg stamped, pacing restlessly. "Then the tragedy at equinox. That was the final blow. . . ."

The dappled warrior stopped himself, glancing quickly at Tek. He had not meant to mention that catastrophe so soon, to spoil her first joy at their meeting—especially in view of the obvious loss of her unborn. Now the damage was done: he had let the news slip out. Tek's eyes narrowed.

"Tragedy?" she asked him. "Tell me of this."

Dagg scuffed one forehoof. Gnats whined, stinging him. He tossed his mane.

"Come." Tek fell in beside him and started up the slope. "Tell me as we walk."

The hillside steepened, its narrow trail threading through tough, spindly trees. Reluctantly, he began.

"After you fled at solstice time, some expressed hope, saying that with 'the pied wych' now cast out, Alma must once more smile—hah!" He snorted. "But the weather only worsened. Teki and I did our best to foster belief that it must be your exile the goddess found so displeasing. Most conceded that you had had nothing to do with the death of noble Sa and that fear for your life—not guilty shame—had driven you away. Feelings ran even higher in your favor when it became known you . . ."

Dagg hastily bit his tongue, reluctant to speak indelicately in view of Tek's obvious miscarriage.

"That is, when your condition became known," he muttered awkwardly, risking a glance at Tek.

She seemed unperturbed, serene in fact. Dagg frowned. Few mares he knew to have lost their young accepted their misfortune so blithely. Even moons later, he knew, many still mourned. Yet Tek evidenced no such deep-felt grief. Though sober and attentive, her expression was not stricken.

"Go on," the pied mare prompted. Puzzled, the young stallion continued.

"The king raged when he learned of your escape. One Companion who had attacked you broke his leg in the fall. Teki could not save him. The other, so they say, barely escaped skewering by the king after his tale of your bungled arrest. What saved him, I think, was his revelation of your—your pregnancy."

Tek nodded. Abashed, the dappled warrior hurried on.

"The news drove the king into a frenzy. He called your union with Jan unholy, the result of your mother's sorcery. He called your expected progeny 'abomination,' which at all costs must be prevented from birth."

Again, Dagg stopped himself, appalled at how badly he had put it, wishing he could snatch back the words which had just passed his lips. His hide flushed scarlet beneath heavy winter shag. Yet still Tek's expression seemed only serious and inward-turned, not anguished. Sadly, she shook her head.

"I cannot understand what the king could have meant. Perhaps no meaning lies in the ravings of the mad. But go on, Dagg. How did the herd respond?"

"Even some of the king's most ardent supporters acknowledged that he ranted then," continued Dagg, "but all still feared to defy him. Korr ordered his chosen to pursue you at once. Luckily, none knew whither you had fled. Teki was questioned, of course, but he professed bafflement at any suggestions that he had aided you, and his young acolytes backed him, every one, all swearing that they had not seen you in at least a day. Teki insisted on open questioning, before the assembled herd, not some secret interview.

"All the acolytes were let go. Even the king, calling for the blood of your unborn as he was, seemed reluctant to harm them. So many had died by now that the welfare of these young ones was doubly precious to the herd. As for Teki himself, much grumbling ensued among the king's loyalists over the pied stallion's being not only your acknowledged sire, but the mate of a 'known outlaw and magicker'—but the healer answered that you were a grown and wedded mare, responsible for your own actions now, and had not sheltered in his grotto since summer last.

"He also reminded all present that he had not shared a cave with your mother, Jah-lila, since before you were born and could scarcely be held accountable for any actions of a mare who chose to live outside the protection of the Vale and its Ring of Law. And when, he asked, had the Red Mare been adjudged an outlaw? She had never stood before Council or king facing charges for any crime. Strange she might be, a foreigner—but not criminal.

"He further called on all to witness his own long and loyal service to the king. Korr could not very well touch him then. Besides, he and everybody else knew that until his acolytes complete their training—years hence—the pied stallion remains the Vale's only healer. The very survival of many present might well hang upon his skill that winter. At last Korr let him go, but the king vowed that as soon as the weather broke, he would dispatch his Companions to hunt you down wherever you might be hiding, even beyond the Vale, if need be."

"And you?" Tek pressed, brow furrowed with concern. "All this you must have heard at second account. Was your absence marked? I lost track of you that night, in the snow. You fell behind. . . ."

Dagg shook his head. "Nay. When I limped home late the following day, I told my sire and dam I had been caught in the storm and wandered for hours, lost, before spending the night huddled in a small, deserted cave: not far from the truth. If they did not believe me, they said nothing to Korr. Blood ties, it seems, still bind them stronger than fealty to a king.

"All the herd attended the grey mare's funeral, despite the cold. Their grief was unbounded. The loss of Sa seemed to burn in the minds of many as a symbol of all that the herd had lost. Few save his Companions paid heed to Korr's words that day: no outbursts, no open rebellion, but a persistent, sullen, smoldering resentment against the king. Cold and starving, the unicorns were growing weary of being bitten and kicked. Attendance at Korr's rallies fell off sharply after that. We needed all our time and energy just to scout for forage. Most simply did not heed the summons of the king's Companions anymore.

"That pricked him. He dispatched his pack to comb the valley for you as soon as Sa's funeral rites were done. When they could not find you, the king had little doubt you had fled to your mother's haunts in the southeastern hills—though Teki and I kept rumors flying of your having hidden deep in the Pan Woods, or even run away wild renegade onto the Plain.

"Some of our allies swore to glimpsing you—or your haunt—on some distant slope of the Vale, crying out to Alma and the spirit of your princely mate to witness your innocence. More than a few of the king's Companions began to doubt the wisdom of actually finding you. We let them go on thinking you were some sort of wych or sprite. From time to time our sympathizers reported ghostly dreams of you mourning the injustice of your fate."

Warming to his tale, despite its gravity, Dagg found himself nearly laughing now. Inventing eerie sightings with which to confound Korr's superstitious followers had proved the winter's one diversion. Such small, delicious victories, he mused, had often proved the only fodder to chew on during the long, cold, hungry nights. Picking the trail beside him in the warm spring sun, Tek joined his laughter easily.

"You rogues. When spinning tales, neither you nor Teki has ever held the strictest regard for the truth."

Grinning, Dagg shrugged. "When the king has champed the truth all tatters with his 'mouthpiece of Alma' nonsense, I hardly see why others should not join in the feast. At any rate, Korr kept his Companions searching the Vale relentlessly for you all winter. Previously, joining the king had meant ease and privileges, better forage and a bullying self-importance in exchange for little actual toil. Now Korr's constant search parties grew so burdensome that many longed to quit his service, but dared not, lest their former Companions throw the deserters upon the mercy of a resentful herd. They kept to their posts now out of fear, not loyalty.

"As equinox neared, the king let it be known that he intended to send a party into the southeast hills at first spring to hunt you out before your time of bearing came. Yet sentiment had shifted so heavily in your favor by this time that the Companions were openly jeered as they set out. The king ought to use his wolves, so some muttered loudly, to seek out new forage for the starving. Many said that you were surely dead. Others feared that did you live, Jah-lila would doubtless protect you with her sorcery."

He glanced again at Tek, but she gave him no indication one way or another regarding her dam's role in the events of the scant month and a little past, merely glanced at him curiously as they continued up the trail.

"You spoke of tragedy," she reminded. "Some great loss during the mighty storm at equinox? Tell me of this."

Dagg looked away, finding the subject almost too painful to relate. But Tek seemed genuinely puzzled. If Jah-lila *had* precipitated the events of equinox, she apparently had not relayed them to her daughter. With a deep sigh, the dappled warrior said:

"At the dispatching of the Companions, the breaking point seemed to come at last. Korr's mate, Ses, had remained silent all this while. Though clearly not approving, she had spoken no public word against her mate. At equinox, though, Ses declared that if the king sent his wolves to hunt you down, she would leave him.

"Her resolve threw Korr into desperation, partly over the threatened loss of his beloved mate and daughter—for with the little filly still suckling, she could not be separated from her dam—and partly, too, because without Lell under his care, his claim to regency would be greatly weakened. Should the remnants of the Council of Elders so choose, they could as easily declare Ses regent as Korr. It was Ses who finally pointed out that were you, Tek, to bring Jan's unborn heir to term, it would be that foal, not Lell, to rightfully own the title of princess.

"Korr grew wild then, declaring 'the pied wych' and your child better dead than left to live. He blamed your dam as somehow the ultimate cause of all the herd's misfortune, calling her deceiver and seducer. Ses took refuge in Sa's deserted grotto. Korr sent his Companions to demand Lell's return, but Ses stood in the egress of the cave and shouted, 'I'll not rejoin my mate while he remains in his madness, and if you take my filly from me before she is weaned, she will die. How will that serve your king?'

"The king's Companions, unwilling to risk injury to either Ses or Lell, could only return—defeated—to Korr. He was furious, but what could he do? By day, while Ses foraged, Lell sheltered in Teki's cave with his acolytes. Public sentiment was now such that Korr dared not risk removing her in Ses's absence. The herd might have been moved to open rebellion then.

"Instead, Korr threw himself into planning the expedition to track you down. He dared not leave the Vale himself—for his position was now so precarious he feared his absence might lend the Council opportunity to declare another regent. On the eve of equinox, he sent his Companions out. In place of the traditional spring pilgrimage to the Hallow Hills, Korr ordered this quest for vengeance instead. Indeed, we'd few uninitiated colts and fillies left by then, and those too sickly for any trek.

"The Companions were to cross into the southeastern hills through the snowbound pass the moment enough snow had melted to make the way passable. Then they were to disperse, combing every inch of wilderland until they found you. My parents were among them, but even they, I think, had begun to scent which way the wind was blowing. Those Companions who remained behind with Korr were mostly old, injured, or sick.

"Great storms had been building in the southeast for days, the end of winter finally in sight. A violent deluge broke at last on equinox eve. Snow-locked mountainsides turned suddenly to muddy slush. Despite the downpour, so my parents tell, the Companions climbed struggling toward the pass. All at once, near the trail's highest point—between one heartbeat and the next—a vast wall of mud hurtled down upon them. The slope above had given way beneath the weight of melting snow and torrential rain.

"A scant few, among them my sire and dam, gained shelter beneath a jutting overhang of stone. They watched in horror as their fellows were swept away. Not one that had been caught by the slide remained to be found. The survivors, fleeing for their lives, returned to Korr and told their tale. Many who listened concluded it must have been a sorcerous storm, conjured by the red wych Jah-lila to punish Korr for seeking her daughter's life. Some are even calling your dam a prophet of Alma now, and Korr the false, blaspheming raver."

The trail had leveled out, threading along the side of the cliff. Dagg spotted the meadow and ravine far below. The pied mare paced silently, thoughtfully beside him.

"I knew nothing of this," she said at last. "If my dam indeed conjured that storm, she has not told me so. Nor has she spoken of the loss of the king's Companions, though I cannot doubt she knows of it. What ensued after the herd received this news?"

"Great mourning," Dagg replied. "Though the king's wolves had been much resented, they were still our blood, warriors of the Ring and loyal to their king—if unwisely so—and kith or kin to many. Their deaths put the herd's loss this winter past at nearly half our former numbers."

"And Korr?" Tek asked.

Dagg shook his head. "The king was devastated, seemed to regard the calamity as divine judgment. He has been silent since, issuing no proclamations, holding no rallies, making no demands. Many see it as a good sign, the beginning of a return to sanity. He moves about solely in the company of his few remaining Companions—most have dared to desert since equinox, and been accepted back into the herd after fitting penance. Ses still remains in Sa's grotto. Korr has neither called for her nor gone to her.

"Most of the winter's survivors are so relieved at the dispersal of the snows, the early warmth of spring, and the green buds growing that they spend their time foraging ravenously and give little thought to the herd's leadership. Their mood, for the moment quiet, seems to be one of waiting. No word has been heard of you, and though most are anxious for news, none have dared come in search since learning the fate of the king's Companions."

Tek smiled at him. "None till you," she said quietly.

Dagg snorted. "As your shoulder-friend, I doubt your dam would see cause to do me harm. Besides, the snow's long melted, and it scarce looks like rain."

Tek let out a great laugh, and Dagg could not help joining her. They had made good progress up the trail. He spotted a cave suddenly, a narrow slit in the cliff's side—it looked like a mere crease in the rock, not the entrance to a grotto.

"Come in; come in," Tek told him, entering. "My mother set out foraging early this morn. I doubt that she is yet returned, but we can wait within, sheltered from gnats and the cool spring wind."

Dagg hesitated, unease gripping him suddenly. He did not relish meeting the Red Mare face to face. Her veiled powers, her foreignness and mystery unnerved him. Lashing his tail, he followed the pied mare reluctantly into the cave. Its upper walls and ceiling clustered with glow-

ing lichens and fungi in rose, ghost blue, saffron, and plum. Their faint
light seemed to brighten as his eyes adjusted. Tek threw herself down
in one corner of the cave. Small heaps of last year's herbs and grass
lay about. The pied mare nodded to it.

"A little of the forage my mother laid in remains, even yet. Eat, if
you will."

But Dagg shook his head, settling himself opposite Tek. Though
weary, he felt no hunger pangs. He smelled the absent Red Mare now,
her unmistakable scent like rosehips and ripening cherries. She had always carried about her that spice fragrance of the magical milkwood
pods. The substance of them, so it was said, was in her very bones,
imparting the unique brilliant mallow color to her coat.

But though the Red Mare's scent was strong, she herself was not
in evidence. Dagg allowed himself a relieved sigh. A respite, then, before he met the magicker. He caught as well an unmistakable whiff of
pan: salty and sharp, an odor he had loathed since having been ambushed as a colt by pans for trespassing their Woods. He could only
conclude that this cave must have been used as a den by the fetid
creatures before the Red Mare chased them out. Politely, he ignored the
stench.

"You spoke of the herd's mood of waiting," Tek said, her own
mood lifting suddenly. Indeed, she seemed almost ebullient now, in
sharp contrast to her gravity of only moments past. "Well, they need
not wait long now. Though I am by no means my mother's confidante,
she has imparted to me this much: Jan lives and at this moment journeys
homeward. He will reach the Vale in ten days' time."

Taken wholly unprepared, Dagg started, restraining himself just
short of springing up. He stared astonished at the pied mare across from
him. Had Tek, too, run mad? His mentor and shoulder-friend watched
him expectantly, eyes bright. She seemed to relish his startlement.

"What . . . are you saying?" Dagg stammered. "Jan is not—he was
killed by gryphons. . . ."

Smiling, the pied mare shook her head. "None of us saw. We could
only surmise—wrongly, it seems, for my mother has seen by her sor-
ceries that he was taken and held captive in a far place by a strange,
two-footed race. Now that he has slipped their grasp, he will be home
soon."

She spoke with such anticipation, such confidence that Dagg was
loath to contradict her. Yet clearly what she was telling him could not
be so. He shifted uneasily. The pied mare watched him amiably, her
expression calm.

"You don't believe me," laughed Tek. "Well enough. Were I you,

I, too, would doubt. I will let Jah-lila convince you when she returns. But I tell you now that learning of my mate's imminent return has sustained me this last moon and some. I can scarcely wait to show him our union's fruit, which will surprise even him, I think."

Dagg blinked. "Fruit . . . ?" he started, stopped. "But—"

Again Tek laughed. "I bore my young at equinox. Can you not see I am no longer in foal? And such young! Such miraculous progeny as never before seen among the unicorns—Jan will be delighted, as I hope you will be, and indeed all the herd. I must return to the Vale with my prince's get as soon as may be, that we may greet my mate at his homecoming."

Tek spoke quietly, yet with unmistakable excitement. Snorting, the dappled warrior shook his head. Wild dreams of reunion with her perished mate and young obviously comforted the mad mare, he thought desperately. The very notion made his skin crawl. He had always believed in facing the truth head-on, even if truth were a shrieking gryphon. Jan was dead, and Tek had obviously miscarried long before term. Sighing, his companion shook herself, seemingly from sheer joy.

"You will see," she told him gently. "As soon as Sismoomnat and Pitipak return, you will behold my prince's get."

"Sismoo—Piti—" Dagg stumbled over the unfamiliar names. "Who . . . ?"

"My sisters," Tek replied, so that Dagg could only stare anew. Sisters? He had never heard the pied mare speak of sisters—yet even in Jah-lila's self-imposed exile, he knew, Teki had not forsworn the Red Mare: neither healer nor magicker had ever taken another mate.

"Ah," the pied mare said suddenly, pricking her ears. "I hear them."

Dagg turned his head toward the cave's entryway. He heard a strange fluting and twittering mixed with hisses and grunts. The sound sent slivers of ice along his ribs as a salty rankness filled his nose. He smelled pans! That was pan-chatter he heard! Tek continued to lounge at ease. Was her madness so deep she did not realize their danger?

His limbs tensed, preparing to vault him to his heels just as a slight, upright figure ducked through the grotto's egress and called a greeting to Tek. The pied mare whistled back the same phrase. The pan child— for it was a child, only a small thing, not nearly full grown—was followed by other figures, one of which was two-footed like herself.

For a moment, Dagg lay frozen, staring at the pans—and then his eyes turned in even greater astonishment to what had followed these goatlings through the entryway, stepping on delicate hooves as docilely as deer. What dream was this? Dagg could do little more than gape. He had never seen such a thing. What stood before him in the entryway beside the pans could only be Tek's progeny, given form perhaps by the Red Mare's sorcery, or by Teki's miraculous herb? Born under the dark moon of equinox—touched by Alma surely, but in blessing or curse?

"Behold," Tek proudly bade, rising to nuzzle her young. "Behold what Jan and I have made: my prince's get, heir to the leadership of the unicorns."

Enemies

☽ 25 ☾

Jan trotted eastward along the silvery strand, the direction he and Ryhenna had been traveling since their rescuers, the unicorns-of-the-sea, had set them ashore many days ago. It had been hard going at first. In the beginning, he and the coppery mare had done far more grazing than traveling, plucking every green shoot and bud they could set teeth upon. Soon enough their pace picked up as his companion's flanks hardened, her wind improved, and Jan's own bruised ribs healed.

Ryhenna grew bolder by the day. Skittish at first, she had started at everything: crabs scuttling across the sand, diving seagulls, beachrunners nimbly skirting the incoming waves. Her years imprisoned in the City of Fire had robbed her of all knowledge of the world outside. Now she took it in with the wonder and eagerness of a filly.

Yet despite her innocence, her youth, Jan reminded himself, she was no filly, but a young mare just coming into flower. A beauty, too. Her odd, coppery pelt flashed in the sunlight, so unlike the hue of any unicorn. Her exotic, upright mane—badly singed at equinox—had since regrown. Now it once more bristled the slim, elegant rise of her neck.

Early on, Jan had managed to chew through the chin strap of her water-logged halter and tug it free. His own, fashioned of silvery sky-stuff, proved impossible to remove without the nimble digits of two-foots to unfasten its closure. The dark unicorn could only snort and shake his head in frustration while the hard, linked loops clapped at his cheeks and muzzle, chafing him.

Though the spring days warmed, nights along the windswept beach remained bitingly chill. Most evenings he and the coppery mare managed to gather a stack of grey driftwood dry enough for Jan to set alight with a spark made by striking the tip of his horn against one heel and large enough to smolder the night through once the flames died down. He and Ryhenna rarely needed to seek shelter in the scrub beyond the dunes.

Ryhenna asked him constantly for tales of the Vale, her appetite insatiable. Jan told her the old lays, the history of his people: how, four hundred summers past, treacherous wyverns had driven the unicorns from their rightful home, the Hallow Hills, far to the north across the Plains. He told her how the princess Halla and her weary band of refugees had first stumbled across the deserted Vale and claimed it for their new home in exile—only to be attacked each spring by marauding gryphons: savage predators with great wings of green or blue.

He did not speak of the rest of the legend, of Alma's Firebringer, prophesied to deliver the unicorns from exile by restoring to them their ancestral lands and driving the hated wyverns out. Questions! His heart was full of questions still. The voice of the goddess had been silent since equinox—yet he could harbor no doubts now it was her own divine spark which burned in him.

He found himself sometimes dreaming of the City of Fire, of its two-footed sorcerers and their mysteries. Yet each day they fell farther behind him. More often he dreamed of what lay ahead: the Vale and all his kith, especially Tek. Memory of their joy on the night of courting more than a half year gone and of the pledge that they had shared made each day he remained parted from her an agony.

Memory, too, of the confused and disordered dreams Jah-lila had managed to send him in the City—of Korr's madness, the herd's starvation, and the pied mare's flight—filled him with unease. How much of their message did he—dared he—understand? No such visions came to him during his and Ryhenna's trek homeward along the silvery shore.

Three half-moons to the day after equinox, Jan noted a change in the beach along which he and the coppery mare trotted. The pale, ash-colored sand began gradually to mix with particles of yellow amber. Barely enough at first to warm the cool silver into dove, before long the shade had strayed into dun, and then to deep, true gold. Jan tossed his head, whinnying, his pace accelerating to a flying canter. Startled, Ryhenna kicked into a run beside him.

"What is it?" she cried.

Alongside them the waves had changed from grey to green. Jan laughed, tossing his head.

"The sand, Ryhenna. It's gold!"

His companion half shied, shaking her mane. "Then, truth, the Singing Cliffs cannot be far! How I have longed to see the groves where thou and thy fellows danced court, the spot where ye were set upon by gryphons, and the beachhead where thou wert swept away. . . ."

She whickered in delight, spurred, pulled ahead of him.

"I scarce can wait. O Moonbrow, let us run!"

Laughing, Jan sprinted to close the gap. He nipped at the coppery mare's flank. She kicked playfully, veered into the foaming surf to cast up spray after spray of shining droplets, then charged back onto the ribbon of golden beach again. Jan pounded after, heart racing, drew even and crowded her back toward the waves.

With a gay shriek, the coppery mare twisted free of him, and halted stiff-legged, panting. Jan wheeled and also plunged to a halt, breathing heavily. His companion stood looking at him with her bright, brown eyes. She laughed again, pawing at the sand with one round, solid hoof, swished her long-haired, silky tail against one flank, her beardless chin held up impertinently. How like and yet unlike a unicorn she was!

Laughing, he shouldered against her. She nipped him lightly, a playful champ—then started back with a cry of alarm as the shadow of some winged thing in the air above fleeted over them. Jan, too, looked up, then wheeled and stared. A blue-pinioned shape was diving toward them out of the cloudless morning sky.

"Get behind me, Ryhenna!" the prince of the unicorns cried, dodging in front of the hornless mare.

Above them, the winged figure banked suddenly, rearing back. Its elongated pinions stroked the air as it touched down with a spindle-shanked, gangling grace on the golden sand. Jan stared. Though all over dusty blue—the color of a gryphon formel—the creature before them was much smaller than a wingcat.

It stood upright on two lanky, coral legs. Its slender neck crooked, head tilting from side to side, examining him and Ryhenna first with one salmon-colored eye, and then with the other. Fanning its rosy crest, the figure before them trilled happily, a hollow cooing from deep in its throat. Red chevrons beneath its pinions flashed as it folded wing. Ryhenna crowded against Jan, her voice hushed, terrified.

"What is it, my lord?" she whispered. "Is it a gryphon?"

Jan whickered with relief. "Nay," he cried, euphoria filling him. "No enemy, but a friend. Greetings, Tlat, queen of the seaherons. Well met!"

The queen of the wide-roving windriders nodded, mincing toward them across the sand. "Greetings!" she shrieked. "Greetings, Jan-prince! Welcome, welcome. We feared cat-eagles had seized you. We feared you lost!"

Jan fought the impulse to rush forward and rub shoulders with Tlat as he would with one of his own people. The delicate herons, he knew, were ever wary of being knocked down or trampled by the heavy hooves of unicorns. The young prince restrained himself, keeping his heels planted and still.

"Not lost," he assured Tlat. "Not seized by gryphons—though I was pursued by them. A terrible storm swept me out to sea. It has taken me all this time to find my way back."

"Ah!" cried the heron queen. "So the cat-eagle spoke truth after all. We thought he lied to save himself. But who is your companion? What is this odd, hornless one that stands beside you?"

Jan blinked, lost for a moment. The darting thoughts of herons shifted like the winds. Tlat stood craning and eyeing Ryhenna. Jan moved aside to allow her a better view. The coppery mare shifted nervously as the other approached, stabbing her bill into the air and fluttering her folded wings with growing excitement.

"Color of sunsets! Color of burning!" the heron queen exclaimed. "Such a hue among unicorns we have never seen. And round feet—not pairs of half-moon toes, but only single ones: solid as a mussel shell, round as the ripe egg of the moon. Amazing! Where is your beard, burning-colored mare? Where is your horn?"

Ryhenna seemed disconcerted, at a loss for words. "I . . . I am no unicorn, as my lord Moonbrow is," she managed. "I am only a *da* from the City of . . . of Two-foots, far to the west."

"Two-foots? Two-foots?" cackled Tlat. "My tribe know something of these. They glide the waves in great hollowed-out treefish. Sometimes we see their windwings on our journeys, but we veer clear lest they hurl their hunting sticks at us. They eat our kind and steal our feathers. They are our enemies, as the cat-eagles are! If you have shared nest with our enemies, non-unicorn mare, then you, too, must be our enemy! Be off!"

The heron queen's agitation grew even as she spoke. Her crest fanned in anger, not welcome, now. Bill cocked, she danced grimly before Ryhenna, ready to fly at her. Hastily, Jan stepped between.

"Peace, great queen of the windriders," he soothed. "Ryhenna's people are prisoners of the two-foots, as was I this winter past. When spring arrived, she aided my escape. Now we are grateful to have come once more among our fast allies, the noble herons, instead of among our common enemies, the two-foots or the gryphons."

"Ah!" clucked Tlat, ruffling. "Ah! I see. My apologies, fiery-colored mare. I spoke in haste. Prisoners! Yes. Did the two-foots steal your horn?"

Ryhenna cast about her helplessly. The other's brash manner had clearly unnerved her. Quickly, Jan addressed the heron queen.

"The two-foots' captives grow no horns," he began, but Tlat's raucous cries interrupted him.

"No horns? How misfortunate—useless! Crippled. Like a broken
wing! My commiserations, imperfect mare."

The dark prince saw his companion's face fall, her frame droop.
She seemed utterly crushed at the heron queen's screeches of sympathy.
He drew breath.

"Indeed it is a great pity, but it cannot be helped. But tell me, Tlat,
what has passed since the storm separated me from my band this autumn
past. Has word reached you of how the unicorns fare?"

The heron queen bobbed, her gaze turning once more to Jan.

"No word," she cried. "Badly, we fear. Winter here was harsh. Too
stormy to risk flying far from our cliffs. Many deaths. Our Mother-the-
Sea did not yield much fish. Much courting this spring, though! Each
hen has chosen her mates and begun to lay. Soon a great hatching will
follow: a great squeaking and crying from the squabs just pipped from
their shells. Then will the flock of the herons be renewed! Then will we
forget the deaths and sorrows of this winter past."

Her words sent a chill through Jan.

"But no word from the Vale?" he asked. "You do not know for
certain how my own people fared?"

Tlat wagged her head, beginning to dance again, her tone dolorous.
"No word. Though the winds have moderated since equinox, we have
been too busy replenishing our lost numbers to think of travel. We fear
your people wintered as poorly as did we, but we have sent no envoys
to inquire. Scouting for cat-eagles and fishing to feed my mates, I spotted you upon the strand. Great will be the rejoicing among the herons
when I bring word of your return!"

Her words, shrieked and croaked in heron fashion, warmed Jan.

"I am grateful, great Tlat, for the ardor of your welcome. Truly the
far-ranging herons are the invaluable allies of the unicorns. May your
consorts be many and your nests bountiful. I would stay longer, enjoying
your company, but I dare not. I must return to my people. Already I
have been absent too long."

Tlat started with a cry, flapping her wings. Ryhenna half shied.

"Too long! Yes! I, too, have been gone a great while. My mates
hunger, their warmth dwindling. Each now sits his nest, incubating one
of my rosy eggs. Soon the hatchlings will pip! I must return. Having
fished, my crop is full. But first, come. You must not depart our shores
until I show you the thing we have been keeping all winter. It put us
to great trouble, but we persevered out of loyalty to our allies, the
unicorns. We knew that you would want us to. I had planned to send

fliers to your Vale soon to alert your people of its presence upon our shores. The cat-eagle we captured. One of those who attacked you this autumn past."

Now it was Jan's turn to half shy in surprise. Captured a gryphon—one of the raiders that had harried him and his fellows upon the strand more than a half year gone? He marveled the gracile seaherons had managed to capture such a formidable enemy, much less hold it prisoner for over half a year. But before he could so much as draw breath to question Tlat, the heron queen had spread her wings to the stiff sea breeze and risen into the air. In another moment, she was out of earshot. Earthbound below, Jan and Ryhenna could only follow.

The windrider flew high and slowly, circling back from time to time. Jan and the coppery mare cantered along the damp, gleaming road of sand between wet green wave and dry golden dune. They passed along the sandstone canyons of the Singing Cliffs. Ryhenna cocked her head to the sweet, weeping soughing of breeze through their odd formations, sculpted by centuries of wind and tide.

They came to a familiar stretch of beach and cliff. Jan recognized the break in the cliff wall, the half-submerged rocks, the deep, uneven trough in the sand where, at high tide, the surf washed through with treacherous force. Here was the point at which, last autumn, he had emerged from the cliffs, felt the gryphon's claws along his back, then been swept away by the furious sea.

He remembered the gryphon—a green-and-gold male—overwhelmed by the same vast wave that had claimed Jan. He remembered glimpsing the other's limp form floating on the waves afterward, seeing it cast back up on shore—perhaps *not* dead. Had the wingcat survived? Something moved upon the rocks just above the waterline ahead. Jan halted, staring at the creature as yet unaware of his gaze, while overhead Tlat veered and circled. The creature's dull golden pelt was sandy and scabbed, his foreparts a mass of shabby green feathers: a gryphon on the brink of starvation.

Jan shook himself. Beside him, Ryhenna pressed against his flank, peering over his back at the wasted predator. The lionlike haunches were sunk in, his rib cage showing starkly through thin, patchy fur. One wing lay folded against his side. The other dragged awkwardly across the rock. The wingcat lay in a heap above the swirling tide. One eagle's claw reached down into the sea. From time to time, the gryphon jerked his submerged forelimb from the water, talons clenched—but always empty.

The wingcat was fishing, Jan realized, as with a weak but triumphant cry, the gryphon at last hefted into sight a small, struggling fish.
With one snap of his hooked, razor-sharp bill, the fish disappeared down
the raptor's scrawny gullet. A moment later, the wingcat returned to
scanning the water, foreclaw once more extended beneath the surface
of the tide. How many fish could he hope to catch thus in a day? Jan
wondered. Surely not enough to keep himself alive. Overhead, Tlat
dipped, cawing and feinting at the fishing gryphon.

"Haw! Cat-eagle! Enemy!" she shrieked. "Look up! Look up!"

The tercel hunched, ignoring her, but she persisted, swooping just
close enough to scatter any fish. At last the starving gryphon raised his
head.

"Take yourself off, you accursed seabird," he rasped. "Has your
kind not taunted me enough?"

"We feed you!" cried Tlat. "Our generosity kept you alive this winter past."

"I never asked for your food!" the gryphon snarled, swiping at her
with sudden, unexpected vigor. Tlat hovered flapping in the air above
him, merrily out of reach.

"You never ask," she shouted, "but you always eat what we bring.
Without us, you would be dead!"

"Better death," the gryphon spat, "than to live, starving and maimed,
on the leavings of arrogant sealice."

With a caw of delighted contempt, Tlat alighted upon a stone just
barely within the gryphon's reach. Her gorge heaved. Had she given
him time, he could have lunged and caught her, but in less than an
eyeblink, she had disgorged three large fish and darted away into the
air again. Jan watched appalled as, driven by hunger too great to deny,
the wingcat snatched up Tlat's gifts and wolfed them down.

Yet the gryphon's own look of disgust told Jan he hated himself
for accepting, for living as a prisoner of the mocking seaherons. *As I
once lived a prisoner of the two-foots,* Jan could not help thinking. A
disturbing sense of empathy touched him. Angrily, he shoved it aside.
This tercel, along with companions, had sought to kill him and his band
half a year ago. Beside him, Ryhenna stood shuddering.

"You do not keep me alive for charity," the wingcat shouted after
Tlat, who now circled overhead, chattering derisively. "I know that well
enough! But your taunts cannot move me, who destroyed the unicorns'
black prince. Surely now my flock will drive the hated intruders from
Ishi's sacred Vale. My life no longer matters, already sacrificed to the
wind-god's almighty glory. I pray only for an end to my misery."

"Kah! Haw! Nonsense!" screamed Tlat. "The first storm of autumn battered your companions to bits. None survived to report the outcome of your raid. Your flock will assume you failed—as indeed you *have* failed. Behold! The prince of unicorns returns, alive and hale, unscratched by treacherous cat-eagle claws."

She wheeled to circle above Jan and Ryhenna. Turning, the wingcat started, green cat-eyes wide. An instant after, they winced, grimacing at the pain his sudden movement had caused his injured wing. Cautiously, Jan moved forward, careful to remain well beyond the wingcat's reach. After a moment's hesitation, Ryhenna accompanied him, still peering with fascination and terror at the wounded gryphon. Jan snorted, lashing his tail.

"What Tlat, noble queen of our allies, says is true, wingcat," the prince of the unicorns flung at him. "Your raid did not succeed, though the sea washed me far. It has taken me a long time to return to the spot where last we met, enemy."

"Great god of winds," the gryphon exclaimed. "It *is* you, cursed prince of trespassers. The sea has not been kind to deliver you back unharmed, while mangling me beyond repair. Have you come merely to mock, as this harridan seabird does, or will you kill me at last and end my shame?"

"I go!" cried Tlat from above. "My mates hunger and my unborn chicks grow cold! I leave you to do with this predator whatever seems good in your eyes, friend Jan. Do not forget it was your allies, the seaherons, who preserved his worthless life to await your vengeance."

"I will never forget your invaluable service, Tlat!" called Jan. "May your flock ever increase!"

Overhead, the queen of the dust-blue herons wheeled, winging swiftly toward the Singing Cliffs. A moment later, she was lost against the hot, flame blue of the cloudless morning sky.

Peacemaking

☽ 26 ☾

Jan stood eyeing the wounded gryphon, who despite obvious weakness and pain refused to cower. The prince of the unicorns had no idea what to do with him. Surely prudence demanded that he kill this savage foe. To attack any grounded wingcat on sight had always been the practice among his people. And yet—

"So, unicorn," the tercel snapped, "did you come merely to gawk? I am Illishar, of the nest of Shreel and Kilkeelahr, kin to great Malar, matriarch of all my clan. I fear no unicorn!"

Were he one of my own people, Jan mused, *we would call him brave.*

The young prince snorted with frustration. Why was it so hard for him to despise this enemy as he should? The tercel's fellows had attacked Jan's peaceful band. This very wingcat's talons had scored his shoulders to the bone. Yearly, the gryphon's kind raided the Vale to steal away the unicorns' newborn fillies and foals.

"Well?" the wingcat taunted hoarsely. "Have you nothing more to say before you end my life, prince of thieves? Or do you mean to take the coward's way and simply leave me? The herons are done with me. Without their fish to add to my own meager catch, I'll quickly starve."

Jan stood silent, considering. The gryphon shifted painfully, hissing. The dark prince felt Ryhenna huddled against him.

"Come, my lord," she whispered urgently. "Let's depart. His hate-filled words frighten me."

"Have you lost your tongue?" the gryphon Illishar shrieked. Jan felt the coppery mare start, flinch. "Or has that silvery chain now clamped shut your jaws? Kill me now, invader—infidel—or else be off! I've little leisure to spend arguing with unicorns."

"Moonbrow," Ryhenna urged him, "let's away."

Jan nodded abruptly and turned. "Aye, Ryhenna. I've long promised to show you all our haunts along the Summer shore. I'll do so now while I ponder what's to be done with this foe."

He started off across the sand, and with a relieved sigh, the coppery mare fell in beside him. Glancing back, Jan glimpsed the tercel sagging as though only anger had kept him upright to challenge Jan. Once more the young prince champed his heart tight against pity. Marauding wing-cats deserved none! Quickening his trot, he led Ryhenna away from his injured enemy, eastward along the shore.

For the better part of the morning, Jan showed the coppery mare the beaches along which he and his fellows had galloped that half year past, the cliffs under which they had sparred, the sparse coastal wood-lands in which they had foraged and bedded and sought shelter against mild summer storms. He described for her his people's alliance with the dust-blue herons and spoke of how he and Tek had courted and pledged. Ryhenna harkened, rapt, but as she walked through the vast courting glade, he heard her soft and bitter sigh.

"Why do you sorrow?" he asked, puzzled.

The coppery mare tossed her head. "I think on the day, not long distant now, when we shall join your herdmates in the Vale."

Jan frowned, moving to stand in front of her. "Ryhenna, I had thought you welcomed the prospect!"

The coppery mare refused to meet his gaze. "I do," she murmured, "and yet I dread it. What will become of me among thy people, Moon-brow? Will I ever dance court in this sacred glade?"

Jan cocked his head, trying to see her better. "Ryhenna, such is my dearest wish," he told her, "that one day you may find in this glade that same joy which I so lately found with Tek."

His companion sighed again, as though swallowing down some hard little pricking pain. "Who among your people would want me?" she said heavily. "Hornless—crippled. Useless. *Imperfect*."

The dark prince fell back a step at her quiet vehemence. "You must set no store by Queen Tlat's thoughtless words. . . ."

"Even though they be true?" Ryhenna finished, turning to meet his gaze at last. "O Moonbrow, dost think I have not always known that while I might one day walk among thy people, I can never be one of them?"

The dark unicorn stared at her, astonished. He shook his head vig-orously. The halter of silvery skystuff clinked and chinged. "Nay, Ry-henna," he told her. "You are wrong."

The breeze off the golden strand stirred the trees surrounding the glade. Ryhenna's coat gleamed fiery copper in the late morning sun. Jan looked away, at the seabirds gliding overhead, at distant herons winging home to the Singing Cliffs from fishing in the bay.

"The sea-unicorns told me—and Jah-lila herself once told me a thing which leads me to hope our rescuer's tale may be true—that my mate's dam was once hornless as you are, born in your City of Fire, but fled and, joining our company, became a unicorn."

The coppery mare's gaze changed, intensified, grew full of such wild longing suddenly that he found it difficult to meet.

"Surely this is but an old mare's tale thou hast spun to keep my spirit up," she breathed. "My own dam used to do the same, but I pray thee to have done. I am no filly to be made docile so."

Again Jan snorted, shaking his head. "I pledge to you, Ryhenna: my mate's dam is a powerful sorceress; if any among the unicorns has power to make you one of us, it is she."

He saw the coppery mare flinch, shuddering. "And if not?"

"If not," the dark prince told her, "then you will be no less welcome among us, admired for your bravery, your counsel, your beauty." The silver halter jingled as he spoke. He made himself say the words: "A horn upon the brow—it is not the world, Ryhenna."

The coppery mare turned away suddenly. He followed her.

"Moonbrow," she breathed, "I fear this above all else: that rejoining old friends in the Vale, thou wilt forget me."

"Ryhenna," the young prince cried. "How could you think it? Such shall never come to pass."

The coppery mare turned again to face him. The breeze sighed through the trees. "Thy mate will reclaim thee," she said bluntly, "and thy duties as prince. *I* am not thy mate—"

Jan shook his head. "Nay."

"Among *daya*," she offered, "a stallion may have many mates."

Again the dark prince shook his head. "But not among unicorns."

She gazed at him, lost. "In the City," she whispered, "I was called thy mate, if only from courtesy. What am I now to thee—what can I be—if not thy mate?"

Her voice was tight, her tone desperate. He moved to stand next to her. "My shoulder-friend," he answered her, "she to whom I owe my freedom and my life. Those among the unicorns who love me, Ryhenna, will love you as well."

"I shall never love any as I love thee, Moonbrow!" she cried.

He nuzzled her, very gently. "Nor I you, Ryhenna," he said. "Tek is my mate. I love her. You are my shoulder-friend, and I love you. I love you both, but differently. And when in a year or two years' time, you dance court within this glade, it will be with one whom you love in a way entirely other than the way that you love me. I am your companion, your friend, Ryhenna, just as you are always and ever mine. Stand fast with me," he said, "and no foe shall ever part us."

The pain so plain upon her features all at once subsided. She whickered low, and champed him lightly once, a comrade's nip, no more. "Well enough then, my shoulder-friend."

He shrugged against her laughing, relieved. Sun overhead was climbing toward noon. He shook himself, snorting.

"So tell me, Ryhenna, what should I do with this gryphon?"

The mare beside him shuddered. "Leave him," she answered. "Leave him to his fate."

Jan sidled uneasily. "By rights, I ought to kill him," he murmured, "as a sworn enemy of the unicorns."

He heard Ryhenna gasp. "Too perilous," she answered quickly. "Weak and starving as he is, Moonbrow, he nonetheless might do thee harm."

The dark unicorn nodded. "Aye. And skewering a crippled foe scarce seems honorable—yet simply leaving him to starve smacks hardly more noble. . . ."

"He frightens me," Ryhenna whispered, "and yet—"

"Yet?"

"I pity him," she finished, glancing at him, "hobbled by his broken wing as surely as a firekeeper's tether once hobbled me. Captive of the herons—and now of us—as truly as once we two were captives in the City of Fire."

Jan stamped, frustrated, lashing his tail. He longed now only to quit the Summer shore and begin the last, short leg of the journey inland toward the Vale. Yet the gryphon's fate stymied him.

Great Alma, guide me, he petitioned silently. *Tell me what to do.*

The air around him hung utterly quiet, silence broken only by the whisper of breeze, the soft sigh of Ryhenna's breath, and the faint, far cries of seabirds fishing. Herons winged swiftly overhead, crops heavy. Some carried more fish, silver gleaming, in their bills. The prince of the unicorns sighed. His goddess remained mute still—or else spoke in words he could not reck.

"We'll feed him until I can decide, Ryhenna," he muttered, trotting across the glade toward the trees and the shore beyond.

🍂

He and Ryhenna spent the early afternoon gathering food for their captive gryphon. Well aware that the tercel needed meat to survive, Jan searched the tide pools for trapped fish. Two of the six he managed to skewer with his horn were of hefty size. Ryhenna meanwhile, at his direction, pawed the wet, golden sand for the fluted clams and rosy crabs that burrowed there, stamping them with her hard, round hooves to crack their shells.

A dead skate, newly cast up by the tide, rounded their haul into a fair-sized catch by the second hour past noon. Jan set about devising a means to transport their gryphon's food to him. The two-foots, he recalled, carried all manner of goods in wheeled carts. Though he and Ryhenna possessed no carts, he mused, they could still drag.

Eventually, the dark unicorn hit upon tangling fish and shellfish in a mat of seaweed and dragging the whole contrivance back to the gryphon on the rocks. Ryhenna suggested that if she lifted the other end of the seaweed clear of the ground, the pair of them might carry it with greater speed. Jan laughed through his teeth, marveling at their innovation as, trotting side to side, he and the coppery mare brought their prisoner his meal.

Despite obvious hunger, the tercel accepted their offering with little grace: screaming and hissing. Ryhenna refused to approach, so Jan pulled the food-laden mat within a few paces of the shrieking tercel by himself, then sprang away to stand with Ryhenna as the wingcat hauled himself laboriously near enough to snag the seaweed and draw it to him.

He fell upon its contents with savage relish. Jan watched, fascinated as the gryphon's razor beak made short work of the skate, slicing and swallowing down the tough cartilage along with the flesh. Strong yet amazingly nimble talons picked lacelike bones from the fish, pried open shellfish, and plucked strings of flesh from the crabs' hollow limbs.

At last, the seaweed mat completely pillaged, the wingcat subsided with a heavy sigh, green eyes half shut. Plainly it had been the most sumptuous meal he had eaten in more than half a year. Behind the dark unicorn, Ryhenna twitched nervously, anxious to be gone, but Jan lingered. Slowly, carefully, he approached the tercel, halted just out of reach. "Earlier this day," he said, "you called my people trespassers. What did you mean by that?"

The tercel stirred, obviously annoyed at Jan's proximity—his very presence—but too sated and contented to raise further protest.

"I called your people what they are, unicorn: thieves," he answered, almost amiably. "The great vale we call the Bowl of Ishi was ours long before you unicorns came."

Jan stared at him. "Yours?" he cried. "How so? No gryphons ever dwelled in our Vale. It was deserted when the princess Halla first claimed it, forty generations ago."

The wingcat's eyes snapped open, then narrowed angrily. "Deserted? Pah!" he scoffed. "It housed the sacred flocks of goat and deer Ishi gathered for my people's use: to provide first meat each spring for our newly pipped hatchlings. But you vile unicorns drove away the tender flocks, profaning the Vale with your presence. Now the formels must hunt your bitter kind in spring, though we prefer the sweet flesh of goats or deer."

The prince of the unicorns stood dumbstruck. The Vale of the Unicorns—claimed by gryphons as a sacred hunting ground? He had never heard of such a thing. Yet ever since the first attacks upon the princess Halla and her followers, gryphon raiders had returned to the Vale every spring. At last, after forty generations of conflict, Jan had learned the reason why.

"Four hundred years have we sought to drive you out," the wounded gryphon rasped. "My own parents died on such a mission two springs past. They flew to kill the unicorns' black prince. Not you, the other one—the one before you. But they failed. Their names were Shreel and Kilkeelahr."

Jan cast his mind back, two years gone, to the time just before his pilgrimage of initiation, when his father Korr had still reigned as prince and a pair of gryphons had nearly succeeded in assassinating the then-prince Korr, his mate and son. The memory was bitter, tinged with bafflement and fear.

"My people slew your father and mother," he told Illishar.

"How well I know that," the gryphon snapped. "When they did not return, we knew they must have perished."

"They came near to killing my sire and dam," Jan added, remembering still. "And me as well."

"Yes!" Illishar replied angrily. "Had they succeeded, they would have been called heroes, perched high in the pecking order once more. Queen Malar would have rewarded them with a prestigious nesting site, a ledge close to her own upon the Cliffs of Assembly, first pick of the kill. A glorious mission. But it failed.

"Thus was I orphaned as a half-grown chick, disinherited by powerful factions within my clan: my parents' enemies. I grew up a nestless beggar, though I am well-born, kin to the matriarch herself. My father was her younger nestmate—but he fell out of favor. That is why he and Shreel were desperate enough to undertake so daring a raid, to win the glory that would buy them back their pride of place. For what is a gryphon without honor? Only a pecked-upon squab. Now I, too, have failed in my bid for glory. The proud line of my parents ends with my death."

Jan let him talk, scarcely daring to interrupt. It had not occurred to him how lonely the gryphon must be. The dark unicorn shook himself. He, too, had spent the winter as a prisoner among strangers. When guarded queries did nothing to stem the gryphon's words, Jan grew bolder, questioning the tercel about his life before the raid, among his own people. Illishar spoke freely, proudly, of the customs of his flock, of their wars and religion, of the constant struggle both within and between the clans.

No single leader ruled, though Malar, the matriarch of the largest clan, was the most ruthless—and therefore the most respected—leader. She was evidently some sort of cousin—possibly an aunt—to Illishar. Jan could not determine quite which. The wingcats counted kin differently from unicorns.

As the afternoon drew on, Ryhenna grew more fidgety, and Jan sent her back to the beach to forage again while he stayed with the gryphon—careful always to remain out of reach of the raptor's beak and claws. She returned as dusk drew on, dragging the ragged tail of a large grey shark, badly picked at by seabirds. Illishar fell on it with ravenous appetite, while the coppery mare grimaced and spat the fetid taste of fishskin from her tongue.

As evening fell and the air grew chill, Jan collected driftwood and struck a fire. The gryphon reacted first with alarm, then awe, and finally delight, drawing close enough to the blazing driftwood to warm himself. On opposite sides of the fire, he and Jan talked on into the deepening dark. Ryhenna hovered nervously, afraid to approach because of the gryphon.

Jan sang Illishar the lay of the princess Halla, of his people's long-ago expulsion from their own sacred lands, the Hallow Hills, by treacherous wyverns, of their long wandering across the Plains until they reached the Vale, seemingly deserted and unclaimed, of their settling for the winter into their new home in exile only to be forced to defend themselves the following spring—and every spring thereafter—against raiding gryphons.

Illishar grew silent, sobered after Jan's recounting. The dark prince lay staring into the smoldering coals of driftwood, flameless now, but still shimmering, red with heat. Ryhenna whinnied uneasily in the darkness behind him. He heard her muffled hooffalls above the calm sea's wash: trotting, pacing. She had not yet lain down.

"A great pity, Illishar," Jan murmured, "that neither of our peoples ever sought converse before: no envoys exchanged, no explanations offered or sought. Much spilling of blood might have been spared, I think, had we chosen to speak before exchanging blows." He sighed sleepily. "My people long only to depart the Vale, though it has housed us well for many years. We wish to reclaim our own lost lands by driving the hated wyverns out."

Wearily, the gryphon nodded, chewing at a stem of seaweed, his crippled wing propped against a stone. "Perhaps you are right, unicorn," he muttered grudgingly, "much though it pains me to admit that one I have long held my greatest enemy might have a point."

A little silence then. The breeze lifted. The waves plashed, lapping. The coals of the dying fire shimmered. Unseen, Ryhenna trotted, circled.

"Greater pity, yet," the wingcat added at last, "that with my wing healed wrong, I can never return to my flock to tell them what I have learned. Nor will your people be eager to believe any word you might speak if such word go against their customed hatred of my kind."

The tercel's words trailed off, his breathing deepening, nearly snoring now. Across the coals from him, the young prince sighed again. "Aye," he murmured. "Unicorns are a boar-headed lot."

✺

He dreamed a dream of gryphons and unicorns sharing the Vale without rancor, wingcats perching the cliffs above, his own people grazing the valley floor below. Here and there, on the slopes between valley floor and cliffs, he glimpsed odd creatures, seemingly half wingcat, half unicorn. Their limbs, torsos, and hindquarters were those of unicorns; shoulders, necks, and heads plumed and pinioned like gryphons. Stroking their great wings, they galloped across steep, grassy slopes and, vaulting into the air, took flight.

He awoke with a start. Ryhenna stood over him, pawing at him with one round forehoof. The embers before him lay cold. Across them, Illishar lounged at ease—alert, awake, but resting. The mat of seaweed lay before him, oddly heaped and twisted. The coppery mare glanced nervously at the gryphon, then pawed Jan again. Cold dawn greyly lit the beach.

"Wake, Moonbrow," Ryhenna hissed. " 'Tis morn."

The dark unicorn rolled stiffly, gathered his limbs under him, but did not rise. Still eyeing the gryphon tercel, the coppery mare backed off.

"All night, I watched," she told him, "to guard thee. Thy foe is hungry still."

Illishar said nothing, watched them, rustling and twisting between his talons the mat of seaweed before him. Jan staggered to his feet, shaking himself. The silver halter rattled. He had not meant to sleep.

"My thanks, Ryhenna," he told her sincerely. "You guard me better than I guard myself."

The coppery mare tossed her head, bleary-eyed. "I go to the glade to sleep," she told him. "Come fetch me when thou wilt."

Jan nodded, watched Ryhenna lope away along the beach toward the grove. The rustle of seaweed drew his attention back to Illishar.

"Your hornless mare would have been little hindrance to me, had I sought to steal upon you unawares," he murmured to Jan.

Walking around the remains of the fire, the young prince drew closer. "You underestimate Ryhenna," he answered. "She held off a troop of two-foot warriors on the white cliffs of the City of Fire. She would make no easy match for you. But if—as you say—it were so easy a task," he asked, "why did you not kill me this night past when you had the chance?"

The tercel shrugged painfully. "What use, Jan of the unicorns?" he asked. "My wing is bent past repair. I will die soon regardless—why prolong my life a few more days on your bones?"

The seaweed rustled. Jan cocked his head, eyed Illishar's nimble digits twisting and plaiting it. "What do you fashion?"

"A net," the tercel replied, spreading it so that the dark unicorn might better see. "To help me fish. Perhaps after you and your mare tire of me and depart—if you do not kill me outright—this net may enable me to live a little longer."

Jan met the gryphon's eye, and for the first time, Illishar looked away. Jan allowed himself the ghost of a smile. "I see you have not yet despaired of your life as wholly as you pretend," he told the gryphon. "Perhaps you yet dream of returning to your people?"

"Vain dreams!" the tercel exclaimed, casting the seaweed net from him angrily. "The bone set wrong. I will never fly again."

Jan lay down on the rocks, still out of reach, but closer to the injured wingcat than he had ever dared to come.

"Among my people," he told Illishar, "when one of our number breaks a limb, our pied healer, Teki, plasters it with mudclay to keep it stiff until the bone can heal. If it begins to heal wrong, he breaks it again. I have seen him do this."

He thought back to the preceding spring, Dagg cracking one forelimb in a slip on a crumbling slope. He remembered Teki's ministrations; himself, Tek, and others flanking the injured warrior by turns, keeping him upright, walking him three-legged, bringing him forage. The memory made him shudder. Even in the warmth and abundant provender of last spring, Dagg easily could have died.

"It was horrible to watch," Jan told the gryphon who lay before him in the rocks, "but my companion survived, and the bone knit strong and straight. Now he runs again as fleetly as before, as though the limb had never suffered ill."

"Why tell me this?" the gryphon cried, spitting a twist of seaweed from his beak. "To torment me? What use for me to hear of unicorns' legs? It is my wing that is broken—my wing! Tell me what good you can do my crooked pinion, unicorn."

The last words were a snarl, full of bitterness.

"I could rebreak your wing, Illishar," Jan said to him, "bring mud to plaster it. You must keep it very still, three half-moons or more, until it heals."

The tercel stared at Jan. "Our two peoples are sworn enemies," he whispered. "You would not do it."

"Call me your enemy no more," Jan bade him, drawing nearer. "I grow weary of our being enemies. The scars your talons left upon my back this autumn past are old scars now, long healed. Time to heal this ancient rift between our peoples as well."

"No!" cried Illishar, shifting as though to drag himself away from Jan. "Even if you spoke the truth and could reset my wing so that it might heal, do you and your mare intend to remain all spring upon this shore? Who would feed me while my pinion mended? The accursed seaherons have given me over."

Jan shook his head. "I will speak to Tlat and entreat her to continue to tend you. Now that spring has returned, the tidewaters teem with fish. The herons can provide for you without hardship. I think they will do so if I assure them you mean to return to your flock and speak for peace not only between gryphons and unicorns, but between gryphons and seaherons as well."

"I have made you no such pledge," Illishar protested angrily, "to speak for peace among my flock on your behalf."

"Think, Illishar," the dark prince urged, "of the glory to be gained. More glory in merely killing an enemy and arousing his people's hatred against yours all the more, or in taming and allying with him, adding his strength and that of all his people to your own? What more glorious tribute could you possibly lay before your leader, Malar, than the prospect of this great peacemaking?"

Illishar twitched unhappily, pondering. His bill clapped shut. "You have a point, unicorn," he managed, unwillingly. "Perhaps—*perhaps*— peace may be possible between our peoples. But the seaherons! Shrieking pests, they have tormented me all this winter past. Their kind has always been a bane to mine. . . ."

"Peace with the herons as well as the unicorns," Jan answered firmly. "Such is my price."

The gryphon tercel sighed, snapping his beak shut once more. At last he muttered, "As you will."

The dark prince whickered, tossing his head. "One more thing I would ask of you," he added, "one more part to my price."

The silver halter jingled. Illishar eyed him suspiciously.

"Remove this halter," he entreated the gryphon. "Surely your talons are dexterous enough to undo the fastening. Bear it back to your people in token of the bargain we have made."

The tercel's green-eyed gaze grew wide, astonished.

"You would trust me so close?" he asked.

The dark unicorn rose, shook himself, shrugged. "It seems I must. I cannot remove this halter on my own. And if you kill me, who will reset your wing?"

Illishar laughed suddenly. To Jan's surprise, it was not the shrill, raucous bird sound he might have expected, but a deep, throaty, catlike thrumming—almost a purr.

"Your hooves and horn are no less formidable than my beak and talons," the wingcat chuckled. "It seems we must trust one another perforce."

Jan nodded and knelt beside the great raptor, bowing his head to one side so that the other could reach the halter's fastening. Illishar seemed to consider a long moment before Jan felt his sharp, unexpectedly delicate talons picking at the buckle. The halter grew loose about Jan's head, but as he moved to pull away, to rise and shake himself free, the other's grasp gently restrained him.

"Be still," the gryphon said. "I am not yet done."

Surprised, the young prince subsided, felt the careful, meticulous touch of the tercel's claws along the crest of his neck, tugging at his mane. The claws released him, and Jan stood up abruptly. The halter slipped free. With a great whinny of triumph, he shook himself, rearing to paw the air, then fell back to all fours again and ducked to scrub either side of his muzzle first against one foreleg, then the other. His face felt oddly uncluttered, light. He was free.

"Unending thanks to you, friend Illishar," he began.

The tercel before him lay running the links of the halter through his talons, eyeing the crescent-moon shaped browpiece with interest. But as Jan raised his head and turned to speak, his attention was seized by the feel of something both light and stiff against his neck. As he rolled his eyes, green flashed at the far limit of his vision. Snorting, shaking his head, he felt the thing, light as a leaf-frond, caught in his mane.

"What have you done?" he asked Illishar. "What more have you done besides what I asked?"

He felt surprise, puzzlement, but strangely, no alarm. The gryphon looked at him and held the halter up.

"You have given me this," he said, "to bear back to my people in token of our pledge. I, too, have given you a token to carry to your flock. One of my feathers I have woven into your mane. Let none of your boar-headed people dare doubt now that you have earned the good-will of a gryphon."

Once more, Jan shook himself, tossing his head. He felt elated and untrammeled. He felt like the strange, wild unicorns—wrongly called renegades—who dwelt upon the Plain, unbound by the Law and customs of their cousins of the Vale. They called themselves the Free People, and wore fallen birds' feathers in their hair.

"Go now," the gryphon told him, "and treat with this Tlat of the shrieking herons. I will prepare myself for your return, when I will allow you to break and reset my wing."

Return

) 27 (

The sky stretched high and blue and clean of clouds. The air was warm, full spring at last. Jan halted, breathing deep. Ryhenna emerged from the trees at his back to stand alongside him. Their three-day passage through the Pan Woods had proved blessedly uneventful: no encounters with goatlings, no ambuscades. The Vale of the Unicorns unfolded below them: rolling valley slopes honeycombed with limestone grottoes. Unicorns dotted the grassy hillsides, grazing.

"So many," Ryhenna breathed. "So many—I never dreamed!"

But to the young prince's eye, their numbers seemed alarmingly scant: almost no colts and fillies, very few elders. Even the ranks of the warriors were thinned. A pang tightened his chest. Eagerly he searched the herd below for someone he knew. Far on the opposite hillside, the healer stood among the crowd of older fillies and foals that could only be acolytes. Jan gave a loud whistle. The pied stallion raised his head, then reared up with a shout, his singer's voice ringing out across the Vale.

"Jan! Jan, prince of the unicorns, returns!"

Jan loped eagerly down the slope, Ryhenna in his wake. Astonished unicorns thundered to meet him as he reached the valley floor. They surged around with whickers of greeting and disbelief, eager to catch wind of him, chafe and shoulder their lost prince. Jan glimpsed runners sprinting off to bear news of his arrival to the far reaches of the Vale. Laughing, half rearing, Jan sported among his people until cries of consternation rang out behind him.

"Look—hornless, beardless. Outcast! Renegade!"

He wheeled to find the whole crowd shying, staring at Ryhenna. The coppery mare stood alone. Jan sprang to her side.

"Behold Ryhenna," he declared, "my shoulder-friend, without whose aid I could never have escaped captivity to return to you."

The crowd fidgeted nervously, then abruptly parted, allowing Teki through.

"Greetings, prince," he cried. "Yonder come your sister and dam."

Looking up, Jan beheld his mother, Ses.

"My son, my son," she cried.

Behind her, Lell eyed him uncertainly with her amber-colored eyes. Jan held himself still as the tiny filly approached, sniffing him over. The sharp knob of horn upon her brow, just beginning to sprout, told him she must be newly weaned. Gazing up at him, she smiled suddenly and cried out,

"Jan!"

Teki began to speak of the winter past. Jan listened, dismayed how precisely his dreams had already revealed to him his people's fate. Sheer madness and bitter waste! Under a sane and reasoned leadership, the herd might have fared the brutal famine and cold with far less loss of life.

"Where is Korr now?" he demanded hotly.

"In our grotto," his dam replied with a heavy sigh. "He grazes only by twilight now, eats barely enough to keep himself alive, though forage is once more plentiful."

Jan bit back the grief and anguish welling up in him. "You say he turned against Tek and drove her from the Vale—why? Why?"

The pied stallion cast down his gaze, shook his head and whispered, "Madness."

"But what has become of her?" Jan pressed. "You say she was in foal?"

Teki's face grew haggard, his eyes bright. "We have no word," he answered roughly. "Dagg, who went in search of her some days past, has not yet returned."

The healer stopped himself, regained his breath. His chest seemed tight.

"We fear she may be dead."

Jan stared at the others, staggered. He turned from Teki to Ses, but his mother's gaze could offer him no hope.

"Nay, not so!" a voice from across the throng called suddenly. "I live!"

The whole herd started, turned. Jan's heart leapt to behold Tek, long-limbed and lithe, her pied form full of energy, loping toward him, flanked on one shoulder by the Red Mare and on the other by Dagg. Others, less plainly visible, trailed them—but the young prince's gaze fixed wholly on Tek.

With a cry, he sprang to her. The press of unicorns had fallen back to let her and her companions through. She stood laughing, no sorrow in her. Her breath against his skin was sweet and soft, her touch gentle, the scent of her delicate as he recalled, aromatic as spice. He nuzzled her, whickering, "My mate. My mate."

She gave him a playful nip, then started back suddenly. "What's this?" she cried. "How came you by this gryphon plume?"

He felt her teeth fasten on it, tugging angrily to work it free, but he pulled back, nickering. "Peace," he bade her. "Let be. I will tell you when you have told me of yourself. How fared you this winter past?"

"My daughter sheltered in my cave," the Red Mare answered, "as safe and warm and well-fed as were you, prince Jan, in the sorcerous City of Fire. You have freed another of its captives, I see, and brought her home with you. *Emwe!* Hail, daughter of fire," Jah-lila called. "Do I guess thy name aright: *Ryhenna?*"

The coppery mare stood staring at Jah-lila. "It is true, then?" she stammered at last. "Ye are the one that erewhile dwelt among my kind?"

Jah-lila nodded. "Born a hornless *da* in the stable of the *chon*. Drinking of the sacred moonpool far across the Plain, I became a unicorn. So, too, mayst thou, little one. Follow, and I will lead thee there."

"I will accompany you!" Dagg exclaimed. He stood transfixed, staring at Ryhenna as though in a dream. Jan watched, taken by surprise, as the other approached the coppery mare. "I am called Dagg, fair Ryh—fair Ryhenna." He stumbled over the unfamiliar name. "The way to the wyvern-infested Hallow Hills is long and dangerous. For all the Red Mare's sorcery, I would feel easier for you with a warrior at your side."

The prince of the unicorns bit back a laugh. Plainly his friend was smitten. After months moping beside the Summer Sea a season past, the dappled warrior seemed finally to have found a mare to spark his eye. The swiftness of it astonished Jan. Ryhenna was now returning Dagg's gaze with shyly flattered interest.

Jan shouldered gently against Tek, nuzzling her, glad to steal a caress while others' eyes fixed on the dappled warrior and the coppery mare. Beside the prince, his mate stood sleek and well-nourished—and plainly not pregnant. Just when her belly ought to have been swollen to its greatest girth, ready to deliver any day, it clearly held no life. An overwhelming sense of loss mingled with his joy at finding the healer's daughter alive and hale.

"Teki told me you were in foal," Jan whispered in her ear. "My love, I am so sorry to see that you have lost it. Later, in a season or two, when you are ready, we can try again."

Shrugging with pleasure against his touch, Tek laughed. "What loss?" she asked. "Nay, Jan. Behold."

Baffled, the young prince of the unicorns turned, following the line of Tek's gaze. It came to rest upon the small figures that had followed her, Jah-lila, and Dagg. Two were unicorns, and two—astonishment pricked him as he realized—were not. The latter were pans, young females both, not yet half-grown. Jan felt his spine stiffen—yet surely such young goatlings must be harmless enough. The two stood calmly beneath his scrutiny, the younger pan pressing against the Red Mare, who nuzzled her.

The other two members of the party were infant unicorns, flat-browed still, hornbuds mere bumps upon their wide, smooth foreheads. Whose progeny were they, Jan wondered? Surely they could not be earlyborns, for though small, each was perfectly formed, surefooted, sound of wind—yet what mares would consent to tryst with their mates so early the preceding summer that they bore their offspring in late winter, before spring forage greened the hills? Madness! The tiny pair gazed up at him with bright, intelligent eyes.

The coloring of them was like none he had ever seen. The young prince shook his head, astonished. The filly was on one side mostly black, with silver stockings and one jet eye outlined in silver. Her other side was mostly silver, black-stockinged, her dark eye black-encircled. The foal was purest white, not a mark or a dark hair on him, and eyes like cloudless sky. The two seemed to shimmer before his gaze: brightening, fading. Tek was laughing at him. He blinked. Slowly, realization dawned.

"Nay," he whispered. "Truth, Tek, these cannot be—not both of them!"

She nodded. "Aye. Born early, by my dam's design—though without my foster sisters' aid, none of us would have survived to greet your homecoming."

"Pans!" Jan exclaimed, turning to stare once more at the young goatlings flanking Jah-lila. "Pan fosterlings?"

The Red Mare nodded. "Aye, prince. Orphaned young, they took me as their dam. Their care has kept me much from the Vale in recent years. Though passing freely among their own kind in the Wood, they know the ways of unicorns as well."

"Emwe," the younger of the pan sisters said to him, gesturing with one hairless forelimb. Jan felt a tremor of recognition. Their speech was like that of the two-foots—more fluting, less guttural—but clearly recognizable.

"Emwe," the prince of the unicorns replied. "Tai-shan nau shopu-cha." *Hail. Moonbrow greets you.*

"Greet-ings," the elder of the two replied, enunciating the words of the unicorn tongue carefully, "great prince of u-nicorns."

All around, nickers of astonishment, alarm from the nervously milling herd—to hear supposedly mute goatlings speak.

"I am Sismoomnat," the young pan replied, "my sis-ter, Pitipak. Our fos-ter dam, Jah-ama, has taught us u-nicorn speech. We al-so speak in the way of our own folk. We are glad to have come among you at last, fair u-nicorns. Our dam has long pledged to bring us to you when time grew ripe."

Swallowing his astonishment, Jan managed a low bow. Perhaps more treaties than he had hoped could be struck this spring.

"Greetings to you both, pan fosterlings of the Red Mare," he answered. "Doubtless you know of the long enmity that lies between our two peoples. Perhaps time indeed grows ripe to resolve our differences. Would you be willing to act as envoys between your people and my own?"

Happily, the young goatling nodded. "It is the task for which Jah-ama reared us. Glad-ly will we bear words of peace between our two tribes."

Beneath the goatlings' smooth, long-fingered forepaws, the black-and-silver filly and the flawless white foal fidgeted, shouldering one another playfully and eyeing Jan with frank, fearless curiosity. The young pans stepped back as the prince of the unicorns moved forward to nose his daughter and son. The nameless filly and foal frolicked against him, their long, delicate legs tangling, their tiny, ropelike tails spiraling with nervous energy. Jan breathed deep, exploring their every curve. Their scent reminded him of Tek—and of himself.

"The foal is Dhattar," Tek told him softly, "the filly, Aiony—"

A low moan cut short her words. Starting up, Jan beheld a dark figure on the near slope. Unicorns fell back, some hissing with disgust. The other did not approach. Moments passed before Jan recognized the haggard stallion. The young prince stared. Could this wasted figure truly be his sire, once the robust and vigorous king of the unicorns? In less than a year, Korr seemed to have aged many.

"Freaks!" he groaned. "Begotten in lawlessness and borne in wychery. They will bring destruction! The goddess's wrath—"

Jan stamped one heel, furious, moving forward to stand between his family and the king.

"What wrath?" he demanded. "Father, what makes my heirs abomination in your eyes? And how is it you claim to know the goddess's will—does Alma speak to you?"

The bony figure stared. "I—nay. I . . . used to think so," he mumbled, shifting uneasily. Then he raised his head, voice growing stronger. "You should never have chosen the pied wych, my son. I warned you sore—"

"My mate is no wych!" Jan retorted hotly. "She is Tek, that same brave warrior whom, before this winter past, you always honored high. Why are you so against our pledge?"

But the dark other only shook his head, muttering. "Nay, it was a long time past, upon the Plain. The wych . . . I never . . ."

As the Red Mare stepped forward, he shied from her as from a gryphon.

"You speak in riddles, Korr." She eyed him steadily.

"Wych! Wych!" the mad stallion cried, rearing, flailing at the air. "See what your wychery has wrought? I trusted you!"

Gazing at him still, Jah-lila never flinched. "My prince," she said, "you and I alone know what befell upon the Plain so long ago, who trusted whom and who betrayed. Honor binds me to hold my tongue until you speak."

"Never!" the haggard stallion shrieked. "Your spells ensnared me once—"

Members of the herd scattered as, for a moment, it looked as though the wild-eyed king might fly at her—but the Red Mare held steady, her gaze fixed upon him square.

"I charge you now," she answered, "for your own honor's sake, speak plain. It is your only hope of peace."

With an inarticulate cry, the mad stallion wheeled, sprang away up the slope. Below, all around Jan the unicorns watched with expressions of anger, or pity, or scorn. Not until the king's form had nearly reached the treeline did the young prince come to himself with a start and spring forward to follow. His dam stepped quickly to block his path.

"Hold, my son. It is himself he flees—and none of us may catch him till he turn and stand his ground."

Jan snorted, dodging, but it was hopeless. His sire's form had vanished into the trees, the thunder of his heels already faded. Restlessly, the young prince paced a circle.

"What maddens him?" he cried.

Ses shook her head. "Only Korr may answer that."

She did not stand aside. The prince's eye fell on Jah-lila, facing him with calm, unfathomable black-green eyes.

"What do you know of this?" he demanded. "Why is my sire in such terror of you? What befell the pair of you upon the Plain?"

The Red Mare's glance flicked after the fugitive king, then turned to rest ruefully upon her daughter Tek. Bitterly, wordlessly, Jah-lila turned away.

That eve was Moondance, the first, so Jan learned, since the sad return of the courting band that fall past. Now unicorns came from all quarters of the Vale to dance in celebration of their newly restored prince and hear his tale. Jan told them of the City of Fire and his captivity there, of his truce with the gryphon and his decision to treat with the pans as well. Finally, he showed them fire. Striking the tip of his horn to one heel, he set ablaze a great heap of deadwood set upon the rocky outcrop of the council rise.

From the far hillside as the flames rose up, one dark and lonely figure watched. Jan recognized the gaunt silhouette against the moonlit sky, but dared not go to seek him yet, lest pursuit drive the mad king entirely from the Vale, where none might hope to find him. With difficulty, the young prince resigned himself for now. Soon, he vowed, he must follow his sire—to the smoking Dragon Hills, if need be—and riddle out the reason for his madness.

Moon reached its zenith in the sky. Jan lay beside his mate and twin heirs. His dam and her weanling nestled nearby. The young pan nursemaids, fallen deeply asleep, sprawled alongside Lell and his own twins. Dagg and Ryhenna, Teki and Jah-lila rested nearby. Casting his gaze out over the slumbering herd, breathing the scent of them and of moonlight and of smoldering fire in the warm spring air, Jan found himself if not wholly satisfied, for the moment at least, at peace. It was good to be back in the Vale and among his people again.

Weariness overwhelmed him. He dozed. *Aye, I have led you a merry round, I know,* the soft, familiar voice within him whispered. *It will not be the last.*

Drowsing, he felt no tremor, no surprise. He floated, suspended as by lapping waves between waking and sleep. Starlight surrounded him. The gryphon feather lifted in the breeze.

Are you willing to accept yet, the goddess murmured, *that you can neither summon nor dismiss me, and that my words must reach you whenever and in whatever form I wish?*

He seemed enveloped by a medium dark as midnight yet infused with light, that was at once both sea and stars, peopled with other travelers besides himself: swimmers sleek and spiral-tusked.

Are you ready to understand that I am the world, Aljan, where all that befalls you is me and my true voice speaking to you—whether I choose the use of words or no? I have not deserted you and can never desert you, prince of unicorns, my Firebringer, Dark Moon.

After

🌙

How my tale has rambled, and how late the night has grown! Truth, I had meant to tell you all, as I promised yestereve—yet I have gotten no further than Jan's return from the City of Fire. Bear with me, gracious hosts, I beg, for I am old, more than thirty winters: a good age for any unicorn, and a vast one for daya among whom I was born.

Ah, well. Summer nights are pleasant, and you have been most tolerant of an old mare's champing: you whom the Vale dwellers so long called renegades, but who justly call yourselves the Free People of the Plain. It is always a joy to sojourn among you. Rest sure, I will tell you what remains of my tale, and all in one sitting, if you will but meet with me upon this same spot tomorrow eve.

Then will I spell you the rest—all of the rest—of the tale of the Firebringer; how Jan drove the hated wyverns from their stolen dens, thus regaining the Hallow Hills for his people, the children-of-the-moon. Of this and much, much more shall I speak. Come again tomorrow, I charge you. This time, faithfully I vow, you shall hear Jan's story to its end.

the Son of
Summer
Stars

For my loving, supportive family.

Contents

Prelude

For a thousand years, the Hallow Hills had been the homeland of the unicorns, held in trust to the goddess Alma. As guardians of her sacred mere, the Well of the Moon, the unicorns called themselves children-of-the-moon, best belovèd of the Mother-of-all. Then wyverns came, white poisonous wyrms, who slew the unicorns' agèd king and fell upon his followers. Proud princess Halla was one of few to escape that venomous end. She and her small, beleaguered band fled south across the wide grass Plain till they found refuge in a broad valley inhabited only by goats and deer. The unicorns claimed this deserted Vale, and here they dwelt four hundred years, awaiting one who would end their long exile, reclaim their lost ancestral lands and drive the hated wyverns out with the goddess's own empyreal fire.

Zod the dreamer called this warrior-to-come the Firebringer: black as the dark between Alma's eyes on the coldest of cloudless midwinter nights. The crescent moon would mark his brow and a white star one hind heel. Wild Caroc prophesied burning blood, sparking hooves and a tongue of flame: a colt born at moondark out of a wyvern's belly and sired by the summer stars. Ellioc, who followed Caroc, claimed he would be no Ring-born unicorn at all, but a Renegade outside the Law. He would storm out of heaven in a torrent of fire, and his advent would mark the ending of the world. But the unicorns called wild Caroc and Ellioc mad. Their strange visions, though recounted long after their distant passing, were scoffed at. Only Zod was believed true seer of the Firebringer, and he, too, by the time of my tale lay centuries dead.

Two nights past, when we assembled here, I told of how, many years ago, I midwived the birth of the Firebringer. I spoke of Aljan, called son-of-Korr, who, while beardless and callow still, made his way from the Vale to the Hallow Hills on pilgrimage and slew a wyvern there. Her poisoned barb set his blood alight. Companions bore him in her severed hide and cast him into the waters of Alma's mere. The deadly venom fevering his blood cooled then, and he rose weak as a newborn foal from the she-wyrm's bellyskin: hooves and horn tempered to unbreakable hardness, his coat burnt black, a slim crescent moon traced into his brow and a white star marking his heel. Thus completing his initiation into the Ring of Warriors, young Jan returned to the Vale and became his people's battleprince.

Night past, I sang you the second cant of the Lay of the Firebringer, how Jan pledged himself to my daughter, Tek, the pied warrior mare, a bond unshakable in Alma's eyes. I recounted his peacemaking among the goat-leggèd pans, the battle he fought with marauding gryphons by the shores of the Summer Sea and how, in the end, he set enmity aside to befriend the wounded wingcat that had once so fiercely sought his life. I told of his sojourn in the far land of the two-footed firekeepers where, upon the sacred cliffs above their settlement, he learned the secret of the flame that smoldered within him. Before Jan departed, trekking homeward with his gift of fire, his hosts dubbed him Moonbrow, but his name among his own folk means Dark Moon.

This even, which marks the last night of my telling, I sing of how Aljan Moonbrow fulfilled his destiny as Alma's Firebrand, returning with his people to the Hallow Hills and casting the venomous wyverns out. My name is Jah-lila. I am called the Red Mare. A seer and a singer and a traveler am I, a midwife and a magicker—fourth and final prophet of the Firebringer. Of my own small role in his triumph and downfall shall I also speak: how Aljan broke the Ring of Law and lost his kingship of the unicorns forever, how he hurtled across heaven on pinions of fire and proved every word of my predecessors true—until here at the last, he has kindled the spark unquenchable, which even now as we dance is unmaking the world.

Serpents

★ 1 ★

New grass, green as gryphons' down, covered the dark earth in fine, sparse filaments. Breeze lifted, and the downy strands rippled. Spring sun warmed the hillside's restless air. Jan halted and shook himself. Sod packed the clefts between the toes of his cloven hooves. He bowed his head, used the long, spiral skewer of his brow-horn to pick the clods away. Sparks leapt when the horn's keen tip grated.

With a snort, the black prince of the unicorns straightened, tossed the forelock from his eyes. He bounded up the steep, grassy slope to catch up his twin daughter and son. Aiony, the filly, glanced back at the sudden pounding of his heels. She reared up nickering, limbs fine as a fawn's, her one side pale silver with black stockings and a black-encircled eye, the other side just the opposite: black with silver shanks and eye. Jan nuzzled her as he came alongside. Aiony pranced and whistled to her brother up the slope, the sound high and sweet as pan-pipes.

"Hey up, Dha! Wait for Jan and me."

The foal Dhattar paused, the same size as his sister but pale as pure cloud. Like her, he sported a nubby horn little more than a promise on his brow. Like hers, his young mane was only beginning to lengthen from its nursling's bristle, the tassel at the end of his ropelike tail barely sprung. He stood picking at the turf with one snow-white heel.

"I *am* waiting," he called.

The prince of the unicorns nickered. Barely weaned, his children already spoke better than most colts half again their age. Jan nibbled his son's withers as he reached him. The white foal shivered happily. Jan snorted, continued moving up the slope.

"Will you tell me what you two are so eager for me to see?" he inquired, for the sixth time.

Chivvying her father's raven-black ribs, Aiony shook her head. Dhattar glanced at her.

"We can't," he answered.

"It's a secret," Aiony insisted.

"A surprise," the white foal concurred.

The prince of the unicorns heaved himself past another slippery place and shook his head. "Well enough, then," he laughed. "Lead on."

The twins bolted, sprinting and chasing as they scrabbled up the rocky hillside. Jan glanced back, startled at how high they had come. The Vale of the Unicorns unfolded below, open meadow hemmed by partially wooded slopes. Far away on the valley floor, Teki the healer stood peering at some medicinal root or herb, his pied black-and-white coloring unmistakable. Around him clustered five or six half-growns— among the few then-colts to have survived the devastating winter that had ravaged the herd barely two years earlier.

The prince of the unicorns gritted his teeth. Half his people had perished in that terrible season of ice and snow—a death toll burgeoned in the prince's absence by one mad usurper's tyranny. A green-tailed, whining fly bit the young stallion's ear, drew blood. Jan rankled and slapped it away with his tail. Korr—his own sire—responsible for so much misery, when a careful policy of scouting and sharing forage would doubtless have saved many who instead had succumbed to hunger and the cold. The prince's ear stung. He shook his head.

"Tell us about the wyvern!"

Aiony came skittering down the hillside. The dark unicorn returned to the present with a start.

"Aye, tell how you slew the wyvern in her den," Dhattar called. "When you were just a colt."

"Like us."

Whickering, Jan shook his head. "Older."

"Lell's age?" Dha ventured.

"Your aunt's only four!" cried Jan. "I was six—three times your age, little goatling kids."

Aiony butted him. Gently, the black unicorn shouldered back. Above him, white Dhattar sneezed amid a swarm of lace-winged flitters. Aiony nipped at her father's flank. Jan shooed her away and began.

"Long ago and many springs past, on pilgrimage . . ."

The tale told itself, unwinding before him like a well-worn path. He hardly listened to his own voice, lost in story, crafting without a thought the internal slant-rhymes and measured cadences of the storyteller's art. His own mate, Tek, was a fine singer of tales, and Teki the healer, her foster sire, one of the best he had ever heard. He had harked the two of them all his life, and never yet dared offer his own recountings to any listeners more critical than his raptly attentive young daughter and son.

"Were you afraid then?" Dhattar broke in, nudged him insistently. "When the wyvern stung, did you fear to die?"

Jan nodded. "Aye."

"But our dam's dam healed you," Aiony was saying. "Jah-lila quelled the she-serpent's poison with the waters of the sacred mere."

Again the black prince nodded, putting his head down, using powerful hindquarters to propel himself up the steepening trail. Dhattar and Aiony spurted ahead as the path led into a dark mass of trees. The black unicorn's skin twitched. View of the Vale behind vanished as firs and cedars closed around him. He glanced at the sky as they emerged once more onto rocky slope, more mindful than ever how they had climbed. The farther from the safety of the valley floor they ventured, the easier prey they made for gryphons.

Yet strangely, for the last two years, not a single wingèd marauder had come. No huge, blue-winged formels—the females—had swooped to steal his people's nurslings, nor had the swifter, lighter tercels struck, their pinions the color of new-sprung grass. The unicorn prince frowned, puzzled, for hunting wingcats would have found ample tender prey. Following that bitterest of winters now two years gone, the Vale had enjoyed early forage, balmy summers, bountiful falls and unseasonably mild winters. *Jah-lila's doing,* the whole herd whispered, *the blessing of Alma's appointed midwife.* The children-of-the-moon had lost no time in getting and bearing new young.

Jan followed his own young, the black-and-silver filly and the snow-white foal, now skirting an outcropping of pale limerock. Truth, he mused, glancing warily at the rocky mass thrusting up from the rich black soil, perhaps the only ill effect of two nearly snowless winters in a row had been a vast increase in the number of serpents: some no thicker than a heron's leg, others stout as a stallion's. The unicorns had begun to watch their tread.

Jan whistled his young. "Aiony! Dha! How much farther?"

Halted on the far side of the outcrop now, the pair whinnied. "We're here."

Jan trotted around the pitted rocks. "When came you here before?"

Dhattar answered, "Never."

Jan turned, perplexed.

"No one brought us," Aiony told him. She and her brother exchanged a glance.

"We came night past," Dhattar continued.

His sister nodded. "Not by hoof. *Looking.*"

Jan cocked his head. "The pair of you slept betwixt your dam and me night past, and never stirred." He turned his gaze from one to another. The twins' eyes watched him with uncanny directness, almost as though they overheard his inmost thoughts. "Are you saying," he ventured, "that you came here, both of you . . . in a dream?"

The white foal nodded, but the black-and-silver filly shook her head. "Not a dream. *Like* dreaming, but . . ."

Her voice trailed off.

"Looking," Dhattar finished. "We came looking."

Jan felt his pulse quicken. Might his children, like their granddam Jah-lila, possess the dreaming sight?

"Do you see things this way," he asked carefully, "things that are real?"

Aiony had turned away, stood surveying the rocks. This time it was Dhattar who answered. "When we saw this place night past, we knew we must bring you."

"Why?" their father asked.

The white foal fidgeted, silent now.

"To show you the serpent," the filly murmured, standing perfectly still.

"Serpent?" Jan's heart thumped hard between his ribs. Quickly, he scanned again, alert for any sign of snakes. Dhattar cavaled.

"Aye, a great long thing," the white foal continued. "Old and ill-tempered. Snows should have killed it winter past." Jan turned to eye his son as he shifted away from his sister, who stood still gazing off into the rocks. "But no snows have fallen, not these two years running," Dhattar went on. "It's dying now, old wrym, but slow and painfully."

"Here it is," the black-and-silver filly was saying.

Turning again, Jan realized that she had left his side. She was moving forward now, picking her way among the rocks. The prince of the unicorns saw a pale form, seething, blue-speckled, coiled directly in his daughter's path. The nadder rose, hissing, flattening its hood. Above gaping jaws, black-slitted pupils dilated. Milky venom hung at the tip of each long, curved fang. The filly stepped fearlessly within the serpent's range.

"Daughter, no!" shouted Jan, vaulting to come between the nadder and its prey.

The serpent struck. The black unicorn felt a fiery sting along one foreleg as he crowded Aiony aside then spun to crush the sapling-thick viper beneath his forehooves. The dying serpent writhed, struck again, reflexively. Jan felt its spine snap as he trampled it. Moments later, all that remained was a nerveless, twitching tangle. The prince of the unicorns stood swaying, staring down at his bloodied foreshank. The double wound below the joint seared his blood. Dizziness swept over him. His pulse throbbed as the nadder's poison crept upward past the knee.

"Daughter, son," he gasped. "Haste down the hillside and whistle for help. Bring the healer. . . ."

Jan felt fiery venom spreading toward the muscle where his forelimb joined the chest. His whole leg ached, nearly numb.

"Off now," he gasped. "At speed!"

The filly and foal remained rooted, their expressions less frightened than curious. "Peace," Dhattar bade him. Aiony answered at almost the same time, "No need."

Jan stared at the pair of them, his heart hammering. "Children, hark me," he choked. "That was a speckled nadder, fat with poison. Without the healer, I'll die."

"But you won't," the white foal told him. "That's the secret."

"The *surprise*," Aiony insisted. "No wyrm may harm you."

"Not since that other serpent stung you," Dhattar added.

"The wyvern," the filly said.

They both gazed at him calmly, expectantly. Jan stood reeling. He had suffered only one other such sting in all his life, from the wyvern queen four years gone while on pilgrimage in the Hallow Hills. Only the magical waters of the moon's mere had saved him then—but that sacred spring lay half a world away: useless. Unreachable. His vision dimmed. Blood beat like slow thunder through him. The speckled viper's venom had nearly reached his breast—but strangely, its progress slowed, the burning diminished.

"You survived the wyvern's sting," Dhattar was saying. "No serpent can fell you now."

"Nor can their stings harm us, your progeny," said Aiony.

His view began to clear. Jan glimpsed his filly shake her mane, her brother nod. "When we beheld the nadder night past, in our vision, we knew this."

"Its sting only burned you a moment," Aiony went on, "and brought no harm."

Jan's sight returned. His balance steadied. Mute with astonishment, he gazed at his twins. Though his pulse still pounded in his chest, the venom's pain had faded, dissipated like cloud. Feeling returned in a prickling rush to his injured limb. Cautiously, the prince of the unicorns set heel to ground.

"We knew you'd not believe us if we simply told you," Aiony said earnestly.

Nervous, the white foal pranced. "We resolved to show you instead."

"We didn't want you to fear," the filly added. "Did you?"

The prince's injured leg bore his weight easily. He no longer felt any numbness. The clot of blood on the shin was drying, matting the hairs. "Aye, children," he answered truthfully. "Very much."

Aiony nuzzled him. "Are you angry with us?"

The prince of the unicorns bent to caress her. "Nay, little one," he murmured, "but you mustn't keep such things from me."

Clearly relieved, white Dhattar nipped him. "We'll not," he said. "You'll believe us now."

Jan gathered his offspring to him and chivvied them gently. "Come. Let's find your dam."

The twins fell in alongside, frisking and shrugging as he picked their way down the steep, rocky slope. The thought did not occur to him till they were nearly to the trees.

"I wonder," he murmured, as they entered the thicket. "Since I am proof against serpents—you two as well—does a way exist that others also might be made proof?"

The trees thickened, blotting out the sky. The prince of the unicorns shook his head.

"Perhaps if I could somehow sting our fellows, as I have been stung. . . ."

Aiony scrubbed her cheek against his flank. "Scratch them with your blood," she told him.

"We could do it, too," the white foal added, "if we weren't so young."

Aiony sighed. "If we had horns."

Ahead of them the trees were thinning. Grassy slope lay beyond. Jan just barely glimpsed it.

"If the herd could be made proof against poison," he mused, "we'd no longer need fear wyverns' barbs—" The prince of the unicorns stopped in his tracks. "We could win back the Hallow Hills!"

Just paces from the wood's edge, Jan stared at nothing. *Win back the Hills?* The possibility rocked him. He had been waiting years for a sign from Alma that the time at last grew ripe to reclaim his people's homeland. Now the goddess had spoken with the mouth of a serpent, slithering out of his children's dreams to leave a bloodmark on his shank. The black prince of the unicorns shook himself, pressed on downslope. He must speak of this with Tek at once. The moment the thought formed in his mind, Dhattar glanced at him.

"Not our dam," he exclaimed. Beside him, Aiony added eagerly, "Lell's the one you must go to now."

Jan turned at the mention of his younger sibling, barely four, a filly still herself. "Why is that?" he asked, baffled. "Where is Lell?"

"With the great green eagle-thing," the white foal answered. "The . . . the . . ." He frowned, searched for the word. "Catbird?"

"Wingcat," Aiony corrected, then turned to nip at her father's beard. "Lell's below us, just beyond the trees—at parley with a gryphon."

Parley

★ 2 ★

T hen Isha, mistress of the sky, turned to Ishi, lord of winds. 'These gryphons, fiercest of all my chicks, shall know a token of my favor.' With one mighty talon, she scratched the earth, creating a valley. With the touch of one wingtip, she brought it life: wooded slopes and grassy meadow. Here the wind god pastured his goats and deer. Here the blue-fletched formels sped each spring to capture first meat for their newly hatched young—until, four hundred winters past, your kind displaced Ishi's sacred flocks. Now the formels find nothing to nourish their squabs but your bitter flesh. *That* is why, little unicorn, this vale belongs to my folk, not yours, no matter how many generations your forebears have trespassed here."

Green-feathered with a golden pelt, the gryphon poised on a jut of rock above the amber filly's head. His coloring clearly marked him a tercel—a male—but so large a one that the young unicorn stood amazed: nearly the size of a blue-winged formel this grass-green raptor crouched. Lell stood motionless, half mesmerized by the tercel's soft, guttural tone midway between a purr and a growl. The prince's sister started suddenly. Not yet half-grown, her slim, straight horn still un-keened, Lell tossed her head, snorted and stamped. Her dam had warned her of wingcats' charming their prey before they sprang.

"A pretty song!" she cried. "But you must trill a sweeter one to capture me." She shook her dark chestnut coat, shaggy from winter yet, unshed. Her pale mane splashed like milk. "Forty generations have my people defended this vale—we shall guard it forty more if need be. My brother the prince shall hear of your intrusion." She ramped. "Wingcats are forbidden here. Begone!"

One corner of the tercel's mouth twitched in what might have been a smile.

"Little unicorn," he answered mildly, "attend. We gryphons are not the ones who trespass Ishi's Vale. But consider: with the birth of your flock's long-sought Firebringer, does not time at last betide you to depart and reclaim your Hallow Hills?"

Lell felt her jaw loosen with surprise. How could this outlander know her people's sacred prophecies? Green as river stones, the crouching gryphon's cat's eyes watched her.

"Tell Prince Moonbrow," he said, "that his shoulder-friend, Illishar of the Broken Wing, flies emissary from my kindred Malar, now wingleader of all the clans. She would parley a peace if, as your brother claims, you truly mean to relinquish this vale."

"We do! We must. He is Alma's Firebringer!" Lell exclaimed, more than a little impressed at her own bravery in answering the huge raptor without a moment's hesitation. The gryphon shrugged. His pinions flexed. The darkamber filly felt the wind they stirred. The sensation made her skin draw. She demanded, "When would your wingleader treat with my prince?"

The tercel clucked. "When the new-hatched chicks are well grown enough to be left in their fathers' care. Spring's end, or early summer."

Lell frowned, thoughts racing. How would her brother, Jan, have responded? "Solstice falls at Moondance this year. Come then," she called up, "on the night of the full moon marking the advent of summer."

The raptor spread huge, jewel-green wings. "So be it. I fly to bring word to my kin before the hatchlings pip."

Pinions fully extended, he stroked the air. Lell's mane whipped. She stood astonished that he should accept her words so readily in her brother's stead. Her heart quailed. An impulse filled her suddenly to bolt, but she stood her ground.

"Tell Jan that in token of faith," the gryphon said, "Malar will bar the formels from hunting Ishi's Vale again this spring, so sparing your young a third year in a row."

Powerful wingbeats hummed. His voice sounded like a cat's purr still. With a mighty bound and blurred thrashing of wings, the tercel was suddenly airborne. Despite herself, Lell flinched. The sweep of his pinions was startling. His shadow passed over her back and flanks.

"We meet again in three months' time, little unicorn," he called, skimming out from the steep hillside and down.

Had she leapt upward then, Lell realized, she could have grazed him. The rush of air dizzied her. Her horn tingled. The blood in her veins sang. Wheeling, she glimpsed the gryphon's back before his furiously threshing wings gained him lift enough to veer, glide upward toward vale's edge. She wheeled again, following his path with her eyes. The Pan Woods lay beyond the top of the rise.

"Lell!" she cried after him, bounding upslope in his wake. "My name is Lell!"

The gryphon neither checked nor turned. Still seeking altitude, his grass-green pinions winnowed the air. He soared away from her. Lell stumbled to a halt. The bright air seemed to burn where he had been. She wondered what it must be like to sail, free as a hawk, so far above the ground. Her withers tightened unexpectedly, aching almost, longing for wings. Grown small, the tercel passed beyond the hillcrest, disappeared from view. Heart still at full gallop, she realized she had been holding her breath.

A sudden drumming of heels brought Lell's head sharp around. The crack of trampled twigs reached her, and the crashing of brush. From wood's edge, scant paces from her, rang out the battle-whistle of a warrior. A moment later, the black prince of the unicorns burst from the trees. Snorting, ramping, he cast fiercely about as though seeking a foe. Lell whinnied and reared, thrusting her young horn toward the empty sky.

"Jan! Jan! Did you see him?" she cried. "My gryphon! He says his wingleader will come parley with us—at summer solstice, Moondance."

❦

The solstice night fell still and clear, with sky above transforming to the dark, even blue of deep water. The round moon, burning silver as it climbed, paled a heaven pricked with summer stars. Pied Tek, the prince's mate, danced in the great ring of unicorns cantering under the moon. White Dhattar and painted Aiony frisked beside her, pummeling one another with their soft weanlings' hooves. The dancers trampled the thick, fragrant grass, kicking and scattering turf. Night breathed warm with coming summer and the panting and sweating of unicorns.

All around her, Tek watched her fellows bowing and turning their heads to scratch their flanks with keen horntips, then reaching to prick the flanks of their fellows. Each full moon since equinox, they had done the same, ever since her mate had spoken of his battle with Alma's serpent and of the magic in his blood. He had vowed to bestow it upon the entire herd. She herself had been the first. Each Moondance since, those already scratched had mingled their blood with the blood of others until after this night, all—from youngest newborn to most venerable elder—would by Alma's grace stand forever proof against serpents and their stings.

The pied mare shook herself for sheer exuberance and danced. She gazed at her weanling filly and foal traipsing ahead amid the swirling rush to butt at Lell with their blunt, barely sprouted horn-nubs. Laughing, the older filly chivvied and nipped at them. They sought refuge behind their granddam Ses. Pale cream with a mane and tail of flame, the mother of Jan and Lell never faltered in her step while the three colts cavorted, playing peekover and tag. Tek whistled Aiony and Dha back to her side.

She spotted Jan ahead of them, emerging from the dancers. He ascended the council rise, a low mass of stone thrusting up from the valley floor. Around it the great moondance circled. Reaching the top of the rock, the young prince halted, his lean stallion's form just entering its prime etched in shadow against the moon-washed hills. *What a wonder I pledged as my mate,* Tek smiled to herself, *scant three years gone, by the Summer Sea.* She admired the crest of his neck, length of his horn, his fine runner's limbs.

Around her, the dance began to subside, moon halfway along its journey to surmount the sky. She halted, gazed about as one by one, unicorns circling her and her offspring strayed to a stop, stood cropping grass or lay down on soft, cushioned earth. Tek, too, lay down with Dha and Ai, not far from Ses and Lell. She sensed the others' expectancy from their skittish prancing, their restive whinnies and snorts. Her own mingled anticipation and trepidation made the pied mare's skin twitch.

On the rise above, her mate tensed suddenly. A ripple passed through the herd. Heads lifted. Necks craned. Gazing into the seamless silver sky, she, too, caught sight: gryphons, a dozen of them in a hollow wedge sailing the moonlit air, dark as cinders, silent as haunts or dreams. Tek's herdmates shifted, jostled, murmured uneasily as the vee descended. A huge wingcat formel occupied the point, the intense blue of her plumage discernible even by moonlight. All were formels, the pied mare realized, save for one flanking the leader's wing, the tips of his green tercel's feathers nearly brushing hers. Scarcely smaller than his fellows, the lone male glided.

Closer they drifted, and closer yet. Their shadows swept the silent herd. Tek felt the hairs of her pelt stiffen and lift. The thud of paws on rippled rock sounded in the stillness as the gryphons alighted on the council rise, first the wingleader, then the tercel beside her, then all the other blue-and-tawny formels of the vee. Tek felt her fellows tense, recoil ever so slightly. Only her mate stood at ease before their enemies, still fanning the air.

The pied mare's ears pricked. "Do you see him, Mother?" she heard Lell whispering. "The green one? My gryphon."

Tek saw the pale mare stroke her daughter once with a motherly tongue. "I see him," Ses murmured. "Be still."

On the rise, the gryphon leader crouched before Jan, her blue feathers sheened with moonlight. Her monstrous wings thrashed vigorously. Tek felt their buffeting even here. The musky odor of raptors and pards reached her, making her flesh draw. Above, Jan stood quiet, waiting until the formel subsided, lashing her lion's tail against one tawny flank. Her feathers roughed, then lay smooth.

"Hail, Jan, prince of unicorns."

The pied mare started. The formel's voice was surprisingly catlike, throaty and smooth, with none of the raucousness of eagles' cries.

"Hail, Malar, wingleader of the gryphons," the prince replied. "Be welcome in our Vale."

Tek heard him perfectly. His words traveled to the rocky slopes, rang ever so softly there. The formels behind their leader stirred, muttering, their green eyes glinting. Only the tercel remained impassive. The gryphon leader cocked her head, eyeing Jan with one cat-slit eye.

"This was *our* Vale once," she said, "entrusted to us by the sky goddess Isha, fold to the sacred flocks of her consort Ishi. Your kind's coming drove those flocks away."

Again, the formels behind her shifted, snapping bills. Tek thought she heard a low-pitched growl. Her own people moved restlessly. She caught sound of a snort, a stamp, a toss of mane. Dhattar and Aiony leaned sleepily against her. Tek bent to nuzzle them, her eyes still on the rise.

"And at our departure," the prince answered Malar firmly, "it is my hope that your wind god's sheep and deer will abundantly return. My people took refuge in this place centuries past. Driven from our home, we never knew we trespassed here. But now our goddess tells us to reclaim ancestral lands. We must depart, but we would not go as enemies. Hear the tale of our first coming to the Vale. My mate would sing you that lay of our long exile and the treachery of wyverns. Ho, Tek! Will you come?"

Tek felt her heart thump. This was the moment she had awaited all evening and dreaded all spring. The warm odor of wingcats filled her nostrils as she rose. Dhattar and Aiony slept. The pied mare's hooves grated on the hard, worn stone as she ascended the council rise. She and her mate exchanged a glance. Jan pressed his shoulder to hers, but said no word. His presence steadied her. The gryphons' beaks and talons glinted. Their moon-shot eyes gleamed.

"Greetings, Malar, queen of gryphons," Tek hailed them. Her voice sounded even enough. Within her ribs, her heart bucked and churned. "I have met your kind in battle time and again and never dreamed to stand at peaceful parley with you. But my mate assures me that two years past, he and your cousin set aside their enmity."

She glanced toward the green-winged tercel flanking the queen. He acknowledged her gesture with a nod, but spoke no word. His wing-leader kept her eyes fixed on Tek.

"I stand ready to make that same peace with you, Queen Malar," the pied mare said, "though we children-of-the-moon have suffered much at the claws of wingcats."

She inclined her head toward her sleeping young, nestled side to side on the grass below, and glimpsed the gryphon leader's headcrest rear, subside. Malar's bill snicked shut. Tek felt her mate's side pressed to hers. He was holding his breath. Behind their queen, the gryphons shifted. One of the formels hissed, but at a sharp glance from the tercel, fell still. Tek felt Jan's breath let out and dared to breathe.

"I would sing you the Lay of the Unicorns," the pied mare told the wingcat queen, "which tells of my people's expulsion from the Hallow Hills. Then the Lay of Exile would I sing, recounting how we found and claimed this unsettled valley, gaining haven from wandering."

Malar seemed to consider, her moonlit eyes half-shut. From the hard clench of Jan's neck beside her, Tek knew his teeth were set. His breath came in little silent spurts. Her own heart thundered.

"In return," the prince's mate continued, "will you sing us your own tales of this vale, that we may learn the whole history of the place we mean soon to leave forever?"

The wingleader of the gryphons glanced furtively at the green-winged tercel beside her. He preened one shoulder, all seeming uncon-cern. Tek saw one corner of the gryphon queen's mouth quirk momentarily into a smile. Returning her gaze to the pied mare, Malar bowed her great eagle's head and moved back to give the pied mare ground.

"So be it," the gryphon leader purred.

Jan, too, fell back, leaving Tek alone on the center of the rise. All around, her herdmates listened. The gryphons waited with up-pricked ears. She felt her mate's eyes watching her. Tek raised her voice and sang of how, forty generations past, wyverns had invaded the unicorns' rightful lands far to the balmy north. Under guise of friendship, the white wyrmlord Lynex had befriended the unicorns' agèd king, then used sorcery to addle the old stallion's wits, blinding him to the wyverns' schemes.

Only Princess Halla had spied the coming betrayal—but her warnings were ignored. In treacherous ambush, wyverns stung to death most of the unicorn warhost, and slew nearly all the rest with fire. Only Halla and her few, desperate followers escaped, fleeing coldward—south—across the Plain. Coming at last upon a vast, deserted vale, the unicorns gladly claimed it, here to spend long exile awaiting the coming of Alma's appointed, who was to lead them back in triumph to the Hallow Hills.

Tek fell silent, the tale run out. Her words rebounded from the distant slope, hung singing faintly under the round white belly of the pregnant moon now poised high overhead. Below, colts and fillies slept beside their waking sires and dams, all recumbent now. Even some of the gryphons reposed, pard-like, their wings no longer ruffled and half-raised, but folded close. All around burned the thousand thousand summer stars which were the goddess Alma's eyes. The pied mare swallowed, throat dry as dust. Her singer's calm broke then, leaving her stranded on the moonlit council rise, confronting gryphons.

Gryphonsong

★ 3 ★

I am that Firebringer," the black prince of the unicorns said, "which our prophets foretold."

Tek fell back as her mate moved forward. She lay down on the council rise, not far behind Jan. The stone held no warmth. The late spring air had cooled. Her mate and Malar faced one another across a low pile of brush to which the pied mare had paid no heed earlier. Jan's words hung in the motionless air. The gryphon wingleader's eyes seemed never to blink. The prince spoke on.

"Time approaches for my people to end our long exile."

The next instant, in one deft motion, he bowed his head and struck the tip of his horn against one heel. A rain of sparks leapt up. The pile of deadwood crackled and caught. Tek realized then it must have been for this purpose that the brush had been gathered. The gryphons' eyes grew wide at the sight of fire, their cats'-pupils slitting. Behind their leader, panicked formels crowded back. Only Malar's nearest companion, the tercel, held steady. He had seen her mate's firemaking before, the pied mare mused, when they had made their privy peace on the shores of the Summer Sea. Ruffled, Malar herself did not retreat, but peered into the crackling blaze.

"How soon? How soon will you depart?" A purr thrummed in her throat. She leaned closer to the warmth.

"Next spring," Jan answered, "once the grass on the Plain is sprung and last year's nurslings are weaned."

The formel raised one feathered brow.

"Suckling mares cannot join in battle," the prince of the unicorns explained. "And battle there will be, despite our having grown proof against the stings of our foes. The Hallow Hills will not be easily won."

Malar stirred beside the fire, lifting one wing to allow its heat to reach her side. She was silent so long, Tek wondered if she had fallen asleep.

"Like you, prince of unicorns," the formel responded at last, "we gryphons now desire peace. We are wearied of raids and your bitter flesh. If you pledge to relinquish Ishi's Vale to our stewardship, we shall nest content."

Turning her head ever so slightly, she glanced back at her dozen followers crouching or reclining behind her.

"But we, too, have a tale to sing, a chorus of the making of this sacred place, ages past at the pipping of the world. Our singer is blood kin to me—and for all that he is but a green-winged tercel, he holds a heart as brave, talons as keen, and a voice as strong as any formel's. Hark now, I bid you, as he raises our song."

The lone male among the gryphons padded forward, skirting his queen and the fire to come directly before Jan. Tek watched as her prince bowed low.

"Hail, Illishar Mended-wing," Jan greeted him. "When my sister told me who among your folk had carried your leader's offer of parley, my heart leapt."

The tercel's stony countenance eased. Tek saw his ruffled quills settle, the golden fur of his flank grow smooth. His voice, like his queen's, was low and sweet.

"So you remember me, Prince Jan."

The dark stallion shook himself. Tek's own ears pricked. She eyed the green gryphon feather tangled amid her mate's long black hair. "How not," he asked, "when I still wear the gift you gave?" His tone was one of genuine gladness and surprise. "You have grown since last we met."

The tercel chuckled. "You also, prince of unicorns. Two years past I was barely fletched, a gangling squab!"

Jan snorted. "A formidable warrior, by my reck."

With a shudder, Tek glimpsed the scars lacing her mate's shoulder blades, indelible reminders of the mortal combat in which he and this tercel once had joined. She glanced at her sleeping filly and foal and felt the pelt rise along her spine. Despite the feather in his hair, to Tek's mind, Jan's battlescars were only one among a cluster of reasons to mistrust these flesh-eating gryphons. Crouched before the prince, the tercel flexed one magnificent wing.

"I, too, suffered in that fray," he murmured. "But you gave me back my life."

"And what befell after I set your bone?" Jan asked.

Tek peered curiously at the gryphon's broad, green pinion, doubting she could ever have dared approach such a dangerous creature, even one with a shattered limb. She and every other unicorn in the Vale, she knew, would gladly have left the fallen raptor to starve. Illishar shrugged, preened a stray feather back into place.

"As soon as my pinion grew strong enough, I made haste back to the Gryphon Mountains to rejoin my flock."

Tek listened. Her mate tossed his head.

"We heard no word of you," he pressed. "Indeed, we have seen no wingcats since, save for your own brief stop last spring. What kept your folk so far from our Vale?"

Tek tensed as, on the far side of the fire, the gryphon formels suddenly ruffled. Two jostled and paced. Another beat her wings in agitation, so that the fire leapt, flared. Illishar's eyes flicked to them, then to his wingleader. Malar returned his gaze impassively, with the barest hint of a nod. The tercel turned again to Jan.

"The flocks have been at war," he said. "Rival clans sought to conquer Malar, but she triumphed in the end. I, too, soared, winning a perch on the high ledge beside her."

Tek saw another glance pass between the wingcat and his queen. Jan stood listening, offering no word.

"Malar is wearied of war," Illishar resumed. "As are we all. When I returned two years past with word that the unicorns might consent to relinquish Ishi's sacred Vale and return to their own lands across the Plain, she pounced at the chance. Others were not so hungry for peace. They sought to seize the wingleader's place."

The gryphon queen behind him shifted. It seemed to Tek that Malar's eyes, still fixed upon Illishar, now shone with inestimable pride. He continued.

"But with my aid and that of all her loyal flock, she has struck her rivals from the sky and pashed their eggs to shards. Mightiest of wingleaders, she soars, and the clans fly united behind her once more!"

Seated upright behind their queen, pinions poised, the formels uttered shrill cries of assent. Tek saw the herd just below the rise tense in alarm, but just as suddenly, the formels fell silent. Malar demurely nibbled one shoulder, as if ignoring their praise.

"Hear my song," cried Illishar, his wings half-raised. "How Isha laid the clutch that hatched all the creatures of the world, and how we gryphons pleased her best of all."

Again fluting whistles from the formels, but more melodic, rising and falling in a complex harmony to the tercel's words.

"Great Isha created her consort Ishi from greenest grass and most golden seed. But he was lifeless, so she closed him in a silver egg, and he hatched out full grown. Half the mottled shell still turns in heaven. Now full, so we see it end-on, beholding only its outward curving edge. A week hence, when it has pivoted, we will see it in profile, the half moon. And in another week's time, on the night of the new moon, we will discern no silver rim at all but instead gaze into the dark mystery of its inner hollow. Blessèd be the goddess and her consort, Ishi!"

Behind him, the formels raised their voices in intricate, effortless accompaniment, the ever-changing position of their wings seeming to accent his words: now lifted, now folded, now outstretched. Only Malar took no part, still as stone, a moonlit sphinx. Shivers feathered the pied mare's limbs and sides. Tek found herself growing rapt as the herd around her. Jan, too, stood motionless, enthralled.

Illishar sang of Isha's gift of the winds to her consort Ishi, of her creation of the Vale for his sacred flocks, lovingly husbanded as first meat for the newly hatched. The tune pulsed and lilted. Tek's heartbeat sped. Her people had no such sinuous music as these gryphons made, the tercel sometimes speaking or chanting while the formels behind him repeated and ornamented his words.

By the time Illishar recounted how centuries past, unicorns had swarmed into Ishi's Vale, forcing out the delectable sheep and deer, leaving only their own unsavory young as rank pickings for the formel's new-pipped chicks, the pied mare was almost on her feet, ready to shout, *No, no! Drive the intruders out*—until she realized with a start that it was against her own kind she would have railed. Groggy, Tek shook herself, no wingèd gryphon, but a four-leggèd unicorn.

The tercel had fallen silent. The formels, too. Dazed, the prince's mate gazed out over the herd, beheld them coming to themselves, stirring slowly like beasts entranced. She had no doubt now how gryphons managed to bewitch their prey. Shaken and stiff, the pied mare rolled her shoulders, extended her neck. Moon hung low on the other side of a sky paling eastward into dawn.

Below her, Lell reclined beside her mother, the only one of all the colts Tek could see who was not asleep. The amber filly gazed at Illishar, eyes following his every move, ears pricked to the rustle of his quills. Head bowed, the tercel fell back to flank his queen, still crouching beside the dying embers of the fire. Malar rose, stretched, fanning her great blue wings and arching her tawny back like a pard. Before her on the rise, Jan stirred, shifting his limbs. Had he stood the whole night? Tek watched him move forward, gait graceful and loose, unimpeded apparently by any fatigue.

"So, Malar, wingleader of the gryphons," he asked, "are we agreed?"

The mighty formel straightened, nodded. "We are agreed, Jan, prince of unicorns. Henceforth, our folk shall be at peace, and next spring your kind will depart Ishi's Vale, returning to your own ancestral Hills."

The slimmest of morning breezes lifted, died. The formel's feathers riffled, then smoothed.

"We take with us in gratitude your songs," she continued, "and leave you ours. We will not soon forget this night's singing, nor the tales that you have taught us. We trust you will remember ours."

She gave a guttural snort, the meaning of which Tek could not readily discern—supposed it might be a laugh, the first the pied mare had heard the gryphon queen utter.

"I would never have guessed that so hoarse-voiced and whinnying a sort as unicorns could honor the sky with such fetching airs—and from but a single throat. What brave and lonely songs you sing! I salute you."

Tek rose, the muscles of her long legs twinging, and stepped to stand beside her mate. She bowed low to the gryphon queen while Jan replied.

"And I salute you, wingleader of all the clans. Song, to my mind, rings far sweeter than war."

The great blue formel nodded curtly, then half-turned, fanning her massy wings again. Behind her, the other formels did the same.

"We must fly," she said. "Our chicks have nestled their fathers long enough. But know this." Malar turned to face Jan over one shoulder. "In emblem of my goodwill, next spring when you march for the Hallow Hills, I will send my kinsmeet Illishar to accompany you."

Beside Jan, Tek felt his start of pleasure, surprise.

"My thanks to you, Queen Malar," he answered warmly. "Your cousin is a mighty warrior. The ranks of the unicorns will be glad of his strength."

Illishar inclined his head. "I shall be as glad to lend it." His mouth edged into a bare hint of a smile. "My wingleader is most anxious that your war against the wyverns succeed, that hereafter Ishi's Vale harbor his flocks in peace, untroubled by wandering unicorns."

Tek saw the expression of the gryphon queen almost imperceptibly sour. Jan gave a whickering laugh.

"I, too, share the great Malar's urgency for the success of our endeavor. Your airborne eyes will be of great value to us, Illishar. We welcome you."

The green-winged tercel bowed his head. At a sign from Malar, her formels rose, some rearing to stand on hind legs as if to stretch, others stroking their wings. Jan's forelock lifted. Tek felt her own mane whipped about her neck. The buffeting grew fiercer. Malar moved a few paces from Jan, seeking room to spring into the air. The other gryphons fell back from her. The mighty wingleader sank into a crouch, half opening her wings, when suddenly a voice from among the unicorns broke the stillness.

"Hold!"

Jan reared and wheeled. Cavaling, Tek turned to see Lell spring to her feet. Before her startled dam could move to stay her, the darkamber filly sprinted for the rise. In three strides and a bound, she had gained the summit. Astonished, the pied mare fell back as the prince's sister hastened to his side.

"Brother, a moment," Lell panted. "I would speak! May I speak?"

Tek watched her mate's baffled eyes scanning his sister. Lell's urgency made her prance and sidle beside him. He spoke quietly.

"Sister, you already speak. What would you say?"

Lell seemed to take his response for leave. She spun eagerly to face the green-winged tercel.

"Illishar Brokenwing, do you know me?" she asked.

The tercel nodded gravely. "Could I forget?" he replied. "You are the prince's sister, with whom I set this parley three moons past."

"Lell," the chestnut filly answered. "My name is Lell. I wanted you to have my name."

The tercel's smile was unmistakable now. "Indeed, Lell Darkamber, I already know it. You called it out to me last spring as I departed. I hope that in three-quarters of a year's time, when I return, we may speak again."

"We shall!" exulted Lell, ramping with delight.

Her mother, Ses, had ascended the rise. She nudged her filly with one firm but unobtrusive shoulder. Lell caught her breath, and with a glance at her dam, managed to collect herself. She swallowed.

"That is, I would welcome it," she answered formally. With a deep bow first to Malar, then to Illishar, she added, "I thank you."

The prince's sister fell back with Ses to stand at the far edge of the rise. Malar crouched again and, with one prodigious leap, launched herself into the air. The gryphon queen rose, wings stroking rapidly at first, then locking to glide as she gained sufficient height. In a bound, green-winged Illishar followed. He seemed to have less trouble rising aloft than his larger, heavier companion. One by one, in swift succession, other formels followed, straining for lift in the windless air. None faltered. In another moment, all were airborne, wafting upward in a ragged vee. They headed south toward the valley's nearer slope. The Gryphon Mountains lay a day's flight beyond, across the Pan Woods that bordered the Vale. Tek moved to stand shoulder to shoulder with her mate.

"Do you see, Mother?" Lell behind her whispered excitedly. "How he flies! How he sang. He remembered my name. In under a year's time, he will return to us. My gryphon."

Baffled, the pied mare turned to watch the amber filly gazing after the green-gold tercel. Her eyes shone like those of some moonstruck half-grown. Tek snorted. Nay, ridiculous! It would be a year or more before Lell could join the Ring of Warriors, probably two or three before she pledged a mate by the Summer Sea. Whickering, the pied mare shook her head, convinced she had misconstrued the other's youthful enthusiasm. She leaned against her mate. Above and to the southwest, the tercel's form and those of the formels grew smaller and smaller yet.

"Do you think he would teach me gryphonsong?" she heard the prince's sister breathe. "Mother, what must it be like to fly?"

Wind

★ 4 ★

A puff of breeze played across Jan's face. The young stallion closed his eyes, relishing it. A moment later, when he opened them, the last of the soaring gryphons were just disappearing beyond the edge of the Vale. Dawnlight illumined the sky, burning it saffron and rose. The few remaining stars winked out. Tek leaned against him. The prince of the unicorns breathed deep, savoring the clean, warm scent of her, pied black as spent night, rosy as the coming dawn. Gently, he nipped her neck and watched his dam, Ses, and sister, Lell, descend the rocky rise. Below, he glimpsed unicorns waking, rolling, rising and shaking off. With a soft whicker, Ses bent to nose Dhattar and Aiony. They stirred. On the rise, his mate beside him murmured.

"Next spring, then."

He nodded. "Aye."

"Good."

He turned, surprised. "You've no fear?"

The warrior mare shrugged, chivvying him. "More relief than fear. Six years have I awaited this trek—since I beheld the Firebringer rush burning from heaven in the vision of my initiation." She nipped playfully at the tassels of his ears till they twitched. "Our folk have waited longer still. Four hundred years."

Her nips grew smarter, more insistent. He half reared, wheeling to fence with her. Laughing, she met him stroke for stroke, their horns clanging loudly in the morning stillness. Breeze lifted, and they broke off, panting. He saw his mate's gaze fall lovingly on Dhattar, up now and harassing Lell. Aiony rolled in the grass at her granddam's fore-hooves, refusing to get up. Around them, other unicorns frisked and grazed. Tek nudged him.

"My thanks for your waiting till the twins were weaned," she murmured. "I'm no strategist like you, no diplomat. Just a warrior—and a singer of sorts. And now a dam. I could not have borne forgoing the coming fray for the sake of suckling young."

She rested her chin at the crown of his head, lips nibbling the base of his horn, beard tickling his cheek. Jan laughed, sneezing, and shook her off.

"Alma chose the time, not I."

He turned to press his muzzle to her. Doing so, he caught sight of a figure just topping the rise. Two figures, in truth—and then he realized it was three. One had the form of a beardless unicorn deep mallow in color, redder than the dawn. She descended the slope on round, uncloven heels, her black mane standing upright as a newborn's along her neck, her tail silky and full.

Alongside her trotted a very different figure, moving upright on goatlike hind limbs. From the square shoulders of this figure's flattened torso hung two nimble forelimbs, one resting easily upon the withers of the red mare, the other swinging with each stride. A small, round head topped the creature's short, slender neck. Her hairless face held dark, expressive eyes. Curving horns and drooping, goatlike ears sprouted amid a shaggy mane.

A slighter, fairer version sat astride the strange unicorn mare, clinging to her brush, making the third member of the trio. Jan heard his mate beside him give a peal of joy. She reared, flailing the air. All around, on the valley floor below, unicorns turned and took note. Their delighted cries echoed the pied mare's:

"Jah-lila! The midwife! The magicker!"

Reaching the valley floor, the red mare answered, "Well met!"

The herd surged toward her and her goatling companions, who waved upheld forelimbs and whistled in perfect imitation of unicorns. Mares with suckling young especially moved to greet them. Jan glimpsed his own filly and foal sprinting with gleeful shrieks to welcome their maternal granddam. They, like most of the colts in the herd, had been delivered by the red mare and the pan sisters, her acolytes.

"Sismoomnat! Pitipak!" he heard Aiony and Dhattar exclaim. The younger pan slipped from her foster mother's back and joined her sister in frisking with them. The red mare waded on through the press, exchanging greetings with stallions and mares, all of whom fell back respectfully before her, even as fellows behind them crowded forward.

Good fortune, the herd murmured, *to breathe the wych's breath, stand in her shadow, tread her track.*

The half-grows, warriors, and elders were old enough to remember the awe in which the herd had, only a few short years ago, once held her—a fear now turned to reverence. She acknowledged them all but never paused, forging determinedly toward her daughter, the pied mare, still standing beside Jan on the rise. He fell back to let daughter and dam exchange caresses and greetings. Jah-lila nickered and called to him.

"Well met, my daughter's mate," she laughed, her dusky voice a deep, sweet echo of Tek's. "My fosterlings and I spied wingcats overhead as we entered the Vale. They kept their parley as agreed?"

The prince of the unicorns nodded. "Aye. Peace is pledged. We are sworn to depart for the Hills at spring."

The red mare nodded, said firmly, "Good."

"How do my foster sisters fare?" Tek inquired.

Jah-lila nuzzled her affectionately. "As you see. They spend much time in the Pan Woods now, midwiving their own folk's young."

"And our allies there?" Jan asked.

The red mare whickered. "Again, very well. The peace you forged in the Woods has been a lasting one."

Below, at herd's edge, the elder of the pan sisters, Sismoomnat, chased half a dozen wildly fleeing foals while Aiony charged Pitipak, trying to butt her off her feet. Lell laughed and circled. Dhattar's coat blazed fire-white among the burning colors of the rest.

"Whence have the three of you come," Tek was asking, "my pan sisters and you?"

The red mare smiled. "From the shores of the Summer Sea," she said. "We watched the narwhals calve. . . ."

Her words were cut short by a long, harsh wail more like a wolf's cry than a unicorn's. Sismoomnat, Pitipak and the foals halted abruptly. Around them, their elders started and wheeled. A haggard figure appeared on the near slope of the Vale, emerging from a dark hollow in the hillside. Jan's heart jolted. He felt Tek beside him sip her breath. Once massy and robust, the tall unicorn at the cavemouth showed sunken flanks, his ribs visible, limbs bony and starved. Black as stormcloud, he loomed in the grotto's entryway. Before him, the herd recoiled.

"Gryphons," the emaciated stallion roared. The cave amplified and echoed the sound. "Wingcats in our midst! First you dance the serpent's dance, then don the quills of our sworn foes. Now you welcome the beardless wych. Traitors!"

He drew nearer, descending the slope half a dozen paces. With shrills of terror, the youngest colts galloped to their dams. The whole herd fell back. Jan spotted Lell standing before young Ai and Dha, pressed close to the pans. He glimpsed Tek's gaze of fury and loathing as she watched the dark figure on the hillside. The prince of the unicorns clenched his teeth and advanced.

"Aye, night past we danced the serpent's dance," he called, "to make ourselves proof against such stings—in honor of That One who made both serpent and the unicorn. We treated with wingcats to win peace ere we depart this vale. And Jah-lila is our honored guest, dam to my mate and midwife to the herd."

He left unsaid the other, bitter truth: that the skeletal figure above was responsible for the deaths of countless fillies and foals before these. Their elders had not forgotten, could never forget, that terrible winter two years gone when this stallion had seized power in Jan's absence and allowed half the herd to starve to death.

"If Alma stands defiled, it is not by us," the young prince continued. "Cry traitor elsewhere."

Jan heard his people's mutters of assent.

"Poison in your blood!" the haunt on the hillside before him shrieked. "You'll never scratch my flank. No serpent's taint to sully me!"

The rumble from the herd grew louder. Dark clouds appeared above the edges of the Vale. Dawn wind blew stronger, gusting now. Sun flickered and flared, backlighting the shadowy thunderheads that moved to encircle it. Jan's ears pricked at restless snorts and whinnies. He heard a mare's voice call out, "Tyrant!"

A young stallion's echoed: "Murderer!"

"Rout him," another shouted. "Cast him from the Vale."

Jan felt hairs lift along his spine. He spun to face the herd. They shouldered and jostled about the council rise, seething with anger, eyes fixed on the hillside above. The young prince reared, struck the sparking stones of the rise with his hooves till they clanged.

"Hold," he shouted. "Hold! Think you that banishment can heal madness? All the herd ran mad that terrible winter—and those who meekly submitted to Korr's tyranny must share his blame. No ruler reigns without the consent of his folk. Had we not rather seek to drive madness from our own hearts? Only then may the herd know peace."

The unicorns subsided uneasily, eyes cast down and askance, unwilling to face him anymore, or each other, or the figure on the rise. Sires gathered their daughters to their sides and nuzzled them. Dams stroked their tiny foals. Drawing breath, Jan turned once more to the figure on the hillside.

"Father—" but the bony stallion cut him off.

"You are not my son!"

The black prince of the unicorns stopped short. Korr's words tore him like a wolf's jaws. Pulse pounding, Jan fought for calm, dismayed that even now, after all this time, his sire could still spit barbs to rankle him.

"You were never my son!" the mad king snarled. "Wild, un-schooled, spurning tradition at every turn. Then you pledged with that strumpet, pied daughter of a wych, and got twin horrors from her womb. I never sired you! You're none of my get—"

"Enough!"

The word burst from Jan, its force bringing the other up short. The young prince of the unicorns shook himself as though to clear a swarm of gnats from his hide. Illishar's feather batted softly against his neck.

"Enough, I say! Two years have you railed against my mate, calling our progeny abomination, yet offered no justification for your charge."

The wind quickened, humming, full of moisture. Stormclouds gusted around the dawn-red sun. Jan snorted.

"Where were you, my sire, when I was but a foal and needed your care? Off ramping with the warriors, haranguing them to endless clashes with gryphons, wyverns, and pans! It was I you shunned then. Not one word or deed of mine was ever worthy of your note."

The old resentment, so long unspoken, roiled up in him now. Jan cavaled.

"Always it was Tek! Her you showered with praise. Tek the warrior, pride of the half-growns, model to all the younger fillies and colts. A stranger would have thought *her* your get and I the fatherless foal. Yet when we pledged, marrying our fates, a bond unshakable under the summer stars—suddenly she was not to be endured, her crimes un-counted, our offspring monstrous. Why?"

The wind blew steadily now, grey clouds obscuring the sun. Jan scarcely heeded it. His smooth summer pelt riffled, teasing his skin. The long hairs of his tail flailed his flank.

"In Alma's name, father, what drives you mad and turns you against me, my mate and young? Speak! If you will but speak, perhaps whatever torments you can be allayed."

The mad king stood gazing at him, eyes wide, rolling.

"Nay," he whispered. "The red wych has cozened you, telling you lies!"

Wind buffeted about them, slapping Jan's forelock into his eyes. The Vale lay in shadow. Thunder growled like a hillcat. Dams and stallions bent over their young, shielding them from the coming rain—but none moved to seek shelter, all eyes fixed on the prince and his sire. Jan glimpsed Jah-lila leaving her daughter's side.

"Korr," she called, "you know as well as I that I have revealed nothing. I have pledged never to speak of the history we share while your silence holds. I honor that pledge still—unlike the oath you once swore me. . . ."

"Never!" the haggard stallion gasped. "You bewitched me there upon the Plain. I was too young to know my own heart—"

"But not too young to give your word." The red mare spoke softly. Her black-green eyes gazed at him without hatred, only sorrow. "Speak of what befell us. Your own silence lies at the root of this madness, not the conduct of any other. Only speak! Be healed."

The gaunt stallion reared, scarcely darker than the stormclouds that towered above. Sudden lightning clashed, followed by deafening thunder. Korr flailed at nothing.

"My mate!" Ses cried. Wind stole her words. "Come back to me. Reveal what troubles you!"

Rain spattered down, stinging as hailstones. Ses moved forward to stand beside the red mare.

"*She* troubles me!" Korr thundered back. "My mate—she is my woe. She stole my heir with her sorcery. Wych!" he shouted above the gale, eyes flicking to Tek's dam, then back to his mate. "You knew. You knew all along. From the time we pledged—you held your tongue and watched. . . ." Again his gaze wavered. "I have no mate, no heir, no son!"

His words had grown so wild Jan could no longer tell to whom the mad king spoke: the red mare or his mate. But the young prince had no time for thought. The king had already launched himself, charging down the rain-slicked slope straight at Ses—or perhaps at Jah-lila. The two mares stood nearly shoulder to shoulder now. Lell cried out and sped forward, as though to fling herself in front of her dam, defend her somehow by coming between her and the mad king's charge.

"No!" shouted Jan.

He vaulted from the council rise, dashed to intercept his frenzied sire. Before him, Ses and Jah-lila parted, sprang in opposite directions to clear the raging stallion's path. Jan managed to veer ahead of Lell, shield her. Korr plunged past in a dusky blur, a waft of rank air, a snatch of bright teeth and a slash of horn. Jan swung his head with all his might, brought his own weapon down with force enough to knock his assailant's skewer aside. The blow clamored, reverberating in his skull.

He felt the bite upon his neck begin to bleed, the long shallow rent across his chest blaze hot with pain. Beside him, Lell—scarcely half his size—dodged, trying to get around him, seeking to fall upon their attacker herself. Korr skidded, wheeled. Jan rushed him, mostly to keep himself safely between his young sister and the king. The black prince slapped hard at his sire with the flat of his horn, pounded him with his heels, driving him back, away from Lell and the others.

At last, with a despairing cry, the mad king shook free, wheeled, fled across the valley floor and up the far hillside. Lightning shattered the sky. Rolling thunder pealed. The wind lashed, flailed. Rain became a downpour. Stunned, the herd broke and scattered, scrambling for haven in the caverns and hollows of the surrounding slopes. Without a moment's hesitation, Jan sprang in pursuit of his sire. Desperately, Tek galloped to intercept him.

"Jan," she cried. "Hold. Forbear!"

The young prince scarcely checked. "Nay," he cried furiously. "Nay, not this time! He'll not evade me more. I'll have the truth if I must chase it to world's edge! Take charge of the herd, Tek—I'll return as soon as may be."

Rain

★ 5 ★

Rain hammered down. Jan's cloven heels bit into the soft hillside, sliding on slippery turf. Thunder crashed. Wind whipped at him. Having long since lost sight of Korr, he gained the trees. Jan shook his head, teeth champed, panting with effort. The downpour was blinding. A glimpse of shadow through the trees ahead. He dodged after it. Tree-boles gave way once more to rocky slope. Above, a gaunt figure struggled to the hillcrest and vanished over it. The young prince redoubled his efforts, loose, wet rocks kicking from under his heels. As he topped the rise, rain pummeled him anew. Snorting, he pitched to a halt.

Below him lay the Pan Woods, home to Sismoomnat and Pitipak's folk, the two-legged goatlings. Until a few short seasons ago, the pans had been among the unicorns' bitterest foes. Now both peoples enjoyed free forage through one another's lands. Gazing down, the prince's eye met nothing but dark woods, sprawling toward horizon's edge through a grey curtain of rain. He listened, but discerned nothing above the deafening downpour. For all the king's haggard appearance, he made swift quarry.

The young prince cast back over one shoulder at the Vale, lying deserted in the rain. He eyed the council rise, empty and small-seeming, about which he and his fellows had lately parleyed and danced. He marked his own cave on the hillside below, where Tek and the twins now doubtless sheltered, and felt a twinge. Impatiently, he shook it off. He would be returning in a few hours—at most a day or two. Just as soon as he had found his sire and wrested his terrible secret from him. Surely then all could be put to rights. Jan set his teeth. Without another thought or backward glance, he plunged over the hillcrest into the dark Pan Woods.

The trees rose thick around him, dripping with moisture. The morning's deluge had subsided at last to a pattering drizzle. Jan trotted along a streambed, seeking tracks. He had combed for hours in widening circles, hoping to come upon his sire or sign of him, or else to encounter friendly pans from whom to ask news or aid.

Jan splashed to a halt in the middle of the stream and bent his long neck to drink. The water tasted cool in the humid summer air. He shook his sodden coat for perhaps the twentieth time. His head reeled. He had not slept in an evening and a day. It was long past noon. Jan stumbled out of the streambed. He had followed it far enough and found no sign. The young prince felt the hollow ache between his ribs, the weakness in his limbs as he reentered the trees. He would have to feed soon, rest.

A glade opened before him, perfectly round, vegetation carefully cleared from its center. Jan recognized it for a pan place, one of their ceremonial circles. A ring of stones enclosed a heap of ash in the circle's heart. Young oats and rye grass sprouted among the trees bordering the clearing. Inhaling the lush, verdant scent, the dark unicorn bent his head, tearing greedily at the fragrant, juicy stuff. Leaves and buds augmented his fare. The hollow in his belly began to fill.

A thicket of firs stood near the clearing's edge. Their strong, resinous aroma beckoned him. Jan nudged aside a spray of boughs and pressed forward, shouldering past outer branches until he reached the hollow interior. The firs stood so close, their spreading foliage so dense, that despite the morning's rain, the fallen fir needles beneath had remained dry. Only when he had sunk down and folded his limbs under him, did the dark unicorn realize how exhausted he was.

His heart rocked against his ribs. Breathing deep, he settled himself into the soft, fragrant carpet. Jan laid his head along his outstretched forelegs. His eyes closed once, opened, closed again. He thought of Korr and resolved to rest only briefly before going on. The gaunt, dark unicorn fled before him in dreams. Hooded serpents swarmed. The young prince twitched, eyelids fluttering, as a viper rose to strike the king. He who had never danced the serpent's dance, never scratched his flank or received the venom-proof blood, cried out as the dream nadder's fangs pierced him.

Jan felt himself racing, sprinting to fend off the serpent's sting— too late. The haggard stallion reared, screaming, then fell endlessly away from Jan into a yawning crevasse. The speckled serpents attenuated into a tangle of stars. The young prince found himself still running, galloping along through dark emptiness high above the rolling globe below. Cold wind whipped his mane. He was crossing a bridge, a precarious curve that spanned the whole sky, arcing ever more steeply down to horizon's edge. In a rush he realized he could not stop, momentum propelling him, hurtling him swift and inevitably toward the end of the world.

❦

Panpipes woke him, their low, susurrous music fluting through the quiet. Jan stirred, groggy. He lifted his head, felt the closeness of fir boughs. Peering through darkness, he realized it was night. In the clearing, just visible through the trees, graceful, two-leggèd figures crouched or reposed about a flaring fire: young pans and old, full-grown warriors, elders, weanlings and infants. Jan glimpsed roots and other forage passing from forelimb to forelimb, dams suckling their young. The guttural clicks and gestures which were the goatlings' speech made little more than a murmur above the crackling of the blaze.

The gentle trilling of their panpipes wove through the summer air. Halfway around the circle Jan spotted the piper. Beside him sat a grey-bearded male, horns ribbed with age, and a bare-cheeked female, skin wizened as willow bark. A much younger pair rose from the circle and approached with forepaws clasped. They bowed low before their elders and handed them sheaves of grass in exchange for garlands. By their rich, sweet scent, Jan knew the flowers to be night-blooming lilies. Their perfume blended with the tang of woodsmoke and the aroma of the trees.

The young couple embraced, forelimbs entwining, and retired to the far side of the ring. Jan heard glad murmuring among their fellows as, each with a gesture and a word, the two elders rose and cast their sheaves into the fire. Red sparks flared up, subsided. Jan could only conclude he had witnessed some sort of joining, perhaps even the pledging of mates, and was swept suddenly, keenly, by memory of his own pledging to Tek almost three years past, by the shores of the Summer Sea.

The young prince shook himself, struggled free of the firs. Time to make himself known. The panpipes still crooned their haunting soft song amid the cheerful hubbub. The two elders resumed their places beside the piper as Jan reached the edge of the glade.

"*Emwe!*" he hailed them, framing with care the difficult, champing syllables of pan speech. "Tai-shan nau shopucha." *Moonbrow greets you.*

He moved forward slowly, so as not to startle them, until the firelight illumined his dark form.

"Have no fear. I am Jan, prince of unicorns, come in peace to seek your counsel."

The pipe player broke off suddenly as the pan campsite erupted in confusion. Jan heard cries of "Pella! Pell'!"—*Look, behold*—and "Sa'ec so!" *Him! It's him.* Sires and dams caught up their young as though to flee. Others snatched and brandished wooden stakes. He saw children quickly gathering stones. The dark unicorn snorted in bewilderment. Peace with the pans had held these two years running without a whisper of strain.

"*Nanapo*: peace," he exclaimed. "I am no foe. I seek another of my race who has fled and taken shelter here."

The pans hesitated. Jan himself poised, determined to run if he must and shed no blood. With relief, he saw the old male rise from his haunches and hold up one forelimb.

"Bikthitet nau," he heard the greybeard urging: *Calm yourselves.* "This is not the same *ufpútlak*—four-footed walker—we encountered earlier. Though dark as the other, *pella*—observe—he does not have that one's wild, unreasoning air. A great green feather tangles this one's mane. And this *ufpútlak* speaks our tongue."

Jan's heart seized at the other's words. He moved a half pace nearer. The pans twitched, pulled back, but did not flee. The greybeard held his ground.

"Elder, have you seen another of my kind this day?" Jan asked urgently. "A night-dark stallion such as I, but lawless, gaunt—it is he I seek."

Carefully, the bearded male nodded. Around him, the goatlings murmured, uneasily. The agèd female, now risen to stand beside her mate, answered, "Such a one came upon us near noon this day. What can you tell us of him?"

Jan drew a deep breath. "He is Korr, king of the unicorns."

Gasps, angry cries rose again from the goatling band. The furrows in the brows of the two elders deepened.

"If he is Korr," the greybeard said evenly, "do you, Jan, prince of *ufpútlaki,* now come to revel in your broken truce?"

The young prince's ribs constricted. "I come seeking him," he answered slowly, carefully. "He is my sire, and he is mad. Having fled our Vale this day, he now imperils not only himself and his folk, but our allies as well. I must find him and return him to the Vale, that his madness may be healed."

More murmuring from the pans. They eyed him, suspicious still. He sensed a slight—if only very slight—easing in the two elders. The fire crackled. The young prince waited. No one spoke. Finally he broke the silence.

"Tell me, I implore you, where I may find him. What deeds of his have made you so wary and put our peoples' hard-won truce in jeopardy?"

Glancing at one another, the elders considered. The rest of the goatlings held silent, watching. At last, the wizened female spoke.

"This midday," she said, "while we rested in the shade of the brittle-blossom trees, this mad *ufpútlak* stampeded among us, cursing us—so we surmise—in his own tongue. None were spared: not elders nor suckling young." Her tone grew hard. "Even children he would eagerly have trampled, had fathers and mothers not snatched them from his path."

Jan felt the blood drain from him at the thought of the mad king charging unchecked among these slight, retiring goatlings, only lately come to trust unicorns. "Did he harm any of you?" the young prince breathed, praying to Alma his worst fears might not prove true.

"Nay," the greybeard replied, and Jan's heart eased. "To our relief, your king drew no blood. We fled and dodged. Our warriors drove him off with volleys of stones—as we shall drive away all unicorns from this day forward! Your king is well-bruised. He fled toward the grassy land that borders our Woods. What do you call it? The Plain."

Jan's breath caught in dismay. The Plain was far more dangerous than the Woods: rife with grass pards that ambushed their prey. Sharp-toothed dogs that hunted in packs. Unicorns, too, roamed the Plain—wild wanderers outside the Ring of Law, of a tribe other than Jan's own. Korr had sworn eternal enmity toward these so-called Renegades. If he were reckless enough to attack Plainsdwellers as he had this goatling band, he would do so at his peril. The Free Folk of the Plain were as dauntless in their own defense as any Ringborn unicorn. Jan set his teeth. He must fly with all speed to intercept his sire.

"My heart grieves with you that this outlaw from my Vale has caused you such alarm," he answered, bowing deeply before the two elders of the goatling band. "My own tribe as well has suffered such inexplicable acts of his madness. A terrible secret haunts his mind. I mean to discover it."

He scanned the pans, gauging their mood, hoping desperately that the damage Korr had done the newborn alliance was not truly beyond repair.

"Meanwhile, I beg you not to let his trespass spoil our peoples' long-sought peace." Jan turned his eyes back to the elder pair. "Korr will be stopped. That I vow. Even now I hasten to call him to account. I ask only that you send runners to my Vale. There you will find my mate, the regent Tek, with her foster sisters, Sismoomnat and Pitipak, and their dam, Jah-lila. Treat with them before you decide to abandon the peace. Tell them I seek my sire upon the Plain and will not rest until I find him."

Silently, the pans deliberated. The elders' eyes roved over the rest of the band, seeking consensus. Jan felt his heartbeats pulsing one by one, his muscles growing taut. At last, the agèd goatlings nodded.

"Very well, Moonbrow," the greybeard replied. "We will do as you ask. The newfound friendship between our two peoples is indeed too precious to be lightly shed."

His mate beside him echoed, "Find your sire, Prince Jan. Our goodwill speed you."

The prince of the unicorns bowed low before them. Their fire, untended, had dwindled to a feeble glow. Jan turned and launched himself, galloping away through the moonlit trees. Alma's daughter, waning now, illumined his path. Behind, he sensed the glow of coals newly stoked and fanned to life again, heard the panpipes resume their plaintive song. He headed west through the still, dark wood, sprinting in the direction of the Great Grass Plain.

Summer

★ 6 ★

Tek stood in the entry to the cave. Moonless night breathed warm around her. Above, a myriad of summer stars flocked the heavens like thistledown. Still discernibly blue, the early evening sky held onto the set sun's light. Nine weeks. The pied mare shook her head. Most of summer flown since the serpent's dance, since peacemaking with the gryphons and, a few days following, goatling envoys.

Snorting, the warrior mare marveled. No diplomat, she had had no fine phrases such as her mate always used to win his enemies' trust. Instead, she had employed her storier's art, reciting the tale of how, two winters past, Korr's derangement had slaughtered nearly half her own people, driven her from the Vale, and imperiled her unborn young. Only intervention by Sismoomnat and Pitipak had enabled Tek and her twins to survive. That seemed to mollify the pans.

She spoke with loathing of Korr and of how, were it not for her faith in Jan, she and others would have fallen upon the mad stallion years ago and driven him from the Vale. In the end, the peace held— but Tek knew it could shatter in a moment if Jan proved unable to capture his sire. Korr had, so the envoys averred, now fled the Pan Woods for the Plain.

Tek gazed up at the summer stars, gradually brightening as evening deepened. Breeze lifted her forelock, and she breathed in the scents of yellowing grass and distant evergreens. The breath became a sigh. She longed for her mate, knew the twins missed him sorely. Where could mad Korr have hidden that Jan must spend moons hunting him? Twice Tek had sent search parties after her mate. Each time they had returned without success.

Night sky grew jet black, its white stars fabulously bright: legend called them Alma's eyes. The piping cry of a mourning-will sounded, high and sweet, from the Vale's far slope. Moments later, its mate answered. Tek turned from the night, back into the cave. Luminous mushrooms clung fan-shaped to the grotto's walls and ceiling, intermingled with phosphorescent lichens. Pale yellow or white, some blue, plum, amber, even rose and brassy green, they cast a glow that was warm and steady.

She did not see the twins and realized they must be in the little alcove at the back of the cave. There a tiny spring welled up. Tek peered around the bend into the dark alcove. Only a scattering of mushrooms here. She spotted the twins. They stood side to side, gazing intently into the black, mirror-smooth water. Their dam moved closer.

"What see you, children," she whispered. "A cavefish?" Neither took eyes from the water. Tek, too, peered down. Painted Aiony leaned against her.

"Nay, Mother," Dhattar replied. "We watch for Jan."

The pied mare laughed. "Watch for Jan—in a cavepool? Your father's leagues distant, on the Plain."

Aiony nodded. "We know. But we find him sometimes, when we watch."

"Water is best," Dhattar continued, "but we see him in clouds and moving grass as well."

His sister shrugged against Tek's chest. "Night is a better time than day, especially when you are wishing for him. That helps us."

Puzzled, Tek bent to nuzzle her. "How do you mean?"

"Stand between us," Dhattar was saying. "Then you'll see him, too."

Still frowning, Tek shifted to bring herself between her twin filly and foal. They pressed against her.

"Look deep," Aiony said.

Eerie sensations flitted through Tek. The pool lay far from still, she realized. Currents swirled below its glassy surface, rippling the image of the stone bottom. The reflected glow of the lichens shifted, trembled.

"Think of him," Dhattar murmured. "He is never far from your mind—or ours—but think of him directly now. School your thoughts."

The pied mare's pulse began, slowly, to pound. Her image in the water before her seemed to grow distant and fade. She felt the twins' warmth, their young heartbeats, more rapid than hers, perfectly synchronized.

"Be at ease," Aiony soothed. "Naught is to fear."

A gathering sense of motion. Tek's heart hammered, then seemed to stop. Time hung suspended as a strong, invisible current began to sweep her more and more swiftly along. She was aware of standing still within the cave beside her young—yet at the same time, some other part of her was galloping free, infinitely swift, like the Mare of the World, who had matched the sun in his race and won her heart's desire. Images of lichenlight in the dark water brightened and shrank, becoming stars. The Vale lay below. Wind buffeted. The Pan Woods raced by, and then the Plain.

Renegades loped across its grassy, rolling back. Starlit grass pards crouched and sprang. In the distance, she caught a glimpse of one who might have been Korr, dark as shadow, but only a glimpse. More Plains-dwellers thundered by, leaping and prancing in a long, snaking dance such as Tek had never before seen. Drawing closer, she heard their snorts and whinnies, felt the drumming of their hooves, caught the scent of their manes and sweat. They vanished over horizon's edge.

The Plain lay empty but for starlit grass. Clear, hornlike notes sounded in the distance, from the throats of thickset, square-nosed oncs grazing unseen. A banded pard prowled by, gave its low, coughing cry. Jan lay in a hollow not twenty paces from it, Tek saw with a start. The prince's eyes were closed. His ears twitched to the sound, but the wind was with him. The pard, never scenting him, padded on.

"Jan," Tek murmured. "Jan. . . ."

Again he stirred.

"Hist. Don't wake him," Dhattar beside her whispered. "Ordeals undreamed of lie ahead."

Aiony nodded. "To find his sire sooner than he knows."

Dhattar sighed. "And chase him longer than he need."

"Ordeals?" the pied mare breathed.

"Fear and anger," the white foal hissed. "Grief and loss. Loneliness. A wound so great it alters time."

Tek's motionless heart started again with a thump. "When will he return . . . ?" she began, baffled.

"Never," the painted filly replied.

A waft of terror swept over Tek. Dhattar nipped her gently. "No fear. You will see him again, but not here. He will never return here. In the Hallow Hills will you behold him, when he scours the wyverns' dens with the fire of the end of the world."

※

The cool of morning woke him. Dawn, not far from breaking, barely paled the sky. The thousand thousand summer stars, winding across the dark like a river of milk, were fading. Jan lifted his head, inhaling the scent of earth and grass that was the Plain, a vast rolling veldt that sprawled from the cool south, where the Summer Sea lapped, northward past the Pan Woods and the Vale to the warmer Hallow Hills and beyond. Somewhere to the eastern south, so rumor claimed, rose the Smoking Hills, home to red dragons.

Still couched, Jan stretched his leg, craned his neck and shook himself. He nibbled at the dew-drenched grass. His throat ached with thirst. He had not come upon water since before yesterday. Food, of course, was plentiful. But danger abounded, too. The rolling land hid many hollows where grass pards might lie. Thrice the sandy-colored predators had sprung at him from the haycorn. Each time he had shied, taken to his heels unscathed. More than once, he had found the bones of unicorns. He kept his ears pricked, avoided places above which kites circled, traveled into the wind whenever he could.

Tracking Korr had proved daunting. The mad king meandered and doubled back. At best, Jan found himself forever a day behind the haggard king. Evidence of struggles scattered Korr's path: two with predators—one in which the pard had lost its life, the other in which the wounded cat had retreated, trailing blood. Worse still were the ambush sites. Jan had found tracks clearly showing where the mad king had charged among small bands of Plainsdwelling unicorns—a stallion and two mares, or a mare with both her half-grown and suckling foals—and scattered them, fencing with those he could catch. Perhaps inflicting other harm which did not show in the tracks.

Sickened, Jan rolled to scrub his back against the loamy ground. He had spent most of the summer chasing Korr all over the Mare's Back, and not once had he spoken to a free-ranging unicorn of the Plain. Often enough he had seen them in the distance, but one glimpse of him and always they fled. He had given up pursuing them. They were fleet as wind and seemed to regard him with a terror better deserved by Korr.

Jan felt the beat of hooves before he heard them, vibrating up through the earth. Three sets of larger heels: warriors, one of whom sounded lighter than the other two—probably a mare. The fourth set was tiny, doubtless a filly or foal. All four headed in his direction at a trot. Jan rolled to get his limbs under him, but did not rise. The sound of their approach drew nearer and nearer yet. Jan waited until they were almost upon him, before he rose from the long grass, calling, "Peace! I am no enemy, but a stranger seeking water. Can you tell me where I may drink?"

With snorts of alarm, the Plainsdwellers halted. The wind was wrong for them. They had not scented him. One of their number nearly bolted, but Jan called again.

"Peace! I need your aid."

The party did indeed consist of a mare, two stallions, and a suckling filly. Feathers of birds entangled their manes. The mare was brilliant crimson, her filly palest blue. The younger and slighter of the two stallions was fair gold, his companion brindled grey. The pair circled forward to protect the mare, who stood to shield her foal.

"Look! Look!" The gold stallion whistled. " 'Tis he of whom Calydor warned: the black Moondancer. Flee!"

Wide-eyed, the grey looked half persuaded, but the mare held her ground.

"Nay," she muttered. " 'T cannot be. Calydor described a haggard stallion of middle years. . . ."

"I am not he," Jan broke in swiftly. "It is he I seek. He has wronged my folk and our allies. I must capture him ere he harms others. . . ."

"Already he has wronged others," the grey snorted. "Pursued, even injured some. Calydor foresaw and warned us from his path. By your speech, you are Vale-born, your hue jet black. What assures us you are not the mad destroyer?"

Jan turned his head so that the green gryphon feather might come into their view. He remembered from a brief encounter on his initiation pilgrimage years ago that unlike his own folk, who dipped only the neck, Plainsdwellers bowed by going down on one knee. The prince of the unicorns now did the same.

"Free People of the Plain," he answered, "I am Aljan Moonbrow, prince of my folk. The one I seek is Korr, our king, though he no longer rules us. For years we contained his madness within our Vale, but now he has broken free. He must be found. This I am come to do."

The golden stallion frowned, suspicious still. The grey seemed somewhat less so, but the crimson mare nodded. The brown and the white feather, each tethered in the long strands of her hair, bobbed.

"Aye, Korr," she murmured. "The one whose name means thunder. . . . All sooth, you are not he," she said suddenly. "I know you now—for I have seen you ere time. Recall you this? You were but a colt half grown, and I a filly about the same age. You had slipped away from your pilgrim band to sing the dead rites for a mare of ours killed by a pard. My dam and I and our companion came upon you. You told us your name. 'Twas—'twas . . ."

She paused, searching.

"Aljan, the Dark Moon!" she exclaimed, triumphant. "We later heard you succeeded Korr. You are now called Aljan-with-the-Moon-upon-his-Brow, are you not? A Moondancer, but fair-spoken, aye. And honorable."

Jan drew back, astonished. Memory washed him—of his initiation pilgrimage four years before, and the Renegades he had met upon that journey—at the end of which had lain the wyvern in her den. The young mare—had she been the filly he had met? She looked so much older now, a mated mare. "I am Aljan," he murmured, still struggling to recall, "though I never knew your name."

"Crimson," she told him, whickering, as though the answer were obvious. She nodded toward the other three. "And these, who were not with me when first we met, are Ashbrindle, my sire." The grey-and-white nodded. "My brother-belovèd, Goldenhair." The younger stallion tossed his head. "And my filly, called Bluewater Sky till she grow wit enough to choose her own name."

Jan bowed his head to each in turn, even Sky, before returning his gaze to the mare.

"Will you aid me, Crimson?" he implored. "I intend no ill against the Free People of the Plain, only to find my sire. Do you know where I may discover him?"

Before him, the three warriors exchanged a glance, seemed to reach agreement. The suckling filly began to nurse.

"Calydor will know," the grey stallion replied, coming forward now. "Ask of him."

Jan looked at him. "Calydor," he mused. "Who is this Calydor?"

"Our prophet," the golden stallion declared. "He recks much and dreams more. He will judge if your words sing true."

"Hist, belovèd," the crimson mare broke in. "Let us speak this stranger fair." She turned to Jan. "Calydor is a farseer. Many call him Alma's Eyes. Were he not our close kin, we might do the same."

The dark unicorn felt his spirits lift. "Where may I find this seer?" he asked. "You say he can scry my lost sire? Will you guide me to him?"

"Water first," the grey brindle replied. "Let us quench our thirst on it." Turning, he whistled his companions to follow. "Come, daughter, filly, and daughter's kin. Time enough to ponder my brother's whereabouts once we have drunk."

Stars

★ 7 ★

Jan trotted beside the crimson mare. Her pale-blue filly pranced along-side. The mare's sire, the brindled grey, led them over grassy, rolling hills, with the mare's brother-belovèd—what did the term mean, Jan wondered: foster brother, half brother?—pale gold, bringing up the rear. The grey-and-white trotted briskly, with hardly a glance behind. He seemed to have accepted Jan, for the present at least, though the younger stallion watched him carefully still.

Only the crimson mare seemed wholly at ease. She had spoken little during their five miles' journey to where a slender brook meandered between two slopes. There they had lingered, savoring the creek's cool-ness, dipping their heads for a second draft as the young sun cleared the horizon and floated free, turning the morning sky from misty white to deeper and deeper blue as it climbed toward zenith. At last, the grey brindle spoke.

" 'Tis well," he said. "You seem no mad raver. I would lead you to my brother, if my companions assent."

The mare and the other stallion both nodded, the pale gold grudg-ingly, barely dipping his chin. So it was the crimson mare the young prince now found himself pacing: the grey ahead, the gold at rearguard, the pale-blue filly frisking and teasing. Morning had grown late, warm, the sun high overhead. White clouds gathered, their shadows slipping over the Plain.

"Tell me of your life here, upon Alma's Back," he bade the crimson mare.

She cocked an eye and replied, "Gladly—but first speak of yours within your Vale. My dam's dam came from there. She said 'twas all proud princes, rules and Law, so she fled to the Mare's Back to win freedom. You call yourself prince, Aljan, yet you seem fairspoken still, not ruled by pride."

He laughed. As they trotted through the long, warm noon and lay up in the shade of steep banks for the hottest part of the day, he spoke of Moondance, of new warriors initiated upon spring pilgrimage, of the yearly trek by those unpaired to find and pledge their mates by the Summer Sea. He spoke of autumn feasting and spring birthing. Of Kindling and Quenching, the herd's winter ceremonies of fire. Crimson listened intently, interrupting from time to time. Jan knew by their silence the grey and the gold were listening, too.

Not until midway into the afternoon had Crimson heard enough. She told then of the Free People, a scattered, far-traveled folk who ranged at will across the Plain. Though some were loners, most traveled in small bands. Plainsdwellers dodged pards, encountered each other at waterholes, whistled greetings to those sighted at distance, and followed one another's spoor to meet and trade news. Alliances formed, endured awhile, then just as easily and amicably dissolved.

The impermanence of such an existence struck Jan as both utterly foreign and oddly alluring. Unbound by any sovereign or herd, each Plainsdweller was completely free—but at what cost? Danger from pards. A life spent in constant motion, rather than settled in a sheltered Vale. *Friendships must be difficult to sustain,* Jan mused. He wondered how mates fared in the rearing of their young.

Yet Crimson seemed to regard the Vale as unbearably confining, circumscribed by rules of every kind. Plainsdwellers had customs, but no Law and no way of enforcing Law had they had any. Far from admiring his status as prince, the crimson mare pronounced Jan's position an unspeakable burden, imposed without consent, to be shaken off at the earliest chance. Who, after all, would not wish to be free as was she? All Moondancers must be mad, she exclaimed, only half in jest, to forgo the liberty of Alma's Back for a rocky, gryphon-haunted Vale.

Six days they roved in search of Calydor, traveling northwest. The Plain became hillier, its terrain more broken. Thunderheads brought showers in the late afternoons. White towers of cloud were building now, Jan noticed as they loped: but too scattered and far to coalesce into a storm. Jan listened to distant thunder growl as the setting sun declined. The wind still smelled dry. Sometimes thunder made the ground tremble—Jan came aware all at once that the tremor he felt was not thunder.

Hoofbeats, he realized. The stamping, tramping cadence of hard heels drumming the Plain, but neither approaching nor receding. It was he and his companions, the dark unicorn decided, who were drawing nearer to the unseen source of that low, rhythmic mutter. With sun just down and sky now a fiery blaze, flushing the scattered thunderheads all shades of melon and rose, the broken landscape of the Plain had grown dusky. His companions' ears pricked, heads lifted and nostrils flared. Their pace quickened.

"What is it?" he asked. "What do we near?"

Crimson tossed her head. "A Gather—'t can only be that! Calydor has called a Gather. I hear them dancing the longdance by water's edge."

Jan caught sound of snorts and whinnies. Evening breeze brought him the warm, unmistakable scent of unicorns. Ahead, the grey-and-white brindle rounded a hillside and halted. Jan and the crimson mare did the same, followed by the others. The prince drew in his breath. Before him, a dark green river snaked through rolling hills. On the far side, in the broad, inner bend of one meandering curve, moved twelve score Plainsdwellers, perhaps more. Their sinuous line recurved and doubled back upon itself, wending and swirling, veering, unwinding, sometimes at nearly full gallop, sometimes in a complicated stamping pattern.

All ages joined in the winding dance. Jan saw elders, mares and stallions in their prime, half-growns, colts and fillies, foals. The Plainsdwellers, Jan saw, were more variegated than his own folk, who were mostly red or blue with occasional greys. Gold and other shades only rarely appeared in the Vale. Among the Free Folk of the Plain, too, hot reds and cool blues cantered by in abundance, but greys and golds seemed nearly as numerous, with a generous sprinkling of dapples and roans, even spotted coats. Feathers adorned the manes of many.

One figure in particular caught Jan's eye—that of the one leading the dance: tall and lank-limbed, with a long neck and horn and a slim, straight muzzle, easily the best dancer, a stallion in his prime. His coat was indigo. Three white feathers tossed in his mane, which was silver, as were his hooves and horn. The evening darkness of his coat was spattered with hoary flecks. They wound upward past one eye before spilling down his neck. Turning at the shoulder, the widening runnel of tiny frosted spots flowed diagonally across his back and meandered down one flank. Pale socks washed three pasterns. The rest of him, almost wholly dark, sported only slight speckling, like stray pricks of light in a summer sky.

Jan studied the other. Twilight was fading, the sun well and truly set. A pale sliver of moon floated amid a river of stars just beginning to become visible. The astral path wandered overhead, arching like a bridge from one to the other end of the world. Scattered to all four quarters, tall thunderheads floated motionless in the distance. Occasionally their thunder growled above the thrumming beat of the dancers' hooves. Lightning illuminated the clouds' interiors, like the diffuse, rosy radiance of cave lichens. Beside him, Crimson suddenly reared.

" 'Tis Calydor," she cried joyously. "I see him there!"

She sprinted down the long, gentle slope toward the river below, her pale-blue filly flying after. Jan sprang in pursuit, heard the grey and the gold coming hard on his heels. Crimson plunged into the smooth green river. Her filly leapt to follow, fording the slow, calm waters with a will. As her dam reached the far bank, Sky clambered out, shook. The mare nuzzled her, then trotted toward the dancers, her filly close behind. Jan swam in their wake, reaching shore half a length in front of Goldenhair and the grey. He paused to shake off, and the other stallions sprang past and up the bank to join their fellows thundering by.

The dark prince bounded after, merged into the long, winding train full of sudden eddies and shifts. Caught up in its wild tempo, he struggled to decipher the intricate patterns of stamping. Eventually he realized that whatever step the dancers executed was chosen by the one leading the line. That one chose the pattern, demonstrated it, and the others repeated it until their leader chose anew. Dancing, Jan noted with relief that though some eyed him with curiosity, none reacted with alarm. Perhaps because of Illishar's feather, he was certain none took him for a Moondancer. Perhaps, too, in the settling dusk, the black of his coat was not so evident.

Evening deepened. The slender crescent moon declined, throwing long shadows. Its pale light glided along the backs and faces of the dancers. At length, their stamping ceased. Halted, the dance's participants stood blowing, shifting to loosen their limbs in the sudden, ringing silence. Panting, Jan heard the distant yip and hoot of Plains dogs scrapping over scavenge. The dance's leader trotted to an open space before the crowd. Behind him, the bend in the river gleamed. Beyond, the Plain sloped moon-sheened to horizon's edge. Above, stars burned. The evening blue with the starlight pattern in his coat shook his pale feathered mane.

"Hail, my fellows!" His voice sounded oddly familiar, though Jan was certain he had never encountered this striking stallion before. "Tonight we gather," he cried, "to foot the longdance, for the dark destroyer roves no more among us. We are free of him. He has fled."

Trepidation seized Jan. Korr no longer upon the Plain? The black prince cast about for his companions. If so, he had no time to lose. He needed one of them to point out who among this press was the seer Calydor. A moment later, Jan spotted Crimson and her filly standing very near the speaker. Ashbrindle stood back a few paces. He did not spy the gold.

"So we celebrate," the star-marked stallion continued, "now that danger is past. Soon our longdance will run its course, praising Álm'harat and her endless Cycle."

Around him, Jan glimpsed half-growns rubbing shoulders, mares nipping after stallions' flanks. Colts and fillies lay down, other, younger ones already asleep. Heat rose in wisps from the Plainsdwellers' backs. The evening-blue unicorn with the starpath markings spoke on.

"But first, respite. I'll sing you a tale. The dark one who lately ramped among us hailed from the distant Vale of Moondance. All our lives have we heard of its warrior Ring, glimpsed its members pilgriming upon the Plain, learnt of half-growns initiated into its warhost—in the name of Álm'harat, yet! Aye, Moondancers do battle to honor The One who makes all life.

"These Valedwellers spare us no love, kick dust on our customs, harry us as Renegades—yet we eschew this witless conflict. The Mare's Back is broad, and we have always found room to dodge them. Until the dark destroyer came, black as a night without moon or stars. He called himself a king. Yet he ruled no one, not even himself. He fell upon us wherever he found us and sought the lives even of fillies and foals in his madness to make war.

"Yet we slipped his grasp. Our ears were keen, our limbs fleet. Dreams gave warning, and we scented him in the wind. We traveled in larger bands, avoiding those places he had last been seen. At length, we drove him from our midst—and, having survived this ordeal, we have begun to think all Moondancers fiends.

"Such is not so. Some of us have sires or dams born to the Ring, who later fled to freedom here. Others have aided such refugees. True, these Ringbreakers disparage the Vale. I little blame them. To speak of it is painful to them. But I will tell you of one I met, many years ago, who was of the Vale and who returned to the Vale, and was no monster, no mad maker of war."

All around, Plainsdwellers shifted and swayed, now pricking their ears, their murmurs quieting. Despite his urgency, Jan found himself listening as the other spoke.

"Many seasons past, when I was a youth with a young beard on my chin, I dreamt one summer under Alma's eyes of a mare: pale as cloud newly warmed by sunset's glow, with a mane and tail brilliant red-orange as the poppy flower."

The dark prince heard sighs, contented murmurs among the crowd, as though the tale were well known, a favorite. Reluctantly, he settled himself, aware that making his way unobtrusively to Crimson or Ash-brindle now through the hush might prove well-nigh impossible.

"She, too, was young," the singer continued. His way of turning, of lifting his head nipped at Jan like a gnat, reminding him of someone he could not quite recall. The star-marked stallion continued. "Gazing upon her in my dream, I sensed that like me, she had never danced the long-dance to its end.

"She lay far to the south, I knew, where the wind blows cool. I set out alone across the Plain. For days I traveled, until I drew near the southern sea that spills green against a golden shore. Tasting salt upon the wind, I halted, knowing Moondancers summer upon that strand. I had no wish to clash with any of that warlike tribe.

"Night fell, and I saw my love, coming by moondark—yet the light of Álm'harat's eyes blazed so, I saw her as well as by day. She moved with caution and with speed, casting about as she traveled, ears pricked, scenting the breeze. She was all my dream had promised: dancer's grace and runner's gait.

"With a joyous cry, I leapt to meet her as one would a long-lost friend, unguarded—and nearly lost my life. She screamed and shied, wholly surprised, then met me with a pummeling of hooves and a slash-ing of horn. I broke off, bewildered. She sprang back, stiff-legged, horn at the ready.

" 'Stand off! Stand off, wild Renegade,' she shouted. 'I seek no enmity with you, but I am a warrior born and versed and can defend myself at need.'

"We both stood wild-eyed, panting, stunned. She, from what must have seemed an ambuscade—I, from the dawning that though she was indeed my vision's mare, she herself had dreamt no such dream. She knew me not, and sooth, what knew I of her? Until that moment I had not even suspected what now stood clear: she was no Plainsdweller as was I, but a Moondancer strayed from her folk. If she searched for another upon the Plain, that other was not I.

"I stammered some halting amends. 'I cry your pardon. I mistook you for a . . . a friend and meant no harm.'

"She eyed me warily. At length she said, 'I, too, seek . . . a certain friend.' She hesitated. Then, 'Perhaps you have news of her.'

"Carefully at first, then with growing ease, she told me of a belovèd companion who had deserted the Vale. Now each night, she said, she slipped away from her band, ventured onto the Plain, intent upon finding her missing companion and persuading her to return. I listened, lost at times. She assumed I knew all concerning her folk, that I had once been one of them, and that I, too, like her friend, had run away.

"I told her I knew naught of her friend, that I, like most of my folk, had been foaled upon the Mare's Back and wist little of her reclusive, warring clan. But I pledged to search and bring word if she would await me nightly on this spot. She was grateful, relieved beyond measure. Venturing the Plain entailed great risk for her. Besides danger from dogs and pards, if discovered, she might have been cast from her band. Simply conversing with me was counted treason.

"The harshness of her people's lives astonished me: hidebound by tradition, imprisoned by Law. How, I wondered, could one raised within such strictures have even conceived this defiance: to dare to follow her own heart rather than the dictates of capricious kings? For all her people's warlike bent, they seemed to my mind to be cowards all, afraid to think and do for themselves.

"This young mare's plan to return her friend to what she believed the safe haven of her Vale was surely bold. Yet in truth, my sympathies were all for the other, the one who had leapt the confines of the Vale and fled to the open Plain. In the space of a heartbeat, I envisioned a plan: that if I could indeed find my love's lost companion, perhaps I and that one together might convince her to remain at liberty upon the Plain.

"She and I parted ere the paling of the stars: she—hopeful but wary still—to return to her summering band; I flush with determination. I scoured the Plain, importuning every passerby for news, imploring those I met to search upon their travels for my belovèd's friend and send me word. Always I returned by nightfall to meet with the poppy-maned mare, bring her what news I had gleaned—maddeningly little, most days.

"She never seemed disappointed, as at first I had feared, only sad, and hopeful still, and patient, ready to wait as long as need be. After we spoke each night, she appeared reluctant to go. So we spoke on, I telling her of my life and my people's ways, she telling me of hers. I learnt more of them from her than ever I could have dreamt.

"Slowly, she warmed to me. I sensed she kept our meetings for more than just the chance of news. I sensed she began to look to me for companionship, that she enjoyed my company more and more. I sang her songs of our folk—I was a young singer then, and my store of stories small. She recited for me those of her own folk's lays that she could recall. Our friendship deepened with each waning night.

"Then at last, word came. A passing band knew of the mare I sought. Another wayfarer spoke of a Gather. The mare for whom I searched would likely gather with the rest to dance the longdance. Excitedly, I told my friend from the Vale. We struck off across the Plain, flying like the wind, and reached the milling celebrants just at dusk. My friend spotted her comrade and ran to her, calling gladly.

"My love's fellow at first mistook her for a new Renegade like herself and welcomed her eagerly to the Plain. Soon, however, my love's intentions became clear. The two mares quarreled, cajoled, discussed and reconciled, each seeking to convince the other to join her. I hung back, uncertain, avid to support the other mare's arguments, yet fearing to intrude. Meanwhile, all around us, the longdance began, its rhythm swelling, ebbing, and rising again.

"At last, my love's friend turned from her and disappeared into the quickening rush. My heart beat hard. Before me, my love stood shaken, confused. Clearly, she had believed persuasion would be easy after the difficult trial of finding her friend. Instead, her comrade had refused to return to the Vale and pressed my love hard to remain. She had spoken convincingly, I saw, touting her newfound freedom. My belovèd wavered. Made bold, I, too, now spoke, declaring my passionate love.

"All around us, our fellows coursed, snorting and plunging, stamping and swirling. Their throb, the tow of their motion overwhelmed us both. She followed me as one lost in a daze. We entered the dance. 'T swept us along, two dreamers caught in currents too swift to swim, too powerful to wake, and we danced the longdance to its end, under the summer stars.

"Briefly, I think, she cast off her Vale and its Ring of Law, entering wholeheartedly into our joyous rite. Perhaps I delude myself. When dawn broke, blinding the stars, our companions scattered, her lost friend among them. She stood unable to follow, and my hopes ended. She must return to her seaside band, she said. She could not go with me.

"I stood speechless, realizing at last why Álm'harat's vision of this mare had never gone beyond the dance. Last eve, which I had thought the dawn of our sweet fellowship upon the Plain, marked its conclusion instead. In dreams the goddess speaks, had spoken true. 'Twas I who had been too lovestruck witless to comprehend. I felt I might die then, the land beneath my heels heave upward, the air became dust, and darkness swallow me.

"Shaking with sorrow, she bade me farewell, and told me that among her folk, mates pledge for life. I had never heard of such a thing. We have all known a few such blessèd pairs, yet I could scarce conceive how one dared hope for such a fortuitous outcome from every tryst, every dancing of the dance. Valedwellers, I learnt, *expect* to pair for life. Yet she had cast even that most venerated custom aside to join with me for but a night.

"And night was done. We could not prolong it, though from that day on, both would be forever changed. She would not skip home to put me coldly from her mind. No day would pass that she would not think of me, just as no hour since passes for me that I do not think of her, dream and desire her. Though that moment filled me with unbearable sadness, never once in all my years have I felt regret. The goddess led me to my love for some purpose as yet hidden.

"Never after have I looked upon all Moondancers as monsters. Warlike and arrogant as a people, perhaps, but this mare that I so briefly loved, and still love, and will love all the days of my life, was not. She was witty, warm, courageous, shy, all traits I can only admire. I trust she, too, has never again thought evil of my folk. Surely the myth that we are all outlaws from the Vale is dispelled from her heart. Perhaps from the hearts of her children. I cannot say, but if Álm'harat joined us for this alone—that we might cast off our peoples' long enmity—it is enough.

"I charge you now as you finish the dance: remember my love. For every dark destroyer, other southlanders abide who are honorable and bear us no ill will. Above all, love one another wisely and well, for what you may hope to be a lifelong pledge under Álm'harat's eyes may endure but an hour. The goddess's ways do baffle us. The night is brief, but the dance is long. So join and accomplish her rite, all you who so desire. It is part of the Mare's great Cycle, which turns all the world and the stars."

As the singer fell silent, bowing his head, the throng surrounding Jan roused themselves. With sudden snorts and wild whinnies, they reared and pranced. Mares and stallions paired off, mock-battling. Small bands of friends cavorted seemingly for sheer pleasure. Yawning colts and young half-growns cropped grass or dozed, oblivious to their elders' energetic frolic. Some pairs had already struck off into the long grass surrounding the clearing. Most still chased and chivvied in the river bend.

In mounting dismay, Jan cast about, aware suddenly that he must find the one named Calydor before he, too, slipped away in this joyous frenzy. Yet, the young prince realized belatedly, he had no inkling where to begin. He could have kicked himself for never having asked Crimson to describe her uncle's coloring. He spotted the crimson mare suddenly, approaching the star-spotted singer, who stood surveying the crowd. He, apparently, did not intend to join his fellows in completing the dance. Jan trotted toward them.

"Hail, my child, daughter to my sib," the dark-blue stallion cried as the young mare shouldered against him with an affectionate nip. "Well met."

"Hail, Calydor," the crimson mare replied above her filly's delighted squeals, "brother to my sire. I bring you greetings."

Jan halted in his tracks.

"More than greetings alone, I see," the singer laughed as he nuzzled her sky-blue foal. "You bring a young Moondancer. Turn and acquaint us, if you will, for he stands not three paces from your flank."

Night

★ 8 ★

Jan came forward. The thin crescent slip of moon was just setting, sinking curve-downward into distant horizon's edge. Soon only summer stars would remain to illuminate the dark. The crimson mare turned with a whicker of surprise.

"There you are, my moondancing friend," she exclaimed. "I sprang ahead to bring word of you to Calydor, but could not catch him ere his tale. Nor could I spot you afterwards. Behold Calydor, brother to my sire."

"Hail, my son, guest to my brother's get," the star-strewn unicorn greeted him.

Jan was struck again by the odd familiarity he felt in the presence of this stallion he had never met before. He and the seer stood the same height, very similar in heft and build. Long-leggèd and lithe, each had a lean, hard dancer's frame. The dark prince bowed in the way of the Vale, dipping his neck.

"Hail, Calydor," he replied. "I seek one of my folk who runs amok, him you call the dark destroyer."

The deep-blue and silver unicorn nodded. "Sooth. Be welcome here. Come, let us retire to the riverbank, and leave the dancers to their sport."

Dozens of unicorns galloped by, some engaged in nothing more than high-spirited games. Others slept, still others lost in the teasing lead-and-follow of mates at play. Jan spotted the brindled grey stallion loping past, following a mare who whistled at him over one shoulder and plunged away into the grass. The crimson mare stood poised, eyeing her fellows. Jan spied the pale gold stallion standing at Plain's edge, watching expectantly. Calydor whickered.

"Go, my child. Enjoy the dance. I will see to Sky. In Álm'harat's keeping, love wisely and well."

With a whistle of gratitude, the crimson mare bowed on one knee and sped away. Her filly hung back uncertain, until the indigo stallion called her. She trotted alongside him as Calydor turned, headed across the trampled grass toward the river's bank. Jan fell into step. The sound of cool, green waters murmured in his ears. Their dark, wet fragrance filled his nostrils. The seer chose a spot at the crest of the bend. The bank here was steep, the river reeds low.

"I dreamt your coming, my son," the starry other said. They stood looking out over the river, the little filly in between. "And well I know of the one you seek."

"Your niece says you are a seer," the young prince replied, "that your folk call you 'Alma's Eyes.' "

The blue-and-silver stallion laughed. "No compliment to my powers, I vow. Only a play upon my name."

" 'Calydor'?" Jan asked. The name was not used in the Vale. "What does it mean?"

" 'Stars in summer,' " the seer replied. "My folk call the stars 'Álm'harat's eyes.' "

Jan nodded. "And mine. But I did not know you for a singer as well. I am honored, having heard your song."

He fell silent, choosing his words. The singer's tale had moved him strangely, though it had told of a mare breaking the herd's Law to run wild renegade. He himself had never seen the wisdom of many of his people's most rigid strictures. Since becoming prince, he had relaxed or discarded a fair number of the oldest and harshest laws. And he had never subscribed to his herd's ill will against the folk of the Plain: another old hatred that made no sense to him.

"My mate is a singer," Jan continued. "Her name is Tek. When I return to her, I will recount your tale."

Calydor bowed his head. "Then 'tis you who honor me. But tell me of the one you seek. Though my dreams speak true, rarely do they reveal all. Much mazes me still about that one, who for two moons trampled the Mare's Back, terrorizing whomever he met."

Jan dug into the riverbank with one cloven heel. The sky-blue filly's head drooped as she leaned against her great-uncle. The young prince gazed off across river and Plain. Images of stars scattered the water's dark, smooth surface so that it looked like a river of night sky threading the grassy hills. The moon had slipped below horizon's edge. Its silver gleam faded.

"I come seeking my sire," the younger stallion replied. "My herd acclaims me their warleader, and Korr was once accounted our king. Three winters past, in my absence, he seized power, leading a mad crusade that cost many their lives. At last his fanaticism was condemned for what it was. He has been outcast since, shrieking curses upon my mate and her dam, upon his own mate and child, and calling Tek's and my offspring abomination. Lately, he railed of some past deed upon the Plain. Now he has fled here, as though so doing can dispel whatever memory from his youth haunts him still. It is time his rampage ceased. This years-long silence must end. It is his silence that has maddened him. If I can but persuade him to reveal this secret he holds, I am convinced he will know peace."

The star-strewn unicorn listened in thoughtful reserve. The little filly leaning against him had closed her eyes.

"I judge you to be sincere," he answered quietly. "No deception shades your voice. Your folk and mine share a long history of enmity, but I see no reason for you and me to perpetuate it. Ask of me what you will."

Jan sighed deeply, and then drew breath, hopeful yet cautious still. "Has Korr harmed any of your folk?"

"Frightened, mostly," the other replied, tossing his head. "By and large, the injuries he dealt were flesh wounds. We are a fleet and wary folk."

Jan nodded, relieved. "Did those who brought news of him to you recount any of Korr's words?"

Sadly, the star-specked unicorn sighed. "Only curses and threats. Those who encountered him called him crazed: violent and inconsolable. Who proffered peace and strove to reason with him suffered worst."

Jan watched the river flowing, swirling the reflected stars. He felt as though Alma's eyes watched him both from heaven and from below. He said to Calydor, "Do I glean rightly that your folk have driven him from the Plain?"

The other nodded. "Dream reached me four days past that a band of young stallions and mares came upon him at a watering place near Plain's edge. He flew at them. At length, they succeeded in driving him from their midst. He struck off into the Salt Waste bordering our grass-lands."

Inwardly Jan groaned. Pursuit of his sire, which had seemed at first a matter of mere hours or days, now promised to stretch on from weeks and months into a season or more. His heart ached to be reunited with his mate and young, but he could not turn back. Korr must be halted and, if at all possible, healed.

"Where may I find the spot at which he left the Plain?" the young prince asked.

Beside him, the blue-and-silver stallion nodded. " 'T lies to north and east, ten days' journey from this spot."

The little filly beside him had lain down on the riverbank. Calydor joined her. Jan folded limb and couched himself as well. His ears swiveled to the snorts and playful whistles of the Plainsdwellers. The drum of heels and their romping cries told him the games and impromptu contests continued. The younger voices were dying down. Other sets of heels, always in pairs, beat away through the grass, accompanied by breathless laughter. Jan was reminded of his own courting rite with Tek beside the Summer Sea.

And yet, so it seemed, these celebrants had no thought of pledging themselves for all eternity under Alma's eyes. Whatever vows they spoke would last but the night, to lapse or renew daily, exactly as they pleased. This baffling custom troubled Jan. How could young know their sires if their parents parted after a tryst? Nonetheless, he realized, Crimson knew her sire. Her brother, the pale golden stallion, knew his sire as well—at least, so Jan had gathered, that his differed from the crimson mare's.

That, too, astonished him, that brother and sister might share but a single parent. Though he could scarce conceive not being pledged to Tek or—more unimaginable still—breaking that pledge, the freedom the Plainsdwellers knew was breathtaking. He could hardly envision such lives as theirs, forever free of the constancy of kings and Law, the touchstone of eternal vows. With a start, Jan woke from his thoughts. The blue-and-silver stallion was speaking.

"Rest here the night, my son. You are weary, having pressed hard these many weeks in pursuit of your sire."

Jan nodded heavily, head drooping, eyes slipping shut. His limbs ached. His ribs throbbed, his spine sore where it flexed. He was weary, but less in body than in spirit. He wanted this business with Korr to be done. He wanted to learn the dark secret that drove Korr mad. Only then, he was sure, might he and his mate and young be free of it. Korr, too, and all the Vale. The young stallion roused himself and reached to taste the rushes at the riverside, aware only now that in his haste to reach the Gather, he had not eaten since noon. The stallion beside him watched.

"You wear a feather in your hair," he remarked at length, "as many of my people do. I have never seen a Valedweller so adorned. Does it signify your rank?"

Jan tossed his head and felt Illishar's green feather slap gently against his neck. In the years since he and the gryphon had sealed their first, tentative truce, it had never worked free. He took it for a good sign. The tender rushes filled his belly, warm and sweet. He turned to Calydor.

"Nay," he laughed. "It commemorates a peace."

The seer's eyes widened, then smiled. The little filly slept slumped against him, limbs folded, chin tucked. She reminded Jan intensely of his twins before they had been weaned. Their horns must have sprouted by this time, breaking the skin and spiraling up. They would be butting into everything now, scrubbing their foreheads against bark and stone to quell the itch young horns always suffered. Beside him, the singer gazed at his grand-niece with the fond absorption Jan recognized in himself for his own young.

"The mare of which you sang," he began, uncertain quite why he was asking—and yet the singer's tale had stirred his curiosity, piquant and strong. "You never forgot her?"

The star-strewn stallion whickered softly, as though thinking back on a memory both rueful and dear.

"How could I?" he breathed. "She was extraordinary. Never after have I been able to view your folk simply as savage warmongers, suppressed by tyrants and imprisoned by laws—but as a tribe not wholly unlike my own, despite very different ways."

Jan snorted. "High time my folk abandoned the worst of our old ways," he remarked, "and adopted new."

Calydor laughed. "How strange you are. A warleader who celebrates peace. A Moondancer who eyes tradition askance."

The dark prince shrugged. He had long since left off wondering at himself.

"But the mare," he continued, "who consorted with you, then returned to the Vale—I have not heard of her. She must have guarded her daring well. In Korr's time, and his father's time, and the time of the queen before him, such a mare would have been cast out had her deeds been discovered."

The older stallion nodded. "I named that very danger in urging her to remain with me, to no avail." He sighed. "Had any way existed for me to go with her and join her folk, I would have. But I could not. Your Law barred me."

Again he sighed, more deeply now, as though resigned.

"Well, 'tis done. One cannot walk another's path, nor halt the turning of the stars, only live and seize what joys one may. I loved this mare. I would do so again, even knowing the outcome."

Jan felt an inexplicable sadness rise up in his breast. He thought of

Tek. Could he ever have so resigned himself to part from her for the rest of his days? The wound was deep enough simply being parted from her for the present.

"You never saw your love again?" he asked Calydor. The other shook his head. "Perhaps she dwells yet within the Vale." Jan frowned, calculating. "She would be about the age of my dam."

"Aye," the star-thrown stallion murmured. "Sometimes I wonder if she will ever break free and return to the Plain, as she vowed to do, when the unnamed task that called her back to the Vale was done. She bade me dismiss her from my thoughts and not to wait for her. Yet I have never forgotten and have waited the years, in hope that one day we once more may meet and dance the longdance to its end."

"The wait may not be much," Jan suggested, unsure why the matter should concern him so. "If she lives, this poppy-maned mare will travel among us when we leave the Vale next spring and trek to the Hallow Hills."

The seer glanced at him. "I have not dreamed of that," he whispered. The night breeze stirred. "Your Vale is hidden from me. The goddess conceals it. I know not why."

Calydor fell silent, gazing off across the river of stars that flowed below them. The soft lowing of far-off oncs haunted the air. The singer's ears pricked, listening. He remained still so long that Jan began to wonder if their conversation were at end. At last the other drew breath.

"After I lost my love, after she turned from me and struck out for the distant sea, I dreamed of her one final time. Álm'harat granted me that. I saw her not as she had once appeared, but older, a mare in prime rather than one just entering the first blush of her youth, still hale and fair, but one who has borne her young and seen them grown. I beheld my belovèd traversing the Mare's Back. I dare to hope therefore that I will see her again, that the promise of our first love may yet be fulfilled, to run shoulder to shoulder all the rest of our days across the wide and rolling Plain."

❦

The broad veldt had quieted, the sound of revelers long stilled. No more contests or further sport occupied the dancing ground. Many of the Plainsdwellers had returned to lie beside their young. Even those yet roving the long grass had hushed. Jan caught only an occasional rustle, a snort or stamp, a breathless whicker. A breeze sprang up, combing the grass, its touch pleasantly light along Jan's back.

He felt at peace, no longer stiff and sore. He turned toward Calydor, drowsing now by his tiny grand-niece, his silhouette against the star-sheened grass so familiar that Jan pondered anew. Of whom did this stranger remind him? The young prince shook his head. His eyes slipped shut. He drifted into dreams only half aware.

He dreamed he saw his dam profiled by starlight. She stood on the lookout knoll high above the Vale, gazing off toward the Plain. The twins stood beside her, horn-buds sprouted, blunt thorns upon their brows. Tek kept watch below them on the slope. All four stood silent. Jan wondered how often they held this vigil, forgetting that he dreamed. Ses murmured to his mate, then turned back to the twins. The wind lifted her forelock, fanning her magnificent mane, washed of all color by the faint light of stars.

"Can you sense him yet?"

Painted Aiony nodded. "Aye."

"Is he safe?"

White Dhattar nodded in turn. "He sleeps."

Tek climbed the slope to join them. "Where is he?"

"At riverside," her filly replied. "Among companions."

"Renegades?" the pied mare asked quickly, forgetting and using the old term for the people of the Plains.

"Plainsdwellers," Ses murmured. Tek nodded.

"A dark-blue stallion all spattered with stars," Dhattar replied. "A river of them flows overhead, and another below. Alma's eyes are every-where."

Beside them, Ses gave a little snort. "Dark blue?" she asked quietly. "How dark?"

Dhattar butted her. "Like indigo."

Gently, she shouldered back. "And the stars?"

"Silver," Aiony told her. "His mane and tail as well. Three hooves wear silver socks."

Her brother scrubbed his chin against his granddam's shoulder. "A seer and a singer and a dancer, like Jan."

Tek shook herself. "Jan is no singer."

Dhattar and Aiony exchanged a glance. Ses said nothing.

"He knows where Korr may be found," Dhattar whispered at Tek, "or where to begin the search."

His black-and-silver sister nodded, shrugging him away from Ses. "He'll lead Jan there."

The pale mare seemed not to hear them. Her expression was distant, deep in thought, eyes gazing toward the Plain. Tek gathered her filly and foal.

"When will he return?" she asked, nuzzling them.

White Dhattar raised his eyes, blue as summer sky, with pupils black and deep as wells. "We said before. He will not return. We will not see him again till the fire from heaven falls."

Tek glanced away, rolling one shoulderblade. She could make nothing of their talk. Their granddam stirred.

"And Korr?" she asked.

The twins turned to her, their faces solemn. They said nothing. Night breeze lifted. The pied mare sighed, missing her mate. League upon league away across the Plain, the sleeping prince shifted and then lay still. He dreamed of traversing a wasteland toward distant thunder. Nearby, a tiny filly's legs twitched, flexed, dancing in dreams. The blue-and-silver stallion beside which she lay nodded over his knees. He dreamed of a mare pale as cloud at first dusk, older now, but still graceful fair, her mane red as sunset, as poppies, as flame, lifted and thrown by the freshening breeze.

_ⅈ_

Jan stirred. Dawn air held still, sky fading into grey. The summer stars had faded from bright beacons to mere specks. The dancing ground lay largely deserted. A few foals and fillies still dozed. Their sires and dams stood by. Others were just emerging from the long grass, mares leading, stallions trotting behind. Many shouldered and chivvied one another fondly, like newly pledged mates. Jan longed for Tek powerfully, and for their twins.

"Good dawn," the blue-and-silver stallion nearby him murmured. Nestled beside him, the sky-blue filly slept on.

"Good dawn," Jan murmured in reply.

Sky above brightened. Those on the dancing ground rose, shook off, some bidding companions farewell. Jan listened to hoofbeats heading off in all directions. Dawn blush touched the horizon, infusing the sky. Crimson loped from the tall Plains grass. Behind her, Goldenhair halted at grass's edge. Farther back, Jan spied others, evidently part of this new-formed group. The pale gold whinnied and stamped. Crimson approached her uncle, bowed low to one knee.

"Good dawn, my child," he greeted her.

She answered him, "Good dawn."

"So you travel with Goldenhair again," he observed.

She laughed. "Always."

"And two companions."

Glancing past the pale gold to the russet mare and the middle-blue half-grown beyond, Crimson nodded. "Newly met. We'll share the way awhile and see if friendship grows."

"Love wisely and well, my child," the seer replied. He nuzzled her filly, already half roused. "Wake, my little child. Fare gently till next we meet."

Sky shivered and stretched, rose unsteadily to her feet then shook off like a wolf cub. Her mother whickered. The filly leapt to her with a glad whistle and began to nurse.

"Ashbrindle fares not with you?" the singer observed.

The crimson mare shook her head. "He has found an old comrade and will not range with us this round." Calydor nodded. Crimson turned to her young. "Come, Bluewater Sky," she said gently. "You fed long and well, night past. We must do a little running this morn before we rest. Then I will show you how to eat grass."

The blue filly stopped suckling and looked up. " 'Rass?" she said, in a small voice, distinctly. It was the first word Jan had heard her utter. Her dam nodded, laughing.

"Aye, grass. How well you speak! Goldenhair will be delighted. Come, let us tell him your new word." She turned, and the filly trotted after her.

Calydor exclaimed, "She will be weaned and hornsprung before you know."

Crimson laughed again, tossing over one shoulder, "Then bearded and grown, as was I!"

"Fare safe, daughter," the star-flecked stallion called after his niece.

"And you, Calydor," she cried. "Fare you well, Aljan Moonbrow. May you Valefolk regain your homeland soon and cease tramping our Plain in a wartroop each spring."

Her voice was light, no malice in it. Jan saw Crimson rejoin Goldenhair and the other two. They stood consulting while the filly suckled. Most of the others had already quit the dancing ground, cantering across the Plain. The sky's rose blush had blanched to white, its stars unseen, but burning still. Sun broke horizon's edge and floated up into the sky. Calydor rose and shook himself. Jan did the same, flexing the stiffness from his legs. He joined the other in tearing a few quick mouthfuls of grass.

"Time to be off," the star-patterned stallion said, "if we mean to catch the cool of the day."

Jan nodded. Pards prowled at dawn, he knew. The two of them kicked into a lope, heading north and east across the Plain.

Calydor

★ 9 ★

At the start of all things, when time was young, Álm'harat fashioned the world and the stars and the dark between. Maker of everything, mother of all, Álm'harat walks among us in mortal shape. Sometimes she appears as a unicorn, a beautiful stallion or a fleet-footed mare, or assumes the guise of a pard in the grass, or wears the wings of a kite upon the air. Life and death she deals, each in its season, advancing her great Cycle that turns all the world and the stars.

"Once she sojourned in these parts as a mare pale as moonlight, who ranged the broad Plain and allowed none to stay her. Such a traveler was she, bearing tales from far lands, that companions dubbed her the Mare of the World. This Mare of the World fell in love with the sun, whose golden mane is burning fire. Feeling that heat, she was smitten and called out to him, but far above, he galloped on. Sprinting the Plain below, she sought to draw his gaze, but still he paid her no heed. So planting herself on the tallest rise, she whistled his name—only to see him race past overhead, aloof and unanswering.

"Undaunted, the Mare of the World asked her fellows, the birds, to fly to the sun and press her suit. They did so, but the sun stallion only flared with laughter, so hotly that some of her envoys' feathers singed and fell fluttering to earth far, far below. The burning sun proclaimed himself too high and fair to return any meager mortal's favor—never suspecting the one who proffered was Álm'harat disguised. He would return her love, he scoffed, only if she proved herself his match.

" 'He means me to fail,' the Mare of the World exclaimed when the birds flew back with their news. 'But I do not concede defeat. Mortal I am—'

"She had forgotten, of course, that she was Álm'harat, for when the goddess dons mortal flesh, she sets aside all remembrance of her true nature, that she may ken the world of her creations as they themselves do. Carefully, she gathered the fallen feathers of her friends.

"'Weave these into my hair,' she bade. The birds complied. 'Though but mortal born,' she vowed, 'a little of Alma lives in me.' So much is true. The goddess burns within us all, even the kite and the pard. 'Your feathers, my fellows, shall speed me like wings.'

"She bade the birds take strands from her mane and tail and wait. Then she traveled east through moonless night with only the light of the stars for a guide. That is why we call them Alma's eyes, for they limned her path through the dark. All night she sped until she reached the rim of the world, where daily the bright sun launches skyward, traversing the arc of stars which spans the vast ether above. There she lay in the long grass like a pard.

"Soon she saw him, the splendid sun, his brilliant fire paling the sky. Night faded. The starpath sparked under his galloping hooves. All heaven caught fire, his radiance infusing the air as he rounded horizon's rim where the starpath ascended. Then the Mare of the World sprang, flying before him, stealing his course. Her shadow fell upon the Plain, racing before the sun. He cried out that any mortal—so he thought— would dare eclipse his light.

"'Catch me if ever you can, proud sun,' she taunted.

"The pinions in her mane lifted to lend her speed. Higher she climbed throughout the morn, as the starpath swelled toward its crest at the apex of the sky. Some stars, by her heels kicked free, fell burning to the earth below. The sun called at her to halt, but she only laughed, her shadow sweeping the Plain. She reached sky's zenith barely ahead of him, her morning's slender lead slipping. As they began the long afternoon's descent down the starpath's arc, Álm'harat whistled to her birds.

"'Time to do as I have asked! Aid me if you love me, friends, for only should I best him shall I win him.'

"The birds rose, carrying the silken strands of the Mare's mane and tail. These they wove into misty nets to hinder the sun. His anger flashed. He sought to sear the billowing webs from the air, but they only melted into rain, damping his fires, despite all shouts and rumbling. All afternoon the birds played cloud-catch with the sun. Unaware still that she was Álm'harat—but feeling the goddess's power within—the Mare of the World ran on, barely two paces ahead of the sun.

"At dusk he caught her, just as they reached the starpath's terminus at the other end of the world. Far from raging now, the sun had calmed, his fires mellowed. No longer white with heat, they simmered yellow, then rosy, then amber. His temper, too, had cooled in the afternoon rains, for during his pursuit, he had deigned to gaze—truly gaze—upon this seeming mortal for the first time.

"The toss of her mane and the long curve of her throat, the plain of her back and roundness of her ribs intrigued him. Her sinewy legs and flashing heels dazzled. Her laugh, when she called, had begun to beguile him, so that when he captured her at last, 'twas no longer anger he felt, but another passion, just as ardent, but no cause for fear. His nips upon her flank were gentle, his words inviting, his touch a caress.

"Yet when he fell upon her, just where the starpath meets the earth and merges with the netherpath—which is also stars, bridging the underside of the world—she ran on. She felt the weight of his belly against her back, the heave and fall of his panting sides, the heat of him infusing her. Her skin glowed, throwing back a cooler radiance borrowed from his. She bore the heft and the heat and the light of him all along the netherpath that curves below, through darkness, seeking dawn.

"All night they sped mated. All night she carried him, and the sacred children of that union are still being born into this world. The Mare reached dawnpoint again, whence their long race had started a full day before. There the netherpath turns upward to touch easternmost horizon's rim and the starpath begins its ascent into daylit heaven. Here the sun at long last, conceding defeat, set her free.

" 'You win, wild mare,' he gasped, breathless. 'Both this race and my heart. Let us pledge forever, body and soul, and never be parted.'

"The Mare of the World smiled, for she had remembered now her nature and her name. 'I am already yours,' she answered. 'I am Álm'harat. You are part of me and of my making. We have never been sundered and never can be, for I am you, and you are I, and the long dance we have been footing circles without end.'

"Álm'harat became herself again, wide as the world and the stars beyond. She became everything that was ever made or has ever been or will be. When the sun no longer saw her as the alluring, willful mare he had chased heaven and underearth to win, he cried out, desolate. But the mother of all things whispered, 'Do not fear.'

"She made an image of herself to be the sun's mate, the same compass as he and filled with his borrowed light. This new creation she called the moon, which strives to travel the starpath ahead of the sun. He must gallop his hardest to catch her up. As he gains, she wanes, spending more and more of her light. When he seizes her, by the dark of the moon, both moon and sun tread the netherpath as one, a time of miracles and strange tidings, when the world sees by the light of Álm'harat's eyes alone.

"Thus has it been for time out of mind. We of the Plain yet wear feathers in her memory. Birds take strands from our manes and tails in payment for their fletch. When Álm'harat created us, she skimmed from the moon some of her shining stuff and poured it into our hooves and horns, into the hearts and minds of all unicorns. Moondancers of the Vale commemorate the goddess at fullmoon, when she fares brightest and farthest from the sun.

"But we of the Plain honor her at moondark, when she and her mate run joined in joy, dancing the longdance to its end. This is the Great Dance, the Cycle unending. Let us live as the maker of all things invites us, as she herself has always done, withholding herself never, sharing favor with all, preferring none of her creatures above any other, loving all wisely and well."

❧

The tales Jan heard and the days he spent in the company of the one the Plainsdwellers called Alma's Eyes were like none he had ever known. The grass grew thinner, shorter, paler, the farther north and east they strove. The green, once so savory upon the young prince's tongue, began yellowing, its sweetness soured. Waterholes became scarce. Once he and his guide sipped from a spring no bigger than a puddle—one they had searched half a morn to find. The soil grew poorer, looser, drier. Dust increased, rimming Jan's nostrils red. As the land grew hillier and grass sparser, he saw scant trace of other unicorns. Calydor's fellows, it seemed, avoided these parts.

The seer spoke of his far-traveled folk, how widely they ranged and seldom they met. He sang of pards and the heroes who had dodged them, of summer storms, flash floods, droughts. The one thing he did not speak of, Jan learned in time, was war. The folk of the Plain had no use for it. Here, those who quarreled either settled their dispute, ignored one another, or parted. Each freeborn unicorn was his own ruler: Plainsdwellers attached little merit to following others and viewed obedience with varying degrees of amusement or disdain.

It occurred to Jan at length that the Vale's lore told mostly of battle: mighty warriors and contests, all struggles ended by force. The Plainsdwellers, he saw, praised heroes who turned foes into friends or averted strife. Keenly aware how Korr's violence must embody for Calydor and his folk all the worst of the Vale, the young prince strove to offer another side, recounting the end of centuries-long feuds with the gryphons and the pans. He held out hope for treaties with the seer's tribe as well. Telling of the herd's anticipated return to the Hallow Hills, he pledged his folk would harry no Plainsdwellers while passing through their lands.

"My son, your herd will not even see us unless we mean you to do so," the other replied. "We will not allow you to bait us. At your approach, we will simply vanish, returning only after you have passed."

The pair of them lay in the long grass near a tiny waterhole they had come across just at noon and there resolved to rest an hour in the heat of midday. Though the year was fast rounding toward summer's end, noon sun could still beat fierce. The young prince turned to Calydor.

"I beg you," he countered, "do not remove yourselves from us. My herd is ready for change. Warlike ways united us during our first, long years of exile. But that exile is soon to end. We must custom ourselves anew to peace."

"Peace which is to follow your war," the seer reminded him. "You mean to wrest the Hills by force, my son."

"As once they were wrested from us!" Jan found himself exclaiming. He stopped, confused, then stammered, "Thus has it been prophesied, by Alma's will. . . ."

The words trailed off. Never before had Jan realized how vainglorious the boast sounded. And yet he knew it to be true—he knew! Calmly, the star-scattered stallion gazed at him. Mirrored in the other's eyes, Jan saw himself for the first time as one seized by war, enthralled by it: ever pondering strategy and measuring potential foes while smugly spouting the goddess's permission for it all. Doubt teased at him, brought him up short.

"My son, none but Álm'harat truly knows the will of Álm'harat," Calydor quietly replied. "But this I do know: the goddess wills much that is beyond our ken. And she is both the maker and the unmaker of the world."

Jan learned much from Calydor of the singer's elusive, wandering folk. By night, the star-marked stallion recited his people's legends, with heroes and heroines all grander than life. Wild paeans to the goddess Álm'harat he chanted, too, as well as passionate ballads extolling the joys of the longdance. The Plainsdwellers, Jan discovered, gathered for such dancing not just in late summer or early fall, but whenever they pleased. The northernmost reach of the Plain, which lay beyond the Hallow Hills, was warm enough, Calydor informed him, for mares to bear their young in any season.

That unicorns might know such freedom astonished Jan. Among the herd, mares conceived only during that season which yielded a spring delivery. No stallion dreamed of asking his mate to do otherwise. Had he and Tek been born upon the Plain, Jan concluded, stunned, he and she might partake of the longdance as often as they chose. Was it really nearly three years since he and his mate had pledged eternal fidelity in their courting by the Summer Sea?

The memory made his blood beat hot—but mates always took care to space their young at least two years apart. Whatever Tek's charms, the young prince would never have considered their dancing again until the twins were weaned—as by now they must be, he realized with a jolt. Fury and longing rose in his breast. Instead of chasing his elusive sire halfway across the Plain, he might have sported the summer beside his mate, renewing their vows.

In exchange for Calydor's godtales and ballads, Jan recited as best he could his own folk's ancient lays—until, on the fourth night, the singer gently told him he much preferred to hear of Jan's own life. The young prince blushed beneath the black hairs of his hide, certain his unpolished rendition must be the cause. Truth, he was no singer: that he knew. Yet here Calydor contradicted him with vehemence and surprise, insisting he had all the makings of a fine singer—timing, cadence, ear—but a heart that clearly joyed far more in spontaneous recounting than rote recitation of histories long past.

At last Jan relented, relating his battle with the wyvern queen, his sojourn among the two-footed firekeepers, his truce with the gryphon Illishar, his pact with the pans, the herd's ordeal during the usurpation of mad Korr, and of Tek, his mate, whose many trials had brought their young safe into the world. Deeply absorbed, the star-flecked seer listened.

"I have no mate, no young," he said at last. "I envy you, my son. Though life upon the Plain allows great liberty, I will say for your Vale that it lends a continuity unknown among my kind. You have friends whom you encounter every day. You do not spend your waking hours trekking from one waterhole to the next. You do not sleep each night in a newfound spot, one ear cocked for pards."

Hearing this, Jan felt a secret triumph, savoring his companion's admission that the Vale might have its merits. The young prince had liked Calydor on sight, sensed his admiration returned. He experienced the oddest camaraderie with the seer, a natural familiarity. Plainly, the older stallion enjoyed his company as well. Jan had never encountered such easy kinship before. It felt uncannily like something he ought to recognize, ought to have known in his colthood but missed somehow.

At last the Plain gave out. A great rift cleft the land as though the whole earth had pulled asunder. A steep slope led down to a flatter, nearly barren expanse, its soil a pale, poor alkaline color. Rounded hills and worn mesas surfaced here and there, slopes striated, alternating bands of soot and light. A chafing breeze blew, smelling of salt and dust. Below, Jan saw only patches of dying grass and leafless thornbriars.

"Behold, my son," the star-strewn seer told him, "the Salt Waste. According to my dreams, 'twas here my folk put the dark destroyer to flight. Legends say that this was once a vast, shallow sea. Some claim seashells and the bones of great fishes can still be found here. I do not know. I have never ventured this place, nor have I any wish. My people call this a realm of haunts, where those who can find no peace withdraw to die."

Jan stared in dismay at the vast wasteland before him, into which his mad king had fled. "How am I to find him?" he murmured. "What hope have I now?"

Calydor turned to him. "See you those mountains far, far to the east?"

The young prince peered through the wavering salt haze, barely discerned a jagged mountain range, white crags nearly fading into the paleness of dusty sky. It hovered before him, almost a dream, resembled a line of great, ridged lizards lying at rest. He nodded.

"See you where the two highest peaks pierce the sky, and the gap plunging between?"

Again, the young prince nodded. "Aye."

"My visions promise that if you keep them ever before you as you go," Calydor told him, "you will catch this dark other whom you seek long before you reach the peaks."

Almost fearing to ask, Jan breathed, "Will I succeed? Will I wrest from Korr the secret that drives him mad?"

The seer's look turned inward. "Yes, my son," he answered softly. "You will see his madness end—but may wonder after if the news you learn be worth the cost."

Gazing off toward the distant mountains, Jan scarcely heard the last of what his companion said. They were not real, he knew, these summits: merely an illusion that floated at the limit of his vision. The true peaks lay beyond horizon's rim, hidden by the curve of the world. This far-off range existed much farther away even than it seemed. Jan gritted his teeth, determined to start at once.

"Little that is edible grows upon the Salt Waste," Calydor was saying. "When you need sustenance, dash open one of the fleshy prickleplants and take care to avoid the spines. The inside is succulent and sweet."

Jan nodded absently, storing the other's words, his thoughts fixed upon the far horizon still. He came to himself a moment later with a start and turned.

"I can never repay your aid and kindness, Calydor."

The blue-and-silver stallion tossed his head. "It was little enough. Until next we meet, my son, I bid you in Álm'harat's name, love wisely and well."

Jan felt a great sadness stab his breast, could not say whence it came. He felt desolate suddenly, as though parting from a lifelong friend. The seer seemed similarly stricken. Jan bowed low to one knee after the fashion of the Plain. The older stallion did the same. Looking one last time into the indigo darkness of the other's coat, the dance of stars that wound across, it almost seemed to Jan that he could see himself lost upon that path of stars. The young prince blinked. The illusion broke.

"Fare well," Jan bade him. "May we meet again."

He turned and began his descent down the soft, crumbling slope to the Salt Waste below.

Salt

★ 10 ★

J an traveled across the barren waste, threading his way through banded hills. His last glimpse of Calydor had come hours earlier. Atop the slope where the Plain began, the other had reared up, whistling a long wild cry of farewell. Halting, Jan had done the same. He had not looked back again, faring on toward the gap in the far mountains, but he sensed the stallion of the summer stars watching him out of sight.

The Salt Waste stretched on and on, its monotony numbing. His eyes reddened, ears filled with blown dust, coat caked with it. Whenever he felt his throat parching and empty belly grinding, he dashed open the nearest spiny plant to taste its sour flesh. Eventually he discovered that outcroppings of what he had mistaken for pebbles were actually plants, their waxy, grey-green surfaces concealing a sweet, juicy pulp. Whenever he found these, Jan ate greedily.

Three days he trekked, sleeping only briefly. Little sting-tailed insects crept out at night. Other animals, too, apparently inhabited this desolate place. Diminutive lizard tracks scampered away over the alkaline dust. Slithering trails of serpents or worms snaked through the sand. Once he came across delicate traces of some sort of minute pig or deer. The little creatures had been feeding on wax-rinds. Their tracks fled northward, the pawprints of some predator, equally tiny, pursuing. The young prince doubted a creature his own size could long survive here.

When, on the fourth day, he encountered Korr's tracks, he nearly stumbled on past, so mesmerized had he become. The wind had fallen the night before, leaving the traces of the night creatures intact. Haze hung in the air. Jan came across a line of cloven-hoofed impressions leading east. He stopped. The imprints were large, unmistakably the king's. They staggered, sometimes curving in great circles, their maker moving little faster than a shamble.

Heart quickening, the young prince started to trot. Crumbling mounds obscured his vision. The dream of white-maned mountains floated coolly before him on horizon's edge. He found where Korr had paused to feed, tearing at thorns. He passed a spot where the king had rested, disturbing the sand beneath the scant shade of a spindly tree. Eagerly, Jan pressed on. Morning hours crept away. The sun was a fever-blaze dead overhead. He cast no shadow. The tracks wove through a meandering maze of mesas and hills.

Abruptly, his ears pricked. He heard slow hoofbeats ahead, much muffled by dust. Jan broke into a lope. He rounded a hillmound, another. The tracks snaked on through the maze. In the stillness, the thud of his hooves, his own breathing, sounded impossibly loud. He rounded more curves. Suddenly the hoofbeats ahead of him faltered. A shrill whistle of surprise reached him, then the hard, random thumps of a warrior leaping and shying.

Jan's heart kicked against his ribs. He bolted into a run. The shrills ahead of him continued, more peals of fury now than alarm. Whistling his own warcry, the dark prince skidded around an embankment to see emaciated Korr, rearing and plunging at a thing that writhed and whipped on the ground before him. Sand flew. Fine dust floated, a smoky curtain on the air. Jan caught a glimpse of long coils pale as salt. Korr charged it. Turning, it massed itself, hood flattened, fangs bared and ready to strike.

"No!" the prince of the Vale shouted. He dashed to interpose himself between the serpent and the king. The hissing creature lunged. The mad king struck at it. "Run," Jan cried. "It's poison!"

Again the viper lashed. The young prince felt its fangs click and slide against his horn as he swept it back. Seething, it gathered itself. Jan gauged himself at the edge of the serpent's range. Korr behind him stood safe.

"Wyrm!" the mad king raved. "Would you impede me?"

Without warning, he plunged past the younger stallion and rushed at the serpent again. Jan leapt after with a cry, threw one shoulder against him. Korr shook him off with a whinny of rage. Black hooves and pale sand flew. Jan saw the viper strike. The dark king ramped and dodged.

"Stop!" Jan exclaimed, colliding with him again. "You've no proof against its sting. Let me!"

With an effort, the young prince managed to shove the older stallion aside. He pinned the serpent's body between one forehoof and the opposite hind heel, then struck its head off with his razor-edged horn. The dead thing continued to flop and bow upward even after he leapt free. Jan turned to Korr. The king stood staring at his own foreshank. Blood ran from a double wound.

"I'm stung," he said.

The prince felt the strength drain from him. His knees trembled. He could not seem to catch his breath.

"No," he whispered. "No. A flesh wound. A scratch, the venom already spent."

The king shook his head, still gazing at the wound. "Deep," he answered. "To the bone." His voice sounded petulant, perturbed. "It smarts and burns." He flexed his leg, then shook it. Blood trickled down.

"Don't," Jan gasped. Dust filled his lungs. He could get no air. Everything tasted of salt. "Stand still. Don't help the poison spread."

Korr tried to put his hoof down, but stumbled. Jan shied, his reflexes strung tauter than a deer's. The king's foreleg seemed unable to bear his weight. He stood three-legged, frowning. He muttered, "Numb."

"Cut the wound," Jan cried. "Bleed the poison out!"

He sprang to rake the tip of his horn across the swelling gash. Runnels of red spattered. The other stallion shook his head, staggered again.

"Late," he remarked. "Too late."

Jan felt a scream tear from his breast as Korr's legs folded. He pitched forward. A grey puff of dust welled up, swirling. The king lay struggling to rise. Jan smote the ground for lack of any serpent left to strike.

"Why?" he cried. "Why did you fly at it? What harm to have let it go?"

Korr's forehooves dug at the sand, uselessly. "It thwarted me," he mumbled.

Jan heard himself railing, unable to stop. "Why did you not let me fend it off? You've no defense from serpent stings—"

The king tossed his haggard shoulders weakly, gave up trying to rise. He murmured, "I needn't listen to you."

"You do!" Jan burst out. The landscape around him reeled. "If not because I am your son, Korr, then because I am your prince! Even a king must obey the battleprince in time of war. . . ."

"Prince," the dark king snorted, refusing to look at him. "You're no prince. I should have let your sib have the office. I should have acknowledged her at the start."

"Lell?" Jan demanded. His sister had been but newly born when

Jan had become warleader. "Lell's barely five years old, still unbearded, not yet a warrior. She's not even been initiated. . . ."

Korr's sudden glare cut short the absurd laugh rising in his throat. "Not Lell," he snapped. "Your other sib. My firstborn. Tek's twice the warrior you'll ever be."

The king's words made no sense to him. Nothing made sense. Time stopped. Jan stood staring at the dark other. Nothing happened. Nothing moved save the airborne dust, which all around them, very slowly, was beginning to settle. The murky air gradually cleared. Jan heard his own ragged, labored breath. His lips and teeth and tongue were numb. He could not speak. Korr rambled on.

"Small matter she was born outside the Vale and by that red wych. She was an heir any prince could be proud of—until you sullied her. I warned you against courting! The pair of you pledged against my will and got your vile get. Ruined now. She'll never lead the unicorns."

The taste of salt swelled, closing Jan's throat. His gorge rose. Pale dust made the other grey as a haunt. Himself, too. "What are you saying?" he managed, barely able to whisper. "What are you saying of Tek?"

Korr examined the sand-caked wound on his leg. It barely bled. "Corrupted," he murmured. "Like all the herd. Jah-lila's to blame. And you. Weanling sop, what have *you* ever done but nuzzle up to gryphons, Renegades, and pans? As though the world were a courtship! You and your peace have betrayed Halla's legacy: eternal vengeance and war till the day we regain our rightful Hills. . . ."

Jan scarcely heard, hardly able to follow the gist of his words. "Are you saying Tek is your daughter?" he gasped. "Your firstborn—my elder sister? Out of Jah-lila? You got foals on two different mares, and the first mare still living?"

The king's head lolled. Roaring filled Jan's ears as he realized the other was nodding. He felt as though lightning had seared him. The agony was uncontainable. Boundless wasteland swallowed his cry.

"Why did you never tell me? Why?"

The king's head, dragging with weariness, lifted once more. The hollow eyes looked at him.

"I tried," he whispered. "When you went with her to the Summer Sea, I warned you against courting. . . ."

"You gave no clear warnings!" Jan shouted. "Only veiled threats that meant nothing. You urged me to choose a mare my own age—you never said Tek was your daughter! Never called her my sister."

The dark king shook his head feebly. "I couldn't. I meant never to speak of it, to . . . to spare her. . . ."

"To spare yourself!" Jan choked. "To spare yourself the shame. You pledged yourself to Jah-lila long before you ever danced the courting dance with Ses by the Summer Sea. You raised me and Lell all our lives without telling us we had a sib . . . a sib by a different mare."

Strength returned momentarily to the withered king. His nostrils flared. "She beguiled me, that wych. No beard, round hooves, mane standing in a brush. She was not even a unicorn! I made no pledge to any unicorn mare. Our sacred pool may have given her a horn, but it could not make her one of us. I left her and returned to the Vale, telling no one that, in my folly, I had consorted with a Renegade. I bade her not to follow me. . . ."

Furiously, Jan cut off the other's storm of words. "Jah-lila is no Renegade. She comes of a different tribe, the *daya* whom the two-footed firekeepers enslave. When she escaped and fled to the Plain, she asked your succor. Drinking of our sacred mere in the heart of wyvern-infested Hallow Hills, she became a unicorn. She is one of us now, and the mother of your heir."

"I never intended—" dying Korr shrilled. "I gave my word to a mere Renegade, to no one. . . ."

"It was still your word," retorted Jan, "the word of a prince's son, the prince-to-be, grandson to the reigning queen. You pledged yourself to Jah-lila, a bond unshakable in Alma's eyes, and then deserted her."

Korr laughed, a dry, wheezing sound. His body tremored as though with cold. The sun overhead blazed shadowless. "Aye, but she found me. Tracked me all the way to the Vale. Who would have thought it? Arrived in foal for all the world to see. Yet she never shamed me, never named her unborn filly's sire. Hoping to tempt me to acknowledge her! Fool. I pretended not to know her."

Again the horrible, airless laugh. Jan's hide crawled. The king continued.

"When Teki sheltered her, all assumed him to be her unborn's sire. Neither he nor she spoke a word of denial. Teki could easily shoulder my blame—he is the herd's only healer, immune to censure. He could sire a dozen foals on a dozen dams and the herd would never cast him out. They need him—far more, it seems, than they needed me."

Korr's voice grew bitter. He sneered.

"Jah-lila haunted the Vale for months, seeking acceptance, striving to lure me back to her side. But the herd never accepted her. I saw to that."

"They accept her now," Jan breathed. He doubted the other heard. "They welcome and honor her."

"At last she departed, self-exiled to the wilderness beyond the Vale.

I thought me done with her and heaved a prayer of thanks. Alma had forgiven me. My granddam the queen had died, my father Khraa become king. I was prince now. I devoted my reign to serving Alma and the Law."

"You served neither," Jan growled. "What you called Law was tyranny; what you named Alma, madness."

Korr ignored him, spoke on, gasping now.

"That very year by the Summer Sea I pledged your dam. She bore you to me the following spring. I reared you sternly, that you might never stray, as had I in my youth. I sought to keep you safe. . . ."

"To keep me ignorant!" Jan cried. "How is it, my sire, you loathe all Renegades so? Did you not once long to be one? Did you not, in your youth, once strike out across the Plain, make promises you spurned to keep—only to think better of your flight and return to the Vale?"

Korr shuddered. The dust on his coat rose and settled. "And if I did?" he muttered sullenly. "I came to my senses with none the wiser. Would you condemn me for mere folly?"

"Not for folly, but for deceit," Jan answered hotly. "You told me I was prince-to-be and deprived a princess of her birthright."

"Aye," the dark king snarled. "The red wych bore her filly in the wild, reared her there two years till she was weaned—then brought her back to the Vale and left her in Teki's care. To shame me! And never a word of who her filly's father was. I made her swear never to tell what had passed between us. All these years, her silence has tortured me, chasing my reason!"

"It is your own silence," cried Jan. "Your own silence that has maddened you."

The other sank, sagged. "But I am dying now. My silence is broken." Salt covered him. He turned glazed eyes toward Jan. His bony head looked like a skull. "So, my son," he grated, "you have wrested my secret at last." His voice was a rasp and a rattle of bones. "Has it been worth the trek?"

Jan stood unable to move, to think. The Waste all around him lay utterly lifeless, motionless, still. He groaned. "How am I to tell Tek?" he wondered, desperate, only half aware he spoke aloud. "How do I dare?"

The haggard king rolled onto his side. His frail head touched the dust, then rose with momentary strength.

"Speak of this to no one," he hissed. "Carry my secret to the end of your days. Jah-lila will hold silent. Her daughter will never rule. The herd will not dream they stand duped by a second son. Tell them, and

you destroy them! They will cast you out, strip you of power. If not
their prince, what are you? Who are you, if not my son?"

Jan stared at nothing, the words of the dark king still ringing in his
mind. Wind hissed about his fetlocks, lifting the sand, stinging him. He
had not felt it rise. It hummed, moaning. The mad king of the unicorns
laid down his head. His body shuddered, tremored, stilled. His stark ribs
rose, subsided, his breathing growing shallower, more labored. Jan stood
fixed, swaying. The wind gusted and whipped. Salt grit beat at his ears,
his eyes and nostrils. His mane and tail thrashed, lashing him.

His fallen sire lay at his feet, unmoving now. Jan scarcely recognized him, so thin and fleshless had he become. Korr's lifeless form lay
like a shadow, a deep pool in the sand. Gazing down at him, Jan felt
oddly disoriented, as though he were beholding a great chasm, a darkness reft of moon or stars. He had no notion how long he stood gazing
into this void. The wind increased, lifting clouds of pale, bitter sand.

Jan stirred, though whether his trance had lasted a heartbeat or an
age, he could not say. He felt numb. His sire was dead. He must complete the burial ritual. The prince of the unicorns bent his horntip to the
sand and drew a circle around the fallen king. Wind blew the shallow
depression in the sand away. Jan tried again, and yet again, to close the
circle, but the wind prevented him. He tried to fill his lungs, to sing the
endingsong:

"Fate has unspoken, one of the Circle. . . ."

Rising tempest stole the words from his teeth. Salt blinded him,
smothered him. Wind battered and deafened him. The world tilted,
steeped in the bitter redolence of ashes and dust. Jan teetered away from
the fallen king, afraid somehow that if he remained, he might fall into
endless, bottomless nothingness. He tried to turn, but the wind drove
him on. He managed one backward glance, and saw fine sand drifted
high against Korr's side. It spilled over, pale grains streaking across the
blackness of him like hurtling stars.

Jan's hooves sank, grit rising to pull him down. He struggled, aware
he must keep moving or be buried in salt. The storm, coming out of the
west, drove him eastward, away from the Plain. Blindly, reluctantly, he
stumbled on toward the dreaming mountains—invisible now—that
bounded unseen horizon's rim and bordered the end of the world.

King's Mate

★ 11 ★

Wind howled. The salt grit stung. He could move no direction other than toward the sandstorm's lee. A weight like that of the world crushed him. How many leagues had he already traveled, one torturous step at a time? Thirst tormented him. He could hardly breathe. His empty belly ached. He tried to halt, to rest, but the gale harried him. Whenever he lay down, dust drifts overtook him within moments, threatening to bury him. He rose and stumbled on.

Time proved impossible to gauge. He had no notion of night or day. The way seemed to be rising, becoming more solid. Fatigue stupefied him. He dared not stop. The ground grew firmer, its shifting granules coarser underfoot. Cold wind cut through his numbness. He felt as though his pelt had been scoured from his hide.

What woke him to himself at last was the sound of his own footfalls. He was walking, slowly, step by step, must have been doing so in a daze for he knew not how long. Numb still from the hours or days that it had flailed him, he realized the wind had ceased. He felt indescribably light. His mouth still tasted of salt. He dared not even try to swallow. But he could breathe. Pitch dark surrounded him. Night, he reasoned: moonless night.

No sound met his ears other than that of his own hooves, scrunching loudly. Each step sank into something loose and rough and pebble-sized, but irregular in shape, and much lighter than riverstones. He felt as though he were treading great piles of cracked acorn shells. He felt muffled, dusty, caked with grit.

Jan halted and shook himself. Sand flew from his coat and mane. He twitched his ears furiously to clear them. The smell of dust rose. He felt light enough to be treading sky, not earth. He became aware of stars, not sure whether they had emerged suddenly or slowly, or whether, perhaps, he had been walking with his eyes shut.

He gazed up, lost in their brightness, trying to recognize a pattern there. They dazzled him, many more than he had ever seen. Too stunned by hunger, thirst, and fatigue, he could find no familiar constellation. He gave up. The scrunch under his hooves gave way to solid stone, rippled and hard. His hoofbeats scuffed, rang, at times struck sparks. Moonless night lasted forever.

After a while, he perceived an utter darkness to one side of him, dividing the night. A faint echo rang from that quarter. To his other side, stars blazed, filling that half of the sky as far above him as he could crane, and as far below as he could peer. The air from that direction felt empty and unimpeded. No echoes rang. A hint of breeze wafted thence, lifting his mane.

Suddenly the starless darkness fell away. He heard a quiet, continuous rushing sound, very familiar to him, but in his daze, he could not think what it was. The susurrous murmur soothed him. He had heard it many times before, he knew, though not for a very long while. A slight pressure lapped against his hooves, a cool ripple, a gentle rill.

Stars burned all around now, above and below. Those beneath him were in motion, winking and wavering, moving past him to a point seemingly only a few paces distant where, converging slightly, they simply vanished. Other stars continuously replaced them, gliding forward from behind, their fixed companions above burning steadily.

Walking among the stars, Jan reached the place where those in motion vanished, and stepped beyond it. Every heavenly light before him hung motionless. The plashing whisper continued behind, quiet, lulling. The coolness streaming against his hooves had ceased. He could not go another step. His eyes slid closed. He realized that he had just lain down. A vast, illumined void surrounded him. He had no idea where he lay. A breath of starwind sighed across him, thin and slight and very cold. He slept.

᭡

Jah-lila stood looking down at the dark pool. Though it was daylight outside the cave, here at the grotto's innermost chamber, no sunlight reached. The phosphorescent lichens from the larger, outward chamber cast little light. Few grew on the smooth ceiling above the spring. The little chamber was dim. Jah-lila gazed into the spring's dark pool. Its surface stirred, but did not break.

She saw the Salt Waste, two dark figures, widely separated and very small, converging. As though she were a kite, she watched, suspended high above. The tiny figures reflected in the pool met. She moved closer, saw the maze of low canyons, a white serpent coiled to strike. She saw the haggard king fly at it, the young prince desperate to save him. The serpent struck. The prince dispatched it. The king stood staring at his shank.

The red mare felt her breast tighten. It was the moment she had feared all the years since she had first sipped of the Hallow Hills' magical mere and become a unicorn. It was the fate she had fought so hard to stay—that the first and only love she had ever known should die of a serpent's sting. She wished then that she might halt, withdraw, end the vision here, but she forced herself on.

Jah-lila gazed deeper into the pool. The image rippled. She heard the words Korr and the one he called second-born exchanged, heard the younger stallion's cries of horror and disbelief. She saw the king collapse, saw the one he had raised from colthood standing stunned. In the dark pool before her, a colorless cave fish slipped through the lifeless form of the king. Korr's image wavered, broke, re-formed. The red mare saw the young prince trying to draw a circle in the dust.

She bent her own horn to the dark pool's bank and traced the semblance of the fallen king into the sand. Completing a circle around it, she scraped dirt onto the likeness with one round, uncloven heel, obliterating it. In the pool before her, wind lifted. Sand began to fly. The burial song rose in her throat. Jah-lila breathed upon the water. She watched the dark prince stagger away.

Softly, painfully, she hummed the endingsong through, then closed her eyes and bent to where the form of fallen Korr reflected. The water felt cool upon her tongue, quenching the song, soothing the parched ache in her throat. She drank a long time, deep, then raised her head. No image lay upon the water. Something brushed her side. Jah-lila turned. Painted Aiony stood nearby, Dhattar peering into the chamber. He came to join them.

"What saw you, Granddam?" Aiony asked her. Dha echoed her. "What did you see?"

"Your father, little ones," she answered.

"He was well?" asked Dhattar.

Jah-lila nodded. "Aye."

The filly spoke. "We've not seen him since he left the Plain."

"He's very far now," the white foal added.

Jah-lila said nothing, lost in thought.

Aiony asked her, "Is our father in the Salt Waste still?"

The red mare shook her head.

Dha's voice was hopeful. "When will we see him?"

Their granddam bent to nuzzle first him, then his sister. "You know well enough," she answered. "Hist now, or your dam will come looking."

She herded them away from the spring, into the outer chamber. Her daughter, Tek, was just coming in the entryway. "There you are," the pied mare exclaimed. "I sought you everywhere. Off, now. Outside. Your granddam has work, and Lell wants to show you the rueberries she found."

She chivvied each gently and scooted them toward the grotto's egress. Beyond it, the daylight shone. Whickering and giggling, they went. The red mare watched them disappear, heard Lell's whistle of greeting, the twins' answering calls. Tek turned to her dam.

"You found him," she said, voice low, urgent with certainty.

Jah-lila nodded. The pied mare closed her eyes, gave an outbreath of relief.

"At last," she murmured. "Safe?"

"Aye."

Her daughter studied her by flickering lichenlight. "Korr," she said softly. "You found him as well."

Again the red mare nodded. She heard the wariness in her offspring's voice, the loathing and dread.

"So Jan has found his sire," she breathed.

"Found and lost him," Jah-lila replied, heart heavy as stone. The lichenlight was far too bright.

Tek stepped directly into her path. "And?"

"And Korr has spoken."

"Then Korr's madness is healed?" The pied mare's words held sudden hope.

"His madness is over," the red mare replied wearily.

"Then Jan will be returning—" Tek cried, full of gladness now. Jah-lila cut her off.

"Nay. Not at once."

Tek stared at her, outraged. "Why not?" she demanded. "What can Korr do to keep him from us still?"

The red mare drew a great breath, spent to the bone. She felt fragile as a bird's egg.

"Daughter," she said. "Jan will return to you; I have promised. In time. I beg you now, let it rest. Farseeing drains me. Let us go outside."

Her daughter pressed against her, instantly contrite. "Forgive my impatience," she murmured. "I miss him so."

The red mare leaned into her daughter's warmth, then nipped her gently and nosed her out the grotto's egress ahead of her. Jah-lila waited until her daughter's shadow passed, muffled hooffalls ringing out on the slope below, heading down. The light of midday stabbed the red mare's eyes as she rounded the bend to stand in the cave's entryway. Lell and the twins' whistles and whickering drifting from far upslope as Lell shouted, "This way!" and the twins insisted, "Hey up!"

Much nearer, on the hillside below, Jah-lila spotted her daughter trotting toward Ryhenna and Dagg. The coppery mare was, like the red mare herself, a runaway from the city of two-footed firekeepers. With Jan's help, she had come to live within the Vale. Drinking of the moon's sacred pool in the Hallow Hills, as the red mare once had done, had given Ryhenna her spiral horn. The pied warrior Dagg, Jan's shoulder-friend, had pledged with her little over two years gone, and their tiny foal, Culu, suckled at her flank.

Idly, Jah-lila watched her daughter converge on the trio downslope as she blinked the sunlight from her eyes. Another unicorn stood by, coat palest cream in the noonday sun, her mane like burning poppies. Jah-lila turned and the chestnut eyes of Ses, Korr's mate and the prince's dam, found her own black-green ones. She whispered, "Jan?"

The red mare murmured, "Alive."

A long pause. Very long. "And Korr?"

Jah-lila gazed at her. "A serpent."

The pale mare started. Her eyes winced shut, her whole frame rigid. She stood racked with a recurrent trembling that might have been suppressed sobs. When she spoke, the red mare scarcely heard. "I feared it."

Silence. The sun beat down.

"I should have told him," Ses gasped suddenly, her voice strangled. "He never knew I knew. So many times I longed to tell Korr all. If I had. . . ."

Jah-lila cut her off quickly, firmly. "No word of yours, however well meant, could have spared him."

The pale mare choked back tears. "I am to blame . . . ," she started.

Jah-lila touched her withers. "Never! Do not shoulder a burden that is Korr's alone. It has lain within his power all these years to speak out, free himself—but always he refused, afraid to confront his past. Till now, at the very end, too late."

At last, the pale mare spoke: "He confided to Jan? Told him of Tek?"

Jah-lila nodded. "Everything. All that he knew."

The pale mare gathered herself, fighting for breath.

"Do not fear," the red mare bade her, "for he will weather it."

Ses set her teeth. "Should we tell the others?"

"Not until your son returns."

The prince's dam opened her eyes. "Should we announce Korr's death?"

Again, the red wych shook her head. "The elders would only declare Jan king. Let us wait. When he returns, he will bring that news with all the rest."

Ses blinked hard. "It will tear the herd apart."

"The herd is stronger than you think," Jah-lila answered, "and primed for change. Your son has seen to that. It was why he had to be their prince, though he can never now become their king."

The pale mare snorted. "Jan's never wanted to be king." Her gaze wandered. "And Lell growing up so reckless wild. . . . All this time you and I have kept our peace. Both held our tongues, praying for Korr to speak, save himself, be healed."

"Can you doubt that had you opened your heart, spoken freely to him, he would have cast you out, and Jan, and your youngest never have been born?"

Ses shook her head and whispered bitterly, "No doubt. But fore-bearing has been hard. So very hard."

Gently, Jah-lila shouldered against her, as much for her own comfort as to lend the other strength. "Never forget that Tek, Jan, and Lell all have their part to play in winning the Hallow Hills."

The red mare stood silent. Above, Lell and the twins were almost out of sight. Below, Tek had reached the other three. The pale mare's sigh was painful, deep.

"He was not so cruel in his youth," she said. "He was magnificent, magnanimous. It was only later, when bitterness consumed him that I could bear him no more. When he grew so cold toward Jan, so heartless of Lell. Before that, for many years, I loved him well."

Jah-lila nodded. "As did I. It is all lost now. Undone by a serpent's sting." Her heart ached. Resolutely, she turned her thoughts ahead. "Let us mourn and ready ourselves," she murmured to Ses. "The end of all is soon to be, and your young Jan-with-the-Moon-upon-his-Brow must lead us there."

World's End

★ 12 ★

Dawn woke him, its greyness paling the air with the first light he had seen in an eternity. Heavy-headed, half-sleeping still, Jan watched the sun emerge from dark caverns housing the netherpath. The fiery stallion leapt onto the steep incline of the starpath, his radiance blazing around him in a burning sphere. Full tilt, he galloped up the endless bowed and rocky path of stars.

The dream passed. Jan found himself lying on a rocky promontory. Sun's featureless disc, inflamed by dawn, floated at eye-level dead ahead. No horizon lay before him, only sky above and mist below. Disoriented, Jan stared. The flat, limitless Salt Waste had vanished, along with its sweltering heat. A cold tang to the air told him he was now much higher.

Sky ahead shone white where the sun burned, paling the stars, but overhead was darkly, intensely blue, almost evening's shade. The trickle of breeze felt thin, the air oddly bodiless. Jan found himself breathing deeply, despite lack of exertion. Below and before him lay nothing but cloud. The narrow promontory on which he lay jutted out into the empty air.

The rock itself was barren black, of a sort he had not seen before. Fused and burned, it appeared as though it had once been thickly liquid, like oozing pitch, then hardened. It felt heavy, utterly solid beneath him, like the substance of skycinders. It echoed faintly, subtly amplifying a low, gentle rustling behind him. Jan realized he had heard it all night as he slept.

Turning his head, the dark unicorn saw the jut on which he lay sloped steeply down to a broad ledge adjoining a sheer cliff face. The ledge narrowed and curved around the cliff on either side. Jan could not see where it led. Down the escarpment's face from above streamed a curtain of water, the stone's featureless blackness visible beneath the swiftly moving glaze.

Reaching the spacious ledge, the transparent fall fanned out, rippling and murmuring, before spilling in wafts of pale spray to the white clouds below. The sheet of water drenching the ledge was less than hoof deep. Jan realized he had felt its coolness against his heels the night before, seen the stars reflected there, slipping over the rim into emptiness below.

Understanding gripped him then that one step farther, or to either side, would have taken him, too, over the edge. He lay on the promontory, breathless, staring at the colorless flow of water washing the cliff. The darkness behind its gleam seemed not solid but empty, holding nothing, not even stars. A pulsebeat or a millennium later, Tek's likeness formed itself before him.

Mottled like the moon she stood, sad seeming, poised as though watching for something beyond her sight. Longing rose in him, and then a tide of nausea. He remembered Korr's words. They clung to him. Salt welled in his throat, choking him. Tek's filmy image rippled in the evermoving glints and shadows of the dark waterfall.

She is my mate! The silent cry rang through his mind. *She cannot be my sister!* His heart knotted. He felt as though it might burst. *The herd will cast me out. And her . . .* His belly lurched. The sky above wheeled. Cold tremors shook him. *What will become of our young?*

For a moment, Tek's image seemed to look straight into him. Brow furrowed, ears up-pricked, she appeared to be listening. Jan flinched and turned away. Shaky with hunger and thirst and the thin air's chill, he gathered his limbs, managed to rise. Despair enveloped him. Before him plunged the abyss.

He stared at the mist swirling far, far below, caught glimpses of dark ridges, all blanketed with the same. When had the Salt Waste given way? He had no idea, no notion how he had come here. It was as though he had stepped from the earth, walked among stars, then crossed back into the world here, among the clouds.

He stood swaying. His shifting weight dislodged a stone. Silently, it plummeted. He found himself thinking, *How effortless, simply to fall . . .*

The clang of hooves roused him. Distinct but distant, they moved at a walk: half a dozen sets, coming from below and around the bend of the broad, wet ledge. The dark unicorn turned, careful, suddenly, of the perilous drop-off. On the black escarpment before him, Tek's image had disappeared. Only darkness loomed behind the falling water.

Above the murmur of the waterfall, sound carried undistorted. Un-

derlying the hooves' faint, rhythmic tramp, the young stallion detected
a thrum of voices. The hard, black rock hummed with the sound, vibrating ever so slightly. Jan felt the sensation as a whisper in his bones.
The hoofbeats neared, climbing toward his level, and the voices clarified. He distinguished words, a chant:

> "Red Halla's royal scouts roved forth,
> Explored the Plain's edge east and north,
> Sought scarlet dragons' Smoking Hills
> Beyond bare Saltlands' bitter rills.
> Four scouts fared forth, fast shoulder-friends,
> Climbed clouded cliffs where world ends,
> And, ragged ranks reduced to three,
> Were warned of wyvern treachery
> By Mélintélinas, lithe queen
> Of dragons languid, long, and lean.
> One scout sped south, strove to return,
> Lest Halla, herd, and homeland burn.
> His fellows fallen, stranded here,
> Have heard no word four hundred year.
> Their daughters' sons bide, yearning yet
> For news of Halla's offspring's get
> That wyrms lie vanquished, Hallows freed
> By valiant victors' distant deed.
> Come outlander with tidings and
> His name shall be the Firebrand.
> More swart than midnight swept of stars,
> The moon athwart his brow bescars.
> One heel whicked white by wyvern stings,
> His flame the final firefall brings.
> We dragons' denmates must remain
> Till Firebrand fetch us home again. . . ."

A line of unicorns appeared around the bend. They were all small-
ish, stocky, with shag thick as the dead of winter. Their beards were
bristling, their fetlocks thickly feathered. Their manes stood up an inch
or two before flouncing to one side. Perhaps half a dozen filed onto the
black, water-washed ledge, all darkish: charcoals, deep blues, an earthen
red. Most were roans, Jan noticed, with a dapple, two brindles.

As they caught sight of him, their words abruptly ceased. Only the
lead unicorn had chanted, the others sounding a harmonious drone. He
was a young stallion, his coat berry-colored, almost maroon, and frosted

with paler hairs. He and his little band stared up at Jan, balanced above them on his slender jut of rock.

"Hail," their leader called up, eyeing him curiously. "Who be you? Be you come for the Congeries?"

The dark prince stared in turn. The last creatures he had expected to encounter so far from home were unicorns.

"Jan," he managed, voice a gluey mumble. Bowing his head made the world reel. "My people call me—"

The words caught in his throat—for he realized that no matter how the herd might hail him, he was not their prince. By rights, Tek should be princess, she who was Korr's secret, firstborn child, his own belovèd mate and the mother of his young. Cold sickness surged in Jan.

"Care!" He heard the other's cry only faintly. "Come down!" As through haze, he saw the maroon start nearer. "Why stand you on the brink?"

The dark unicorn felt his balance right, grasped only then how close to falling he had just come. Unsteadily he picked his way down the rocky slant to the broad, drenched ledge. The young maroon gazed frankly at his flowing mane, lightly fringed heels, at his midnight coat and silky beard. Behind, the others murmured and stared. Jan realized only then that the frayed remnants of Illishar's feather still hung amid his hair.

"I be Oro," his hosts' leader was telling him, bowing in turn, "come for the Congeries. But what manner of unicorn be you, with a falling mane and pelt so dark and fine? What people be these of whom you speak? Whence hail you?"

"I—" Again, Jan faltered. Never before had he hesitated to declare himself Korrson, born of the Vale. Now such an admission appalled him. "Storm drove me across the Salt Waste," he stammered, "from the Plain. . . ."

Not a lie exactly. His head throbbed. The world receded. His knees felt dangerously weak.

"The Plain?" Oro's voice vibrated with sudden urgency. "You hail not of here but from beyond?"

The others buzzed excitedly. Jan could not discern their words above the plash of running water.

"What is this place?" he gasped, locking his legs to keep from falling. "Where have I come?"

Oro cocked his head. "Dragonsholm—or, as those in the time of Halla called it, the Smoking Hills."

Jan raised his head, turned to gaze at the small, shaggy unicorns before him.

THE SON OF SUMMER STARS

"What do you know of Halla," he panted, "ancestral princess of my folk?"

He saw the maroon unicorn's eyes widen.

"The Hallows!" those behind Oro exclaimed. "An he claim ancient Halla, then he hail of the Hallow Hills."

Jan shook his head, careful not to unbalance himself. "Nay, though I have pilgrimmed there. I am from the Vale," he said slowly, "many leagues to the south. There my people settled after Halla's defeat."

Again the hubbub, mixed with cries of consternation. "Defeat? Halla defeated—slain?"

"Not slain," he explained, "but forced to flee." His forelock had fallen into his eyes. He tossed it back. "Within the year, my folk intend . . ."

The sudden hush that fell was deafening. Most of the party started and drew back, some nearly touching the clear curtain of water behind. Only Oro held his ground, staring up wide-eyed at the dark unicorn's brow. Jan saw others' anxious glances, heard excited whispers:

"Come outlander with tidings, and/His name shall be . . ."

"Firebringer," Jan murmured, "so my folk call me."

Still staring, Oro drew near. He quoted softly, "More swart than midnight swept of stars,/The moon athwart his brow bescars. . . ."

He seemed to come to himself, bowed deeply before Jan. His voice, at first uncertain, gained in strength.

"Be most welcome among us, swart Firebrand, outland born, moon-browed. Come below! Sing at our Congeries, whither we, already over-due, now hasten."

To the rear of him, his fellows began ducking hurriedly into the flat darkness behind the shallow waterfall. Jan blinked, stared, unable at first to comprehend what he was seeing. Swiftly, one by one, Oro's band walked straight into the dark, sheer stone—over which the clear water-curtain streamed rippling—and disappeared. The roan maroon was the last to go, backing away from Jan. His joyous words rang ghostly above the water's patter.

"All Dragonsholm must hear your news! Four hundred year have we awaited it, and you."

The Netherpath

★ 13 ★

"We ourselves hail of the Hallow Hills," Oro was saying, "four hundred summer ago."

He trotted alongside Jan. Moments earlier, as the dark stallion had followed the mountain unicorns from the ledge, he had found himself passing not into solid rockface, but through falling water, which sluiced the dust from his pelt, into the narrow opening of a steeply slanting cavern. Promising rest and sustenance below, Oro and his fellows sprang with careless agility along the dim, rocky path—at times less a tunnel than a shaft. Jan followed as nimbly as he could.

"We be the Scouts of Halla," the young maroon continued, "descendants of the original four dispatched to gather news of wyrms when that verminous race first squirmed its way with honey-tongued lies into our own far Hallows. One of the four died, and another departed again to bring word to our waiting princess. We do not know if he succeeded, or what befell if indeed he managed to warn her of wyvern treachery in Dragonsholm before their flight to the Hallow Hills. You say the wyrms defeated Halla? That she fled north to some place called the Vale?"

Jan nodded, weariness weighing him. It was nearly all he could manage simply to stay on his feet.

"Each winter at Congeries we sing of Halla's deeds," Oro informed him, "and of the tragedy which parted our ancestors from her so long ago. We honor the line of Halla yet and hail the far Hallows our true home."

Jan looked at the shaggy maroon trotting just ahead, negotiating the treacherous terrain with ease. "Did neither of your two forebears ever depart?"

Oro shook his head.

"What held them here?"

The other snorted. "Wounds," he answered. "Exhaustion. Then young. Then age." He sighed. "None of us born after have ever seen the far Hallows."

"Have your folk never traveled thither since?" A furrow creased the dark unicorn's brow. "Did none ever seek to find the Hallow Hills?"

"The Saltlands form a daunting barrier," the young maroon replied. "After our progenitors died, none knew the way. Moreover, the shifting steeps to western south be at times impassable."

"Only at times?" Jan felt the furrow on his brow deepen. Though till now too few in number to reoccupy the Hallow Hills, forty generations of his own folk had pilgrimmed there. The resignation of Halla's Scouts to remain so long from their ancestral lands puzzled him. "Then what keeps you here?"

"Our hosts keep us," his escort replied, clearly misunderstanding his meaning entirely. "They have sheltered us since our first forebears came. They subsist a rare long while. Many who greeted Halla's original scouts be living still."

"Hosts?" Jan inquired.

"The red dragons," the maroon-colored roan answered, "who settle these steeps, which be drenched in swirling clouds of their slumbering breath. By their grace, peaks hereabouts hold stable and still, that we need not fear."

The dark unicorn shook his head, not understanding. His companion chatted on.

"All summer we forage the lower scarps, where the bristlepine and the rock lichens green. Each winter we climb to the cavemouth and take the netherpath to a Congeries, where we feed upon the cave straw, the waternuts and milky white mushrooms that flourish below. Many pass the time in the Hall of Whispers, singing of Halla and of other heroes for our own and dragons' ears."

"The red dragons," Jan murmured. Hunger and thirst had fogged his memory. Slowly, he recalled. "They who once cherished our enemies the wyverns before those wyrms rebelled and fled, seeking refuge in our Hallow Hills, which they overran. Before that battle, Halla sent her scouts to consult the dragons' queen, Mélin . . . Mélintél . . ."

"Yea, Queen Mélintélinas," Oro exclaimed. "You do wit of our red dragons, then."

"Too little," the dark prince of the Vale replied. His mouth tasted of cobwebs and dust. "Tell me of them."

"They be vast," the young maroon responded, "and spend their lives

underground, lost in what we deem slumber, but they call contemplation. Betimes they wake, but only rarely do they stir."

Jan turned to study his comrade. "Will I see them?"

Oro sighed and shook his head. "Unlikely. Most of my kind live
whole lives without setting eyes on them, so deep do our dragons lie.
No unicorn could pass into these mountains' fiery heart unscathed."

The dark unicorn considered. "How do you know of them, then?"
he asked his shaggy guide. "And they of you?"

"We hear them," the young stallion replied. "They speak to us at
Congeries. Their words reach us in the Hall of Whispers. All winter
they hark our songs, our tales, while they meditate and dream."

Jan found himself scarcely able to take in his companion's words,
so far had thirst and hunger dulled him. The maroon-colored scout rattled on, and the dark unicorn of the Vale heeded as much as he could.
This descent by what Oro called the netherpath was often precipitous.
The tunnels themselves looked like gigantic worm hollows eaten into
the dense black rock.

Lightwells provided illumination. From time to time, the tunnels
passed beside breaks in the outer wall, allowing views either of sheer
canyons or drifting cloud. Once from such a view, Jan spied distant
fountains of steaming water shooting skyward, accompanied by rumbles
like thunder. The tunnels themselves occasionally shook. As Jan and his
companions descended deeper, the lightwells grew rarer, then altogether
ceased. Soon the only light came from cave lichens, glowing pale shades
of blue and amber, yellow and mauve. In places, small luminous creatures like crickets meandered the walls.

Though Jan frequently heard the soft plash of water, the tunnels
themselves were warm and dry. A gentle heat radiated from the black
rock itself, which carried sounds softly yet distinctly—over great dis-
tances, it seemed. Several times, the party passed cavernous cracks lit
by a shifting, reddish glow. Gazing down into one, Jan saw very far
below a sluggish river of fiery stuff. When he asked what it was, Oro
responded, "Dragonsflood."

The path they traveled, though steep, was well worn. Generations
of hooves had smoothed even so hard a surface as the ringing black
stone. Other tunnels beside which they passed seemed long abandoned,
coated along their interiors with pale, smooth, crystalline stuff. Lichens
did not grow there, nor cave crickets crawl, but the iridescent crystal
conducted light, providing a ghostly glimmer along such tunnels' length.
Passing the first of many, Oro snorted as if catching wind of something
foul.

"Those hollows once were wyvern ways, before our dragons cast them out. Slithery wyrmskin contains a volatile oil which rubs off as wyverns glide, leaving behind a shining trail which hardens over time."

Jan nodded, little needing the other to tell him so. He had discovered as much during his first pilgrimage, when a wyvern queen had lured him underground and tempted him to betray his folk. The wyvern dens underlying the Hallow Hills were thickly coated with such shimmering crystal.

"We do not tread there," Oro added, hurrying past along their own dark, winding path. "Wyrmsoil be flammable, the hardened residue as well. During their sojourn here, the wyrms lay ever in danger of fire."

Jan stumbled, sluggish. The trail led endlessly down and down. Unlike the pliant heels of Oro and his fellows, his own fire-hardened hooves clanged and sparked against the ringing black rock. He marveled at these small unicorns' deft maneuvering along the rocky steeps. They seemed more shaggy, curl-horned sheep than unicorns. He himself had to place each step with utmost care lest he plummet into crags the bottom of which he could not see but which sounded, from the echo of falling scree, interminably deep.

At last the trail leveled off. Before them lay a great cavern, vast in its expanse. Entering, Jan could not discern whence the dusky illumination came. Much of the dimly lit chamber was shrouded in darkness. Oro's companions hurried to either side where, the prince of the Vale realized, a large assembly of other unicorns waited expectantly among the shadows. All faced inward, toward the chamber's heart, and all, so far as Jan was able to discern in the murky light, resembled one another as closely as Oro and his band: small, dark, shaggy brindles, dapples, and roans with halfstanding manes.

His maroon-colored guide was leading him forward, out onto the chamber's wide floor, which, Jan saw, was littered with great pebbles, all roughly round, some smooth as riverstones, some faceted as bees' eyes. Of many colors they gleamed—deep amber, darkest blue, violet so pure it was nearly black, swarthy gold—but reds predominated. Most, especially the larger stones, ranged in hue from dark crimson to wine red, from russet and ocher to vermilion and scarlet. They reminded Jan of the dim, smoldering coals of a fire long perished.

Among the stones lay crystalline pillars, smoothly irregular in shape, all fallen on their sides, some with bulbous knobs at either end. Other crystal forms resembled rotted treestumps, overturned. These squat, pearlescent masses were full of openings. A long trail of them wound snakelike across the chamber's length, most nested one against another, others lying askew. Large, semi-transparent leaves or shells lay everywhere, brittle as fanclams and more numerous than the jewels.

They, too, were mostly red, looked almost like enormous fish scales. Blearily, Jan's eyes swept the trove, unable to take it in.

"What place is this?" he mumbled, stumbling to a stop as Oro halted at the chamber's heart.

Magnified, the echo of his voice leapt away from him on every side, less jarring than a shout, but just as penetrating. Jolted, Jan listened to the sudden sound's reverberations, already dying. Leaning near, the maroon stallion scarcely breathed, though the prince of the Vale heard him distinctly as mothwings beating against a leaf.

"The queen's vault," he answered, "known as the Hall of Whispers. Peace, now. I must announce you."

They stood among the jewels and shards and crystal boles, very near a massive oblong boulder. One end formed a great flattened dome. The other tapered to a ragged, broken point. Two smooth, symmetrical hollows gaped from the translucent dome, one on either side of the tapering cone. At dome's crest, between the hollows, dipped an oval depression. It was filled with clear fluid, sparkling though absolutely still, its dark, reflective surface smooth as skin. Jan gazed longingly at the well-spring. His parched throat burned.

"Hail," Oro beside him said, without so much as raising his voice. Nevertheless, his words filled the chamber. Those assembled at the chamber's periphery responded, "Hail."

Each must have spoken no louder than a murmur, yet the collective ring was strong and clear. Jan thought he detected other voices, too— deeper and more resonant than unicorns'—lost among the rest.

"I beg you forbear our latecoming," the young maroon continued. "Rockfall day past delayed our climb. Then, just as my fellows and I reached Streaming Ledge hard by the veiled ingress to the netherpath, we met a stranger on the brink of dawn."

Again the echoing murmur, curious, even excited now. The ranks ranging the vast hall's edge shifted and stirred. This time Jan could not distinguish words, but once more he sensed, blended amongst the others, strangely timbred voices which were not of his own kind.

"By me he stands," Oro announced, his timing and cadence clearly that of a singer, "an outlander called Firebrand, with the moon-marked brow. He comes from beyond, over Saltland and Plain, bearing news of lost Halla, our sovereign princess, and the wretched wyverns who wrested from her the Hallow Hills."

The uproar that greeted these words was deafening: shouts of surprise, exclamations, disbelief, calls for Oro to explain. Jan flattened his ears, overwhelmed by the rolling waves of sound. Beside him, the young maroon stood calmly, undismayed—perhaps even a little pleased—by the upheaval his news had occasioned. An instant later, the tumult vanished as voices infinitely fuller and stronger than any unicorn's spoke, extinguishing all other clamor.

"Welcome," the first of these new, resonant voices said, and others echoed it. "Welcome. Welcome . . ."

The words seemed to come from all directions. Casting his gaze, the dark unicorn strove to locate their source.

"Welcome to Dragonsholm, Firebrand." A fourth voice spoke. Others chorused, "Firebrand. Firebrand . . ."

Their pure, even tones filled the hall like the calling of oncs or the belling of hounds, richly pleasurable to harken. Jan felt no fear of these unseen speakers, wherever they might be. All were female, he sensed. The timbre of their voices, so much more powerful than those of his own folk, somehow told him so. He sensed, too, that regardless of how near they sounded, in reality they lay many leagues distant, the black rock carrying their words to him and his to them.

"Hail, red dragons," he answered, "holders of the Smoking Hills, hosts to the Scouts of Halla, my people's long-lost kin."

Around him, the hushed unicorns stirred, ears up-pricked, listening. Oro stood no longer at his side, Jan realized. He glimpsed him just joining the edge of the crowd. The prince of the Vale stood alone by the great crystalline boulder with the pool in its crown.

"You are called Firebrand," a dragon voice said.

Another, speaking just on the heels of the first, asked, "Are you the one?"

"The one of whom the Scouts have spoken," still another voice continued, "destined to lead them back to their Hallow Hills?"

"You have traveled far," still others added. "You must be weary."

"I am Aljan," the dark unicorn answered, and indeed, he felt nearly mazed with weariness, unsure how many hours or days he had gone without water and food. "My folk call me Firebringer, and Moonbrow." But not prince. He would not tell them the folk of the Vale called him prince. "It is they I mean to lead in retaking the Hallow Hills. As for the Scouts of Halla, I cannot say."

"Tell us this tale," the dragon voices responded.

"The tale of you."

"The tale of your journey."

"All season lies before us."

"It must be a wondrous tale."

Jan felt his knees growing weak. The dark room spun. He heard murmurs of concern from those in the shadows, saw Oro start toward him.

"But sip first," the voices of dragons invited. The maroon stallion halted, hesitated. The dragons lilted on.

"Sip."

"Sip of the queen's pool beside you."

Turning, Jan tried to focus on the natural basin of water in the huge white boulder's crown. Oddly, though its surface lay perfectly still, it seemed to bend and shift somehow, as though currents beneath its surface created eddies. As he bent to drink, the depression's shallow bottom appeared to recede from him. He caught glimpses of comets and suns, of unicorns hurtling across a field of stars—or was it a starlit Plain?

Jan shook his head. He closed his eyes, sure that fatigue was causing him to dream. His mouth touched the water, and he was surprised to find it warm, not cool. As the water filled his mouth, the fantastic notion came to him that he was drinking stars. He swallowed once. The pleasantly tepid fluid seemed slightly thicker than water, its taste mildly acerbic, yet at the same time like balm. He had prepared to draw in long drafts, but strangely, after the first sip, he felt entirely satisfied.

❦

He had been speaking, he knew, for a very long time. Jan felt wholly detached, free of hunger, thirst, and fatigue. Time seemed suspended. The sea of figures before him shifted and changed, Oro's the only one he was able to distinguish with certainty. His own voice, filling the vast, dimly lit chamber, sounded unlike himself, like the voice of another, a singer's cant from the one with whom he had traveled upon the Plain, the one with the star-flung coat. What had been his name? *Summer Stars*.

The dark unicorn had no idea how long he had spoken, telling the unseen dragons and the shadowy Scouts before him everything about his people's history, how lying wyrms had defeated Halla four hundred summers gone, driven her and her small surviving band from the Hallow Hills. How they had come upon the Vale after long wanderings and taken refuge, there to grow strong and numerous again, in preparation for recapturing the Hollow Hills.

He spoke of his own life, how he had been reared by the king of the unicorns and, in his youth, faced a wyvern queen in her den. His hooves now struck sparks, his horn, hardened by wyvern sorcery, grown keen and hard enough to pierce even the toughest wyvern bone. He had dwelt half a year with two-footed firekeepers, learning the secret of their flame. His folk all hailed him Firebringer. Forging alliances with gryphons and pans, he had made his herd proof against wyvern stings. This coming spring, they would leave the Vale and march into wyvern-held Hallow Hills to retake them in Alma's name.

He spoke of the king of the Vale run mad and of pursuing him across the Plain. He spoke of his mate, pied Tek the warrior mare, a singer, wondrously fair, firstborn child to the late king who, serpent-stung to death upon the Waste, left the Vale in his daughter's charge. Queen of the unicorns she reigned, though she did not yet know it. Mother to twin heirs, a filly and foal. The only thing he did not reveal was his own parentage, never naming himself Son-of-Korr or prince. Despite his oddly calm, loosened-tongued state, he could not bring himself even now to face the horror spat at him by dying Korr, that he and his mate shared a single sire.

The voices of dragons spoke no more. The Scouts of Halla listened rapt. When he spoke of Tek, they cheered. Jan had no awareness of the passage of time, speaking on as in a dream. Neither night nor day penetrated the depths of Queen Mélintélinas's Hall. Figures among the crowd came and went as he spoke. He felt no need for food or drink or sleep. At times, he realized, he had ceased to speak, and the Scouts of Halla spoke, or sang, or chanted their own history: the journey of their four ancestors over the Plain, across the Salt Waste to the Smoking Hills.

Here, from Queen Mélintélinas, they had learned the wyverns' secret past: that wyrms had stolen dragonsfire, seeking to seize these dark steeps for their own, only to be driven off at last by the red firedrakes who once had sheltered them. The wyrms had wandered then, surviving the Salt Waste and the wide grass Plain until they slithered into the Hallow Hills and lied their way into a truce with the unicorns who dwelt there—all the while planning to betray them and seize their lands as once they had striven to seize the red dragons'.

The voices of Oro and his fellows sounded through the cavern in long, resonant notes. While one singer chanted a melody, four or six others droned a background chord which changed as the song progressed. These airs—some solemn, but many lively—filled the chamber's vast expanse. Jan marveled how the great hall enhanced sound and channeled it, so it seemed, to all the depth and breadth of the Smoking Hills. He imagined his words and those of the singers reaching out along all the netherpaths to wash against the ears of dragons slumbering, or perhaps listening, far underground.

At last he became aware that all voices had ceased, his own and those of Oro and the rest. A silence pervaded the dusky chamber that was neither cold nor ominous. Jan felt suspended still, untouched by thirst, hunger, or fatigue. Once more Oro stood beside him near the great crystalline boulder. The shaggy throng of mountain unicorns that once had kept their distance had moved closer now. A new voice spoke, one the dark unicorn had not heard before: a dragon's voice.

"Well sung," she sighed, and the echoes whispered, "Sung. Sung . . ."

A murmur passed through the crowd. Jan heard gasps of "The queen! The queen!"

"Aye," she answered. "You have wakened me, and the song your words have woven has entered my dreams."

The dark unicorn heard Oro's delighted, breathless laughter, saw playful nips and gleeful chivvying exchanged among many around him, though all seemed mindful of decorum, at pains to maintain a respectful hush.

"Of one singer I would hear more," said the dragon queen, her strange voice penetrating yet mellifluous, "the outlander who calls himself Aljan. Oro, who escorted him on the netherpath, guide him, I pray you, to my chamber below."

Jan sensed a sudden change in the hall. The unicorns around him froze, caught in their breath with expressions of uncertainty, even alarm. He himself felt nothing, neither terror nor joy. Beside him, Oro tensed.

"Great queen," he began, as if straining for calm.

"Peace," she bade him, almost gently. "Has he not drunk the dragonsup? Would I send for him if to do so would bring him harm?"

Her words seemed to calm the Scouts, though glances still darted among the company. The young maroon swallowed.

"And I, great queen?" he asked, nearly choking as he glanced at the shallow, fluid-filled depression in the dome of the huge crystalline boulder beside which he and the dark prince stood. "Am I, too, to sup?"

"Not yet," she answered. Jan sensed amusement just beneath her tone, saw Oro heave a soundless sigh of relief. "Do but lead him as far as safely you may, then instruct him the way to journey's end."

The words rang briefly in the still chamber. A moment of silence followed. Then quickly, quietly, the crowd began to disperse. The scores, perhaps even hundreds of small, shaggy unicorns moved near silently, melting back into the shadows to exit the great hall, through what egress the dark unicorn could not see. Soon he discerned from an almost indistinguishable change in the soft echoes in the chamber that he and Oro now stood alone.

"We must depart," the maroon beside him breathed. "First we must climb a little, and then descend a very long way for you to reach the queen."

The roan stallion led Jan to the far side of the immense chamber.

The dark prince spied an inclined path leading up the wall toward a tunnel above. Oro started up. Jan followed, pausing in the tunnel's entry to gaze back down at the vast chamber below. The scattering of huge jewels, the pale, pillar-like shapes all lying fallen, the great, reddish scales, and the enormous oblong, irregular boulder with the fluid-filled depression in its crown all altered suddenly in the dark unicorn's view.

They no longer appeared to lie in random, orderless scatter. They were, he realized, the scales and bones of some great animal, its flesh long gone, its spine forming a winding trail across the floor. Bones of four great limbs splayed to either side. Toppled ribs lay in between, among the jewels and scales which must have adorned the creature's hide. Its skull, Jan perceived with a start, was the oblong boulder, resting jaw downward, empty eye sockets the symmetrical, gaping hollows. The little pool gleamed darkly in the—apparently natural—depression upon its brow. Jan could not guess the source of the liquid forming there. Gasping, he gazed at the huge reptilian skeleton below.

"What is that?" he managed. "Whose bones?"

His guide glanced at him quizzically. "The bones of Mélintélinas, late queen of the red dragons. Did I not tell you this be her lair?"

"Late . . . ?" Jan shook his head, trying to clear it. He felt stunned, stupid still. "But is not Mélintélinas the queen who has summoned me?"

Oro shook his head, turning to travel on. "Nay. That be her daughter, the new queen, Wyzásukitán."

The Dragon Queen

★ 14 ★

"The Hall of Whispers served as the old queen's audience hall," Oro panted, champing to moisten his mouth in the hot, dry air. "It be sacred to the dragons, but we have always stood welcome there. Our hosts tell us our Congeries honors the memory of the queen they mourn still."

"Mélintélinas," Jan murmured. "To whom Halla sent envoys four hundred autumns past?"

The other nodded. "The same."

"When did she die?" the dark unicorn asked. "I thought firedrakes lived centuries."

Oro nodded. "Queen Mélintélinas reigned twelve hundred year and passed into eternity scarcely a hundred winter past. Her successor, Wy-zásukitán, be young—as yet unpaired—but very skilled in dragon-lore. . . ."

The walls of the tunnels through which they descended grew warmer, their dull golden glow becoming brighter. Wafts of steam curled by, passing in gentle gusts. Jan was aware of the heat, but it did not truly reach him. He felt no flush beneath the skin, no prick of sweat. His heart did not pound, nor his breath labor. It seemed to him he could embody the very heat of the sun and suffer no ill.

Beside him, Oro's thick roan coat ran with sweat. His ribs heaved. His speech came short. Sometimes he stumbled. At last he halted, staring ahead down the sloping path. Jan halted beside him. The fog had dissipated. Below them lay a lake of fire. Air shimmered above it. Beneath, liquid spurts of yellowish white mingled with sluggish swirls of sunset orange and molten red. A series of small, black islands, very closely spaced, formed a kind of path across—if one were very sure of foot.

"I can fare no farther," Oro gasped. "Heat fells me. You, though, be shielded by the dragonsup. Forge on across the cinder isles. The hold of Wyzásukitán lies beyond the brimstone sea."

Jan bowed to his host, seeking words of thanks, but found himself unexpectedly tongue-tied.

"Farewell for the present, Scout," he heard himself say at last. "I trust to rejoin you shortly."

Oro also bowed, very low. "Fare you well, Firebrand," he answered gravely. "I and my folk await your return."

Abruptly, he swung and stumbled back up the trail. Jan watched the dark roan stagger, reeling almost, then rally and press on. Jan watched him disappear as the trail rose, curving away and passing into other, higher chambers. Oro's halting hoofbeats gradually receded. Motionless, Jan listened until they faded at last. Then he turned and headed down to the lake of fire.

The air about it shuddered with heat, the burning fluid Oro had once called dragonsflood, fiercely incandescent. The feather in his hair smoked slightly, fragrantly. Yet, he felt no fiery blast as he crossed the black and cindery shore. Near its edge, the glowing brimstone had darkened and solidified into a fragile crust. A great gust of heat shook the ground, rumbling like the breath of some immense creature beyond the subterranean lake of fire. Its sun-bright surface wrinkled, rippling.

When the tremor had passed, Jan stepped out onto the first of the minuscule islands. Its pitted surface grated and clanged beneath his heels. Little showers of sparks fell into the radiant substance of the lake and disappeared. The dark unicorn moved cautiously, sometimes retracing his steps. The lake stretched on, its low, dark ceiling lost in shadow. Such must be the birthplace of the sun, he mused, whence mares of smoke and stallions of fire blazed forth to charge heaven.

He saw lake's edge ahead. At first it seemed but a far distant darkness upon the gleaming surface, but as he approached, Jan realized it was neither a cluster of islands nor floating slag, but the limit of the brimstone sea. He stepped from the last island onto the cinder shore, which rose gently toward a cavernous opening in the wall of rock ahead. The ceiling soared higher here, the gigantic cavern mouth smoothly oval in shape.

Another glow lit the chamber beyond, steady and reddish. Jan walked toward it, up the beach. Pale smoke trailed through the crest of the entryway in a steady, tendriled stream. Another great sighing, accompanied by rumbling and shaking. The smoky mist redoubled. The dark unicorn halted till the quake subsided, then moved forward again.

The black, pitted pebbles crunched and shifted beneath his cloven heels. He reached the great entryway.

"Welcome, Firebrand," the creature before him sighed. "For you I gladly suspend my contemplation. Enter and be welcome. I have awaited your coming four hundred years."

※

The dragon queen sprawled, inestimably vast, filling the great chamber before Jan. She was long and sinuous and covered with jewels. With a start, the dark unicorn noticed huge leathery wings, red as the rest of her, draping her back. Puzzlement made him frown. Living as they did, so far underground, he would never have imagined the red dragons to be wingèd. The old lays mentioned no powers of flight, and the remains of the old queen, Mélintélinas, had borne no wings.

Wyzásukitán looked at him. Her head was wedge-shaped, the muzzle long and slim, with flaring nostrils through which her hazy breath steamed. Two long mustachios, like those catfishes bear, sprouted below each nostril. They floated fluidly on the air as the dragon moved and turned her head. Her ears were slim, like gryphons' ears. A row of spiky ridges ran from the top of her head down the back of her neck, along the spine and tail to the tip, which ended in a flattened wedge.

Her body was covered by a myriad of ovate, interlocking scales which shimmered, reflecting the light of the lake of fire. Innumerable round and faceted stones encrusted her scaly skin. Of every color, though red predominated, they caught and held the light, burning like distant fires. Her massive hind limbs bore immense, pardlike claws. Her forelimbs, smaller and more delicately made, sported taloned toes of a size to crush a unicorn in a single snatch. Her breath moving through her lungs and throat did so with a hollow rushing like surf.

Upon her forehead, above the great ruby eyes, a circular depression lay, like a shallow bowl. In size and shape, it exactly resembled the slight hollow in the enormous skull of the late queen, from which he had recently sipped. The natural dish in Wyzásukitán's brow gleamed, a dark, clear liquid pooling there. The firedrake kept her head perfectly level, he noted, as if on guard against spilling the precious contents. Jan bowed to her.

"Hail, Wyzásukitán, queen of red dragons," he said.

"Hail, Aljan Firebringer," Wyzásukitán replied. Despite the harsh susurration, her voice was surprisingly melodious. Her steaming breath smelled of resin and spice. "Before her end, my mother spoke of your coming."

"What word did Queen Mélintélinas say of me?" Jan asked, surprised. Oddly, he felt no fear.

Wyzásukitán exhaled another cloud of fragrant breath and lowered her head, turning it slightly, only very slightly, to one side. "She told me one of your kind would come from beyond, bearing news of my great enemy, Lynex."

The dark prince nodded. "Lynex the wyvern king was driven from the Smoking Hills by your mother, Queen Mélintélinas, four hundred winters gone." Jan recited what he knew. "He and his folk wandered the Plain until they reached the Hallow Hills, at that time homeland to my folk. Lynex inveigled his way into the good graces of my people's then-king, despite protests by his daughter, the princess Halla. When the wyverns slithered into limestone caves hard by my people's sacred mere, the Mirror of the Moon, Halla, her suspicions roused, sent scouts to find the Smoking Hills whence these white wyrms had originally come. Her scouts parleyed with your mother the winter's length. She kept two here and sent the third back with warning of the wyverns' treacherous ways. . . . But surely Halla's scouts informed your people of all these things," Jan broke in on himself, "when first they arrived four hundred years ago."

The huge dragon nodded, her breath swirling about her. It rose toward the chamber's distant ceiling. Jan guessed it eventually reached the surface of the hills to drift in the dense fog that gave the region its name.

"Yea," Wyzásukitán answered. "So they did. And the two who remained here at my mother's behest became founders of the line that dwells here yet. Their chanting fills our meditations with beautiful song. We have lain very still these last four hundred years, harkening it." One shoulder moved: perhaps a shrug. "In that regard," she breathed, "your Scouts do for us much as the wyrms once did."

"The wyverns were singers?" Jan exclaimed.

Again the red dragon nodded. "They patrolled our dens, kept them free of vermin. They ate our dead. But we prized them for their songs and the stories that they told, which nourished our dreams."

"They call themselves your cousins," the dark prince told her.

Wyzásukitán snorted. Her breath swirled. "They are no cousins of ours."

"What do the red dragons dream?" Jan asked.

The dragon queen sighed. "Much in the heavens and under the earth. We live a long time, by your counting, and have no need to hurry about our affairs. Much time we spend in contemplation, envisioning what will come and what is and what has already passed—but I stray. I was

asking of Lynex. We have heard no news of him since your late princess's scouts arrived. Tell me what befell after the one who departed
returned to the Hallow Hills."

Jan nodded. "He warned Halla of wyvern treachery. But too late.
The wyrms had already bred. Come spring, they attacked, killing most
of the herd before driving Halla's small band of survivors away. These
wandered until they found the Vale, which has sheltered us for forty
generations. But our time there is almost out. My folk mean to return
to the Hallow Hills within the year, to wrest them back from Lynex and
his crew. We are told he lives and rules the wyverns still. In the way
of his kind, he has grown more heads than the single one with which
he started. We hear he is seven-headed now."

"And seven times more treacherous, to be sure," mused Wyzásukitán.

"Why do the red dragons hate the white wyrms so?" Jan ventured.
"You lived in harmony so long. What trespass caused you to cast them
out?"

"Harmony would be too strong a term," the dragon queen replied,
voice darkening. "Suffice to say we dwelled without enmity until the
advent of Lynex. Lynex was different from other wyrms. His tail bore
a poison sting, unlike the blunt tips of his fellows. He used this barb to
hunt live prey, including his own kind. He ventured aboveground to
stalk the shag-haired goats and bred with others of his kind to produce
more sting-tailed wyverns, killing those of his broods that bore no
stings."

Wyzásukitán turned her head, remembering.

"He and his folk conspired many seasons, while we slept unaware
of the plots fomenting around us. Lynex led his sting-tailed wyrms to
kill or drive away all other wyverns. But we suspected naught until
Lynex and his followers began to prey upon my people's pups, carrying
off eggs from the nest and stinging to death the newly hatched, then
dragging away their bones."

The firedrake's eyes smoldered, her beautiful voice growing tighter,
more harsh.

"Lynex declared himself king of wyrms and cousin to dragons. Master of fire he styled himself, porting coals about in a golden bowl. My
mother awoke at last and roused her kith to drive the wyrms away.
Lynex fled, and all his poisonous tribe. We trusted winter's cold aboveground to kill them—but they huddled about their king's firebowl and
escaped to trouble your tribe as once they had troubled my own. My
dam held herself responsible for this wrong. It weighed upon her, and

upon my people. Four hundred years have we lain in contemplation since, considering how best to fashion a remedy."

"Remedy?" Jan asked. "Have you discovered one?"

The dragon queen turned. "To understand that, Firebrand," she answered, "you must understand my kind." Again she shrugged, at once both languid and restless. "Behold my wings. My mother was already well into her prime, as we dragons count time, her wings long shed, when your late princess's scouts arrived."

The dark prince listened as Wyzásukitán's folded wings rustled softly, shifting.

"She had flown her mating flight a hundred years previous and would lay eggs from that tryst to the end of her days. She had no wings anymore, nor had any other of her kith, for as you may know, among my kind, only the queen and her consort ever breed. My mother's consort had long since flown. They always do, after the nuptial flight. Where a queen's consort flies, we do not know, for none ever return. We are a female race. A male is born among us only once in a thousand years."

Before him, the great dragon's voice warmed, gentled.

"They are black, these firedrakes, most beautiful to behold. My own consort is so much younger than I," murmured Wyzásukitán. "My mother hatched him only shortly before she died. He will not be ready to fly for three centuries yet. So darksome fair, he will make the perfect sire to all my progeny. My wings, how they ache from disuse! They are ready now, and I long to try them."

Realization jolted Jan. "Your . . . your consort," he stammered. "He is your sib? Your own mother's child?"

The dragon queen flexed her massive, bat-form wings. "Of course. It is always thus among dragons."

A bitter taste rose in Jan's mouth. He thought of Tek, his late sire's own uncounted daughter, Korr's first, unspoken child. Wary of offending the dragon queen, Jan swallowed hard. Yet such a union as she described was unconscionable among his own folk, even if his and Tek's pledge had been undertaken innocently, neither knowing Tek's secret parentage. Yet once done, it could never be undone: Dhattar and Aiony were the living proof. Shaken, Jan found his tongue.

"You say Lynex, too, bred with his own kin?" The thought repulsed him.

Again Wyzásukitán nodded. "As did your own scouts upon their arrival here."

"What?" cried Jan, shocked. "How do you mean?"

Ever so subtly, the dragon queen cocked her head. "There were only two," she answered quietly, "two that remained. They have had no contact with others of your folk these four hundred years. How did you imagine they had multiplied if at first sib had not pledged with sib?"

Jan's mind reeled. He felt his knees lock. How was it he had not deduced something so obvious? Inbreeding explained the striking resemblance among all Oro's folk: modest stature, stocky build, dark roan or dapple coats, those odd, half-standing manes. Jan shook himself, staggered. Numbly, he strove to collect himself, to bring his awareness back to the firedrake's lair. He opened his mouth to speak. But the dragon queen spoke first.

"Your thoughts return to your Vale, I see," she said, "and to those you cherish there. Come." She bowed her head to the chamber's floor. "Gaze into me, and you will see what is and is to be."

Jan breathed deeply, trying to clear his head. Shaken still, he approached the dragon queen. Her mouth was easily great enough to engulf him in a single snap, yet he felt no fear, only his own turmoil roiling within. Despite her reptilian shape, he doubted somehow that dragons ate flesh. Steaming, her fragrant breath enveloped him. Her enormous, ruby-colored eye watched him as he leaned to peer into the dark pool of her brow.

The King's Uncounted Daughter

★ 15 ★

Tek stood in the entryway to the cave, gazing off across the Vale. Equinox was upon them. Brief summer had run its course. Soon days would last shorter than the nights. The tang of fall seasoned the air, though the grass grew green, not yet goldening, and evenings had not turned chill. Tek watched the long shadow of the Vale's sunward side advancing toward the far sunlit slope. Unicorns still grazed the hillsides, or ramped and frolicked on the valley floor.

The pied mare stood keenly aware that all she surveyed she beheld for the last time in season. Never again would she gaze upon the Vale on summer's ending day, autumn's eve. Come spring—whether or not her mate had returned—she and the herd must depart for the Hallow Hills. The creeping shadows overtaking the Vale advanced. Tek sighed, longing for Jan, heart filled with something akin to despair. Neither he nor she had expected his absence to stretch so long. Jan's chasing his crazed sire had only achieved what Korr had striven toward all along: to part her from her mate and him from her.

The pied mare set her teeth. She loathed the dark king with all her fury. Though as a filly and young half-grown she had enjoyed his high favor—exactly why, she had never known—she had always mistrusted him, kept her distance. About the time of his son's initiation, she and Jan had become shoulder-friends, and still the dark king had smiled his approval. Only when Jan had grown old enough to eye the mares had the king's mood inexplicably darkened—though never toward Tek, only toward his son. She had steered well clear of Korr then, never dallying with the young prince before his father's eyes.

Still, she never could have imagined the king's rage upon her return from the Summer Sea when he learned of the sacred pledge she and

Jan had shared, a vow unshakable in Alma's eyes. The king had railed wildly against her then. When her burgeoning belly made plain that she was in foal, the dark stallion's ravings tipped into madness, and he had sought her death. Fleeing the Vale, she had taken refuge with her then-outcast dam, Jah-lila, who had used sorcery to defend her and midwive her young.

Again the pied mare breathed deep, the bare hint of a smile quirking her mouth. How the world had turned since then: now Korr was the hated outcast, Jah-lila the honored insider, advisor to the prince. Tek herself had returned in triumph, her eminence second only to that of her mate. Quietly, she studied the darkening Vale, which she had ruled all summer as prince's regent. The herd trusted her, gladly followed her word. She had won their respect on her own merits. That she was daughter to the red wych and dam to the prince's heirs only enhanced her station.

Tek's smile slipped, faded. A frown of frustration wrinkled her brow. Where was he? Where was her belovèd Jan? Weeks had passed since the scouts she had sent had brought back any useful news. At first, when summer had been new, she had waited. But when, after three days her mate had not returned, she had dispatched runners into the Pan Woods to look for him and his quarry. Her foster sisters, the young pans Sismoomnat and Pitipak, had set forth as well. All had returned with tales of Korr's senseless terrorizing of the Wood. It had taken weeks for Tek to reparley the peace with all the goatling tribes.

She had realized then that Jan dared not return unsuccessful. The goatlings expected—indeed had demanded, and she confidently promised—that the dark marauder be captured and punished for his trespass against the unicorn's allies. The pied mare shook her head. She had never considered herself a diplomat. She had none of Jan's glib grace, his quick understanding. Still, she had evidently succeeded, for the pans had held their truce and agreed to wait the outcome of the prince's quest.

Meanwhile, the prince's mate had learned, Jan had followed his sire onto the Plain. Again, Tek tasted despair. That limitless expanse gave Jan everywhere to search, Korr anywhere to hide. The herd's lack of ties with the Plain's few, scattered wanderers troubled her as well. For centuries her own folk had hated and feared these wild unicorns, believing them outcasts and rebels from the Vale. Tek knew differently, yet still felt the greatest unease at Jan's venturing among such unknown folk. Outside the Ring of Law, who knew what customs they might keep? That the Plain was also home to great, banded pards and savage grasscats filled her with dread.

Despite all dangers, Tek had found no dearth of volunteers to scout the Plain. The first to set out had brought back nothing. The Mare's Back was simply too vast for outlanders to track either friend or foe. She instructed her next scouts to seek out Plainsdwellers and ask their aid. But, as she had feared, the ones most of her own folk still stubbornly called "Renegades" shied clear of dwellers of the Vale—and again her scouts returned thwarted.

Her resolve only strengthened, she had called on Jan's and her own shoulder-companion Dagg to lead the next search, and this expedition had at last borne fruit. Dagg had encountered Plainsdwellers, and though he clearly lost no love for ones he considered Ringbreakers or descendants of such, he had approached politely as many times as needed to persuade them. In the end, he had learned what he had come to learn: that Korr had rampaged across the Plain. The Free People called him the dark destroyer.

Jan, too, apparently because of his similar coloring, had at first been mistaken for Korr and been shunned. At length, he had managed to gain the trust of a party of Renegades even as Dagg and his fellows now had done, and convinced them that he sought to contain the mad stallion, not repeat his crimes. Dagg had learned of the long chase Korr had led his friend, how Jan had sought and received aid of a seer or singer known as Alma's Eyes. But when Dagg had eventually caught up with this one, the young prince had already left him, vanished away into the Salt Waste on the trail of the king.

"It was odd," Dagg had said. "When first I saw him in profile, by moonlight, my heart lifted with joy. I thought he was Jan. They have the same legs and frame, the same muzzle and mane. Their voices, even some of their gestures, echo in the most uncanny way."

The dappled warrior had snorted then.

"Of course, by day, none could mistake the two. The seer is an evening blue speckled with stars. His manner of speech is that of the Plain. He is older than Jan, not quite Korr's age, and spent ten days in Jan's company."

Again the dappled warrior had snorted, remembering.

"After their parting, so I gather, this Alma's Eyes went among his people singing the history of Jan and the Vale. Jan, it seems, recounted a number of our lays to him, which allayed much of the Plainsdwellers' mistrust. Korr's acts clearly had stirred much ill feeling against our folk."

Dagg shrugged, sidled, seeming almost chagrined.

"I believe the links Jan forged during his sojourn upon the Plain will serve us well come spring. Jan, so it seems, made a fair enough singer to catch the ear of this Alma's Eyes, who recounts nothing like our own formal singers of the Vale—and yet, a kind of wild beauty haunts his song. His folk admire him, and through him, Jan."

Tek laughed quietly to herself, thinking of her mate. He had always revered her singer's gift, declaring himself reft of any skill. Yet she had always suspected he, too, harbored the bent. How he loved the old lays, remembered them flawlessly, remarking even the slightest variation from one recitation to the next. He spoke with ease before even the greatest throng. What if until now, his musical nature had manifested solely through fiercely expressive dancing? She had always known him to be as much a singer as he was a warrior, a peacemaker, a dancer, and a prince.

Someone moved beside her on the slope before the cave. She started, remembering belatedly that she shared this stony spot with Dagg. The dappled warrior moved closer to her. She did not turn her head, the image of his robust frame, pale eyes, grey mane, and yellow coat firmly imprinted on her mind. The grey spots flocking his withers and hindquarters thickened into stockings on all four legs. He rubbed shoulders with her companionably. She leaned, shouldering him in turn. Quietly, unselfconsciously, Dagg voiced her greatest fear:

"What if he does not return? What if Jan does not appear by spring? What then?"

She shuddered, sighed. "We must honor our pact with the gryphons regardless. We must leave the Vale and press on to the Hallow Hills."

"The herd will follow you, and gladly," Dagg told her.

Tek shrugged, smiled. "In Jan's name."

Here Dagg surprised her. He shook his head. "For your own sake. You are a great warrior. Our folk would charge with you into the wyverns' jaws for that alone."

She felt a little thrill of gratitude, of pride, tried not to show it. "Now that Jan's blood makes us all proof against their stings, such a charge should prove easier."

Dagg chuckled softly. "I doubt you delude yourself thinking our task will be accomplished with ease."

"First we must see the herd safe through winter—Alma grant us another mild one, I pray, for the sake of our fillies and foals." Tek frowned, thinking. "Kindling marks the opening of winter, and Quenching its end."

She gazed down at the valley floor where, in the lengthening shadows of evening, beneath a blue, brilliant sky, her twin offspring ramped whinnying along with Lell and with Dagg's firstborn, Culu. Barely a year and a half old, the suckling foal sported forequarters of intense, true yellow shading to brilliant salmon at the rump, exactly the hue of the sundog for which he was named. The pan sisters Sismoomnat and Pitipak chased the four colts amid much whistling and squealing. Ringing their swirl, Jah-lila, Ses, and Dagg's mate, Ryhenna, stood, shooing stray tag-players back into bounds.

Tek eyed the coppery mare, who, like her own dam, had been born outside the Vale to a hornless race, but who, upon joining the herd, had drunk of the sacred waters of the moon's mere deep within the Hallow Hills and been transformed into a unicorn. Ryhenna's coppery coat exactly matched the hue of her standing mane. Her tail fell full and silky. Like Jah-lila, she was beardless, lacking tassels to the tips of her small, neat ears and feathery fringe to her fetlocks. Instead of being cloven, her hooves were solid rounds.

Yet despite such differences, Ryhenna had been welcomed into the Vale even as Jah-lila now found welcome, hailed as Jan's savior for aiding his escape from her own captors, the two-footed firekeepers. Ryhenna's transformation had been celebrated in myth and lay, her copper-colored horn admired, and with her mate's aid, she had set about learning the ways of a warrior with a will. Jan had declared her mistress of fire, and she presided over Kindling and Quenching, the herd's newly created ceremonies at winter's beginning and end, striking the sparks from which all the torches of winter would burn.

"By winter's end, before we march," Tek said to Dagg, "we must all harden our heels and horns that we may smite the wyrms' bony breastplates without shattering our weapons."

Dagg nodded. "Come spring, it will be time."

The game below had broken up. Tek watched the figures moving up the hill toward her, colts and fillies frisking still, the mares moving more leisurely. Lell pranced alongside Sismoomnat, the elder of the two pan sisters. The pied mare caught a snatch of their conversation as they ambled by, Lell tossing the milk mane from her eyes, Sismoomnat resting one forelimb on the dark amber filly's withers with a trace of a smile. Tek, too, smiled. Lell reminded her more than a little of Jan as a colt: hot-headed and passionate, fiercely intelligent but ruled by her heart.

"His wings were broad and green, and his voice so lilting sweet. He vowed to return to us, come spring, and accompany us to the Vale."

Sismoomnat nodded gravely as Lell halted and began to graze. The young pan bent to pull and collect grass seed in one upturned, hairless paw.

"You must introduce him to me when he returns," she murmured. Tek turned her attention back downslope. They were discussing the gryphon Illishar. Still. The pied mare marveled at it, that the green-fletched wingcat could have so captured Lell's curiosity. Nothing seemed to distract her from speculating when he would return, expounding the magnificence of his flight and the sweetness of his song. She would prattle thus to any who would harken until their ears well and nearly withered. Tek regarded Dhattar and Aiony, accompanied by Pitipak, the younger pan. The three of them had begun another game on the slope. She heard white Dhattar saying, "Nay, we'll not see him at all this winter."

Aiony added, "Save in dreams."

Pitipak made a small sound, as of sympathy. Tek's ears pricked, but she dared not interrupt with questions. Like as not, such would only quiet her offspring completely, or loose a torrent of observations too tangled for Tek herself to sort. Quietly, their dam eavesdropped.

"He talks to the one with the red jewels now," Aiony was saying.

"She's older than we," Dhattar laughed, "and goes about things very slowly."

Chasing him around Aiony, Pitipak nearly caught him. The black-and-silver filly dodged away now, as well.

"She's been sleeping a long, long time."

Tek turned her mind away, unable to follow their thread. Almost certainly, she knew, they were discussing Jan, but she lacked any context with which to make their words meaningful. Reluctantly, she contented herself with the assurance he was alive and hale. Ryhenna came up the hillside now, followed closely by her young one, Culu. With an affectionate nip, Dagg left the pied mare's side. The coppery mare whistled a greeting to Tek before nuzzling her mate. The little foal began to suckle. Jah-lila and Ses came up the rear. They, too, spoke quietly as evening neared.

"I have often wondered where in the wide Plain he might be found, but of late the more intensely," Ses was saying, head down, tone barely above her breath. "Then, on a sudden, to have news of him after so long, that he is well, a singer. . . . I had always suspected—"

Her words broke off as she and the red mare drew close to Tek. Schooling her expression to betray nothing, the pied mare listened in surprise. Ses spoke of Jan, of course—who else? Yet, despite her obvious strong emotion, her words rang somehow odd in reference to her son. Puzzled, Tek glanced away and harkened without seeming to.

"Both you and I have forfeited much for the welfare of our young," Jah-lila murmured to Ses.

The pied mare felt a telltale frown creasing her brow and dismissed it. Her own dam, she knew, had forgone a place in the herd for nearly ten years in order that her filly might be raised among them as Teki's daughter. Tek—and all the Vale—now knew that the stallion whose namesake she was had not been her sire. To this day, the red mare continued to conceal that one's identity. Some nameless Renegade was all the account Tek had ever been able to wrest from her.

Of her own dam's sacrifice, the pied mare was well aware. But what of Ses? Did Jah-lila refer to the public repudiation of Korr by his mate when, during that terrible winter, his madness had threatened even Lell? Yet Tek had the strongest feeling that Ses's unknown deed must have been to Jan's benefit, not Lell's. The pale mare's eyes were closed, as if in pain.

"I count the days till Jan's return," she whispered to Jah-lila. "Though I could do no other and keep my offspring safe, I have held this silence far too long. By Alma's eyes, Red Mare, I swear when next we meet, I'll tell my son the truth."

❦

Jan felt himself returning. He became aware of the dragon's den again, of the awful glare of the pool of fire, of its intense heat. Neither troubled him, though he was vaguely aware that he should long since have swooned. Dimly, in the back of his mind, he tried to remember what had caused this strange imperviousness—dragonsup?—but his thoughts were fluid, shifting still, and the query refused to come to the forefront of consciousness. Instead, a new need suddenly kindled there, bright and imperative: to learn the meaning of his mother's vow. *I'll tell my son the truth*. He had no inkling what she could mean.

"What is this?" he demanded. "What have I beheld?"

Before him, the languid dragon stirred. Great lids slid down over garnet eyes, then up again. The pool upon her brow rippled and stilled. Her vast body stretched away across the chamber, enormous claws of her toes tightening. Her monumental, rose-colored wings flexed. The resulting gust fanned the steam of her breath in curling eddies about Jan. She chuckled very quietly, deep in her throat, at his sudden urgency, all trace of his former reticence gone.

"None but your home and friends, the unicorns of your Vale," she answered, chiding. "I should have thought you would have recognized them."

The dark unicorn let his breath out, chastened. "Your pardon," he offered, then tried again. "What I meant to ask is: is what I see upon your brow that which is, or are these images your own inventions, conjurings. . . ."

"Lies?" Wyzásukitán inquired mildly.

"Dreams," Jan countered.

Again the red dragon chuckled. "You see what is. I see it, too, but it is no dream of mine. We dragons do not dream, in that sense. We contemplate that which is. The only conjurer here is you, invoking upon my brow those things you most desire to see."

Jan frowned, unsatisfied. "But is it real?" he whispered. "Or only imagined by me?"

Wyzásukitán shrugged. Her massive wing moved, glittering. Her head remained perfectly still. "Does it feel real—or imaginary?"

"Real," Jan answered, unhesitating.

The dragon queen nodded, closing her eyes again and inclining her head almost imperceptibly. The strange water upon her brow lapped, smoothed. "Then trust it as real, for I believe the truth, however harsh, is what you long to see above all things, even above soothing lies. A courageous wish, and a most unusual one. Álmaharát-elár-herát, whom we call the Many-Jeweled One, or Her of the Thousand Thousand Eyes, has chosen you well for her purpose. You have seen what is and what has been. Come. Look again. I will show you now what is to be."

Kindling

★ 16 ★

J an gazed deep into the dragon's pool. The Vale lay below him in a gryphon's eye view. He leaned closer, perception skimming lower through the air. Frost rimed the grass, brown stubble now. Wisps of snow sifted down, floating like feathers. Sky hung grey, early dusk drawing on. Jan watched his fellows gathering. When he spied the great heap of brushwood on the council rise, he knew the day could only be solstice, the start of winter.

His herdmates below looked well-fed, pelts thick and warm. Nearly all the many fillies and foals would be weaned by spring. *When the herd must depart,* Jan heard himself think, unsure if he spoke aloud in the distant dragon's den. *I must return by then,* he thought. *I must lead them.* The notion filled him with dread, not of the task itself, but of the other that must accompany it: disclosure of Korr's unspeakable secret.

Far below, Tek stood upon the council rise. She was a striking sight, bold black and rose, her particolored mane lifting in the slight, frigid breeze. The herd around her assembled joyously. How regal she looked, like a princess, like a queen. *She is their queen,* he thought. *Leader of the herd now that Korr is gone—and not as my regent, but in her own right: undeclared princess of the line of Halla all the time that I have ruled.*

Watching her, Jan felt terror and longing war within his breast. He did not know, suddenly, how he would bear yielding his station as prince. For honor's sake, and out of love for Tek, he could consider no other course. Yet its taste rose bitter in his mouth—for another thing he must relinquish, too. And this he could not face at all: abandoning his mate, renouncing her. *Not Tek, my belovèd!* It was inconceivable.

Mounting panic took him by the throat. He gasped, shuddering. The image in the dragon's pool wavered, obscured by snow. Frantically, Jan strove to still his roiling thoughts. Gradually, his inner clamor quieted, breathing eased. The images in the pool clarified. He gazed into them deeply, desperately. The scene below offered distraction, lifted him out of his turmoil and pain. His last awareness of the dragon's den and his own identity faded as he grew wholly absorbed.

Tek spoke to the assembled herd, and they danced the great ring-dance, trampling the snow. Much later, when the dance had ended, Tek again addressed the herd. Her foster father, Teki the healer, came forward and sang the lay of Jan's winter captivity three years past and of his eventual return, bearing the secret of fire in his hooves and horn. Impervious to solstice chill in their thick winter shag, the resting herd stood harkening, or lounged at ease on the frosty ground.

Teki's lay done, Tek called on Ryhenna to stand beside her on the rise. Dagg's copper-colored mate had fought at the prince's shoulder during his escape from the two-footed firekeepers. She too, like Jan, had trod upon the burning coals Jan had kindled that day, tempering her round, solid hooves to sparking hardness. Each year since the herd had acclaimed her its priestess, she had kindled the great bonfire that would burn all winter long.

Calling on Alma now, thanking the goddess for her gift of fire, the coppery mare reared and dashed her hooves against the stones on which the dried tinder rested. Sparks flew. Ryhenna rose and struck again, again. Whinnying, she cavaled, stamping her hind heels. All the herd whistled with her. More sparks. Some flew into the midst of the tinder and caught. Smoke curled up, then little tongues of flame. When the bonfire had become a blaze, Tek called members of the herd to come forward.

In twos and threes, unicorns approached the council rise. Each bore a dried branch clenched in teeth. Carefully, they dipped their brands into the flame, then raised them burning aloft. The firebearers sprang away at a gallop, ploughing through snow, seeking their grottoes before the firebrands guttered. Each grotto, Jan knew, housed a similar tinder pile beside a cache of stores. Here borrowed flames would burn all season, warming the herd, that none need ever again suffer privation from hunger and cold. Guardians would tend the great bonfire on the council rise until the birth of spring.

Jan found his viewpoint pulling back from the Kindling, buoyed like a gryphon on a rising wind. The images before him blurred, altering. He seemed to have traversed many miles in a single breath. Vague impressions of Pan Woods and Plain swept rapidly beneath him, then the rises and ripples of the Hallow Hills. He began to descend, rushing earthward. Below, he glimpsed the Mirror of the Moon, the unicorns' sacred pool, hard by the expanse of broken limestone shelves housing entry to the wyverns' dens.

The next heartbeat found him within. Long caverns twisted through the white limestone, all coated with a crystalline glaze. As the pale wyrms slithered, their tiny scales sloughed, volatile oils from their skin rubbing off, forming silvery trails. Over hundreds of years, the trails had thickened into layers which caught the lightwells' gleam, diffusing it, to lend a dim glow to the dens even in their deepest parts. The translucent patina had a resinous odor. Jan knew it to be fiercely combustible. One spark could set the whole warren alight.

Jan found himself in the deepest recess of the vast network of interlocking tunnels. A great wyvern lay curled in his lair, unaware of the dark unicorn's distant observation. This wyrm was the largest Jan had ever seen, larger even than the three-headed queen he had battled as a colt. Jan guessed that this creature must be very old, for wyverns grew throughout their lives. At the tip of his poison tail, seven barbs glinted. Two badger-broad forepaws, his only limbs, scratched absently at his vitreous belly, stretched taut by a recent meal. Old scars disfigured his breast.

The wyrm had seven heads. Realization seized Jan with a start. Each head possessed a hood, bristling whiskers and dozens of needle-sharp teeth. The eldest, central pate was also the largest. It lay dozing, long neck stretched along the ground. Other heads twined about it. Two were nearly half as large. These also slept. The rest were smaller, younger, wakeful. Of them, the final, seventh nob was a mere slip, whining and nibbling at its own gill ruff. Its three companions stirred restively, glancing about the room as if on guard. A firebrand smoldered smokily nearby, only the smallest stack of twigs heaped by for future fuel. Furtively, in whispers, the four smallest heads argued.

"Why must *we* always keep watch," the next-to-smallest complained, "while the large ones sleep?"

"Silence!" the fourth-largest head hissed. "You'll wake the One."

The complainer and its closest companion both hissed and turned to eye the largest pate, which slept on, unperturbed. The tiniest sniffed at a fellow's gills, parting colorless lips for a tentative nibble. The second-to-smallest spun and snapped at the tiny head, driving it back. The fourth-largest clucked at the other three, then cast about suspiciously, eyeing the egress to the wyrm king's den as if impatient for some visitor. The second-largest countenance, flanking the One, stirred. All four of the small aspects riveted their gazes upon it for a few heartbeats, then lost interest when it made no further move.

"Where in all the burrows is the kindling?" the fourth-largest demanded. "Our brand's near burnt out."

"Do you think it was the peaceseekers, waylaying the wood gatherers again?" the fifth-largest nob ventured.

"Peaceseekers!" the next-to-the-smallest growled, then spat. "Stingless grubs."

The tiny head hissed furiously, a tangle of sounds that might have been, "Stingless! Stingless!" Its three waking comrades ignored it.

"It was when our queen died, five seasons past," the fifth-largest muttered, "that was when our fortunes fell."

The next-to-smallest one beside it harrumphed. "They were wretched before."

"Hardly!" the fourth-largest snapped. "While our queen lived, she kept the barbless freaks in check."

"Verminous peaceseekers!" its companion, fifth-largest, snarled.

"We were never cold then; that I'll grant," the next-to-smallest face conceded.

"Peace! Peace!" the tiny head hissed as though it were a curse.

"Killed by those thrice-cursed unicorns," the fourth-largest head murmured.

Its slightly smaller companion added, "Our gallant queen. Priestess of the divine fire."

"She never let our torch grow cold," the second-to-smallest added.

The tiny head alongside hissed out, "Torches. Cold."

The gazes of the four small waking faces flicked between the egress and the guttering fire. The one largest pate dozed on, as did the two middle-sized heads that flanked it. The larger of those uncoiled its neck, turned upside down. Again the four small heads froze, silenced, until their medium-sized fellow again lay still.

"Cursed be the night-dark prince of unicorns," the fourth-to-largest whispered. "When he slew our queen, we lost our heirs as well."

"All those ripe eggs, ready for hatching," the fifth-largest lamented. "Tramped under his cloven heels."

"His and his shoulder-friends', the pied one and the dapple," the next-to-smallest added.

The fifth-largest continued, "Two dozen sharp-pricked little prits. Had they but hatched, they'd have quelled and mastered all these stingless freaks!"

"Eggs, prits," hissed the littlest head. "Freaks!"

"Yes, stingless," the fourth-largest head of the wyrmking echoed. "That's all the wyverns were before we hatched. When our folk slaved among the thrice-cursed dragons, none bore a sting. We, Lynex, were the first. We bred our line into a race of wyverns—independent, strong!—not those cringing wyrms our folk had been. We made our followers hunters, capturers of prey, no longer puling scavengers, eaters of the dead."

Another head took up the thread. "And for years upon years, our line bred true. We ourself sired most of the eggs our females laid. The stingless ones were few and easily destroyed. But now the One grows old and sires no more. The eggs the unicorns crushed were our last brood. Now stingless ones hatch nearly as frequently as those with stings! Some females refuse to eat such young, hide them away instead to keep them safe."

"The old queen knew how to find and devour them," its companion beside it interjected. "But she is dead now, and the One has lost interest. He dozes his hours away, content to let others address our woes. . . ."

"But others do not remedy as they ought," another interrupted. "The stingless peaceseekers are becoming a troublesome faction. They speak out against the spring hunting. They themselves seek only carrion to eat—"

"Carrion!" squawked the next-to-smallest head, and the fifth-largest spat, "Filth!"

"They refuse to take fellow creatures' lives!" the fourth-largest ranted. "Pledge not to hunt living prey!"

The voices of all four of the smaller heads had risen, becoming both louder and more shrill. They hissed and squabbled among themselves until the two middle-sized heads—flanking the largest, still-sleeping visage—jerked awake. Clear, crystalline eyes fixed on the smaller four, the middle-sized pair rose hissing.

"Stingless freaks," one crackled.

Its mate echoed, "Witless ones, more like."

"Still your prating tongues before you wake the One," the second-to-largest muzzle cautioned, reaching to sink its fangs into two of the smaller four in turn. All of the little heads leaned frantically away, but the necks of the middle-sized heads were longer.

"No more talk of peaceseekers and unicorns," the third-to-largest head commanded. "Such dross troubles the dreams of the One. Our late queen is gone, but our fire burns on."

"Hist! Hist!" the youngest head broke in. Behind, the fire was nearly out.

"Quick, lackwits!" the second-to-largest pate snarled. "Feed the flame. If it dies, the One will snap you four off at the chins and devour your brains."

"You were ordered to watch," its companion, the third-largest, berated. "A fine mess you have made of it, too. This torch is the last in all our dens, to be hoarded and tended with utmost care!"

Frantically, the four smaller heads snatched up tinder and twigs to add to the dwindling fire. At first it seemed they had smothered it, but then smoke curled up and bright tongues of red and yellow burst across the fuel. The two middle-sized maws snicked and snorted, the four smaller pates sighing with evident relief. Five of the wakeful, coherent heads turned to cast angry, hopeful looks toward the chamber's egress.

"Where in all the dens is the wood gatherer?" the third-largest demanded of the one beside it. "Could it be the stingless peaceseekers again? You know they preach life without reliance on fire."

The second-largest muttered. "Fire savages the blood. Fire first gave us stings and a taste for live meat. . . ."

All five watching the door continued to grumble. Behind them, the wyrmking's one great, original head dozed on. Meanwhile the littlest face watched the bright, short-lived flames consuming the last of the firebrand's fuel. For a few moments, the fire guttered, fizzing, then shrank still further. It became a blue flicker, vanished in a waft of pungent smoke. Sudden chill swept the room. The nostrils of the five other waking heads flared. Gasping, they wheeled to gape at the shadowed remains of the burnt-out branch. Not a sound broke the stillness but the tiny maw's whimpers.

The eyes of the one great head snapped open, stared for a moment at the newly darkened chamber. The only light now illuminating the den was a distant lightwell's feeble glow. Lynex's central head reared on its muscular stalk. All around, the other crania writhed, wailing, even the second- and third-largest. The great head ignored them, glaring straight at the empty fireledge, now nothing but ashes and char. The wyrmking's knifelike claws dug into his gleaming belly below his savagely scarred breast.

"Which?" he growled, voice deeper than any Jan had ever heard. "Which one of you let my fire go out?"

❧

Jan felt himself in motion again, rising, pulling aloft. He left the crystalline dens of wyverns beneath the Hallow Hills and crossed the Plain, traversed the Pan Woods. He found himself hovering above the Vale once more. The snows had passed. Another ceremony, similar to the Kindling that had marked winter's onset, was now under way. Again unicorns circled the great bonfire, still burning. The air had warmed, cool yet, but with the promise of balmier days ahead. Some of the herd were already shedding their heavy shag. It had been another mild winter, Jan could see: thanks, no doubt, to the weather wych, Jah-lila.

After the dancing, Teki again ascended the council rise. This time he sang of Tek's flight from the Vale, how his foster daughter had carried Jan's unborn offspring through bitter snows and taken refuge in the wilderness with her then-exiled dam. He praised the pan sisters Sismoomnat and Pitipak who had delivered Tek and described the torrential floods that had overwhelmed the murderous warparty Korr had sent against her in the spring.

That had been the ending of Korr's power, if not his madness. Jan had returned from captivity among the firekeepers just as Tek and her newborns had made their own return. The lay ended with the reunion of mates and Jan's embracing his twin filly and foal. Many of the youngest listeners had drifted into sleep. The fire priestess, Ryhenna, addressed the herd, reminding them that once moon reached its zenith, the bonfire would be tended no more, its flames allowed to flicker out, coals left to cool.

This night, however, she added new words, urging all full-grown unicorns to sharpen their hooves and horns, then tread as she now trod upon the embers rimming the dwindling tongues of flame. Into these she dipped her horn, holding it in the swirl of fire that it, like her fire-hardened hooves, might toughen beyond all previous strength, the better to pierce the wyverns' bony breasts.

Eagerly, all of fighting age complied: newly initiated half-growns, seasoned warriors, elders, a dozen of whom formed the Council which confirmed all kings' judgments and granted each succeeding battleprince his right to rule. First Tek, then Dagg, then Jah-lila and Ses, followed by Teki and the rest, bent to run keen ridges of spiral horn against flint-edged heels, honing both edges in the same smooth stroke, then came forward to join Ryhenna.

Those colts and fillies and suckling foals still waking looked on with longing. Too tender for war, they were forbidden to sharpen their hooves and horns. At last, the long procession ended. Their elders, weaponry now tempered, returned from the council rise and lay down among their offspring to doze the weary night till dawn.

Jan watched the moon climb, pass zenith, decline. The whole valley lay silent, still—except for furtive movement atop the rise. Jan beheld his own sister Lell, barely five years old, not yet initiated, clumsily keening her hooves and horn. At last achieving a respectable edge, she crept forward, ears pricked and eyes darting. Gingerly, she stepped onto the bonfire's coals, dipping her young horn into the last red wisps of flame.

"I don't count what Ses says," Jan heard her muttering between clenched teeth. "I *am* ready. I'm not too young. I mean to be a warrior, and I might as soon begin by battling wyverns. She'll not keep me from this fray."

"Bravely spoken," a voice behind her quietly replied.

The timbre was a low, throaty growl like the purr of a hillcat. Lell jumped stiff-legged as a startled hare and whirled. Silhouetted, a gryphon sat on the council rise. Jan himself was amazed. He had not observed the other's approach, nor heard his wings. The tercel had alighted in utter silence, cat's eyes dilated in the blazing moonlight.

"Illishar!" Lell hissed, her joyous whisper just short of a shriek that would have wakened others and given them both away.

"The same, little one," he replied. "I bid you hail. Only lately arrived, I wished not to disturb your folk."

"You are most welcome," Lell answered fervently, then hesitated, casting a glance at her sharpened hooves, then over at the fire. "I beg you," she burst out softly, urgently, "do not speak of what you have just seen. . . ."

The wingcat smiled. "I see naught but a gracious filly who, waking at my approach, arose to welcome me."

Lell eyed him fiercely. "I mean to be a warrior," she said. "Jan would let me. I know he would! If he were here—I mean to join this fray against the wyrms."

The green-winged tercel nodded. "So I see. And now, little one, may I beg a boon? Fall back, if you will, a pace or two and allow me a place beside your fire. My flight this day has been long and chill."

Lell stumbled back from the bonfire hurriedly, allowing the gryphon space to move into the glow of the coals. He crouched, then stretched himself, forelegs laid upon the ground, wings not folded, but raised, the better to catch the fire's heat. Jan heard the deep, steady rumble of his purr. Lell stood awkwardly, seeming not to know what next to do. The gryphon beckoned her.

"Step closer, little darkamber," he bade. "Do not grow cold on my account. Rest and tell me of your warrior dreams. I, too, sought to join my clan's battleranks against great odds. I succeeded, as you see, and have won a perch high on the ledges beside my leader's wing."

Lell happily approached and lay down facing the green-and-gold tercel. Jan marveled at his sister's lack of fear. She treated Illishar as she would her own folk, appeared to regard him as no different from a unicorn.

"Gladly," she answered. "I welcome your company."

The gryphon bowed his head in a flattered nod. "And I yours, little darkamber, for I sense that like me, you mean to win your way to the ledges of honor among your flock."

Spring

★ 17 ★

Spring, Jan saw, and no longer first spring. A month or more had passed since equinox. Watching in the dragon's pool, Jan felt uneasiness. He saw the future Vale spread green below him, his fellows grazing its hillsides, their winter shag long shed. But he saw no sign of himself, no indication that by the time predicted in this foreseeing, he had returned. And he would need to be returned by spring if he were to lead the march to the Hallow Hills.

Jan saw his sister Lell high on the Vale's grassy steeps. She looked older, less a filly than a half-grown. Her legs had lengthened, as had her neck and mane, her horn no longer a colt's blunt truncheon, but a slim flattened skewer, pointed and edged. Standing on a rocky outcrop overhanging the Vale, she looked a young warrior. Illishar sat beside her. His feline form—huge almost as a formel—dwarfed his unicorn companion. Lell had not yet reached a half-grown's size, but she had attained the shape, leaving fillyhood behind. Within the year, Jan felt sure, she would be initiated. How soon, he wondered, before she joined the courting rites by the Summer Sea?

Breeze lifted Lell's mane, her face grown longer and more slender, a young mare's. Beside her, Illishar's raised wings cupped the breeze, one curving above Lell's back. He and she watched a group of warriors sparring far below on the valley floor. Jan spotted the black-and-rose figure of Tek directing the exercises, the dappled yellow and grey of Dagg alongside her. Lell tossed her head.

"They won't let me join in," she said. "They say I'm too young. Jan would never exclude me so! So every day I watch them, then steal off and practice by myself."

Illishar stretched to let breeze riffle his feathers. "So, too, did I in my youth—until I had won me a spot among the formels. They would not grant it willingly. I had to prove myself beyond all quarrel. They called me a little, useless tercel squab, keen enough for hunting, perhaps, but never so much as considered for a perch beside the wingleader or for serious war." He laughed his throaty, purring laugh. "I proved every one of them wrong."

Lell turned to him. "We don't do that. Among my folk, we don't discount our he-colts. All half-growns are expected to become warriors. Besides, with unicorns, it is the stallions who are heftier."

Again Illishar laughed. "I know! Such an odd and fascinating flock. Though Malar did not deem my joining your war a savory task, I relish it, for I have learned more of your folk in one short moon than ever I could have done in a lifetime otherwise."

Together they watched the maneuvers below. Tek and Dagg's shrill whistles reached the heights. Jan had never seen the warriors so crisp. He felt a surge of pride, gratitude to Tek and Dagg, then regret that he was not to be among them. He shook it off. The herd need fear naught from lack of practice or skill when they met the wyrms. He could not have trained them better himself.

"You see? You see?" he heard Lell whispering. "The left flank doesn't swing fast enough. They must wheel more sprightly if they're to close the trap ere wyverns flee. When Jan arrives, he'll chase them into step."

Beside her the green-winged tercel nodded. "My flock employs similar stratagems, but ours are all airborne."

"Will you teach me?" Lell asked him. The other laughed, eyeing her wingless shoulders. Lell sighed heavily. "I wish I could fly."

"Become a gryphon, and you shall," her companion teased. The darkamber filly whickered and kicked at him.

"I want you to teach me another lay!" she cried.

"What?" the tercel reared back in mock surprise. "I have already taught you Ishi's Hatching. It is the talk of all your flock. Next they will say you are my acolyte."

Lell shook herself. "I would not mind a bit. I want to learn every song I can ere you must go." Her tone abruptly saddened. "After we fight the wyverns, you'll return to your mountains, and I'll not see you more."

The gryphon folded his wings, some of the feathers just brushing Lell's back as they closed. "No fear, little darkamber," he told her. "My pinions are strong. We gryphons do not let friendships lapse. But touching on your coming war, is it not high time your herd departed?"

Lell nodded, her eyes on Tek far, far below. "We all hoped Jan would have returned by now. But he has not come. So Tek waits. But I heard her telling Dagg we can bide no more than another fortnight before we must begin our trek. I think we should wait! Yet all the herd champs to face the wyverns. We have been waiting four hundred years."

Jan felt himself rising away from the Vale. The air around him thinned and darkened. His view dimmed. He had the brief sensation of hurtling through stars, then of sudden descending. He became aware of himself underground once more, beneath the Hallow Hills. Lynex the wyvern king lay in his barren chamber, all seven snaking heads wakeful now. Despite the absence of fire, the den was lighter than it had been. Illumination from the lightwells had the warmer intensity of spring. The wyvern heaved his scarred and bloated form upright to stare at the charred fireledge. The single greatest head among the writhing tangle of necks pulled transparent lips back from splintery fangs.

"First these stingless peaceseekers," it snarled. "Then my queen slain. Now the last of our fire burnt out." Its voice was deep, all gravel and broken flint.

The tiniest head struck out at nothing, flattening its hoodlike gill ruff, hissing, "Burnt out. Burnt out!"

"No thanks to *you*," one of the middle-sized pates muttered, glaring at the smaller ones.

The little nob turned, spat at its companions. "You!"

"Silence!" roared the one great head.

Five countenances flinched, but the sixth, the tiniest, turned and hissed. The large head snapped savagely at the little thing. With a shriek, the tiniest nob ducked. The great head eyed each smaller one in turn.

"I hold you all responsible," it snarled. "I might still cull the lot of you and rear a new crop of secondary skulls—ones with brains this time!"

The last words were a shout. Again the smaller heads cowered. None spoke.

"If only my queen lived still, she would know what to do. Winters have been so cold. Our torch dimmed, and the stingless freaks thwarted the wood gatherers. How they must have celebrated when they learned the torch was out. 'Devour them all!' my queen would have said."

The great head turned away, muttering. The half-dozen subsidiaries watched, all turning in unison as their leader wove. Jan was reminded suddenly of pacing among his own kind, or the random pecking of nervous birds. The wyvern shifted from one thick, badger-like forepaw to the other. Knifelike nails bit into the chamber's crystalline floor.

"So many of them now," the great head continued peevishly. "Their mothers hide them from me. They even breed. Whole nests of stingless

THE SON OF SUMMER STARS

offspring from stingless progenitors! There must be a way to find and seize them."

"A way," one of the two middle-sized heads echoed warily. The great head ignored it.

"Perhaps we should command loyal followers to hunt them, harry them from one end of the warren to the other," the companion middle-sized pate suggested softly.

Two of the other nobs nodded vigorously. "Harry them! A clean sweep."

"Yes," the great head mused, picking at the ancient scars on the royal breast. "Yes. A sweep." Abruptly the One frowned. The smaller pates tensed. "But not all with stings can be relied upon. Most have nieces or nephews who are stingless, sisters or brothers, even daughters and sons! Some have gone so far as to begin to believe the ravings of those . . . those barbless lunatics."

"Ravings," the tiniest maw fizzed. "Lunatics!"

"How do they stay alive?" the wyvern king's largest pate exclaimed. "They will not hunt living prey. They must eat carrion!"

"Carrion!" the littlest head spat.

"What sort of existence is that for a wyvern?" the largest nob growled at a middle-sized head.

"No existence at all," it responded hastily.

Preoccupied, the large one turned away. "They are reverting to what we once were, when we dwelled among the thrice-cursed red dragons: stingless rubbish clearers, eaters of the dead!"

"Never again!" one of the small pates echoed.

Its fellows joined it: "Such indignity."

"The degradation."

"All our woes are the unicorns' doing," one of the middle-sized muzzles ventured. "Had they not deprived us of our queen, the stingless ones would never have multiplied."

"We must wreak revenge against the unicorns as well," the other middle-sized nob added.

The largest, central head considered. "That we must," it murmured. "But they only come in spring, and only a score or two, to keep their nightlong vigil by the wellspring atop the limestone steep. Truth to tell," he mused, "they come a few weeks after equinox. It is that time now."

The wyvern king reared suddenly. The other heads jerked in surprise.

"The stingless traitors can wait," Lynex's oldest pate said sharply. "We'll arrange an ambush for the unicorn pilgrims instead. My loyalists shall have the meat—and I'll know my supporters by who agrees to taste this living prey. Once we have feasted, time enough to fall upon the stingless and their collaborators!"

"Yes! Yes!" the other nobs rejoiced. "We'll lie in wait for unicorns along the path to their vigil pool. They will never sip its healing draught! We'll rend the flesh of our enemies, then devour our own kind—stingless cowards and any others not wyvern enough to use their stings."

The seven-stranded laughter of the wyvern king echoed through the limestone hollows. Again Jan felt himself lifted, drawn up through tons of earth covering the wyverns' dens, out into the light and air again. A blur of motion, the momentary feel of rushing. He found himself hovering above the Vale once more. Spring had advanced another half moon. Tek stood upon the council rise. Dagg and Ryhenna, Teki and Jah-lila, Ses, Illishar and Lell flanked her. Once more the whole herd stood assembled.

"He is not yet among us, but he will return," Tek told them. "We have waited as long as we dare. To delay more would betray his vision. I doubt not that Jan will rejoin us, but our march must now begin. We have just-weaned colts and fillies among us. This trek will last the remainder of the spring. It will be new summer when we reach the Hills, where wyverns wait our hooves and horns!"

Shouts of approval rose from the press. The cry of "Jan, Jan the prince!" went up, while some—more than a few—shouted, "For Tek! Tek, regent and prince's mate!"

Aye, Jan thought with sudden bitterness. *They* should *cheer her, for she is their rightful battleprince, not I.* Regret seized him, and envy. *Would that I were wholly other than who I am,* he thought, *some Renegade, even, not the late king's son. Sooth, I could gladly give my office up if only I might keep my pledge with Tek.* He shoved his painful thoughts aside. It was all hopeless. Below him, Tek cried: "Away, then. To our homeland! To the Hills."

She sprang from the council rise, her mane of mingled black and rose streaming. Her companions on the rise sprang behind her: red Jah-lila, painted Teki, dappled Dagg and his copper mate, Ryhenna, dark-amber Lell with the milk-pale mane, and her mother, Ses, the color of cream with a mane like crimson fire. Illishar rose into the air in a green thrashing of wings. Sunlight flashed on his golden flanks. Beneath, the herd surged after Tek, all eager to depart the Vale, hearts bound for the far Hallows.

Jan became aware of an echo, oddly hollow, as though originating deep underground. His view of the herd climbing the steeps of the Vale shrank, grew distant. Before them, he knew, lay the Pan Woods and the Plain. Once more he pulled back, traveling at speed. It seemed that darkness fell, until he realized he had merely come to himself in the vast and sunless dragon's den. Glare of the molten firelake flickered across the pool of water in the red queen's brow. The chanting that had drawn him from the Vale echoed somewhere overhead, in the caves above. Awareness of himself and of Wyzásukitán once more faded as his mind floated upward to the source of the sound:

"Now fare we forth, far Hallows bound. . . ."

Jan beheld the Hall of Whispers, burial crypt of Mélintélinas. He saw the Scouts of Halla dispersed among the old queen's bones. Oro stood by the great skull with its pool of lustrous, dark water. He led the chant, bidding his comrades come forward one by one, take a single sup from that pool, which seemed never to run dry. Having sipped, each shaggy unicorn filed away across the great chamber, disappeared into shadows beyond the gleam of the dragon's jewels. Their recitation never faltered.

> "When time betides, a way be found.
> Afar, ancestral comrades call.
> We answer ably, ardent all. . . ."

Their words puzzled Jan. They moved with orderly determination, as though embarking upon some quest. *Far Hallows bound*—could Oro's fellows truly mean to cross Salt Waste and Plain? He distinctly remembered the dark maroon telling him no egress led from the Smoking Hills. How, then, did the Scouts intend to leave? Though the unexpected possibility of allies buoyed Jan, his skin prickled—for even if Oro and the rest managed to win free of these mist-enshrouded mountains, how would they avoid deadly wyvern stings?

Unease swept him. He struggled, but found himself unable to rouse from this dream of the future unfolding before him in the dragon's brow. The Scouts of Halla vanished from view. Lost in the underground caverns of the Smoking Hills, their chanting diminished, finally ceased. Darkness awhile. Then he beheld the Plain rolling before him, drenched in the sunlight of middle spring. He had no inkling how much time was to have passed.

Before him, two groups of unicorns converged. The first, led by Tek, her particolored rose and jet unmistakable among the orange reds and sky-water blues, the occasional grey or gold. Narrow at the head, flaring, then tapering toward the rear, the herd flowed across the green grass Plain. Young occupied the center, flanked by their elders on every side. The steady, deliberate pace, Jan observed, enabled even the youn-

gest to travel untaxed. Half-growns frisked and sparred along the
fringes. Plainsgrass around them rippled and bowed.

The vast warband of the Vale moved toward another group, far
fewer, but much more widely spaced. The foremost of these stood dark
blue with a silver mane. Jan recognized Calydor with his star-bespeckled
coat. To one side stood the seer's niece, Crimson, and her pale-blue
filly, Sky. Crimson's belly looked heavy and round, in foal again. Her
companion, Goldenhair, was nowhere to be seen, but Jan spotted her
father, Ashbrindle, on Calydor's other side. Numerous Plainsdwellers
flanked them. They stood awaiting the Valedwellers' approach.

Tek whistled the herd to a halt. Dagg flanked her, Ryhenna a few
paces behind. Her mother, Jah-lila, stood at her other shoulder with Lell,
Teki the healer, and Dhattar and Aiony with Ses well back of them all.
Above, Illishar circled, his shadow passing over them from time to time.

"Hail, Free People of the Plain," the pied mare called. "I am Tek,
regent and mate to Aljan Moonbrow, our prince. We come in peace and
seek no quarrel."

"Hail," the star-strewn seer replied. "I am Calydor, singer and farseer among my folk, who call me Alma's Eyes. Some here have met
your mate. I bid you safe travel."

"We seek to pass through your lands on our way to our ancestral
home, which we mean to wrest from treacherous wyverns," Tek continued. "Have we your leave to pass?"

Calydor tossed his mane. "Though your goal is known to us, none
here may grant you leave—for the Plain is not ours. We lay no claim.
Rather, 't claims us, the People of the Plain. Pass freely, as we do, and
ask no leave."

The pied leader of the unicorns bowed her head. "I thank you,
Calydor, and all your folk. I pledge my herd will not trouble yours as
we pass. My mate has come before us and told our tale. Should any
among you care to join our cause, my folk stand eager to accept allies.
Once we have won back our Hallow Hills, all who fought alongside us
will be welcome to share our newfound home."

Snorting, stamping, and a tossing of heads among the Plainsdwellers
followed. Jan's ears pricked, but he could not be sure he had heard a
whicker or two, quickly bitten off. Solemnly, Calydor shook his head.

"I thank you, Regent Tek, for your generosity. I know of none
among my folk who would join you. We of the Plain are not reft of
homeland. We stand content. Any of my fellows are, of course, free to
embrace your cause. Perhaps in time some will make such wishes
known. But we do not generally savor war. The vastness of the Mare's
Back settles our disputes. If others offend us, we leave them. But we

wish you well for the sake of your mate, who impressed me greatly as an honorable wight."

Watching, high above them in dreams, Jan warmed to Calydor's praise. Yet he sensed consternation among his own folk at the Plainsdweller's reply. Most of those from the Vale, Jan suspected, had simply assumed these ragtag vagabonds would rush to join the herd's battle march, praising Alma for the privilege. That their herd's sacred quest might be viewed with cool detachment by outsiders baffled some. Jan himself could only smile. He admired Tek's calm, collected response.

"So be it," she said warmly. "We welcome any who join us and bid fair weather to the rest. One other favor I would ask. My folk have traversed the Plain many times on yearly pilgrimage to initiate our young. But those bands numbered only warriors and half-growns, no elders or weanlings or suckling mares. The host before you moves far more slowly. We need guides to show us shelter from wind and rain, help us ward away pards and find sufficient water. Would any among you consent to the task?"

Jan sensed interest stirring among the Free People of the Plain. Calydor stepped forward.

"I myself will gladly escort you," he answered. "I wot these parts well. Many of my companions may choose to accompany. We are, I confess, most curious, having heard many rumors of you, but rarely met Moondancers face to face.

Tek nodded. "Very well," she said. "Let us share path for as long as may be."

With mixed eagerness and hesitation, the two groups merged, colts and fillies boldest, half-growns boisterous. Full-growns and elders on both sides approached more warily. Yet the two groups did mingle, exchanged tentative questions, greetings. Only one among the Vale-dwellers did not stir, Jan noticed presently. One mare poised motionless. Others eddied around her, yet she remained rooted, eyes riveted on the star-strewn seer who, joined by his brother, niece and niece's daughter, stood treating with Tek, Dagg, Ryhenna, Teki, Jah-lila and various Elders of the Vale.

Calydor caught sight of her suddenly. She stood not many paces from him. Glancing up, his gaze fell upon her. He froze. He had not marked her before, Jan realized. She must have stood screened from his view during Tek's initial greeting, or perhaps the pied mare had held the seer's whole attention. But he glimpsed the other now. Jan saw the silver-flecked stallion's eyes lock on hers. Half a dozen heartbeats, the pair of them stared mute. The mare's fiery mane, red as poppies, beat against the pale ivory of her pelt.

With a start, she wheeled and loped away. Not a word or a whistle, not a backward glance. Unnoticed by the others, the stallion's eyes yearned after her. Plainly, he could not desert the parley. But why, Jan wondered, had the mare not joined them? As one of the youngest of the Council of Elders, she was entitled, indeed expected. Jan's brow furrowed. The pale mare's conduct baffled him. He would have thought her eager to speak with Calydor, learn all she could from the seer of the time he had spent with Jan. But she had fled away. The young prince could not fathom it. For the red-maned mare had been Ses, his own dam.

Oasis

★ 18 ★

A passage of time. Jan knew not how long. He had lost all awareness of the dragon's den and of his own body, wholly absorbed in visions of events to come. He knew only that time had elapsed between the last future scene he had observed and the new one now beginning. The Plain still, but night shadowed. A brilliant moon shone down. Tall grass swayed and whispered about a series of meandering waterways and interconnected pools. Jan spied unicorns of the Vale camped all around, most lying up near the largest waterhole. A few Plainsdwellers mingled with the herd. Others lay off in the tall grass or under trees flanking the fingerling pools.

Sentries, both Valedwellers and Plainsdwellers, stood alert for pards. The fillies and foals lay surrounded by elders. Jan harbored no fear for them. Scenting the slight, sighing breeze, he found it free of all odor of predators. Nevertheless, he was keenly aware that this oasis—so vital to his folk—formed a maze of rills and rises, troughs and groves and irregular pools. Despite the sentries' diligent watch, almost any creature—even one large as a unicorn or pard—might steal past undetected if it moved stealthily and luck ran with it.

Shadows, movement among the trees. Far from the main camp, which lay barely within view through the close-spaced trees, Jan detected motion. Two small figures fidgeted among the treeboles, one black-and-silver, well camouflaged by mottled moonlight and shade, the other wholly white, pale ghostly as a dream. With a start of surprise, Jan recognized the tiny pair: Aiony and Dhattar, his own filly and foal. They stood taut, listening, straining to see through the moonblaze and shadow. Jan heard rustling.

"Here she comes," Aiony whispered to her brother. He nodded with a little snort.

A third figure emerged from the trees, larger than the first two, but still much smaller than full-grown. For a moment moonlight glanced across her. Jan was able to discern the darkamber coat, the milky mane of his sister Lell. For a moment, Jan thought he sensed another presence, something larger than all three of them, moving behind Lell in the darkness of the trees—but the moment passed. No scent, no sound, no further hint of motion from that quarter. Lell shook herself.

"There you are," she hissed. "It took me best part of an hour, stumbling about dodging sentries, to find you."

Jan saw his son's legs stiffen, his coat bristle. "We told you the pool shaped like a salamander."

Lell snorted. "They're *all* shaped like salamanders," she answered, exasperated.

Dha's mouth fell open as though to make some reply, but his sister murmured, "Peace. They come."

The darkamber filly and Dhattar both turned, moving closer to each other and to Aiony.

"I'm not sure this is wise," Lell muttered, her sudden caution surprising Jan.

"You wanted to see wyverns," Dhattar responded.

"Aye, but in secret?" his young aunt inquired. "Years from now, when we tell the tale, no one will believe us."

Aiony nodded, rubbing her cheek against the older filly's shoulder. "They will believe us, rest sure."

"Should we not inform Tek? As regent . . ."

"She deserves our loyalty and trust," the younger filly finished. "Aye. No doubt. Had we informed her, she would surely have kept her head and acted well."

"But what of others?" Dhattar picked up his sister's thread. "The herd's hatred of wyverns goes back centuries. Even now we march against those still loyal to Lynex who hold our homeland from us."

Lell's gaze turned inward, considering. "You fear if we told Tek, she might not believe us?"

Aiony laughed softly. "Not that. Nay, never that."

"If we told her," Dhattar replied, "she must consult the Elders. Others would learn of it. Soon all would know."

"You fear Tek might not be able to restrain our folk from falling upon these wyverns?"

Dhattar shrugged. "Perhaps. These wyrms are defenseless, after all."

"Not all of them," Lell countered. "You said some of them have stings."

"To which we are impervious," Aiony replied. "Nay, theirs is the greater peril. Our mother rules by the herd's goodwill. Why strain her regency by inviting strife?"

Lell set her teeth, deep in thought, and cast one furtive glance over her shoulder as though searching for something behind them in the dark. Jan detected nothing. Evidently neither could Lell. A moment later, she returned her attention to her young nephew and niece.

"Well enough, then. I will watch—but mark me, I'll raise the alarm if they offer the least . . ."

She did not finish the phrase. Across the narrow finger of water, a form appeared, translucent as ice. Blazing moonlight cut through its reptilian shape, illuminating sinews, suggestions of organs and the shadows of bones. The oily, fine-scaled skin gave off a rainbow sheen. Long-necked, the creature's body sported two wide forepaws before tapering away into a lengthy tail. The form was joined by another of its kind and another still. The nostrils on their long, tapered muzzles flared at the scent of water.

Standing just at trees' edge on the opposite bank, the three colts stood motionless. Scarcely the length of a running bound separated the three wyrms from them. Clearly parched, the newcomers hesitated only an instant before slithering toward the pool. Two bent eagerly to drink, but the third caught sight of the young unicorns reflected in the water. With a little shriek, it jerked upright. Its two companions did the same.

"Unicorns!" one hissed. "Warn the others—"

"Peace," Aiony called, her soft voice carrying easily in the still night air. "We mean you no harm."

The three across the pool hesitated, clearly torn between two terrors: that of remaining and that of fleeing without tasting the precious water. The middle one, slightly larger than the others, seemed to rally.

"What do you mean?" it demanded. "Are your folk not enemies of my kind? How is it you offer peace?"

"We are Lell Darkamber, king's daughter," Aiony replied, nodding to the filly at her side, "and Aiony, princess-to-be, and my brother, Dhattar, prince-to-be. We war only against followers of Lynex, who will not yield our rightful lands."

"We are seers, my sister and I," Dhattar went on. "We know you have deserted Lynex and fled the Hills, and that you hold him as much an enemy as do we."

Across the pool, the three wyverns gaped in surprise. Jan discerned all at once that they were younglings, far from fully grown. *Of course,*

he reasoned. *They would have to be.* The only stingless ones to have
survived among the wyverns had hatched since the death of the wyvern
queen.

"It is true we are no friends of Lynex," another of the white wyrms
admitted. "He sought to destroy our kind. Now he lies in wait for your
pilgrims along the moon lake's path. We fled rather than join that treachery. We are done with Lynex and his sting-tailed ways. We long only
for a peaceful life which harms no one. We seek new dens in a new
homeland."

"Show us your tails," Lell called. "We must be sure."

Unhesitatingly, the wyvern trio held up the blunt, stingless tips at
the end of their whiplike tails. The darkamber filly nodded, satisfied.

"Well enough," she said. "Drink and go your way. We three will
not harm you. But mark you take all pains to avoid our sentries, for if
you draw their notice, my companions and I cannot pledge your safety.
Few of our fellows distinguish wyrms with stings from those without."

The three wyverns hesitated a long moment. Sheer fatigue seemed
to decide for them, and they dipped their muzzles to the pool, drawing
the water in desperate draughts. At last, the eldest raised its head.

"We thank you," it offered. "We have long suspected our legends
calling your kind lackwits and fools to be untrue. Till now, we have
had no truth with which to dispel them. Rest sure that our talespinners
will remember this deed, how unicorns spared us and offered us water,
allowing us to journey on unscathed."

"The rest of our number must drink," another of the wyverns hissed
urgently.

"Fetch them," Lell replied. "We will stand watch."

Quick as a flinch, the smallest of the wyrms vanished into the trees.
Of the remaining two, the younger spoke.

"Five summers gone, your warriors slew Lynex's queen and gave
our kind the chance we needed to multiply and grow. Unwittingly, perhaps. Still, we owe you that."

"Our sire and dam slew her," Dhattar told them, "with their
shoulder-friend, Dagg. They only did so because she meant to kill them
and would not let them go."

"Our flight from Lynex has succeeded," the other wyvern replied,
"solely because he dare not send loyalists to hunt us down while marshaling his forces to ambush you. We knew we must seize this, our one
chance of escape, lest he fall upon us and devour us as he means to do
with you."

Aiony and Lell glanced at one another. "He may find himself surprised instead," the older filly answered.

"But where will you go?" Aiony asked the two wyrms suddenly. "You must find shelter by summer's end."

The pair twitched in despair. "We know nothing of the world beyond our dens. We knew only that we must flee or die. We cannot guess where our trek will lead, only that it must be far from Lynex and his murderous kind."

"Hark me," Aiony replied. "My sib and I have seen your destination in dreams. You must circle back the way you came, for no haven lies before you. Travel north and west instead, and you will find dens in plenty by summer's end. This I vow. You must trust our word. Had we meant you harm, we had raised the alarm by now."

The two wyverns gazed at her uncertainly until a rustling behind made them turn. Other wyverns emerged from the trees, heads darting cautiously. Catching sight of the pool, they hastened to the bank, drank eagerly and long.

"Look into the water," Dhattar murmured to Lell. "I'll show you the wyrmking in his lair."

Lell looked deep, and as she did so, Jan felt his perception merge with hers. Through Lell's eyes, he saw the moonbright pool, its still surface disturbed by the touch of many wyverns. Lell heard their soft lapping, the rustle of bodies, quiet hissing of breath. Jan watched her reflection ripple in the pool beside Dhattar's. Their images pulled apart and re-formed into new shapes: Lynex's den, shot through with moonlight. The white wyrmking towered above a cringing, single-headed underling.

"Gone?" the central, largest pate demanded, and its secondary heads echoed, "What do you mean, gone?"

"Escaped, my liege," the messenger whimpered. "Fled to the Plain. Not a stingless one remains in all our dens."

"Fled?" the great head of Lynex raged. "They had no right! They were mine. My subjects. Mine to banish or destroy. So hungry—I have grown so very hungry, waiting on these unicorns. Where now is my feast?"

The messenger cowered before Lynex as the wyrmking's half-dozen smaller aspects ranted, "Hungry, hungry! Longing for the feast!"

Jaws snapping, heads writhing above the scar-laced breast, the iridescent white form reared up, roaring its rage. Suddenly the great central head whipped around, returned its gaze to the messenger now creeping away.

"Halt," Lynex spat. "You do not have leave to go. Did you not mark your king hungers?"

The other gave a terrified cry. "No, no, my liege! I am but a messenger. Mercy. Mercy, I beg you! . . ."

Frantically, the little wyrm dashed for the den's egress. Quicker than thought, the wyverns' seven-headed king lunged. Brilliant moonlight from a lightwell glanced across him, breast scars gleaming between the stumpy forepaws' powerful, extended claws, teeth like broken fishbones, all seven mouths agape. Sickened, Lell heard the messenger shriek. Dhattar set his hoof down in the pool, breaking the image.

"We needn't watch more," he told her softly.

Jan felt his sister's silent sigh. She shook herself, heart thumping inside her ribs, voice tight with outrage.

"He's evil," she whispered. "He eats his own kind."

Dhattar nodded, then glanced away. The stingless wyverns had finished drinking. Jan observed them: all were noticeably plumper, more nimble, less weary. Aiony nodded gravely to the foremost among them. Apparently they had been speaking softly for some time.

"We will not forget, little black-and-silver. Seeking these dens which you describe, we will praise your name, and think no more ill of unicorns."

"Have a care how you depart," Aiony answered. "All the herd does not feel as we. One day, perhaps, we will pledge truce with stingless wyverns—but for now, this must be but our own, privy pact. Avoid our sentries and depart in peace, guided by Alma's eyes."

Softly as running water, the wyverns slipped away. Jan marked only the barest rustle of grass as they withdrew. That, too, faded. Lell looked at Aiony.

"They're smaller than I thought."

Dhattar nodded. "Those were but youths, and stingless. The ones with stings are older, far greater in size. Our warriors will have no easy task."

"Truth," another voice behind them murmured, a deep, throaty purr like a grass pard's thrumming.

Dhattar and Aiony jumped and wheeled. Lell did not, merely cast a glance over one shoulder at Illishar just emerging from the trees. His massy, wingèd form was as graceful moving along the ground as it was in flight.

"You unicorns are a fearless lot," he chuckled. "I wonder you don't all perish before you're grown."

Aiony laughed, nipping the tercel gently on his great eagle's foreleg. "You move very silent, Illishar."

"And you are not quite the all-seer you think yourself, little moonshadow."

"We're young," Dhattar answered matter-of-factly. "We'll see more clearly in time." With one curving talon, the gryphon pulled a wisp of grass from the white foal's mane. Gently, Lell champed her nephew by the crest of the neck and shook him, then did the same to Aiony.

"I thought best—since you'd sworn me against informing your dam—to bring a warrior fierce enough to defend us at need."

Jan felt relief flooding him to realize Illishar had guarded the young trio the whole while.

"Come," the gryphon said, turning. "Night grows late. Were we to stay longer, we would be missed. Let us see if we are as clever at slipping back through the sentries as we were at slipping out."

Dhattar and Aiony on either side, Lell bringing up the rear, the three colts followed. The shadow of the grove swallowed them. Before them, barely in sight, the main body of the camp lay off across the tall grass. No sooner had the four companions vanished from Jan's view than two new figures emerged from the trees. These, too, had apparently concealed themselves and watched. Deep cherry red, Jah-lila shook her standing mane and turned to her fellow, the star-covered stallion Calydor.

"Sooth, their power astonishes," he remarked, "and in view of their age—foaled but three summers gone?"

The red mare nodded.

"This deed bodes weighty for their folk."

Jah-lila smiled. "When it becomes known. But that will not be for some seasons yet."

"Only three years in age." Calydor shook his head in disbelief. "The Sight runs strongly in their blood."

The red wych eyed him wryly, murmured, "On both sides. Now ask me what you will."

The star-marked seer snorted. "Will you aid me? Will you do as I ask and arrange a meeting? She will not converse with me in others' sight, or even look on me. She flees when I approach. I must speak with her. I must."

The red mare's black-green eyes grew merry. "Have I not always brought you word of her whenever I traversed the Plain? Let you know she was well and had borne two healthy colts and fared happily among her folk?"

"You told as little as you could," Calydor snapped. "You never told me her station, that she had pledged as prince's mate and borne him heirs."

The red mare shrugged, gazing off into the trees in the direction Illishar and his three companions had gone. "I had my reasons." Her gaze turned back to the other. "Tell me, now that you have met, what think you of Jan?"

"A fine young stallion, deft dancer, gifted singer—as different from the raver that sired him as I can imagine."

"And Ses's other child?"

"Brave as a pard, that one," Calydor exclaimed. "She'd make a fine 'Renegade.' "

Jah-lila whinnied with laughter. "High praise."

The blue-and-silver stallion shifted impatiently. "Enough chat, Red One. Will you aid my cause? Will you persuade her to meet me, in secret if she must?"

The red mare turned, eyeing him fondly and shaking her head. "No need, old friend. Ses has already come to me, entreating me to devise this tryst. Wait a little. She will come."

Jan saw the blue-and-silver stallion start, frame rigid, eyes moonlit fire. Jah-lila nipped him affectionately and meandered away into the trees.

"I'll leave you to her." Her words floated softly back over one shoulder. "And wish you best fortune."

The shadows took her. Her form vanished. Ears pricked, breath short, Calydor gazed into the moon-mottled grove. The hairs of his pelt lifted as though he were cold. Night breeze blew balmy. His long, silver whisk tail swatted one flank. He snorted, tossing the pale forelock back from his eyes, and picked at the loose soil near the riverbank with one hind heel. Before him, a figure coalesced, a mare of moonshine and smoke. With a curious mixture of purpose and hesitation, she moved forward. Unseen, many leagues distant, Jan recognized her instantly. The star-lit stallion called her name. Turning toward him, Ses halted. He drew near, choosing each step.

"Too long," he breathed. "Too long, my one-time love."

She eyed him sadly. "Perhaps," she murmured. "I, too, have felt the years."

"Why did you not come to me," he entreated softly, voice scarcely steady, "as once I begged? Were your Vale's walls so high, so fast you could not win free till now?"

Again, her sad-eyed gaze met his. "I had a daughter and a son to rear. A mate with whom to keep faith."

"A mate who betrayed you, and all your folk," the seer rasped, "who nearly destroyed his own herd, then tried to do the same to mine."

Ses cast down her eyes with a bitter sigh. "He was not always mad," she breathed. "I loved him well. Why did you not come to me, if you were so determined?"

Her words were a plea. She turned, unable to look at him. He gentled, drew closer.

"Knowing my coming could spell death for us both?"

She moved away. He gazed across the dark, motionless pool, every lumen of the sky mirrored there.

"The Red Mare brought me word of you," he murmured. "At long, odd intervals: that you had borne fine foals, that you seemed happy. She would not bear my messages."

Ses gazed at the shadows. "Jah-lila never told me she had found you—I suspect she knew I could not have borne such news. Parts of my life in the Vale brought me great joy: my children, aye. But always there was regret."

The cream-colored mare with the poppy-red mane turned to face him.

"I never dreamed she brought you word. She did not speak of her journeys to the Plain. I never asked her to find you or speak of me. I thought you had forgotten me."

Again he moved nearer. "I have spent my life remembering you." This time she did not draw away. Still he only gazed, as though not daring to touch lest she vanish, a dream. After a time, he said, "She bore me only bits and snatches, as though hearsay, claiming she was exiled from the Vale and did not know more."

"She was exiled," Ses murmured. "But she is a seer and knows far more than what her own eyes tell her."

The silvered midnight stallion sighed. "I, too, am a farseer. A fine one. Yet I could never find you in my dreams. Still all these years, I never lost hope that one day you would come to me."

The pale mare's laugh was bitter. "I asked Jah-lila to contrive this rendezvous that I might appeal to you to keep your distance. None yet know the fate of my mate. . . ."

"What of it?" Calydor cried, voice hoarse with astonishment. "You cast him off! Three years hence. The Red One told me this."

"Because his madness endangered my child. That does not leave me free to pledge another. We of the Vale do not treat lightly the swearing of eternal vows."

Calydor whickered, in bafflement and despair. "Here we make no such pledges. You could leave your folk. . . ."

"Do not say it!" Ses hissed. "Not while my youngest remains a child. Calydor, do not tempt me."

"Your herd poises on the brink of war," the farseer replied. "Of course I will tempt you. I will tempt all your folk. Do not go! Do not hazard your life. Remain with me upon the Plain and what need then for your hallowed Hills? Let the wyverns have them."

The pale mare's countenance hardened. "You forget the wrong done my people so many years ago."

"Centuries. To unicorns who are all long dead."

"Lynex of the white wyrms is not dead," she answered. "He holds the Hills in triumph still. For the righting of that ancient wrong my son was born."

"Had you but left your folk and come with me," Calydor besought her, "then he had been *our* son."

Ses started, turning. "Ours?" she whispered, barely audible. "Do you not . . . ?"

But the other ran over her words. "A dozen nights and days Jan and I spent in one another's company, trading our peoples' tales. All I learned of him I have sung across the Plain. What goodwill you find among us now is due largely to news of his peacemaking. Sooth to look at him, save for his color, one would never guess him to be scion to that warmongering sire. Would he *were* my son!" Calydor exclaimed. "Would ever I had sired a son so fine."

The pale mare stared at him for a long, long while. Her chestnut eyes revealed nothing. At last she spoke:

"Rest sure that once this war is done and Lell is grown, I will turn my thoughts to the Plain and to you. I promise no more. Until then, I beg you, keep clear."

The blue-and-silver's reply was quiet and full of pain. "Here we stand on the verge of summer, just three days' journey from the Hills. On the morrow, Tek and her warriors press on, leaving behind colts and fillies too young to fight, elders too frail, nursing mares and the halt and infirm to shelter with us at oasis till your messengers return. This much my folk have promised yours. And if a few hotheads have joined your lackwit crusade, as many among your own ranks mean to desert: those who have lost their stomach for this war or who, like us, cannot comprehend its end. You could be one of those, my love. The pair of us could be away before your sentries were aware."

Firmly, the pale mare shook her head. "Not while my son lives. Not while Korr's fate remains unknown. Not while my daughter is yet too young to fend for herself."

Calydor smiled. "That last will not be long," he mused. "A precocious one that."

"Like her brother."

"She reminds me of the bold young filly in the lay of the mare and the pard."

Ses's head snapped up. "Mare and pard?" she inquired testily. "What mean you by that?"

The farseer only smiled, reciting offhand. " 'She who saw her enemy couched in the grass, and loved him for his beauty and his grace, and charmed him there, despite himself, and lived to tell the tale.' You might do well to keep one eye upon your fearless daughter, love," he said. "Young as she is, I think her heart already stolen, and the thief yet unawares."

A little silence grew up between them. Moon moved across heaven and the waters ever so slightly. The sky rolled a hair's breadth, tilting the stars.

"How can you go?" he asked. "How can you fly to war with your son not even here to lead the fray?"

"Have you seen him?" she queried. "Have you seen Jan in your dreams? If Jah-lila sees, she will not say. The twins see him, but all they can say is that he speaks with one all covered with jewels, deep within the earth or sky. I know not what they mean. Do you?"

Calydor shook his head. "I have not seen him."

Ses snorted. "Fine seer you."

The star-strewn stallion tossed his head. "I foresaw the dark destroyer, and the peacemaker who followed. I foresaw you, so many years ago. And I have seen much of weather and of pards that have threatened my people over the years." He shrugged. "I know not why I cannot see your son. One viewer cannot behold everything. I am but one among Álm'harat's many thousand eyes."

Ses gazed at the camp, dimly visible through the dark line of trees bordering the pool. "I must return," she sighed. "Three days' hard travel lies ahead, and beyond that, battle. The twins vow Jan will return at need. I trust soon to see my son again." Already she was moving toward the trees. "Go hale and safe, Calydor, that we may meet again after this war."

"Swear you will come away with me then," he whispered, "so I may bear the wait."

But she said nothing. Only wind murmured. She vanished into the dark of the trees. Calydor discerned no trace. As though a haunt, she had turned once more to mist. The Plain lay utterly silent save for the faintest breath breeze. Somewhere in the distance, he heard a pard cough. Above him, the moon, silvery gibbous, blazed like the greatest of Alma's eyes among the summer stars.

The Scouts of Halla

★ 19 ★

Gazing into the depths before him, Jan realized it was not near-summer sky he saw, but the darkness of the waters on the dragon queen's brow. Glimmers there were not stars but gleams reflected from the lake of fire. All view of future events faded. He knew himself to be in the den of Wyzásukitán. How long—an hour, an evening? He had no sense of time. Still he felt neither hunger nor fatigue, thirst nor intensity of heat. He had not been with the dragon long, surely. No more than a few hours at most.

The clear fluid of the pool before him trembled, sudden ripples traversing its surface, shaking apart the stars. Dragon's breath swirled about him like fog as Wyzásukitán sighed, lifting her head. The dark unicorn fell back a pace as the massive reptilian queen now gazed down upon him from a great height. The long muscles beneath her taut, jeweled skin flexed. Her wings and limbs and tail arched, rid themselves of stiffness. Again she sighed, and her white breath shot out like jets of cloud.

"What troubles you, prince of unicorns? I sense your disquiet."

Jan gazed up at her steadily, refusing to let her vastness overwhelm him.

"I am grateful for this foreseeing which you have granted, great queen," he answered, "but uncertainty chivvies me. Is what I see before me only that which *can* be—or that which *will* be, which *must* be?"

"I grant nothing," Wyzásukitán murmured in her measured, guarded way. She sounded quietly amused. "You behold only what you yourself are capable of beholding."

Abruptly, she fell silent. Jan waited a long moment. When she did not continue, he made bold to say, "You have not answered my question, great queen."

The red dragon betrayed not the slightest affront. She seemed only interested, perhaps approving. "You must answer it yourself, dark prince. What is it you see?"

The dark unicorn hesitated. "What I see has the feel of truth. . . ." The words trailed off. The dragon waited. "Yet if what I see has not yet come to pass, then it can be neither true nor false."

Wyzásukitán's mouth quirked, suppressing a smile.

"Oh?" she asked, so softly he almost did not hear. "Is it the future that you see?"

"Aye," he answered tentatively, then with conviction. "Aye. It *is* the future—no mere dream."

"Ah," the red dragon queen sighed. The steam of her breath rose toward the ceiling in roiling columns as she drew the long syllable out. "What troubles you, then?"

Jan felt a sudden crick of frustration. Was she toying with him? Suddenly he wondered, then shook himself. Nay, truth, he was sure she was not. He suspected her of being deliberately obtuse, while at the same time certain there was no malice in her. She was not questioning him merely to amuse herself, though he sensed his answers somehow amused her. Quashing a sudden urge to reply in kind, he drew breath and tried again.

"I wish to know if what I see is possibility or certainty. Do I see but one of many paths the future may take, or do I see the surety of what will without question come to pass?"

The dragon's jewel-encrusted browridge lifted. Her nostrils flared. "Consider. If what you saw were mere possibility, why should that trouble you?"

Jan thought a moment before replying. "If mere possibility, why bother to observe it?"

Wyzásukitán's great shoulder shrugged ever so slightly. "To spy a goal toward which to strive—or a warning of perils to avoid?"

The dark unicorn frowned. "Perhaps."

"Now consider this," the red queen continued: "if what you saw were indeed predestined, unalterable?"

Jan shifted uneasily. "Then I am most troubled."

She watched him. "Why?"

"Because I do not see myself in these scenes-to-come. Where shall I be? Am I not my people's Firebringer? Must I not journey among them to the Hallow Hills and lead their preparations to battle the white wyrms?"

"Must you?" the dragon replied. "Is that indeed foreordained? Are you privy to the last step of every dance set in motion by Her of the Thousand Jeweled Eyes?"

Her look grew suddenly less detached. Inquisitive. Penetrating, even. Jan felt his discomfiture grow. "Nay," he answered. "Alma reveals little of her plans. What I learn I invariably glean in snatches, glimpses."

"Yet always she has guided you?"

He nodded. "Even when I myself remained unaware."

"Then what uneases you?"

Jan frowned, trying hard to frame the words. "I sense somehow, gazing into your brow, that time slips away. That I should hasten back to my folk before their hour of need."

"You believe that the hour does not yet betide," answered Wyzá-sukitán. Doubtfully, Jan considered. Nay, of course not. Why caval so? None of what he had foreseen had yet come to pass. All lay in the offing. Ample time remained to rejoin the herd. Ample time. Did it not? The dragon queen shrugged. "Perhaps you do not see yourself among your folk because you do not wish to be among them."

The dark unicorn gazed up at her, baffled. The dragon gazed down.

"Might your absence have less to do with inability to rejoin them than with your refusal to do so?"

"Refusal?" Jan exclaimed, astonished. Outrage pricked at him. "Refusal to rejoin my folk—to accept the destiny toward which I have striven all my life?"

Wyzásukitán evidenced no surprise. Gently, she said, "Another thing troubles you, Firebrand. A duty unbearable holds you back from your folk."

Jan stared at her, her great gleaming form vast and beautiful above him, the light of the lake of fire winking and glancing off her jeweled skin like a thousand summer stars. He felt his unease collapse into terror.

"I don't know what you mean," he stammered.

She looked at him. "Indeed?" she asked. "You do."

"Nay, I . . . ," he started.

"Say me no nays," she answered curtly. "It is your mate, is it not? Tek, the rose-and-black mare who leads your herd. You love her. You long for her. Yet you fear reunion. Admit why that should be, Aljan of the Dark Moon. Tell me why you refuse to rejoin your mate."

Jan's head whirled. The cavern seemed to tilt. He felt himself falling helplessly through infinite space.

"It is not . . . not Tek," he managed, lock-kneed, swaying. The careening chamber steadied, stilled. He breathed deep. "Not Tek I fear, but what I must do when next we meet. What I must tell her. . . ."

The dragon inclined her head. "That is?"

Words choked him. "That she is Korr's heir before me, my own sister by half, sired by my sire, the king's secret firstborn daughter, queen of the unicorns."

He scarcely believed he had gotten it all out. He stood panting, unable to look at Wyzásukitán. He stared off across the huge chamber toward the lake of fire. It rippled, shimmered, not silent, but making low roarings from time to time, its thick, molten flux moving at cross-currents. Hissing sounded, fiery vapors venting, and the thick fizzing of spattered drops. Blaze and shadows played against the chamber's walls. He felt his whole being in a state of tumult like the lake.

"Trust what you feel," the firedrake told him. "What rises in you at this news?"

Anguish. Fury. Nausea. He could admit to none of them. "I don't know."

Above him, Wyzásukitán turned her head to one side and eyed him askance. "Do you mean to renounce your kingship to Tek? To renounce her as your mate?"

"I don't know!"

He had no inkling what he intended to do. He had lived all his life believing himself to be prince, only to discover the office belonged to Tek. He had no right to rule. Tek deserved the truth. Deserved her birthright. The love he bore her was so great he felt his heart might burst. Yet how was Alma's prophecy ever to be fulfilled if he renounced his leadership?

But deep within his inmost soul, he knew that none of those considerations really mattered. What appalled him most was that in revealing Tek's parentage, he must lose her. Despite vows sworn by the Summer Sea, no matter how unbreakable in Alma's eyes, regardless the fruit of that innocent pledge, how could such a union be allowed to stand? What joy to rejoin the herd if nevermore might he claim Tek as his mate? That their bond, meant to last a lifetime, must now end was what he truly could not face.

"I don't know," he told Wyzásukitán, his voice a ghost. The great dragon was bending down again. Her huge head came to rest on the chamber floor before him.

"Then gaze once more into my brow," she replied, "and find your answer there."

The dark water drew him, shot through with images. He moved toward it, unable to resist. Below, he saw the dark, rilled expanse of the Smoking Hills, their cinder-black tors thrust up like antler tines. Snow dusted the peaks and the deep crags which never saw the sun.

Slopes sheered away into dragon's breath. Valleys opened below. Jan could not understand how he himself had breached these barrier cliffs. No egress seemed possible for any wight devoid of wings.

He heard their chant before he saw them, strung out single file like an endless line of roan-colored ants. They moved in unison, hooves all falling at the same time, till the black stone rang with the beat of their song:

> "So soon the Scouts of Halla, we
> Fare forth to fill our destiny:
> On hardy wyrms to hone our horns,
> Unite in arms with unicorns
> Who march the Mare's Back; thus we must
> Endure the deadly Saltland dust
> As firedrake allies ope the way,
> Behold our Firebrand's battle day. . . ."

The chant rolled on and on, each step bringing the winding train of unicorns closer to the impassable ridges. Jan distinguished Oro at the head of the lengthy queue, which seemed to consist solely of brawny half-growns and warriors in their prime. The dark prince of the Vale recognized them instantly as a warhost. But where did they intend to go? Surely they could not mean to join Tek's host trekking across the Plain, for how could they hope to escape the Smoking Hills?

Yet as he watched, something caught his eye. Oro and the others moved almost as in trance, impervious to cold. Though their movements were measured, their expressions remained alert. No somnolent marchers, these. Was it only their singleness of purpose which made them appear invulnerable? Higher they climbed and higher, more shaggy goats than unicorns. Steadily, unhesitatingly, they scaled nearly vertical steeps and descended precipitous slopes. Jan marveled at their tirelessness, traversing the sheer paths in their snaking file hundreds of unicorns long.

Even so, he surmised, they were approaching a spot where they could proceed no farther. Oro and the front of the line had already reached it: a flat plateau falling away into a deep canyon, overlooked by a tall pinnacle. For the unicorns now assembling on the plateau, no means existed to move forward. The drop into the adjacent vale was sheer. No way to skirt the rift, for it was hemmed by unscalable scarps, the tallest a conical peak poised at one end of the canyon. Its sharp yet massive point rose above the others like a thick, curved horn.

How did the Scouts mean to cross, Jan wondered? When all had assembled, Oro stood near plateau's edge, his back to the steep, un-bridgeable valley. Jan could not make out his words, though the others all listened attentively. They stood in perfect stillness, so utter as to seem preternatural. Not one so much as stamped a hoof for warmth. Oro turned to gaze at the rift before them, then at the pointed peak rising to one side. Jan noted the cone's asymmetry, the side facing the valley undercut, so that the pinnacle seemed to hang above it, tons upon tons of incredibly hard, black rock.

A faint tremor shook the ground. Jan felt its thrum even in the air. The mountains seemed to mutter almost imperceptibly, then subside. Oro and the others drew back from the plateau's edge. Another tremor, more forceful this time. Echoes and sharp reports as of a great cracking and straining rebounded from the far side of the valley. Oro's band crowded tightly together in the center of the plateau. Again, the tremor stilled. Silence then, save for the cracks and groans, as though the fabric of some immeasurably vast tree, twisted by wind, were slowly, ever so slowly, breaking apart.

None of the warriors upon the plateau whinnied in fear. None cavaled. They all watched, Jan realized, eyes fixed on the tall peak leaning above the valley. Jan stared at the peak. It was vibrating. Slightly at first, then more and more insistently, it created a shudder in the air. The shudder grew, like a wind slowly building, until it buffeted but made no sound. The groaning started again, so low it was nearly below Jan's range, a deep, thunderous keening like nothing he had heard before.

The next tremor, when it came, was so sudden, so violent, even Jan, floating bodiless above, flinched. The black, snow-covered cone tore from its base, plunging down into the deep crevasse with a concussion that seemed to rock the world. A gout of smoke or steam shot up from the base of the shattered peak, which appeared to be hollow. A hail of cinders and dust rained from the sky.

The valley swallowed the peak and ceased to be as the fallen mountain filled the rift from edge to edge. Thundering rubble continued to quake there, shifting and seething. The broken peak's conical base, which had not fallen, now rumbled and broke apart. Explosive blasts of earth and smoke. Jan glimpsed something moving in the heart of the disintegrating base, a huge shining thing, reddish in color, crawling or flowing along like a slow river, or the side of some immensely vast creature in motion under the earth, a creature that had lain dormant so long it had grown larger than its original tunnel, a creature shifting in sleep, or waking and stretching sleepily before moving off in search of more spacious dens.

Oro and the Scouts of Halla were in motion, too. As soon as the first force of the blast had passed and the rubble now filling the former valley settled, every unicorn waiting upon the plateau sprang forward. They dashed headlong across the quaking new stretch in a sweeping charge while smoking grey cinders pelted out of the sky, covering them with a dusting of grey.

The Scouts of Halla were across the rift. As they reached the far side, Jan realized with a start that the hills were gentler here. Beyond, he saw, lay the waterless Salt Waste. Wind blew in the direction of the Waste, pursuing the sprinting unicorns. Cinderfall grew heavier, the ground's trembling more ferocious. Had Oro's band not surged forward precisely when they did, Jan saw, they would never have managed to cross. Brightness infused the ashfall. Some of the cinders glowed. Some were not cinders at all, he grasped, but droplets of dragonsflood.

A bright fountain spewed from a rift in the ruin of the fallen peak's broken base. Beneath welled a molted tongue of red that spilled slowly to the shallow depression's floor. Once the fiery flood had wound across, all passage would be blocked, at least until it cooled. How long would that take, Jan wondered—days? Weeks? The Scouts of Halla fled on toward the Salt Waste across the foothills of Dragonsholm. Their heels raised a cloud which mingled with the falling ash.

Battle

★ 20 ★

S*ummer*. The suddenness of transition startled him. One moment Jan had seemed to be wheeling over the snow-capped Smoking Hills, air obscured by clouds of dust and smoke. The next, he found himself leagues upon leagues away, the wide, green Plain rolling beneath, a clear cloudless dawn sky above, the Hallow Hills before.

Unicorns of the Vale lay in the tall grass, gazing toward their unreclaimed homeland. Tek, flanked by Ryhenna and Dagg, couched at the crest of the rise. Jah-lila, Teki, and Ses waited close behind. The rest of the band reclined below them, well hidden. No colts lounged among the band, no ancient elders or suckling mares. Warriors only made up the great warhost, nostrils flaring to scent the breeze, ears swiveling to catch every sound. Thick haze hung low in the sky far to the east, its source beyond horizon's edge. It tainted the sunrise orange-red, a fiery light bathing the Hallow Hills. The dappled warrior beside Tek shifted.

"No sign of him," he muttered. "Where is he? He set out an hour since."

"Grant him time," Ryhenna soothed in the strange, lilting cadence of her former tribe, the *daya*. "Dawn breaketh only now."

The pied mare turned, called softly. "What is that haze in the east? Can you tell?"

Below her, the red mare lifted her head. "Naught that will affect us here. It comes of the Smoking Hills."

"A blood-bright dawn," Teki the healer beside her murmured. "Will the weather hold?"

"Aye," the red mare told him. "It will."

"Blood-stained but beautiful," the pale mare, Ses, beside them whispered. "Its red light illumines the hills. So they appeared on the eve of my initiation, years ago."

"When thou sawest thy vision of the Firebringer?" Ryhenna inquired.

Ses nodded, wistful. "And other things."

Tek turned back to the Hallow Hills, glowing crimson in the dawnlight still. "Where is Jan?" she barely breathed. "Why has he not returned?"

A shrill cry fell from above, piercing as a kite's. The pied mare started, felt the warhost behind her stir. Her gaze darted skyward. A moment later, his shadow passed over her, and she was able to glimpse Illishar, his hue so well matched to the green sky he had approached unseen. Circling, he began to descend.

"At last!" Tek heard Dagg exclaim. "Once the wingcat reports, we can devise our best means of attack."

The wyverns lay concealed, hidden behind boulders and rocky outcroppings. The ravine formed a box canyon, its banks gentle at first, but whoever ventured its narrow passage found the sides soon steepened to precarious slopes. The wyverns often drove game here: deer and boar, bands of antelope that had strayed from the Plain. No game drives now since the first of the year. Instead, they had waited, king's loyalists ever on watch for unicorns, those thrice-cursed skulkers of the Vale who never failed to steal into the Hills sometime during the spring.

"What a ruin," the first of two wyverns sheltering behind a single boulder hissed. "This dawn marks summer's first day, and where are the unicorns? They never came."

"Nor will they," its companion muttered, smaller than the first, and more slenderly made. "They died out or gave up or lost their way. The sum is, they come here no more."

"Precisely," the first wyvern muttered. "We've frittered all spring on this fruitless task, when we might have been coursing young fawns and cracking their bones."

This larger wyvern was of a bluer cast than the more slender one. Its tail was longer, the sting upon it more wickedly barbed. A rudimentary second head was budding from one shoulder, no more than an offshoot, its features still indistinct, mouth sealed shut, the bulbous, bruise-dark lids of its nascent eyes not yet open. It writhed fretfully against the thicker stalk of the bluish wyvern's primary neck. With one blunt, badger-like claw, the ice-blue wyrm petted it, humming.

"This ravine makes a fair enough game-trap," the slimmer, more pearl-colored wyrm was saying. A summer hopper flicked through the air. With a snap, it downed the long-legged thing. "I've run down onc and springer here, even a Plainscalf once."

Its two-headed companion nodded impatiently. "As have we all. But now we must let game pass unmolested, lest we spook any phantom unicorns that might wander near."

"The king has lost his wits," the pearl-colored wyvern murmured, sniffing the grass in search of other hoppers. "Ever since the queen was slain."

"*There* was a wyvern," the elder wyrm exclaimed. Its rudimentary nob slumbered now against its collarbone. It scratched its main pate's gill ruff with one knife-nailed badger claw. "She'd have thrown the king down and taken his place, had the unicorns not finished her."

A scarlet earthworm wove through the grass. The bluish wyvern stabbed after it, but missed. Its companion studied a yellow butterfly fluttering about its head.

"Then we'd have fire still," it answered. "She'd have shared it among us again. It was only the king's edict—and his fear—that forbade each of us keeping our own fire, as we used to do. All those winters lazing beside a burning brand! That's what made us strong. It's lack of warmth caused all those stingless prits to hatch."

The yellow butterfly fluttered near. The pearlescent wyvern clapped its jaws, but the next instant spat, shook its head and pawed its muzzle to dislodge the clinging yellow wings. "Uch! It tastes of saltclay and sulfur."

Its companion chuckled. "No doubt. What you say of fire is true as well. Now that the king's let his own brand die, our last flame is gone. Unless we find another source, no more stinging wyrms will hatch of our broods. Mark me."

"The stingless ones," the pearly wyrm added. "You heard they fled? Aye, across the Plain. Six days ago."

Its bluish companion turned. "Fled? I thought they were in hiding."

"Nay," the slender wyvern assured it. "Yet not one stinging loyalist was sent in pursuit—lest we miss the unicorns! Time enough to track peaceseekers once we've dealt with His Majesty's unicorns—what is this sudden fascination? He says he sees them in his dreams. Says he feels them watching him."

"Unicorns," the bluish wyvern scoffed, glancing at the ravine's grass-covered slopes dotted with boulders and slabs of exposed stone. "We'll never see another. . . ."

"Hist!" his companion snapped, suddenly alert. The pearl-colored wyvern's gaze was fixed downslope. The larger wyrm heard grunts and

whiffs of surprise from fellows massed behind other boulders on both
their own and the facing slopes. Only those hiding lower on the near
hillside were visible to the bluish wyvern. They, too, had become instantly attentive. Alongside, the pearl-colored wyvern breathed a single
word: "Unicorns!"

Downslope, filing into the canyon, came a party of unicorns. Late
morning sun blazed down. The breeze sighed balmy, just a bare trace
cool. A robust young stallion led, his yellow dappling into grey along
shoulder and flank. Only a few others in the band appeared, like him,
to be warriors in their prime. Most seemed youthful half-growns. They
traveled cautiously, eyes darting, ears up-pricked. The wyverns waited
in fevered silence until the last of the band, a slim, coppery mare, had
entered the confines of the sloping ravine.

"Now!" the pearl-hued wyvern screamed, rising to plunge down the
slope in a streaking slither. "Drive them deep into the canyon. Trap and
devour them!"

The bluish wyvern also lunged. All around, its fellows dodged from
behind boulders and coursed toward the hapless unicorns, who wheeled
and whistled in alarm.

"They're mostly striplings!" the bluish wyvern cried. "Helpless
prits. Sting them to death and drag the meat to the king!"

It saw its own kind across the ravine, pouring down the opposite
slope toward their prey. But what was this? Instead of scattering in
terror, the unicorns were massing. Racing toward them, the two-headed
wyvern heard the party's leader, the grey-and-yellow dapple, coolly
whistling orders, saw the coppery mare and young half-growns beside
her swinging to form themselves into an outward facing ring, horns
bristling to meet the wyvern onslaught. Here was no motley band of
colts. Those wyrms who reached them first were skewered and tramped,
fell back with screams of surprise, hisses of rage.

"No matter!" the ice-blue found itself shrieking. "No matter they're
warriors. We're larger than they. We outnumber them. Use your stings!"

Its own tail lashed to scourge the dappled stallion ramping before
him. The unicorn braced for the coming blow, did not so much as dodge.
He held his place in the outward-facing ring, hooves set, horn aimed.

"See how your blood burns at this!" the ice-blue wyvern shrilled,
bringing its tail barb down like a flail.

The yellow stallion shuddered, shrugged the stroke aside, then
lashed and lunged. The bluish wyvern drew back, surprised. All around,
its snarling companions swarmed. None of the unicorns broke ranks.
The blue wyrm saw them repeatedly stung, but though they flinched,
they did not fall. The battle became a grunting, panting shoving-match,

wyverns pressing in against the circle, horned warriors refusing to buckle.

"Our stings have lost their power!" the pearly one beside it cried, panic beginning to edge its voice.

"Our horns have not," the copper-colored mare beside the dappled stallion retorted, lunging. Her horn pierced the pearlescent wyvern through one shoulder. It sank, writhing, colorless blood streaming down its pale hide. Its badger claws pawed ineffectually at the wound.

"I'm pierced!" it shrieked. "Pierced through the bone! The unicorn has rent me!"

"Our weapons are keener than once they were," the dappled stallion panted. One flailing forehoof landed a stunning blow to the wounded wyvern's skull. "And tempered by fire. Your fibrous bone no longer dulls and chips our skewers."

Beside the stallion, the copper mare bent to finish the fallen wyrm. With a shriek, the bluish wyvern beheld others of its folk struck down by these half-grown colts, these stripling warriors. It reared to flee. The dappled stallion sprang. The bluish wyvern felt searing pain cleave its breast. *Pierced,* it realized, stunned. *Riven.* Already its awareness ebbed. *Run through the heart.* The cartilaginous breastplate that had protected its kind for centuries worthless now. *Our stings, useless. Our king's fire, burnt out.*

Sky above burned impossibly blue, not a cloud or a wisp obscuring the sun at zenith. Something circled there. A kite? No. Too large. Too green. Not the right shape at all. This creature's lower half looked like a pard. The wyvern's thoughts evaporated. Dimly, it felt the dappled stallion pulling his skewer-like horn free of its breast. Faintly, it felt itself fall. Distantly, it heard the high-pitched cry of the pard-bird overhead. Around the dying wyvern, its companions began to flee.

New whistling arose, not from the ring of young unicorns in the heart of the ravine, but from elsewhere on every side. The wyvern's transparent eyelids sagged. Unicorns, many more of them, streamed into the ravine from the entryway. A pied rose-and-black mare charged at their head. Other groups poured over the tops of both slopes, one led by a black-maned, mallow-red mare, the other by a poppy-maned mare pale as flame. These two bands converged on the fleeing wyverns while the third, larger mass swept up from the ravine's egress.

Trapped, the dying wyvern thought, astonished still. *Trapped even as we had hoped to trap them.* Screams from the wounded. The concussion of falling bodies. The dying wyvern's eyes slid shut. Battle's din, ever more furious, receded to a gentle buzz. The wyrm felt, barely, as from a great distance, the tramp of heels and the slither of bellies passing over it. *Overwhelmed by innumerable, invulnerable enemies,* it thought. *The utter absurdity. The waste. When our king bade us lie here in wait for unicorns, we, too, should have fled.*

🐚

"It will be a rout, then," Jan whispered, gazing into the illuminated darkness of the dragon's brow. His conclusion startled, confounded him. "Who would have believed it could be so? I had always thought recapturing the Hills would be arduous, a mighty struggle. . . ."

He let the words trail away as Wyzásukitán stirred.

"Oh, a rout is it?" she asked him gently.

Her smoky breath flowed and swirled about him. Across the dark pool, fleeing wyverns fell beneath the heels and horns of the unicorn warhost pursuing them across the Hallow Hills toward their limestone dens flanking the cliffs where the sacred moonpool lay. The dragon queen turned her head ever so slightly.

"You think it will be a rout?" queried Wyzásukitán. "You suspect your folk can win back your Hills so easily they have no need of you?"

The dark prince shuddered, considering. Did he truly believe these predictions, then? Dared he trust the visions? Had he gradually, without realizing, come to accept the images as the sure and certain future? But were they, he wondered? Would the events portrayed here come to pass in time, regardless of his own actions or failure to act? Dared he relax into such a soothing complacency?

"Nay, I . . . ," he started.

"Watch," the dragon queen murmured.

The images upon her brow intensified, their colors deepening, becoming brighter. Jan felt himself drawn in the way that had become so familiar during his brief stay with the dragon queen. How long had it lasted—a few hours? Half a day? How far into the future lay the events that he observed? He ceased to wonder as the view pulled him back into its depths. As before, he merged with it and lost himself.

He floated in the air above the Hallow Hills. The wyvern warriors who had lain in ambush in the box canyon had all broken ranks, seeking to flee the steep-sided ravine. Unicorns pouring over the sides fell upon them without mercy, the whistled orders of Tek and Dagg, Teki and Jah-lila, Ryhenna and Ses sounding clearly above the din: shrieks from the wyrms, the clash of hooves and horns, groans from the dying, panting and snorts.

Bodies littered the canyon, impeding the long-legged unicorns. The wyverns, with their slithering gait, snaked over and between mounds of the fallen. Ineffectual stings forced them to fight with teeth and claws.

The few who managed to escape the ravine flashed away faster than coursing rainwater. The unicorn warhost gave chase, managed to cut a fair number down as they fled across the open, rolling hills, through broken scrub and groves of slender trees.

The fleeing wyverns' screams had evidently been heard, for out of the limestone shelfland adjoining the moonpool cliffs poured fresh waves of stinging wyrms. Shrieked warnings of the invaders' seeming invulnerability only confused the rescuers, who attacked the unicorns in the traditional manner, with their stings. The battle changed from a chase to a series of pitched skirmishes as the two surging warhosts broke apart into dozens upon dozens of smaller assaults and combats.

Morning passed. Noon sun, coolly ablaze in the deep blue sky, declined to middle and then late afternoon. The great black stain upon the air to the east continued to grow, filling that quarter, and then that half of the sky. It chased the sun like a dark, enveloping mass. Watching it, the wyverns groaned. "An omen, an omen!" Jan heard some crying. "A darkness from out of the Smoking Hills. Surely it marks the end of the world."

Wyverns fell. Unicorns, as well—but far fewer than the wyrms. Repeatedly, small bands of a half-dozen unicorns maneuvered to surround one of the huge, stinging wyrms. More than a few had double heads, they were so old. The ring of warriors then pressed in on the wyrm, striking and slashing, pummeling with hooves and stabbing with horns, while the wyvern lashed ineffectually with its barb, snapped needle teeth, and raked what unicorns it could with the knifelike claws on its broad, stub paws.

Even seasoned warriors working in concert took a long time to bring down each large, fierce wyrm. And for every wyvern felled, it seemed another, fresh foe emerged from one of many entryways to the wyverns' subterranean dens. Jan glimpsed Tek and Dagg consulting, Ryhenna and Teki leading others to guard the larger entryways, prevent wounded wyverns from escaping back underground, and kill new wyrms as they emerged.

The strategy achieved only partial success. The crumbling limestone of the wyvern shelves made precarious footing for even the most agile of unicorns, and so many entries pocked the surface of the shelves that the guardians could not ward them all. Jan saw many more wyverns enter or emerge. Yet the pied healer and the coppery mare stemmed the flood of wyverns, slowing the pace of reinforcements and hindering safe retreat.

"Where is their fire?" Jan heard Tek crying to Dagg. "Why do they not use it against us?"

"And where is their leader, the wyrmking Lynex?" the dappled stallion whistled back. "Is he too craven to show his seven faces? Would he but show himself, and this whole struggle could be settled here and now!"

"Lynex, you coward!" Jan heard Tek shout down into the largest entryway. "I'd battle you myself, wyrmking. You stole these lands from the late princess Halla centuries ago. You have lived so long only that we unicorns might grow strong enough to take our homeland back again. Show yourself! Come out and face me if you dare!"

As if in answer, a low rumble sounded from the wyverns' dens. The hollow, deep-throated sound rose from the depths like the howl of stormwind. Thrumming followed, as of mighty limbs pounding the earth. The soft swish of slithering bellies whispered under the concatenation of noise. Startled, the unicorns fell back. The next instant, two dozen of the largest, most powerful wyverns Jan had ever seen rushed from the entryway, fanning out in a great semicircle and beating their paws upon the ground.

The earth shook with their thunderous drumming. Barbed tails thrashed like willow withies whipped by storm. In unison, the white wyrms roared. Each was nearly the size of the huge, three-headed queen Jan had slain years ago in his youth. Not a one of them did not have double heads, and two had third heads sprouting at the base of their necks. All around them, from other egresses, a flood of wyverns poured, all enormous, unwounded and unspent.

Late afternoon sun hung westering. Panting, their coats foaming with sweat, Tek's warriors stared at the advancing wyrms. Lines of blood streaked some of the unicorns, where wyvern teeth or claws had found their mark. The legs of some trembled, whether from tension or fatigue Jan could not tell. He knew none shook from fear. They had fought full tilt for hours, since before noon. Now, though they gave ground slowly before the howling, stamping wyrms, not a one of them fled.

Suddenly from the entryway, into the half-ring created by his score of gigantic bodyguards, another wyvern emerged, larger even than they. His seven heads arrayed, all their gill ruffs fanned, teeth bared like seven nests of thorny splinters. His long, seven-stinged tail lashed, doubling back upon itself. Massive paws, their nails like swords, impaled the air.

Lynex loomed above his own bodyguards. Gazing at the immense wyrmking, Tek gasped, appalled. Pale skin blazing opalescent in the afternoon sun, the scarred and ancient wyvern was easily twice the size his three-headed queen had been. Turning his baleful, seven-faced gaze toward Tek, the wyvern leader snarled.

"Coward?" the largest among his seven pates rumbled. "Little unicorn, you misjudge."

The visages wove and intertwined, bobbing and slithering one against another as they spoke.

"Do you imagine me a doddard, an old spent thing?" the second-largest face demanded. Its companion, nearly as large, spat, "Think again!"

"Behold my personal bodyguards," the fourth-largest commanded. Beside it, another, only slightly smaller, added, "We have not yet even begun our battle."

"What matter our stings no longer fell you," the second-smallest countenance inquired, "or that our fire burnt out?"

The tiniest maw hissed and slavered, snapping frantically at nothing. "Coward. Doddard. Bodyguards," it gurgled. "Battle! Stings and fire!"

"I am old beyond counting, hungry and powerful," the monstrous central head roared. "I have waited a long time for you. Prepare to die, puny, brazen upstarts. Killers of my queen. We seized these hills from your ancestors centuries past—and we do not mean to give them up!"

With a shout like rolling thunder, the colossal wyrmking, his bodyguards and all his followers surged forward. Tek stood stock-still, as though riveted by indecision or fear. Steep, precarious shelfland rose before her, the cliffs of the moon's mere behind. With a jolt, Jan realized what it was his mate surely already saw: if the wyverns succeeded in driving the unicorns back against those cliffs, the wyrms could crush them there and devour them all before the sun had set.

Flight

★ 21 ★

Rally!" Jan shouted, voice echoing hollowly in the vast chamber of the dragon queen. "Tek, rally them—form the crescent and the wedge. Don't let the wyrms drive you against the cliffs!"

The image before him wavered and rippled apart. Jan's awareness wrenched back to his surroundings: the dragon's den, the impossible heat and wavering glow of molten fire. The dark unicorn blinked as Wyzásukitán abruptly moved, lifting her brow high above the young prince's vision. He stared at her, startled and angry that she should snatch his view of Tek and her peril away. Ramping, he opened his mouth to speak, but Wyzásukitán spoke first.

"Tell me what you have seen, dark prince," she bade. White smoke of her breath wreathed her whiskered muzzle.

"I see my mate and her band in jeopardy," Jan answered shortly. "I charge you, lower your brow once more...."

The dragon queen eyed him, brow held regally above, not inclining her head the least measure. She studied him intently, gaze neutral, without malice, but no longer leisurely languid and amused. "Tell me your feelings, dark prince. What at this moment do you feel for your mate?"

"Love, longing, concern," Jan said without a moment's thought. "I see danger and would be there to defend her."

"So you would return to your mate?" Wyzásukitán asked. "And to your folk, whatever the consequence?"

"Aye, of course!" the dark unicorn cried, stamping. Sparks flew. The answer seemed so clear to him. He could not believe he had wandered in such confusion until now. He must return to Tek, rejoin the herd and accept whatever destiny Alma had prepared. The dragon queen looked at him.

"And will you tell your mate Korr's secret?"

Jan nodded. The answer did not come happily, but come it did and without hesitation.

"And your folk?" Wyzásukitán pressed gently. "You will tell them as well?"

"Of course," the dark unicorn answered. "I'll not live a lie, asking Tek to surrender her birthright that I might keep power not mine to hold."

"You will renounce your kingship?" the dragon queen sighed, white breath curling among her floating whiskers.

Jan nodded. "Aye, for love of her. And for Alma, who is what is: all truth, the Truth of everything that exists. Tek's parentage is what it is. So, too, my love for her. I must be true to both, and to myself."

The queen gazed down at him, her thousand thousand jewels glinting in the golden light of the molten lake that seethed beyond chamber's egress to the rear of Jan. He moved toward her, deeper into the chamber, his heart grown calm, at peace within himself.

"Why do you not ask that I lower my brow?" the dragon queen inquired. "Do you not wish to resume your gaze?"

Jan shook his head. "Nay. I wish only to return to my folk. I must winter with them their last season in the Vale, cross the Plain with them and join them as they fall upon the wyverns. It matters not that I may no longer serve as battleprince. Tek, as queen, must rightfully lead and rule them. Gladly will I march at her side, free of the silence and secrets Korr used to deceive us all."

"You would return, then?" the dragon queen asked.

He nodded. "Tell me what path I must take to depart these steeps and return to the Vale. All fall and winter lie before me. I must use that season to best advantage in broaching this terrible news to Tek and the herd by the time spring breaks and we cross the Plain to the Hallow Hills."

Wyzásukitán shrugged, flexing vast shoulder blades. Her huge, bat-like wings lifted a trace, rustling, their crusted jewels dragging the golden ground.

"Aljan Firebrand," the dragon queen replied, "no pass leads from Dragonsholm to return you to your Vale."

Jan frowned. "Somehow I found my way here from the Salt Waste. A way leads out again. It must."

Slowly, carefully, the dragon queen shook her head. The dark water of her brow never spilled. "None you could ever tread again."

The furrow in the dark unicorn's brow deepened. "Given time, I could find it," he answered, moving closer. "With your aid, I could find it more quickly."

The dragon pulled back, turning her head to eye him. "The path by which you came exists no more," she answered simply. "The rills of Dragonsholm continuously shift as my kind turn over in their dreams. On rare occasions, one of us changes her den. Then the earth shudders for many leagues. Peaks fall; valleys open and fill; new ridges heave up. These Smoking Hills are in constant flux. The way you found endured but briefly. It is no more."

Jan felt cold. "How long before a new way opens?"

Again the dragon shrugged. "Impossible to tell."

"But I must return to the Vale," the dark unicorn protested, "while autumn's yet new. I would be with Tek before the snows and use the coming winter to accustom the herd to the news I bear."

Wyzásukitán lifted her great, lithe form higher from the ground. First she tensed, then relaxed her huge forelimbs, her hind limbs. Her long tail stirred. "Fall is flown, Aljan. Winter, too. And so as well the spring. This day marks the first of summer, Firebrand."

Jan stared at her, badly confused. "You jest," he cried. "No more than a few hours have passed since I came to you. . . ."

"Indeed?" she asked. "I never jest. And I tell you now, you have stood with me all winter and all spring, and with Oro in the Hall of Whispers all fall before."

The dark unicorn shook his head. "Nay," he insisted. "It is but hours. I have not hungered or slept. . . ."

"You drank the dragonsup from my late mother's brow: all that remains of her waking dreams. It eased your hunger and fatigue, your thirst, your vulnerability to heat and cold. How else did you think, Firebrand, to stand before me in my den beside a lake of molten stone?"

Jan gazed up at the red dragon queen, speechless. She drew breath and sighed white clouds before continuing.

"I bade Oro and his warriors also sip before I sent them off, that they might gallop the whole way to your far Hallows, without pausing to eat or drink or rest. The hour grows short. Your people stand in urgent need, and time betides you to return."

"Time, time . . . ," Jan murmured. "How long have I stood dreaming here?"

"As long as it took the events which you witnessed to unfold," the dragon queen replied.

"Then what I saw, all that I saw . . . ," he groped.

"Was occurring as you watched," Wyzásukitán replied. "Your sense of time has been suspended by the water of my mother's dreams. You experienced these months as we dragons do, in a long, fluid reverie devoid of time."

"What I saw," Jan tried again, "the battle. . . ."

"Is no prediction," the firedrake answered, "rages even now, this moment, as we speak."

The dark unicorn felt his skin prickle. He demanded, "Tek's peril?"

"Is real. Is happening now."

A jolt like lightning coursed his blood. "Then I must go to her!" he shouted. "At once—"

He wheeled as though to dash from the dragon's den, recross the lake of fire, find his way to the surface again. The red dragon called to him.

"Hold, Aljan. What you saw in my brow was unfolding even as you beheld it. How long, do you think, to reach her, even if you ran day and night, never resting?"

He pitched to a stop, heart dropping with a sickening plunge. "Too late?" he demanded. "Do you say I have come to myself too late? That the children-of-the-moon will perish or triumph without me, locked underground, leagues parted from them, my destiny failed, unable to save or even join them in their hour of gravest need?"

His last words were a cry of agony as he realized: he had tarried too long, lost in his own chaos. His mate would succeed or die without him, his people win back the Hills or lose them in his absence. He was destined to participate in nothing, contribute nothing to this pivotal juncture in his people's history. Even if he eventually escaped the Smoking Hills, how would he dare rejoin his folk? His colts perhaps half-grown by then, his sister already a wedded mare, his memory in the mind of his own mate dimmed, his people's recollection of him faded, his destiny forgotten, unfulfilled. He would be recalled only as the one who had failed Alma's sacred plan, her would-be Firebringer who had never managed to accomplish her end. The dragon queen above him was laughing gently.

"Too late?" she chuckled. "High time, more like. Time your charming Scouts trotted back to their Hallows. They are a sweet-voiced tribe in sooth. Their songs have raptured my fellows these many years. But we have lain too still for far too long listening, entranced, holding steady these precarious steeps."

Jewels flashing, no malice in her, she smiled at Jan. He understood then that she was laughing at herself.

"My sisters have all outgrown their dens. Even my mate-to-be. He is young yet, still wingless, not ready to fly—though my own wings ache. Time I ventured a practice flight. Exercise, so they say, strengthens the sinews."

Her great eyes blinked. She paused considering.

"I shall find my betrothed a plaything," she murmured. "Some pale exotic wyrm fetched from far lands, one that will live long and sing for his delight."

She glanced at Jan.

"We dragons, as you know, do not eat flesh."

Wyzásukitán rose to her fullest height. The curve of her spine brushed the chamber's ceiling.

"Too late, Firebrand?" she asked. "Too late to fill your destiny? Never, Dark Moon of the unicorns—not while I have wings."

Her great leathery pinions unfolded, spreading across the cavernous roof. The innumerable jewels of her dark reddish hide gleamed, brilliant as night sky crowded with summer stars. One huge forelimb reached toward him, her claws spread wide. Jan had not even a moment to flinch before her gigantic talons closed about him, impossibly strong. They could have crushed him in an instant, he realized, yet he felt no fear as they curled snugly about him and lifted him easily from the cavern floor. He sensed the last remnants of the green feather in his hair vanish in a blazing flash.

Wyzásukitán's huge hind limbs flexed. Her shoulders, braced against the chamber's ceiling of curving stone, shoved upward with a mighty heave. The cavern broke apart in a shuddering roar as the dragon queen leapt free of earth. Rocks and boulders showered around them as the dragon shot upward. Jan found himself cradled against her jeweled breast, sheltered from falling debris. The hot ichor that beat beneath her scales pulsed slow and steady as the heartbeat of the world.

As the mountain fell away around them, Jan felt the outer air. Below, the lake of fire fountained skyward, no longer contained by rock. Molten stone rained all about them like liquid stars. The dragon's vast wings stroked and oared the wind, rising with effortless power into the darkening sky. Jan saw the Smoking Hills far below, jagged and black and wreathed in white mist. Rivers of fire flooded the ridges as far as he could see. The mountain from which Wyzásukitán had just burst was only one such peak which spouted fire.

Sun had already set upon the Smoking Hills, plunging them into darkness save for the ember-bright glow of dragonsflood. Wyzásukitán veered in a hurtling rush toward the west, where dying sunset flamed scarlet still, a distant, unseen conflagration. Smoking cinders and flaming chunks of rock arced around them as they flew. Jan realized they were climbing higher, and higher yet, rising above the burning dust and ash.

The farther they rose, the more frigid the wind became. Though he felt its bite, Jan did not mind the cold, or the airlessness of atmosphere attenuated almost too thin to breathe. The dragon queen's heart hammered. Her great lungs labored even as her stroking wings maintained their powerful, even rhythm. She was soaring aloft, coursing westward, chasing the sun. The Smoking Hills raced far, far below. Tiny peaks burst and spattered fire. Crimson rivulets threaded the black landscape.

The Salt Waste rushed beneath them, racing along at impossible speed. The upper ether through which they lanced had grown so thin there scarcely seemed to exist any wind. The rising cloud of ash and dust fell away behind them as they flew. The world shrank. Above, the sky darkened, air thinning into nothing, stars beginning to prick through the crimson blaze that colored the sky. Slowly, it grew more tawny. They left the crimson behind. The Salt Waste receded and the Plain rolled underneath.

They were drawing nearer the western horizon, closer to the Hallow Hills. The vanished sun appeared, unsetting, rising above the western horizon as though it were the breaking dawn. Sunlight streamed across the Plain, turning the sky not scarlet, but gold. Time seemed to reverse as they sped westward from first evening into dusk into very late afternoon.

From high, high above in icy space near the limit of the air, Jan looked down to see a host of unicorns galloping far in the distance ahead, much closer to the edge of the Hallow Hills than he and Wyzásukitán. Members of the host were all dark in color: ink blues and reddish roans, charcoal dapples and deep-golden duns. A roan maroon led them.

They raced with the energy of warriors still fresh, newly embarked, yet Jan knew they had been traveling for—how long: hours? Days? He knew only that sipping from the late dragon queen's dreams had fortified them in the same manner it had fortified him. He wondered if they had any notion of passing time. Or did they journey in reverie, a blur, as he himself had journeyed through three-quarters of a year deep in the darkness of the dragons' halls?

He watched the late, late afternoon sun floating infinitesimally upward, growing gradually younger and brighter with each passing moment. Its strong yellow light illumined the distant Hallow Hills. He felt the rhythm of Wyzásukitán's wings change, descending now. The warband of unicorns far ahead and below had just left the rolling Plain. The Scouts of Halla were streaming into the rills of their ancestral land.

❧

The wyverns pressed forward relentlessly, the white wyrmking at their head screaming his hatred for unicorns. Tek braced herself, determined not to be driven farther back. Already her warriors around her were dangerously bunched. They had no room to pivot and dodge, none to charge to one another's aid. The wyverns had them pinned against the moonpool cliffs, escape to either side so narrow that few unicorns could have survived a dash for freedom. The rest would have been overtaken and cut down. Better far to make a stand. Indeed, it was their only hope.

The pied mare glanced to left and right, surveying the battle. Dagg fought shoulder to shoulder with her, his mate, Ryhenna, on his other side. She spotted Ses farther back and to the left, the cream-colored mare with the flame-bright mane holding her ground in a press of other unicorns against the surge of oncoming wyverns. Tek searched the opposite way, glimpsed her own dam, Jah-lila, even farther distant, flanked by her foster father and namesake, the healer Teki.

The unicorn warhost stood spread in a long, shallow ribbon against the moonpool cliffs, more wyverns pouring from their holes and rushing toward them at every moment. Coldly, clearly, Tek grasped Lynex's strategy: with luck, he hoped to break through the unicorns' ranks and splinter them, then surround each smaller group and overwhelm it. Barring that, she knew, he planned to grind them against the cliffs until their line thinned and collapsed.

The extent to which her troops had allowed themselves to become stretched was not good, the pied mare saw. No helping it now. Her only viable tactic was to form them into an outward-facing crescent strong enough to resist the momentum of the wyvern advance. Then, carefully, she must pull the tips of the crescent inward, massing and thickening the formation before bulging its forward edge into a point. Perhaps, just possibly, she could then drive this wedge into Lynex's army, thus breaking it in two.

But they stood a long way from there yet, she acknowledged grimly, even as she whistled to rally the herd. She heard others take up the cries, pass them on in shrill piping that rose above the grinding noises of battle. Raggedly, the crescent began to form.

Scarred Lynex, amid his double-dozen huge bodyguards, reared at the heart of the onrushing mass, driving his followers with shrieks and threats. Despite all the foes her warhost had slain so far, Tek realized, as many more faced them now, fresher, larger, wilier and older than any they had fought earlier in the day. The new onslaught's force was tremendous. Again and again, Tek hurled herself forward, fighting furiously. Half a dozen wyverns fell before her hooves and horn. Dagg and Ryhenna protected her shoulder. Overhead, Illishar harried and stooped.

Others of her band did not fare so well. The pied mare spied places where the ranks of her defenders had grown perilously thin. The crush of fighters impeded reinforcements from reaching those spots. She saw Ses standing at one such point, nearly the sole defender. How much longer could she hold out? To the other side, Teki and Jah-lila worked feverishly, marshaling warriors to strengthen the line.

The crescent had stalled coalescing into the wedge needed to drive the wyrmking's hoard apart. Tek whistled the rallying cry again, again, but the exhausted unicorns were faltering. Before them, Lynex, three times the size of any other wyvern on the field, hooted his glee.

"Smash them, crush them!" his largest head shouted.

"Rip them, rend them," the two middle-sized pates flanking the main one cried.

"Snap them, slash them, bite and devour them," three of the smaller maws ranted, while the littlest nob gabbled and hissed: "Smash, rend, slash, devour!"

The wyverns were breaking through. Tek saw the line waver in two places. Ses leapt toward one of the weakening points, spurring on comrades with her whistles and cries. Ryhenna sprang to join her. On the opposite side of the pied mare, Teki and Jah-lila forged toward the other spot at which the warhost's ranks were in imminent danger of giving way. Too slowly. Defenders crumpled beneath the wyverns' teeth and claws. The crescent was staving in. Tek felt her own heart quail. The healer and the red mare would never reach the breach in time.

"Dagg, go!" she shouted, giving her shoulder-friend a slap on the rump with the flat of her horn.

The dappled warrior sprinted toward the buckling formation's edge, shouldering his way across the fray, whistling encouragement to those who still lived and desperately fought on. Tek returned to the struggle before her. She dared not follow Dagg's progress even a moment more. His absence and Ryhenna's created a gap in the ranks around her. She leapt forward to fill the breach.

The seven-headed wyvern king towered above her, his immense bodyguards writhing. They bore down on Tek like a mountain falling. Illishar swooped, dived, trying to strike at the wyrmking's heads, but his double-headed bodyguards battered the gryphon tercel off. The pied mare found herself unable to hold her ground. Notwithstanding her furious charges, she was being driven back, step by step. How many more before she found herself against the cliff? Her folk around her, she knew, found themselves in the same case: hemmed in, incapable of breaking free.

"To war! To war!"

The cry rang out from behind the wyverns whom they faced. Faint at first, it strengthened suddenly as the wind turned and carried the resonant war chant to the pied mare's ears full force. Unicorns. Unmistakably a warcry of unicorns. Beyond the wyrmhoard, a raising of dust and a thunder of heels. The words grew nearer and louder yet.

"We be the Scouts of Halla! In the Firebrand's name we come. Aljan-with-the-Moon-upon-his-Brow has summoned us to your aid, Queen Tek. Wyzásukitán hastened us from the Smoking Hills. The wyverns! The wyverns! To war!"

A flood of unicorns crested the wyvern shelves. Smaller than the common run, all were dark roans, deep blues and greys, brick-red dapples, brindles of tarnished gold, their leader a young stallion of frosted maroon. The pied mare could only gape as the shaggy strangers stampeded down the limestone slopes like a cascade of maddened hill goats. Tek wasted not one moment of the wyverns' panic. As the white wyrms spun, shrieking, she whistled: "Forward! Strike hard, warriors of the Ring!"

Around her she saw, felt, heard her own folk plunge ahead with renewed vigor, rushing to meet these unknown allies who called her queen and claimed to come from Jan. The wyverns, caught between two closing pincers of unicorns, screamed in terror, their ranks disintegrating.

"A trap!" the deserters shrilled.

"Stand your ground, you bloodless fools," shouted the wyrmking's central head. "We outnumber them still!"

In full rout, scattering for their lives, his troops ignored the command. The Vale's warhost, rumps no longer against the cliff, joined the newcomers in pursuing and skewering as many as they could. Few wyrms managed to clamber back into their caves, for the rush of newcomers had swept them downslope, away from their dens' entryways. For the first time since the arrival of Lynex, Tek began to feel—not just hope, but truly feel—that the unicorns might carry the day.

Upstart

★ 22 ★

Lell galloped across the Hallow Hills through the late afternoon light. Signs of battle lay everywhere. Strewn upon the summer grass, in the meadows and little stands of trees, upon the grassy, broken slopes and beside the streams, lay carcasses of the slain. Mostly wyvern, the half-grown filly noted with relief. Her folk were prevailing, then—or had been earlier. Sun hung low over the western horizon, its light a warm, golden amber, not yet deepened to crimson. She would have to hurry. Lell turned her eyes from the slain and galloped on.

She had left the oasis where suckling mares, weanlings too young to be initiated, the old and the infirm had remained in the Plainsdwellers' charge, there to await news of the battle's outcome. But Lell had not waited. Five years old, she was of age to join the warriors. Had a pilgrimage been made this year, she would have been initiated. But Jan had not returned and the herd had been deep in plans for war. The harsh winter of three seasons past had slain every other filly and foal her own age. The herd would brook no pilgrimage of one.

What, then, the prince's sister fumed, was she to do—wait till she was a doddering mare and the sucklings at last grown old enough to join the Ring? She refused to wait! Jan would never have allowed such a travesty—and in his absence, she would not permit the most glorious battle of her people's history to pass her by. Besides, she reminded herself smugly, the twins had said she *must* go. They had come upon her as she had been preparing in secret to slip away. She had feared at first they meant to stay her, report her to Calydor, sound the alarm.

They had done no such thing, only said they had come to aid her, knew where the sentries stood and what path was best to avoid their eyes. They said they had come to tell her Calydor was occupied elsewhere and that now was the ideal time to slip away. He would not miss her for hours, perhaps until morning, if she went straightaway. Then they told her the route to the Hallow Hills, as glibly as though they had fared it themselves.

"But we *have* fared it," Aiony had told her, though Lell had breathed not a word of her thoughts aloud.

"Night past," Dhattar continued, "we followed the path of past pilgrims in dreams."

Lell had long since abandoned hope of grasping the twins' meaning when they spoke of their dreams. Instead, she had accepted their aid gratefully, tucking the course they described away into memory honed by Illishar, like the rhyme and meter of a lay. *This is what Jan would have wanted me to do,* she found herself thinking, a bit uncertainly— and then with more confidence, *at least, this is what Jan himself would have done were he in my case.*

And the way had not proved so very hard to follow, after all. She fared only half a day behind the warriors. They had departed the previous afternoon, she the following morning. Grass trampled and earth turned by their passing remained for Lell to follow. She pushed relentlessly, resting but briefly before pressing on.

Where was Jan? The thought beat at her unceasingly as she ran. *Why had he not returned?* She felt as though she must make up for his absence somehow, must go in his stead. None of the others could be relied upon, the twins cautioned, not even Calydor. Though a seer, he had not dreamed what they had dreamed. He would not believe them, they feared. And telling him would spoil Lell's chance to go. Tek would need *her,* they insisted, no other. She must kindle fire. She must join the fray before sunset, must fly like the wind with the heart of a pard. She must not yield.

Lell set her thoughts aside as she came to a rocky rise. White limestone and black earth marked a difficult trail. From somewhere beyond, the amber filly heard, the din of battle rose. Her limbs trembled. She had run since dawn. It was not fear, she told herself, and began to climb.

The slope was steep and slippery. Scree tumbled continually from beneath her hooves. At times the hillside lay bare before her, devoid of scrub; at times it wound through trees. Choosing her footing, she climbed higher. Panting, she tried to scan the path ahead. Oddly, what she most feared was not wyverns, but her own folk, Illishar's airborne eyes, especially. That he might spy her before she reached the fray and swoop to thwart her only hardened her determination. Though she had often confided her intention to join the warriors, somehow she doubted he would approve so readily were he to encounter her here, now, preparing to fling herself into battle.

Panting, she reached the top of the precarious slope and ducked into cover of the trees. The noise of war seemed much closer now. Cautiously, she made her way through the grove toward it. The trees around her were odd, their aroma smoky and sweet. Never before had she seen trees with such scabrous, twisting trunks and bluish-silver leaves in the shape of crescents, hearts and rounds. The limbs were all sprouted in rose-colored buds, some already burst open into flower. Their odor was smooth, milklike, soothing. The most tempting thing she had ever scented.

Milkwood, she realized suddenly. The magical trees grew here alone, on the moonpool cliffs of the Hallow Hills. Jah-lila had eaten of these buds in her youth, Lell knew, when the red mare had first become a unicorn. Ryhenna, too. Their properties were marvelous. Famished, Lell sampled a spray of buds. She had barely eaten over the last days of hard travel, and not at all today. The savor of the buds was sweet without cloying, creamy as mares' milk. A cool tang ran through her. It made her both shiver and long to taste again.

The sounds of battle grew more insistent. The amber filly tore herself away and sprang on, trotting now, seeking the source of the din. Ahead of her, the trees thinned. She scented water. She found herself on the shore of a pool, perfectly round and perfectly clear. White limestone sand made up its bank and bottom, falling away into a blue spring that roiled and bubbled. Strangely, the surface of the pool lay perfectly still, mirror-smooth. Lell started, understanding where she was.

"The Mirror of the Moon," she whispered, naming the sacred mere about which initiates kept night-long vigils, into which they gazed to glimpse their own futures, and from which they drank in solemn ceremony, becoming warriors of the Ring.

Lell shivered again, parched with a day's waterless journey, and yet at the same time cold. Slowly, respectfully, she approached the mere. Bending, she drank—not the single, ceremonial sup of the newly initiated, but a great draught. The taste was sweet. The amber filly stared into the crystal waters, searching for some vision such as Dhattar and Aiony beheld each time they glanced into any puddle or stream. But she saw nothing. No fate. No destiny.

Lell skirted the pool's edge. The clatter of battle grew steadily louder. She reached the far side of the mere. Leaving the moonpool behind, the amber filly hurried deeper into the trees. Presently, she saw grove's end, open sky beyond turning deeper and deeper gold with the advancing sunset. The milkwood plateau dropped away in an almost vertical cliff. Below lay the wyvern shelves, sloping in broken ledges to the south, toward the Plain. Caves pitted the soft, white stone.

Across this rocky expanse, the battle sprawled. Wyverns and unicorns clashed and charged across the crumbling surface. Lell saw unicorns pursuing wyrms, surrounding them. Hemmed by inward-facing rings of warriors, the captured wyverns reared and snarled, fighting with tooth and tail and claw. Horned warriors dodged and darted, feinted, struck. Others guarded entry to the caves.

Snorts and shouts sounded above the clash: shrill whistles of warriors, screams from the wounded, groans from the dying, curses, triumphant yells, the thump of heels upon the rock. A fine white dust hung above the fray, stirred by the ceaseless scritch of bellies and tromp of hooves. Sky was the color of goldenflower. Black shadow of the moon-pool cliff crept slowly across the shelves.

Lell watched, mesmerized. Shaking, she was unaware of fear. She picked out the black-and-rose form of Tek below her, rearing and stabbing at a two-headed wyrm. Far ahead of the pied regent, the amber filly glimpsed the red mare, Jah-lila, and the black-and-white pelt of the healer, Teki. They seemed engaged in cutting off retreat to the south. Far from them, on the other side of the field, Lell saw Dagg's grey-dappled figure fighting alongside the coppery form of Ryhenna. They made up part of a ring surrounding a pair of wyverns, one of whom lay wounded.

To their flank, separated from them by a great distance, Lell saw her dam, Ses. The cream-colored mare ramped and reared, mane tossing along the curve of her neck as bright as poppies, as flame, despite the late afternoon's advancing shadow. Her mother's back was to the cliffs. Lell watched without the slightest qualm of being spotted. What troubled her more was how she was to descend that sheer, near-vertical slope and join the fray.

The gold in the sky was taking on a tinge of fire. Scanning aloft, she did not see Illishar. Fear seized her. Then she found him—on the ground, beak and one claw buried in the throat of a massive wyrm. He was dragging the lifeless form upslope. When he cast the slain thing across an entry, blocking it, the warriors that had been guarding that cave sprang away, freed to other tasks.

The field swarmed with unicorns the amber filly did not recognize: odd roans, all brick and slate, lapis and ruddy sienna. Darting and springing about like deer, they maneuvered the treacherous footing of the wyvern shelves undaunted, fighting with ferocious energy. One among their number, a dark maroon, fought alongside Tek. Lell caught his cry above the din:

"For the queen! For the queen, in Halla's name!"

Her own people's shouts were "For Jan, the Allmother's Fire-bringer!" and "For pied Tek, regent and prince's mate!"

Who were these strange little shaggy unicorns? Allies, clearly. They bore down on the foe with a fury her own folk strove gamely to match. The white wyrms they fought twisted and struggled, lashing and some-times bowling hoofed warriors off their feet with powerful sweeps of their otherwise useless tails. The amber filly, gazing upon the seething turmoil below her, had no idea how to interpret it. Were the unicorns winning? She hoped so.

Yet at the same time, she had the uneasy feeling the battle might still go either way, as easily tipping in the favor of the wyverns as not. Dusk was fast drawing on. What would happen at nightfall? Would the two sides fight on? Would darkness return the advantage to the wyrms? If they managed to slip safe belowground under cover of darkness, the amber filly reasoned, they could easily hide in the earth for as long as they chose. Would Tek dare risk leading a second assault down into the twisting maze that was their dens?

It was their sheer size, more so even than their numbers, Lell re-alized, which might determine battle's outcome. The stinging wyrms were easily three and four times the size of the youthful, stingless peace-seekers she and the twins had aided three nights before. These wyverns were old, toughened, loyal to their king. Some had double heads. Larg-est of all loomed their seven-faced sovereign, massive Lynex, unmis-takable, far larger than the bodyguards that ringed him. Furiously, Tek, the dark maroon and others of the stranger-unicorns threw themselves against the wyrmking's protectors, trying to break through. Already three of the royal guards had fallen.

Lell came to herself with a start. Would her brother, Jan, have stood gaping so, like a witless foal, when there was a task to be done? Sky above was turning from golden to amber. She must kindle fire. No time to lose, for the twins had told her she must bring fire to the battlefield before the setting of the sun. Clumsily, Lell bent to strike the tip of her horn against one flinty heel. A spark leapt up, flared, then fell to earth and died. Nervously, Lell tried again. No spark this time. A third strike. This time two sparks glowed, but each snuffed out in midair before reaching the ground.

Tinder, she realized. She must use tinder to catch a spark, nurture it. Frantically, the darkamber filly cast about her for something dry and fine. Dead grass or shredded bark, anything would do. Below her, the battle raged on. Overhead, the sky blazed, the fiery tinge intensifying with every second that passed.

Wyrmking

★ 23 ★

The pale mare tossed back her poppy-colored mane and lunged again at another wyvern, piercing the fibrous breastplate beneath its skin and bringing it down. It writhed and thrashed, already dead. She felt its sting glance heavily against one flank. The wyvern's colorless blood ran down her horn, soaking her brow, burning. Ses slung her damp forelock out of her eyes and fought on.

The clatter of battle rattled around her. The sun hung low, already hidden by the limestone cliff overlooking the wyvern shelves. The Mirror of the Moon lay on that forested plateau, she knew. She killed another wyvern. Were the wyrms being routed? She did not know, fought the more fiercely to keep from having to think. She had kept her thoughts from many such thorny mires of late—quandaries such as what she would do after this war, when Lell was grown. When she was free.

What would she do if Jan never returned? Nay, he must! Alma had shown her in the vision of her initiation night that she was to bear the long-awaited Firebringer. Surely he would appear. The only mystery was when. But what then? Dared she tell him the truth, as she had sworn to Jah-lila she would do?

She thought once more of that secret she had hidden from him and all the world since before his birth. Why had she done so? Self-preservation, surely. And at the urging of the Red Mare, who had assured her over and over that Jan must be born unto the Ring and reared as prince-to-be. Her own status as prince's mate had meant little to Ses. She had kept silent to protect her son and to spare her mate, whom she had truly loved—hoping ever against hope that he would one day free himself of the dreadful guilt that had ridden him to his death.

And yet, more than for any other reason, she had held her tongue for Lell. On the night of her initiation, long before either of her children's births, Ses had seen not only her destiny to bear the herd a Firebringer, but another to come after him: a wingèd thing. What her filly's dream pinions might mean, the pale mare could not guess. But she had named her daughter Álell. *Wing*. Regardless of her firstborn's fate, the poppy-maned mare trusted her filly was safe, secure in the care of the Free Folk of the Plain, three days' journey from this war.

She fought on. The dust of battle rose all around, a white haze. The figures surrounding her seemed pale as haunts. Sky above now edged from golden into flame. The unicorns had secured most of the entries to the wyverns' dens, she saw, preventing retreat back under the earth. The wyrms lay slain by heaps and dozens about the shelves. Her own folk's losses, she noted with relief, were fewer than the wyrms'. The unicorns had formed a solid line, pushing the wyverns slowly, inexorably toward the Plain.

The wyrms' resistance was frenzied. After initial panic at the arrival of the stranger roans, some among the wyvern horde had rallied. Had they yielded, or rushed headlong with their companions for the Plain, Ses was certain Tek would have spared further bloodshed and let them go. But all who remained refused surrender. Seven-headed Lynex, surrounded by bodyguards, shrieked with multiple shrill voices at the remains of his horde to fight to the death and not to yield.

Where was his fire, the pale mare wondered? All her life she had heard of wyverns hoarding flame, stolen from the red dragons so many years ago. Yet the foe had not used the deadly stuff even once this day. In dousing the wyrmqueen's flame years past, had her firstborn robbed the wyverns of all they possessed? She could not say. She only knew Lynex wielded none as he towered above the wedge-shaped attack formation led by Tek.

His bodyguards writhed and reared, striving to keep Tek's warriors at bay, but one by one, the double-headed guardians were being seized and pulled down. Of the great scarred wyrmking's original score, only a dozen remained. The odd-colored strangers, who called themselves Scouts of Halla, rallied around Tek, aiding her assault against the seven-headed wyrm. They fought tirelessly, like creatures possessed. Their leader, a small maroon stallion, conferred with the pied mare and followed her commands, singing out to his followers in a ringing chant that was nothing like the piercing whistles Vale unicorns used.

For what did Lynex wait? Why did he still fight on? Ses could not fathom him. The golden-orange sky above grew more and more intensely flame. A sudden commotion interrupted her thoughts. She wheeled, half expecting to find wyverns had broken her fellows' ranks, gotten behind her somehow. Instead, she saw a unicorn stallion come charging around the cliffside onto the battlefield. He cast feverishly about with the look of one taking no part in the fray, but desperately seeking among the fighters.

He was tall and lean and long-maned. The gloom of the cliff's shadow muted his coloring. From the toss of his head, from his gait and stance, she thought for one wild instant he was Jan. Then the actual hue of his coat registered: midnight blue scattered with silvery stars. A shock went through her: Calydor! What could his purpose be? Like his fellows, he had refused to join this fray, agreeing only to ward those of the Vale too young or old or infirm to fight. Spotting the pale mare now, Calydor sped toward her.

"Ses," he cried. "Is she here? Is she with you?"

With the wyvern directly before her now dead, the pale mare turned to meet the Plainsdweller.

"What do you mean?" she panted. "Whom do you seek? Why are you not with Lell and the others?"

Searching still, the star-covered stallion pitched to a halt. " 'Tis your daughter I seek! We discovered her missing the morn after your warhost departed."

"Missing?" exclaimed Ses. "What, how . . . ?" Her balance reeled.

"We combed the oasis, but found no trace—no pards," he told her quickly. "I am certain she followed the host. Did she catch you up? Have you seen her?"

"Come to enter the fray?" Ses cried, fear thudding against her heart. "My Lell is no match for these monstrous wyrms! She's but a filly— and each of them larger than a full-grown warrior. . . ."

Hastily, she, too, began to scan the battle. The wyrmhorde teetered on the brink of overthrow. In time, the unicorns' steady forward push would surely overwhelm them. But time, she realized, noting the brilliant color of the sky, might be what the unicorns did not have. As soon as the sun sank away, all odds might change. If Lynex could hold on just so long. . . . Beside her, the star-strewn stallion spoke.

"You have not seen her? She is not among you here?"

"Nay," the pale mare gasped, nearly frantic now, aware that simply because she had not laid eyes on Lell amid the day's mayhem did not mean her daughter had not hurled herself foolishly into the fray. Even impervious to wyverns' venom, the amber filly could still easily have been torn to bits by their teeth or claws. Calydor's brow furrowed.

"Mayhap she did not last this far," he murmured. Ses wheeled to stare at him. He swiftly added, "She may have had sense enough to abandon her wild scheme, to turn back, and I missed her. By my reck, even with pards, she's safer on the Plain than amid this slaughter...."

Sudden shrill whinnying caught their attention. Whirling, Ses saw one of the wyrmking's bodyguards deserting, thrashing to break free of the attacking unicorns and make its escape. Scouts of Halla fell upon it as it rushed by. Frenetically, it shook them off. Several gave chase while the rest sprang after Tek, who now pressed forward in a fury, fighting toward Lynex as the sunset sky caught fire. The wyvern king and his ten surviving guards cursed their fleeing companion.

The enormous wyrm was coming straight toward her, Ses realized with a start. A day of battle had dulled her wits. She felt Calydor spring past her to intercept the wyrm, moving with a grassbuck's strength and speed. Coming as it did from one who once so coolly championed flight over combat, his action caused her an instant's surprise. Then she saw that pressed as the pair of them were, so close against the limestone cliff, no room remained for flight.

Ses sprang after the blue-and-silver stallion. She dived at the great wyvern's tail, impaling its poison tip as it swung around toward Calydor. Her horn grated, sparking against the ground. It occurred to her what risk the singer had taken, venturing the battlefield in search of Lell, unprotected as he was from white wyrms' stings. As the pale mare pinned the wyvern's tail, the star-strewn stallion stabbed upward under its gaping jaw. Already the other of its two heads lay dead.

Once more realization came: Calydor did not possess fire-tempered hooves or horn, could not have pierced the bony breastplate protecting the monster's heart if he had tried. She heard the wyrmking's guardian give a high-pitched scream. It stiffened. Calydor shook free, sprang away from the dying creature's flailing claws as it toppled. Ses braced herself, kept her horn firmly planted in the creature's thrashing tail lest the Plainsdweller be struck by a reflexive sting.

"Look to your leader! Hie, Tek! Tek," Calydor was shouting, sprinting suddenly toward the black-and-rose mare. Ses, too, leapt away, leaving the wyvern for others to finish. She had seen what Summer Stars had seen: Tek and her battlemates smashing through the ring of bodyguards at the weak point opened when the traitor fled. The Scouts formed a blunt wedge that shoved into the opening, forcing the guards farther and farther apart. The wedge then split, each half continuing to press outward, creating a corridor.

Down this corridor charged Tek. Bugling her warcry, she hurtled at Lynex like a striking hawk. The wyrmking caught sight of her, reared back, but with a mighty leap, the pied mare caught his third-smallest head in her teeth. She gave a savage shake, like a wolf pup snapping a rock squirrel's neck, then let go and dropped to the ground. There she half crouched, stance ready, horn aimed. The king of the white wyrms convulsed. A cry sprang from six of his throats. The third-smallest head lay limp, slain. The Scouts of Halla strove gamely to keep Lynex's remaining bodyguards from closing ranks and pinning Tek inside their ring. Ses pounded across the corpse-strewn field, hot on Calydor's heels.

"Wretch! Wretch," keened the wyvern king. "A hundred years and more have I tended that head."

Tek's words rang boldly over the din of battle. Ses made them out with ease.

"I'll snap all seven like buds from a stalk," the pied mare returned. "Four centuries have my folk suffered exile because of your treachery! Now we mean to put that wrong to rights and drive the last wyrm from our Hallow Hills."

Another of the wyrmking's bodyguards broke from its companions and strove to flee. The Scouts of Halla pressed to hem it in. It writhed and flailed across Ses's path. Ahead of her, Calydor's way was also blocked as he fought to reach the corridor and Tek.

"Hoofed grass-eater!" scarred Lynex shrieked. "Little whistling nit!"

"A warrior of the Ring am I," Tek threw back at him. Ses's ears pricked. The pied mare shouted on. "Mate to the prince and mother of his heirs. Regent in his absence, I am your fiercest enemy. Scheming, deceiving tyrant wyrm!"

Once more she sprang, from a standing start, with a vigor that astonished Ses. About the great wyvern's central pate, his lesser crania darted, wove. The pied mare seized one of these in teeth, a nob larger than the first she had killed. It screamed and tore free. Tek landed, instantly sprang again. Lynex reared, lifting his faces above the reach of her teeth. Tucking her chin, she stabbed the injured head deep in its cheek. A sharp shake of her horn as she fell to earth reversed the slash into its eye. The wounded visage wailed, bleeding great streaks of near-colorless blood and entangling itself among the wyrmking's other necks and heads.

Again he bellowed, so loudly the pale mare's ears flinched. Ahead of her, Calydor had made his way around the knot of Scouts attacking the fleeing bodyguard. She strove to follow him. Now the star-strewn stallion fought forward through the throng of unicorns that had once formed the corridor allowing Tek in to reach Lynex. The crush of battle was closing that opening, warriors backing and sidling into one another. The blue-and-silver stallion hurled himself into their midst. Ses shouldered after him. Beyond them—not far, but almost unreachable because of the press—Tek faced the wyrm.

His rippling tail, like a mighty rapid, swept toward the pied mare, its seven-stinged tip brandished to flail at her. Tek overleapt it, slashing down in the same motion, and Lynex roared. One massive forepaw, broad as the mare's ribcage, swung its saberclaws. Tek ducked, dodged, twisted, and ran it through. The bladelike claws of the other paw scored her shoulders. She pivoted and sprang free, laughing. Ses saw blood welling into the wounds Tek did not even seem to feel.

The pied mare speared the wyrmking through the side. With a snarl, his great head swooped, sank its splinter-fangs into her shoulder. Tek struck him off with one forehoof, slashing a long, shallow wound across his throat. Ses watched his torn gills begin to bleed. The pale mare flung herself against the mass of unicorns grappling with towering wyrms. Calydor still forged ahead. She sought to trail just behind, squeezing through what gaps he managed before the surge of battle closed them. Beyond the shifting, near-impassable wall of warriors, the pied mare taunted the wyrms' seven-headed king.

"Surrender, Lynex," Tek roared. "Give up this fight. Swear never to return, and I will let your folk depart."

"Never!" the white wyrm shrieked. "Not while I live will I allow my people to retreat." He struck at her again with one massive forepaw. Nimbly, she dodged away.

"Your bodyguards desert you! How long can you hold them to certain death?"

"Where is your mate?" the king of wyverns snarled, his huge, main head darting to snap at her. Tek ducked and sidestepped, avoiding the clash of needle-like teeth.

"On errands more pressing than pricking at you, wyrmking," she answered. The unwounded maws of the great wyvern laughed. He slithered after her.

"Jan, who killed my queen—was he too great a coward to come himself, but must send his mate to face my wrath?"

"One warrior mare among my race is more than a match for you," Tek spat, lunging after one of two midsized heads flanking the main one, champed it by the gill ruff.

She got one foreleg over it, compressing its windpipe in the crook of her knee. With a squall of terror, Lynex tried to wrest his second-most-ancient head from her grasp. The pied mare held on with teeth and limb, her other legs braced. Ses saw the wyvern's near forepaw pinned against his body by the taut downward stretch of the captured pate's neck. His free paw tore at Tek but, too stubby and short, it could not reach around his scarred and bony breast. Tek dragged the head down, bowing her own head and leaning all her weight onto the forelimb that pinned it.

"Surrender," the pale mare heard Tek grate. "Yield, wyrmking, or you lose this head as well."

The huge white wyrm began to scream. His massive body rocked, trying to shake the pied mare free. Ses saw Tek let her standing limbs buckle, setting her down hard on the ground. The wyrm's secondary head remained pinned in her folded forelimb, gill ruff held fast in her strong, square teeth. Maddened with fear, the three auxiliary nobs as yet unscathed flung themselves high and wide, shrieking, while the main head swooped, attempting to catch Tek in its jaws. Teeth still clenched about the captured pate's gill ruff, the pied mare pointed her horn at the main head, keeping it at bay.

Off to one side, Ses became aware of flashes of copper and yellow-grey. Ryhenna and Dagg had seen Tek's danger. As Calydor and she herself did, they, too, were struggling to reach their shoulder-friend. Beyond, Ses caught another glimpse: Teki and Jah-lila also fighting toward Tek. The maroon-colored leader of the Scouts of Halla battled hard at the edge of the ring of bodyguards. All strove to converge on Tek's contest with Lynex—yet none, Ses feared, would be able to reach her. The crush was so great, finding space to plant a hoof, much less wedge one's body, proved nearly impossible. Beyond, pied mare and wyvern king fought in an open space. The sky above blazed like burning grass.

With a roar like stormwind, Lynex heaved. His massive body undulated, then torqued. With a powerful wrench, the wyvern king rolled. The force snapped the neck of his own head captured in the pied mare's teeth. Unable to loose her grip in time, Tek was jerked through air and slammed hard to the ground. She lay a moment, motionless and stunned, as the wyrmking pulled free of her, three of his seven heads now dangling uselessly. Slowly, he reared up, paws raised, his dozen saberclaws bristling.

Ses heard the red mare shouting her daughter's name. Tek stirred groggily. Clearly the breath had been knocked from her, perhaps even ribs cracked. Hissing, Lynex swayed above her, savoring victory. The pied mare rolled painfully to her knees, shook her head, then struggled up. She stood unsteadily. Ses whinnied, barreling forward in Calydor's wake. To one side, Dagg's battle yell rose above the tumult, echoed by Ryhenna's. Ses saw the pair of them plunging toward the pied mare at desperate speed. Beyond, the pale mare glimpsed Tek's foster father, Teki, vaulting over the fallen, her dam, Jah-lila, charging alongside.

Ahead of them all, at the battle line, the Scouts' maroon-colored leader chanted orders to his troops. On every side, bodyguards toppled, pulled down. Unicorns hurtled toward their injured leader like a thunder of forkhorns spooked by storm. And none of them, Ses knew suddenly, with certainty, would reach her in time. She saw that Lynex understood this. The congestion of fighters and the piling of bodies around him was too great. The pied mare was his. He was sure of it.

"Another moment, mare, and your flesh becomes my feast," he crowed.

Ses saw blood trickle from Tek's nostril and stain her beard. Head slightly lowered, she gazed up at Lynex. She stood three-legged, favoring the forelimb she had used to pinion his second-eldest head. Ses saw her snort blood in a fine scarlet spray. Her limbs tensed, braced, almost crouching. Her mouth moved. The pale mare was never sure after if she had heard the words, or only understood them from the framing of Tek's lips and teeth and tongue.

"Well enough, wyrm," the pied mare snarled at him, green eyes leveled in a gaze of pure hatred, without a hint of resignation or surrender. "Try to take it, if you dare."

The wyrmking lunged. The black-and-rose mare reared to meet him. The sun set. Evening sky was the color of fading roses. A shrill cry halted everything. Or rather, nothing halted. It only seemed to halt. Ses felt herself frozen in time, still struggling forward like all her companions, the wyvern bodyguards falling around her, swarmed on and skewered by the Scouts of Halla. The high sound that had cut—was still cutting—the air was not a scream, the pale mare realized, but a whistle, a wild piercing battlecry shrilled by one younger and smaller than any other warrior on the field.

Turning—so slowly, it seemed as in a dream—Ses caught sight of her long-leggèd amber filly with the mane pale as milk galloping full-tilt down the cliffside above with a burning brand clutched in her teeth. The white limestone cliff rose nearly vertical. Showers of scree cascaded from Lell's hooves. The brand in her teeth flashed and crackled, its flame orange, its buds so newly lit that Ses could still discern their shapes: hearts and rounds and crescents for the leaves, five-petaled roses for the flowers. The milkwood's resinous sap popped, fizzing as it flamed, the smoky mingles of white and grey, smelling at once milk-sweet and tart as pitch.

Halfway down the precipitous slope, Lell sprang. The milkwood blazed as she hurtled, seemed almost to fly, sailing down toward Tek and the wyvern king. She came to earth far short, but she had gauged her leap to land her not on hard limestone but atop a heap of slain wyverns. The next instant, she sprang again, for the packed crush of living unicorns this time. Still piping her warcry, the amber filly dashed across their jostling backs, pounding hard for Lynex, milkwood brand flaming in her teeth.

Surprised, momentarily distracted, the wyrmking hesitated, turning his central head's gaze from Tek toward Lell. To one side of him, Dagg and the leader of the Scouts dragged down the last defender blocking their path. Ryhenna thundered after them. To the wyrmking's other side, Jah-lila broke through the wall of fallen bodyguards, her black horn slicked with wyverns' blood. Teki vaulted in her wake. Just ahead of Ses, Calydor struggled over the motionless form of another fallen guard. It lay within their power to reach Tek now, the pale mare realized.

The king of the wyverns seemed to reach the same surmise. He turned back toward the wounded mare. She ramped and feinted before him. Heaped bodies ringed them like a barricade. Ses saw that with her injured foreleg, Tek could not flee, could not hope to climb that mound of dead unaided. She could only stand defiant, pawing the air. With a howl, the huge white wyrm lunged. Ahead, as she scrambled upward in Calydor's wake, Ses saw Lell spring over the barricade of the slain, past Tek, swift as wind, light as wings, the firebrand blazing above her head. Full gallop, she scaled the belly and scarred breast of the king of wyrms and flung the firebrand in his face.

The wyvern leader roared, arching, knifelike nails clawing at his main head's eyes. The other three remaining heads screamed and strained as if hoping to tear free of the wyrmking's massive body, which tumbled backward, writhing. Lell plummeted to the ground as the scaly slope on which she had stood abruptly snatched itself away. Gaining the crest, Ses observed Jah-lila below seize the nape of her daughter's neck in teeth and haul her bodily away from thrashing Lynex as though Tek were a weanling filly. Teki shouldered from the other side, helping the red mare drag her daughter up over the fallen bodyguards. Dagg and the leader of the Scouts sprinted across to lend their strength. Among the four of them, they managed to half-lift, half-herd the injured mare to safety.

Lell, sprawled on the limestone near Lynex, was already scrambling to her feet. Ryhenna tried to go to her, but the furious thrashing of the wyvern's tail between them drove her back. The wyrmking keened and rolled, scattering the resinous firebrand into a thousand flaming shards. These were strewn by wind and the wyvern's looping, sweeping tail into a broad arc.

"My eye! My eye, you little, cursèd wretch," the king of the wyverns howled.

Sparks flew within the open space where he and Tek had lately dueled. Flames caught the wisps of summer-dry grass that sprouted in the crevices of the wyvern shelves. A semicircle of fire sprang up along the periphery of the open space. It stretched from far to Ses's left all the way to where Tek and the others had disappeared over the mound of the fallen. Spreading fast, the two ends ran around behind the wyrm as though seeking to join. Barely in time, Ryhenna sprang out of its path.

On the far side of the open space from Ses, beyond Lynex and Lell, the two running trails of fire met, completing a ring. The dance of fire, low enough in its initial seconds for a unicorn to have sprung over, rose almost instantly to above head height. Within its circle, the wyrmking flailed, his cries subsiding. Panting, he rose, collecting himself, tail coiling, one eye of his great head wizened shut. The other heads whimpered. He turned his one-eyed gaze toward Lell. With a cry, Ses plunged toward her filly. A curtain of flame roared before her, blocking her path. The pale mare pitched to a halt, ramped helpless on the mass of wyvern dead, gazing into a ring of fire in which Lynex and her daughter now both lay trapped.

"I'll see you rue saving your queen," the white wyrm snarled.

Lell backed away. "Not till you wyrms rue that ever you stole our lands from us."

The amber filly's voice was steady, her expression wary, but unafraid. Ses tried to call to her, bid her flee, but the crackling flames drowned out her voice. Lynex lunged at Lell. She dodged, sought to skirt him. Behind him the ring, newly joined, had not yet flared unleapable. The wyvern's tail swung, lashing, driving her back. The amber filly struck at the stings, but they were far too swift and powerful. She had to spring away to keep from being bowled over. Lynex swept his tail in a leisurely arc, herding her. One badger paw extended to intercept her as she rounded the fire ring's inner curve.

Instead of dodging, Lell ran straight for the paw, then veered suddenly inward. Ses saw Lynex, lunging, lose his balance as he missed. His broad paw dipped into the fire. Howling, he snatched it out. Again Lell scaled the scarred slope of his breast. All four of his remaining heads bent to gape at her, but instead of fencing with her horn, she wheeled and kicked like a mountain calf, striking one of the smaller skulls smartly in the jaw. Shards of teeth fine as fishbones flew, glinting by firelight.

Sky above was the dark of flushed, sweet grapes. The burning ring lit the wyvern shelves in a yellow blaze. To one side, Ses saw Tek shouting, fighting to break past Jah-lila and Teki, Dagg and the leader of the Scouts, all of whom held her back from going to Lell. Within, the wyvern's newly wounded head slapped and flailed, preventing his other maws from striking. Lell flew like a woodshare away from Lynex. A woodshare with nowhere to go. All around burned the impassable wall of fire.

With a savage bellow, Lynex crushed his own wounded pate in the jaws of his largest visage. The little head ceased writhing. The great one opened its jaws. The smaller fell nerveless from its grasp. With a howl, the wyvern sprang, both paws extended. Lell ran for the wall of fire, as though she meant to dash headlong through it. The wyvern's tail swung round to prevent her. The amber filly skidded, avoided it, and leapt. But as she entered the wall of fire, the seven flails of wyrmking's tail coiled about her, plucking her back.

"Lell! My child!" Ses screamed as she saw her filly's coat catch fire. The pale mare sprang toward the flames. Calydor vaulted to block her path.

"Nay, my love! Don't sacrifice yourself. To save her would take wings!"

He would not let her by. Ses fought him, bit, pummeled wildly with her hooves. To no avail. He held his ground. She could not get past. Ryhenna had joined him. They were holding her back. Above the din, she heard Tek's desperate cries. Beyond Ryhenna and Calydor, beyond the curtain of fire, Ses saw her filly struggling to free her legs from the wyrm's long, twining tail, which only tightened, dragging her closer to Lynex's daggerclaws and gaping jaws. How much time had elapsed, the pale mare wondered—a heartbeat? Two? Was it possible Lell did not yet feel the fire? Her mane and coat blazed. The amber filly arched suddenly, a cry breaking from her. Ses cried out as well, as though she herself burned.

A sound that was like none she had ever heard before, half pard's roar, half eagle's scream, cut the night. From the darkness of fading sky above, a figure dropped, lit up by firelight, its great wings green as new-sprung grass. They beat about the wyrmking's heads, boxing, buffeting them. Ses saw the tercel's golden-furred paws slash into the wyvern's shoulder and breast. His eagle's claws closed about the throats of the two still-living smaller heads.

One of the wyvern's huge forepaws struck at Illishar. Powerfully thrashing wings kept it at bay. With a yell, the gryphon struck at the wyrmking's one remaining eye. The wyvern shrieked, contorted. Illishar leapt free of him and snatched Lell from his thrashing tail. She shouted, writhed, flame spreading from her to his feathers and pelt. His talons bit into her shoulderblades. Ses saw his pard's claws dig into her flank. She was nearly half-grown, at the very edge of his ability to carry.

Illishar, too, was screaming now, his burning wings battering the air, straining against a weight that nearly dragged him down. With furious strokes, he bore her up. Ses felt the wind of his wings, heated by flame, fanning the ring of fire. Wailing and squirming, the blinded wyvern tossed below. The burning filly writhed in the tercel's grip. He dragged her through the air, barely clearing the curtain of fire. Shrilling, keening, he fought his way upward, higher into the darkening sky. Flames licked across his belly and green-fletched throat.

The white wall of the limestone cliff loomed. He strove for altitude. Lell's screeches tore the night. She seemed to gallop through sunless sky. Fire ran all along their limbs. Illishar cleared the cliff, cleared the trees. He staggered low across the canopy of the milkwood grove, an erratic series of plummets and heaves. Far below, Ses lost sight of them. The light of their burning flickered, played eerily through the trees, lighting the air above. All at once, it vanished utterly, plunging the grove into darkness again as though the pair of them had, surrendering at last, fallen from the sky.

Endingfire

★ 24 ★

The darkness out of the Smoking Hills swallowed the last hint of dusk. Sudden night, devoid of stars, fell. The ring of fire encompassing Lynex lit the battlefield, upon which every creature now stood arrested save for the wyrmking, who floundered mewling. No sound save that thin, oddly vigorless wail and the crackle of flame. Tek leaned against her dam and foster sire, her off forelimb swollen, badly strained. That pang, and the ache of her bruised ribs and slashed shoulders was as nothing to the pain she felt for Lell and Illishar, who only scant moments before had disappeared beyond the clifftop, their terrible light abruptly doused. Grief crushed the pied mare's breast.

From the blackness above came a mighty rushing, as of wind. Tek felt a stirring reft of coolness, a waft as hot as sun-burned rock. Another noise now, louder than the ceaseless rush. This second sound belled like a mighty trump, calling, calling in long, clear notes that shook the earth. The notes drew nearer, nearer at incredible speed, as did the rush. The hot wind increased. All came from above, from the strange black cloud that had swept all day from the Smoking Hills and at last devoured the sky.

A blast of fire shot through the darkness overhead. The immense tongue of flame flared, subsided, was replaced by another, and another yet, each gout nearer. The unicorns, still motionless upon the battlefield, gaped. Their enemies, who also poised, craned upward. The darkness parted, and out of it, a dragon swooped. She was vast, vaster than any creature Tek had ever beheld, red in color, and embedded with thousands of flashing jewels which scintillated in the light of her fiery breath.

The dragon descended, impossibly huge, the size of a mountain.

Each note she trumped was followed by a roaring spurt of flame. Without being aware, Tek found that she had recoiled, fallen back, as had every living creature around her, whether unicorn or wyvern. Only the wyrmking remained where he lay, rolling and moaning insensibly within the ring of fire. The rush of the dragon's wings as she approached scoured everything in her path. Tek slitted her eyes, tightened her nostrils, folded her ears against the hard, gritty gusts.

The mighty firedrake came to rest with a concussion that shook the hills. The heat of her drove both unicorns and wyverns back. Her jewels flashed and winked like innumerable stars or eyes. Her scales seemed to glow of their own accord. Her huge, membranous wings remained raised above her back, only half folded. One great foreclaw tightened upon the earth, tearing great troughs in the soft limestone. The other remained clutched loosely, cradling to her breast something Tek could not quite see.

Most of her immense form was lost from Tek's view by darkness and the rolling slope of the land. Forelimbs on the wyvern shelves, tail resting upon the Plain, she settled before the burning ring encircling Lynex. The dragon peered at the wounded wyrmking. Her magnificently finned and whiskered head was larger than his entire body.

"Lynex," she sighed, expelling a billow of burning breath. "Lynex, do you know me?"

Her finished air swirled whiter than cloud, her words surprisingly melodious, despite the harsh susurration. Slowly, painfully, the wyrmking recoiled. Of his seven heads, only the central, largest pate still moved, eyes sightless and shattered. The other six dandled.

"Mélintélinas," he croaked. "Red dragon queen! I feel your heat."

The dragon shook her head. "Mélintélinas is dead," she whispered. "She did not live to see your end. It is I, her daughter, Wyzásukitán. Your queen."

"Wyzásukitán," hissed Lynex, dragging himself upright, sightless eyes questing fruitlessly to perceive her.

The great dragon's head nodded. "Aye. I am she who, four hundred winters gone, nearly fell victim to your jaws when, steeped in treachery, you decided dragon pups were fit food for your kind, that eating a living dragon's flesh could make you, like us, mistresses of fire."

She shifted, moving closer.

"Full-grown firedrakes, of course, you feared to molest. But new-hatched pups, these you stole and devoured while their nurses dreamed. Not even the royal nest was safe from your predations, for only the flesh of a queen's heir, so you determined, suited your own nobility."

The dragon's voice was hypnotic, her face impassive.

"So you sought to roll from the nursery that egg which housed my mother's heir. But the queen's sleep was not so deep as other dragons'. She woke. I hatched to find not nurturing attendants but a predator. I struck, defending my own life until my dam could save me. It was my tiny eggteeth and infant claws which scarred your icy breast."

The red dragon's enormous talons upon the ground tightened, crushing the powdery stone.

"You slipped my mother's traps and escaped the Smoking Hills. She ordered all your kind driven forth, expecting the lot of you to perish in the arid cold aboveground. But you had stolen fire and borne it with you. Thus were your kind able to survive and flee the Smoking Hills."

She turned. Ruby eyes studied him.

"Thus were you able to make your way across the Salt Waste and the Plain. You came here to trouble these unicorns, to steal their lands from them."

The firedrake's jeweled wings tensed, spread, stretching to their full extent.

"My mother, having flown her nuptial flight, had lost her wings and could not follow you. Nor could her earthbound sisters, since among my kind only unwed queens and their mates have wings."

Wyzásukitán hissed, her breath steaming.

"But I have always known what task I must perform before relinquishing my maidenhead. I have been a long, long time growing my wings, Lynex. Four hundred years have I contemplated this tryst."

The white wyrm rolled, sprawling, seeking to crawl away from her, toward the far edge of the burning ring.

"No," he groaned, then half shrieked. "Mercy! . . ."

"What mercy had you for a new-hatched dragon pup?" the queen of the red dragons inquired, her enormous presence glittering above him in the hot light of the fire. "What mercy did you show these unicorns, and their ancestors? What mercy did you grant any of your own kind who spoke out against your ruthless ways?"

She reached for him.

"Ah!" cried Lynex, shrinking and writhing as her great forepaw entered the ring of fire. "Let me go! Let me go!"

The queen of the red dragons shook her vast head. "Never," she answered. "My mother made that mistake. I shall not repeat it."

"What do you intend to do with me?" the white wyrmking shrieked, struggling uselessly against the dragon's grasp.

Wyzásukitán eyed him, and with a snuff of her strange white breath, doused the fire surrounding him. Flame jetted from her nostrils then, in steady, controlled spurts, illuminating the night.

"My mate-to-be is young yet," replied the dragon queen. "It will be hundreds of years before he is ready to fly. Till then, he needs a plaything. Something long-lived to amuse him as he grows." Lifting her head, she shot a great gout of fire across the sky, then bent to examine her prize. "Lynex," she inquired, "can you sing?"

"No!" the wyvern screamed. "No! No!"

His howls grew softer as she lifted him high into the air and turned her attention from him to her other forepaw, the one she cradled to her breast. Carefully, she lowered it to the ground. The enormous talons opened. A unicorn stepped free. Tek felt her own heart kick against her side. Jan! Her mate stood upon the limestone shelves, whole and unscathed. Scanning the battlefield, his eyes found her. Their gazes locked. Bending before him, the dragon laid her head upon the stone.

"Sip again, Firebrand," she urged. "One last dragonsup to protect you from your own fire."

Tek's mate bent his muzzle to the dragon's brow. The pied mare noticed for the first time the shallow depression, perfectly round, like a little Mirror of the Moon. Dark waters swirled there. She saw Jan drink.

"My thanks to you, Dark Moon," said Wyzásukitán, her white breath smoking, "for rousing me from my long sleep and guiding me here. Dance fire now through all the stinging wyverns' dens, that none may ever return to trouble you. Fare well."

Lifting her whiskered head, she scanned the unicorns. Around her, Tek saw her new-met, shaggy allies all stood with heads bowed. The dragon queen smiled.

"And fare well to you, proud Scouts of Halla, who lately dwelt among my kind. My sisters and I will miss your beautiful singing. We must find us other songs to haunt our dreams."

Her ruby eyes found Jan again.

"Firebrand, I take my leave. May the light of Her of the Thousand Jeweled Eyes illumine you."

Pulling herself upright into a crouch, the vast dragon sprang skyward. Her breath flared out in mighty bursts of flame, coruscating in the air, which hung thick and dark, full of particles. She coursed upward, as though to overleap the strange black cloud. Lynex's wails and cries receded. The darkness swallowed them. The great belling notes of the dragon's voice shot away to the northeast, back toward the Smoking Hills.

Tek stirred, saw Jan ramping, striking his heels and his horn to the ground. Sparks flew up, showering, setting the bone-dry wisps of grass ablaze. He dashed for the largest entrance to the wyverns' dens, the one through which Lynex and his bodyguards had emerged. A swarm of burning stars swirled in the wake of Alma's Firebringer as he disappeared into the cave.

Tek heard a roar, as of some resinous substance kindling all in a flash. Fire spouted from the mouth of the wyverns' dens, accompanied by roiling smoke. Tek saw smoke and flame begin to pour from other openings. Within moments, every lightwell in the porous limestone blazed with preternatural light. Crashes and rumbles, as of tunnels collapsing or bursting. The battlefield rocked. Tek heard those wyverns who yet remained screaming in fear.

"Let them go! Let them go," the pied mare shouted as the white wyrms slithered like stormwater toward the Plain. "Let the dogs and grass pards finish them!"

Her own folk milled, but held their ground. The shelves trembled and jarred. Pain in her side bit deep.

"That was Jan!" she heard Dagg beside her exclaim. "Jan, in the hand of the dragon queen."

"The holy Firebrand," Oro beside him whispered.

The dappled warrior turned to the shaggy stranger. "He's gone down into the wyrms' dens and set them alight."

Dazed, Dagg took a step in that direction, as though he half meant to go after his friend. The red mare Jah-lila called, "Hold. We cannot follow."

A dark grey ash began to fall. Tek realized for the first time that the mysterious black cloud was descending, enveloping them. It was made of cinders, tiny particles of soot. The stuff felt warm and gritty, feathery at first; then heavier and heavier it fell. It caked her ears and mane and the lashes of her eyes, coated her pelt and the pelts of her fellows. It covered the earth upon which they stood. Beside her she heard Teki the healer breathe,

"Álm'harat spare us. It is the end of the world."

The Son of Summer Stars

★ 25 ★

Jan's hooves sparked against the flammable crystal lining the wyverns' dens. As he galloped deeper through the twisting warrens, everywhere his heels touched was set alight. The fire ran after him through the caves, casting a blinding glare and billowing heat which did not trouble him, any more than had the airless cold above the ashcloud or the fever of the molten firelake. A tireless velocity carried him through all the length and breadth of the wyverns' dens, always faster than the fires he danced. Its flaring brilliance illumined his course.

He galloped through caverns and chambers, needing no guide. Alma showed him ever and always the way. All the dens through which he passed stood empty. He became aware presently that they were collapsing behind him, the superheated tunnels cracking and shattering, giving way in a series of terrible concussions. This would go on for a long time, he knew. Even after he departed these grottoes, they would burn for days.

The glory of Alma sang in his blood. Fire like the sun gusted beneath his heels. The moon upon his brow gleamed. He felt unbounded by physical body, unencumbered by space and time, keenly aware that before the new could be born, the old must be scoured away. He felt the agent of both that imminent demise and the coming rebirth, at one with all things, with Alma. It seemed the fire he danced was the great Fire, the One Dance that circled the world and the stars, the Cycle of All Things.

When at last his exultation waned, he understood that the dragonsup was ebbing, his divinity passing. Mortality returned. Time to make his way aboveground. He veered upward. As he emerged from the burning maze, air's coolness washed like a long drink of water against his skin. In the darkness of falling ash, he could not tell if it were day or night. A dim, round orb that might have been either moon or sun gleamed wanly overhead. Canted off to one side, it threw only the slenderest of light. Ash lay thick upon everything, changing the look of the land, painting it grey ghostly as the realm of haunts. He found he was not lost, knew himself to be at the southernmost edge of the wyvern shelves, where they intercepted the Plain.

The Mare's Back, too, lay deep in cindersnow. He shook himself, dislodging a soft cloud of the fine, feathery ash from his pelt. Moments later, it began to coat him again. He turned northward, toward the Hallow Hills and the cliff beneath the milkwood groves where the heart of the battle had raged, certain that soon or late, if he followed this course, he would rejoin Tek.

🍂

Barely awake, Lell lay listening to the soft lap of the water supporting her. The world around her stood dark and very still. Ash was falling onto her half-closed eye. It piled in a downy heap on her eyelashes. She blinked, stirring. The water felt deliciously cool after the terrible sensation of burning that had troubled her dreams. She rolled, floundering, and found herself in shallows. Her folded limbs touched bottom, her knees and hocks in contact with coarse, shifting sand.

"Get up," she heard Aiony saying faintly, but quite distinctly, from somewhere nearby.

Dully, the amber filly struggled to untangle her disobedient limbs. A moment later, she was able to stand. The scent of milkwood blooms wafted all around her, their aroma heavy and all-pervading. She felt the tingle of the milkwood buds she had eaten, and the resinous smoke she had inhaled, suffusing her blood.

"Pull Illishar out of the water," Dhattar's soft voice chimed. "The moon's mere has seen to his burns, just as it did yours—but he's not awake yet, and it's time he came out."

Lell stood trembling, feeling the soft weight of ashfall. It clung damply to her pelt. There was no shaking it off. So thick were the cinders sifting out of the sky that the world seemed dark as twilight. Was that the moon shining above her, or the sun? She saw Dhattar and Aiony standing at the edge of the circular mere. The pure pallor of the white foal's pelt and the silver of Aiony's pied coloring seemed subtly, inexplicably, to glow.

"Where am I?" Lell muttered thickly, snorting to get the ashmud from her nostrils.

"The Mirror of the Moon," Aiony replied, her voice strangely far-sounding, "where Illishar bore you to douse the flames. He knows naught of its healing powers, but he knew it was water, the closest to be found."

"Illishar!" Lell gasped, fully awake now, her heart giving a sharp, silent thump. "Where . . . ?"

"Behind you," Dhattar replied.

Lell wheeled unsteadily, spied the gryphon tercel floating half submerged in the clear surface of the mere, which was littered with milkwood flowers, she saw. The ashfall did not seem to affect the pool's clarity. Instead, inexplicably, the cinders appeared to vanish upon contact with the waters, which remained crystal clear, the mere's sandy bottom still snowy white, unsmirched. Its whiteness glowed almost as distinctly as Dhattar and Aiony.

"Pull him out," Dhattar was telling her.

Lell waded to the unconscious wingcat, bent to grasp one splayed, water-logged wing in her teeth. She backed toward shore. He drifted amazingly easily, supported by the mere. She managed to drag his head, neck, and most of his shoulders onto the shore. He twitched, sputtered, but did not wake. A bright silvery substance spattered his throat and chest. It coated most of his pelt and much of one wing. Curious, Lell bent to sniff. The fur and feathers there smelled odorless and new.

"What is it?" she stammered.

"The bright spots?" Aiony asked.

"Where the fire burned him and the mere healed him," Dhattar replied.

"Healed you as well," Aiony continued.

Lell glanced down at herself. She, too, was covered with patches of pale new hair. She stared at it.

"Burned?" she murmured, mystified. It had been a dream.

"The mere saved you both," Aiony replied, earnestly, distantly. "Illishar's scorched pinions and pelt have come back silver. Your own burnt hair has sprouted gold."

Lell turned to stare at the twin filly and foal. They stood quietly, only a few paces distant, still glowing softly, oddly in the dim ashfall. Lell shook herself, felt the ash upon her pelt dislodge. None, she realized suddenly, was settling on either Dhattar or Aiony. It was falling through them.

"The ash . . . ," she exclaimed.

They glanced at one another. "It hasn't reached us yet," Aiony said.

"How are you come here?" Lell whispered, too stunned to think clearly.

"We're on the Plain," Dhattar replied, "with the Plainsdwellers and the rest. We're three days' journey from you still. The ash won't reach us for hours yet."

Lell could not take her eyes from them. Their translucent brightness fascinated her. "But where—how . . . ?"

Aiony shrugged. "We stand by an oasis pool, gazing into it. We see you and Illishar, the Mirror of the Moon."

"We watched the battle thus, earlier," Dhattar went on. "We only called you now to wake you, urge you to come out. It was time, and you were very deep asleep."

"The battle," Lell gasped, casting about her suddenly. "How goes the battle?"

"Peace," Dhattar answered. "It's won. Wyverns routed and Lynex borne away. Jan is returned. All's well."

Her mind a tangle, Lell half turned, but Aiony called, "List. You need not go down to them so soon. Rest. Illishar will want you by him when he wakes. Ample time betides. The Hills are won, the old age slain, a new age about to be born. Sleep. Regain your strength."

Her voice faded, retreating further and further as she spoke. Her image and that of Dhattar grew thin, finally vanishing altogether. Only ashfall drifted where the pair had stood. The amber filly felt her trembling limbs give way. How foolish to think she could have taken another step. Of course she must stay with Illishar, must tell him everything when he woke.

"Illishar," she murmured, bending over him. The slumbering gryphon stirred. Soft growling or purring sounded deep in his throat, but his eyes remained shut, limbs loose, his breathing steady. Her own eyes slid closed. She sank into sleep with one cheek pressed against his feathery breast.

❧

The end of the world lasted three days' time. For all that while, the grey ash fell, gloaming the sun to a pitiful light weaker than the moon and stealing all warmth, so the days were cool and the nights chill dark. Cinders covered all the Hallow Hills and the wyvern shelves and the Plain beyond as far as any eye could see. And by the close of that period, these things had been achieved: Jan emerged from the wyverns' dens; Lell and Illishar awoke and descended from the moonpool to rejoin their folk; Ses gathered her filly to her with joyous cries, then bowed in gratitude before her gryphon rescuer.

Jan found his mate, and told her all—in confidence, away from others' ears. Still ignorant, his kith and folk and shoulder-friends embraced him, full of marvel and delight. He promised to give them the tale of his year's adventure as soon as the herd could be reunited and cinderfall had ceased. Meanwhile, the gloomy grit sifted down and down, drabbing all hues, making ghostly the world. Most of the slain lay beneath the milkwood cliffs, heaped upon the wyvern shelves where fighting had been fiercest. Those limestone hollows collapsed in a grinding roar of smothering fire at close of the second day, consuming their dead. Other wyrmsmeat Jan and Tek ordered brought to the same spot to be burned. The unicorn dead they carried to the ancient burial cliffs and laid out beneath the sky.

By afternoon of the third day, the ashfall began to thin. As evening neared, the red mare Jah-lila stood upon a rise overlooking the Plain and called in a storm. All night fell the warm, hard rain. Sun rose undimmed on the following morning, the first real dawn since the ending of the world. The Scouts of Halla gazed upon their new homeland, admiring its splendor at the break of day. Then they departed, pledging to return ere summer's end with their elders and young, whom the red dragons had secreted safe away during the late upheaval in the Smoking Hills. Oro bowed low to both Tek and Jan, then turned and chanted to his band, singing them into single file across the green and rolling Plain.

The Mare's Back, too, had been washed clean by recent rain, free of the haunt-grey dust which had shrouded it. Calydor also took his leave, along with Tek's runners, bearing news of the warhost's victory and summoning those of the herd awaiting at oasis. On the twelfth day after the battle which had marked the close of the Era of Exile and begun the Age of the Firebringer, the herd's colts and fillies, suckling mares and their foals, ancient elders and the halt of limb entered at last into the Hallow Hills, lush with verdant foliage and summer grass.

Jan and Tek greeted their twins, and Ryhenna and Dagg their tiny son with relief and joy. The Plainsdwellers, to no one's surprise, evidenced little interest in the herd's newly won lands. Jan suspected they now regarded the Hallow Hills as both battlesite and gravelands, sacred and terrible, and not to be trespassed lightly. Those who ventured the Hills escorting new arrivals took their leave hastily, almost precipitously. Tek and Jan spoke their thanks and let them go. Calydor had not been among them. His absence puzzled and saddened Jan. But he had long since learned how strange were the ways of the Free People. They came and went capriciously, often as not without farewells.

Jan called the herd together on the fourteenth day, moondark, the time of portents and miracles. On the open meadow below the milkwood cliffs that housed the sacred mere, he sang them the lay of his journey through Pan Woods and across the Mare's Back in pursuit of Korr. He sang freely, in the manner of the Plain, of his travels with Calydor, his overtaking the mad king. His voice was strong and sure and omitted nothing, not dying Korr's revelation of Tek's parentage, not his own lost wandering across the Salt Barrens, not his encounter with Oro in the Smoking Hills, nor his sojourn belowground with the Scouts of Halla, nor his long rumination with Wyzásukitán.

Nothing he told his folk was by that time news to Tek or his closest kith. He had told them all in private, days before, starting with his mate. He had watched her hark to his news with tangled emotions: relief to discover at last her unknown sire, horror to find him to be Korr. And she had answered nothing, neither flying at Jan nor cursing, nor weeping, nor fleeing, nor falling into frozen gloom, nor any of the other wild responses he had dreaded. Instead, she had only stood beside him and nuzzled him, till he had cried out in helpless exasperation,

"And knowing this, what will you do?"

"I will think on it," she had told him quietly. "Come, love, let us bury our dead."

So they had done, while the cinders fell, till the rain of the midwife washed clean a world newly born of ashes and dust. Now Jan told the rest of his folk as well. Their reaction was stunned silence. Yet none cried out in condemnation against him or Tek. Any outrage was for Korr, and he was dead. Rather, his people heard Jan to the end. Doing so, he realized, because they loved him for his deeds alone. Prince or Firebringer mattered not.

Finishing his tale, Jan turned to me, Jah-lila, to verify my daughter's parentage. I did so, affirming that I had indeed loved the black prince of unicorns in his youth, a year before he had taken the pale mare Ses as mate. I had encountered him upon the Plain shortly after my escape from captors far to the south. Not yet then a unicorn, I had known naught of unicorn ways. Korr had pledged himself to me, but later broke the vow, deserting me upon the Plain and returning to his folk, sure I would be unable to follow him.

But follow I did, already in foal, and found him in his Vale. He pretended not to know me, to mistake me for a Renegade. I saw that should I attempt to lay a claim on him, he would declare me outlaw and cast me from the herd. So I called Teki, who sheltered me, my mate. In exchange for my silence, Korr allowed me to remain. I pledged never to reveal my knowledge of him until he himself had spoken. Still the prince's mistrust and fear begrudged me any peace. I left the Vale, exiling myself. When my daughter was weaned, I brought her from the wilderness and left her in Teki's care, that she might be reared within the herd and perhaps one day reclaim her birthright.

Jan bowed to me as I concluded, then turned once more to address his folk:

"A year ago, I knew nothing of these things. Until his dying words, I was ignorant of Korr's deception. When I succeeded him as prince, I did so in good faith, believing myself to be his heir. But I am not. Tek is the late king's firstborn. It is she who must reign now in his stead. Though I have been your prince, I cannot become your king. I call upon the Council to proclaim Tek queen. Would that you follow her as loyally as you have followed me."

The herd stood silent, like wights amazed. Plainly few had realized until this moment the import of Jan's revelation that Tek, not he, was the late king's heir. Slowly at first, and then more vigorously, murmurs of affirmation rose. They swelled, never quite becoming cheers—for Korr's treachery and the wrong my daughter had suffered could be naught to cheer—but serving as clear and unmistakable approval. The children-of-the-moon accepted my daughter as ruler in Jan's stead. The pied mare stepped forward.

"I accept with gratitude your acclamation," she told them warmly. "Though Korr was my sire and I his eldest-born, I would not impose myself upon you without your assent. You and I have looked to Jan as our leader these last five years. I would not take him from you to advance myself. But if you will have me, then gladly will I serve as queen."

Her head came up, nostrils flaring, particolored mane thrown back.

"After four hundred years in arms, we find ourselves at last at peace, and sovereignty reverts from warleader to queen. But hark me. I'll not reign without Jan at my shoulder. Battleprince no more, consider him now harbinger of this new peace that we have won. Let the title he has so ably borne remain. As my first edict, with our Elders' leave, I proclaim him forever prince of the unicorns."

This time the cheers were thunderous. Members of the herd threw back their heads, pealed forth wild shouts, struck hooves to earth and drummed up sparks. The din took some little time to subside. That done, Tek bowed her head and stepped back, yielding once more to Jan.

"Know this as well," her dark prince bade them. "Neither Tek nor I harbored any suspicion of her lineage when we pledged one to another four summers gone. Korr concealed this knowledge from us, and Jahlila bought her daughter's safety and place among the herd with a vow of silence to Korr."

Jan squared himself before his folk.

"For my own deed, I accept no censure. If trespass has been done, be it on Korr's head. With pure intent, I swore myself under summer stars, by light of Alma's thousand thousand eyes. Such a covenant cannot be foresworn. It is unshakable. I will not regret it now. Nor will I abandon Tek and the twin issue of our deepest joy."

Blacker than starless night he stood, head high, beard bristling in the wind.

"What has passed between us can be neither recanted nor denied. It is done. No word or feat can now undo it. Tek was my mate. She can be mine no more. Yet though we never again summer beside the Sea or bring forth new progeny, she remains the only such love I will ever know. I'll seek no other in her stead. Though I sire no more young till the end of my days, I will never pledge my heart to another."

The herd stood speechless, thunderstruck. Not a murmur or a snort disturbed the hush. Doubtless none had yet reasoned through the full consequence of the blood Jan and Tek believed they shared. Bemused or troubled glances, expressions of cautious approval, rank distaste, even dread passed like wildfire among members of the herd to hear Jan preparing to renounce his sacred marriage vow and the reason therefor. My daughter came forward to stand at Jan's shoulder again.

"I, too, concur," she announced. "Though I remain barren from this day forth, I'll neither disown my past nor plight any other suitor my troth. Can you accept this of me and continue to call me queen? Will you honor the now severed bond betwixt me and my one-time mate, who cherish still the offspring we once, unwitting, bore? Can you spare ill will against our young and welcome them as my heirs? Among us all, their innocence is absolute."

Again, silence. Then gradually, murmurs—not grudging, only thoughtful. Beside the healer, Teki, who once to safeguard me and mine had called himself my mate, Dhattar and Aiony chivvied, the black-and-silver filly snorting at flitter-bys, the white foal scrubbing his young horn against one knee. They paid no mind to anything else, as though unaware or unconcerned or, perhaps, already certain of the day's outcome. Acknowledging them as their future princess and prince, the children-of-the-moon could feel no hardness of heart. In muted tones, but without cavil, the herd assented. Tek closed her eyes. Jan touched his cheek to hers, then drew breath.

"So be it. Tek, I therefore renounce. . . ."

I gave him no time to complete the phrase.

"No need!" I cried. "No reason to abjure your vows, no need to wonder at the welcome of your heirs or forgo future young."

The young prince stumbled to a halt. Frowning, so puzzled I could not hold back my joyous laugh, he and his queen turned to look at me.

"Children, forgive my holding tongue till now, for I meant all the world to know your mettle. Aljan Moonbrow," I declared to him, "called also Firebringer and Dark Moon, you have spoken earnestly in the belief that Tek is our late king's firstborn child and you, his secondborn. The former is true. The latter, not. You are *not* half brother to your mate. She is not your sib. You and Tek are no kin whatsoever to one another. No blood ties you. Henceforth let none ever question your union or your offspring already born or as yet unborn."

Jan stared at me like a sleeper startled from his dreams. Beside him, his pied mate shook her head as one kicked smartly in the skull, half stunned. Jan roused.

"What?" he murmured, hoarse. "How can that be?" His voice gained strength. "What do you mean: Tek and I share no blood? Have you not confirmed her as Korr's heir? How is she then not sib to me?"

Smiling, triumphant, I held my peace, for it was not mine to answer now. I glanced toward Ses, who flanked me on that meadow's slope, and as we had already agreed, she stepped forward to face the prince, her child.

"Because you are not Korr's son, my son. My mate who reared you was never your sire. You are not king's get."

Her voice was collected, decisive, clear. Before us, the whole herd rippled, some shying in surprise, others sidling, snorting. I heard whinnies, whickers of disbelief, manes tossing, tails slapped, hooves stamped. Ses waited them out. A look passed between her and Tek, the young queen's so intent, it was almost a plea. When the pied mare spoke, though, her words were calm.

"Tell us how this may be."

"I loved another," the pale mare said. "The summer before I swore myself Korr's mate. He was one of the Free Folk. We met and loved upon the Plain after their custom, without exchange of any vows, and then we parted."

She met Jan's eyes.

"That autumn, when I pledged to Korr, I knew not then that I carried a foal. I meant my pledge. I intended to be his lifelong mate and bear his heir. It was not to be. I bore you to my lost Renegade come spring and carried you to term. You did not drop early, as others thought."

The pale mare glanced at me, then down, away.

"Except the midwife, who understood. When I guessed her secret in turn, each of us held silent after, protecting our own and one another's children from a capricious ruler. In time, I brought Lell, too, into the world, sired by my mate, the king."

She found Lell with her eyes. The half-grown filly, her dark-amber coat merled now with gold, stood pressed against the shelter of Illishar's folded wing. Like hers, his sandy pelt was brindled now, his grass-green fletching silver flecked. Amazement lit Lell's gaze, but she watched her dam without condemnation or grief.

"I will tell you this," continued the poppy-maned mare, addressing her son once more. "Though I spoke no pledge to my wild love of the Plain so many years ago, his memory has haunted me. Korr's death pains me deep. I loved him well. Had he renounced his madness and deceit, willingly would I have returned to him."

Her gaze lifted, skimming the assembled unicorns toward the unseen Mare's Back beyond.

"But Korr did not. Now he is dead, and I am free. The Hallow Hills are won, and my daughter grown beyond colthood faster than I could have dreamed. I find my thoughts straying to the Plain, ever and always, night and noon. There, the one I once loved awaits me still."

Her voice grew quiet. I had to prick my ears to hear.

"I long for him I so lately found again, who guided us across the Plain, shared battle with us, and begged me to depart with him, as I nearly did so many summers past when instead I chose otherwise, returning to the herd to swear my pledge to Korr."

Watching her red mane furl and toss, I could only approve the coolness with which she spoke, shirking none of the blame, but neither shouldering any not hers to bear. My daughter leaned against her mate, still staring at Ses. Beside her, the pale mare's son stood dumbstruck, as did all the herd before them. I thought the jaws of some might brush the ground.

"Korr not my sire?" he whispered, stammering as one struggling against a gale. "If not Korr . . . , then who?"

"Calydor," his dam replied, "whose name means Summer Stars."

Aftermath

Such, then, were the things that befell that day, so soon after the dawning of an age, the re-beginning of the world. Ses bade her young daughter and her son brief farewell, departing for the Plain in search of Calydor. She swore to return often, and she has kept that vow. Jan, too, vowed to venture forth upon the Mare's Back before next summer's end to find them both and learn more of the stallion that had sired him. This the dark prince did, sojourning time and again in the company of Summer Stars, who taught him more of the lay-chanter's art, so that Aljan Moonbrow is renowned among you—O dwellers of the Plain— as a singer of tales. But I thought you should know him as his own folk do, a warrior prince and a peacemaker.

For accords with the gryphons and the pans were but the start of his alliances. He traveled far across the Plain as Tek's envoy, forging pacts with many tribes. The unicorns are done with war. My daughter's reign has been a long, lazing dream of peace. Truly a new world her Dark Moon has made, and is making still. For though I am ancient, very near to Alma now, the world is young. Aljan and his mate are but elders. Many seasons lie ahead before they ascend the starpath to merge with the summer stars.

Thus the Battle of Endingfire initiated the passing of the old and set in motion the new dance that is still becoming, even as we speak. No more than a moon after, Jan stood upon the moonpool cliffs, gazing up into dusky heaven thick with distant suns. The infinite expanse of the void encompassing those myriad stars seemed to enter him, pervading his senses and filling him with a deep, lulling wonder. He became aware of a presence, vast as the starry sky. Only a moment passed before he knew her.

"Alma," he whispered.

The presence answered, "Aye."

"Where have you been?" he asked her.

She laughed gently, silently, within his mind. "With you," she answered. "Always. Even when you do not know it."

Inwardly, he felt his ears prick with surprise. "Your voice sounds like the dragon queen's."

"I am many voices," the goddess told him, "that never cease to speak."

He turned to her within himself. "Why did you not tell me?" he asked. "Why did you let me believe myself prince?"

Again, amused laughter. "But you are prince," the presence replied.

"By acclamation," he retorted, "not by right. Prince at my mate the queen's behest."

The goddess answered nothing, only smiled.

"Why did you never give me any inkling Korr was not my sire?" Jan demanded, stung.

The other's air of tolerant amusement never faded. "Why should I concern myself with that?" she asked indifferently. "Have I not said before I do not make kings or rings of Law? Those things are yours to make or to unmake, exactly as you choose."

Jan held his silence.

The deity asked, "Is being my Firebringer not honor enough?"

The dark prince flushed, chagrined—then let it go, unable to muster true affront.

"Aye: born out of a wyrmqueen's belly," he murmured, recounting the old prophecy, "foaled at moondark, and sired by the summer stars." He paused, considering. Alma's eyes burned very bright all around. Finally, he said, "I did not lead the battle against the wyverns."

The goddess whispered, "Did you not?"

Jan shook his head. "Tek did. Nor did I carry the brand against Lynex. That deed was Lell's."

The goddess nodded. "But you wakened the dragon that bore him away and danced fire through all the stinging wyverns' dens, expelling them from my Hallows forevermore."

Still troubled, Jan felt his brow furrow. "What sets me apart?" he breathed. "All the fire I ever found, I gave away: now my people's heels can all strike sparks. Their fire-tempered horns have grown as keen and hard as mine, their blood as venomproof."

Again the other nodded, laughing. "Of course. Did you think I had intended otherwise? Flame is not the only fire." Her tone turned almost stern. "You have brought your folk another spark far greater than any flame. You have opened their eyes to the world, Aljan, shown them lands and peoples formerly beyond their ken. You have whistled them out of their cramped, closed, inward-facing ring and led them into my Dance, the Great Circle and Cycle encompassing all."

· She seemed to sigh, not with sadness but with joy.

"Such has always been my plan for the unicorns, that they dwell in harmony among my other favored children. You drove the followers of Lynex out because they would have none of that peace. Nay, flame has not been the greatest of my gifts to you. Knowledge, Aljan, that even now remakes the world. Knowledge is the fire."

Dusk had wholly faded now. Sky above had darkened to true night. The full moon, barely hidden by horizon's edge, was just beginning to rise. He knew he must return to his folk for the dance, and yet he did not stir. Gazing heavenward, he felt the goddess recede, not departing, merely withdrawing from his uppermost awareness. She was everywhere, he knew, in the heavens, in the stars, in dragons and unicorns. In him. He could not lose her. The knowledge warmed him to the heart.

See how I have whiled the night away! My friends, I never meant to keep you all so long. I thought my telling of Jan's tale would fill but two short nights. Instead I have talked each of three long evenings into dawn. Forgive me. I am an old mare, much given to prattle. In this age of peace, with no foes to conquer, no battles to plan, each day unfolds free of war and woe. What is there to do but talk, dream, love, and dance in celebration of this new age I midwived in by birth of the Firebringer at moondark under Alma's thousand thousand eyes?

Hail, dwellers of the Plain! I will let you go. Your kindness goes beyond counting to have harkened to me so long. Close cousins to my adopted herd, you know so little of us still. Hostilities between our two tribes have long since ceased, yet we see you too seldom, though your kind may pass as freely into the Hallow Hills as members of my herd now cross the Plain. Ere Jan, such amity could never have been. Yet he was not always the great peacemaker and singer you esteem. In his youth he was a battleprince, by Alma blessed: a warrior, a dancer, a bringer of fire.